LORE OLYMPUS

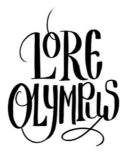

VOLUME ONE

RACHEL SMYTHE

NEW YORK

Lore Olympus: Volume One is a work of fiction. Names, places, characters, and incidents either are the product of the author's imagination or are used fictitiously. Any resemblance to actual persons, living or dead, events, or locales is entirely coincidental.

Published in the United States by Del Rey, an imprint of Random House, a division of Penguin Random House LLC, New York.

Del Rey and the House colophon are registered trademarks of Penguin Random House LLC.

Portions of this work originally appeared on webtoons.com.

LIBRARY OF CONGRESS CATALOGING-IN-PUBLICATION DATA
Names: Smythe, Rachel (Comics artist), author, artist.
Title: Lore Olympus / Rachel Smythe.
Description: First edition. | New York : Del Rey, 2021
Identifiers: LCCN 2021008087 | Hardcover ISBN 9780593160299 (v. 1) |
Trade paperback ISBN 9780593356074 (v. 1) |
Barnes & Noble edition ISBN 9780593359358 (v. 1)
Subjects: LCSH: Mythology, Greek—Comic books, strips, etc. |
Graphic novels.
Classification: LCC PN6727.S54758 L67 2021 | DDC 741.5/973—dc23
LC record available at https://lccn.loc.gov/2021008087

Printed in China

randomhousebooks.com

4 6 8 9 7 5

Book design by Edwin Vazquez

To my family, friends, and fans.

CONTENT WARNING
FROM RACHEL SMYTHE

Lore Olympus regularly deals with themes of physical and mental abuse, sexual trauma, and toxic relationships.

Some of the interactions in this volume may be distressing for some readers. Please exercise discretion, and seek out the support of others if you require it.

*"WHILE YOU ARE HERE, YOU SHALL RULE ALL THAT LIVES
AND MOVES AND SHALL HAVE THE GREATEST RIGHTS
AMONG THE DEATHLESS GODS : THOSE WHO DEFRAUD
YOU AND DO NOT APPEASE YOUR POWER WITH
OFFERINGS, REVERENTLY PERFORMING RITES AND
PAYING FIT GIFTS, SHALL BE PUNISHED FOR EVERMORE."*

— HADES TO PERSEPHONE

*HESIOD, THE HOMERIC HYMNS, AND HOMERICA
BY HESIOD; HOMER; EVELYN-WHITE, HUGH G.
(HUGH GERARD), D. 1924*

EPISODE 01: STAG, YOU'RE IT

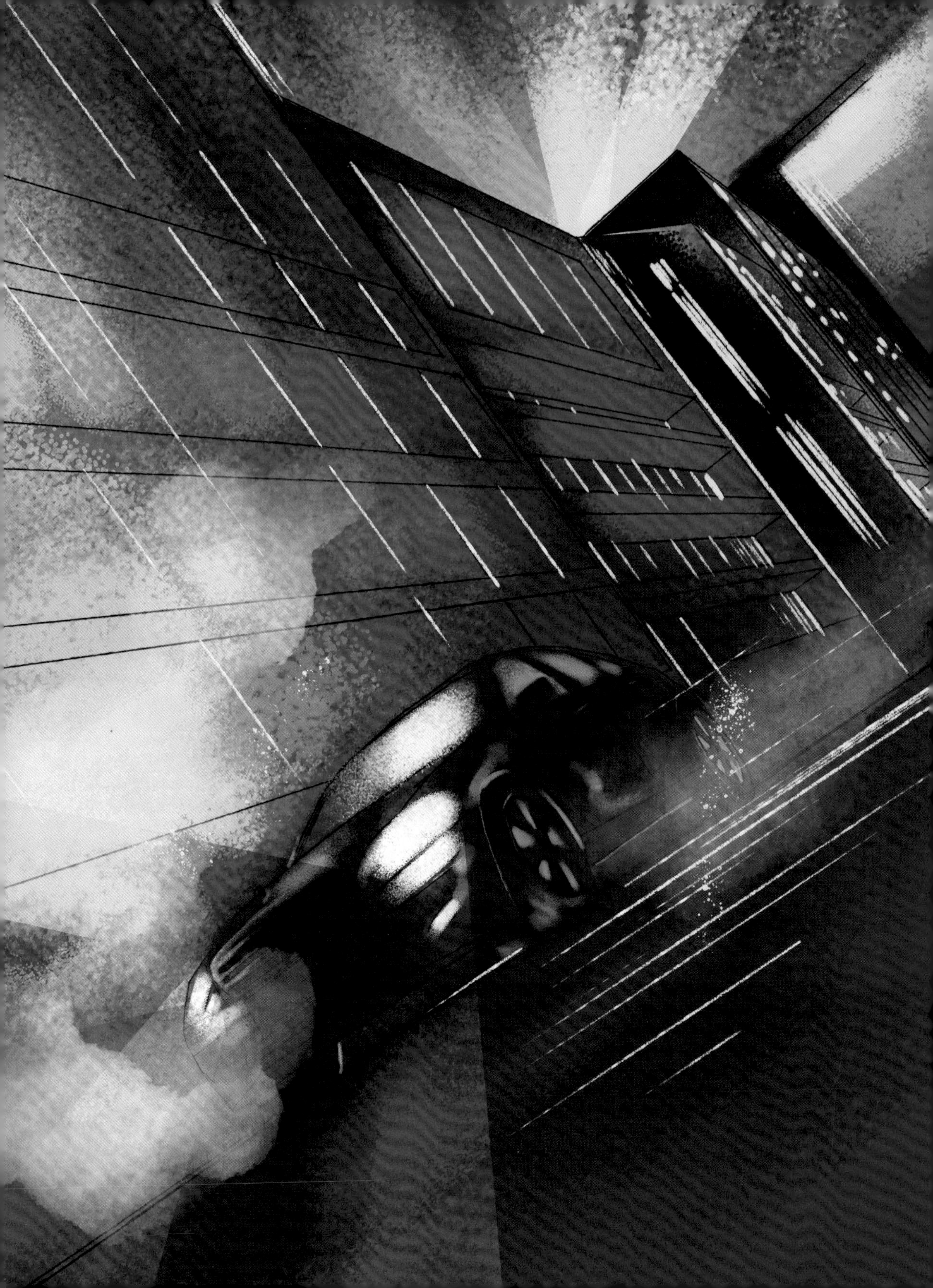

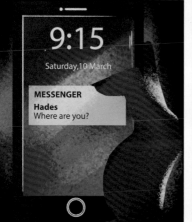

9:15

Saturday, 10 March

MESSENGER
Hades
Where are you?

HA!

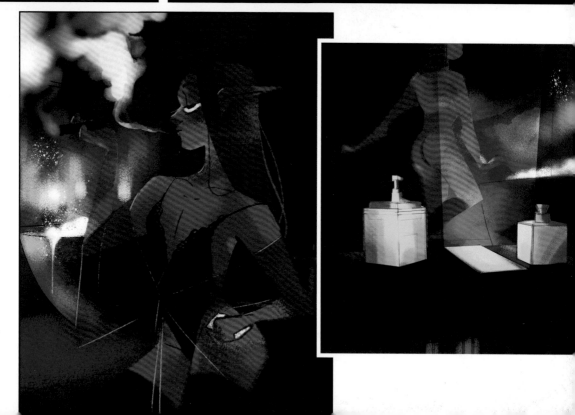

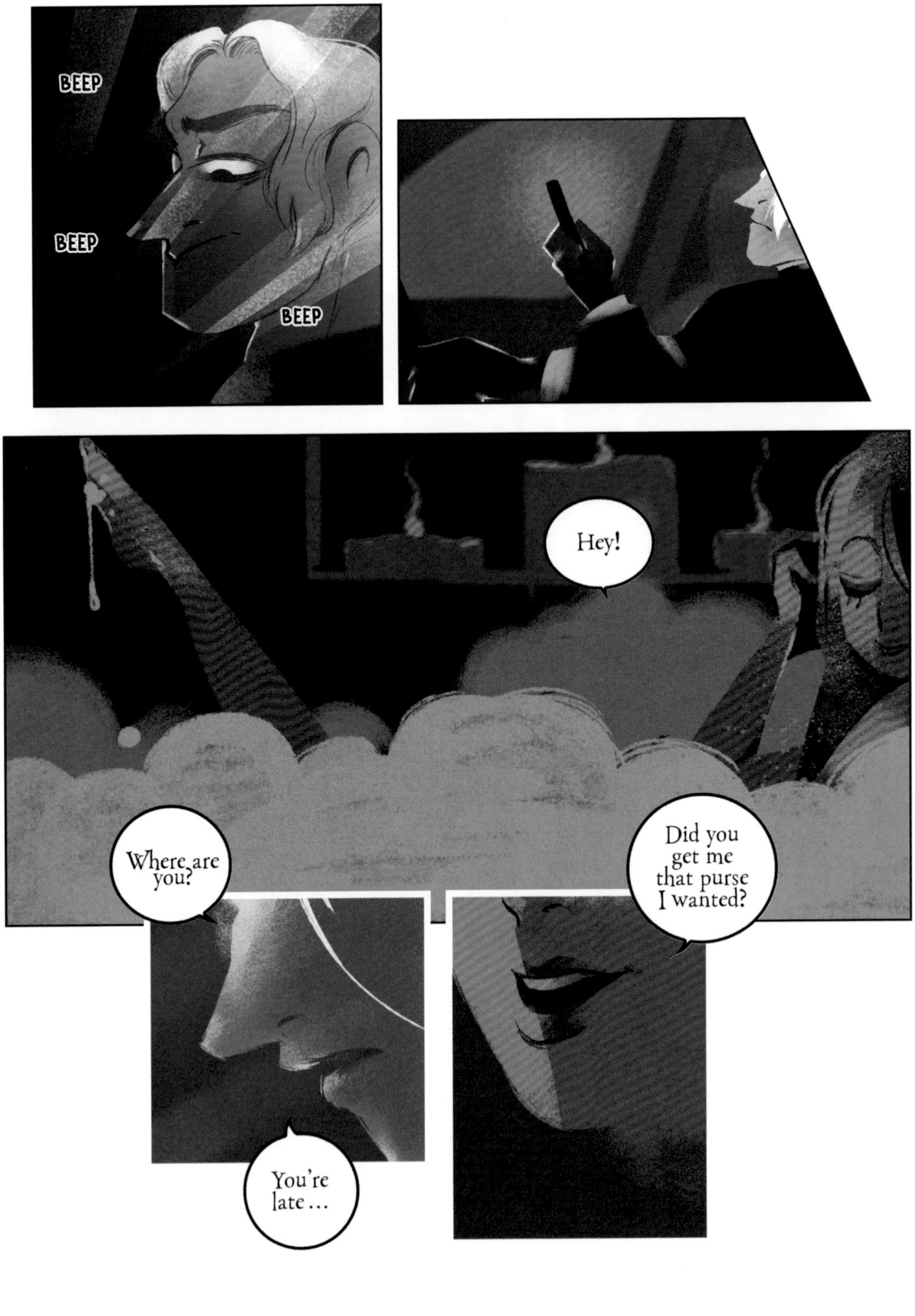
BEEP
BEEP
BEEP
Hey!
Where are you?
Did you get me that purse I wanted?
You're late ...

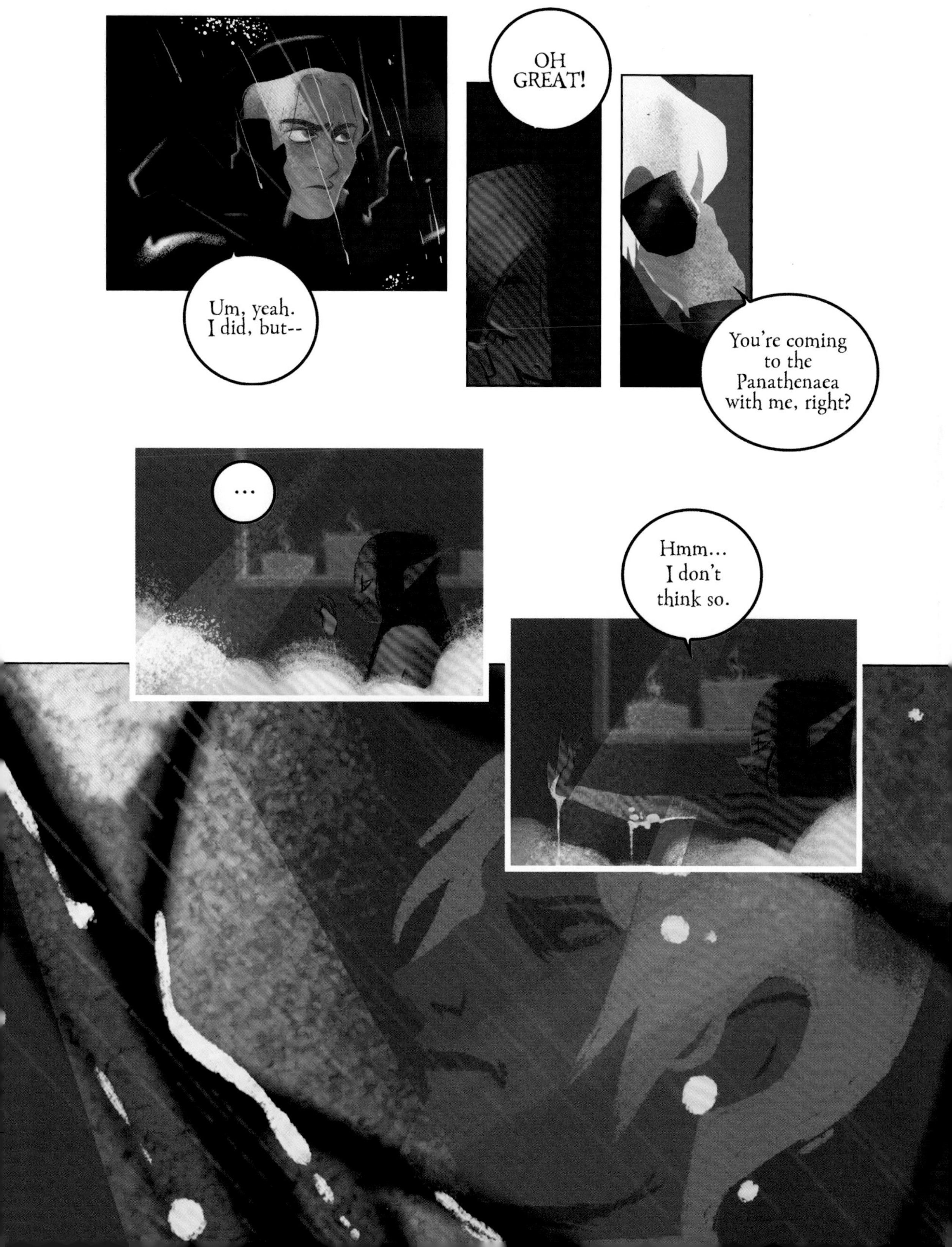
Um, yeah.
I did, but--
OH
GREAT!
You're coming
to the
Panathenaea
with me, right?
...
Hmm...
I don't
think so.

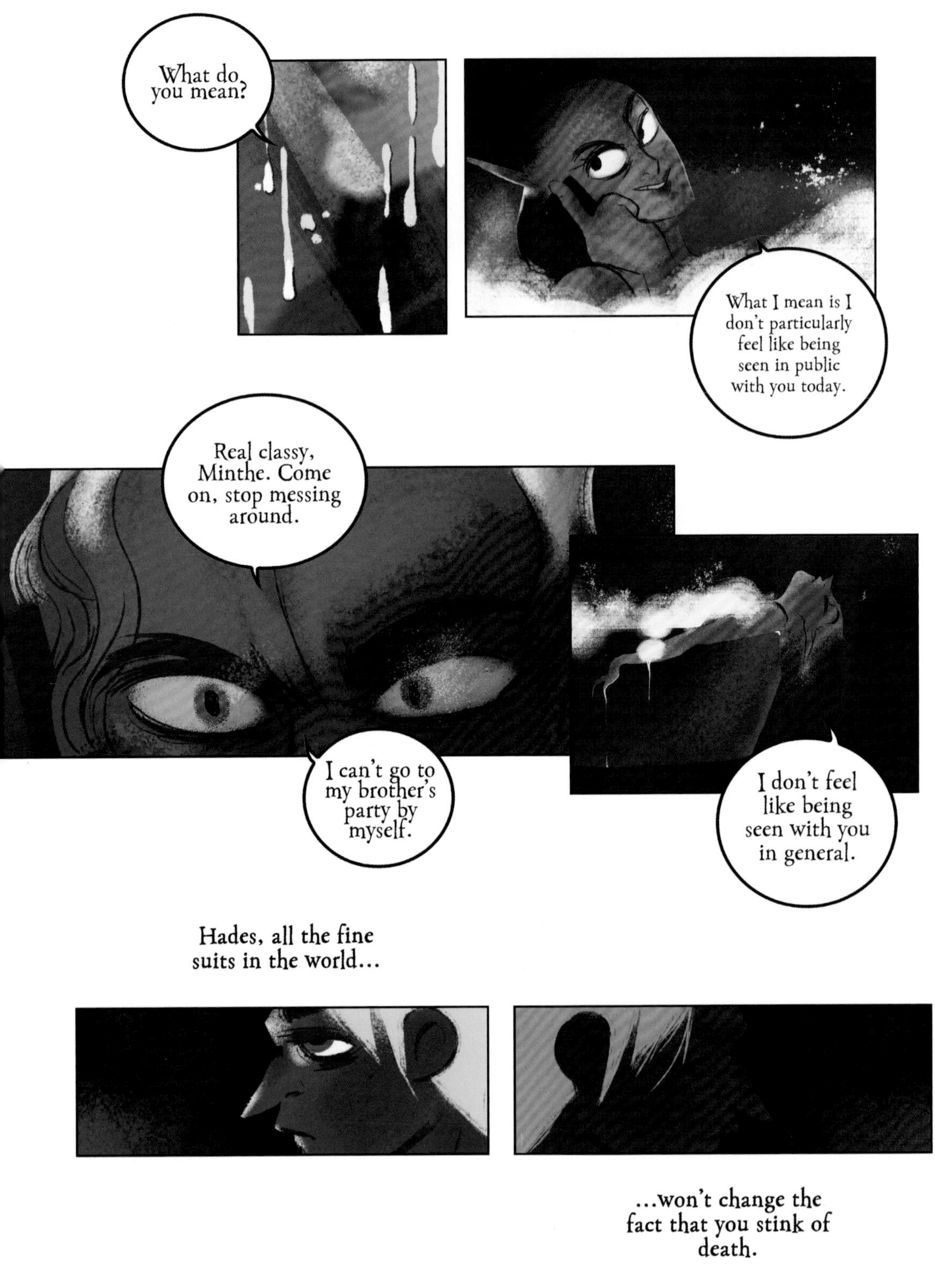
What do you mean?
What I mean is I don't particularly feel like being seen in public with you today.
Real classy, Minthe. Come on, stop messing around.
I can't go to my brother's party by myself.
I don't feel like being seen with you in general.
Hades, all the fine suits in the world...
...won't change the fact that you stink of death.

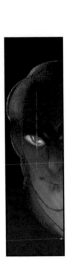

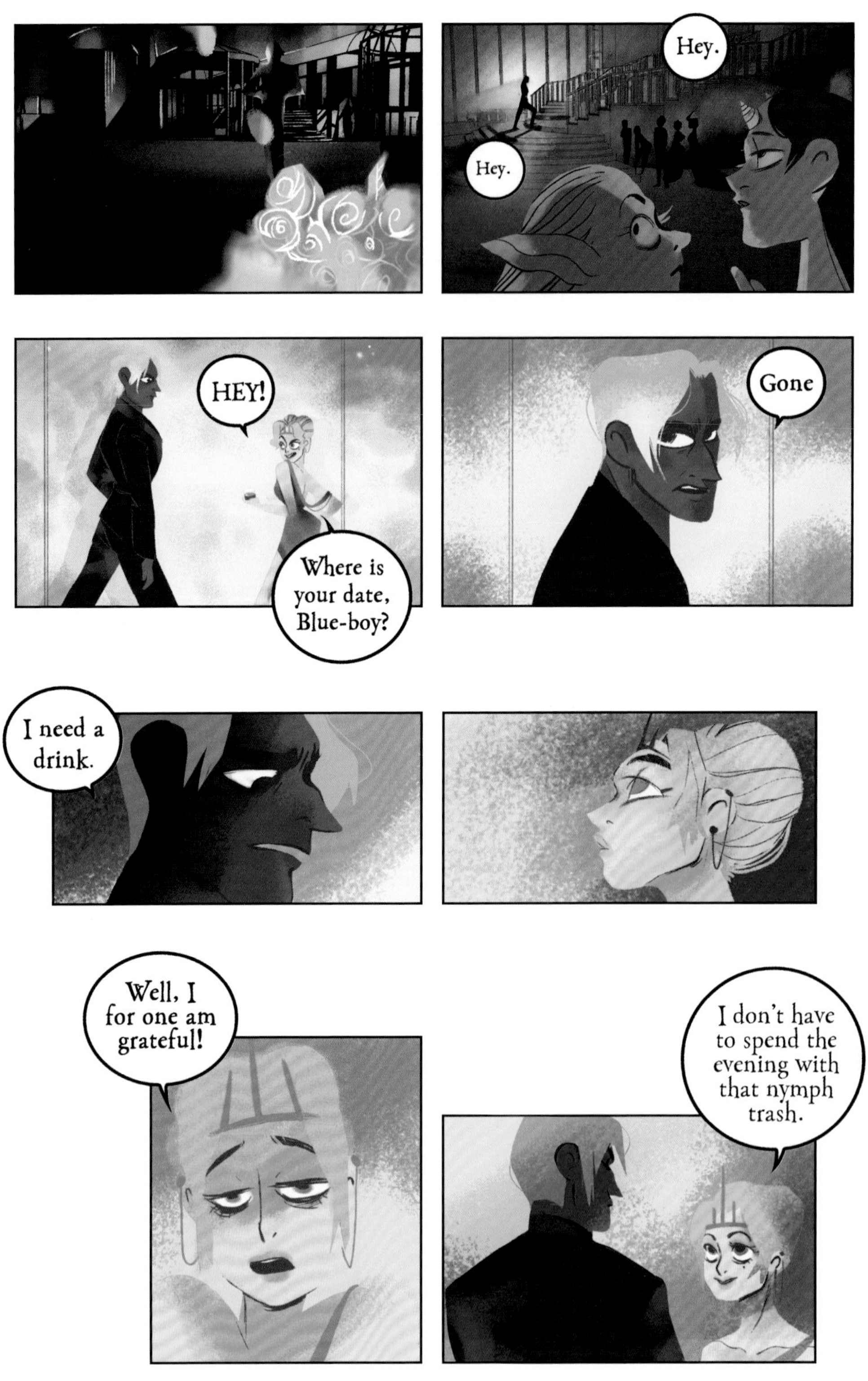
Hey.
Hey.
HEY!
Where is your date, Blue-boy?
Gone
I need a drink.
Well, I for one am grateful!
I don't have to spend the evening with that nymph trash.

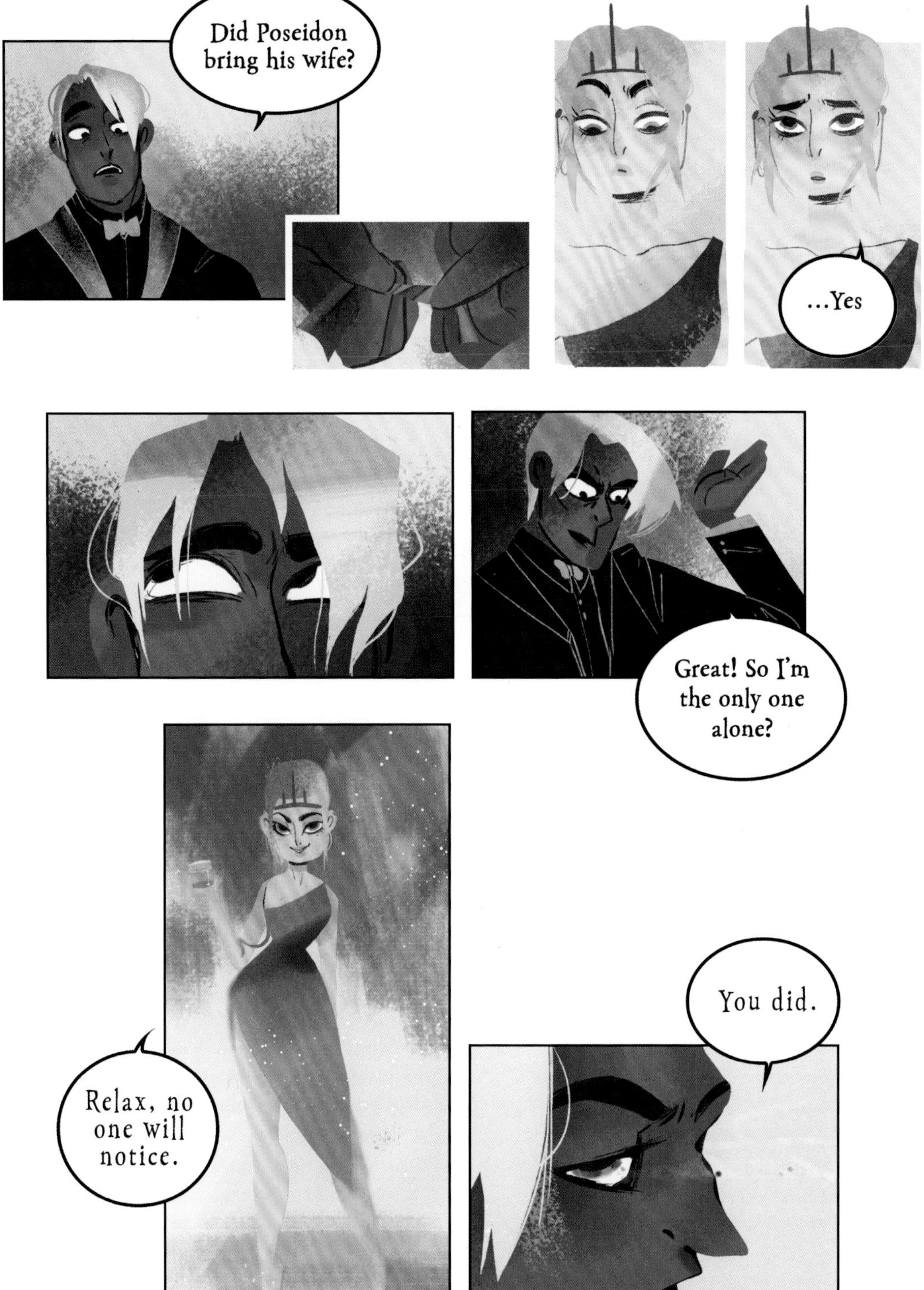
Did Poseidon bring his wife?
...Yes
Great! So I'm the only one alone?
Relax, no one will notice.
You did.

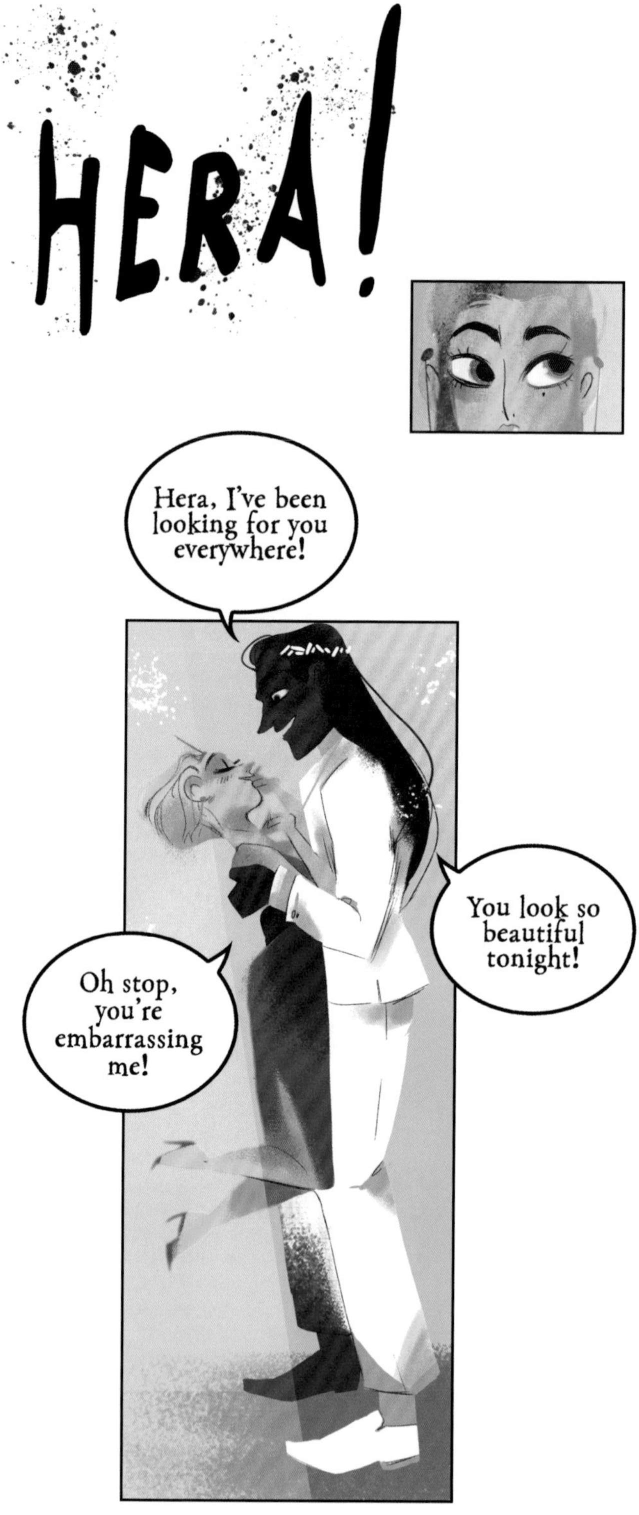
HERA!
Hera, I've been looking for you everywhere!
You look so beautiful tonight!
Oh stop, you're embarrassing me!

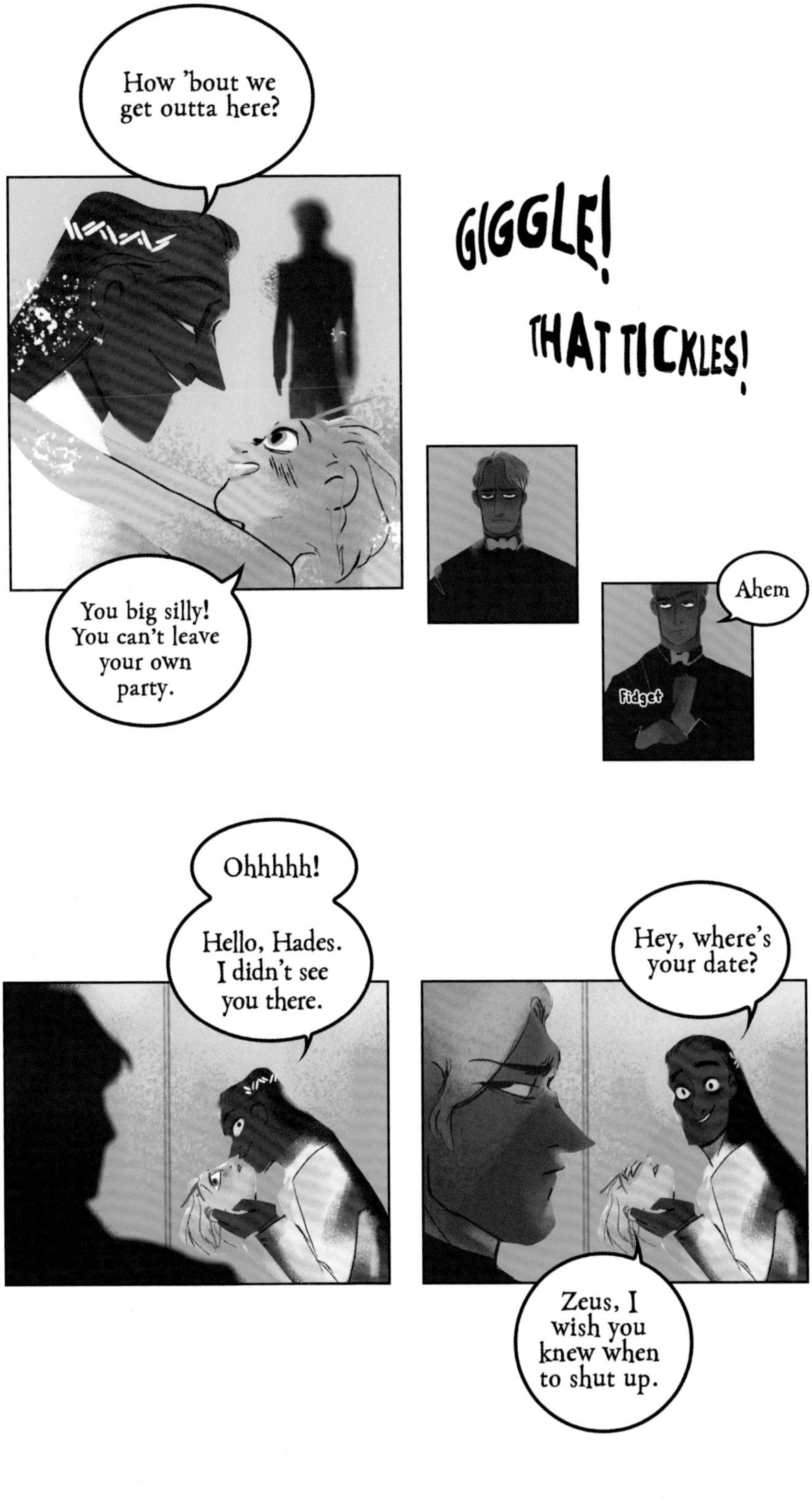
How 'bout we get outta here?
GIGGLE!
THAT TICKLES!
You big silly! You can't leave your own party.
Ahem
Fidget
Ohhhhh!
Hello, Hades. I didn't see you there.
Hey, where's your date?
Zeus, I wish you knew when to shut up.

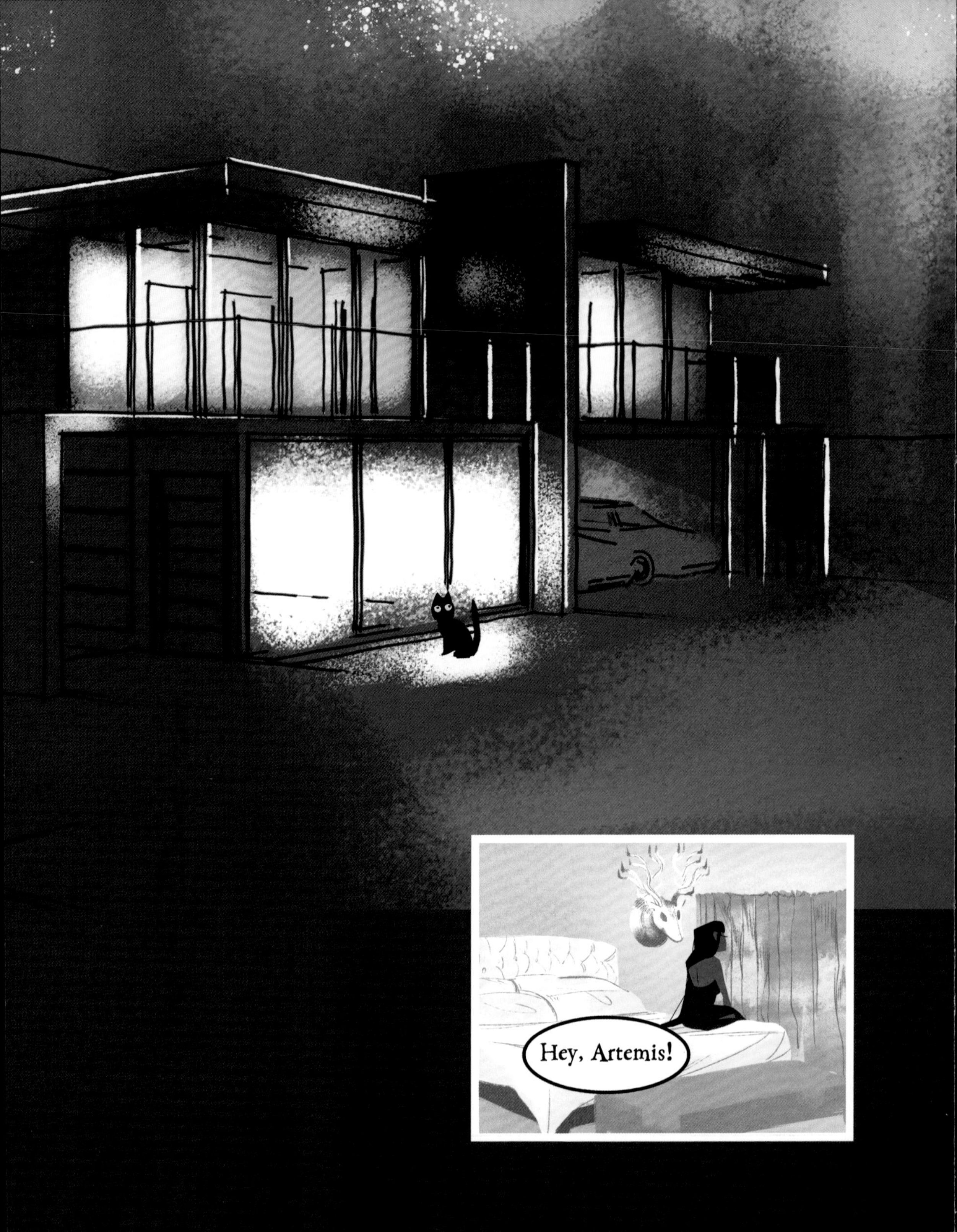
Hey, Artemis!

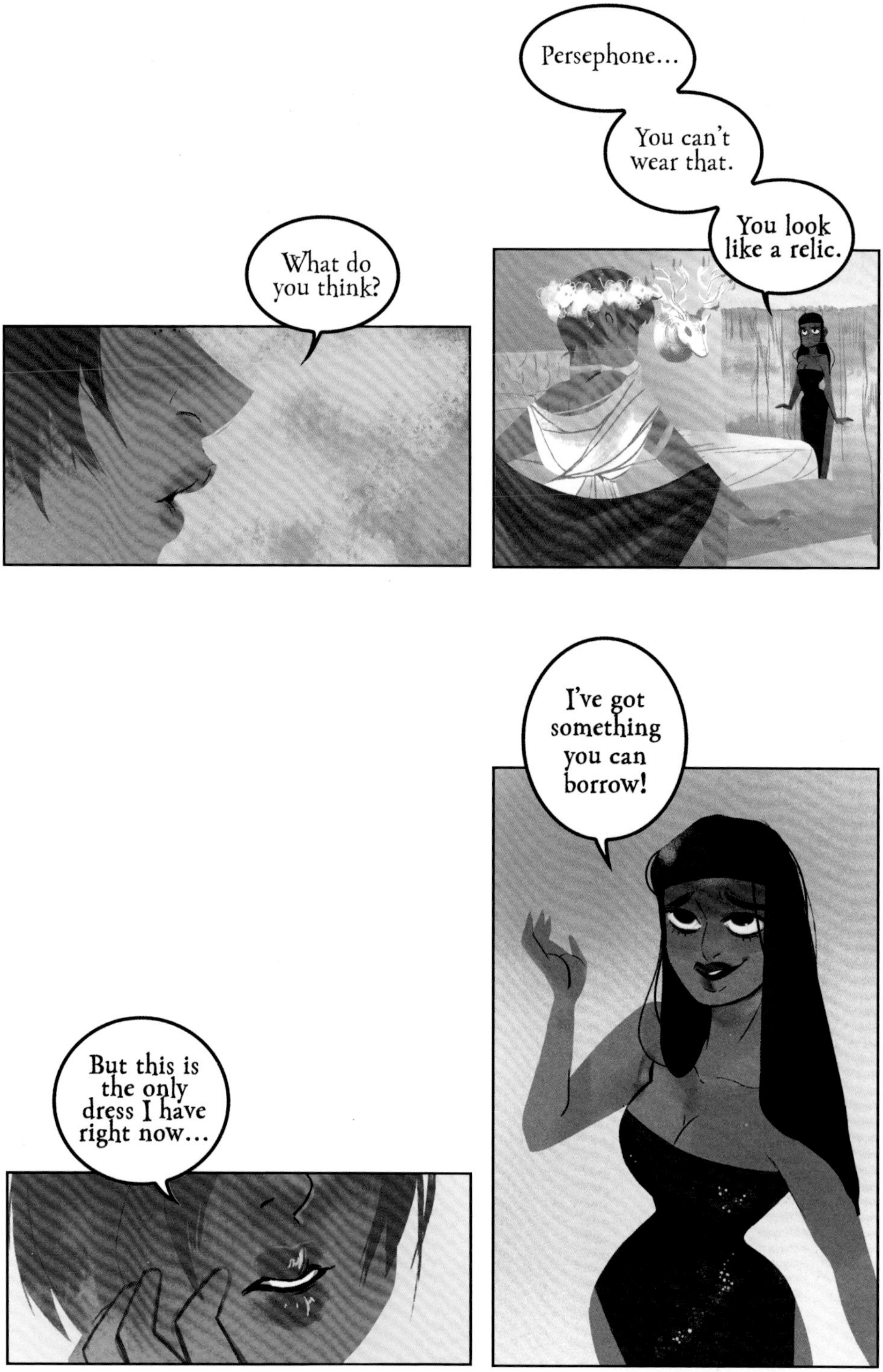
What do you think?
Persephone...
You can't wear that.
You look like a relic.
But this is the only dress I have right now...
I've got something you can borrow!

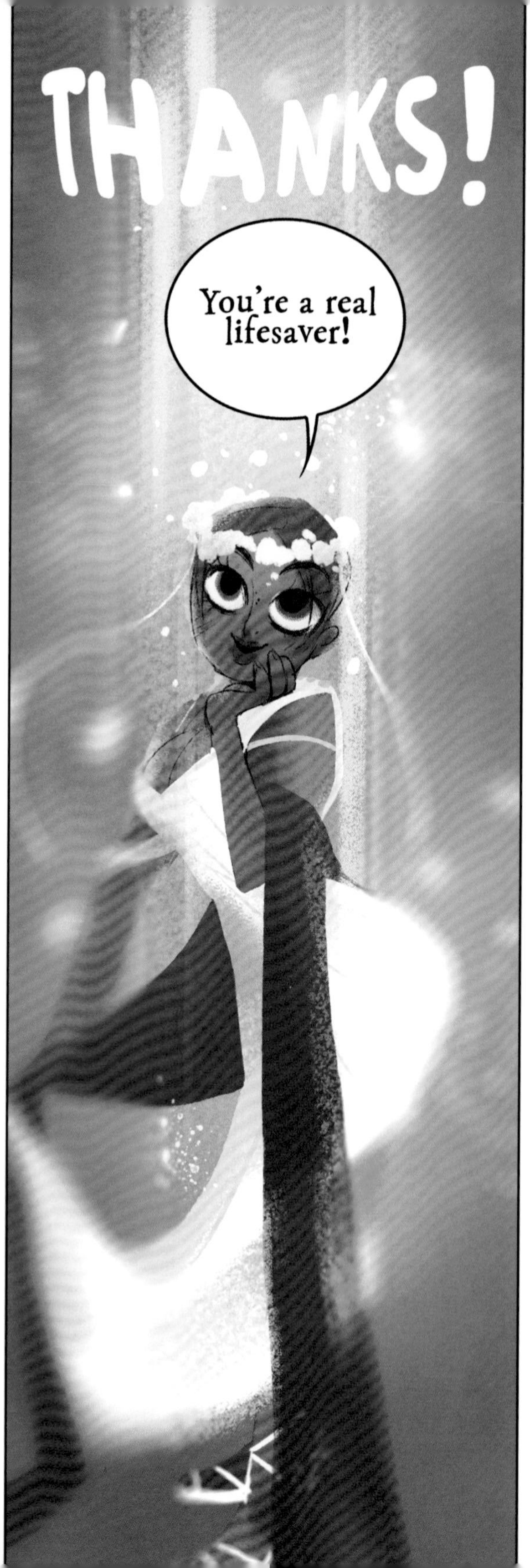
THANKS!
You're a real lifesaver!

EPISODE 02: WHO IS SHE? (PART I)

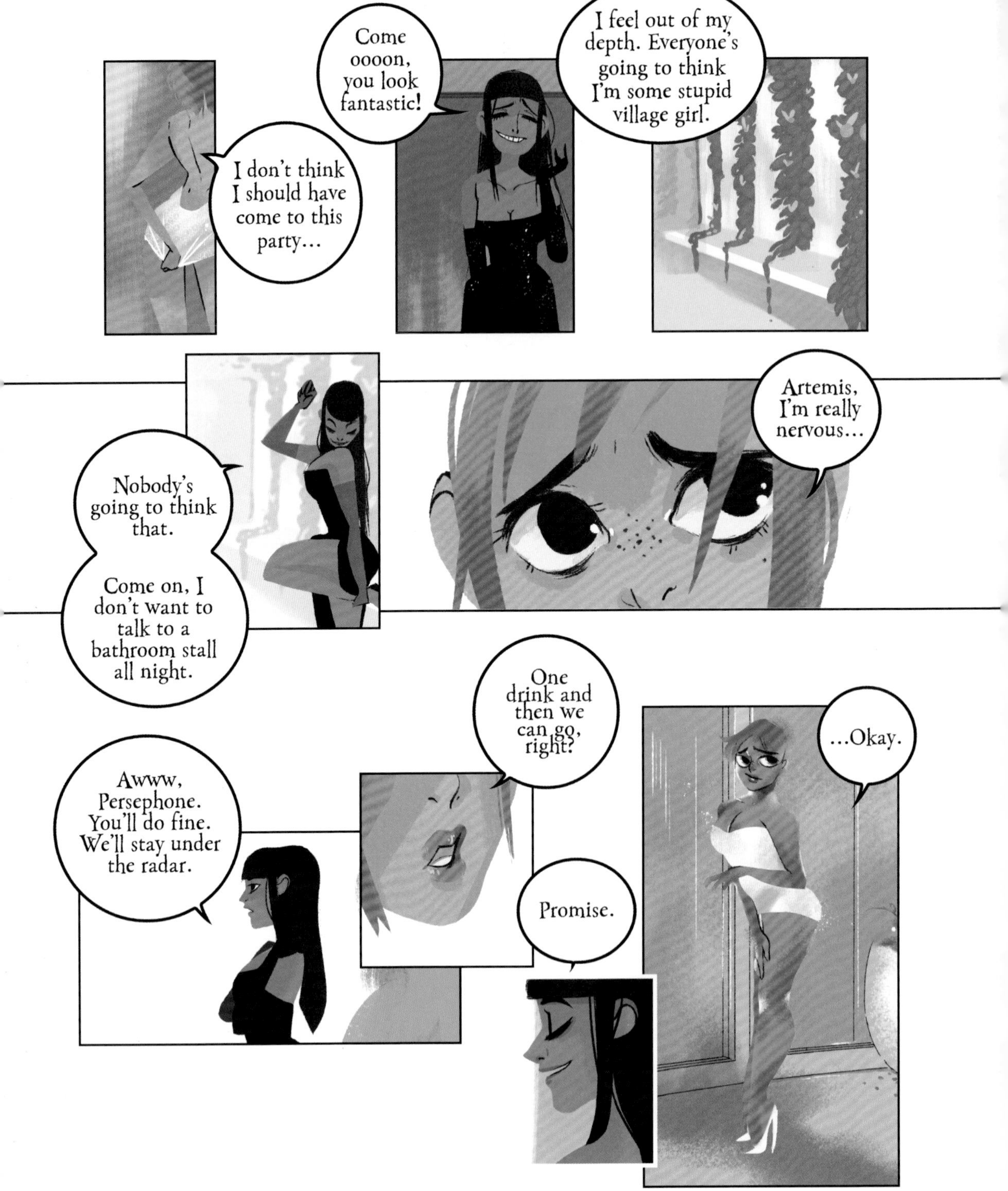
I don't think I should have come to this party...
Come oooon, you look fantastic!
I feel out of my depth. Everyone's going to think I'm some stupid village girl.
Nobody's going to think that.
Come on, I don't want to talk to a bathroom stall all night.
Artemis, I'm really nervous...
Awww, Persephone. You'll do fine. We'll stay under the radar.
One drink and then we can go, right?
Promise.
...Okay.

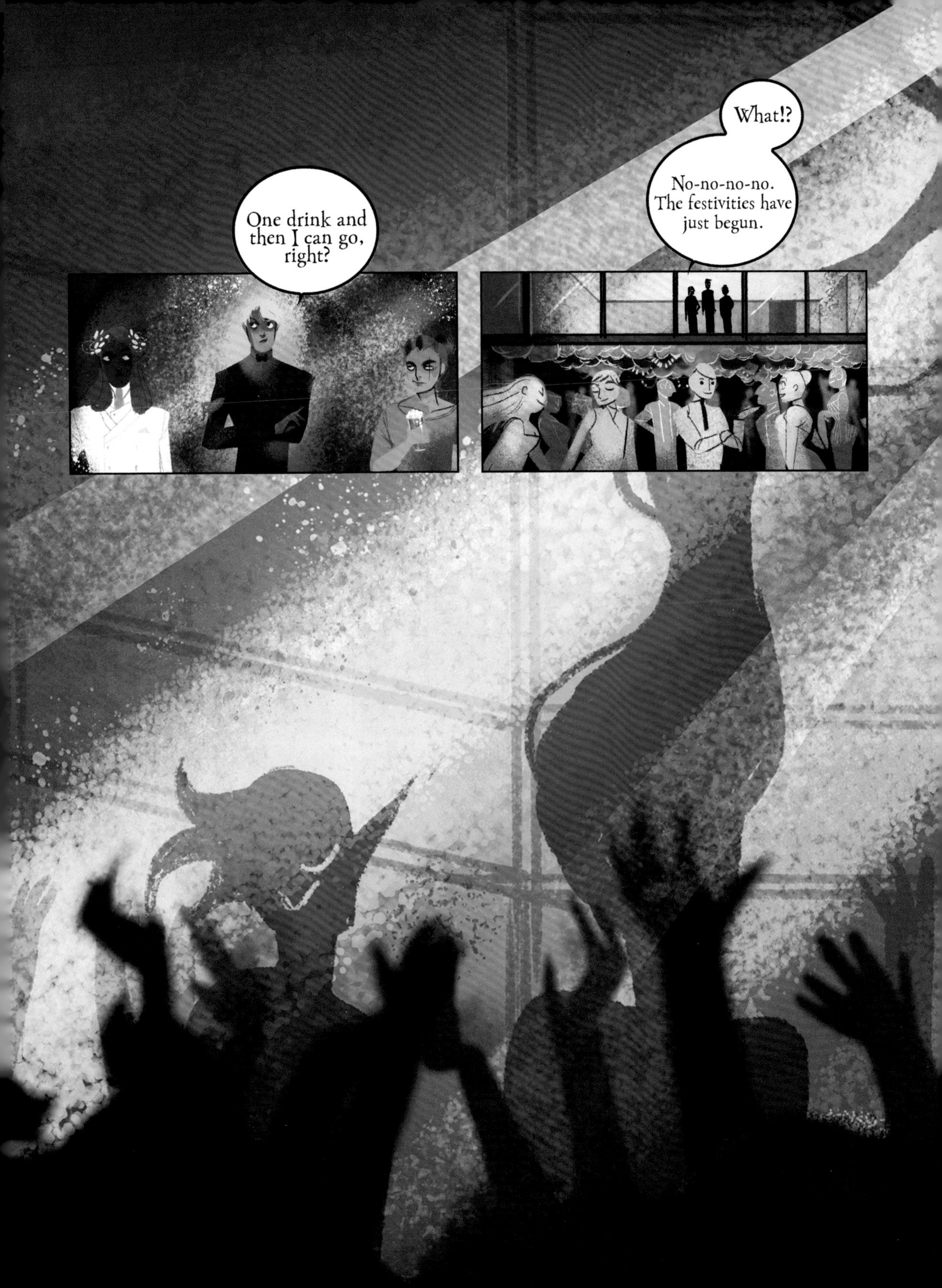
One drink and then I can go, right?
No-no-no-no. The festivities have just begun.
What!?

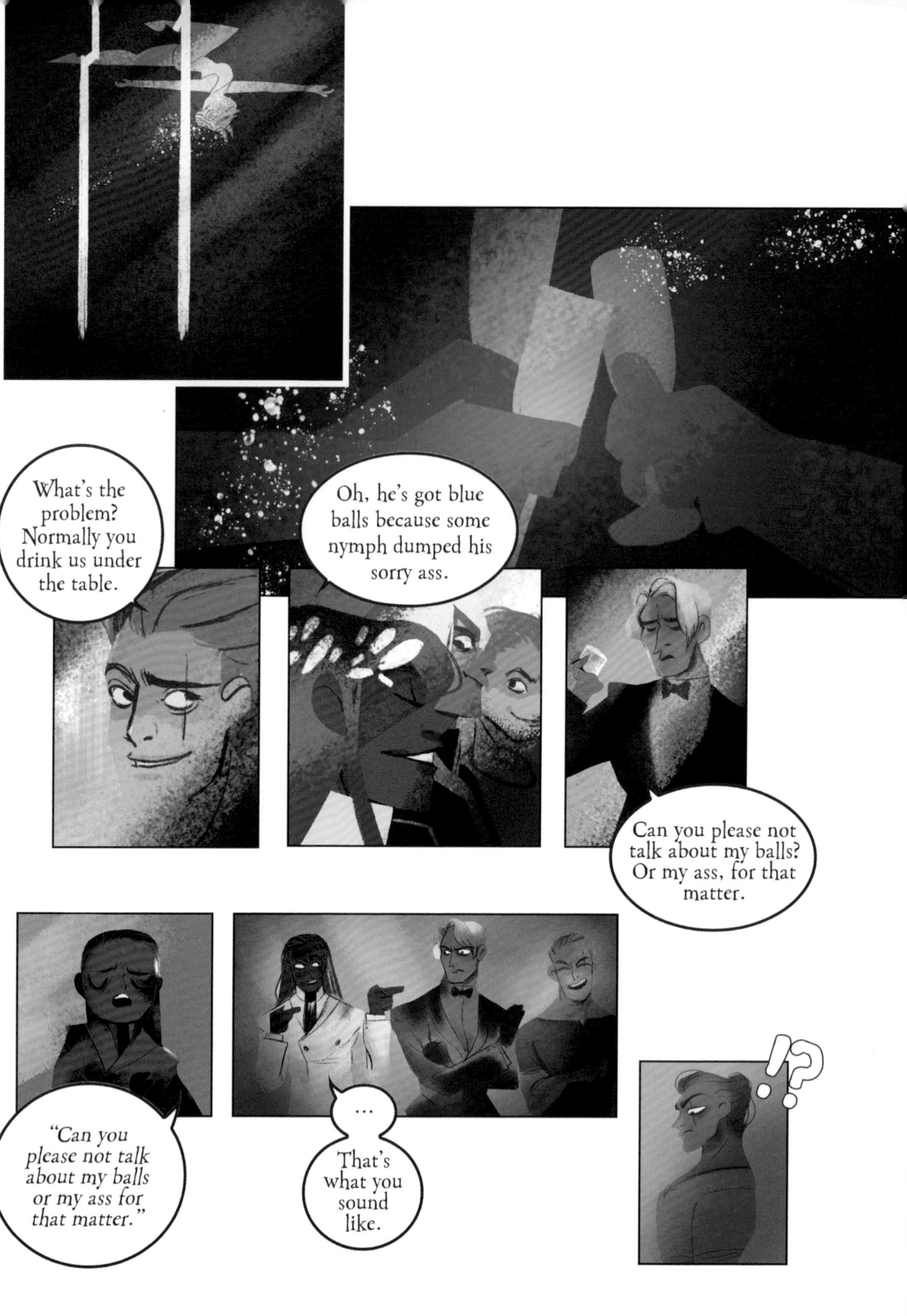
What's the problem? Normally you drink us under the table.
Oh, he's got blue balls because some nymph dumped his sorry ass.
Can you please not talk about my balls? Or my ass, for that matter.
"Can you please not talk about my balls or my ass for that matter."
...
That's what you sound like.
!?

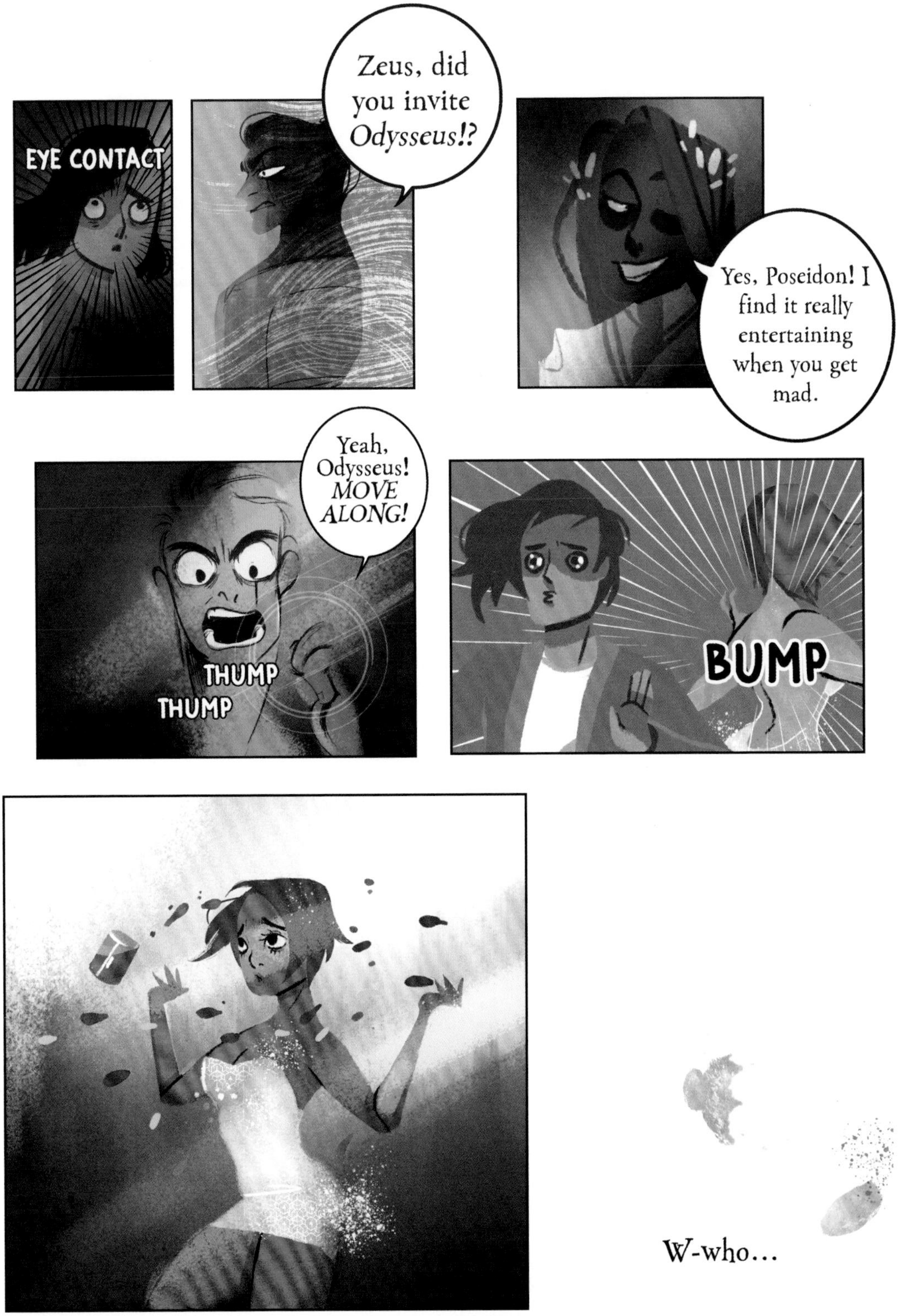
EYE CONTACT
Zeus, did you invite Odysseus!?
Yes, Poseidon! I find it really entertaining when you get mad.
Yeah, Odysseus! *MOVE ALONG!*
THUMP
THUMP
BUMP
W-who...

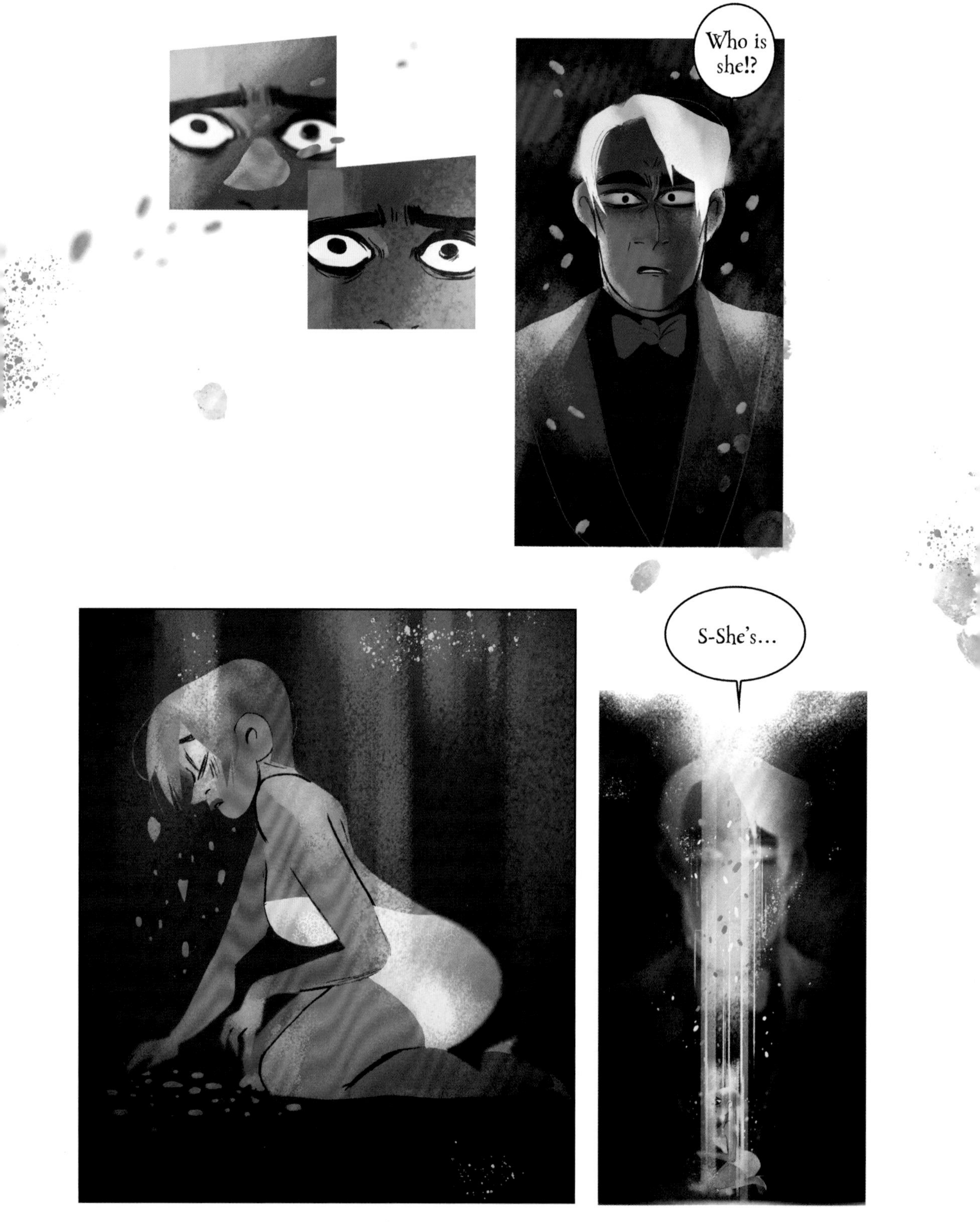
Who is she!?
S-She's...

She's
beautiful.

EPISODE 03: WHO IS SHE? (PART 2)

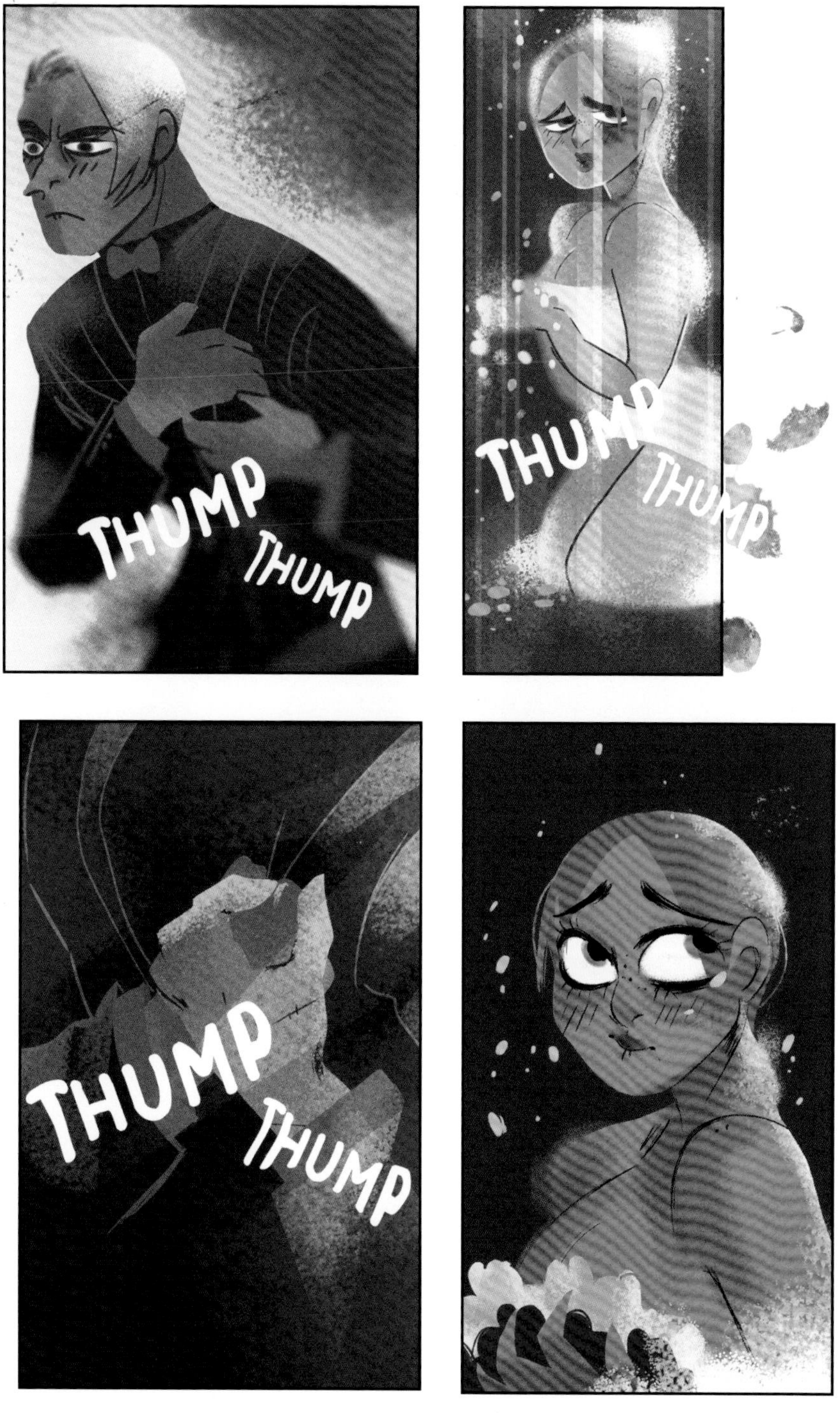
THUMP
THUMP
THUMP
THUMP
THUMP
THUMP

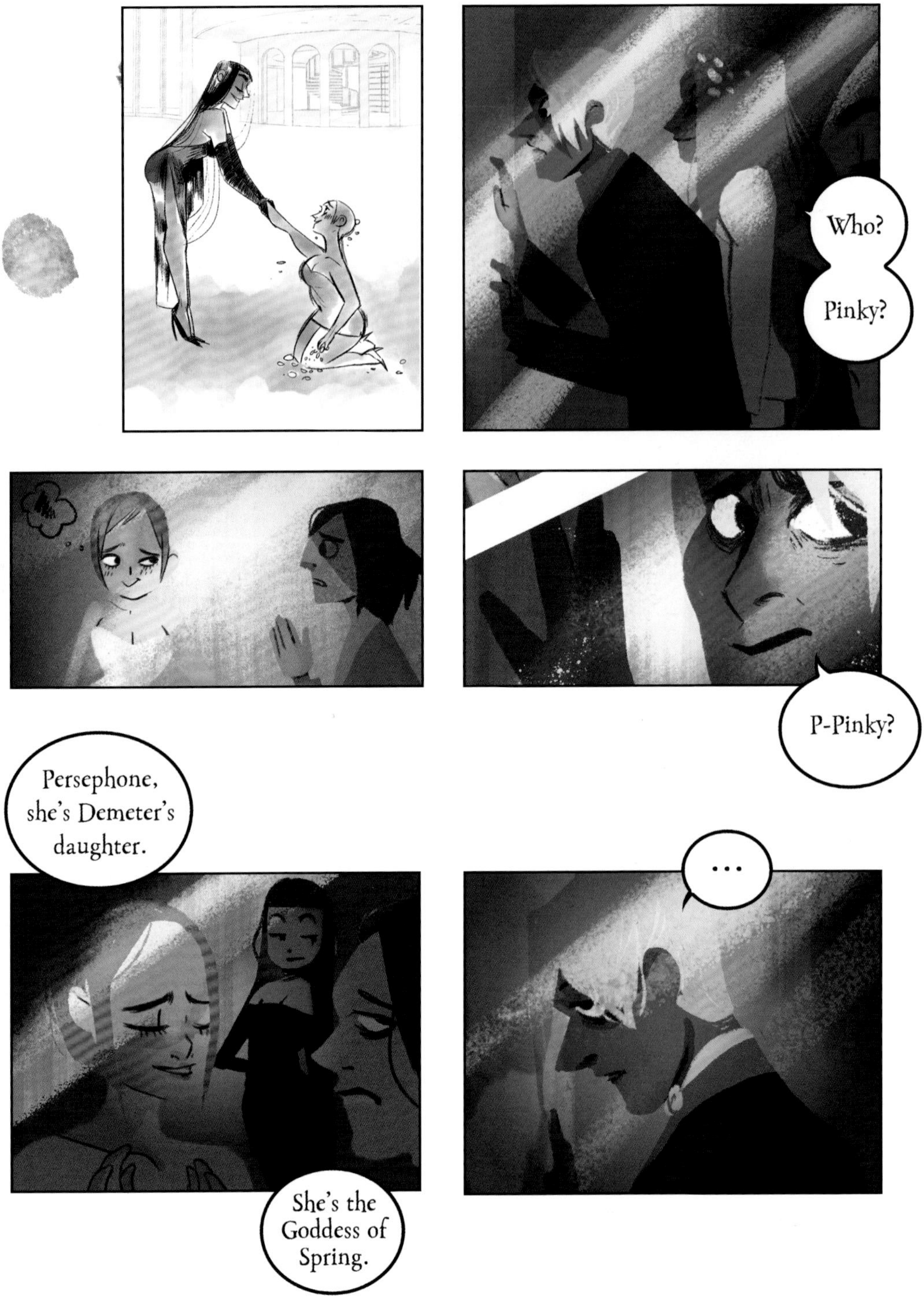
Who?
Pinky?
P-Pinky?
Persephone, she's Demeter's daughter.
She's the Goddess of Spring.
...

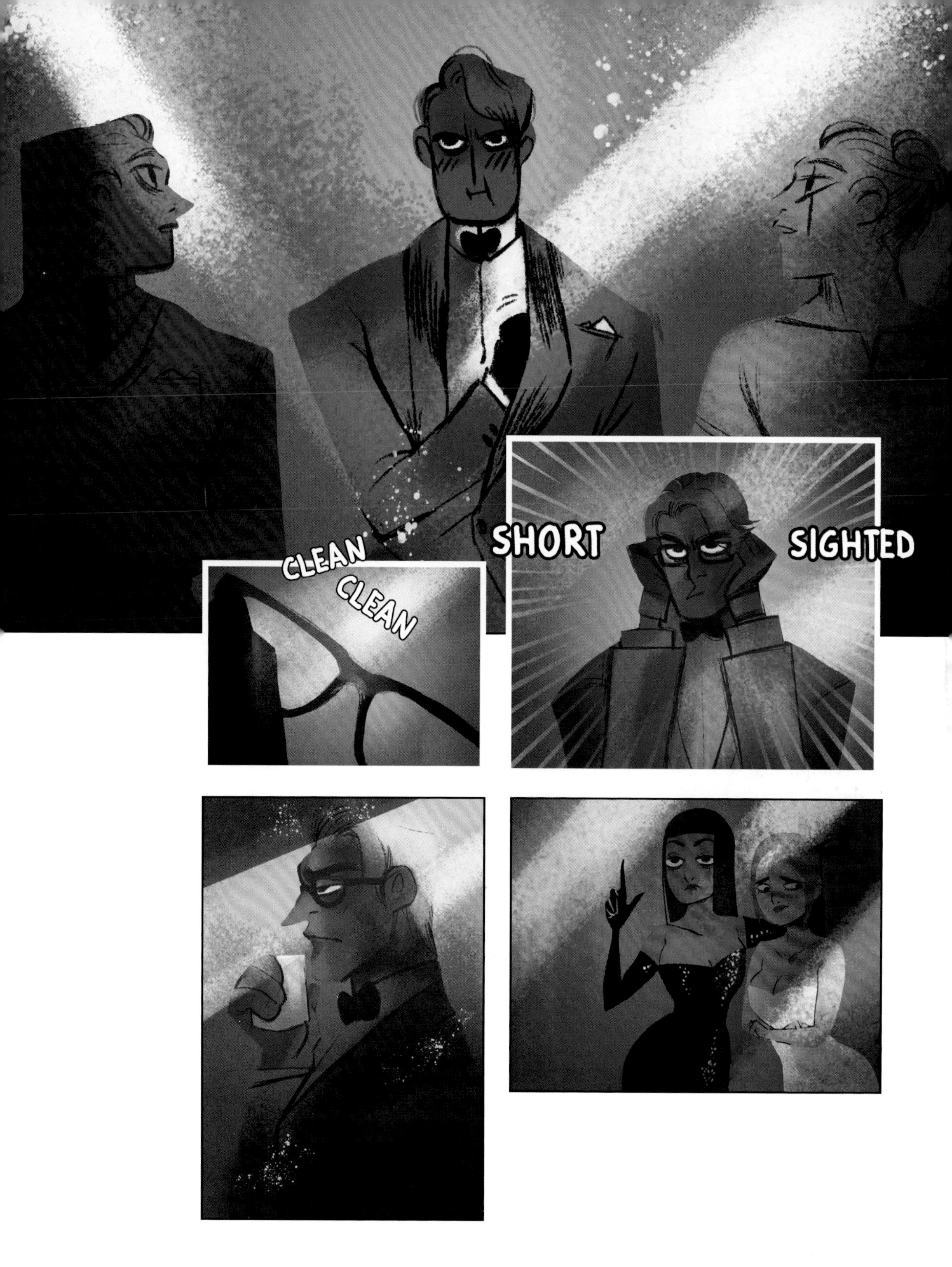
CLEAN
CLEAN
SHORT
SIGHTED

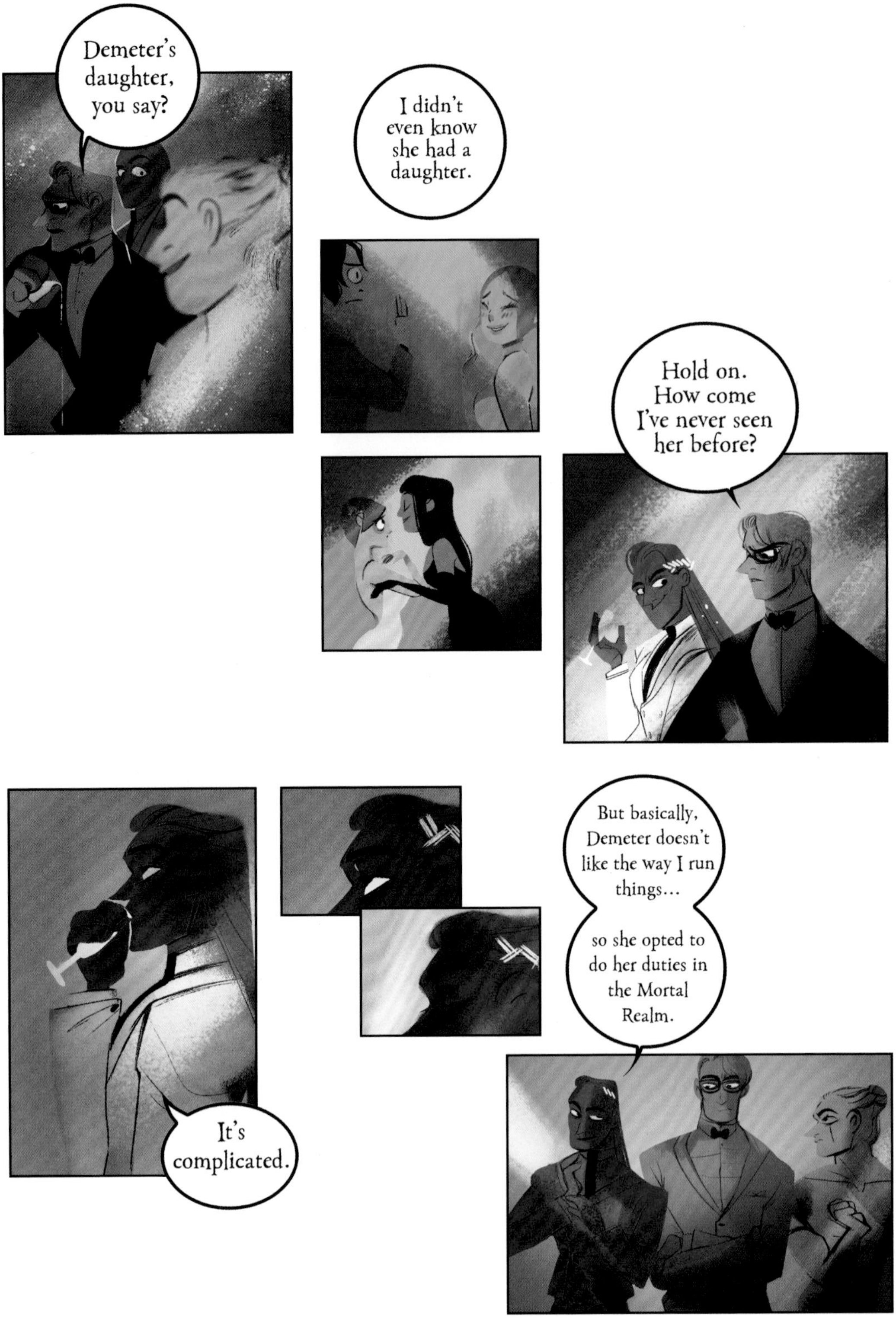
Demeter's daughter, you say?
I didn't even know she had a daughter.
Hold on. How come I've never seen her before?
It's complicated.
But basically, Demeter doesn't like the way I run things...
so she opted to do her duties in the Mortal Realm.

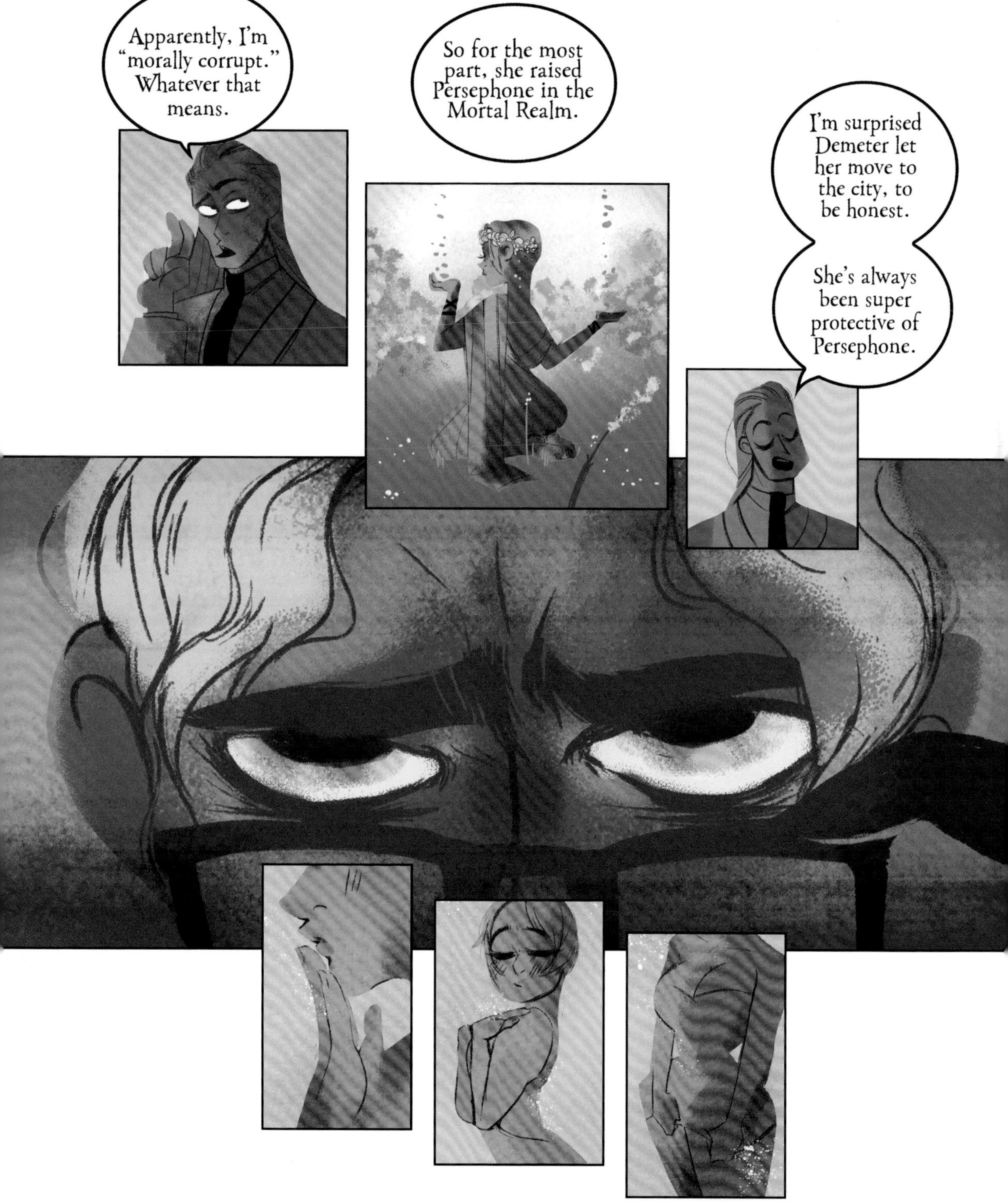
Apparently, I'm "morally corrupt." Whatever that means.
So for the most part, she raised Persephone in the Mortal Realm.
I'm surprised Demeter let her move to the city, to be honest.
She's always been super protective of Persephone.

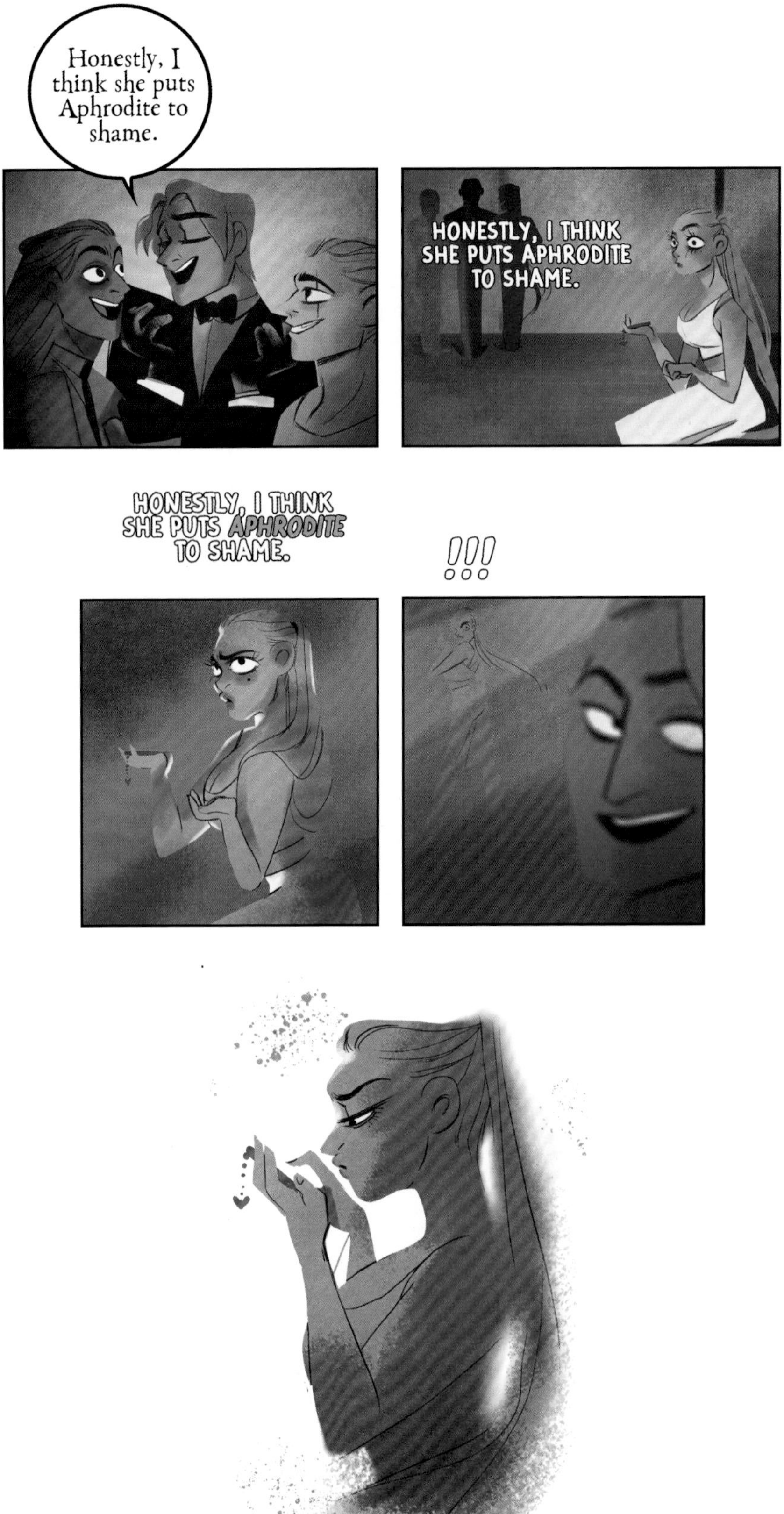
Honestly, I think she puts Aphrodite to shame.
HONESTLY, I THINK SHE PUTS APHRODITE TO SHAME.
HONESTLY, I THINK SHE PUTS APHRODITE TO SHAME.
!!!

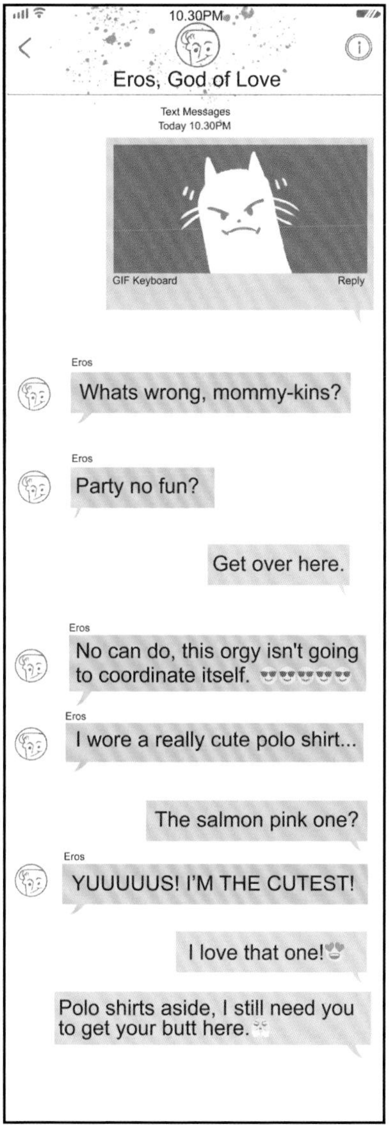
10.30PM
Eros, God of Love
Text Messages
Today 10.30PM
GIF Keyboard
Reply
Eros
Whats wrong, mommy-kins?
Eros
Party no fun?
Get over here.
Eros
No can do, this orgy isn't going to coordinate itself. 😎😎😎😎😎
Eros
I wore a really cute polo shirt...
The salmon pink one?
Eros
YUUUUUS! I'M THE CUTEST!
I love that one!😍
Polo shirts aside, I still need you to get your butt here.

EPISODE 04: WHO IS SHE? (PART 3)

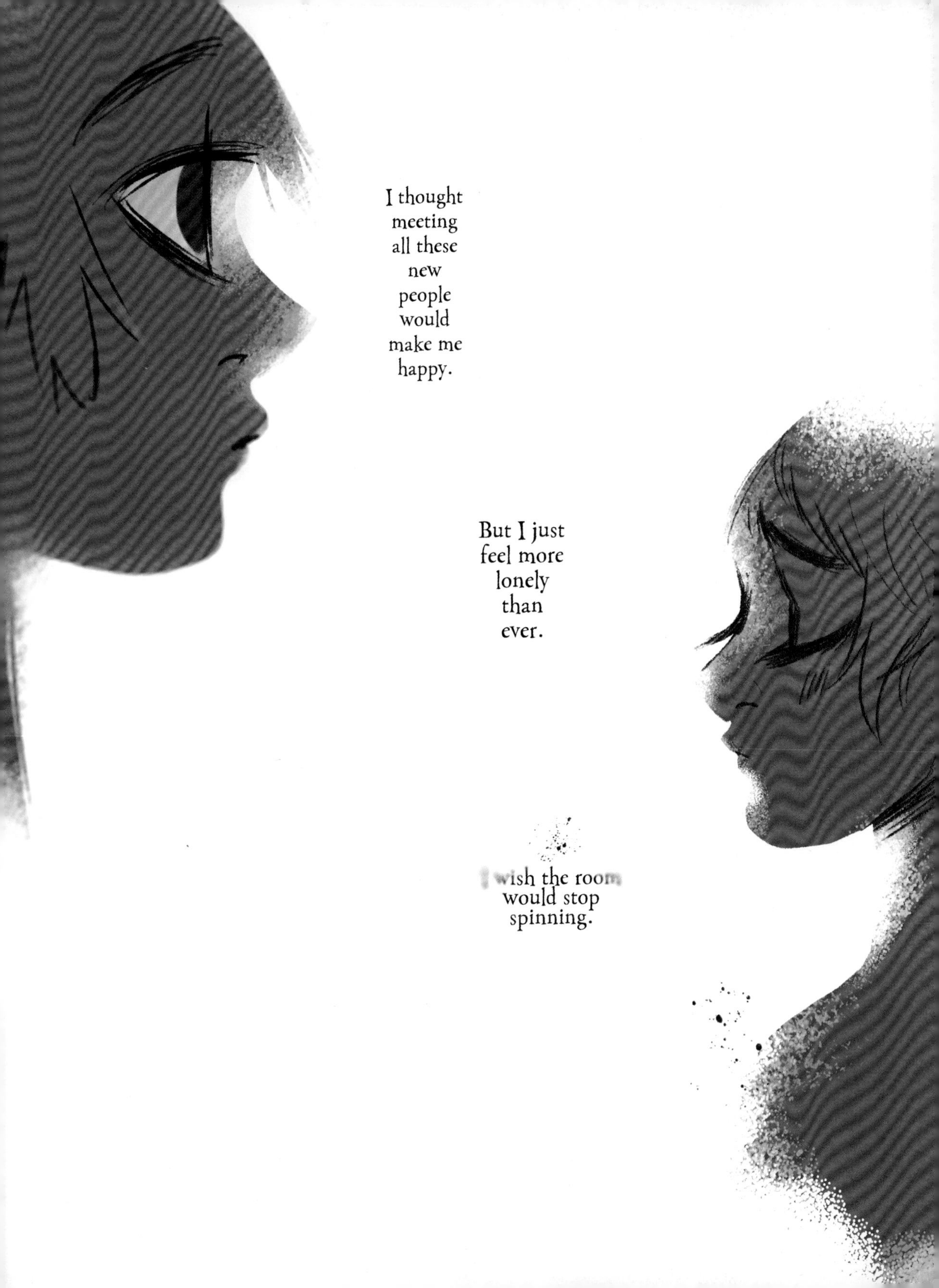
I thought meeting all these new people would make me happy.
But I just feel more lonely than ever.
I wish the room would stop spinning.

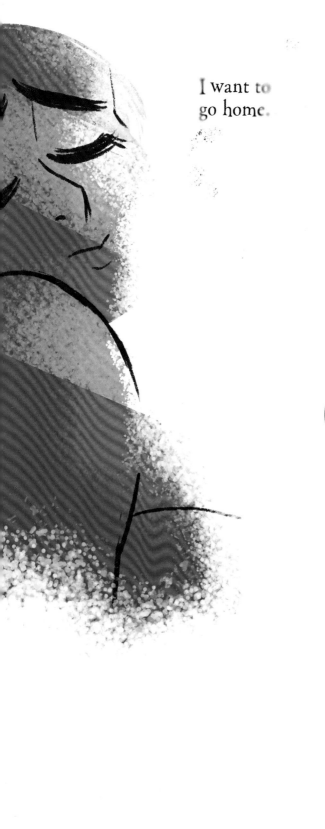

I want to
go home.

I'm very
sorry about
all of this.

But as far as I'm
concerned…

...Aphrodite's word is law.

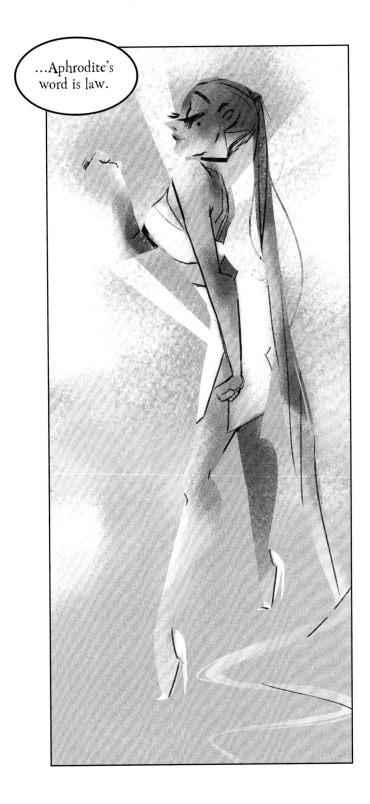

EPISODE 05: SWEET REVENGE

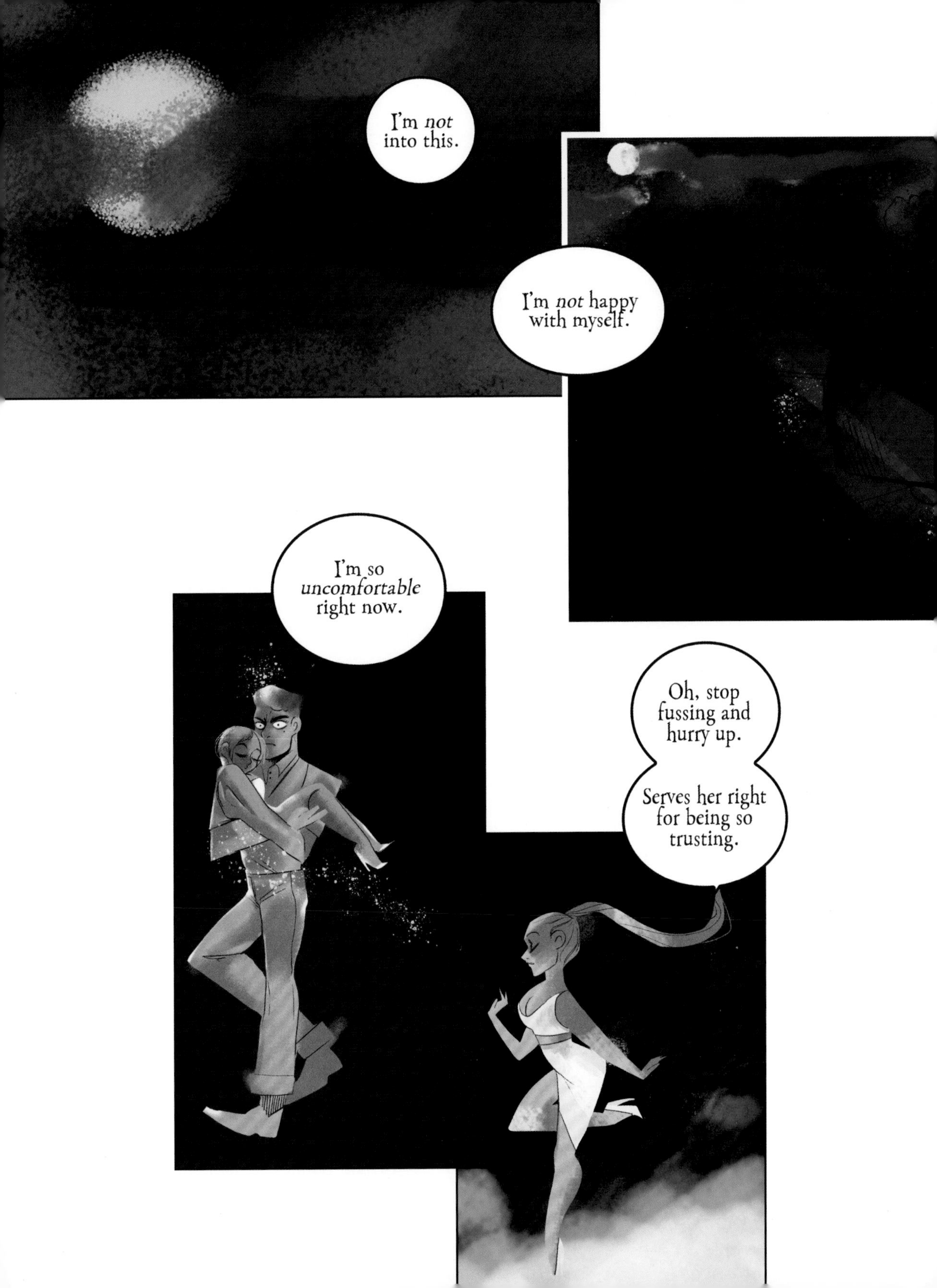
I'm *not* into this.
I'm *not* happy with myself.
I'm so *uncomfortable* right now.
Oh, stop fussing and hurry up.
Serves her right for being so trusting.

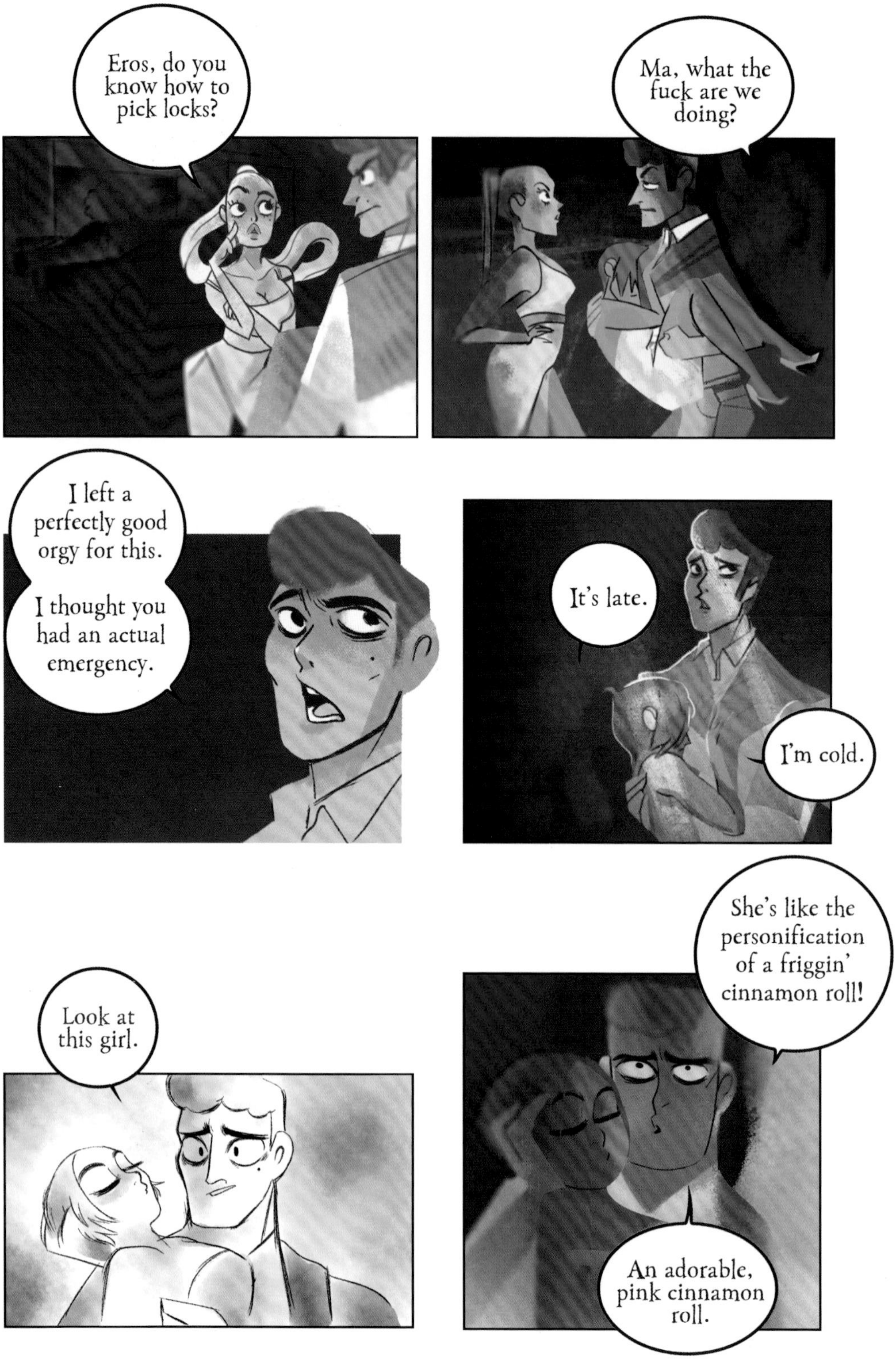
Eros, do you know how to pick locks?
Ma, what the fuck are we doing?
I left a perfectly good orgy for this.
I thought you had an actual emergency.
It's late.
I'm cold.
Look at this girl.
She's like the personification of a friggin' cinnamon roll!
An adorable, pink cinnamon roll.

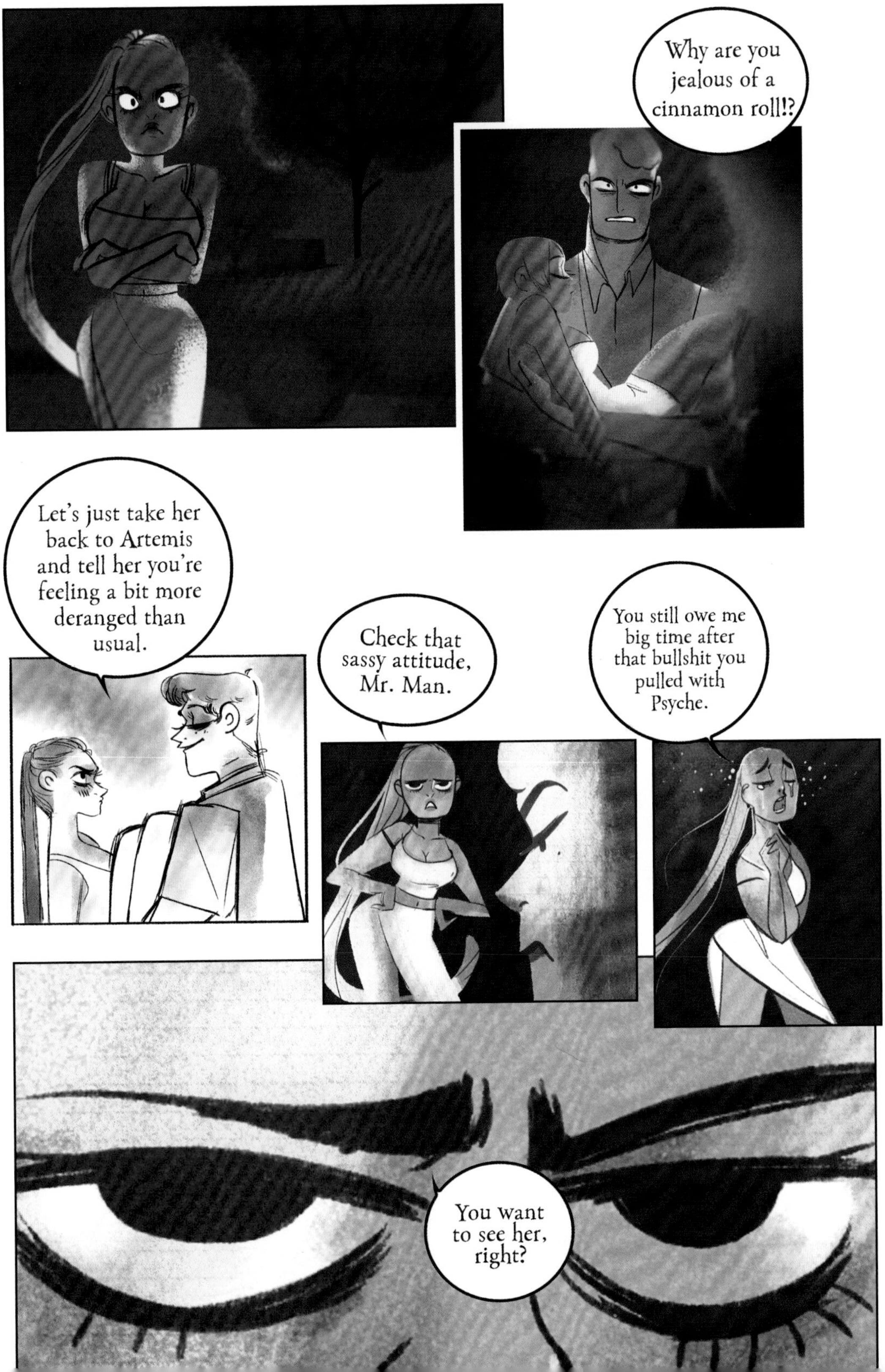
Why are you jealous of a cinnamon roll!?
Let's just take her back to Artemis and tell her you're feeling a bit more deranged than usual.
Check that sassy attitude, Mr. Man.
You still owe me big time after that bullshit you pulled with Psyche.
You want to see her, right?

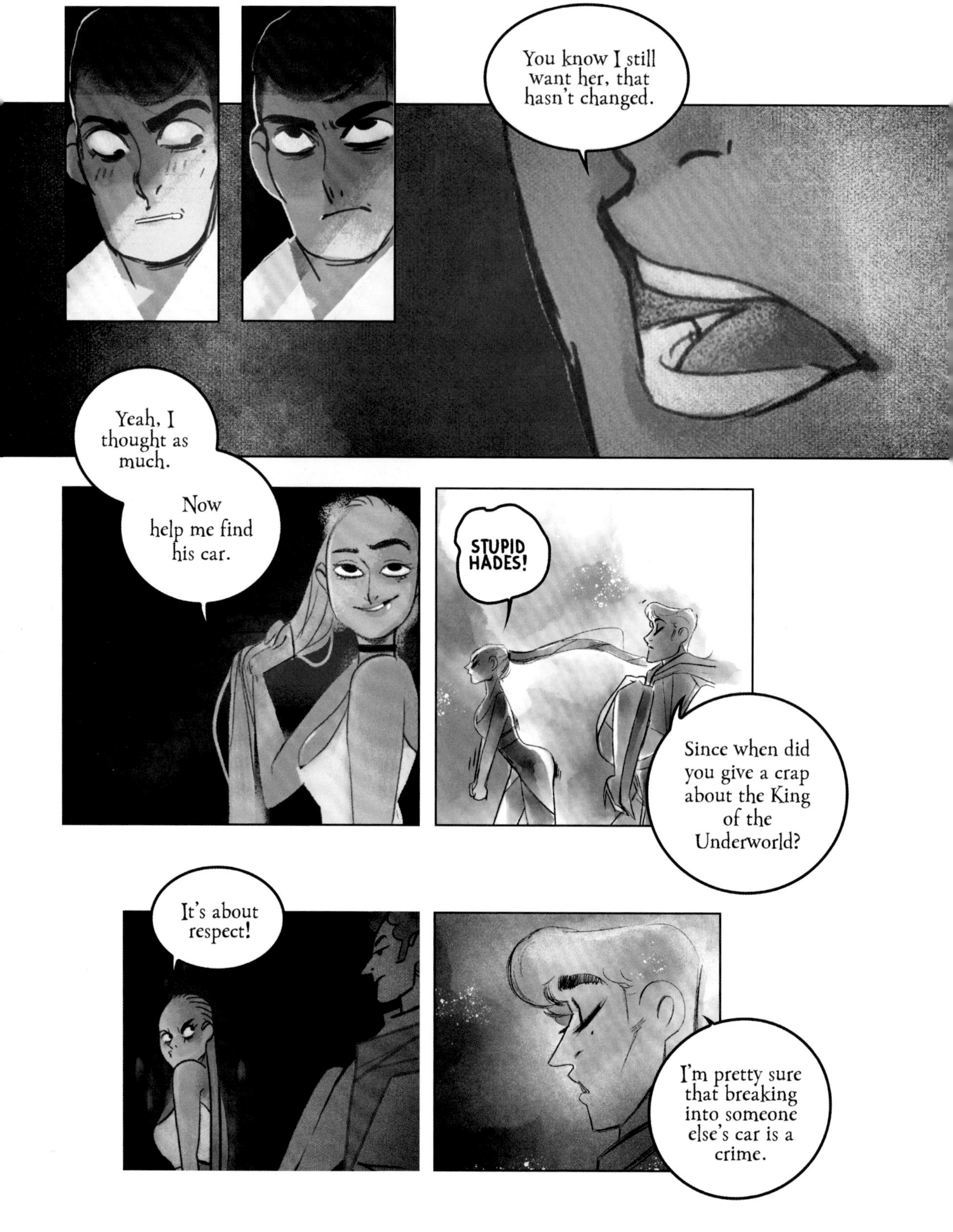
You know I still want her, that hasn't changed.
Yeah, I thought as much.
Now help me find his car.
STUPID HADES!
Since when did you give a crap about the King of the Underworld?
It's about respect!
I'm pretty sure that breaking into someone else's car is a crime.

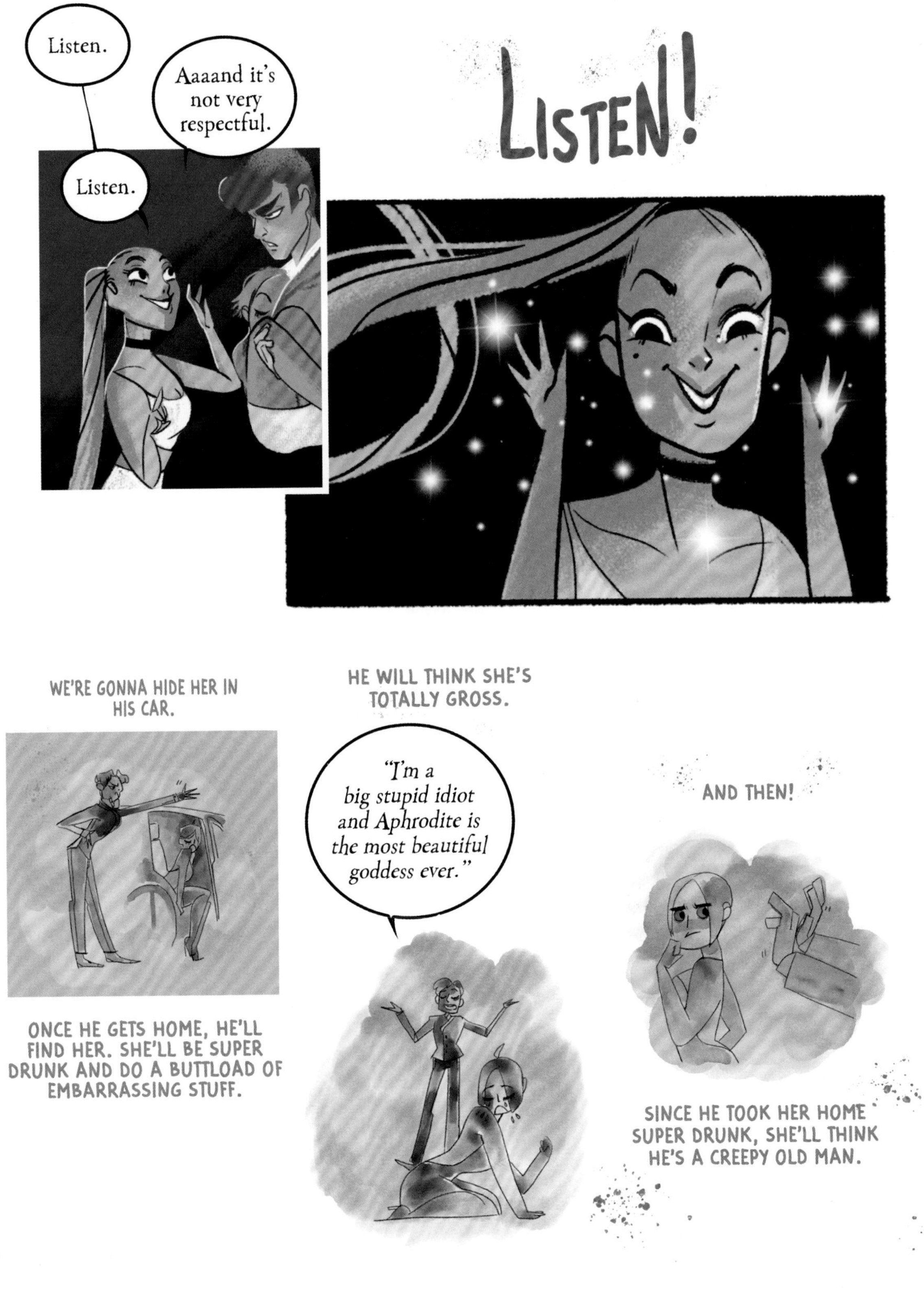

Listen.
Aaaand it's not very respectful.
Listen.
LISTEN!
WE'RE GONNA HIDE HER IN HIS CAR.
ONCE HE GETS HOME, HE'LL FIND HER. SHE'LL BE SUPER DRUNK AND DO A BUTTLOAD OF EMBARRASSING STUFF.
HE WILL THINK SHE'S TOTALLY GROSS.
"I'm a big stupid idiot and Aphrodite is the most beautiful goddess ever."
AND THEN!
SINCE HE TOOK HER HOME SUPER DRUNK, SHE'LL THINK HE'S A CREEPY OLD MAN.

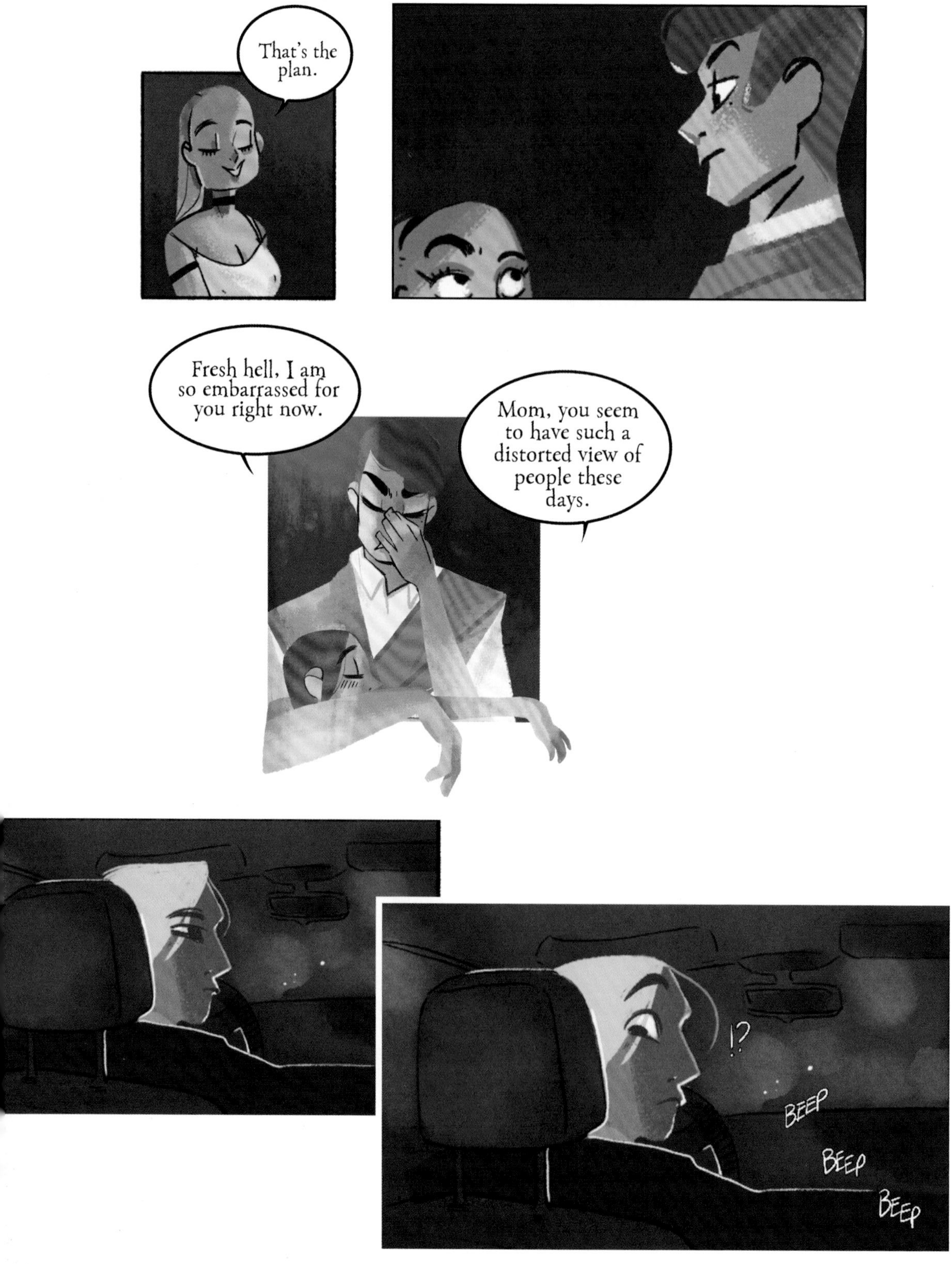
That's the plan.
Fresh hell, I am so embarrassed for you right now.
Mom, you seem to have such a distorted view of people these days.
!?
BEEP
BEEP
BEEP

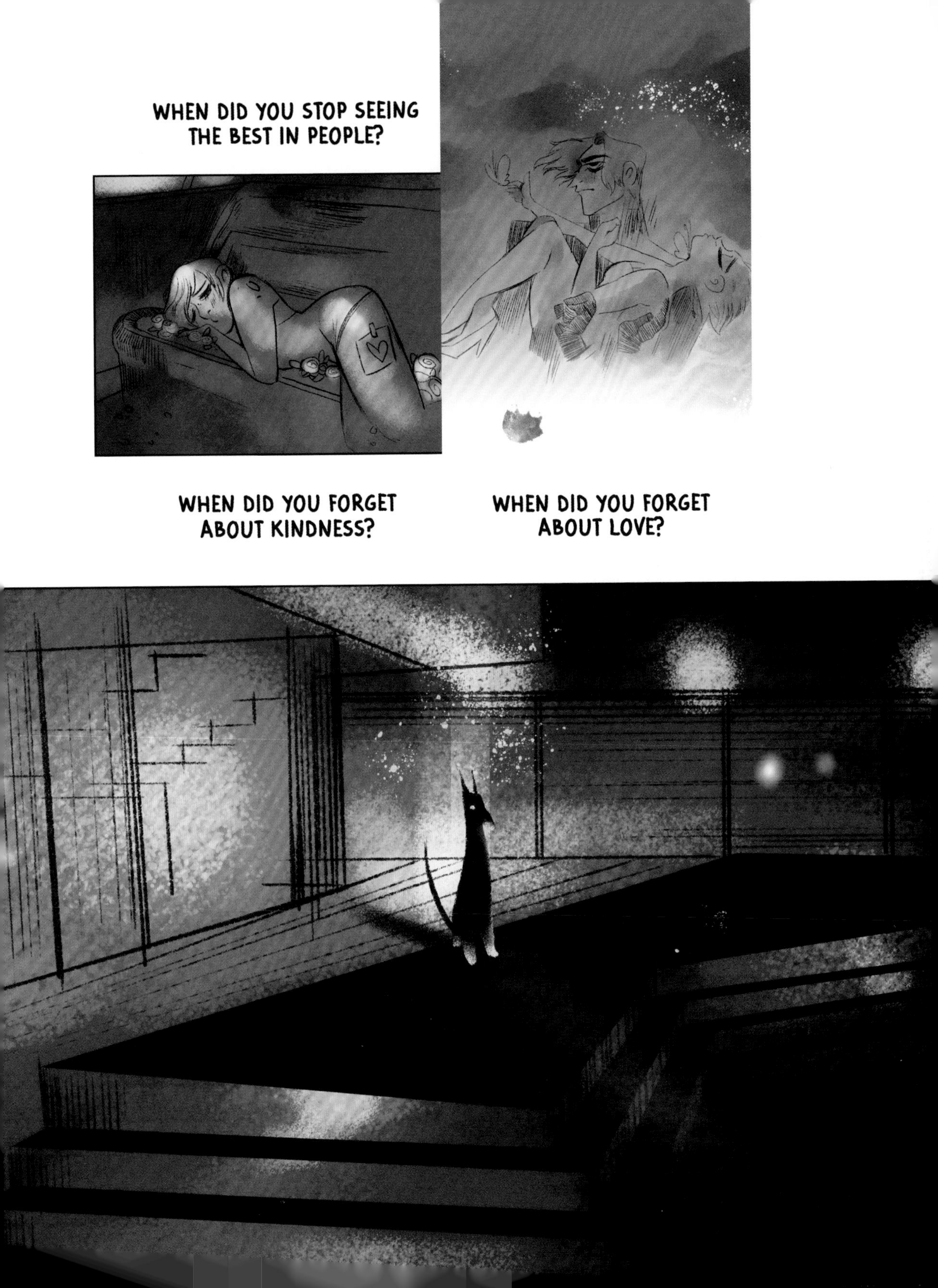
WHEN DID YOU STOP SEEING THE BEST IN PEOPLE?
WHEN DID YOU FORGET ABOUT KINDNESS?
WHEN DID YOU FORGET ABOUT LOVE?

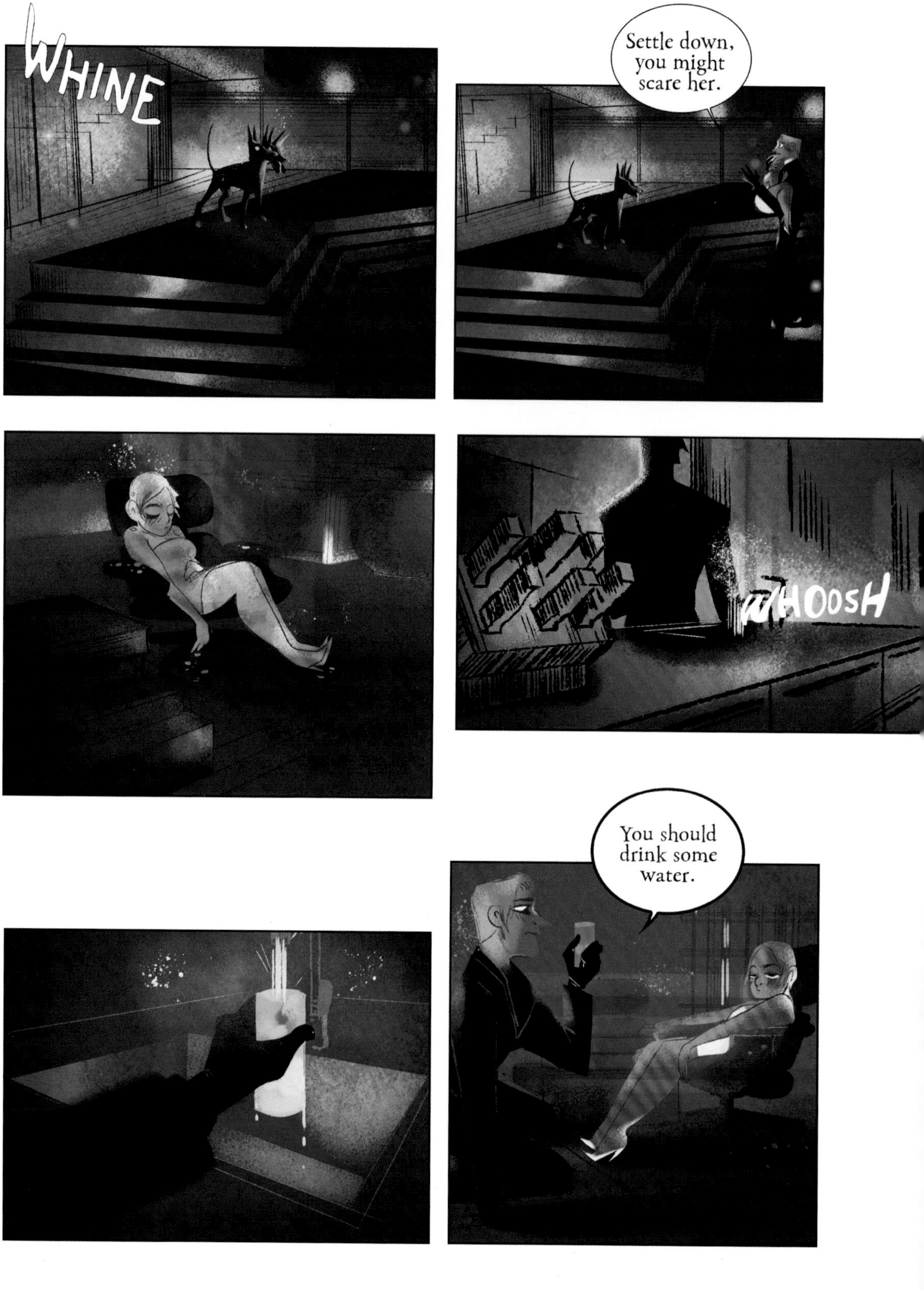
WHINE
Settle down, you might scare her.
WHOOSH
You should drink some water.

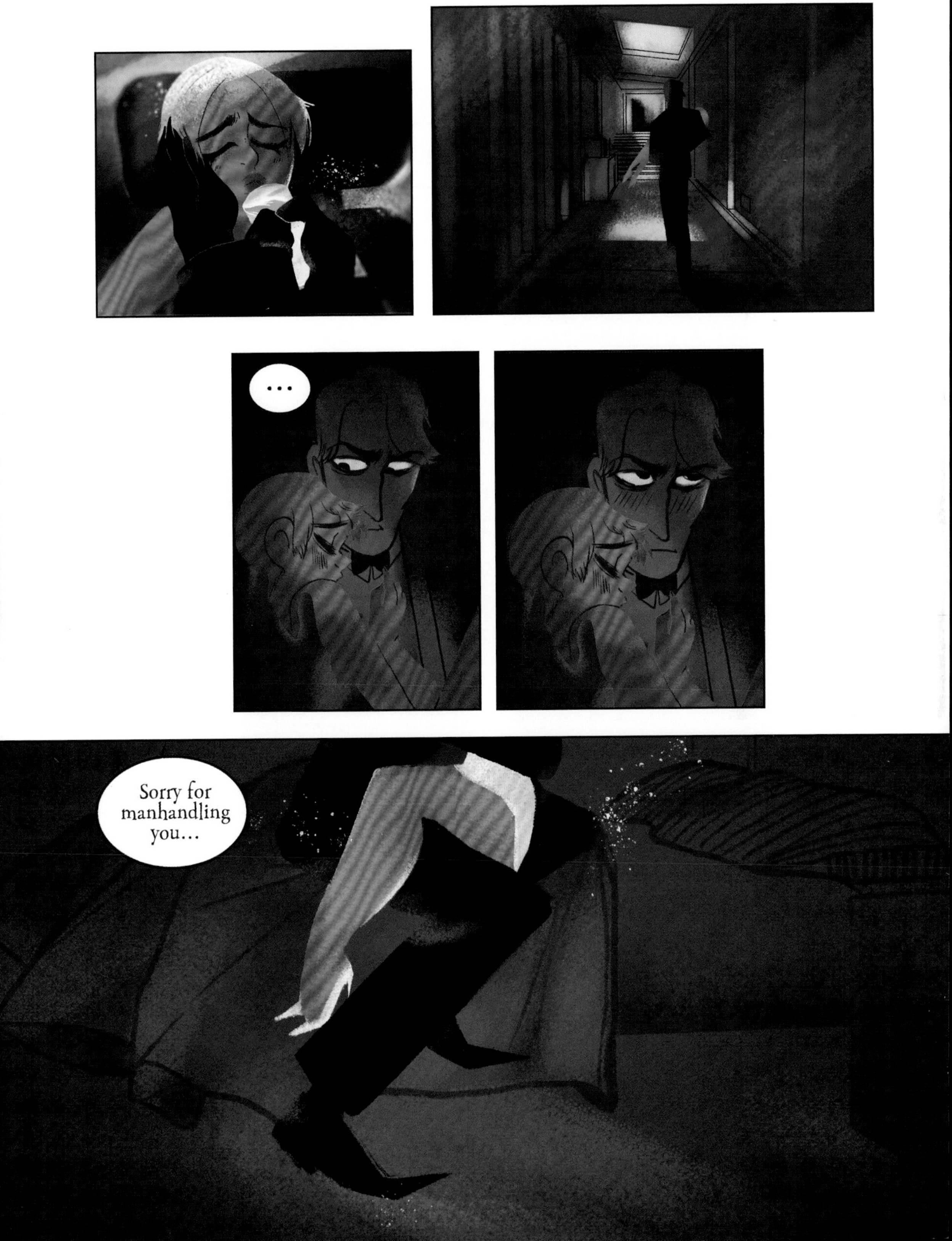
...
Sorry for manhandling you...

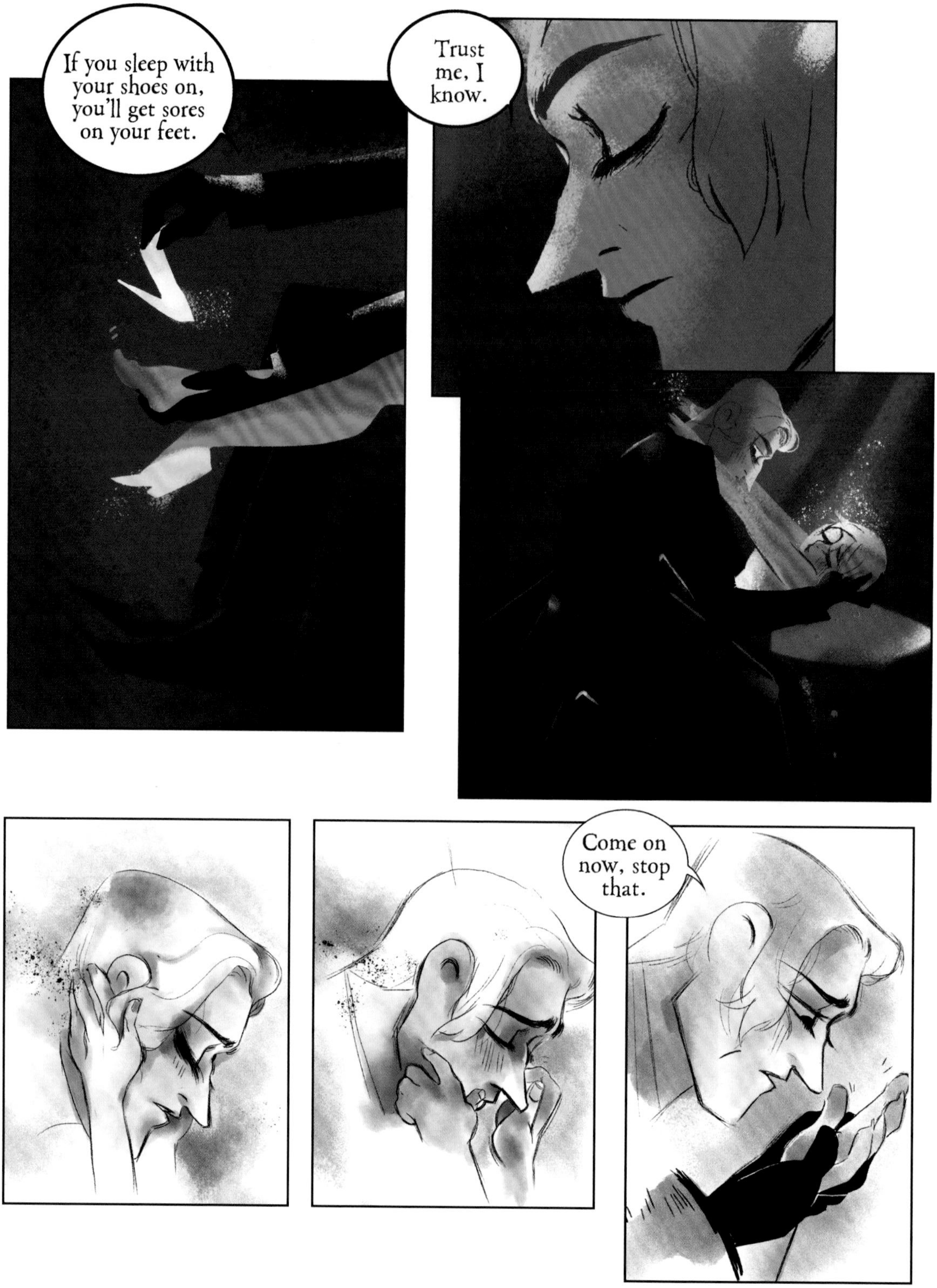
If you sleep with your shoes on, you'll get sores on your feet.
Trust me, I know.
Come on now, stop that.

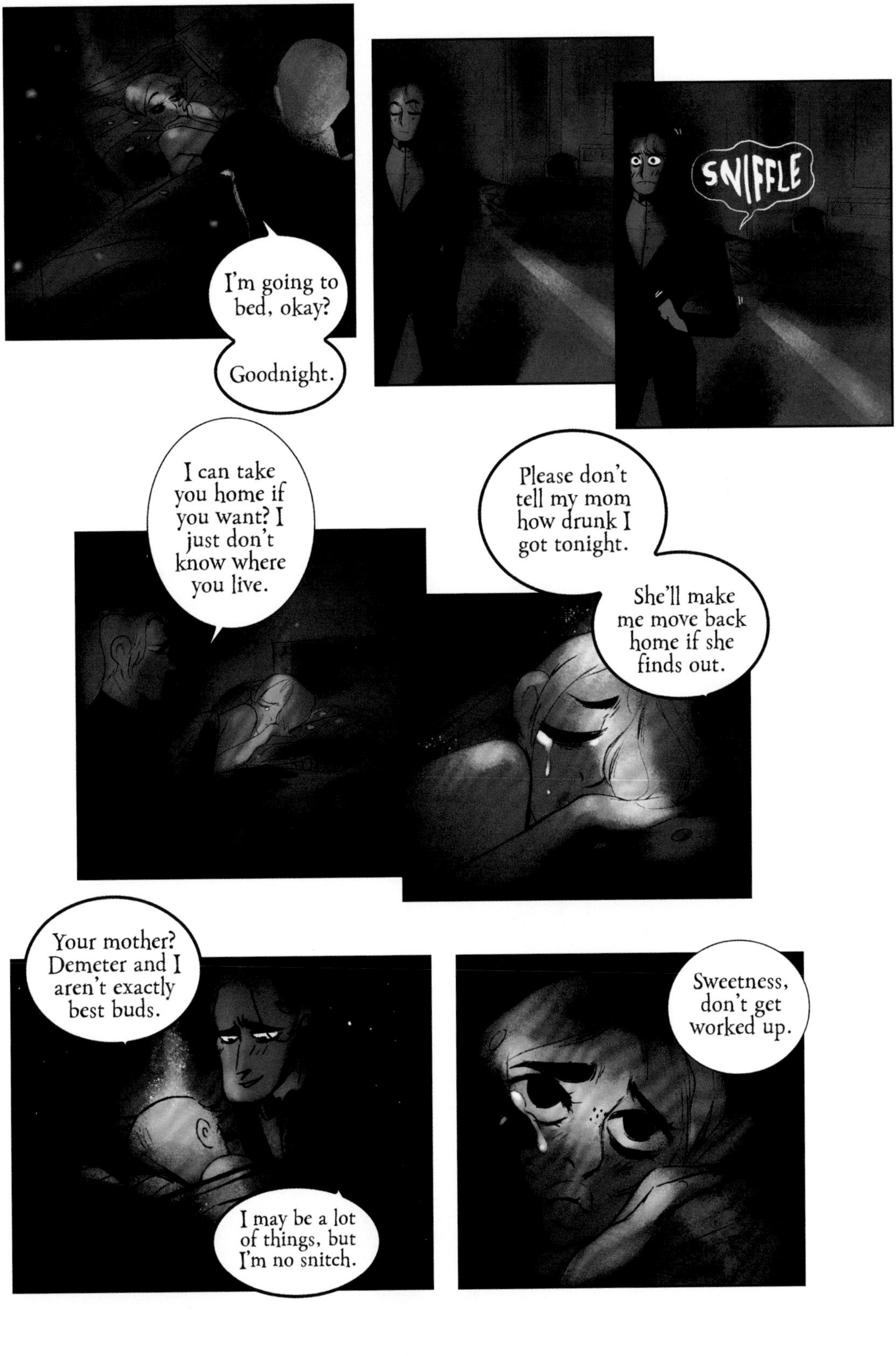
I'm going to bed, okay?
Goodnight.
SNIFFLE
I can take you home if you want? I just don't know where you live.
Please don't tell my mom how drunk I got tonight.
She'll make me move back home if she finds out.
Your mother? Demeter and I aren't exactly best buds.
I may be a lot of things, but I'm no snitch.
Sweetness, don't get worked up.

Everything will seem 1000 times better in the morning.

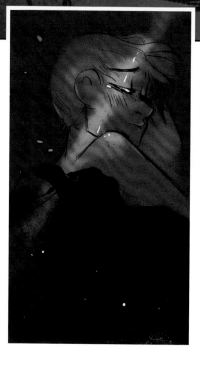

This is all my fault.

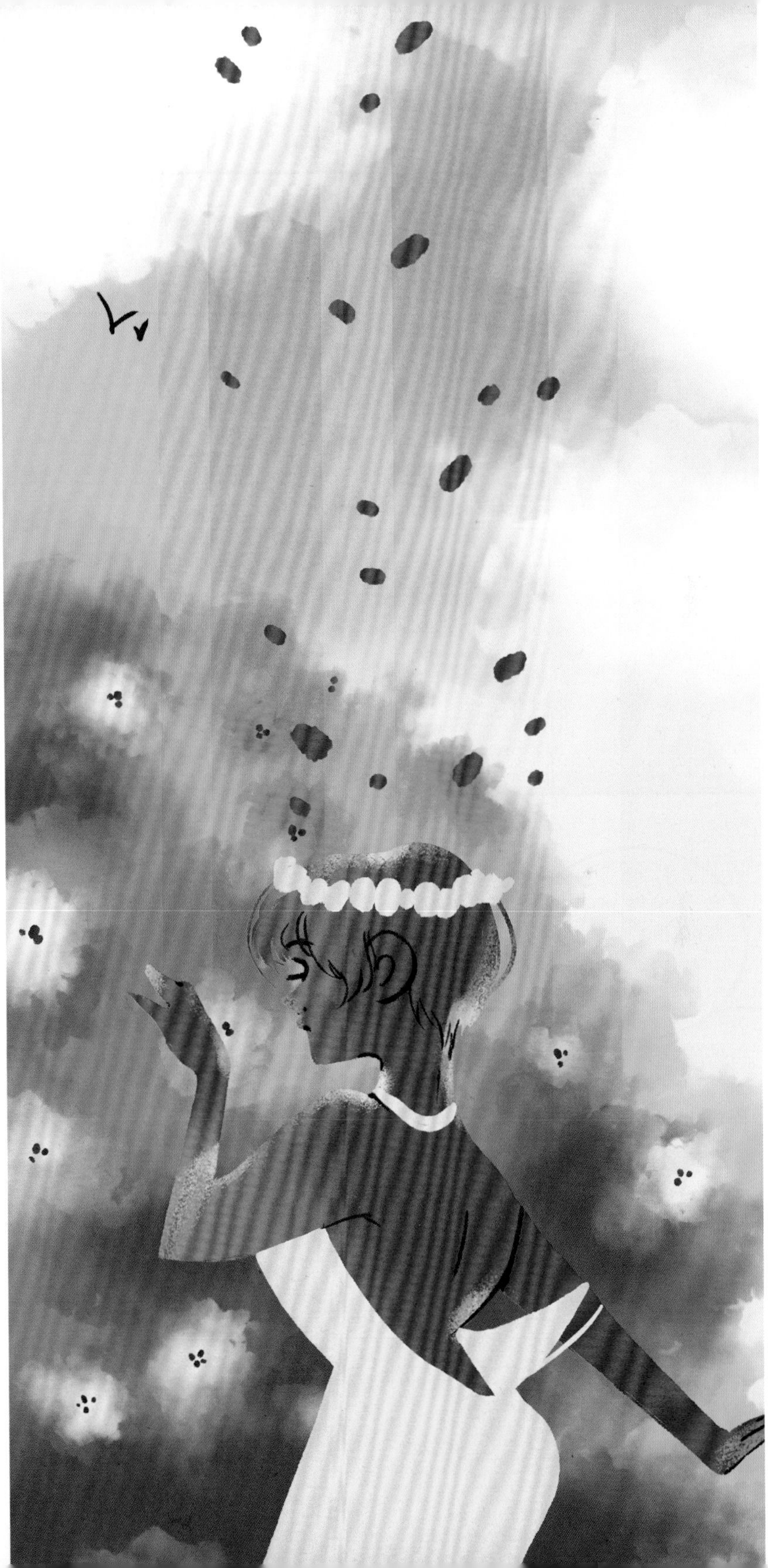

PERSEPHONE

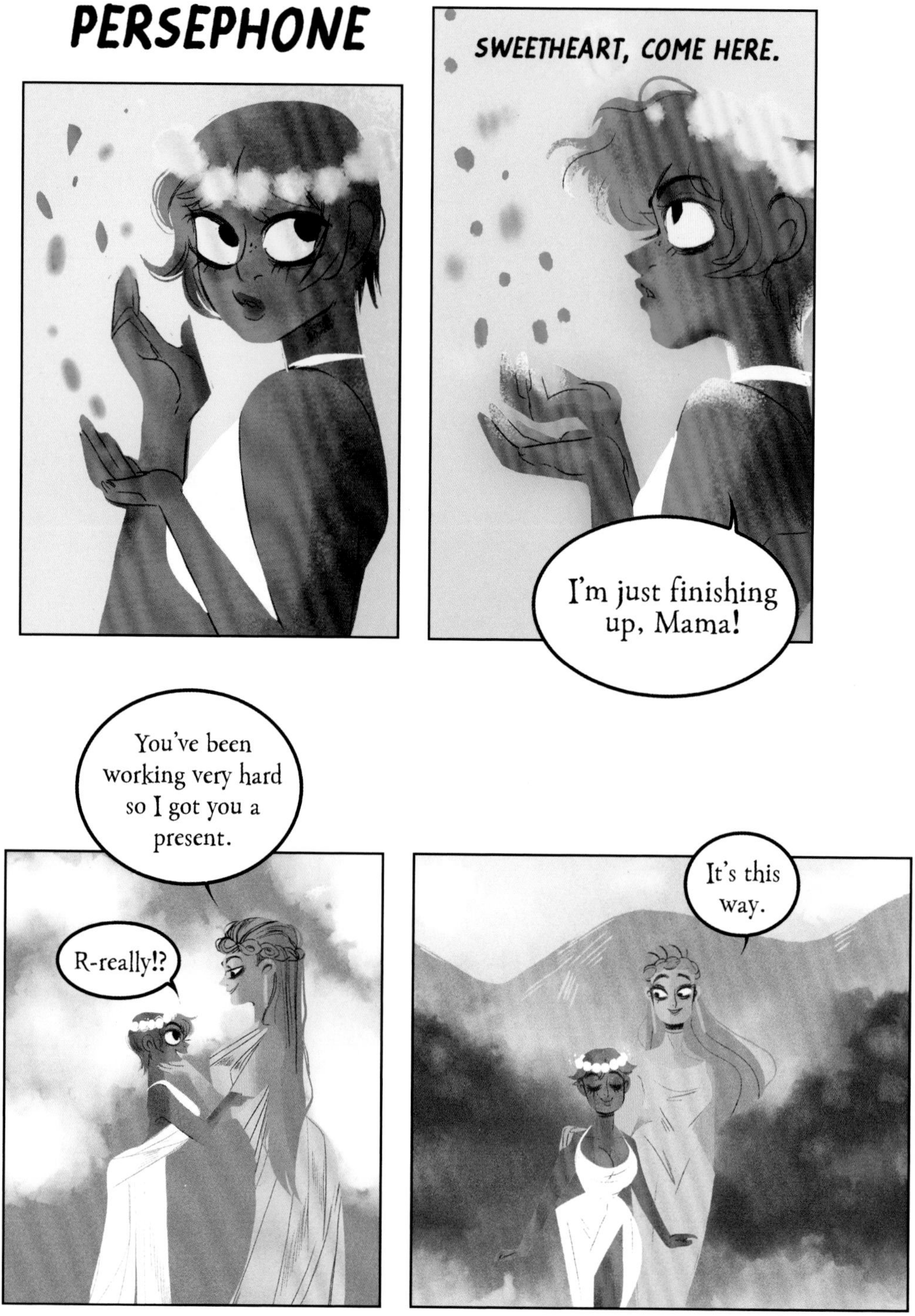
SWEETHEART, COME HERE.
I'm just finishing up, Mama!
You've been working very hard so I got you a present.
R-really!?
It's this way.

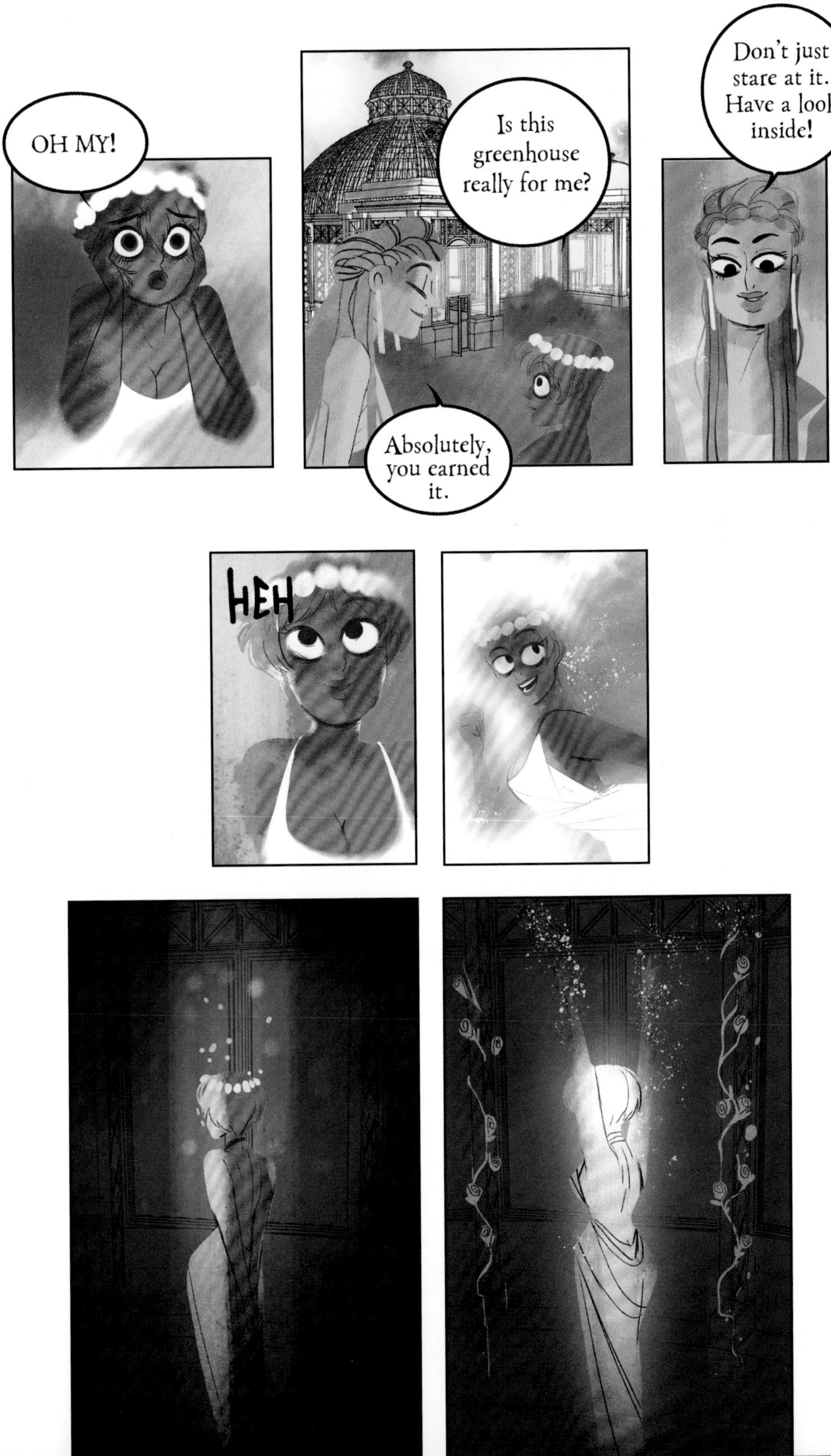
OH MY!
Is this greenhouse really for me?
Absolutely, you earned it.
Don't just stare at it. Have a look inside!
HEH

I think I'm ready to leave now...

But I can't...

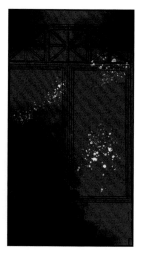

There is no...

THERE IS NO DOOR!

I took the doors away.

MAMA, NO!

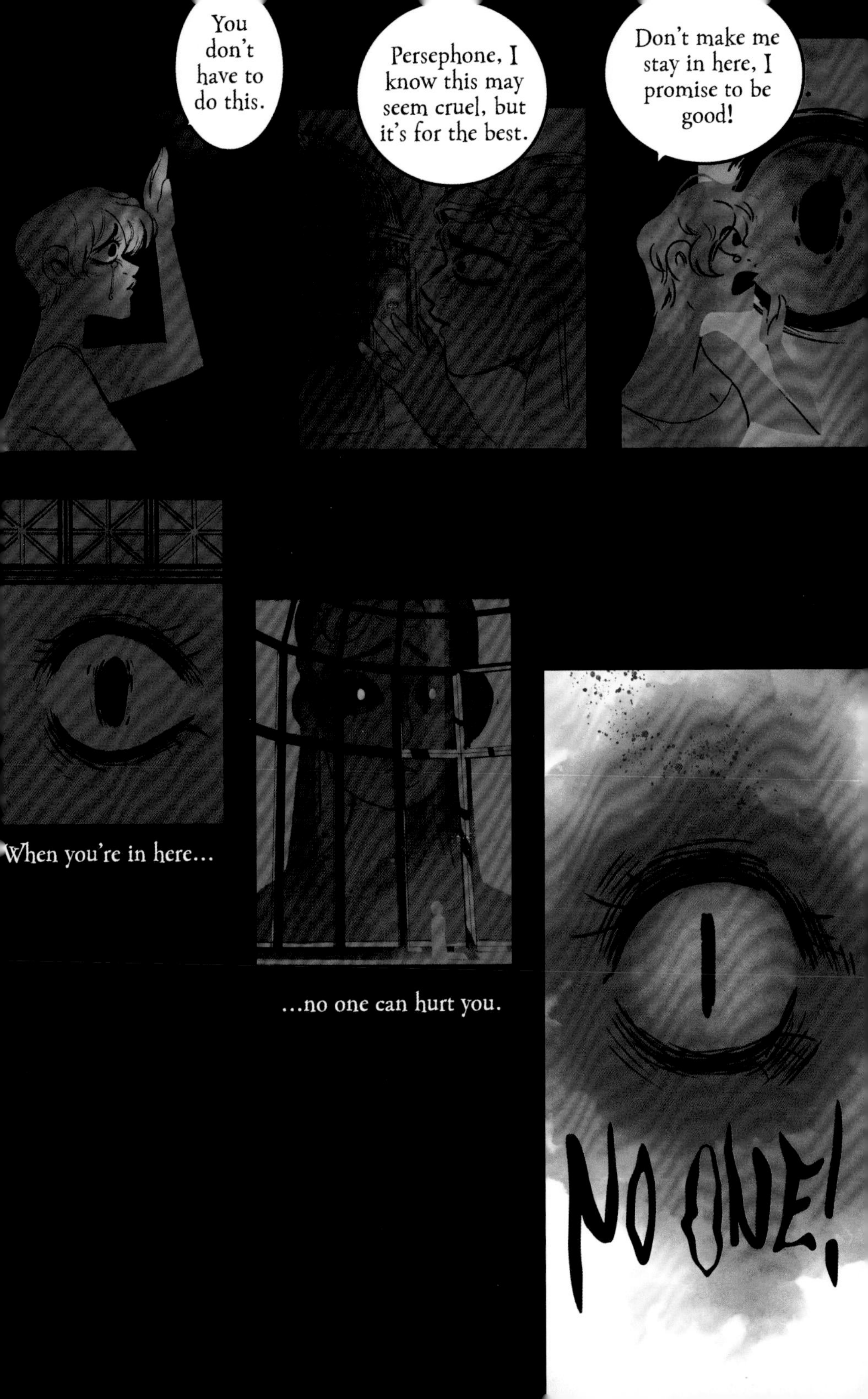
You don't have to do this.
Persephone, I know this may seem cruel, but it's for the best.
Don't make me stay in here, I promise to be good!
When you're in here...
...no one can hurt you.
NO ONE!

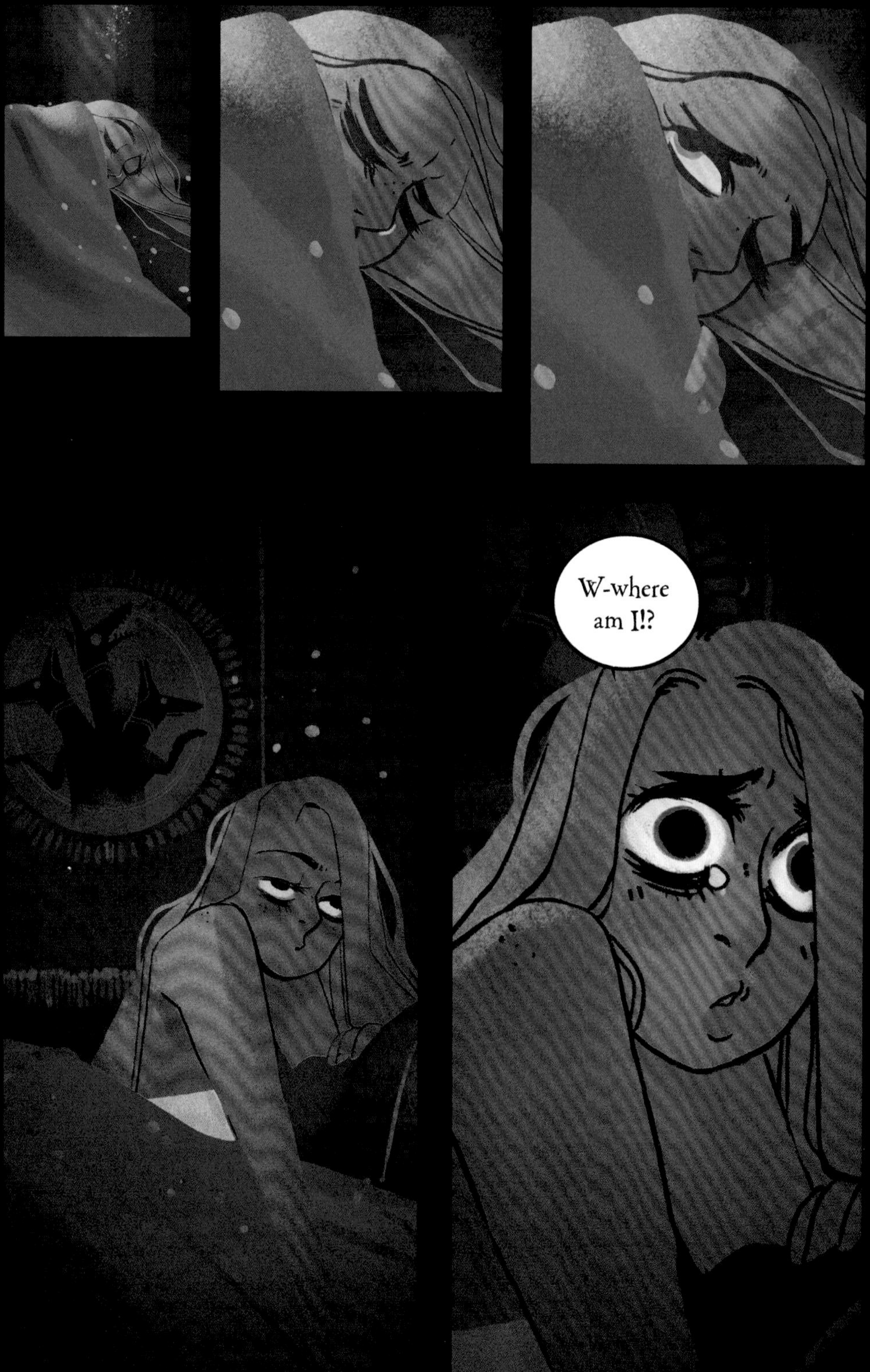
W-where am I!?

EPISODE 06: THE GREENHOUSE

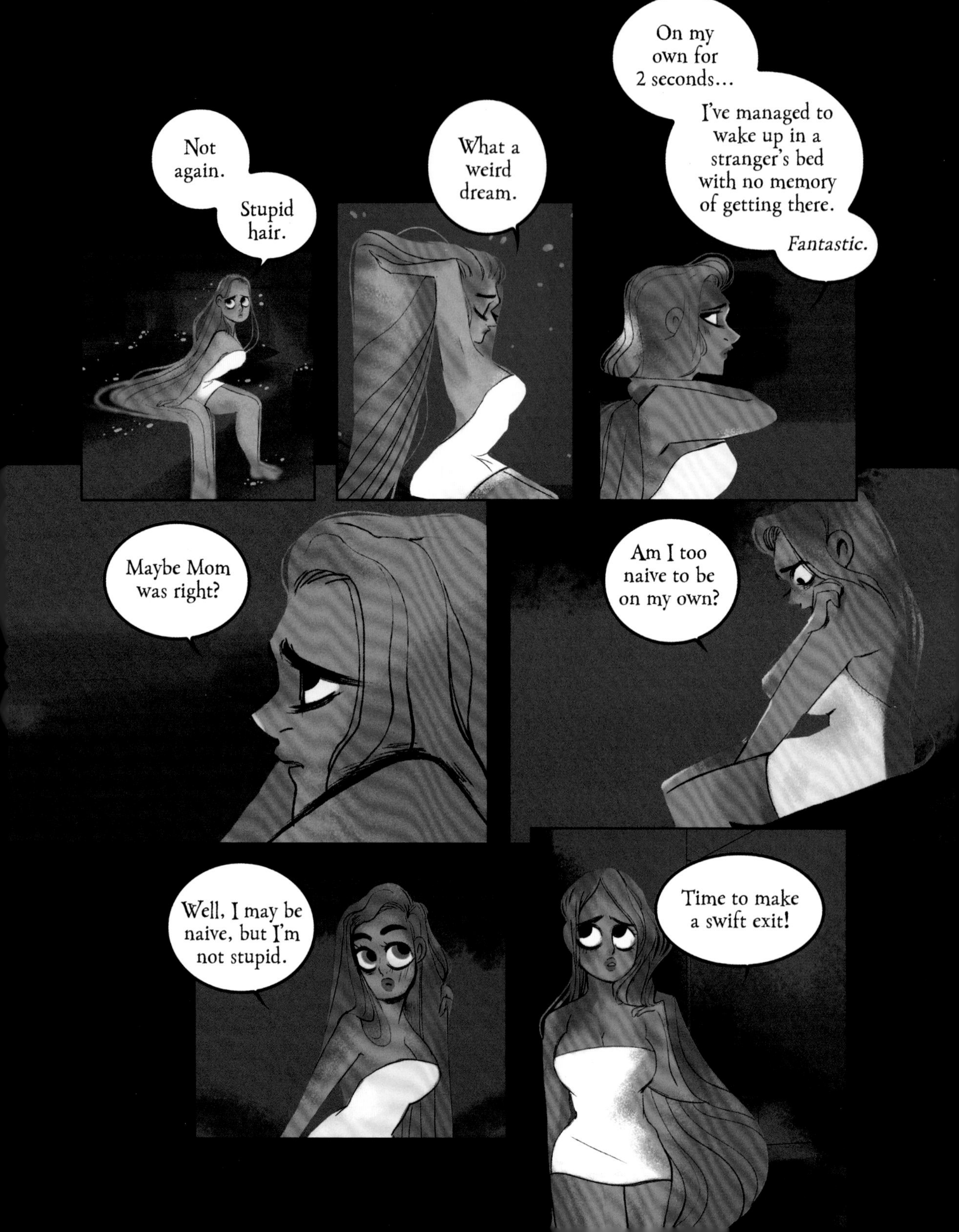
Not again.
Stupid hair.
What a weird dream.
On my own for 2 seconds...
I've managed to wake up in a stranger's bed with no memory of getting there.
Fantastic.
Maybe Mom was right?
Am I too naive to be on my own?
Well, I may be naive, but I'm not stupid.
Time to make a swift exit!

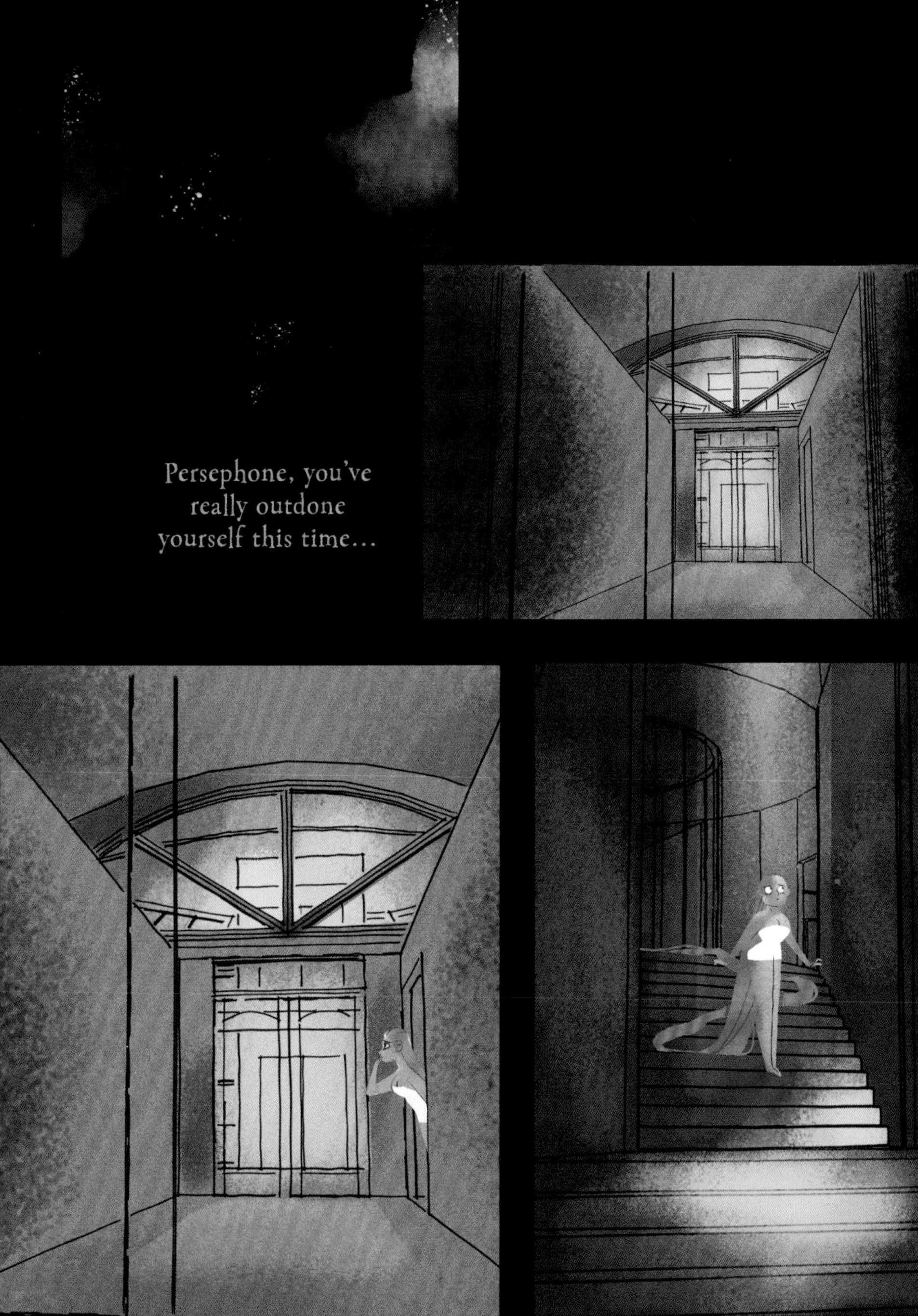
Persephone, you've really outdone yourself this time...

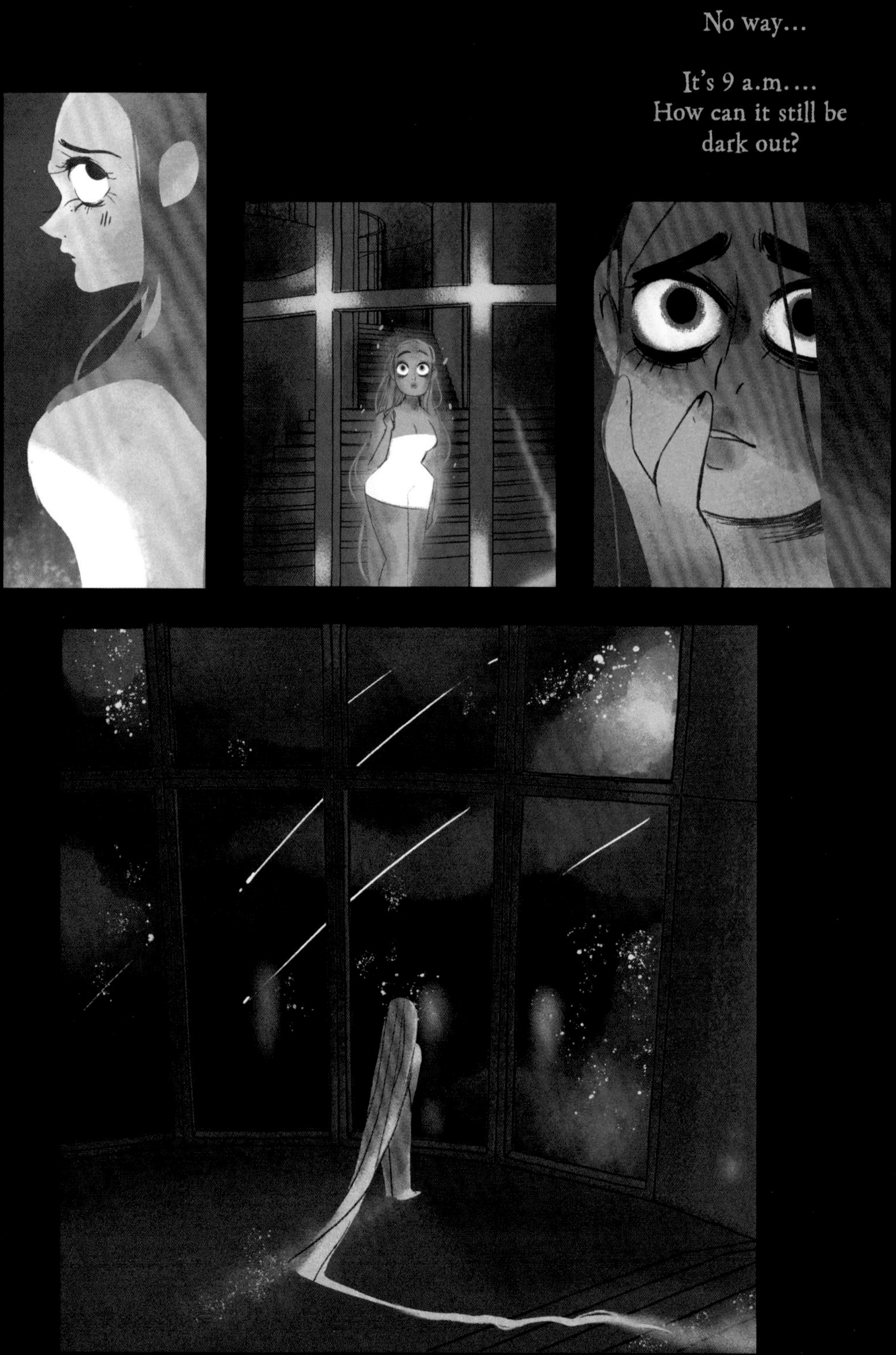
No way...
It's 9 a.m....
How can it still be dark out?

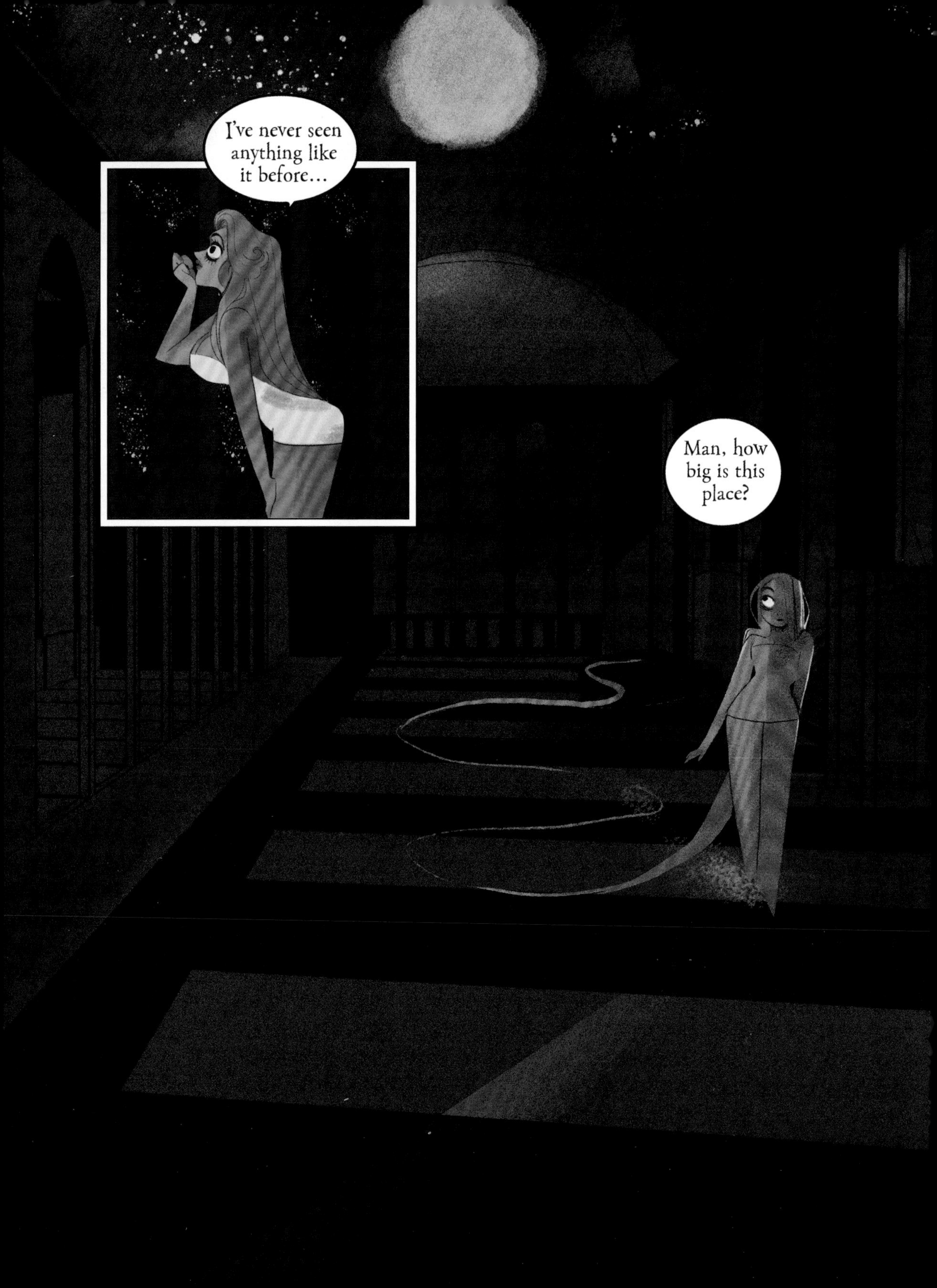
I've never seen anything like it before...
Man, how big is this place?

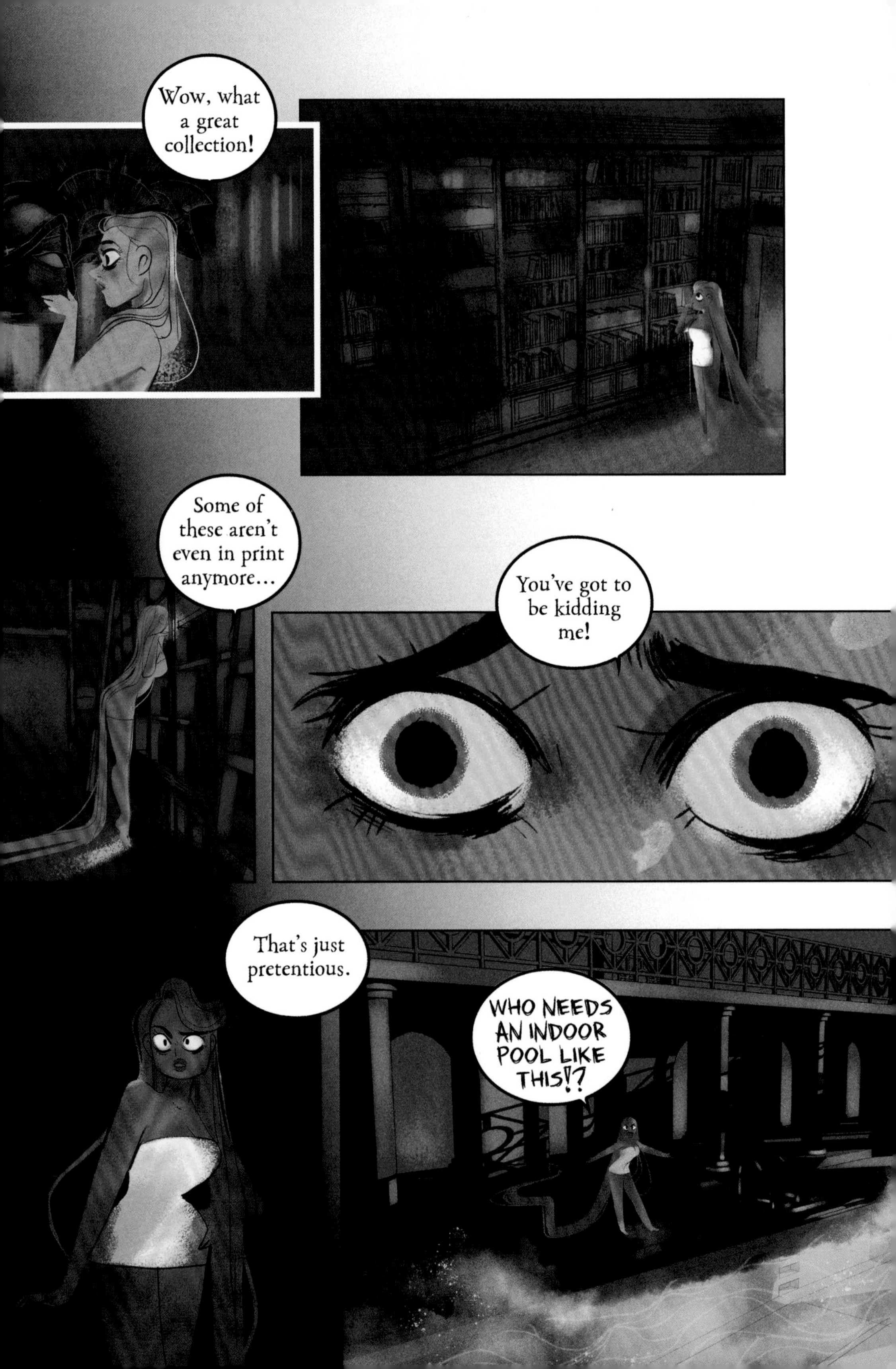
Wow, what a great collection!
Some of these aren't even in print anymore...
You've got to be kidding me!
That's just pretentious.
WHO NEEDS AN INDOOR POOL LIKE THIS!?

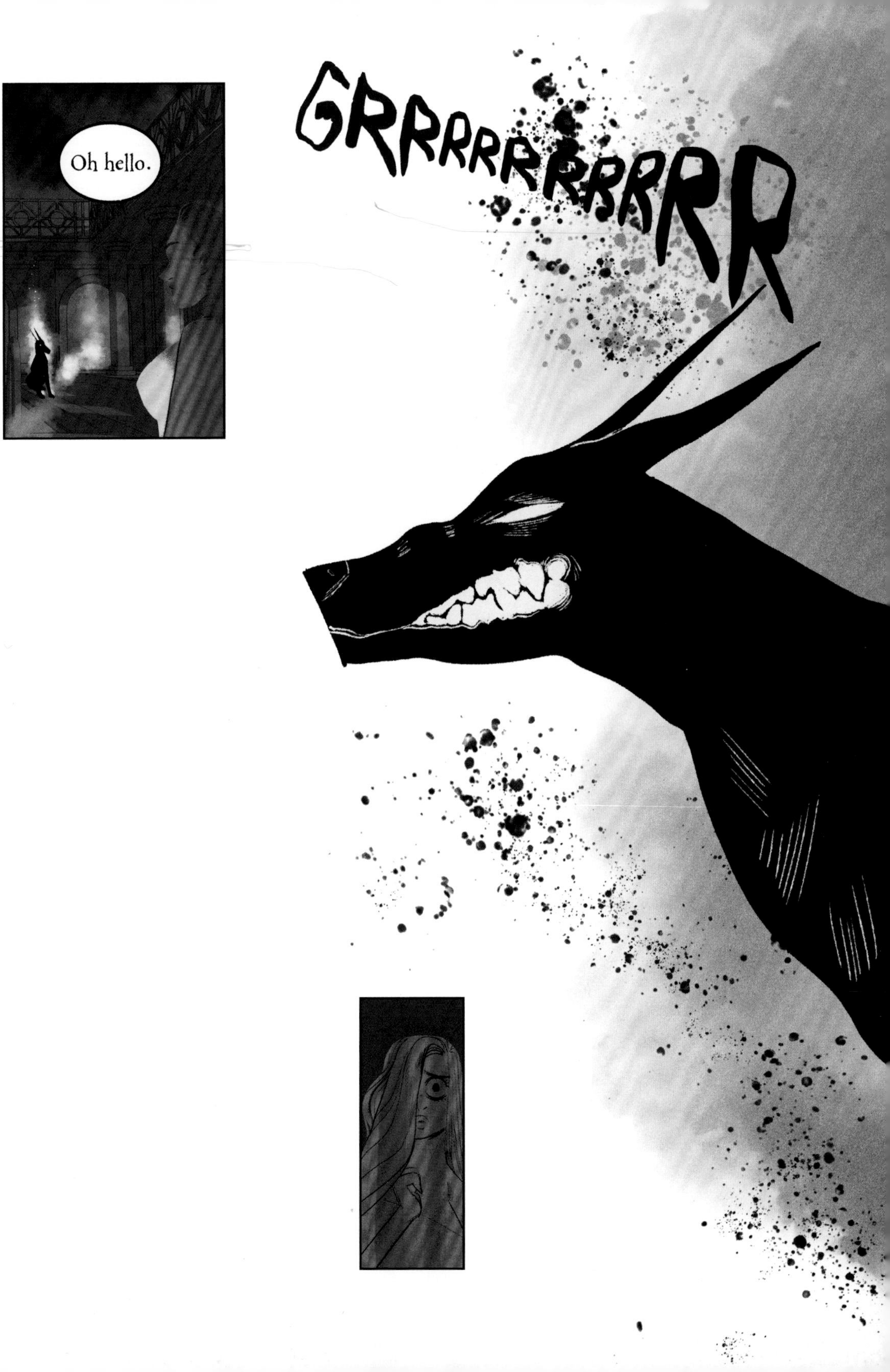
Oh hello.
GRRRRRRRRRRR

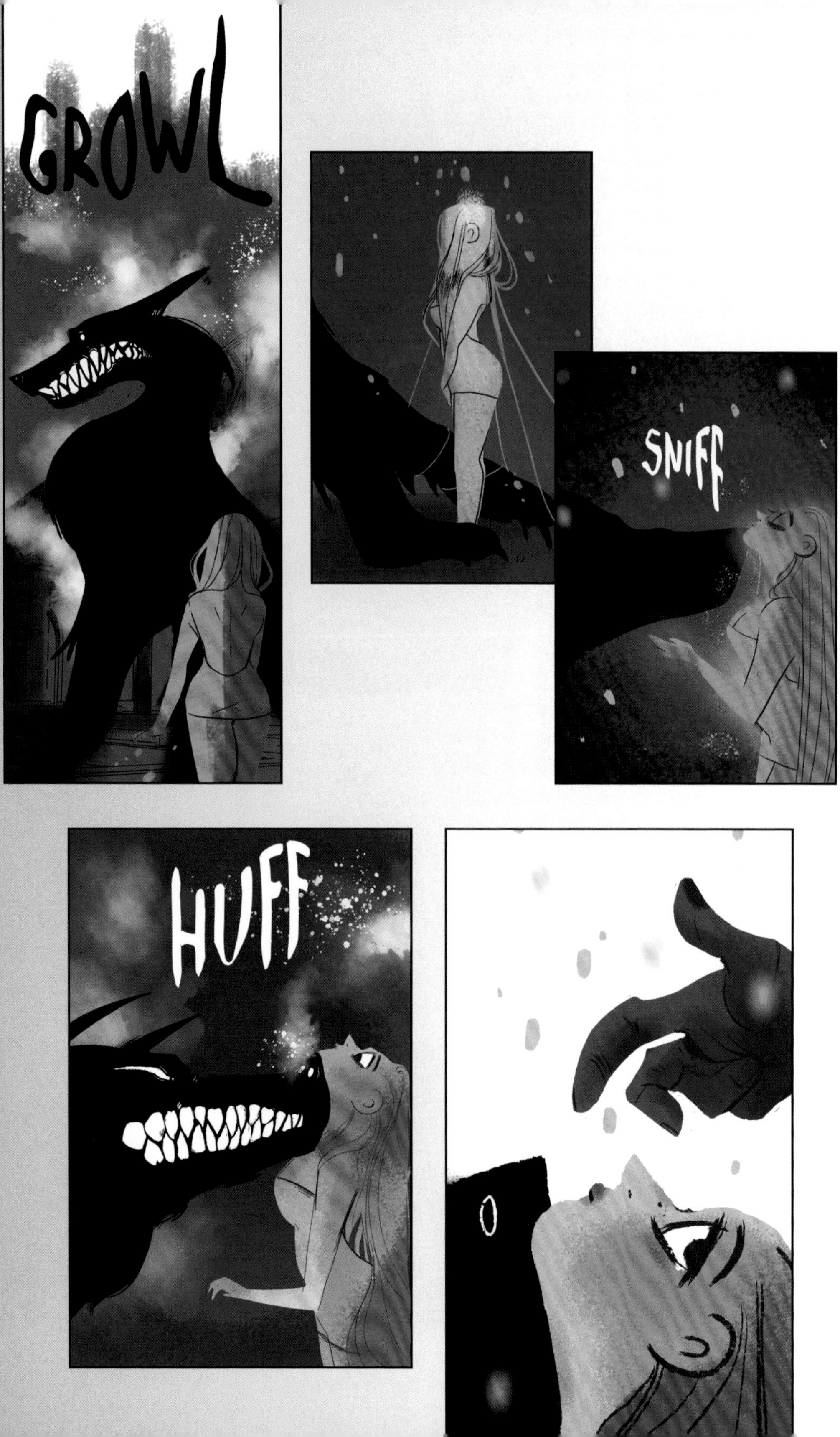
GROWL
SNIFF
HUFF

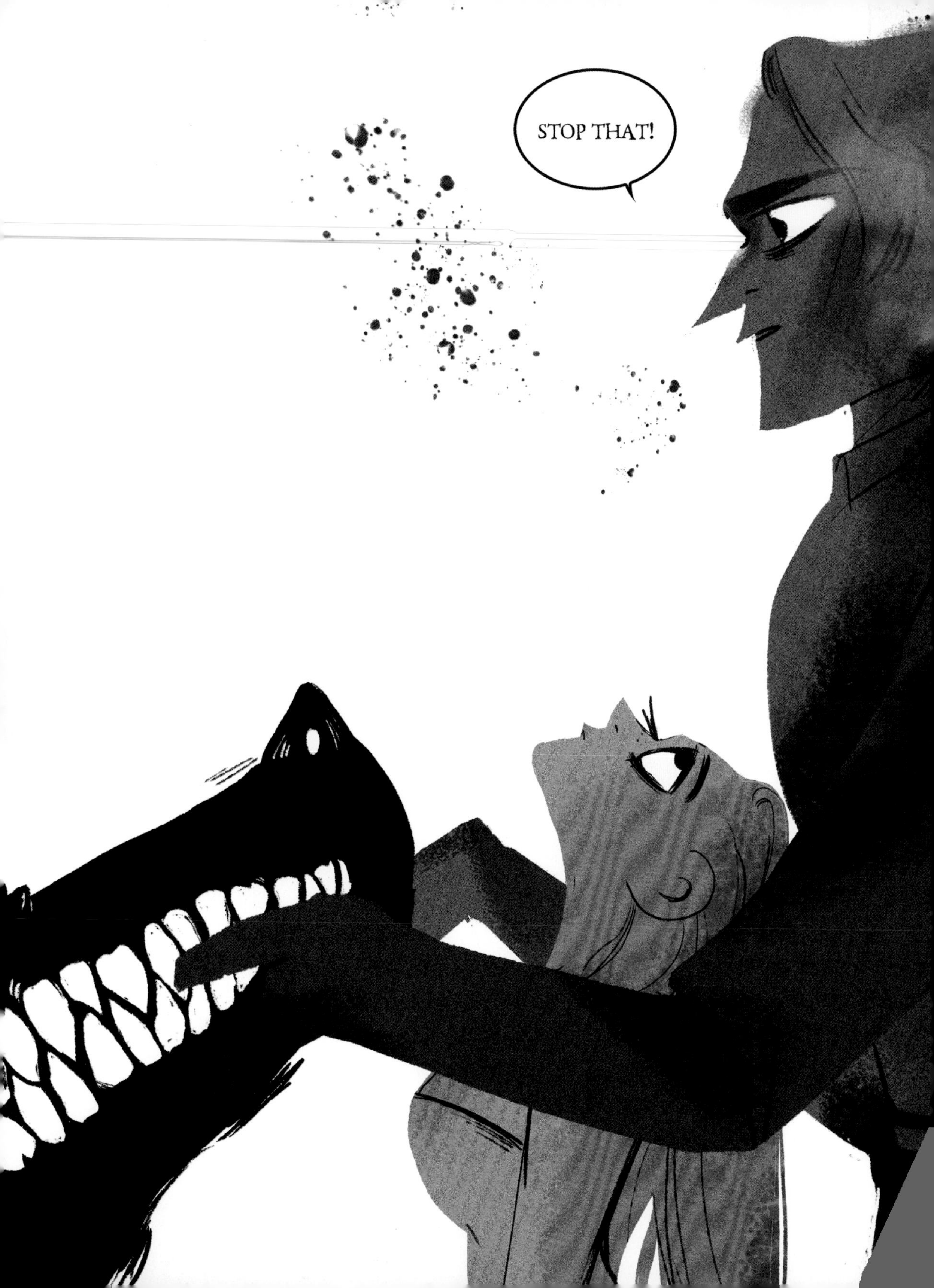
STOP THAT!

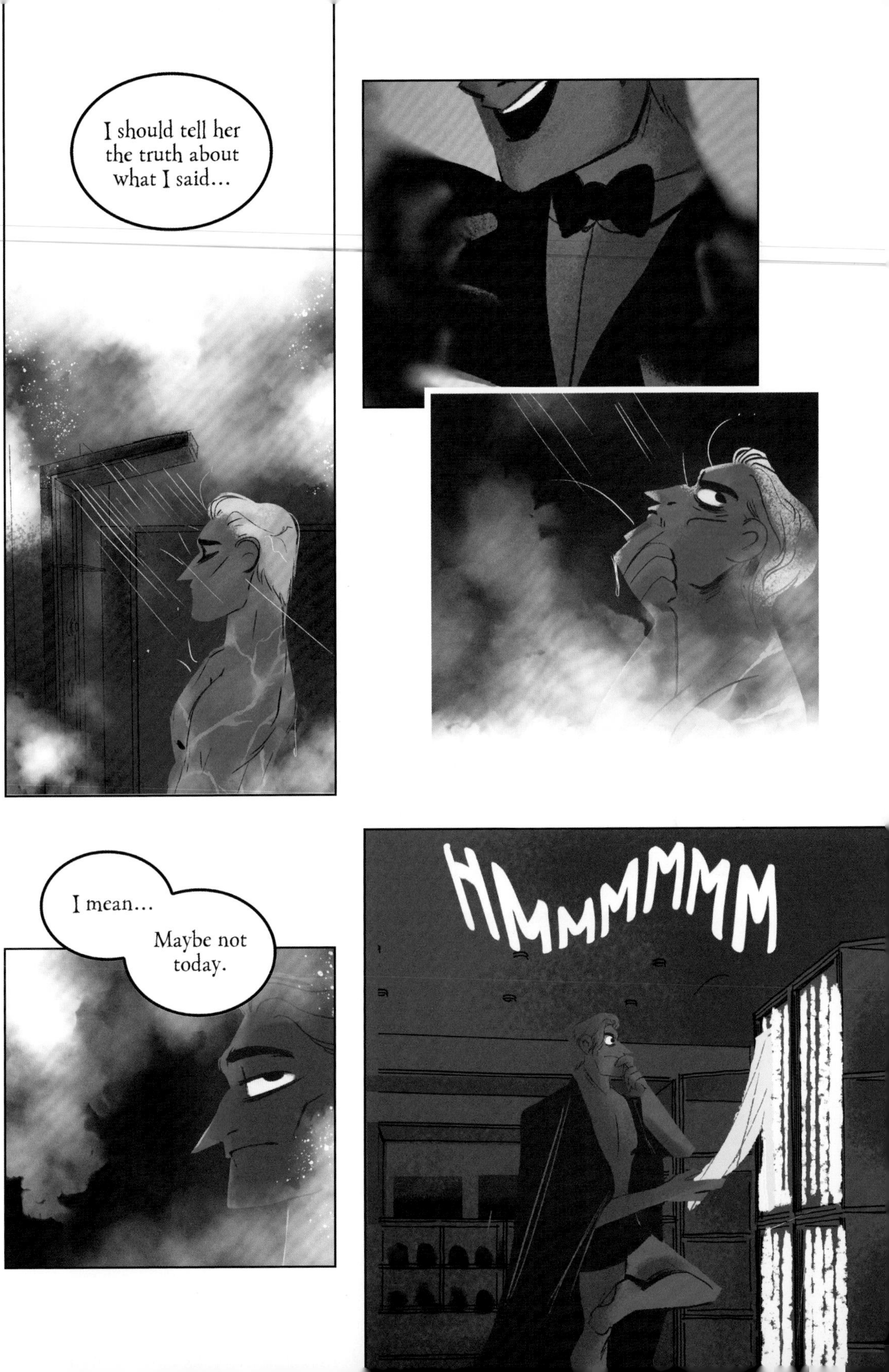
I should tell her the truth about what I said...
I mean...
Maybe not today.
HMMMMMM

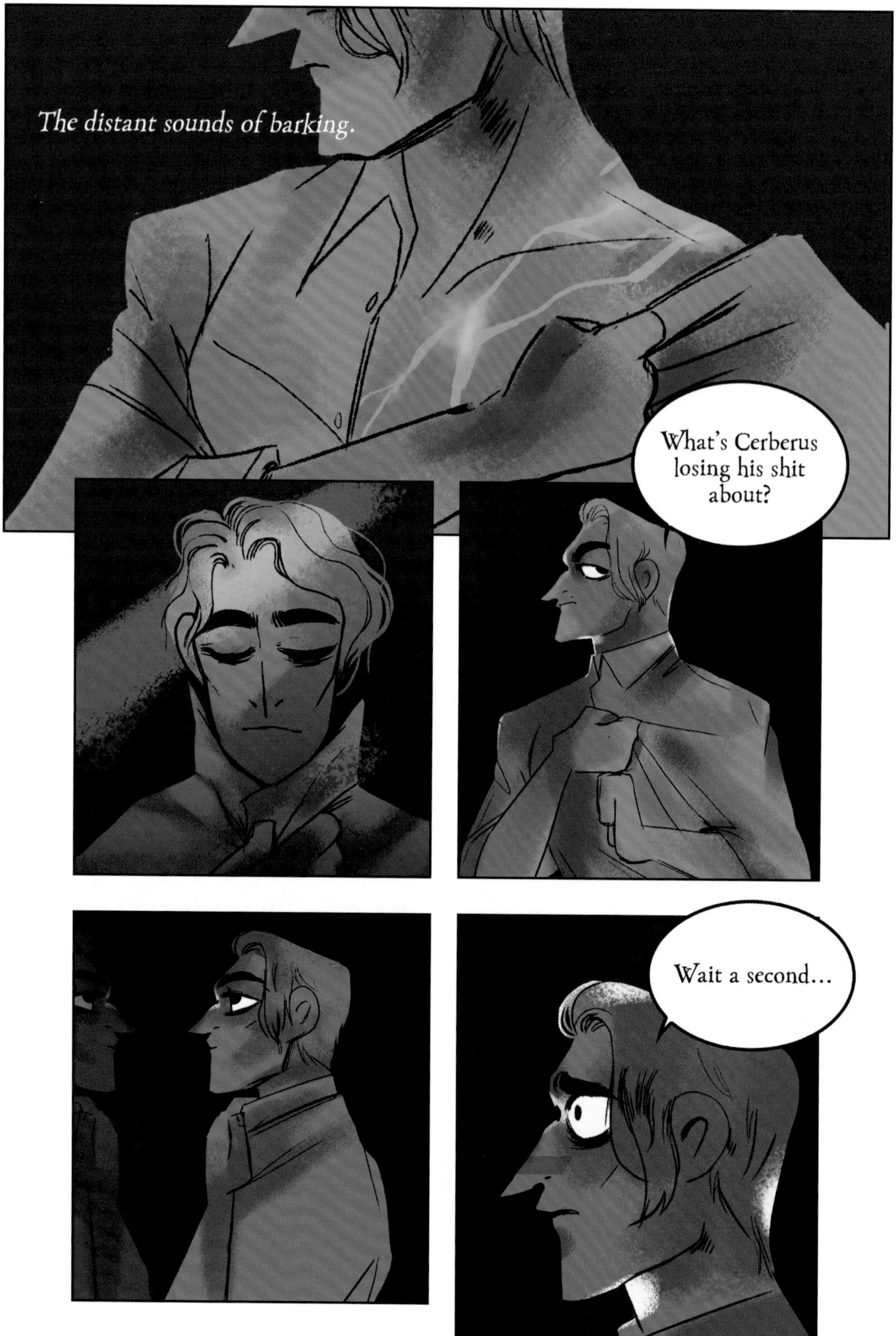
The distant sounds of barking.
What's Cerberus losing his shit about?
Wait a second...

EPISODE 07: A VERY GOOD BOY

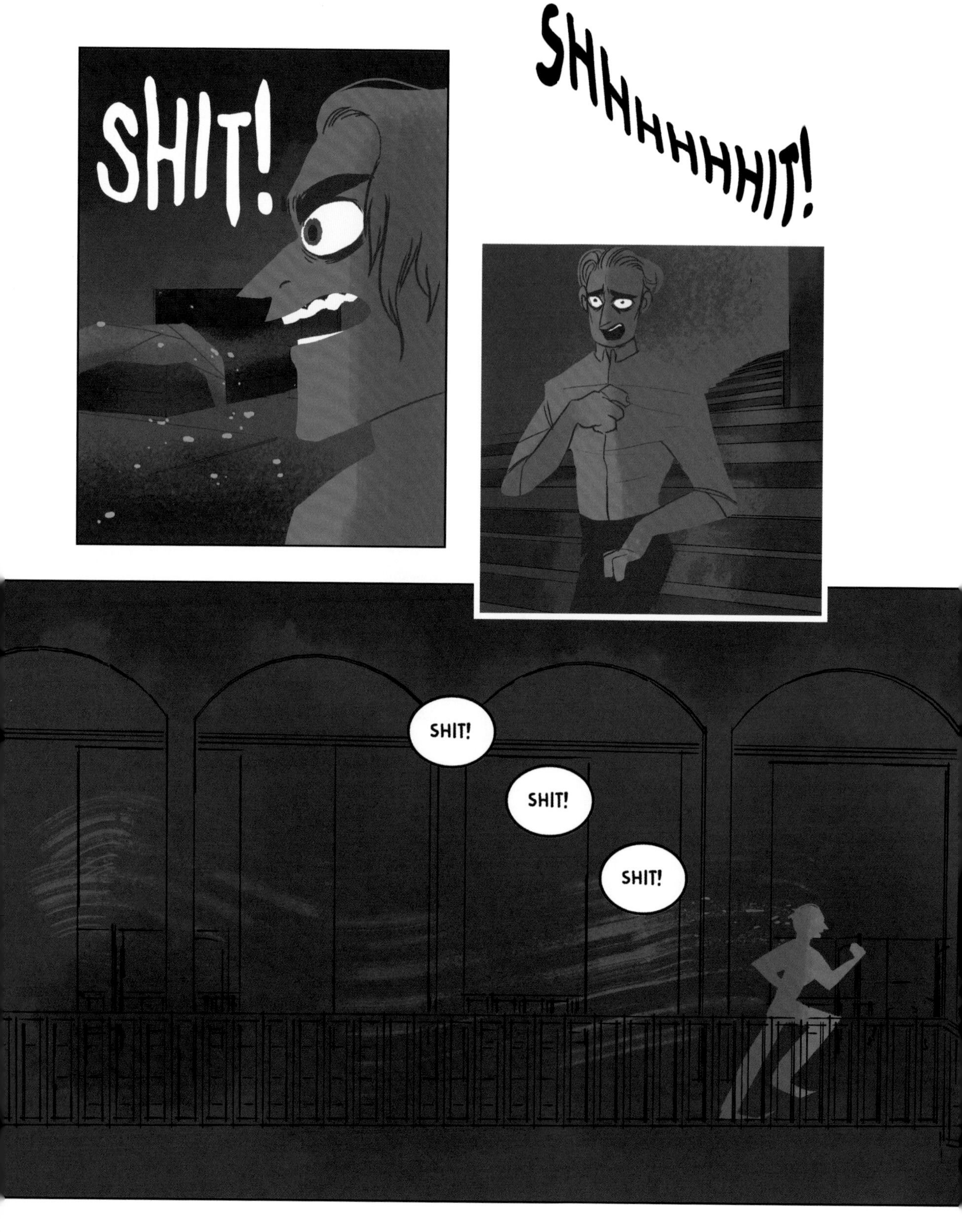
SHIT!
SHHHHHHIT!
SHIT!
SHIT!
SHIT!

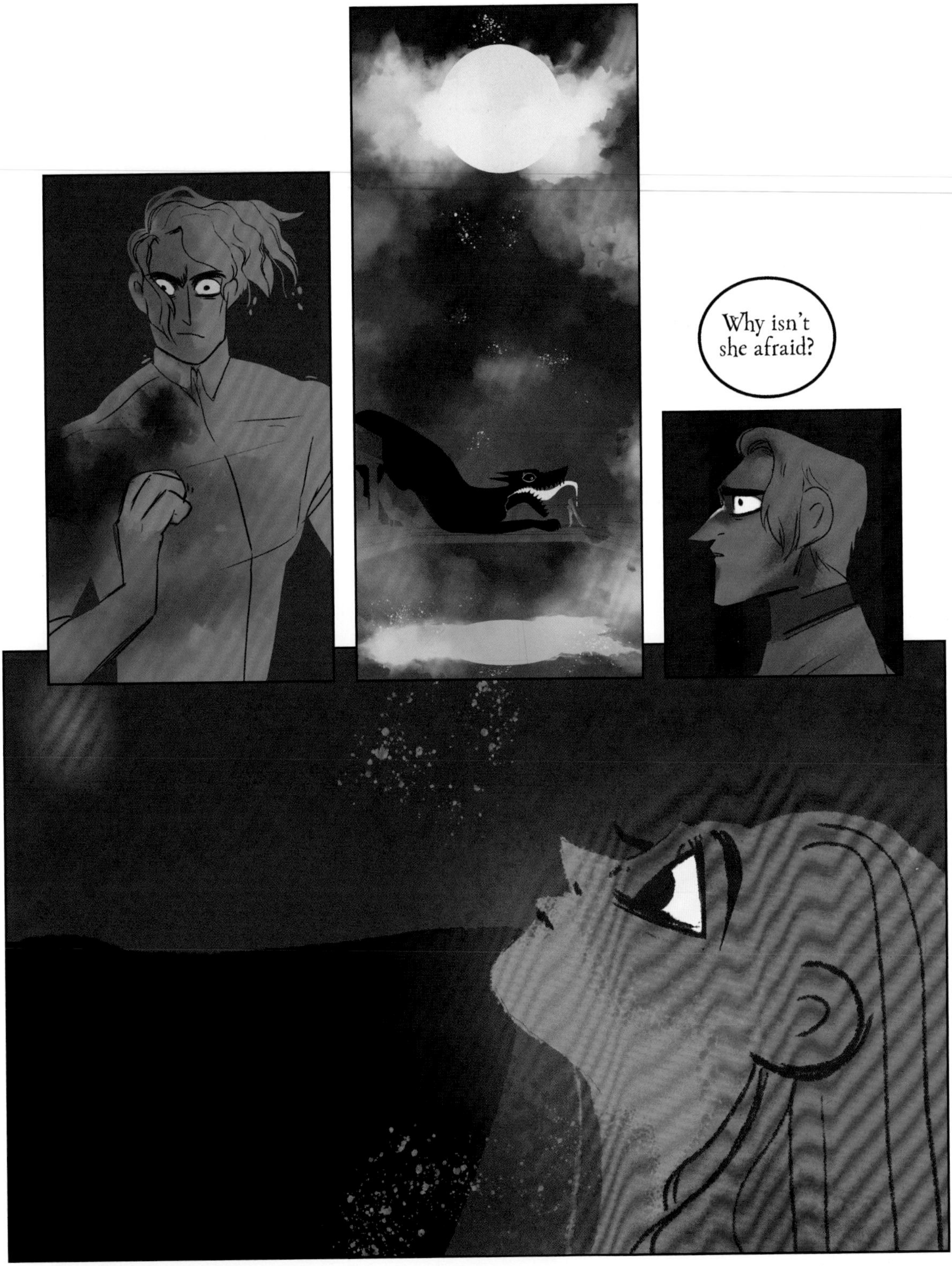
Why isn't she afraid?

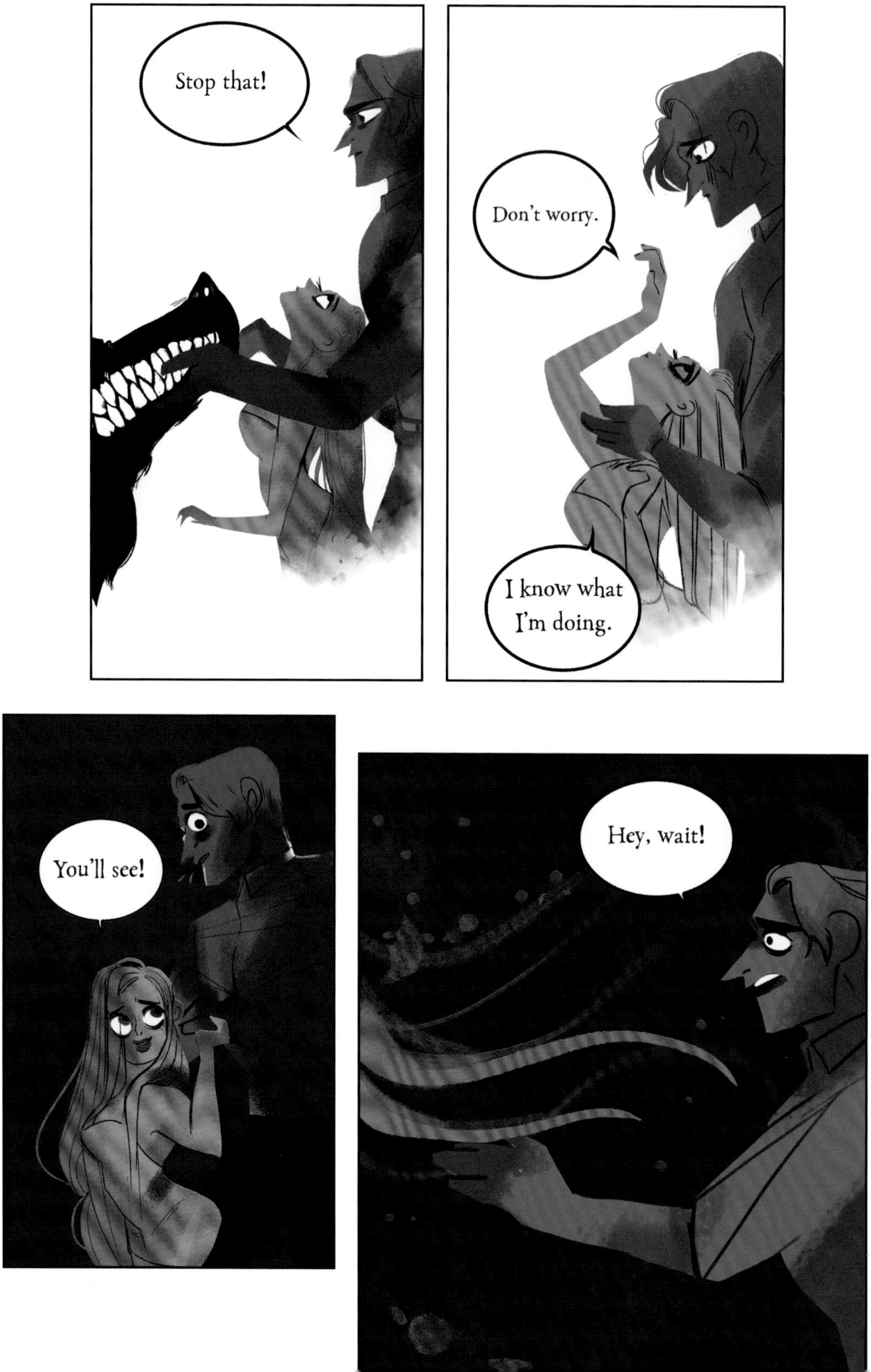
Stop that!
Don't worry.
I know what I'm doing.
You'll see!
Hey, wait!

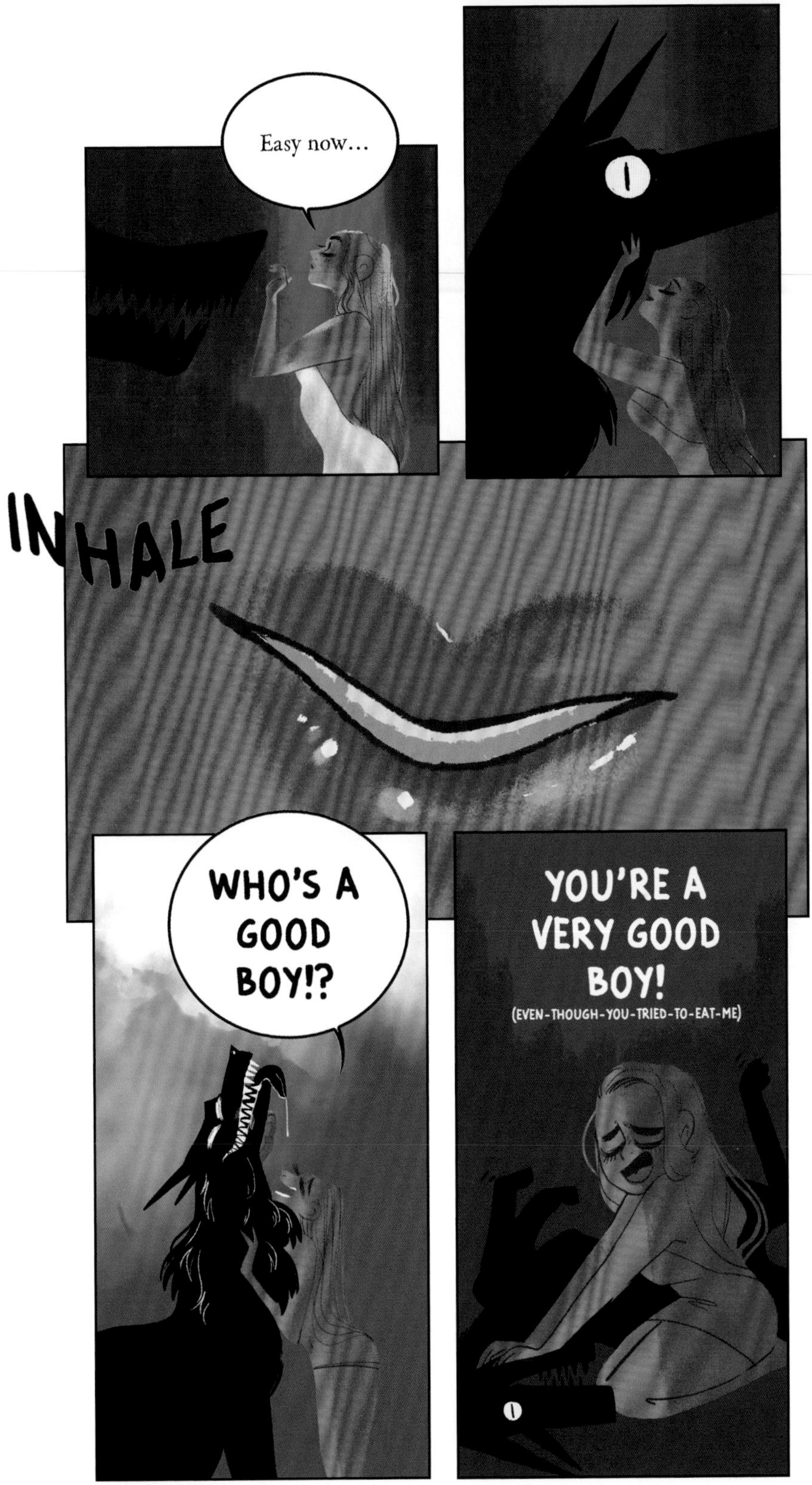
Easy now…
INHALE
WHO'S A GOOD BOY!?
YOU'RE A VERY GOOD BOY!
(EVEN-THOUGH-YOU-TRIED-TO-EAT-ME)

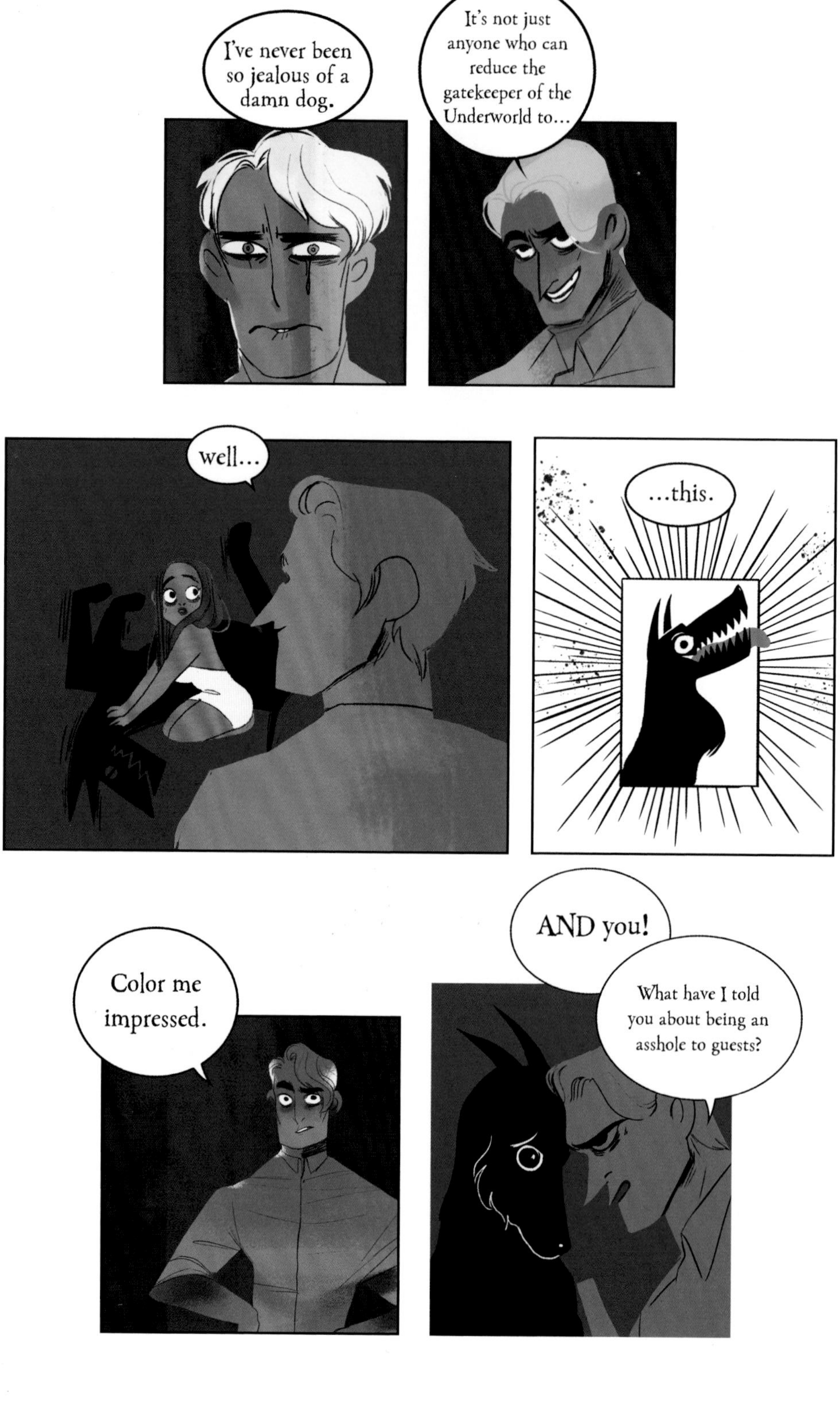
I've never been so jealous of a damn dog.
It's not just anyone who can reduce the gatekeeper of the Underworld to...
well...
...this.
Color me impressed.
AND you!
What have I told you about being an asshole to guests?

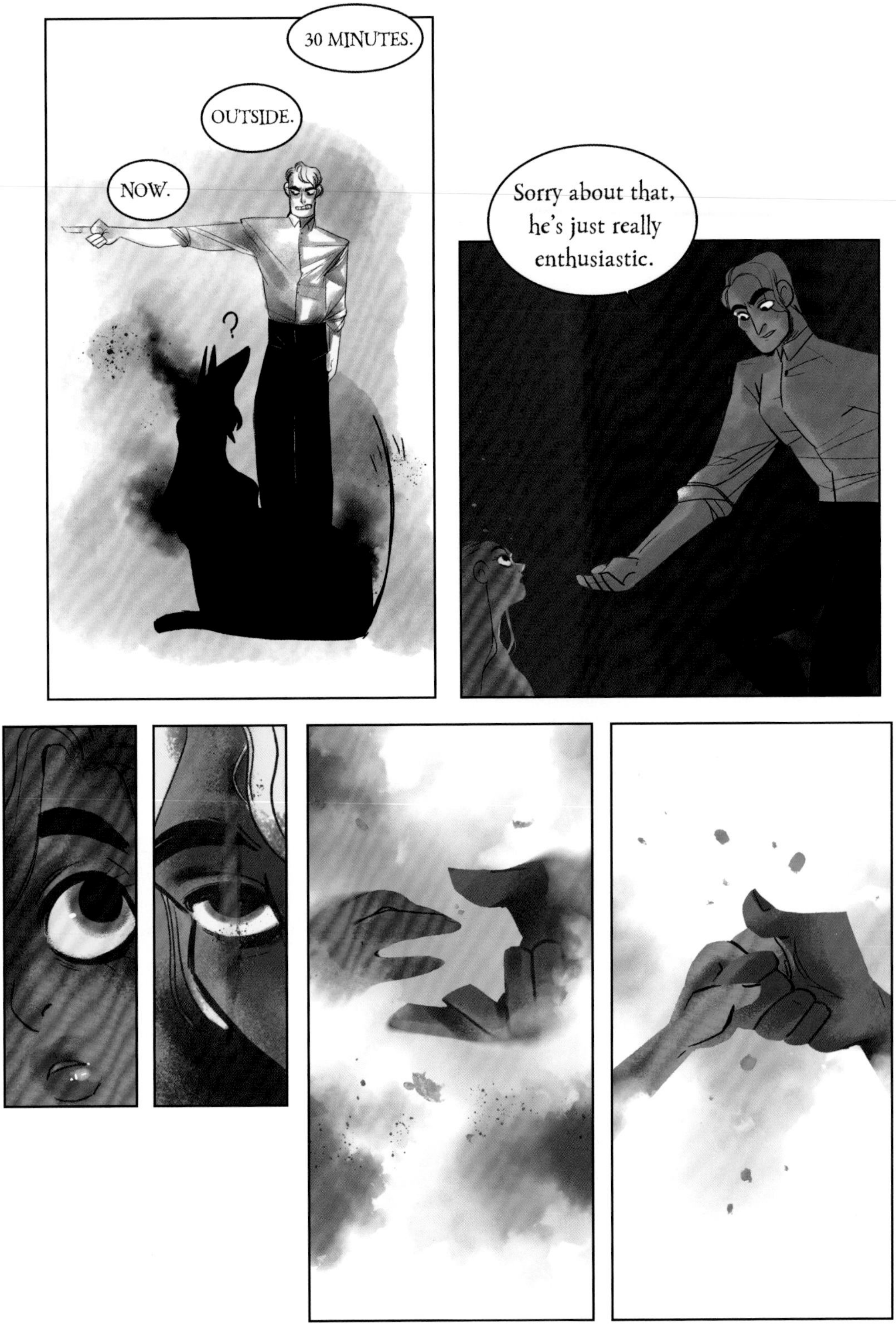

30 MINUTES.
OUTSIDE.
NOW.
?
Sorry about that, he's just really enthusiastic.

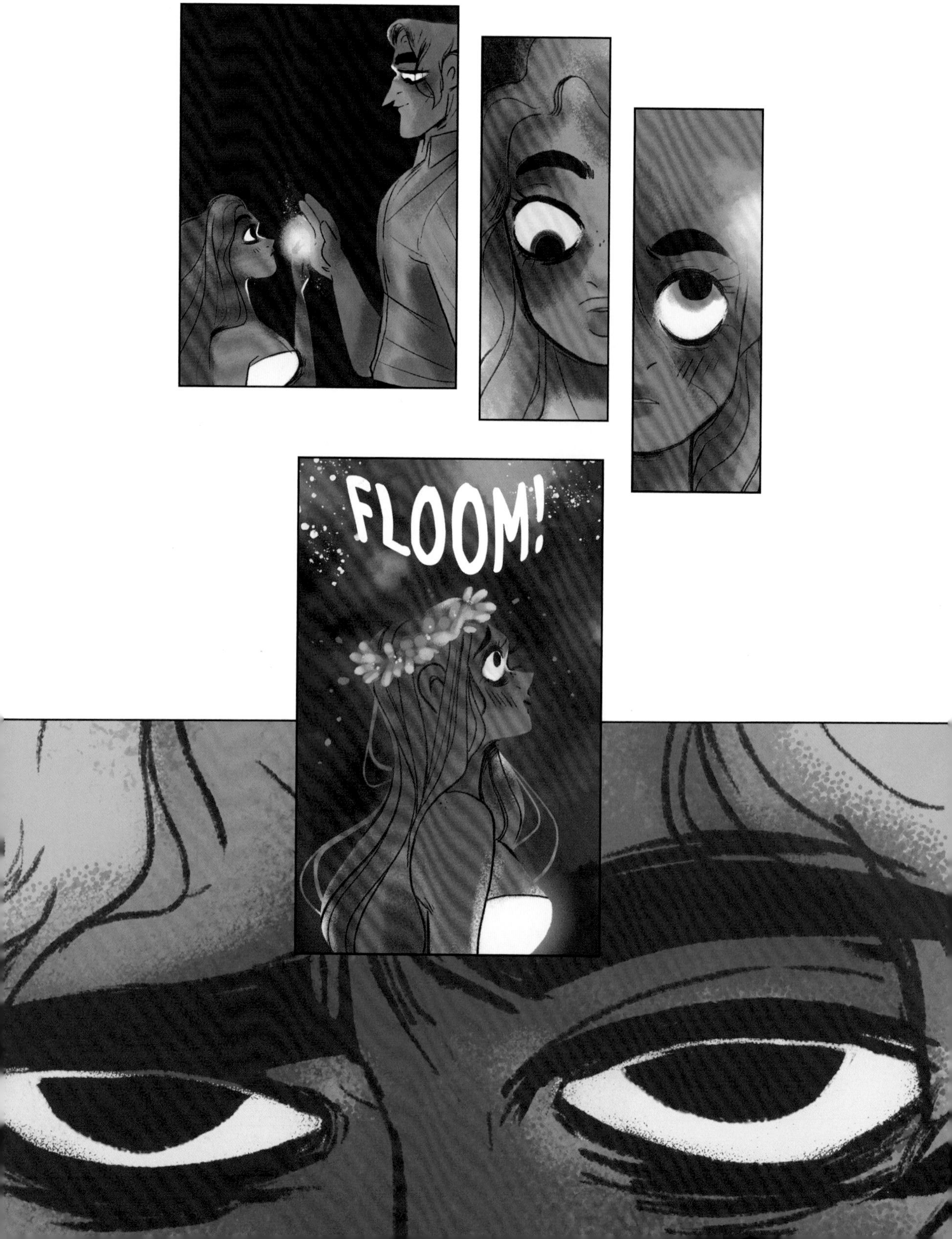
FLOOM!

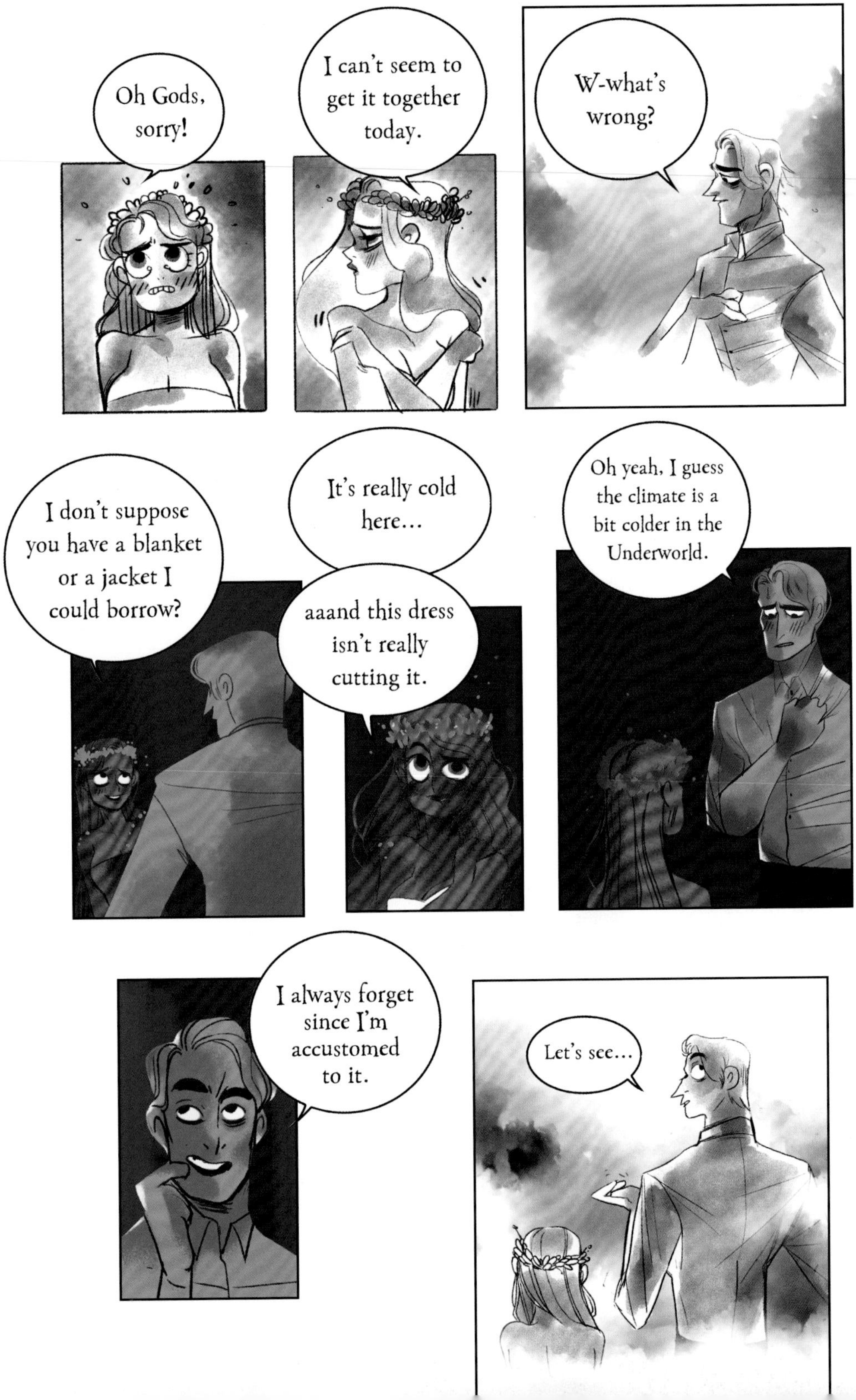
Oh Gods, sorry!
I can't seem to get it together today.
W-what's wrong?
I don't suppose you have a blanket or a jacket I could borrow?
It's really cold here...
aaand this dress isn't really cutting it.
Oh yeah, I guess the climate is a bit colder in the Underworld.
I always forget since I'm accustomed to it.
Let's see...

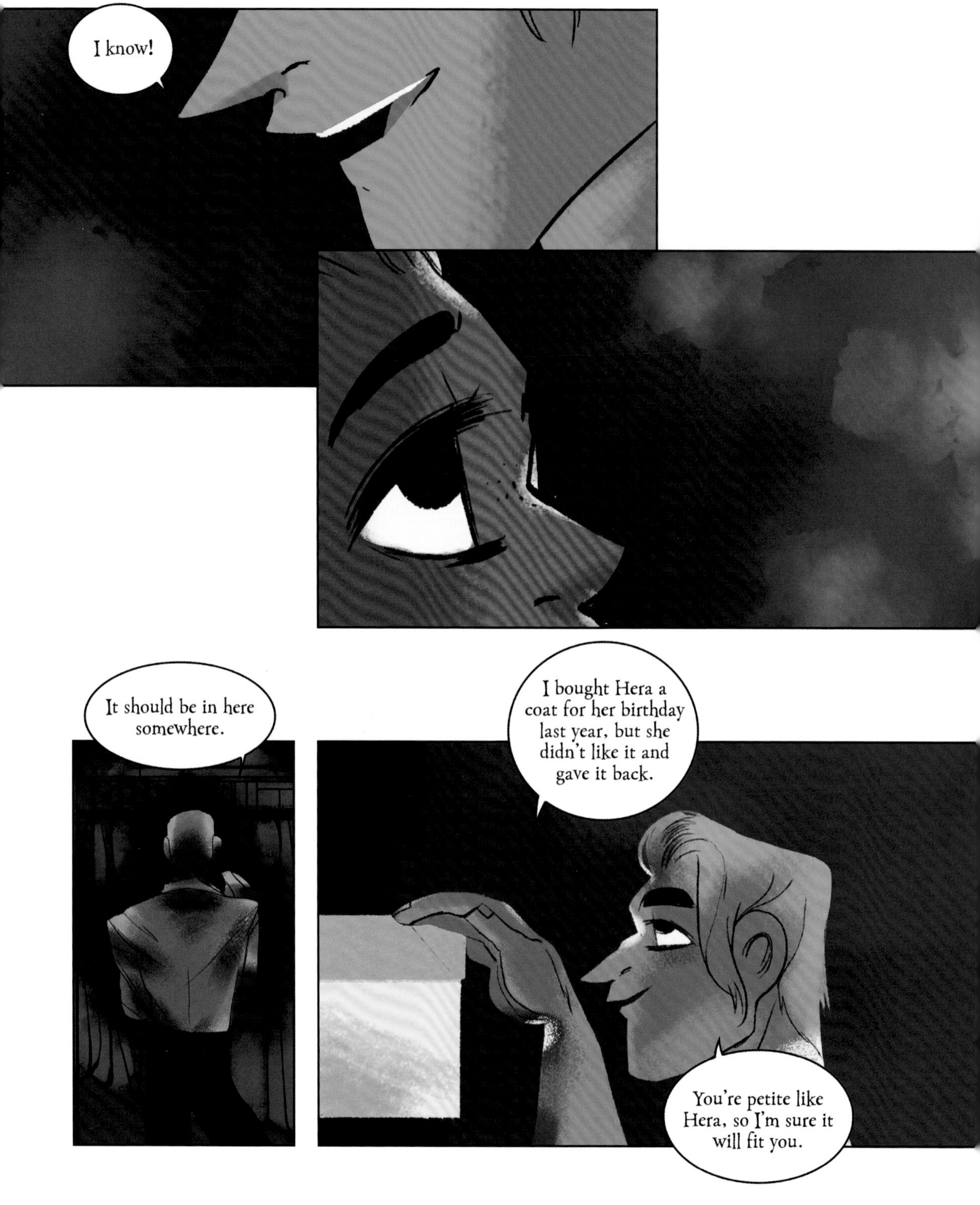
I know!
It should be in here somewhere.
I bought Hera a coat for her birthday last year, but she didn't like it and gave it back.
You're petite like Hera, so I'm sure it will fit you.

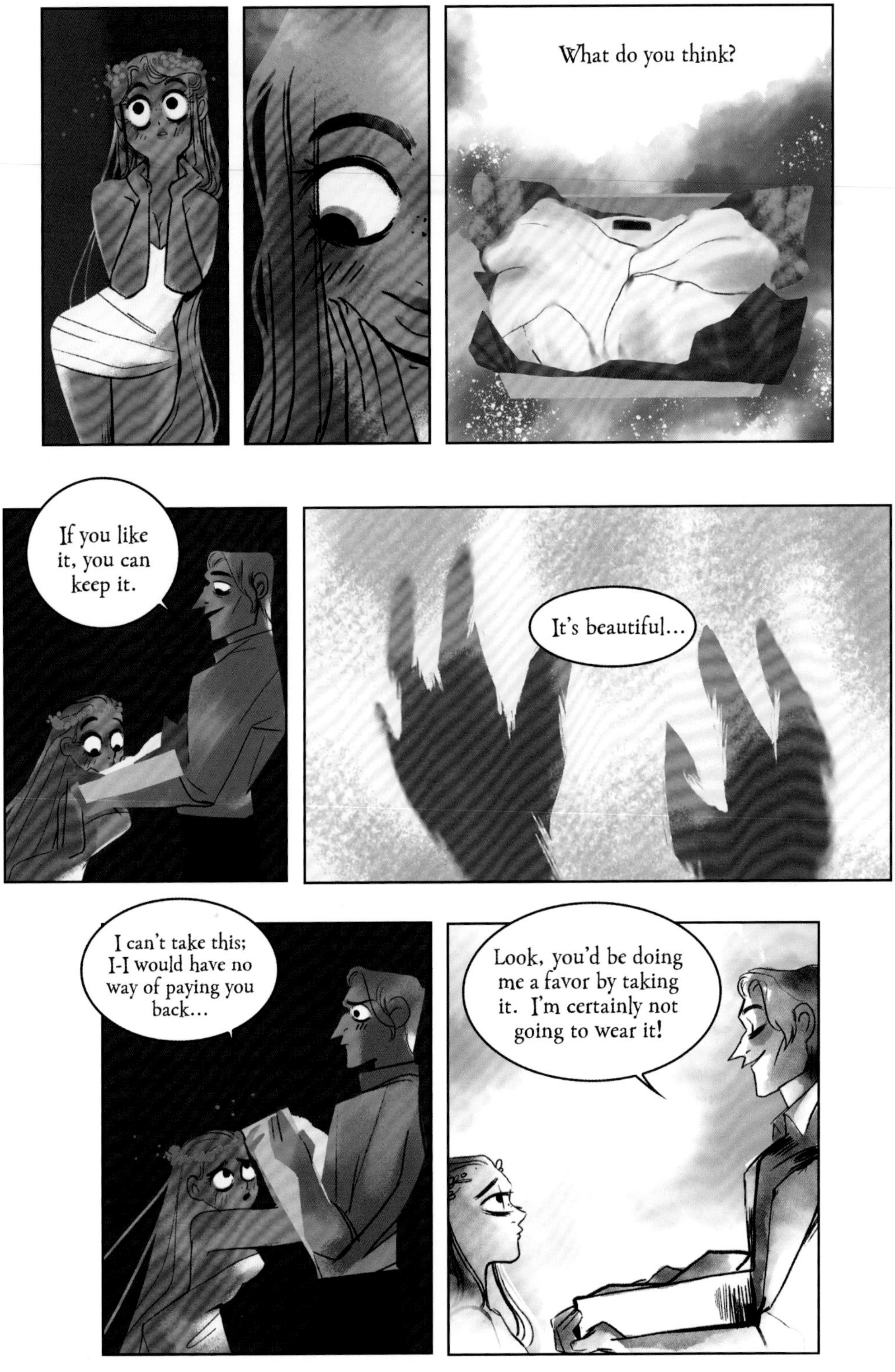
What do you think?
If you like it, you can keep it.
It's beautiful...
I can't take this; I-I would have no way of paying you back...
Look, you'd be doing me a favor by taking it. I'm certainly not going to wear it!

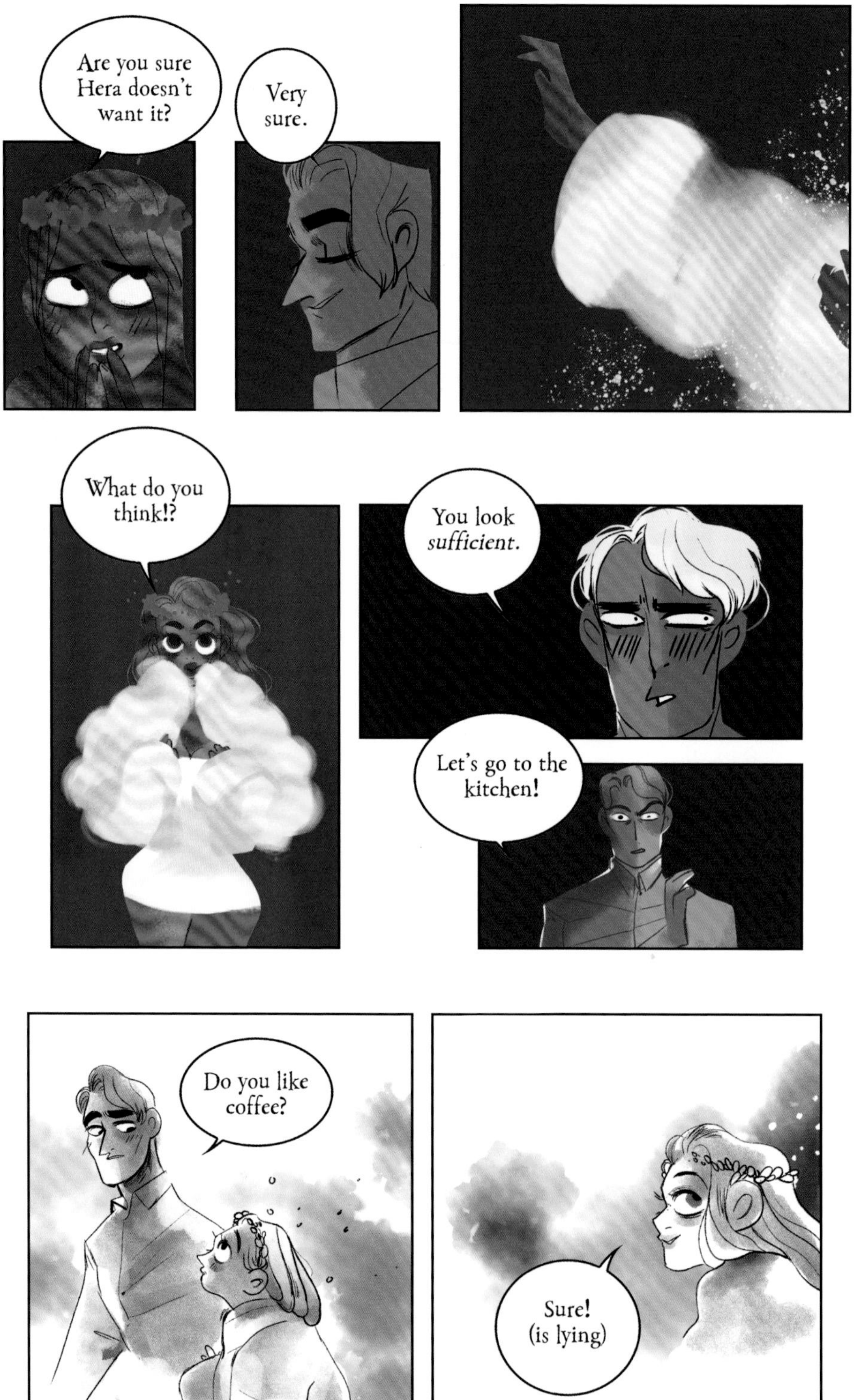
Are you sure Hera doesn't want it?
Very sure.
What do you think!?
You look *sufficient*.
Let's go to the kitchen!
Do you like coffee?
Sure! (is lying)

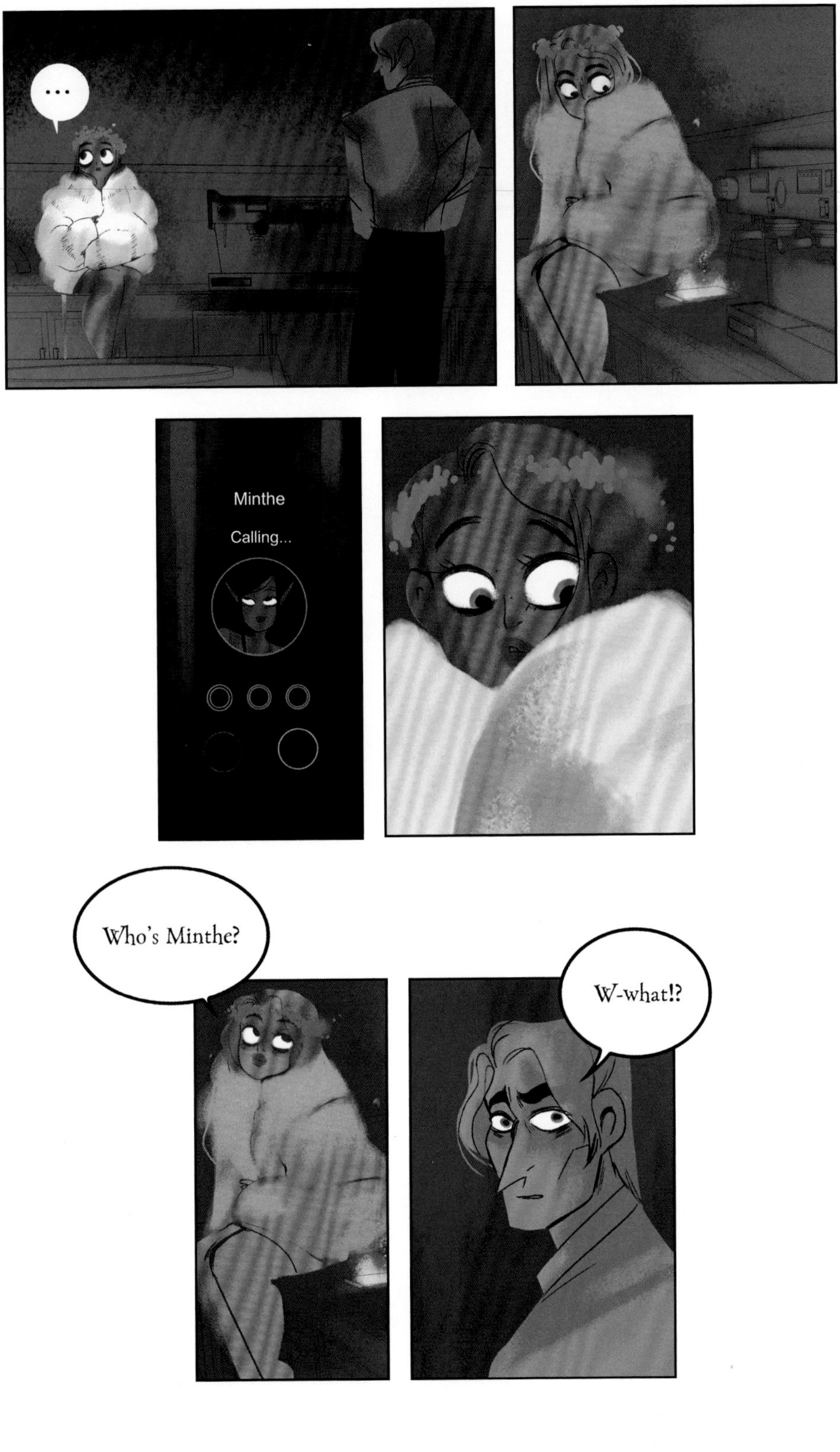
...
Minthe
Calling...
Who's Minthe?
W-what!?

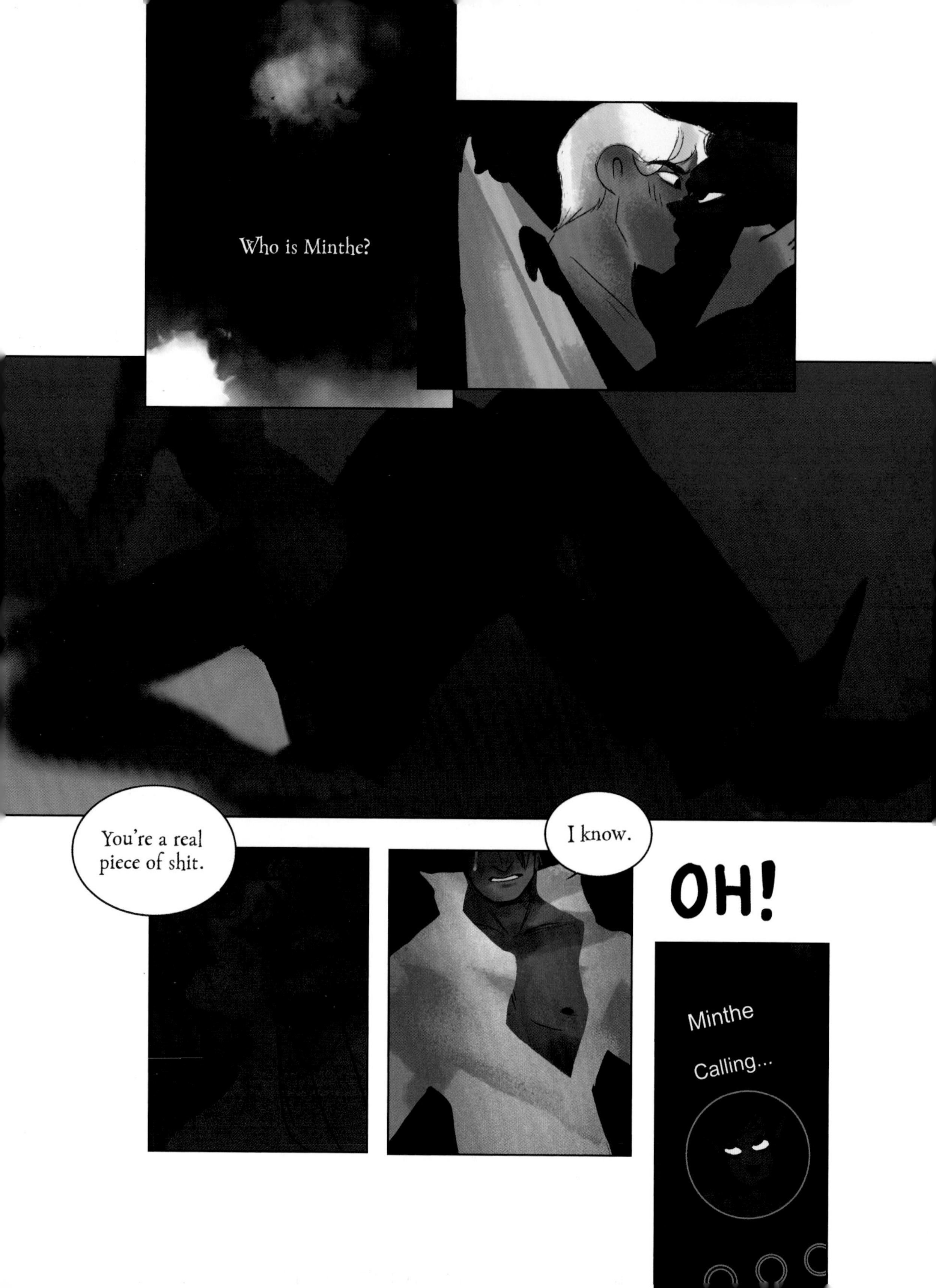
Who is Minthe?
You're a real piece of shit.
I know.
OH!
Minthe
Calling...

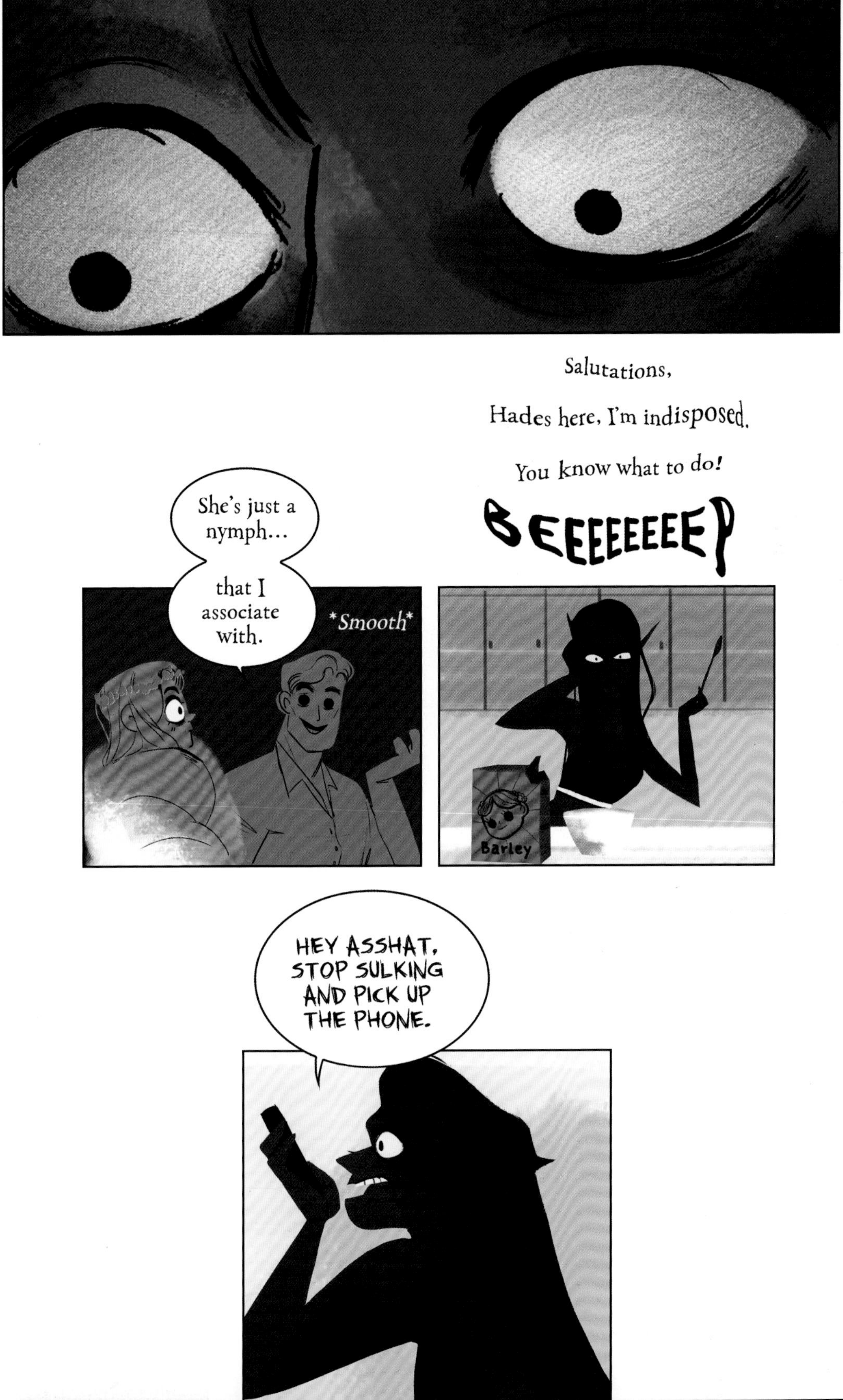
Salutations,
Hades here, I'm indisposed.
You know what to do!
BEEEEEEEP
She's just a nymph...
that I associate with.
Smooth
Barley
HEY ASSHAT, STOP SULKING AND PICK UP THE PHONE.

EPISODE 08: HANDFUL

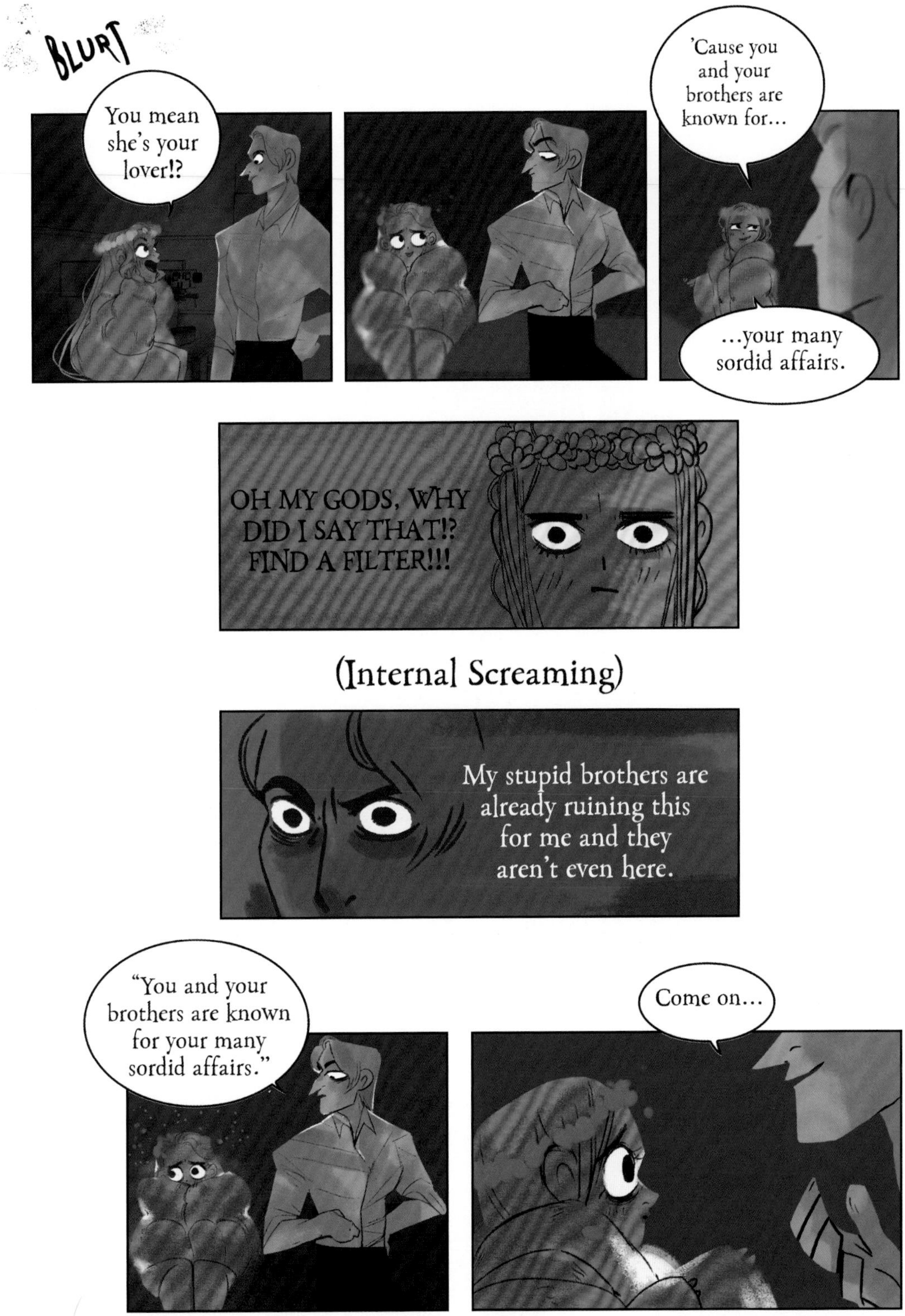
BLURT
You mean she's your lover!?
'Cause you and your brothers are known for...
...your many sordid affairs.
OH MY GODS, WHY DID I SAY THAT!? FIND A FILTER!!!
(Internal Screaming)
My stupid brothers are already ruining this for me and they aren't even here.
"You and your brothers are known for your many sordid affairs."
Come on...

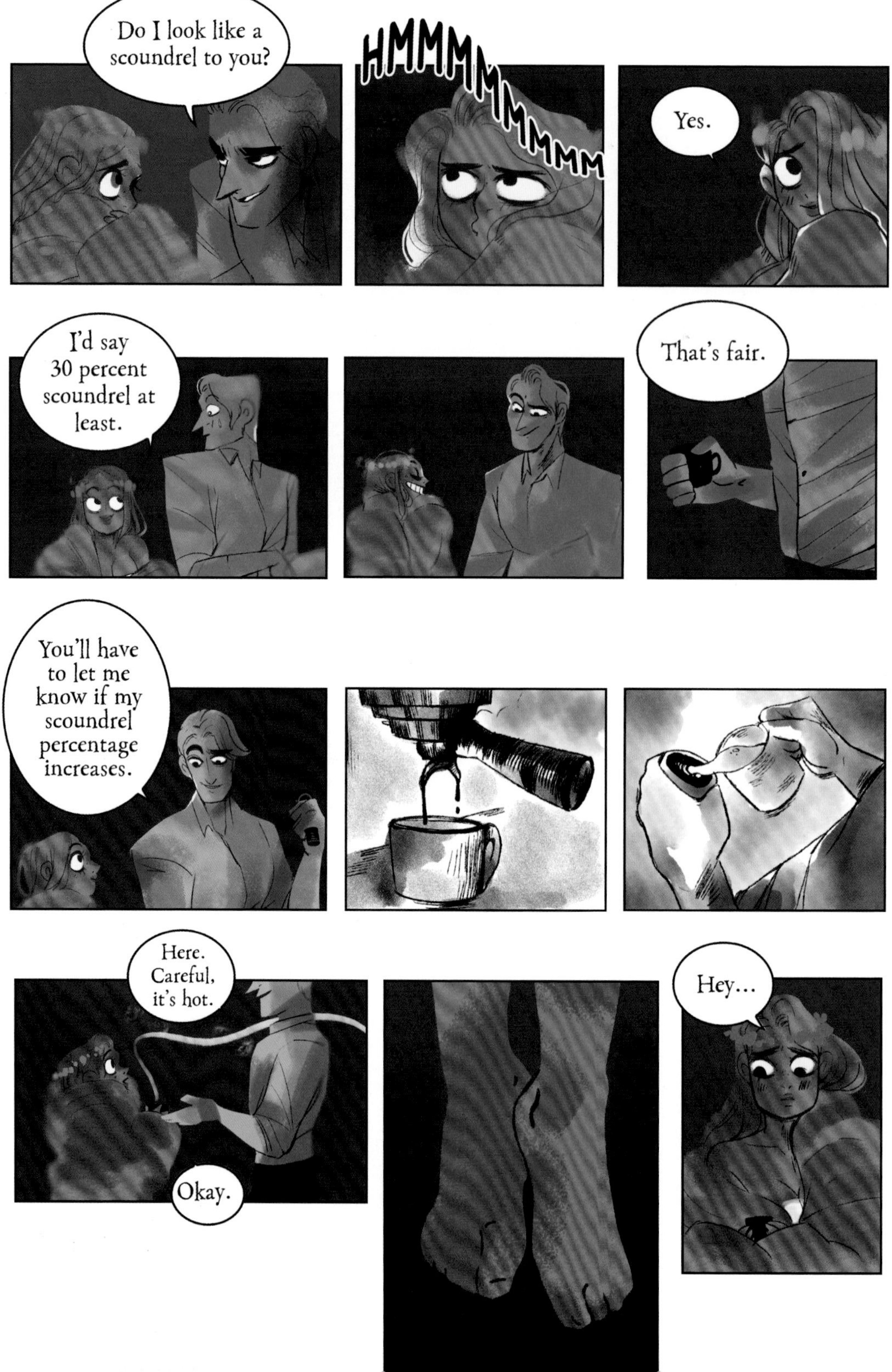
Do I look like a scoundrel to you?
HMMMMMMMMMM
Yes.
I'd say 30 percent scoundrel at least.
That's fair.
You'll have to let me know if my scoundrel percentage increases.
Here. Careful, it's hot.
Okay.
Hey...

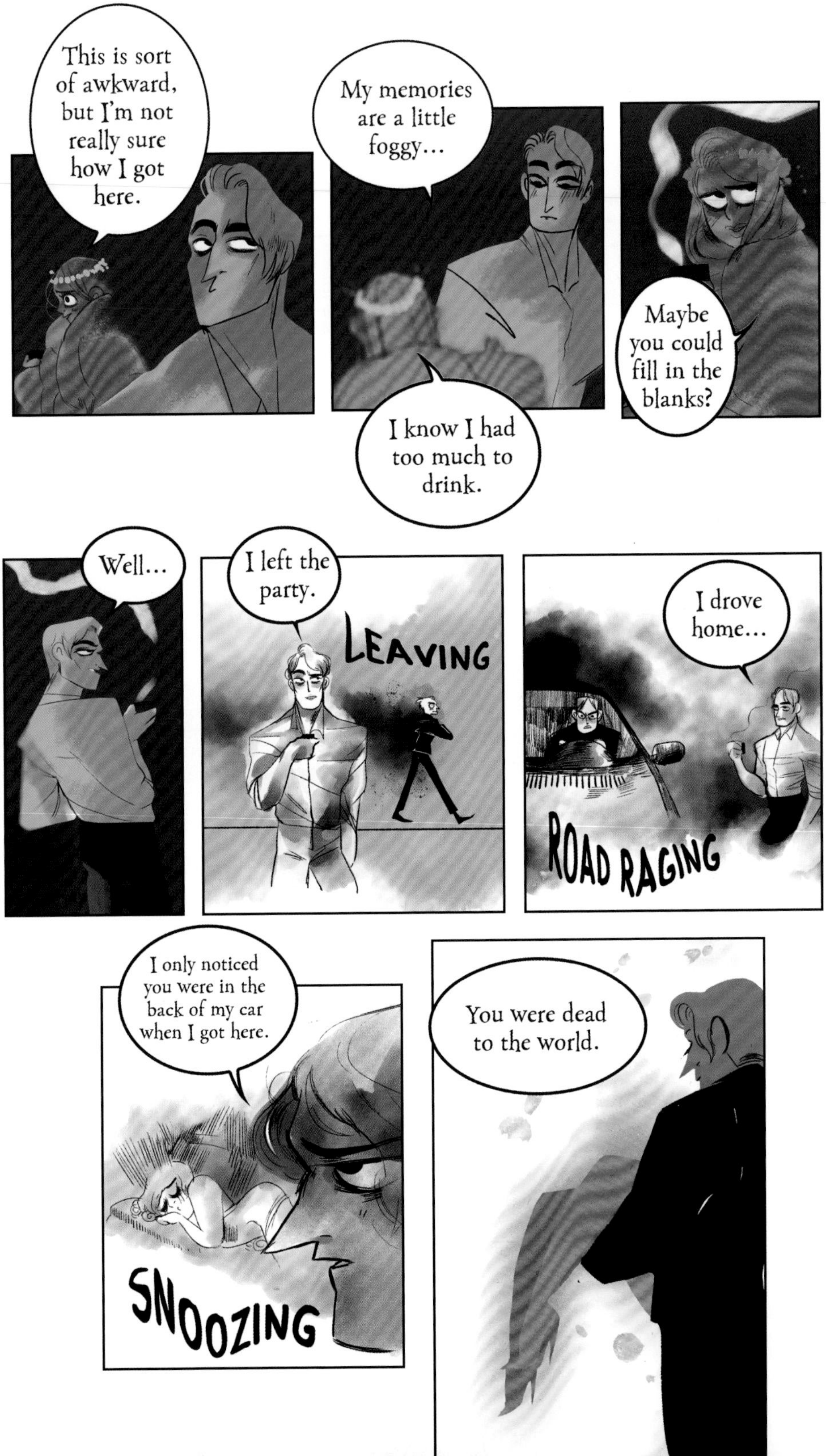
This is sort of awkward, but I'm not really sure how I got here.
My memories are a little foggy...
I know I had too much to drink.
Maybe you could fill in the blanks?
Well...
I left the party.
LEAVING
I drove home...
ROAD RAGING
I only noticed you were in the back of my car when I got here.
SNOOZING
You were dead to the world.

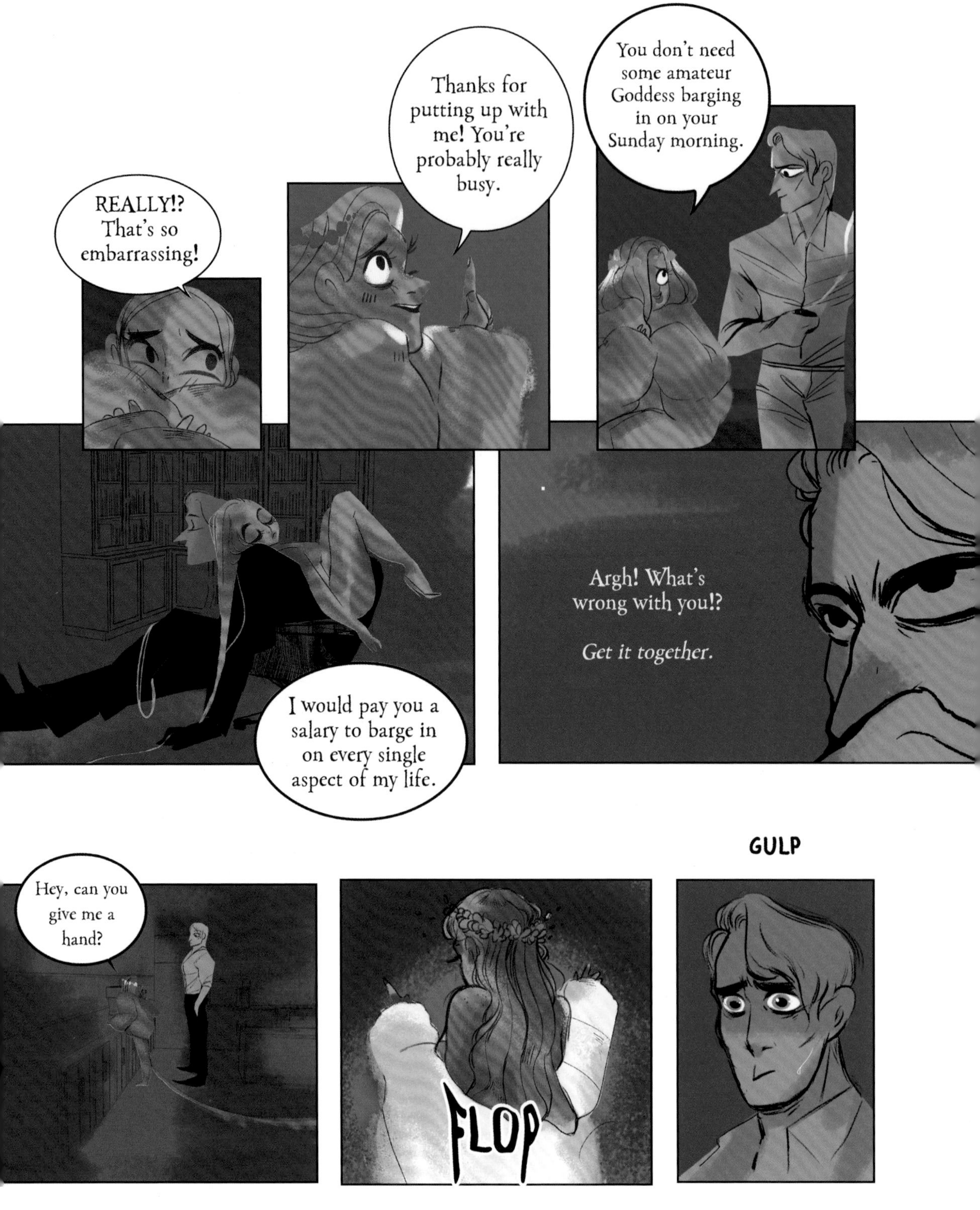
REALLY!? That's so embarrassing!
Thanks for putting up with me! You're probably really busy.
You don't need some amateur Goddess barging in on your Sunday morning.
I would pay you a salary to barge in on every single aspect of my life.
Argh! What's wrong with you!?
Get it together.
GULP
Hey, can you give me a hand?
FLOP

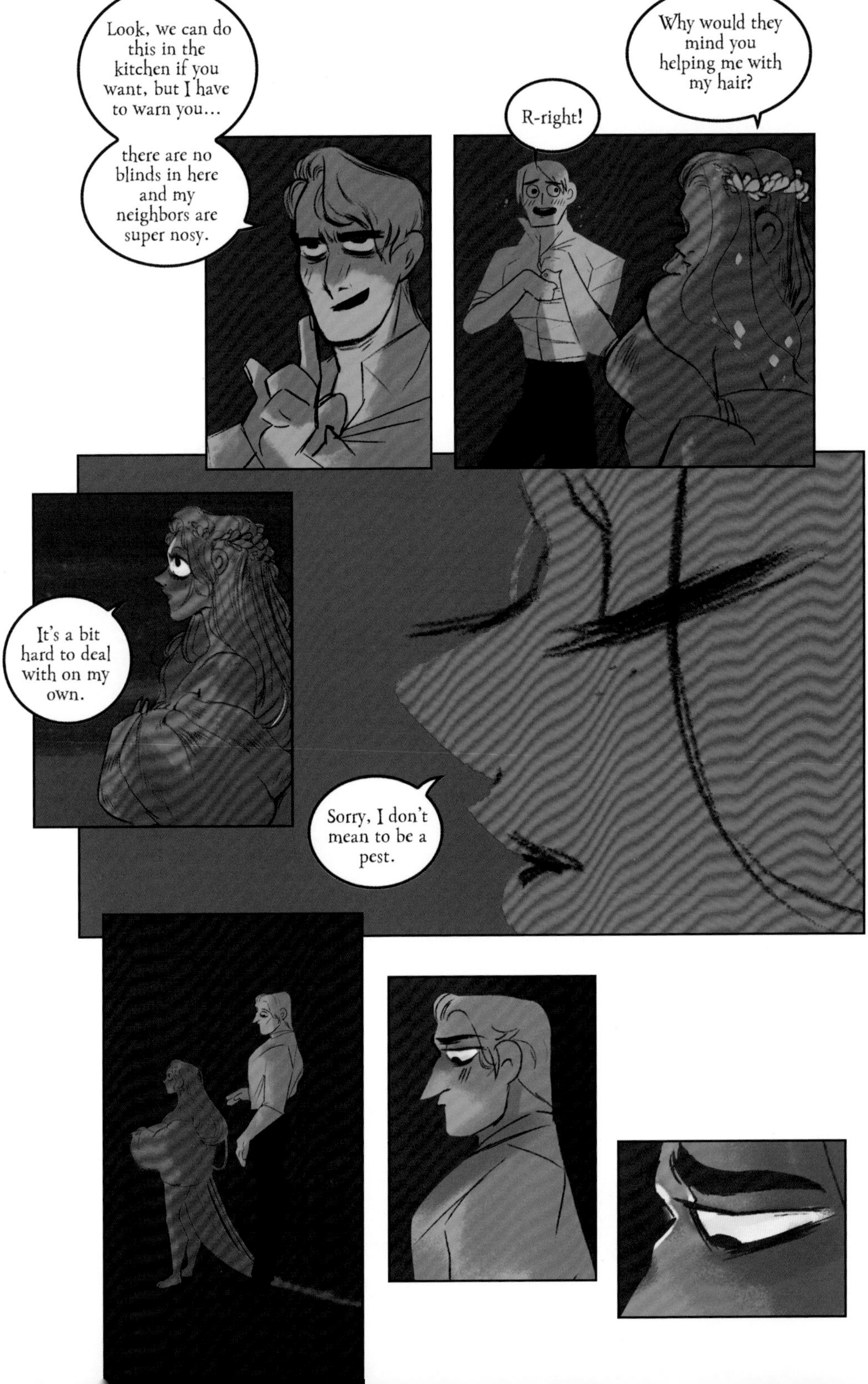
Look, we can do this in the kitchen if you want, but I have to warn you...
there are no blinds in here and my neighbors are super nosy.
R-right!
Why would they mind you helping me with my hair?
It's a bit hard to deal with on my own.
Sorry, I don't mean to be a pest.

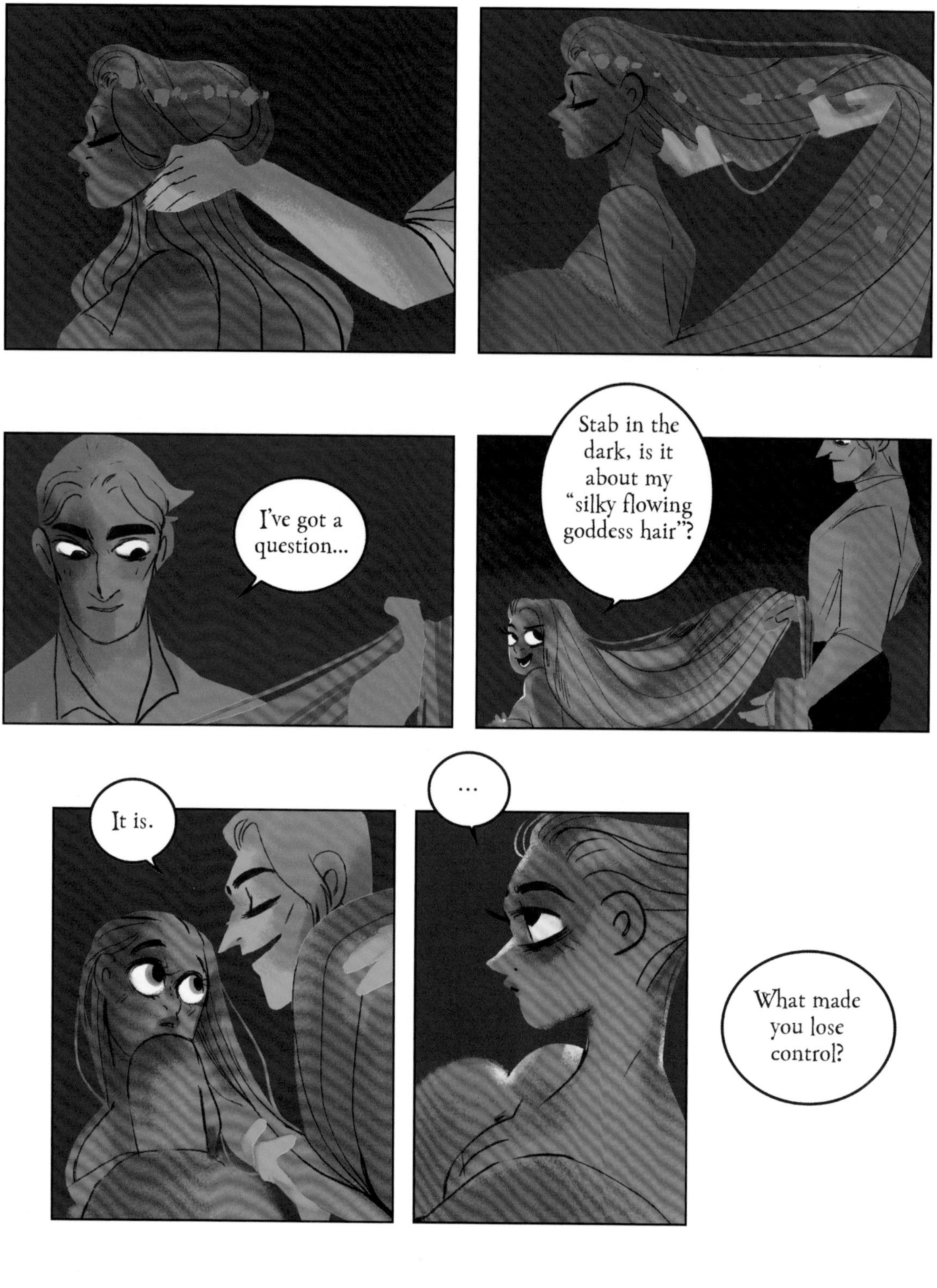

I've got a question...
Stab in the dark, is it about my "silky flowing goddess hair"?
It is.
...
What made you lose control?

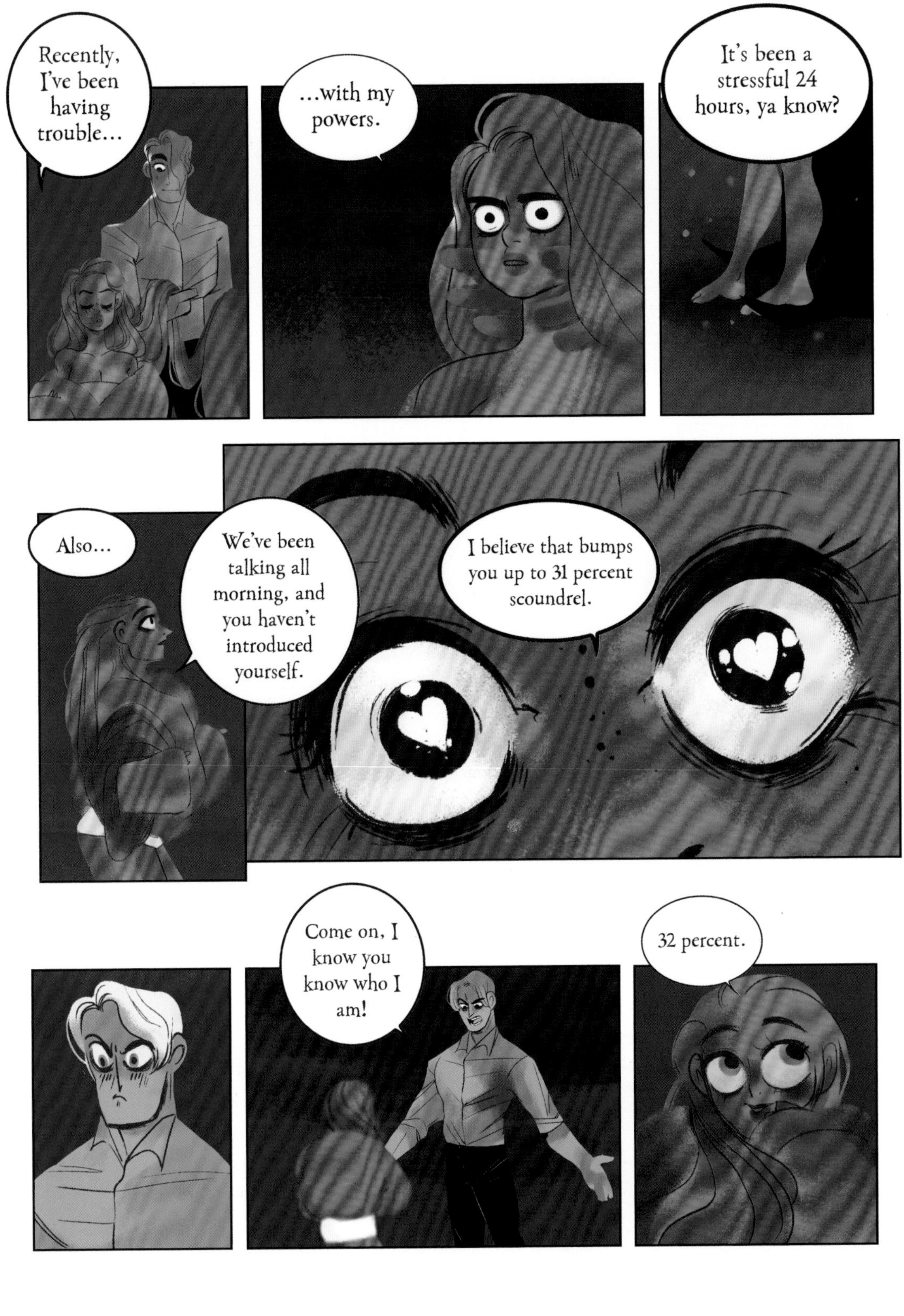
Recently, I've been having trouble...
...with my powers.
It's been a stressful 24 hours, ya know?
Also...
We've been talking all morning, and you haven't introduced yourself.
I believe that bumps you up to 31 percent scoundrel.
Come on, I know you know who I am!
32 percent.

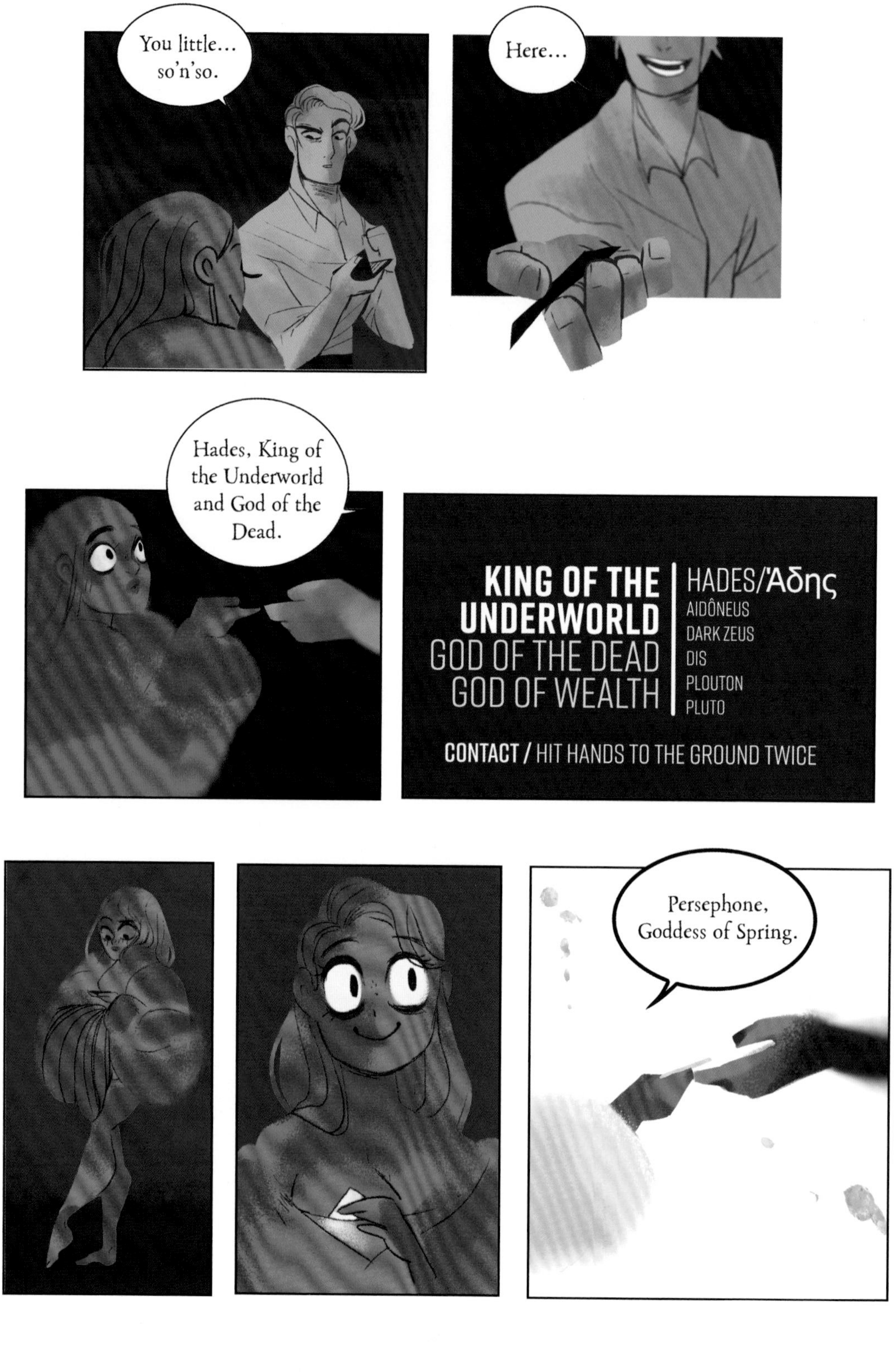
You little... so'n'so.
Here...
Hades, King of the Underworld and God of the Dead.
KING OF THE UNDERWORLD
GOD OF THE DEAD
GOD OF WEALTH
HADES/Άδης
AIDÔNEUS
DARK ZEUS
DIS
PLOUTON
PLUTO
CONTACT / HIT HANDS TO THE GROUND TWICE
Persephone, Goddess of Spring.

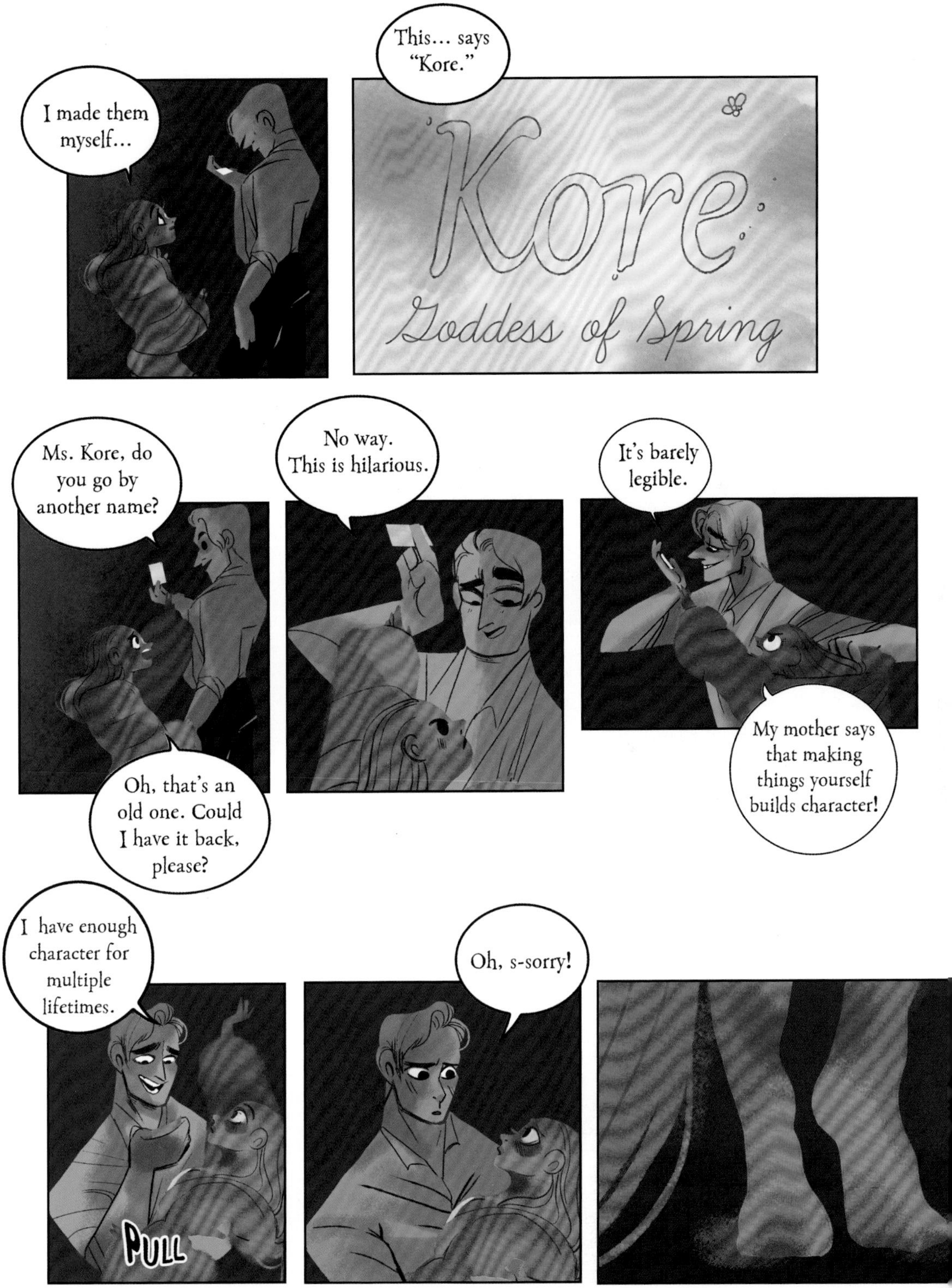
I made them myself...
This... says "Kore."
Kore
Goddess of Spring
Ms. Kore, do you go by another name?
Oh, that's an old one. Could I have it back, please?
No way. This is hilarious.
It's barely legible.
My mother says that making things yourself builds character!
I have enough character for multiple lifetimes.
PULL
Oh, s-sorry!

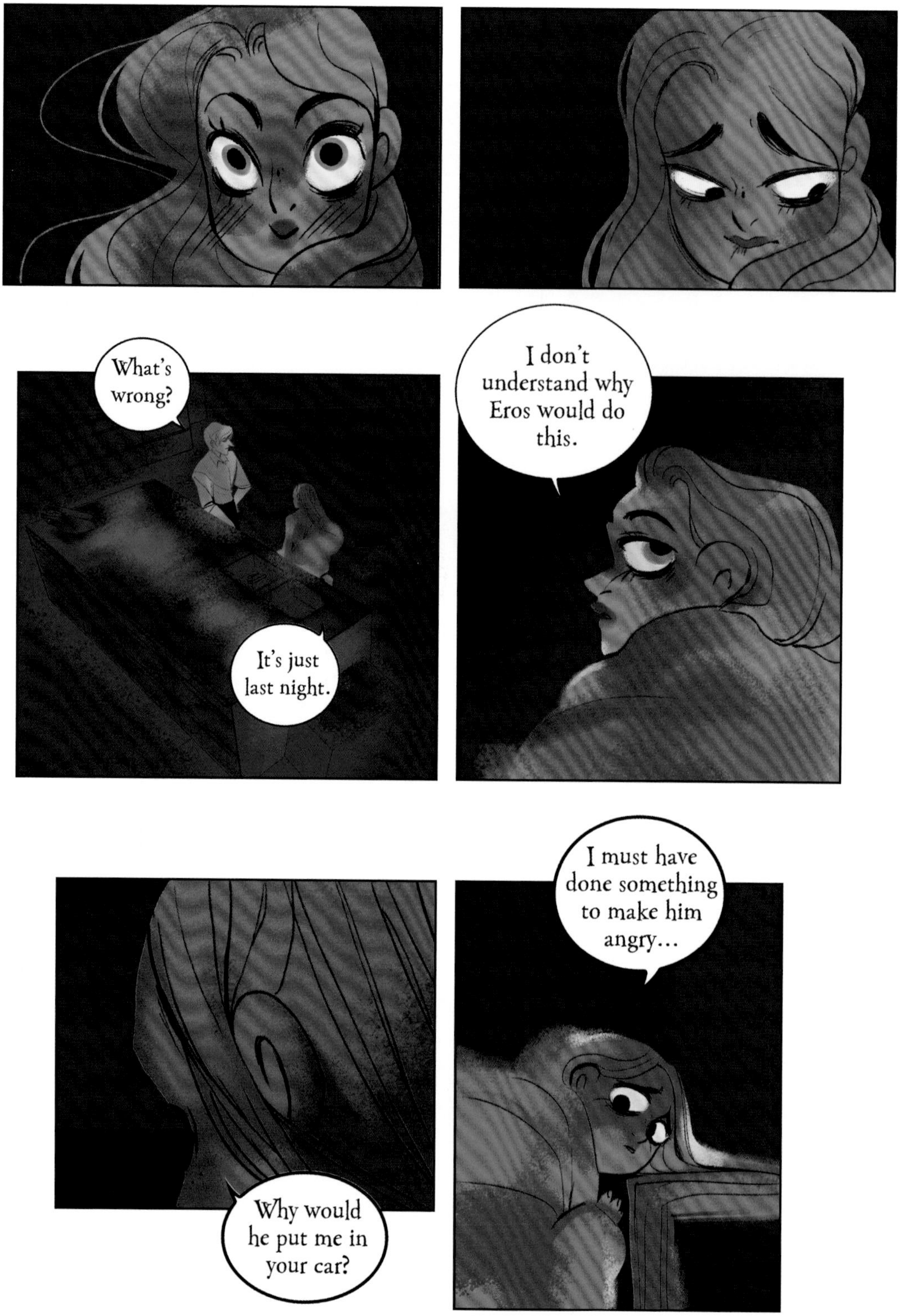
What's wrong?
It's just last night.
I don't understand why Eros would do this.
Why would he put me in your car?
I must have done something to make him angry...

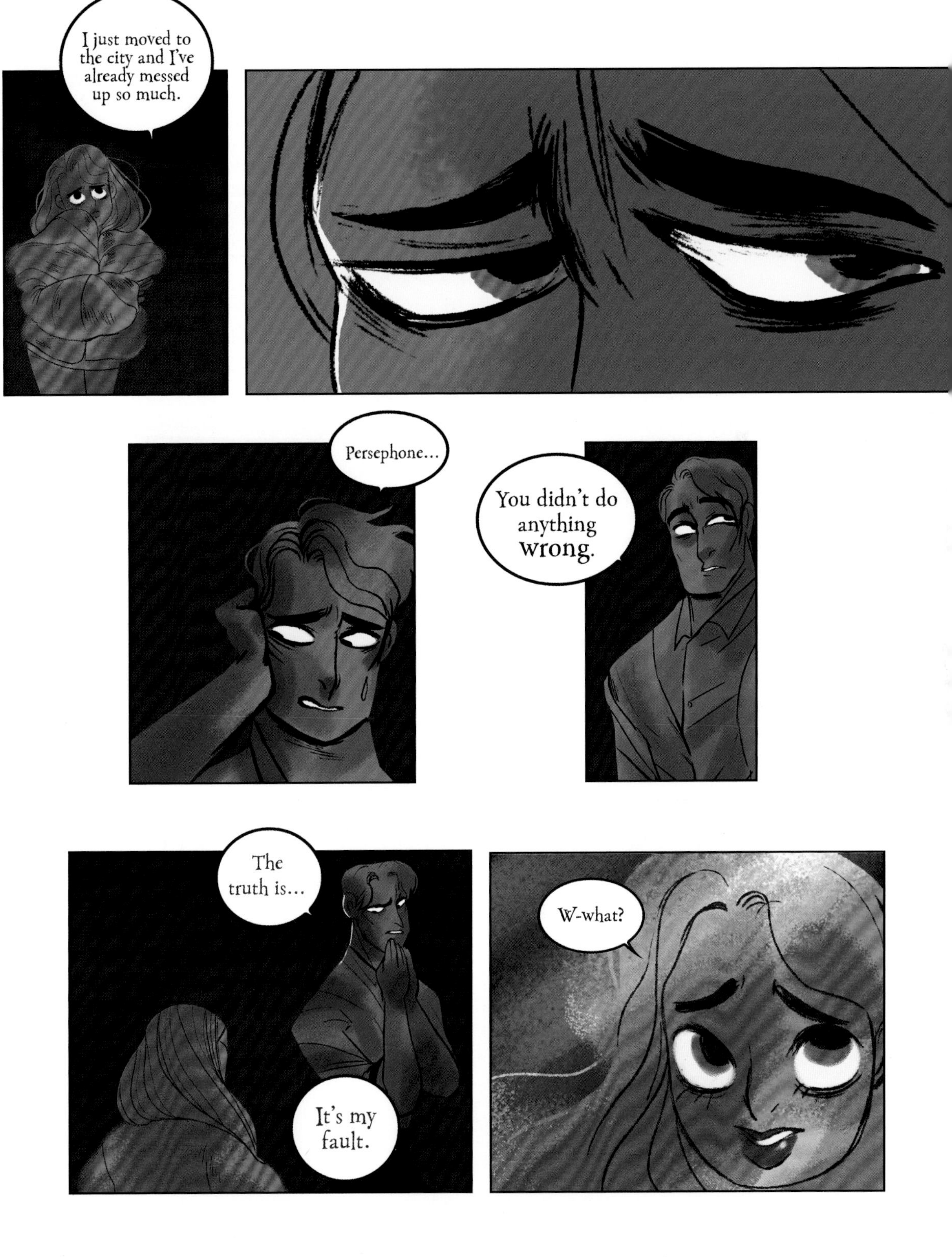
I just moved to the city and I've already messed up so much.
Persephone...
You didn't do anything wrong.
The truth is...
It's my fault.
W-what?

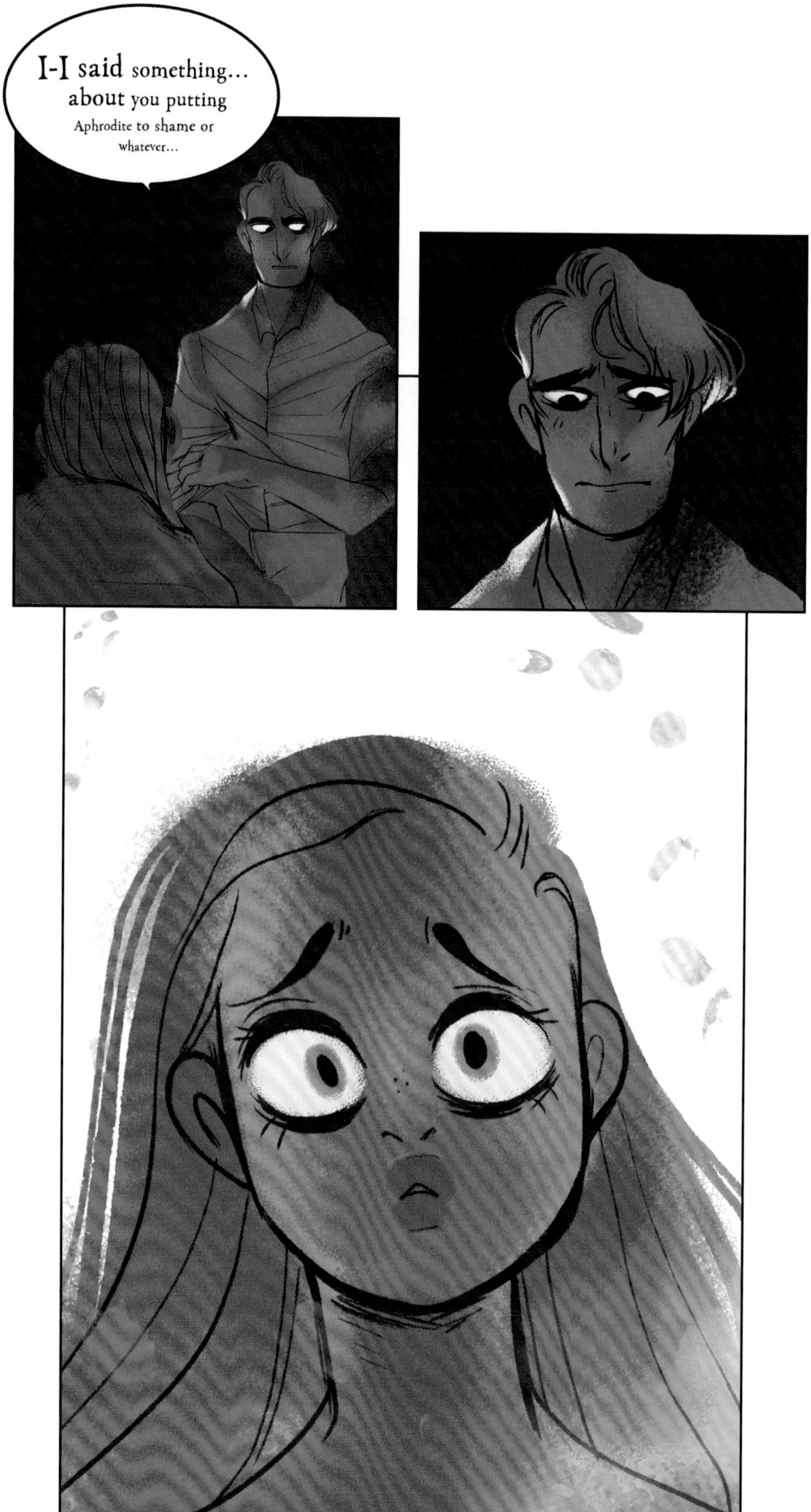
I-I said something... about you putting Aphrodite to shame or whatever...

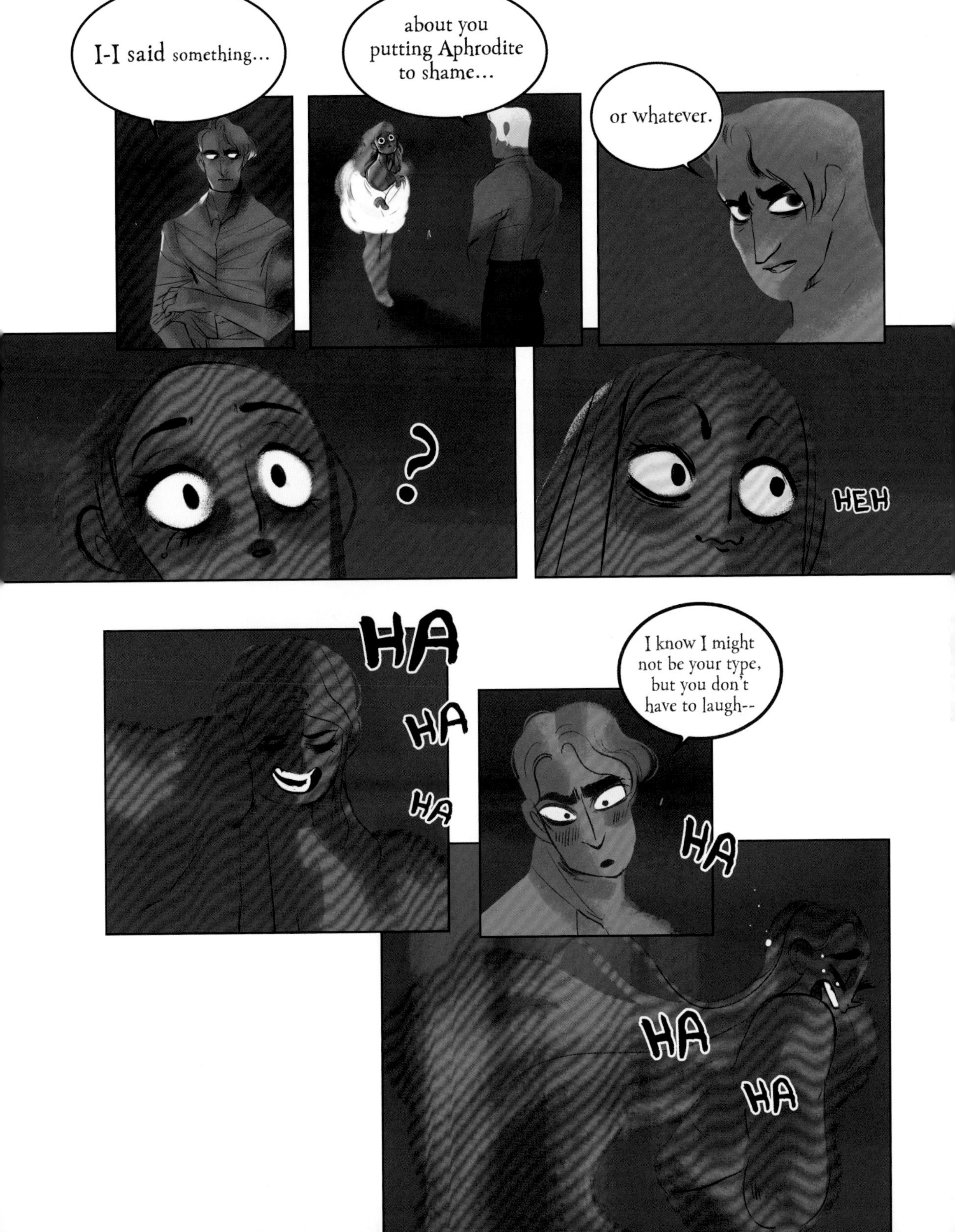

I-I said something...
about you putting Aphrodite to shame...
or whatever.
?
HEH
HA
HA
HA
I know I might not be your type, but you don't have to laugh--
HA
HA
HA

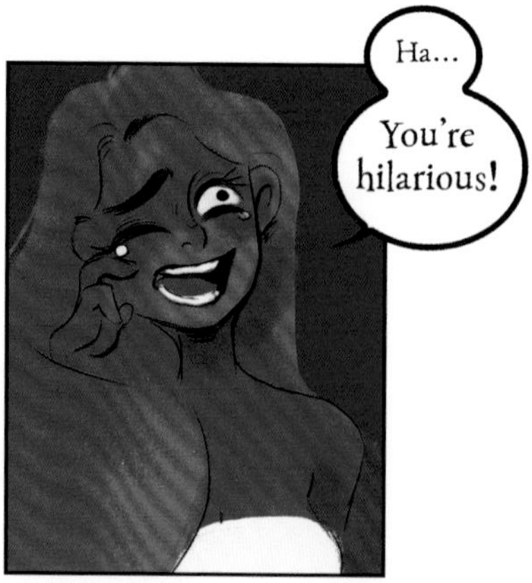
Ha...
You're hilarious!

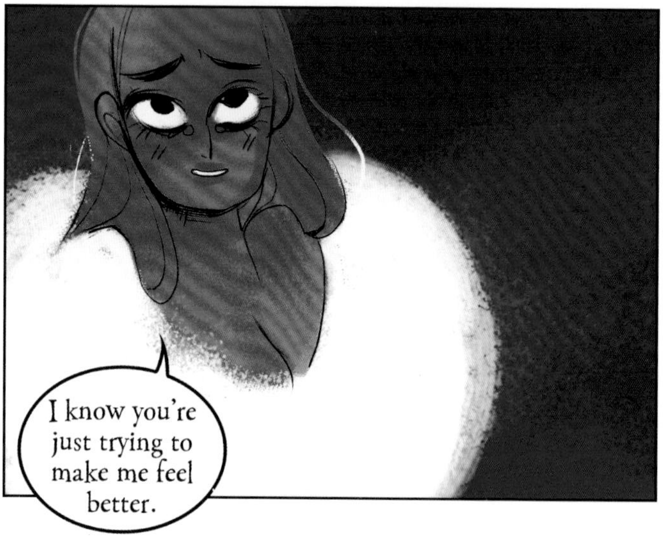
I know you're just trying to make me feel better.

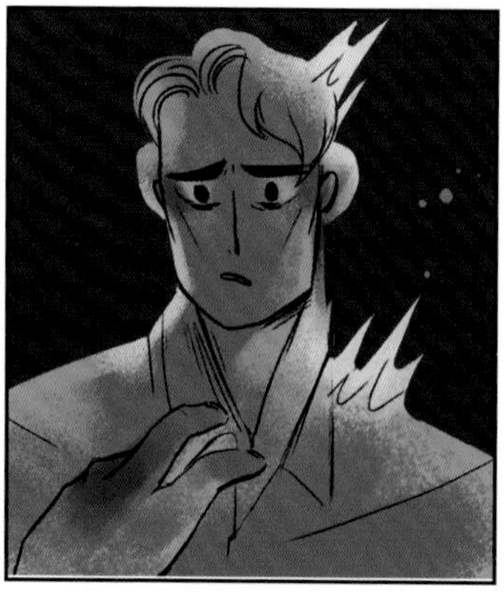

EPISODE 09: GONE TO THE DOGS

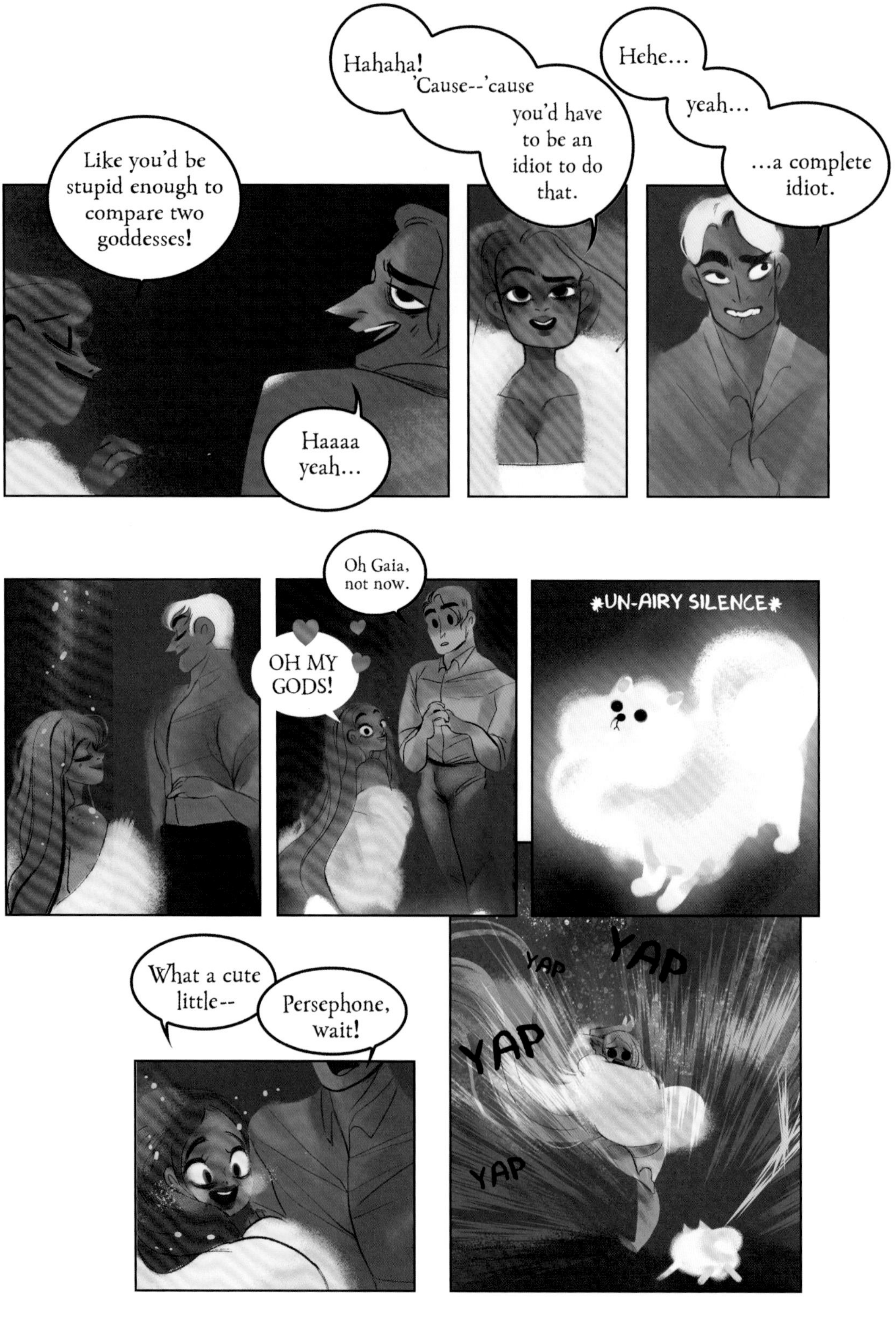
Like you'd be stupid enough to compare two goddesses!
Haaaa yeah...
Hahaha! 'Cause--'cause you'd have to be an idiot to do that.
Hehe... yeah... ...a complete idiot.
Oh Gaia, not now.
OH MY GODS!
UN-AIRY SILENCE
What a cute little--
Persephone, wait!
YAP
YAP
YAP
YAP

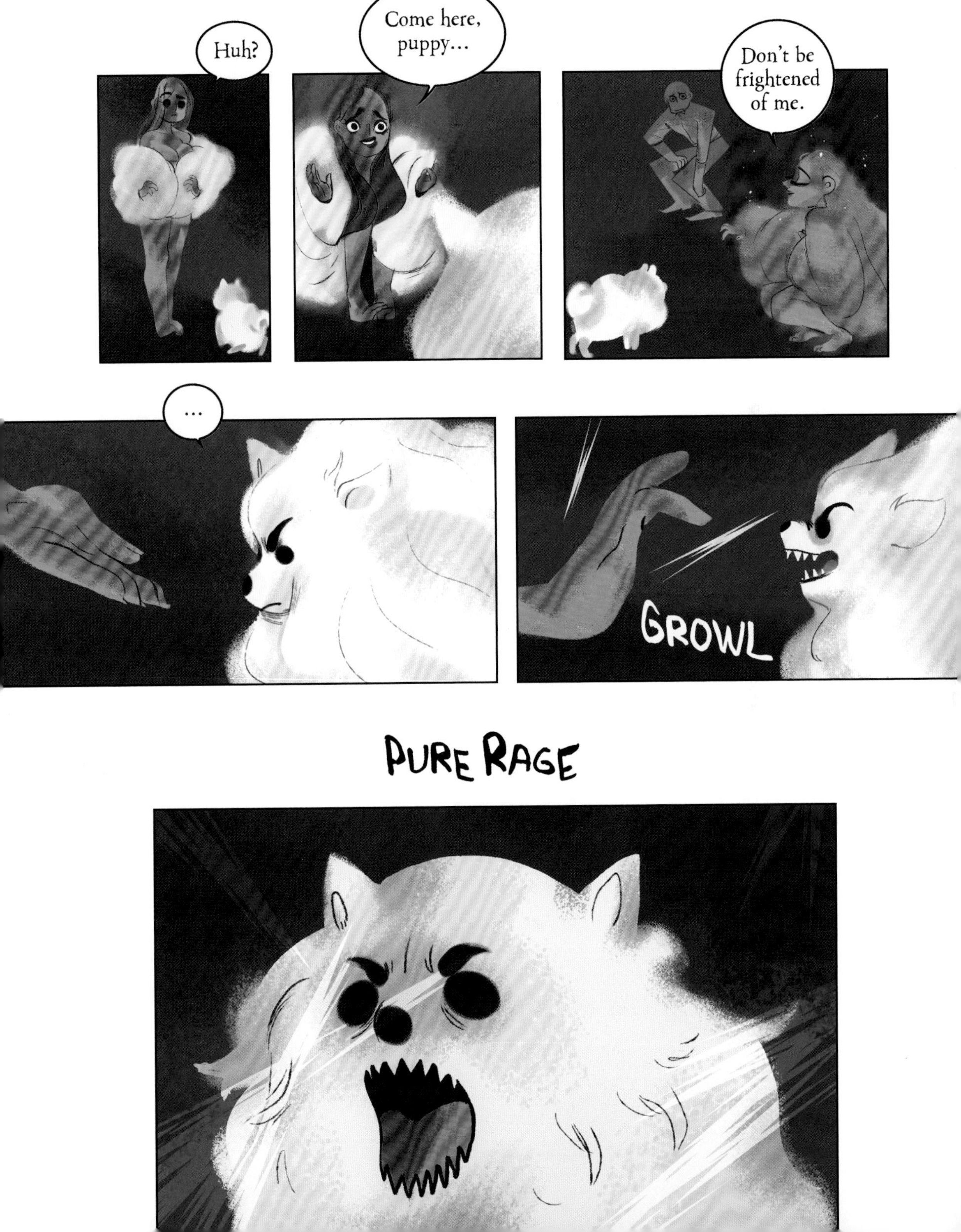
Huh?
Come here, puppy...
Don't be frightened of me.
...
GROWL
PURE RAGE

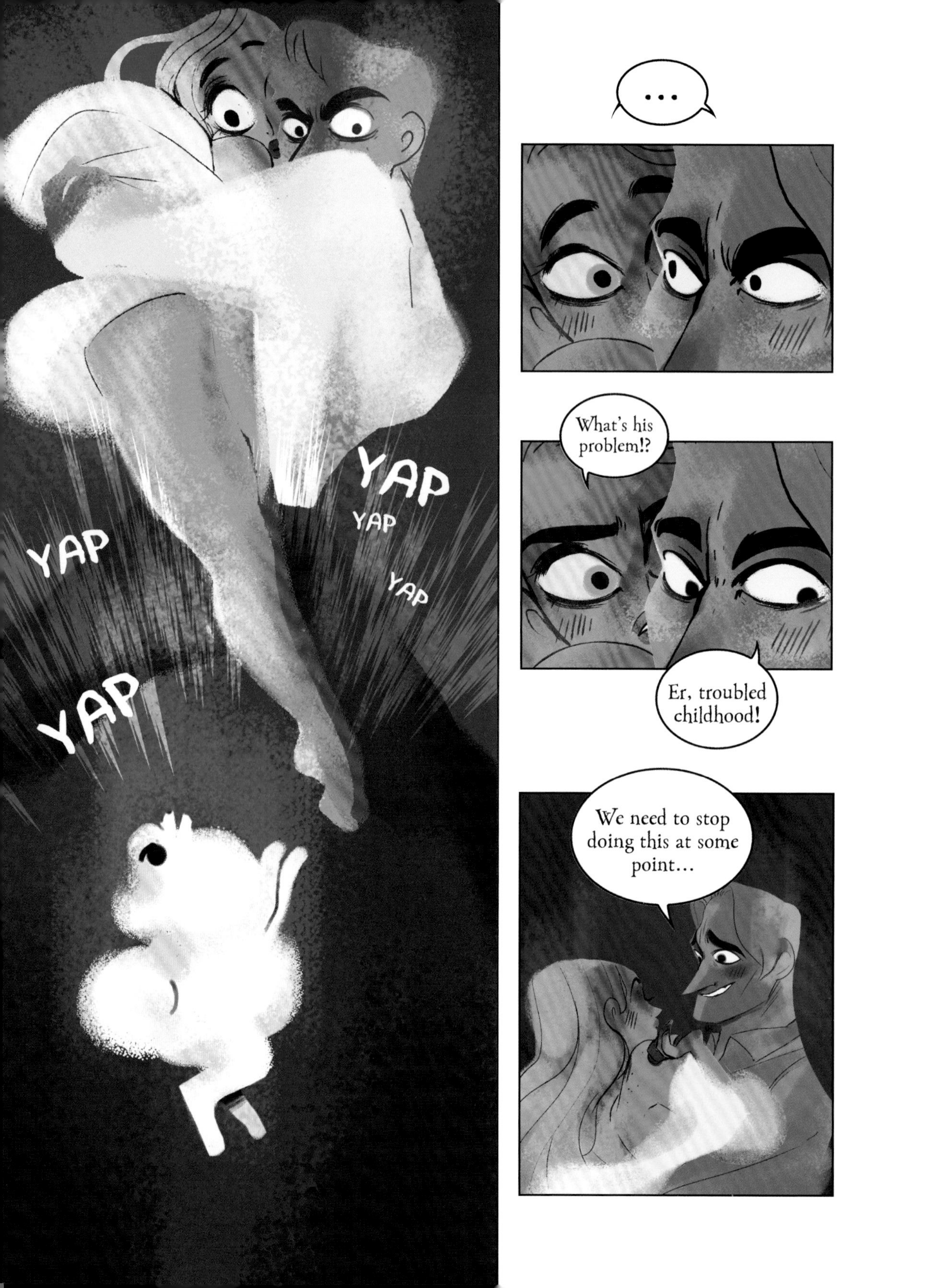
YAP
YAP
YAP
YAP
YAP
...
What's his problem!?
Er, troubled childhood!
We need to stop doing this at some point...

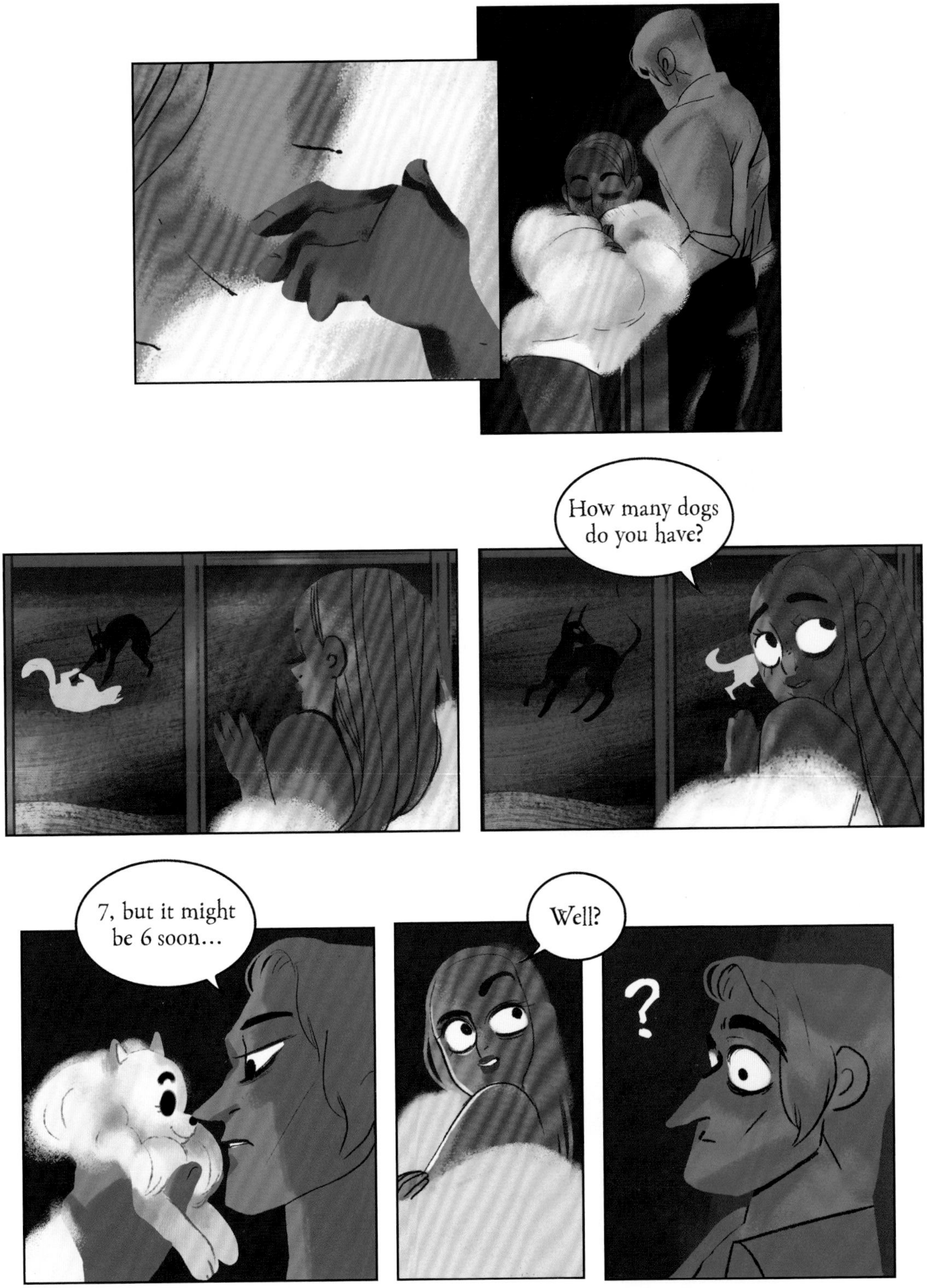
How many dogs do you have?
7, but it might be 6 soon...
Well?
?

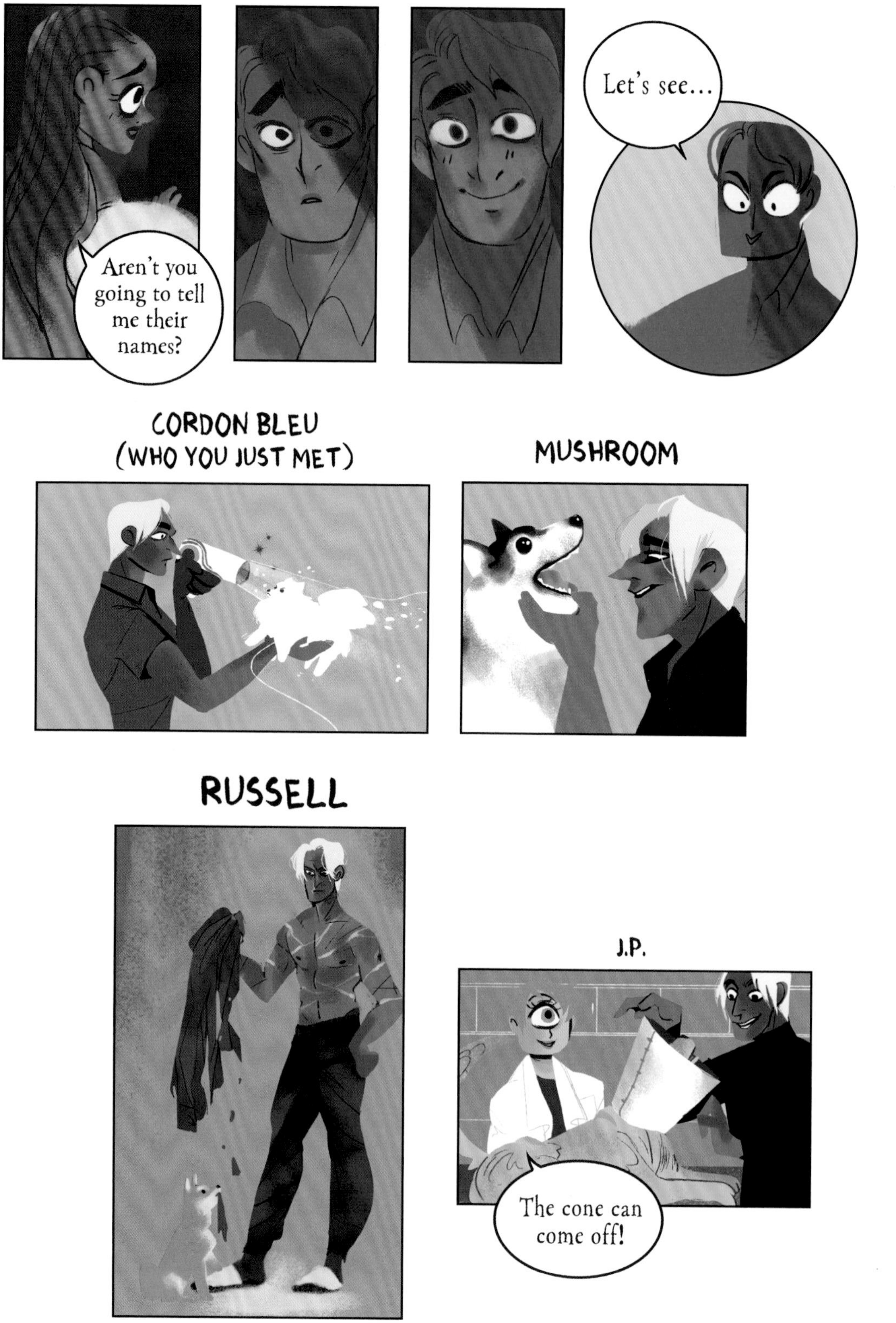
Aren't you going to tell me their names?
Let's see...
CORDON BLEU (WHO YOU JUST MET)
MUSHROOM
RUSSELL
J.P.
The cone can come off!

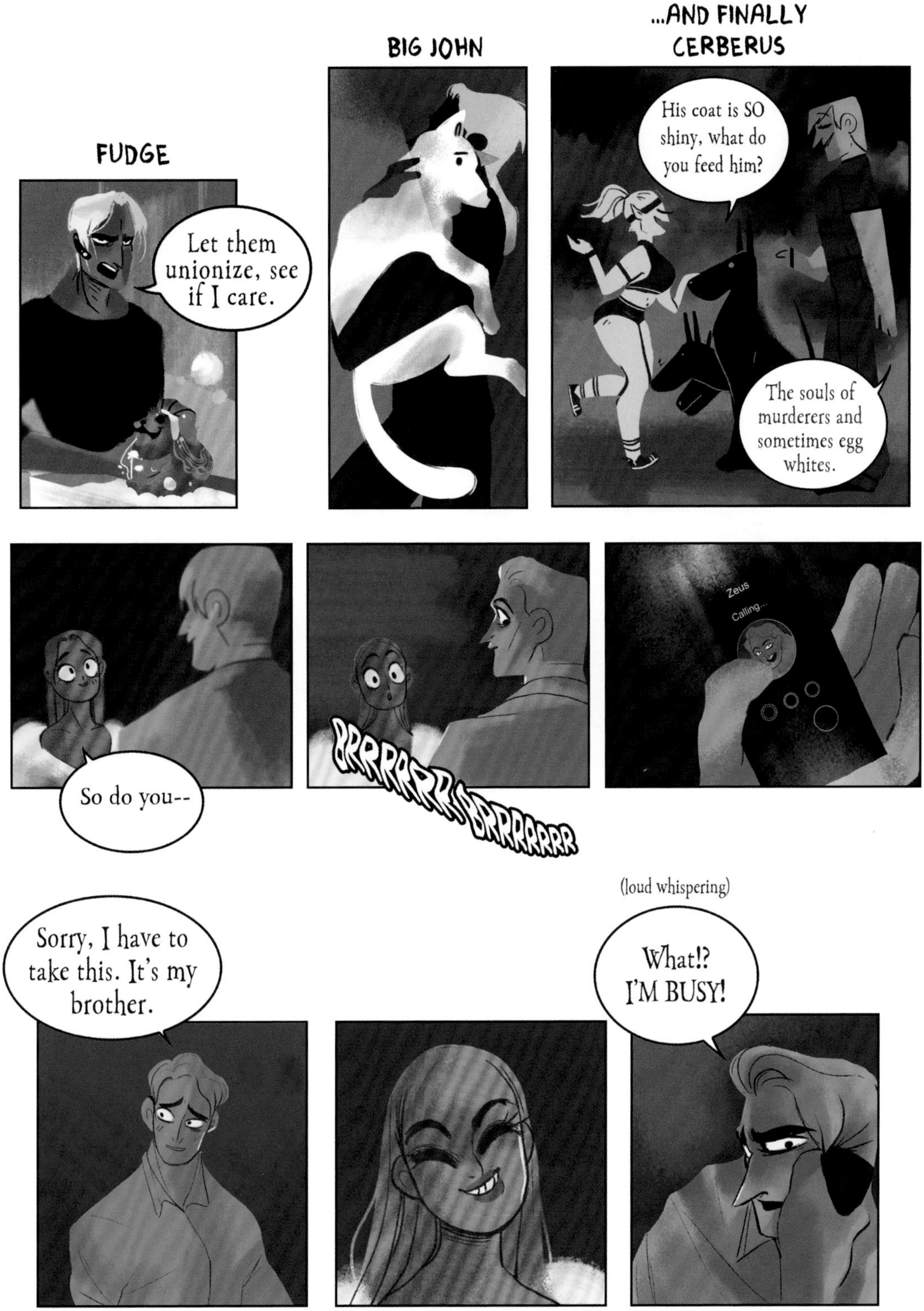
FUDGE
Let them unionize, see if I care.
BIG JOHN
...AND FINALLY CERBERUS
His coat is SO shiny, what do you feed him?
The souls of murderers and sometimes egg whites.
So do you--
BRRRRRRR BRRRRRRRR
Zeus
Calling...
Sorry, I have to take this. It's my brother.
(loud whispering)
What!? I'M BUSY!

(loud whispering)

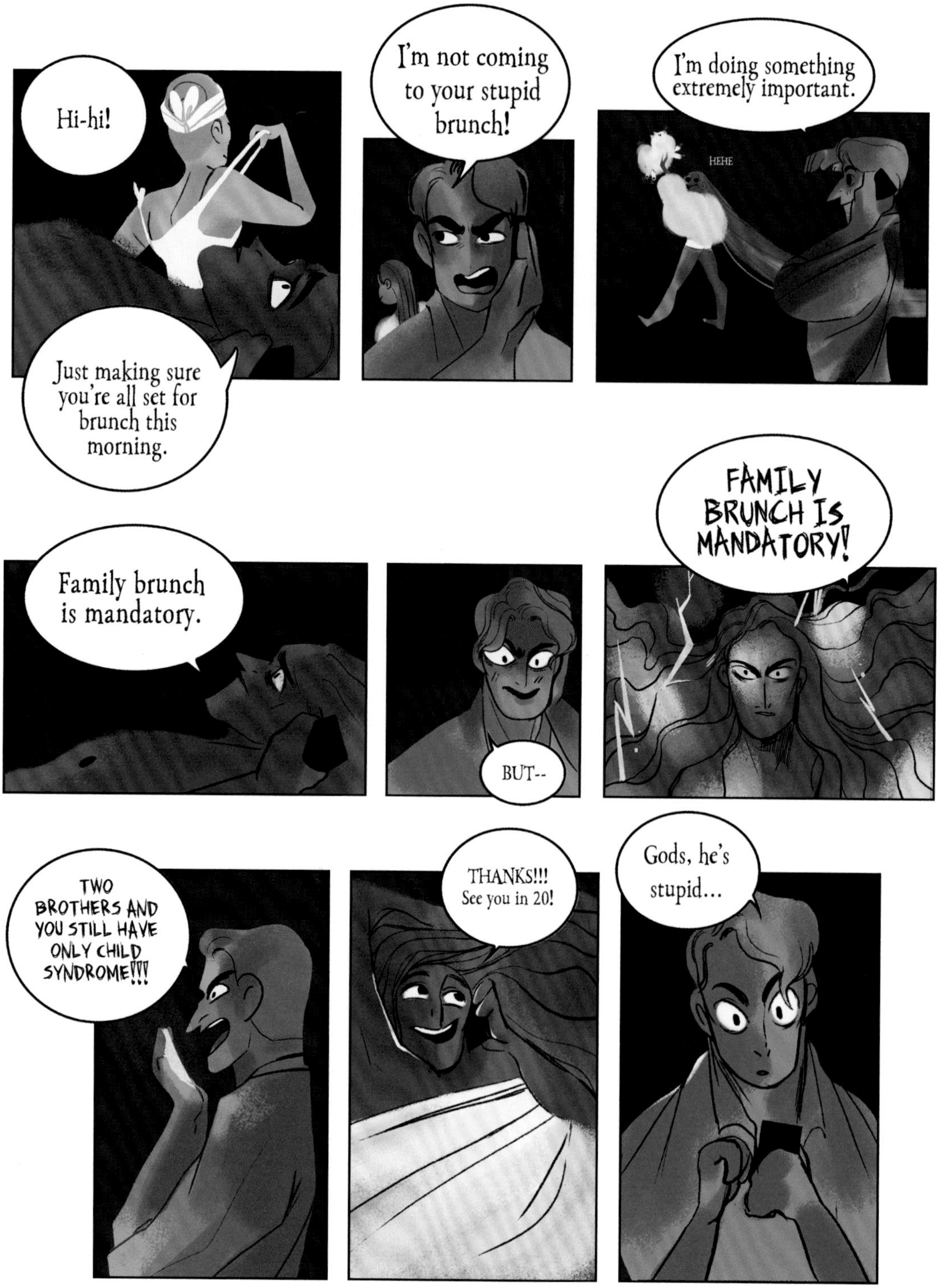
Hi-hi!
Just making sure you're all set for brunch this morning.
I'm not coming to your stupid brunch!
I'm doing something extremely important.
HEHE
Family brunch is mandatory.
BUT--
FAMILY BRUNCH IS MANDATORY!
TWO BROTHERS AND YOU STILL HAVE ONLY CHILD SYNDROME!!!
THANKS!!! See you in 20!
Gods, he's stupid...

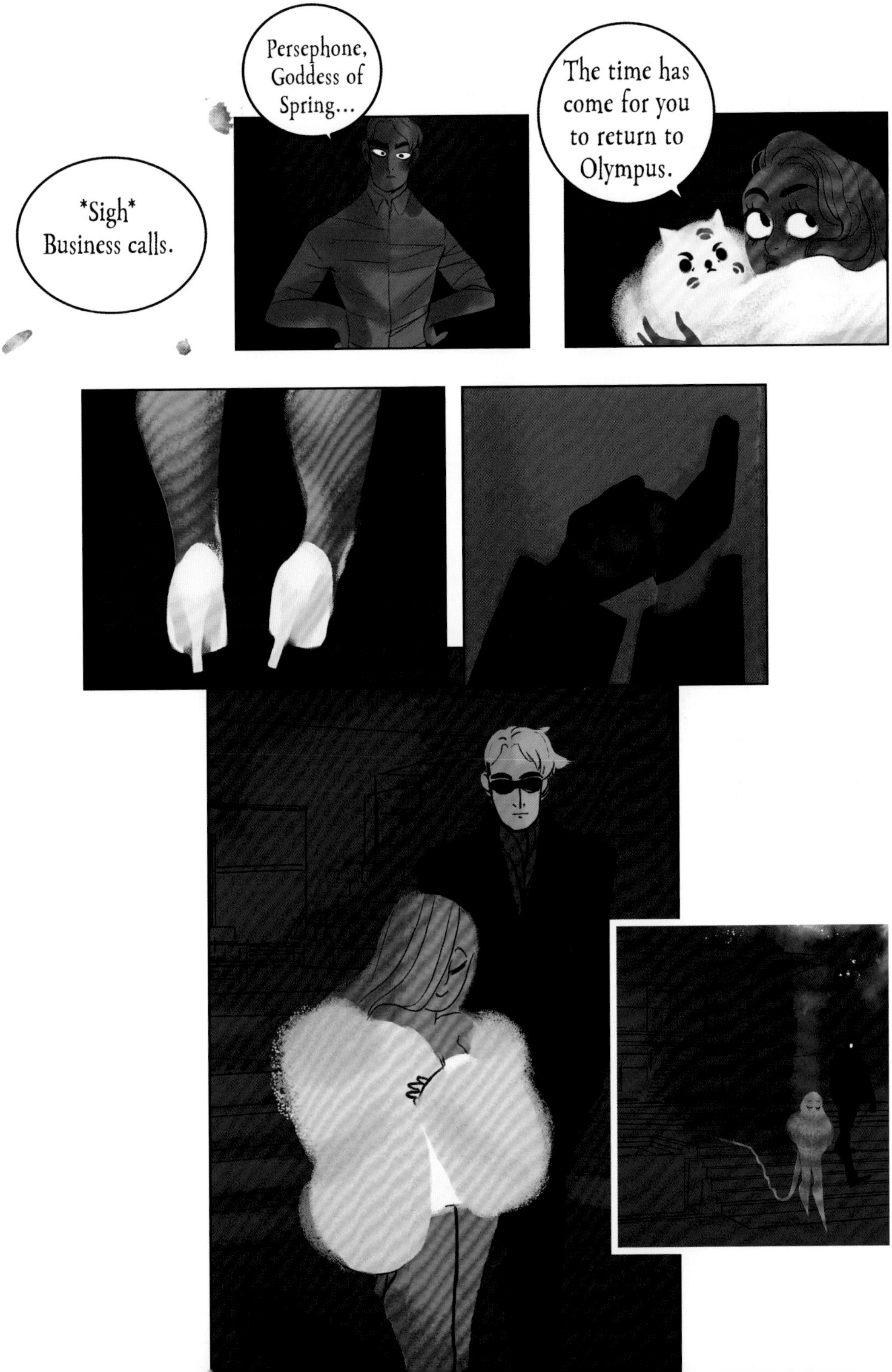
Sigh Business calls.
Persephone, Goddess of Spring...
The time has come for you to return to Olympus.

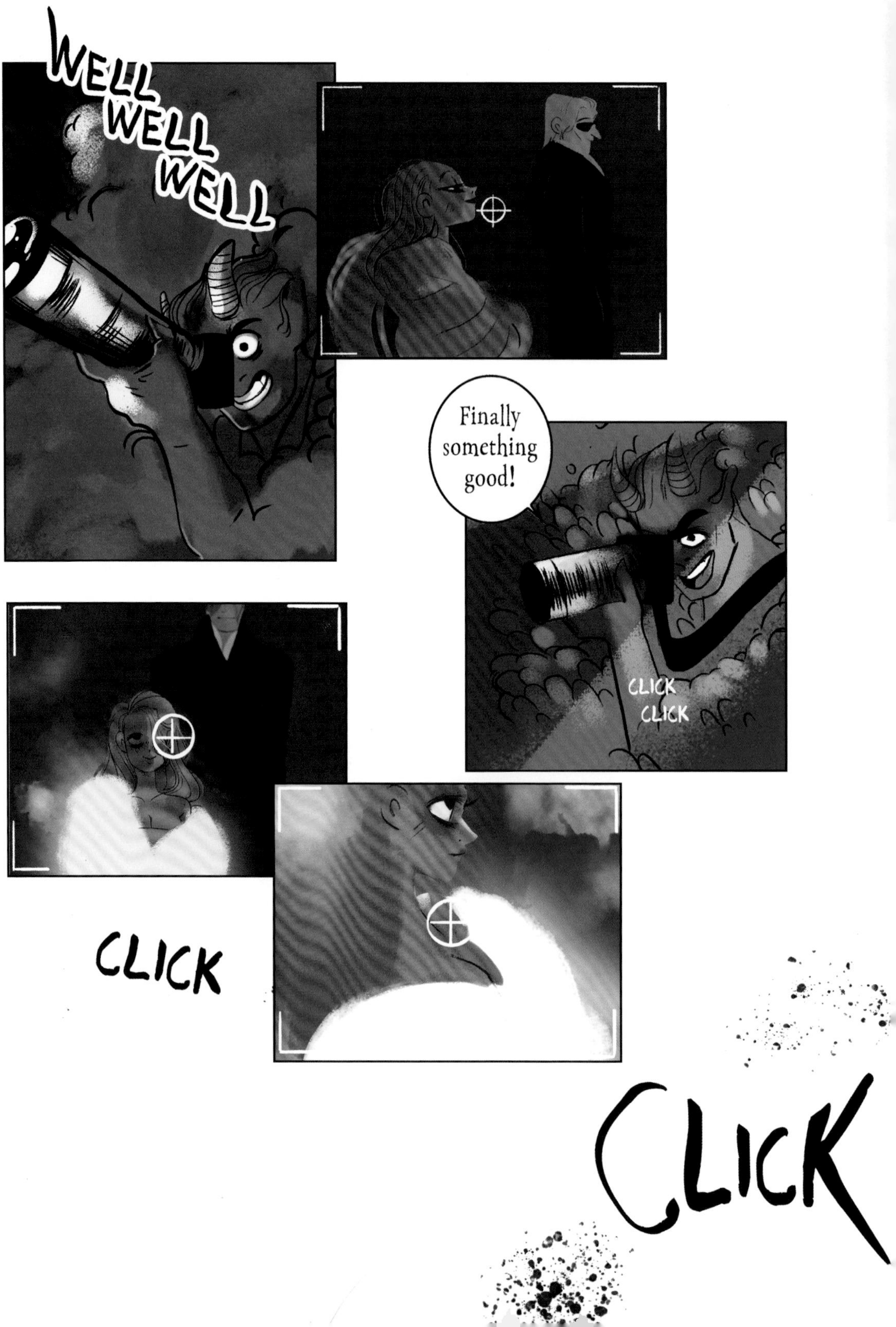
WELL WELL WELL
Finally something good!
CLICK CLICK
CLICK
CLICK

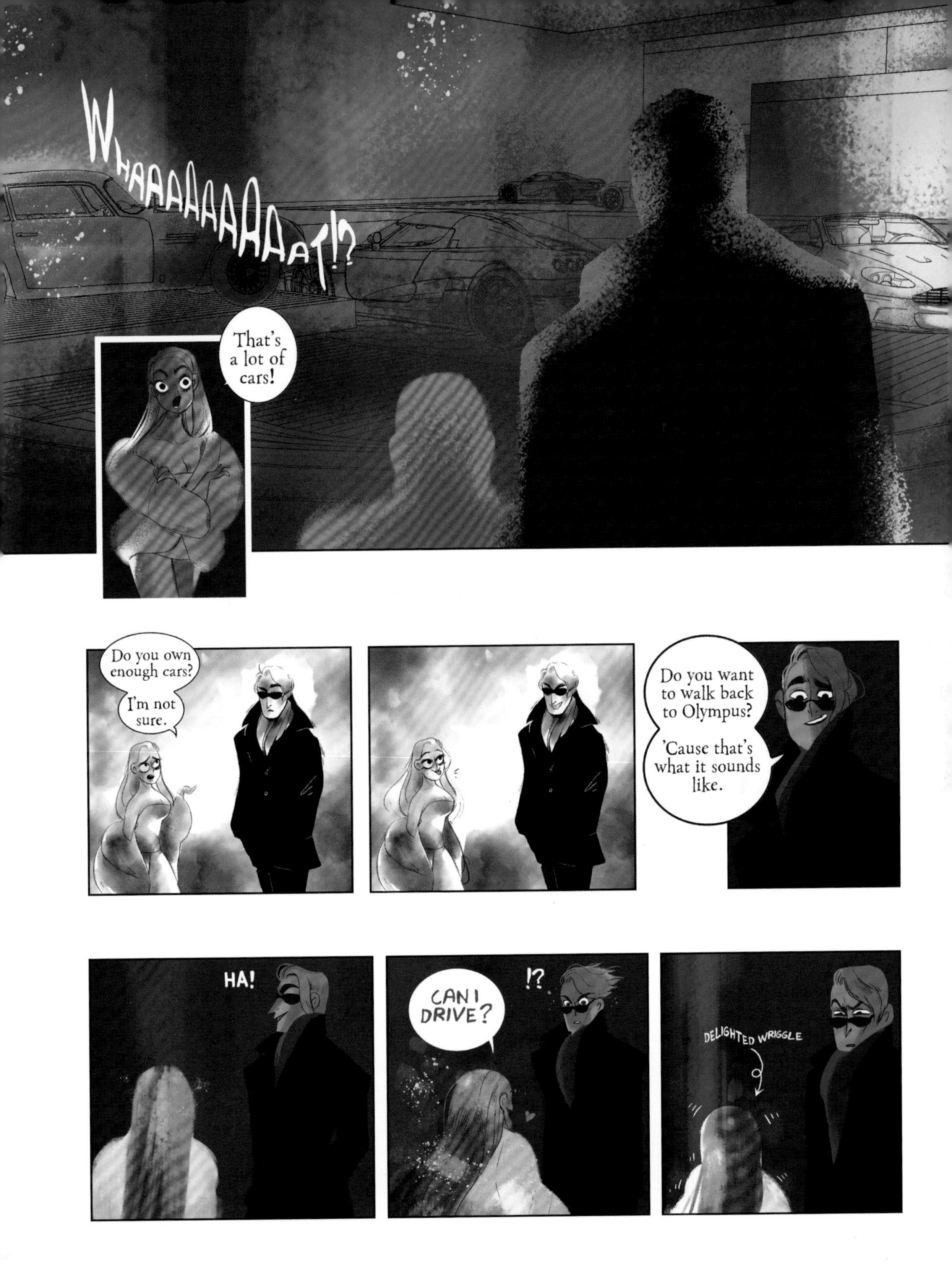
WHAAAAAAAAAAT!?
That's a lot of cars!
Do you own enough cars?
I'm not sure.
Do you want to walk back to Olympus?
'Cause that's what it sounds like.
HA!
CAN I DRIVE?
!?
DELIGHTED WRIGGLE

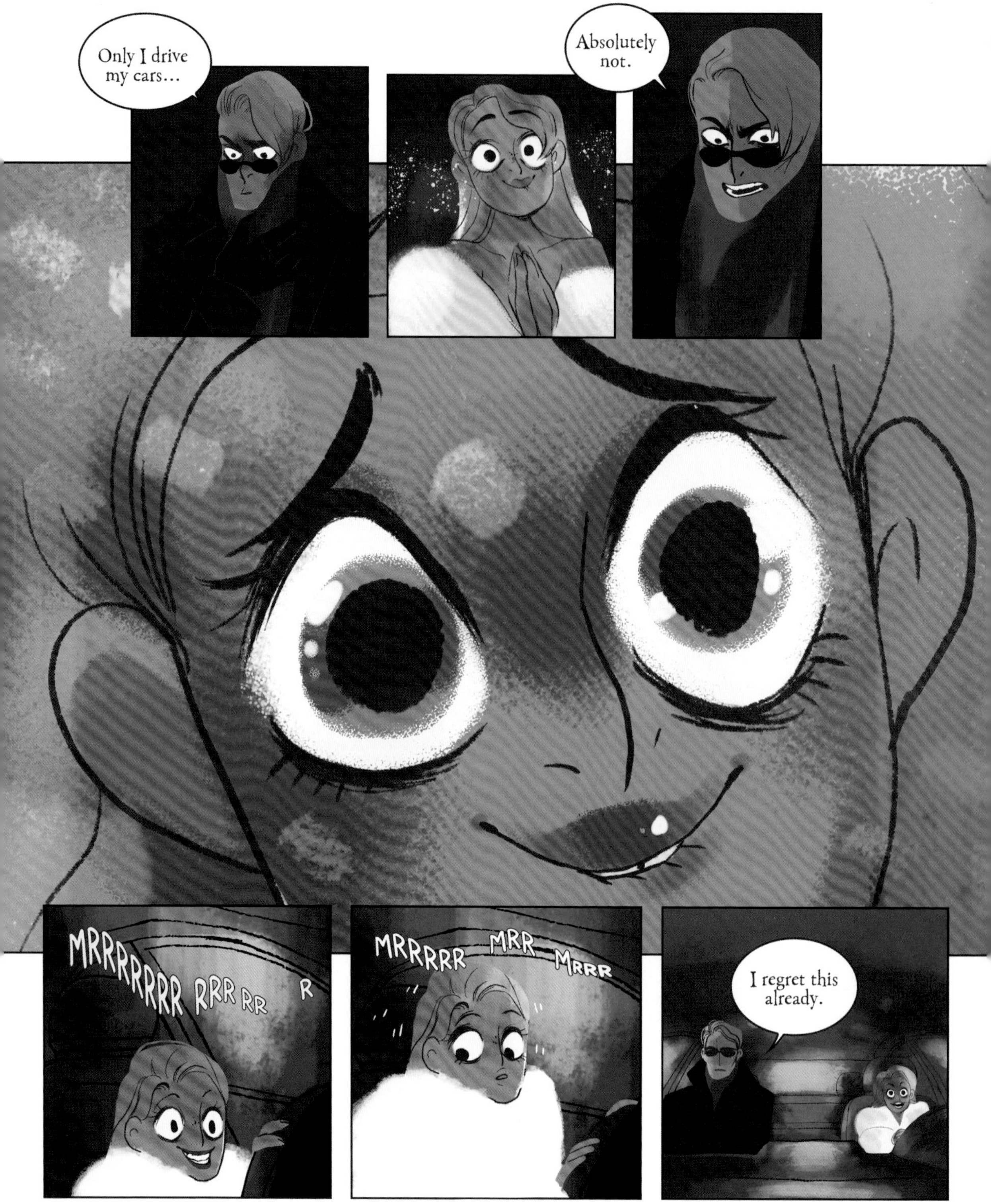
Only I drive my cars...
Absolutely not.
MRRRRRRRR RRR RR R
MRRRRR MRR MRRR
I regret this already.

EPISODE 10: DISEMBARK

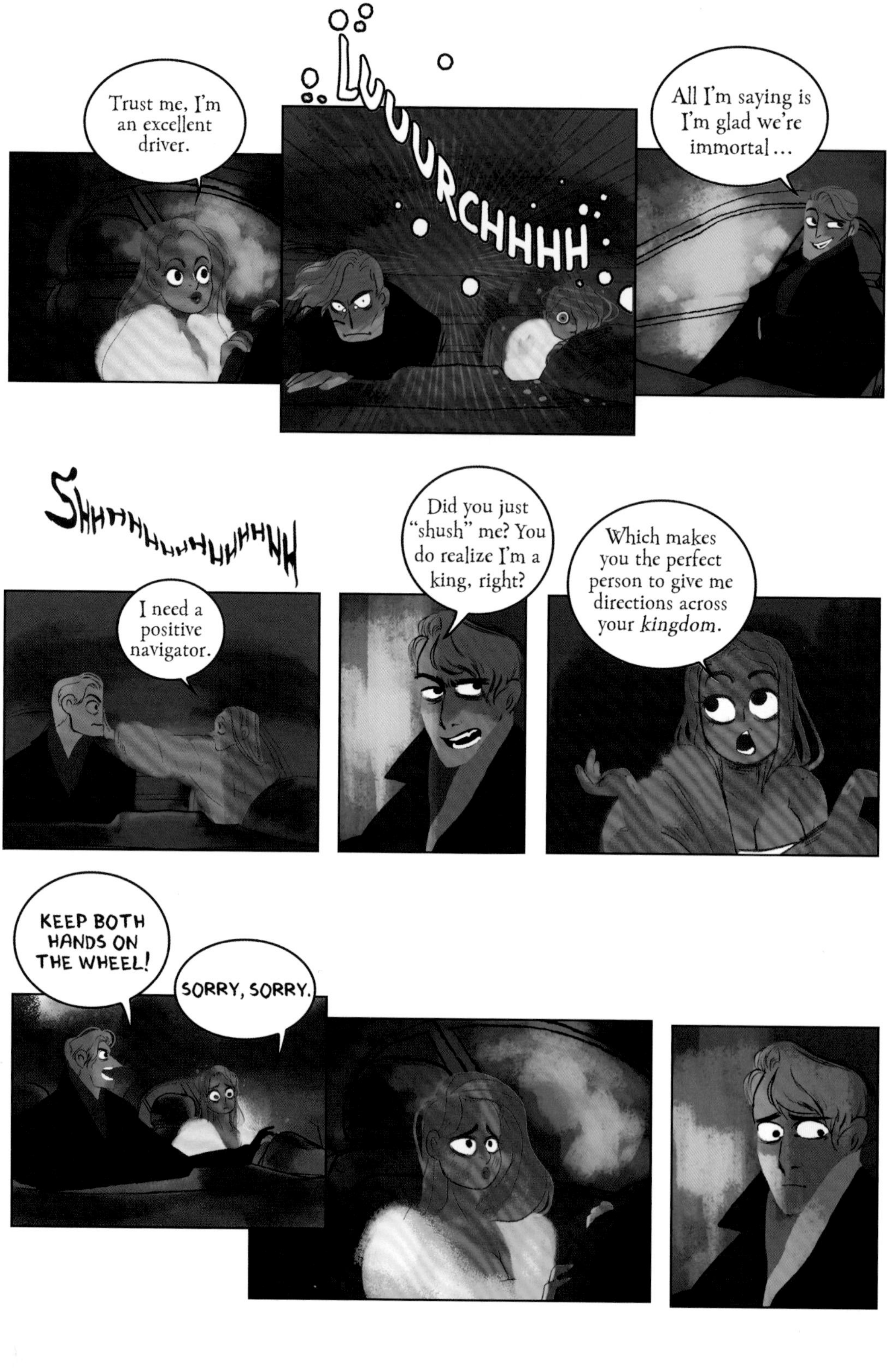

Trust me, I'm an excellent driver.
LUUURCHHHH
All I'm saying is I'm glad we're immortal . . .
SHHHHHHHHHHHHNH
I need a positive navigator.
Did you just "shush" me? You do realize I'm a king, right?
Which makes you the perfect person to give me directions across your *kingdom*.
KEEP BOTH HANDS ON THE WHEEL!
SORRY, SORRY.

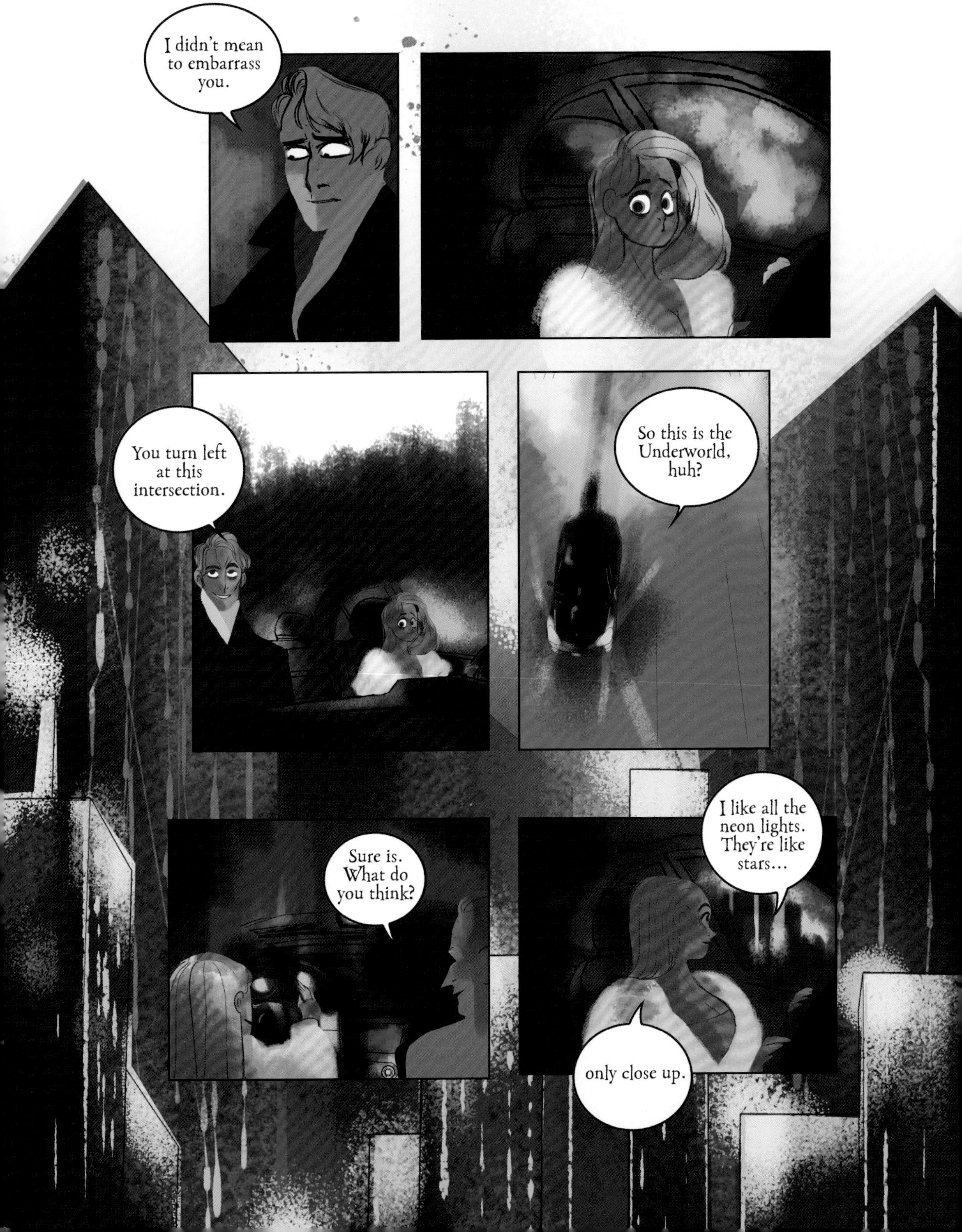
I didn't mean to embarrass you.
You turn left at this intersection.
So this is the Underworld, huh?
Sure is. What do you think?
I like all the neon lights. They're like stars…
only close up.

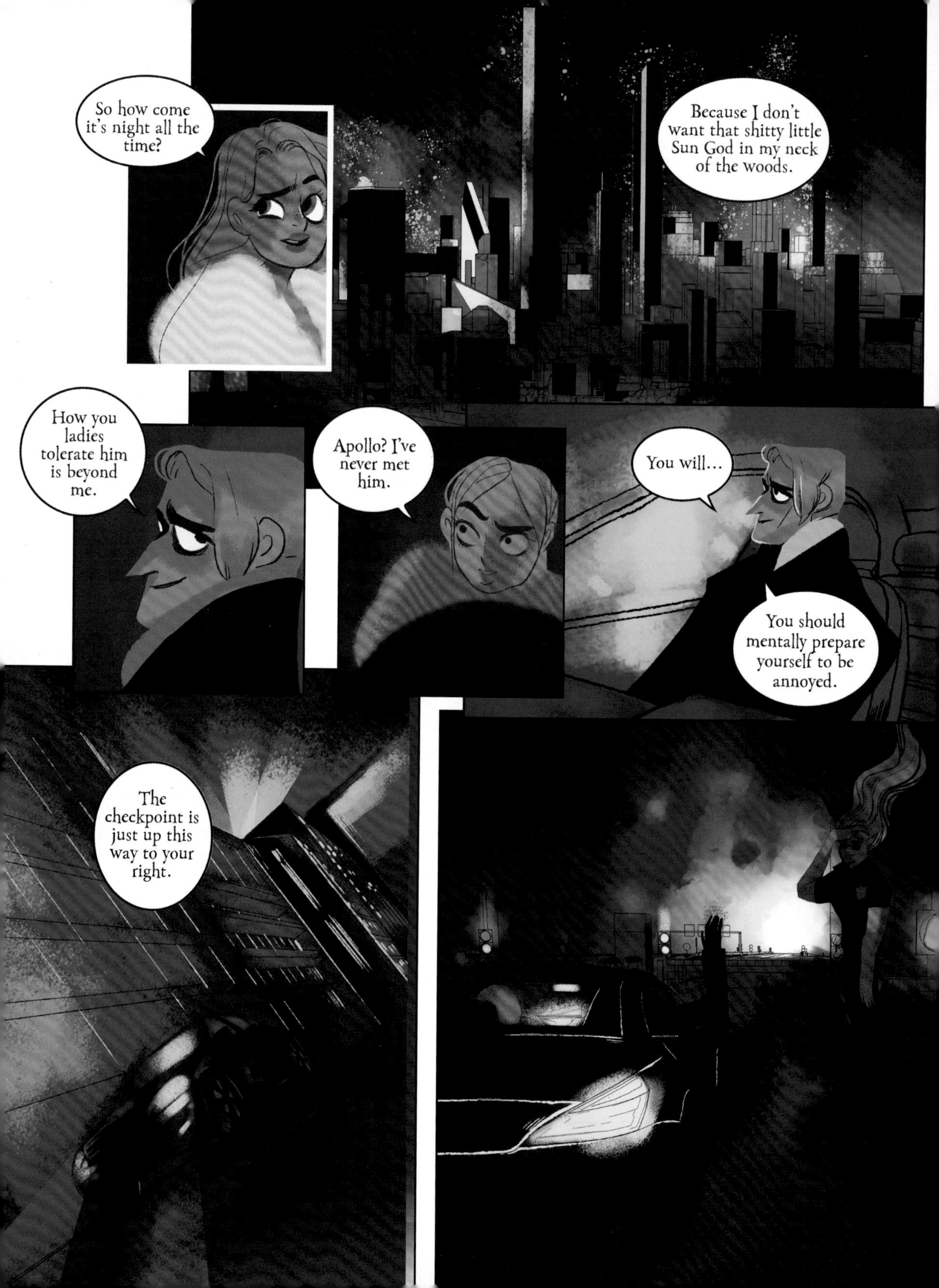
So how come it's night all the time?
Because I don't want that shitty little Sun God in my neck of the woods.
How you ladies tolerate him is beyond me.
Apollo? I've never met him.
You will...
You should mentally prepare yourself to be annoyed.
The checkpoint is just up this way to your right.

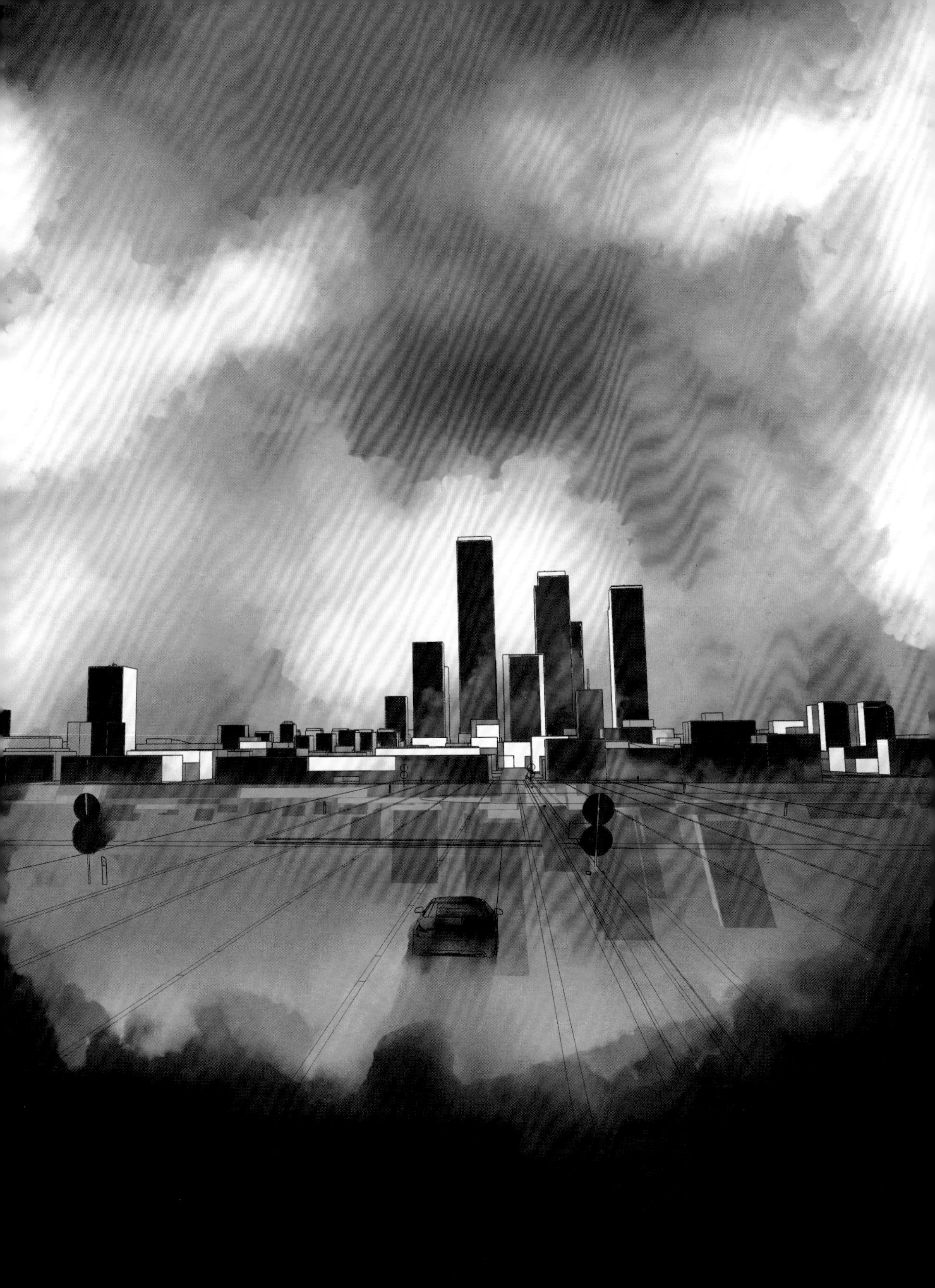

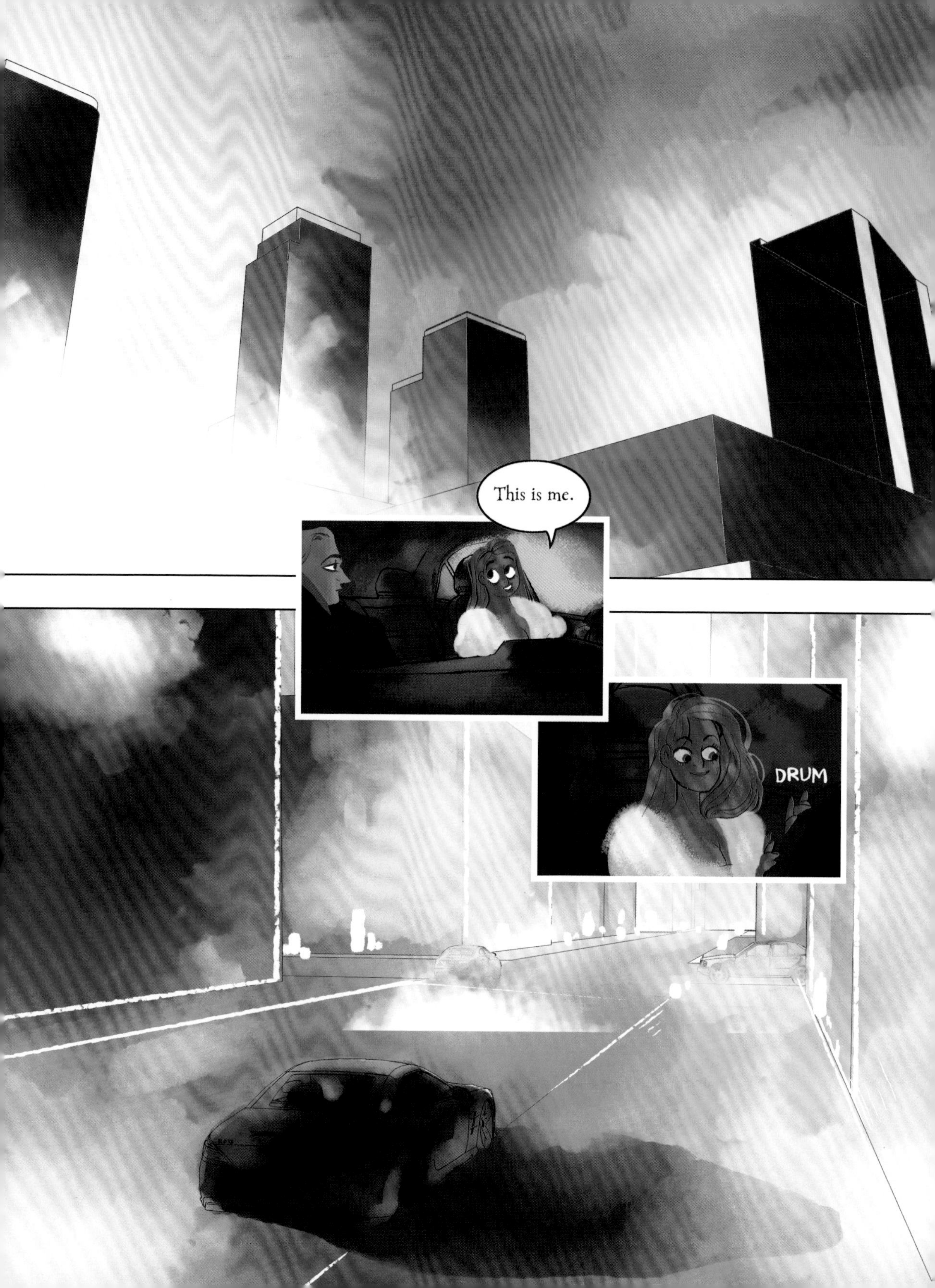
This is me.
DRUM

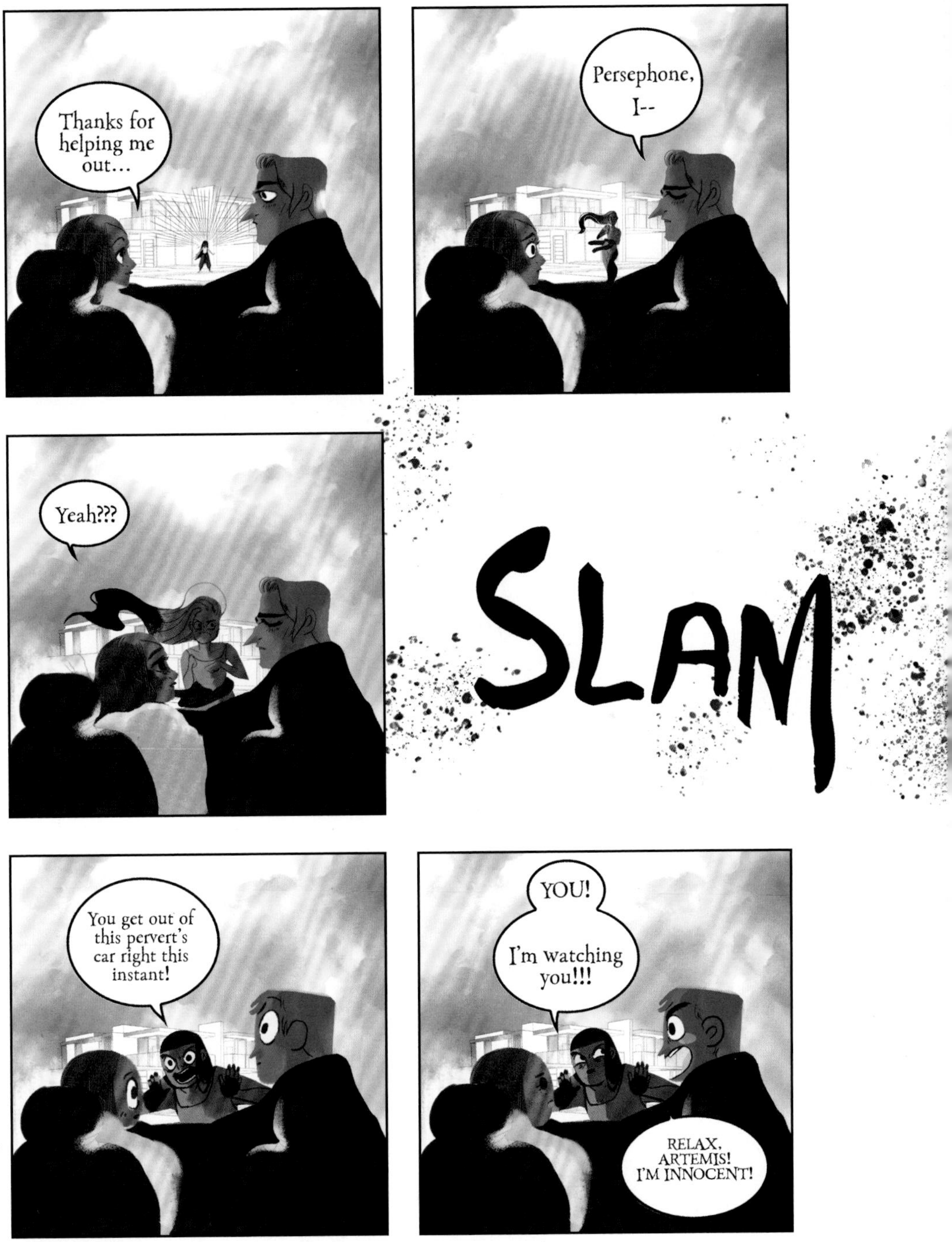
Thanks for helping me out...
Persephone, I--
Yeah???
SLAM
You get out of this pervert's car right this instant!
YOU!
I'm watching you!!!
RELAX, ARTEMIS! I'M INNOCENT!

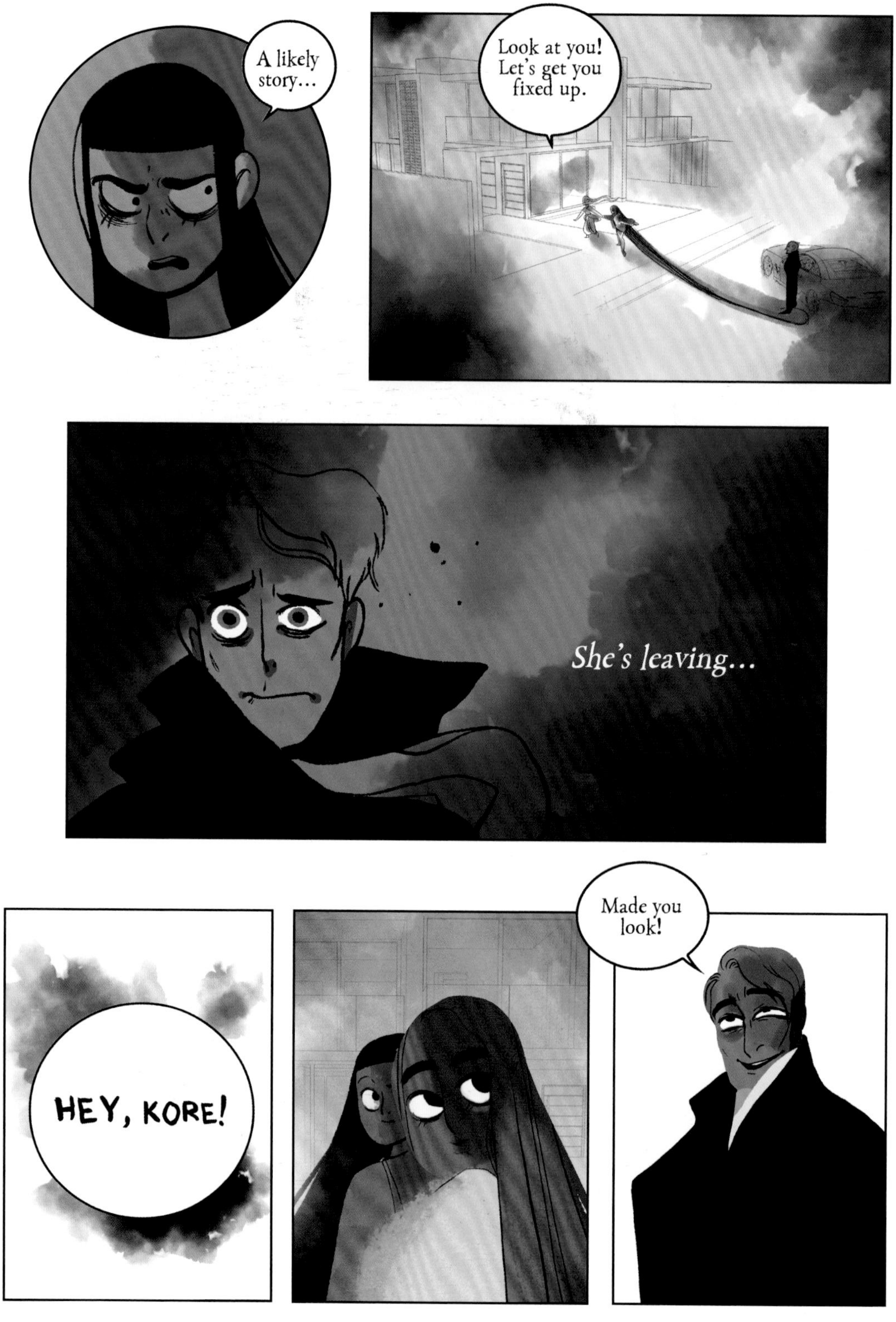
A likely story…
Look at you! Let's get you fixed up.
She's leaving…
HEY, KORE!
Made you look!

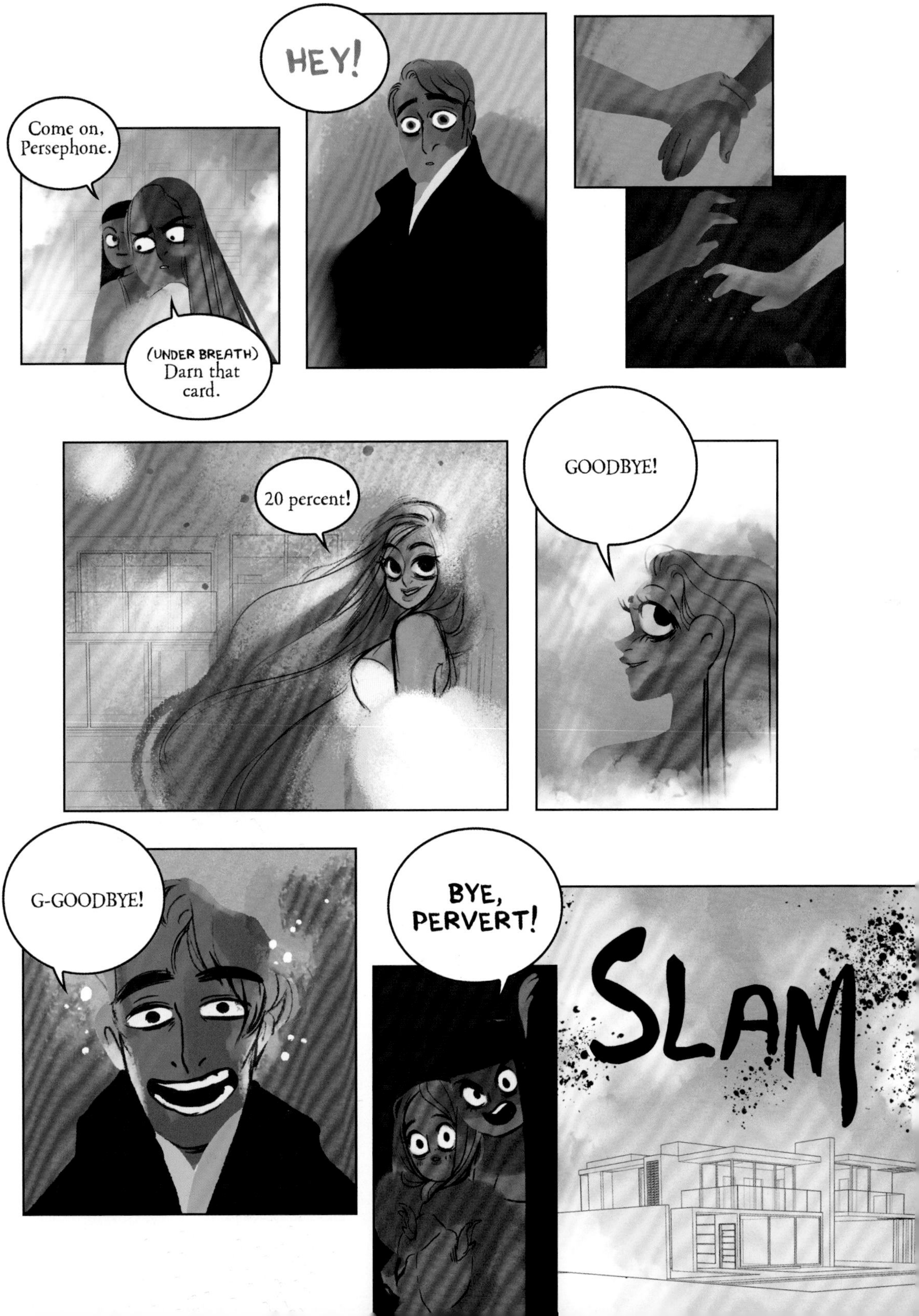
Come on, Persephone.
(UNDER BREATH) Darn that card.
HEY!
20 percent!
GOODBYE!
G-GOODBYE!
BYE, PERVERT!
SLAM

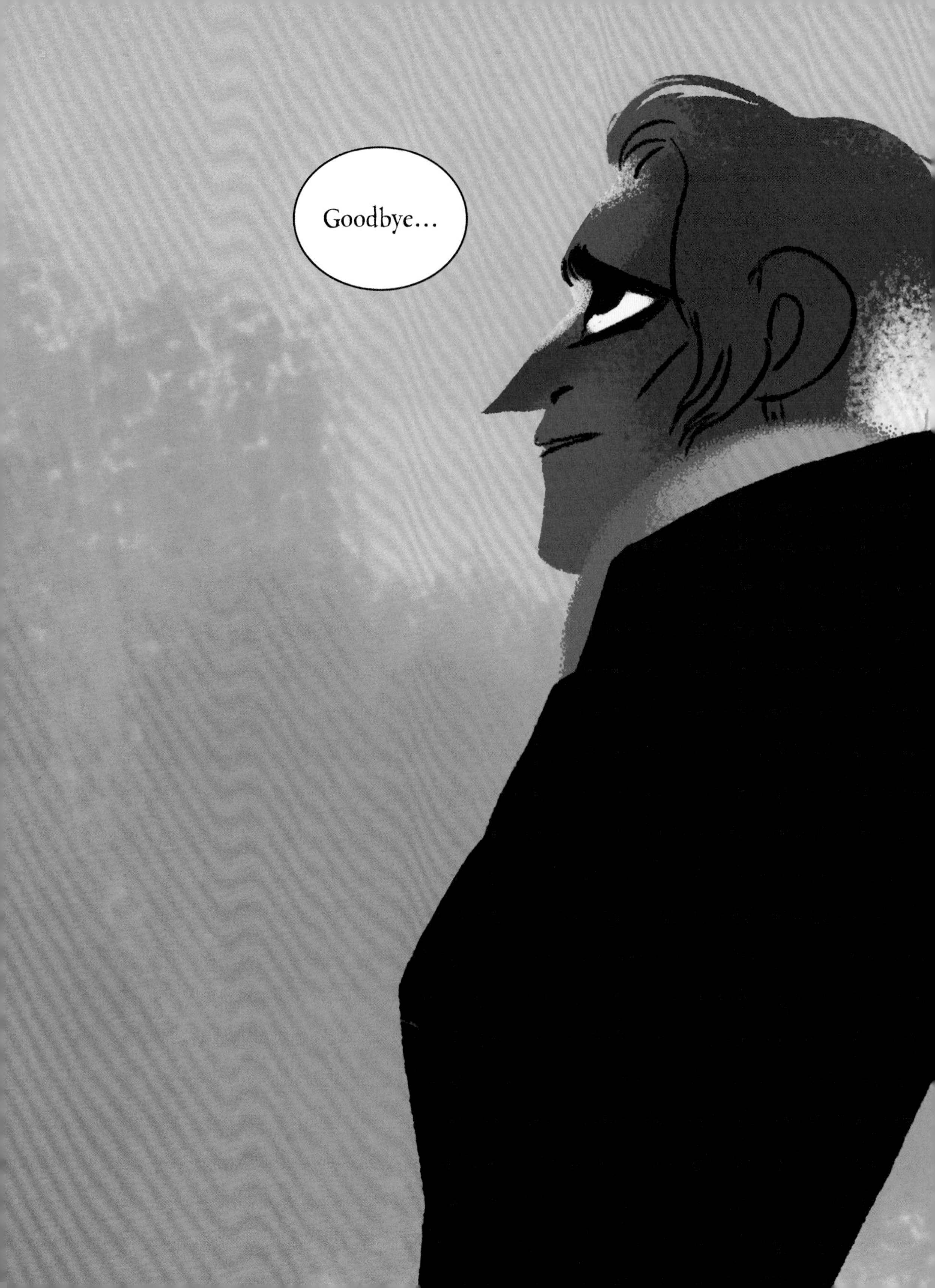
Goodbye…

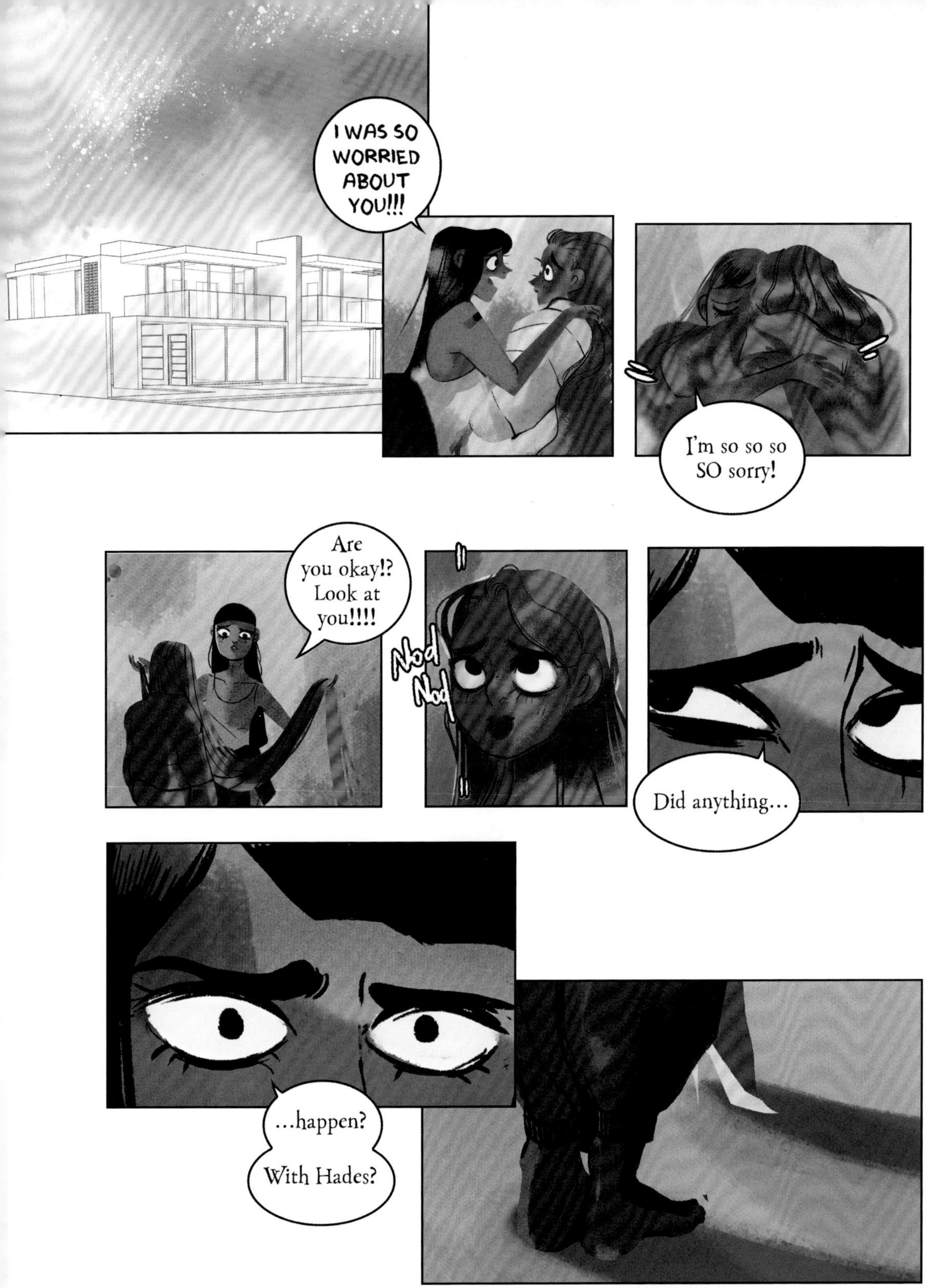

I WAS SO WORRIED ABOUT YOU!!!
I'm so so so SO sorry!
Are you okay!? Look at you!!!!
Nod Nod
Did anything...
...happen?
With Hades?

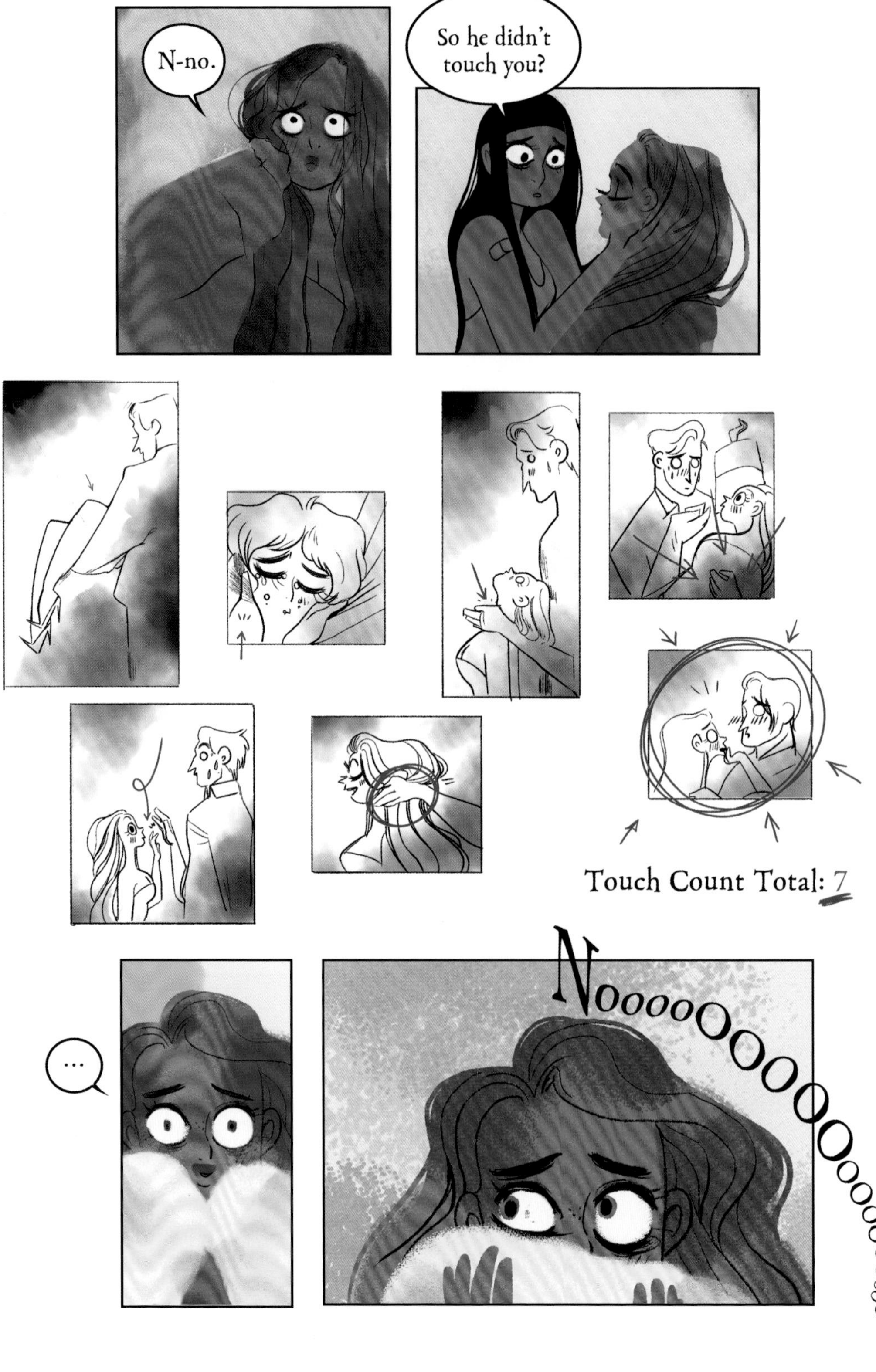
N-no.
So he didn't touch you?
Touch Count Total: 7
...
NoooooOOOOOOOooooooooooooooo

EPISODE 11: UNSUPERVISED

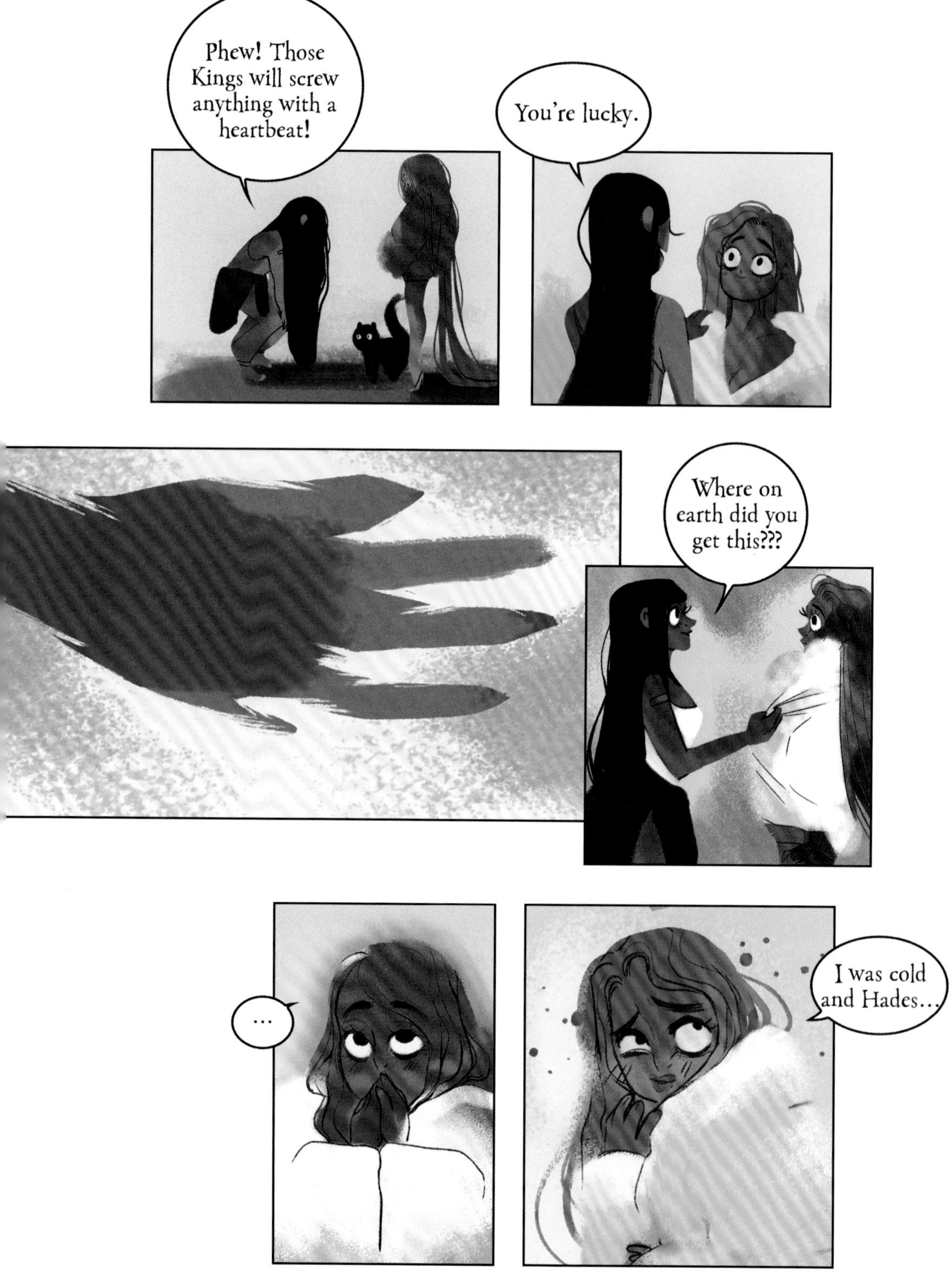
Phew! Those Kings will screw anything with a heartbeat!
You're lucky.
Where on earth did you get this???
...
I was cold and Hades...

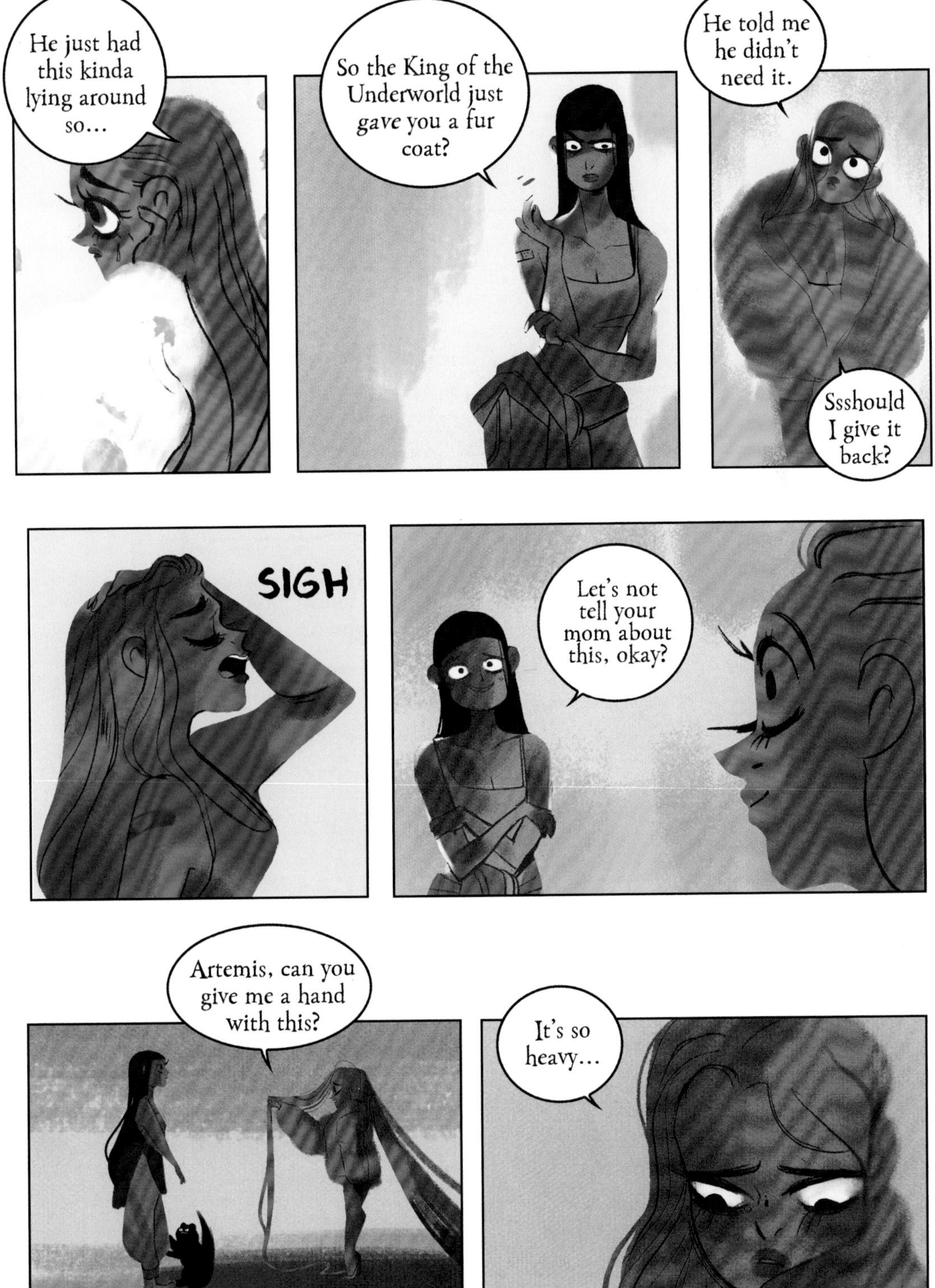
He just had this kinda lying around so...
So the King of the Underworld just gave you a fur coat?
He told me he didn't need it.
Ssshould I give it back?
SIGH
Let's not tell your mom about this, okay?
Artemis, can you give me a hand with this?
It's so heavy...

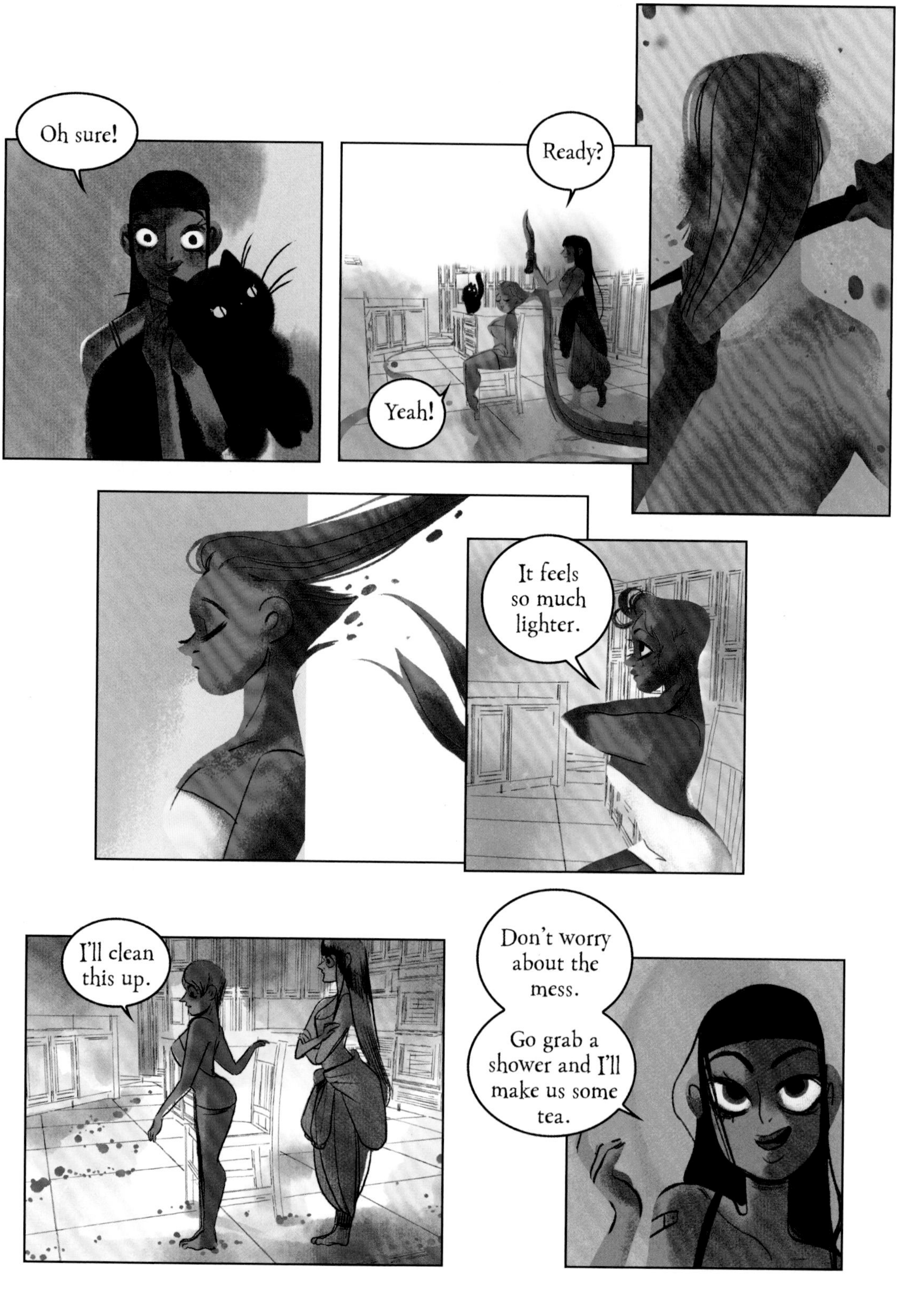
Oh sure!
Ready?
Yeah!
It feels so much lighter.
I'll clean this up.
Don't worry about the mess.
Go grab a shower and I'll make us some tea.

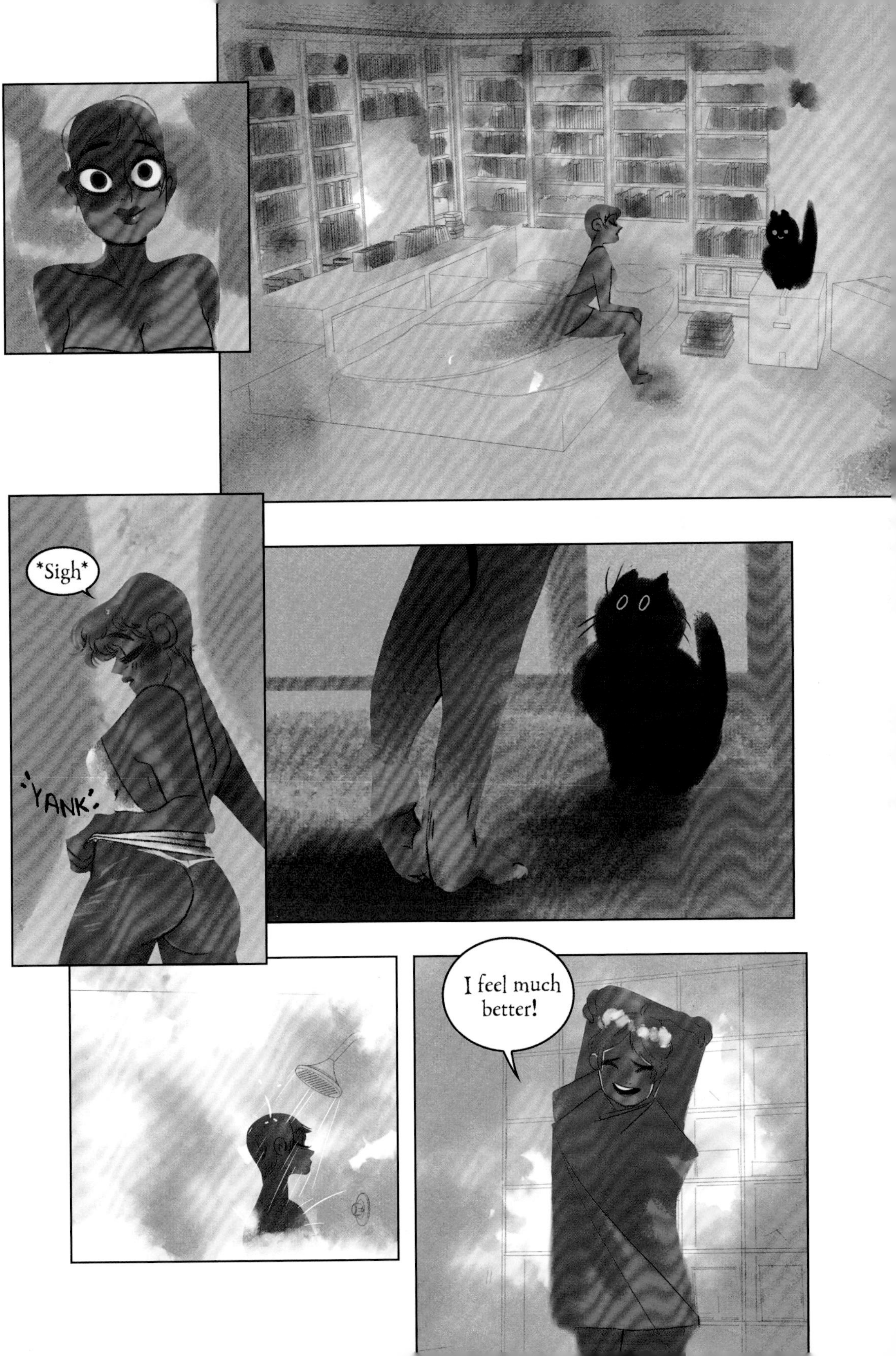
Sigh
YANK
I feel much better!

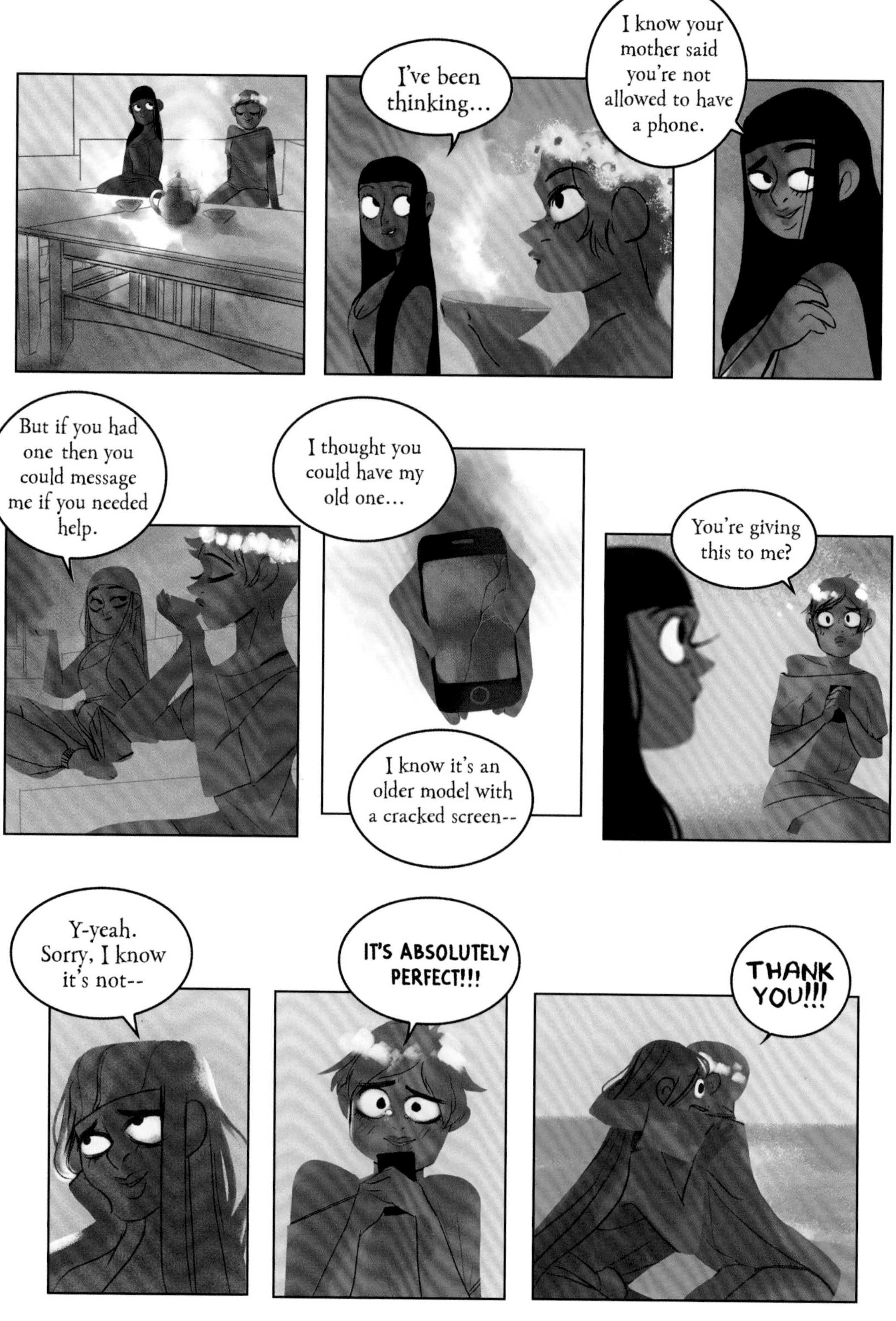
I've been thinking...
I know your mother said you're not allowed to have a phone.
But if you had one then you could message me if you needed help.
I thought you could have my old one...
I know it's an older model with a cracked screen--
You're giving this to me?
Y-yeah. Sorry, I know it's not--
IT'S ABSOLUTELY PERFECT!!!
THANK YOU!!!

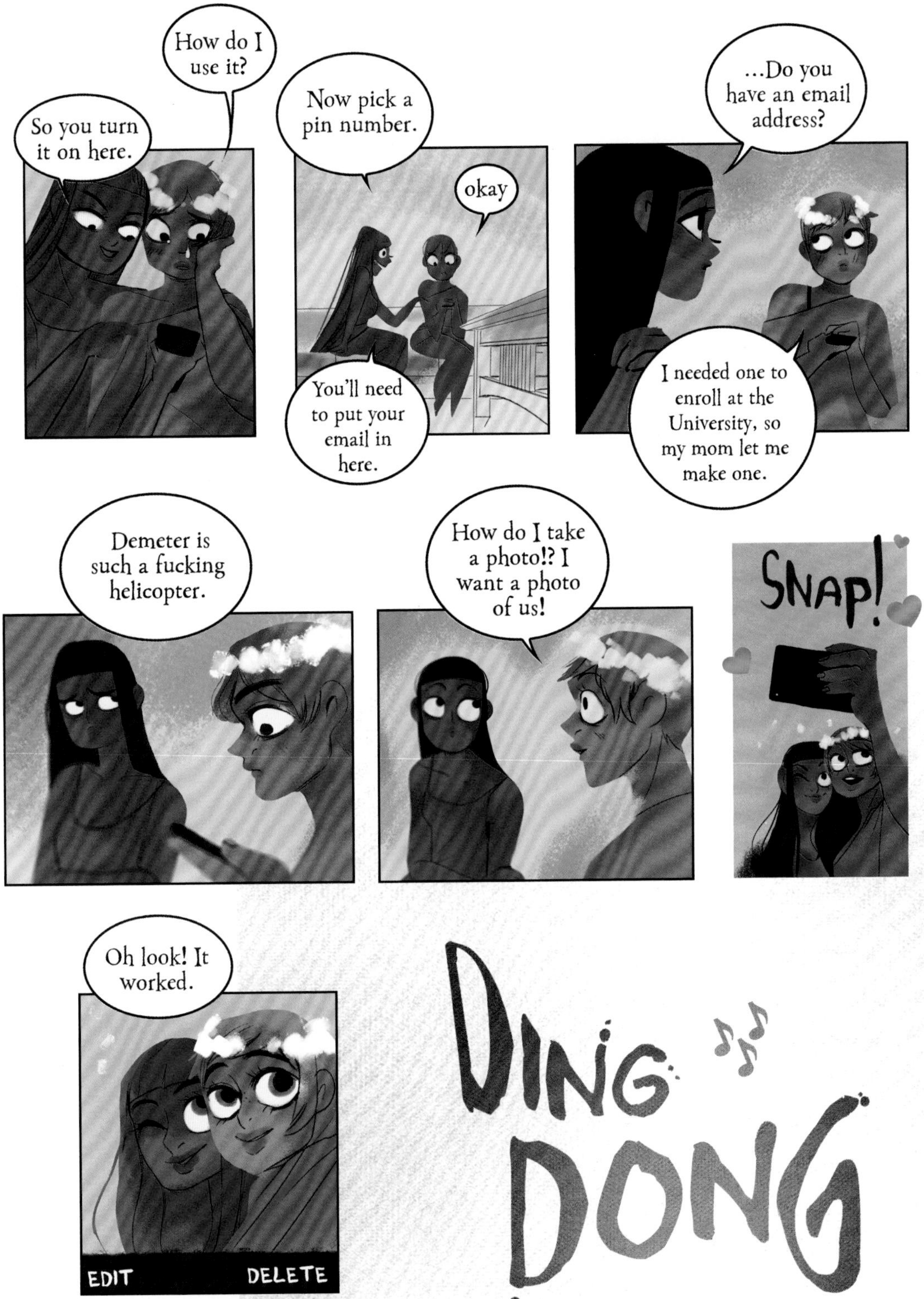
So you turn it on here.
How do I use it?
Now pick a pin number.
okay
You'll need to put your email in here.
...Do you have an email address?
I needed one to enroll at the University, so my mom let me make one.
Demeter is such a fucking helicopter.
How do I take a photo!? I want a photo of us!
SNAP!
Oh look! It worked.
EDIT
DELETE
DING DONG

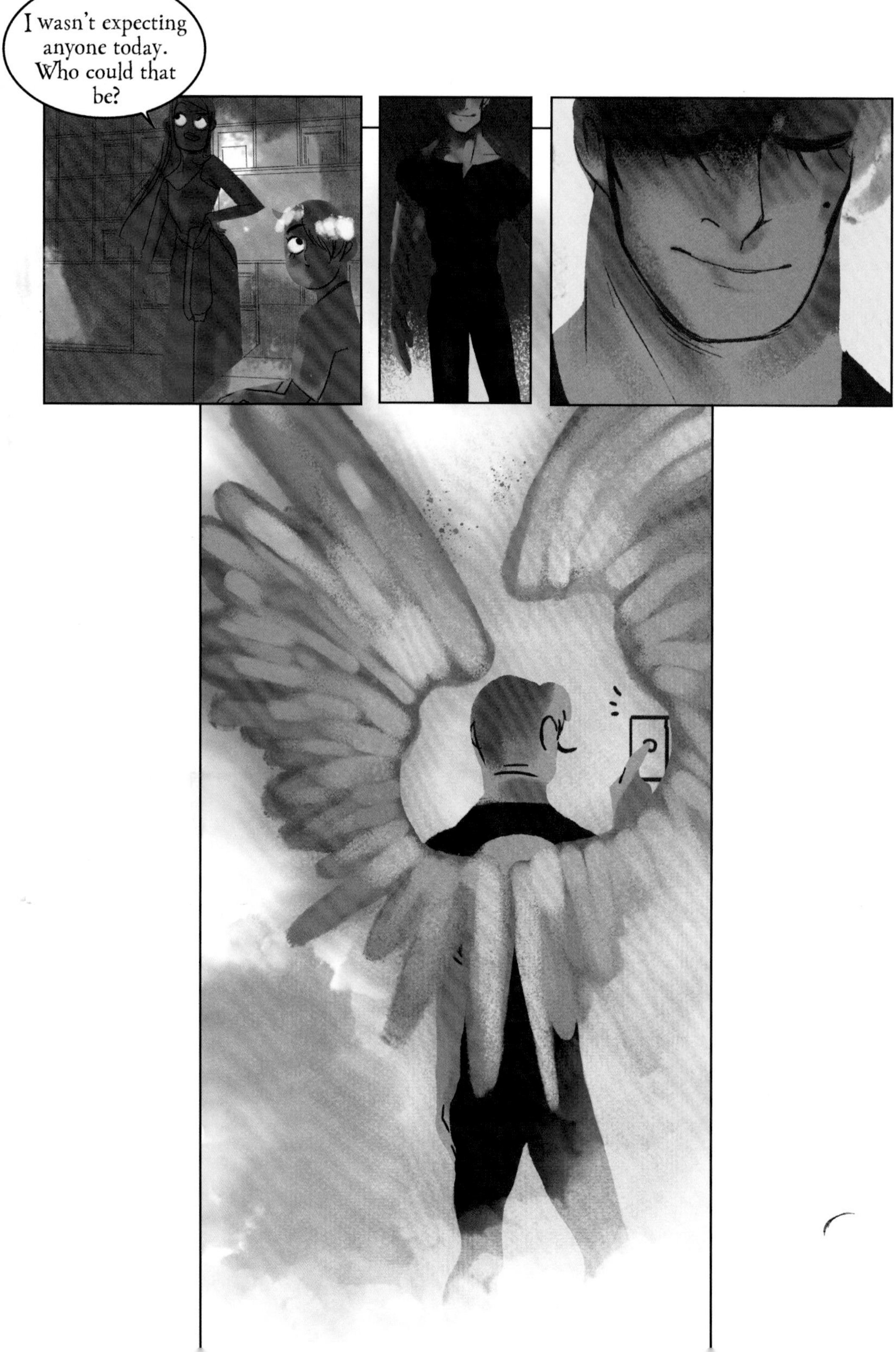
I wasn't expecting anyone today. Who could that be?

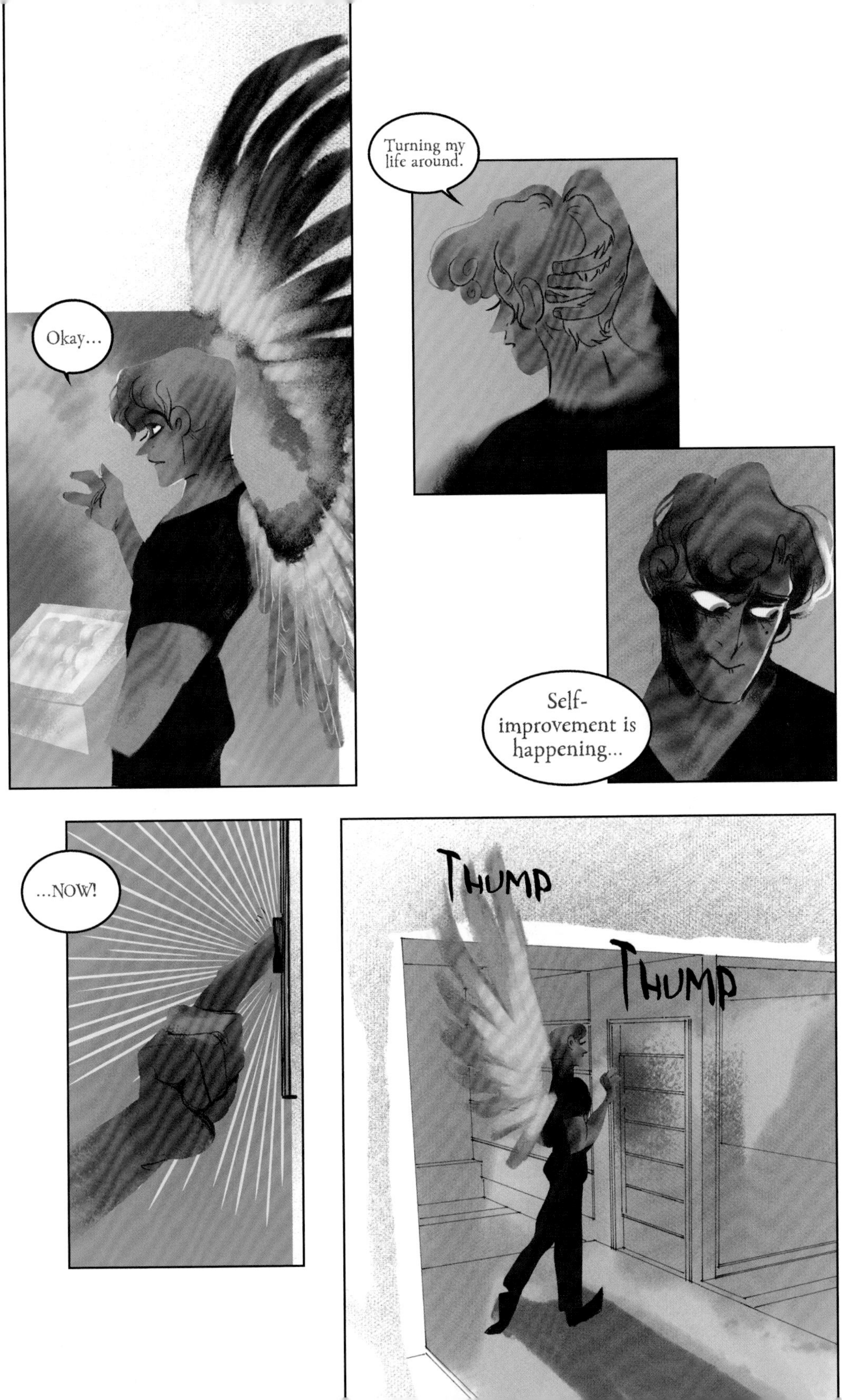
Okay...
Turning my life around.
Self-improvement is happening...
...NOW!
THUMP
THUMP

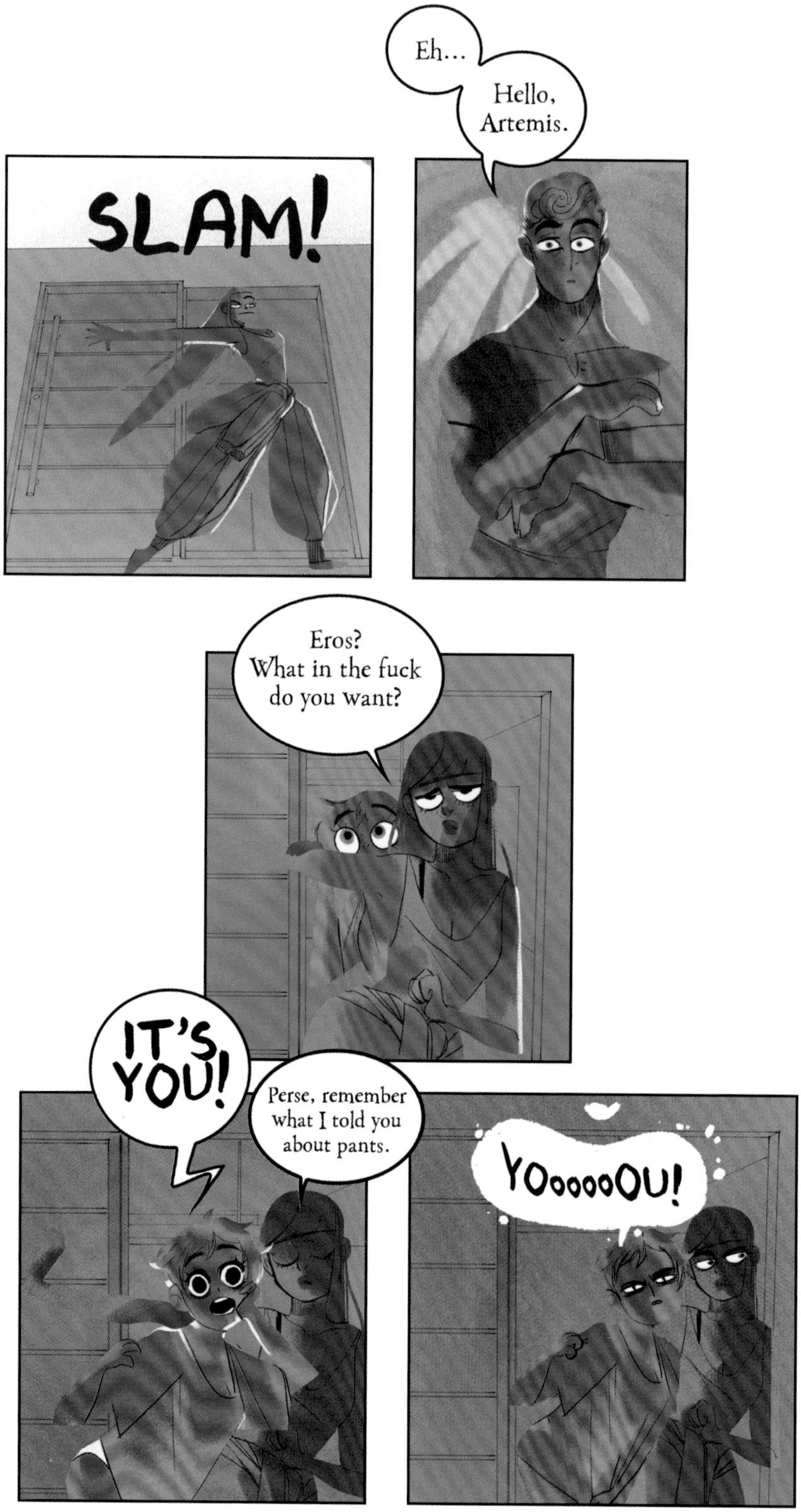
SLAM!
Eh...
Hello, Artemis.
Eros? What in the fuck do you want?
IT'S YOU!
Perse, remember what I told you about pants.
YOooooOU!

EPISODE 12: *Rose-Colored Boy* ♡

xox

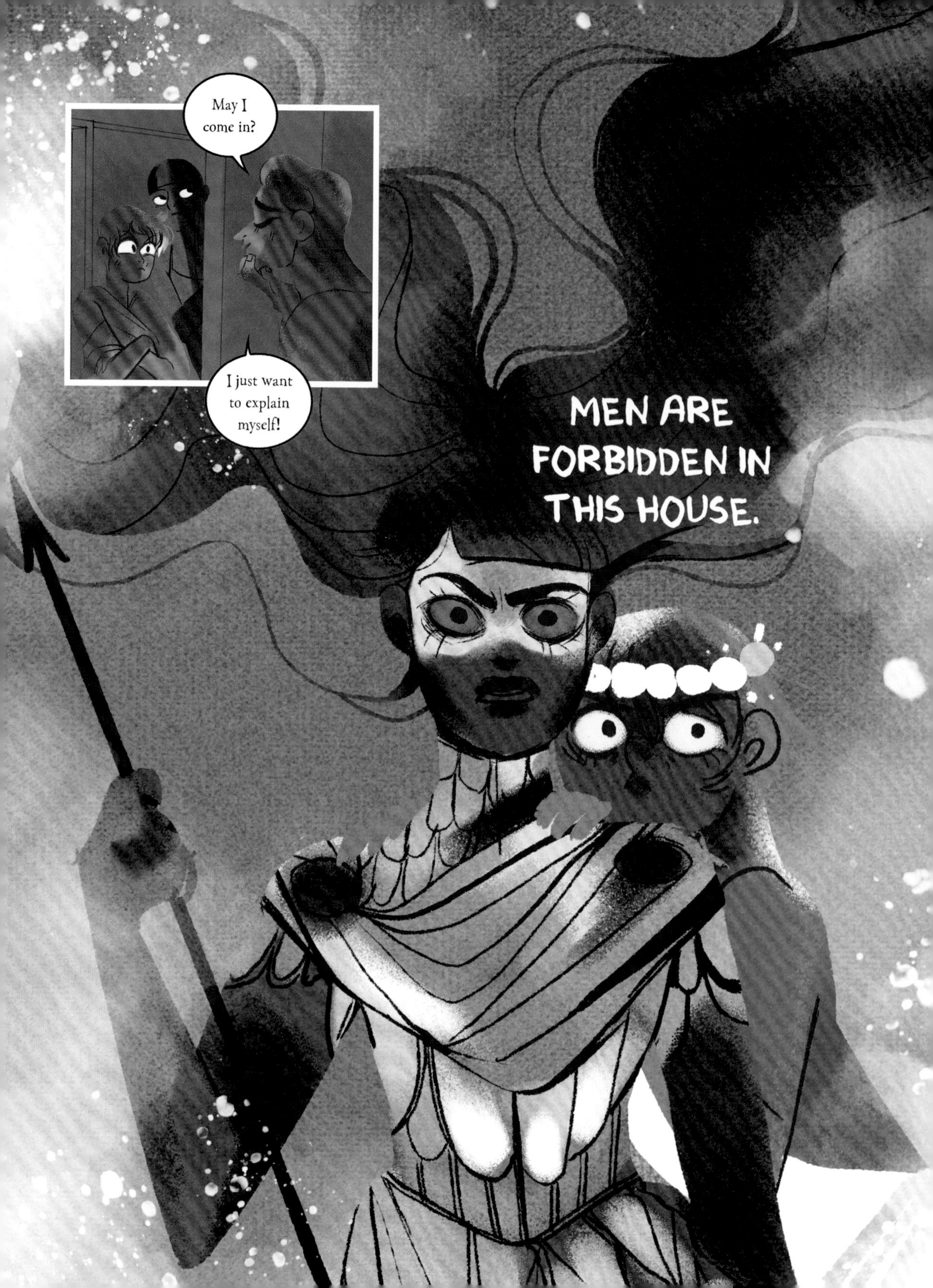
May I come in?
I just want to explain myself!
MEN ARE FORBIDDEN IN THIS HOUSE.

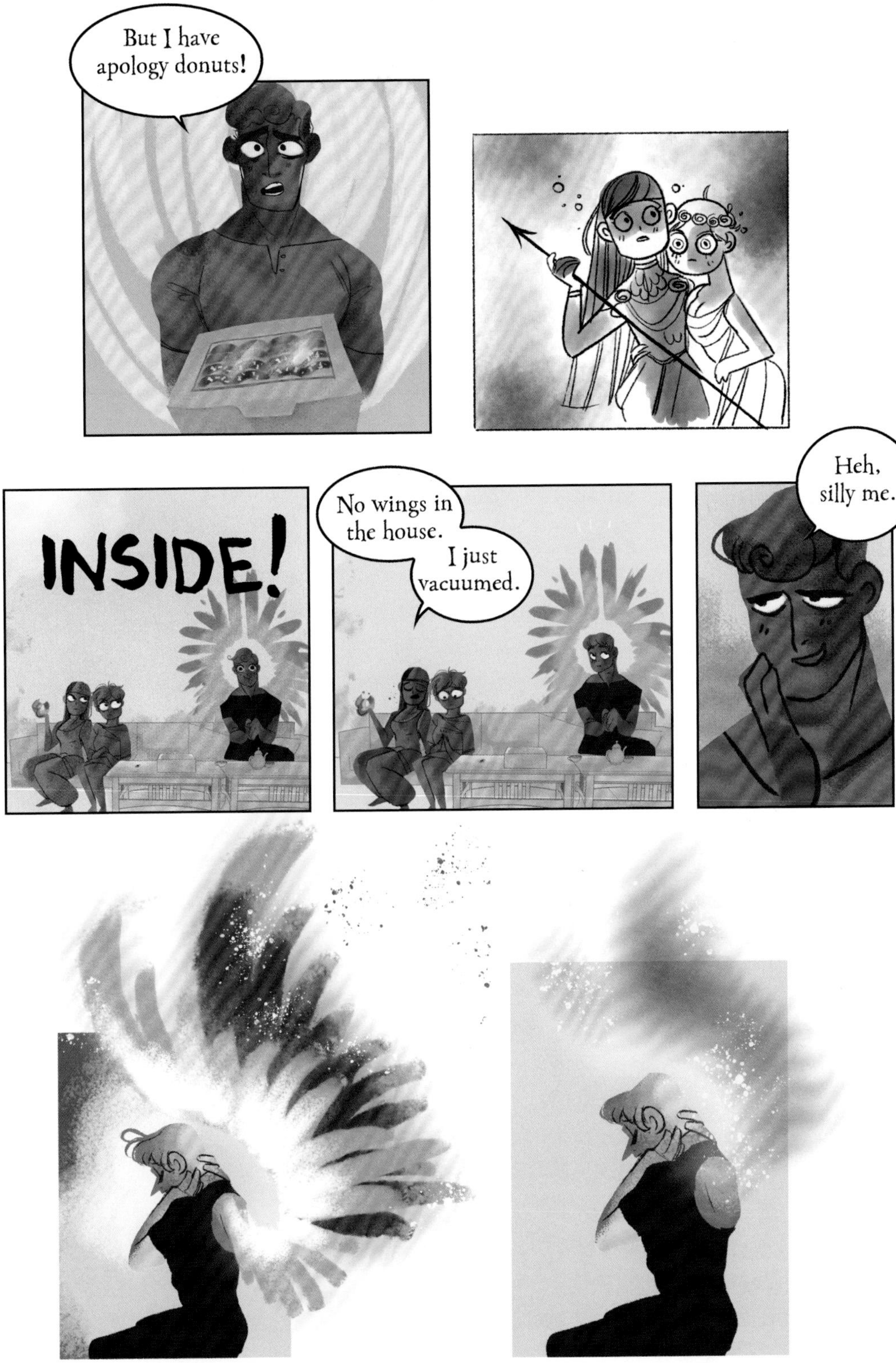

But I have apology donuts!
INSIDE!
No wings in the house.
I just vacuumed.
Heh, silly me.

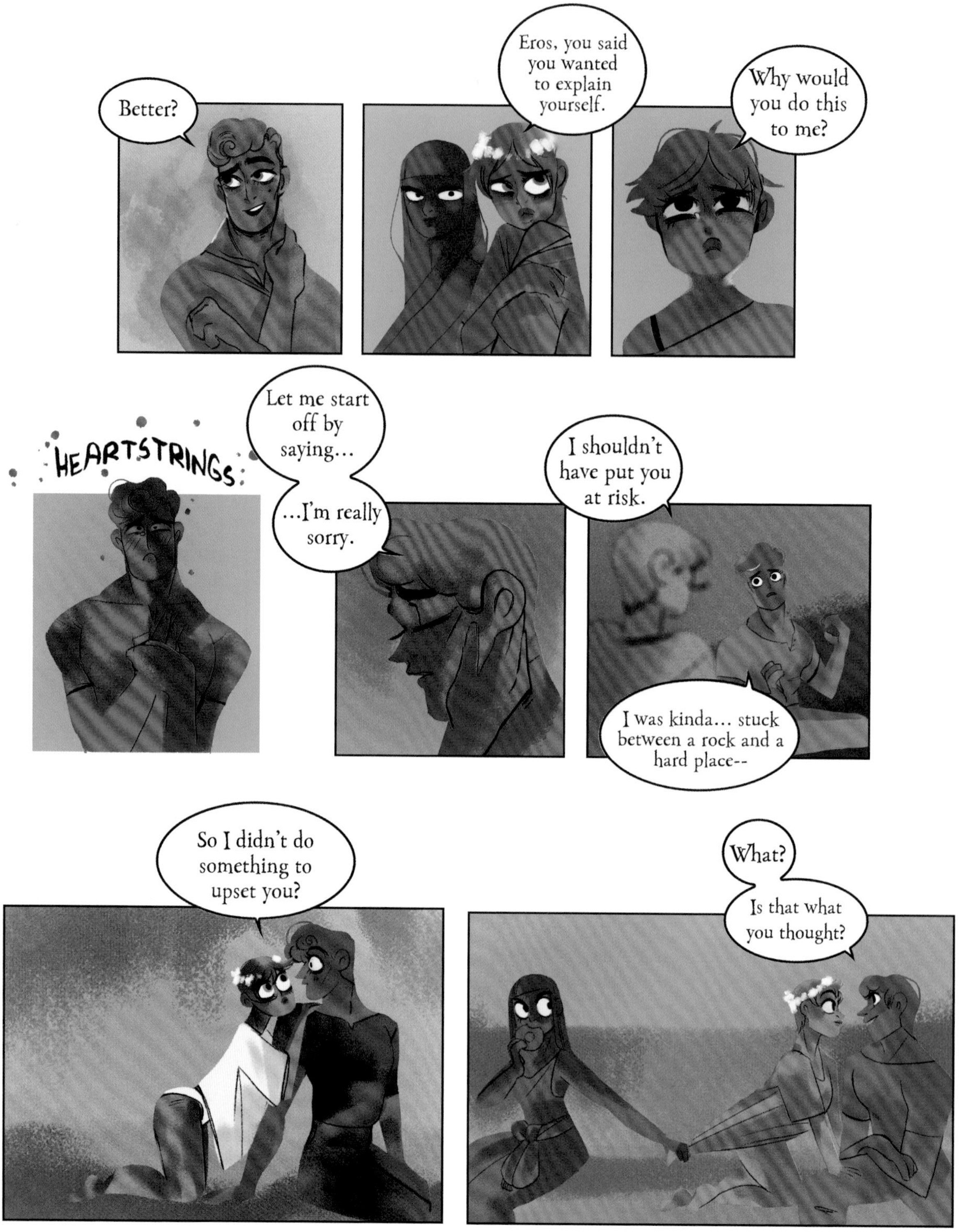
Better?
Eros, you said you wanted to explain yourself.
Why would you do this to me?
HEARTSTRINGS
Let me start off by saying...
...I'm really sorry.
I shouldn't have put you at risk.
I was kinda... stuck between a rock and a hard place--
So I didn't do something to upset you?
What?
Is that what you thought?

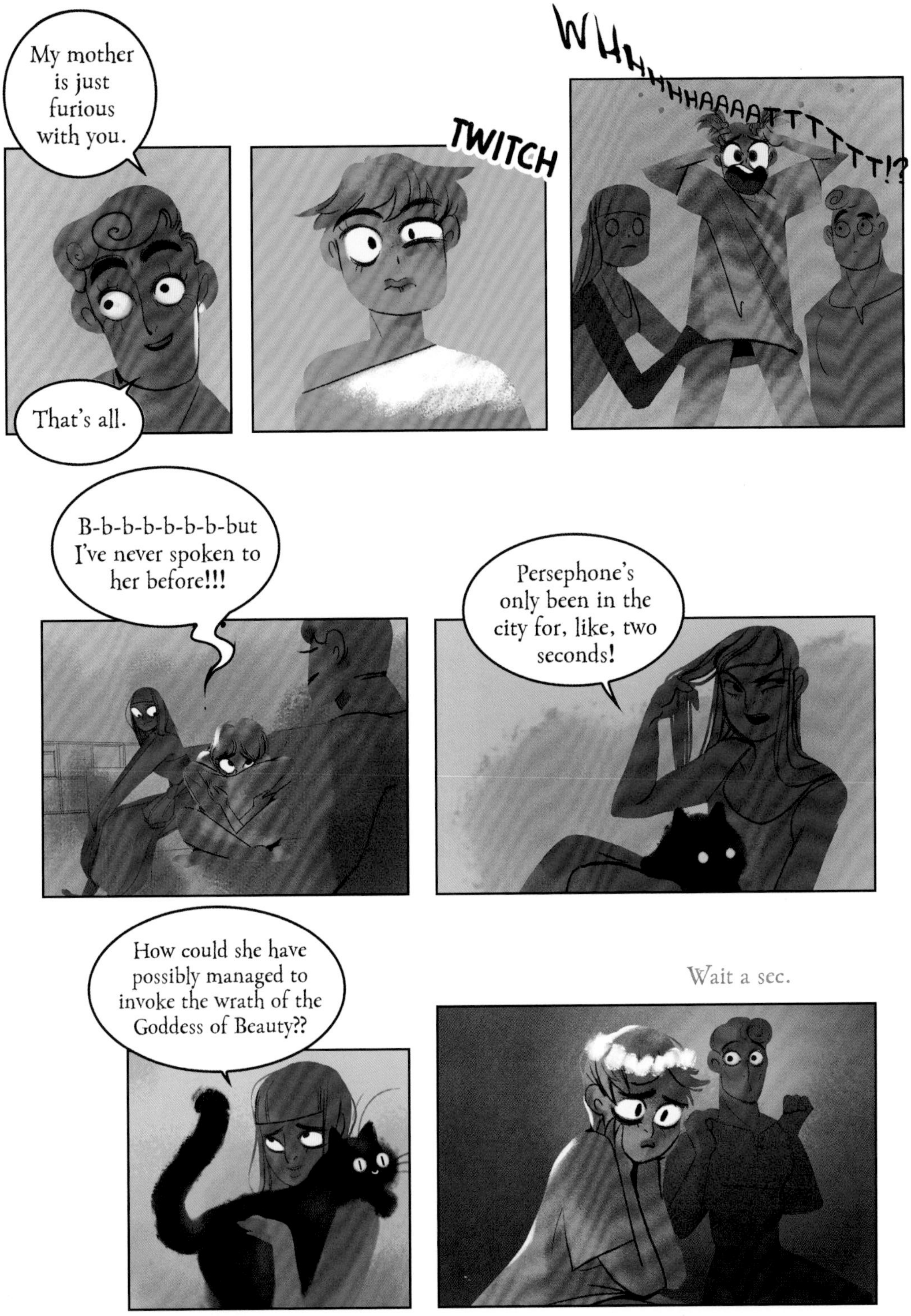
My mother is just furious with you.
That's all.
TWITCH
WHHHHHHAAAATTTTTTT!?
B-b-b-b-b-b-b-but I've never spoken to her before!!!
Persephone's only been in the city for, like, two seconds!
How could she have possibly managed to invoke the wrath of the Goddess of Beauty??
Wait a sec.

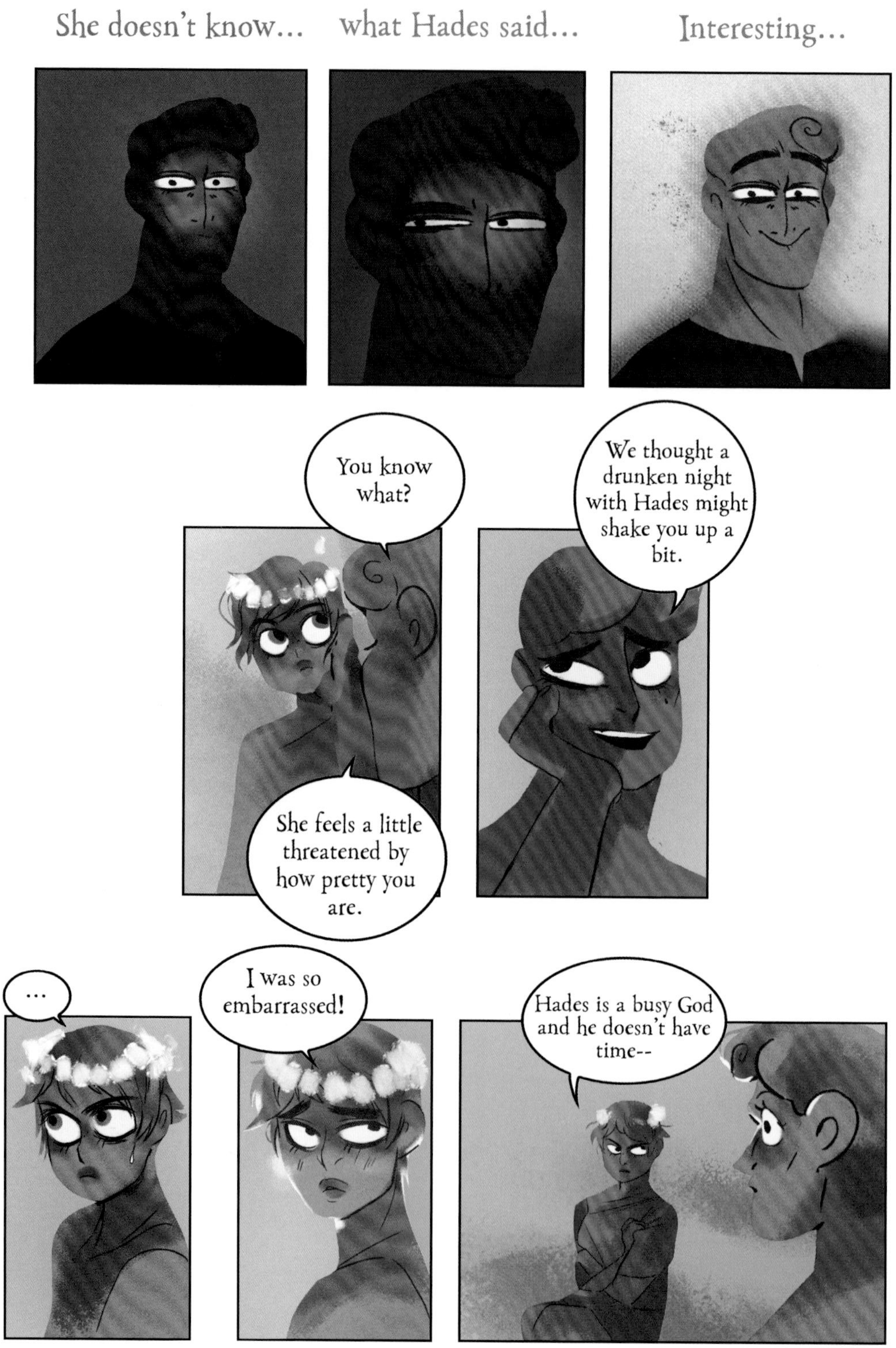
She doesn't know...
what Hades said...
Interesting...
You know what?
We thought a drunken night with Hades might shake you up a bit.
She feels a little threatened by how pretty you are.
...
I was so embarrassed!
Hades is a busy God and he doesn't have time--

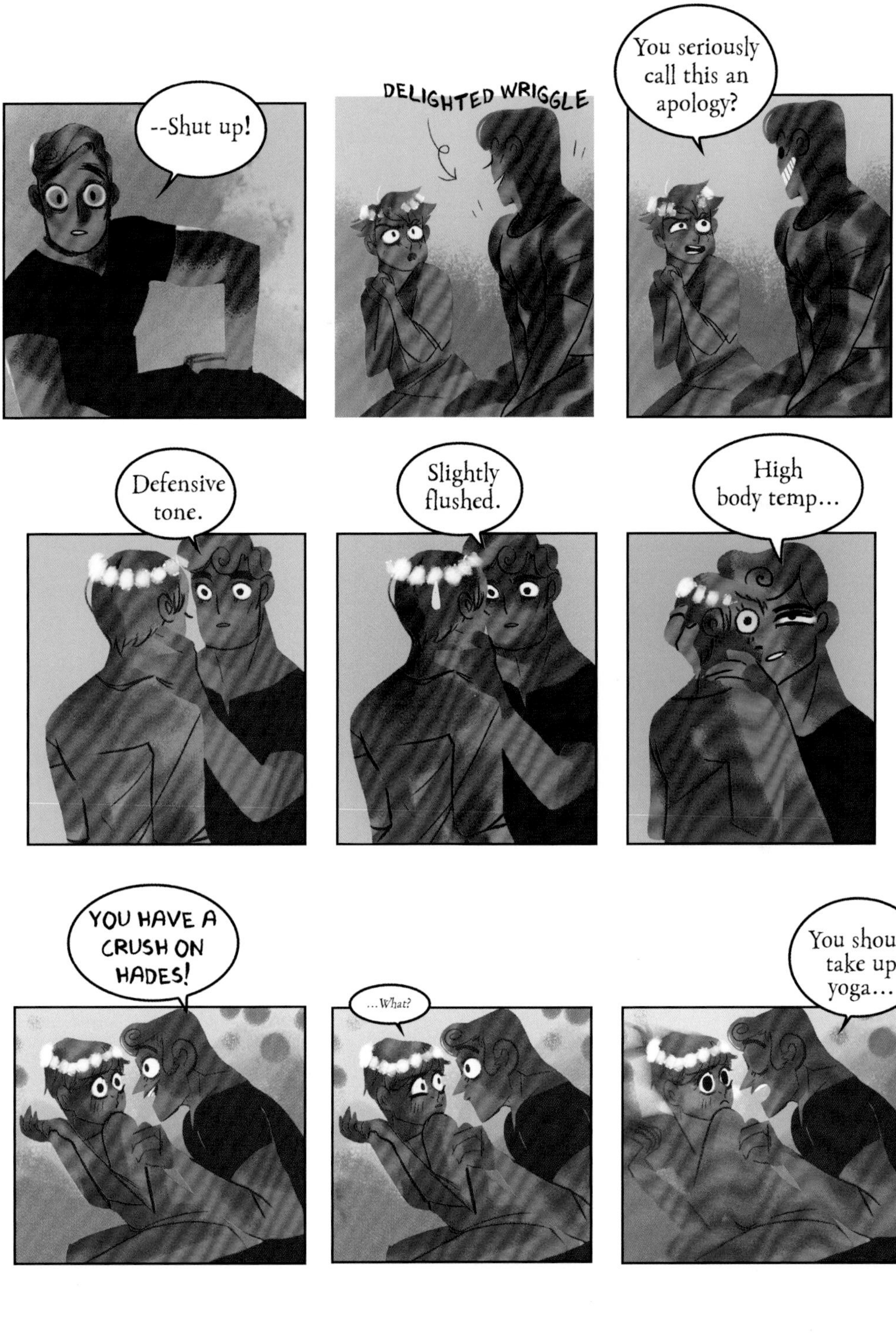
--Shut up!
DELIGHTED WRIGGLE
You seriously call this an apology?
Defensive tone.
Slightly flushed.
High body temp...
YOU HAVE A CRUSH ON HADES!
...What?
You should take up yoga...

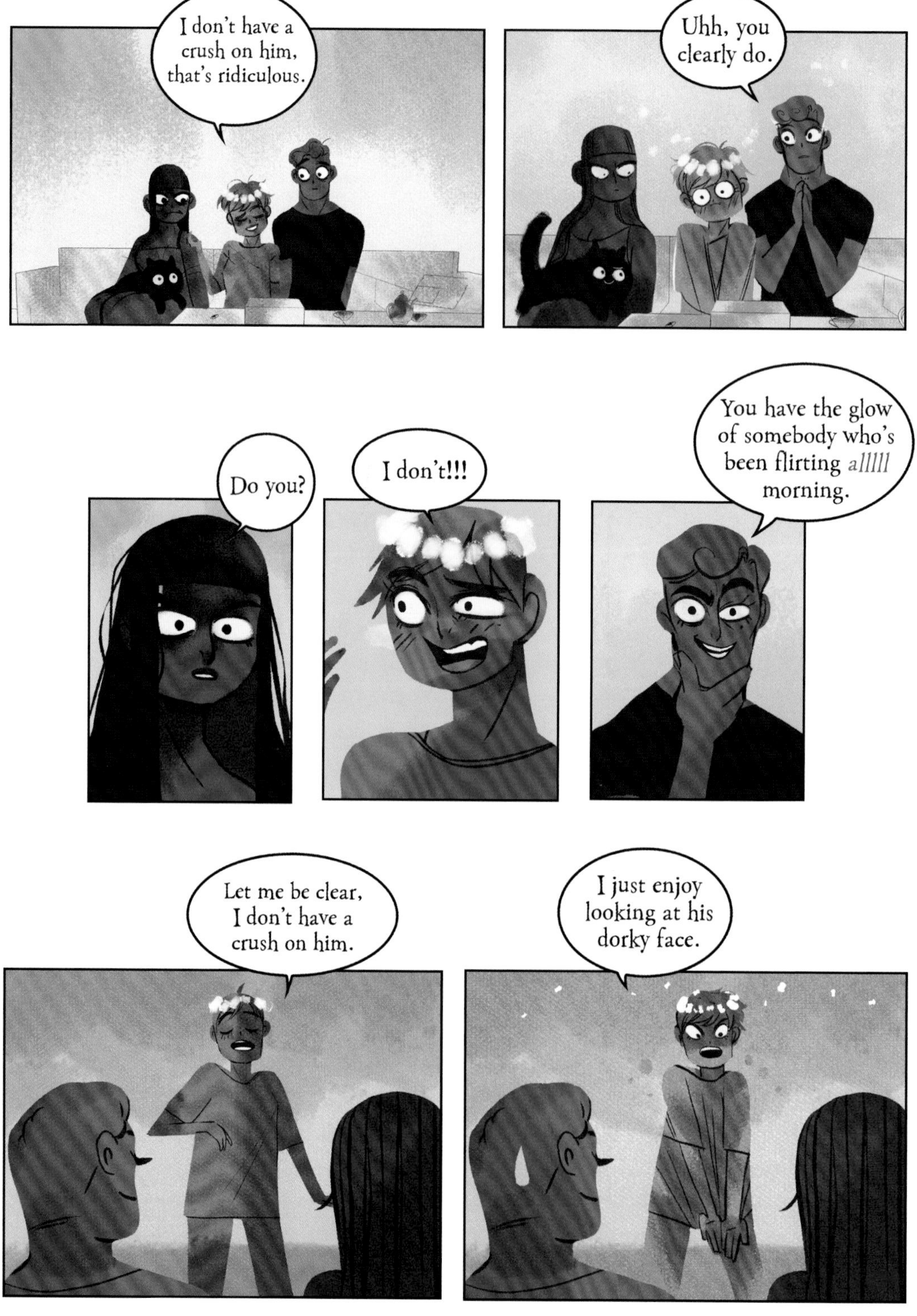

I don't have a crush on him, that's ridiculous.
Uhh, you clearly do.
Do you?
I don't!!!
You have the glow of somebody who's been flirting *alllll* morning.
Let me be clear, I don't have a crush on him.
I just enjoy looking at his dorky face.

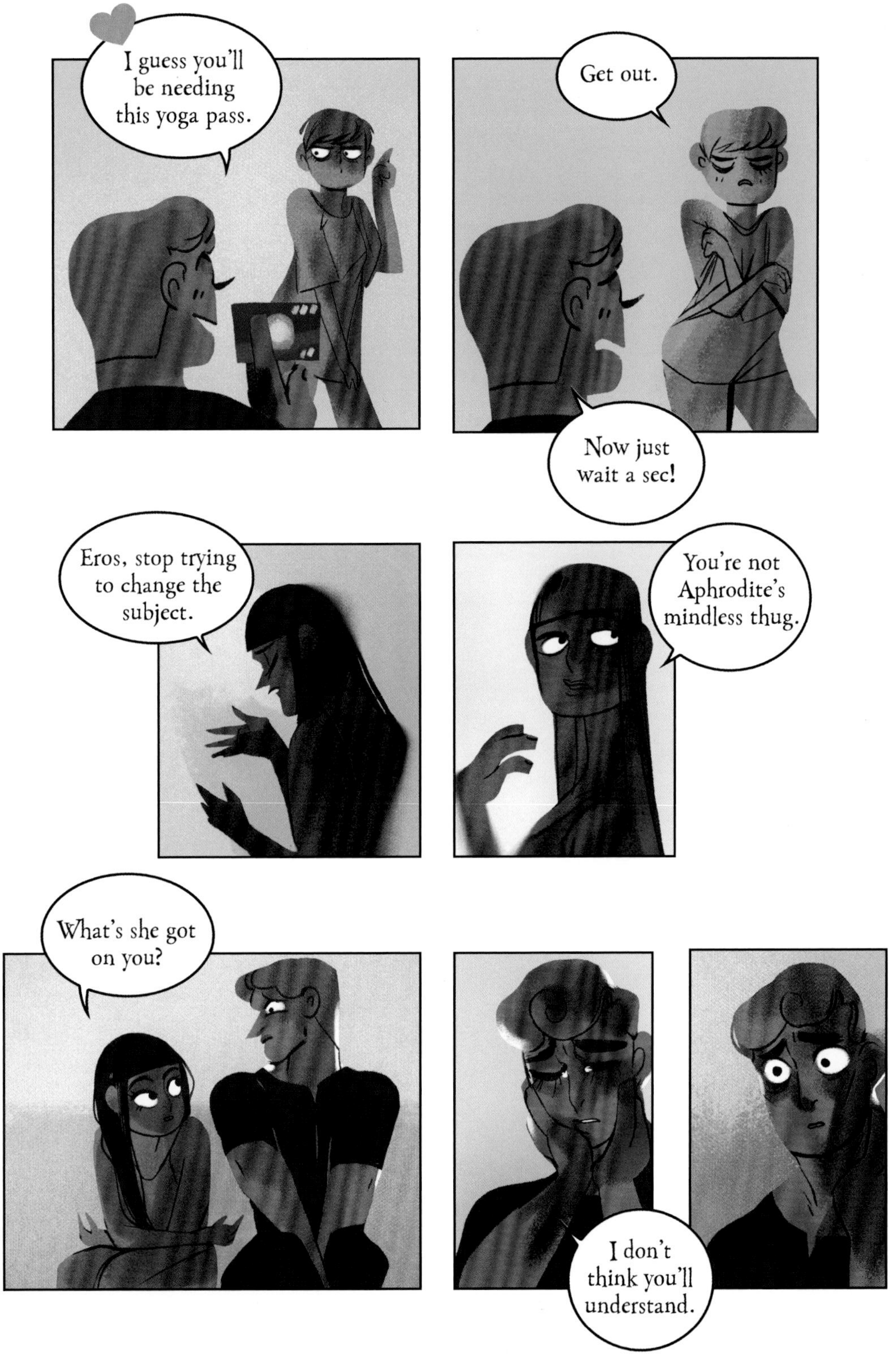
I guess you'll be needing this yoga pass.
Get out.
Now just wait a sec!
Eros, stop trying to change the subject.
You're not Aphrodite's mindless thug.
What's she got on you?
I don't think you'll understand.

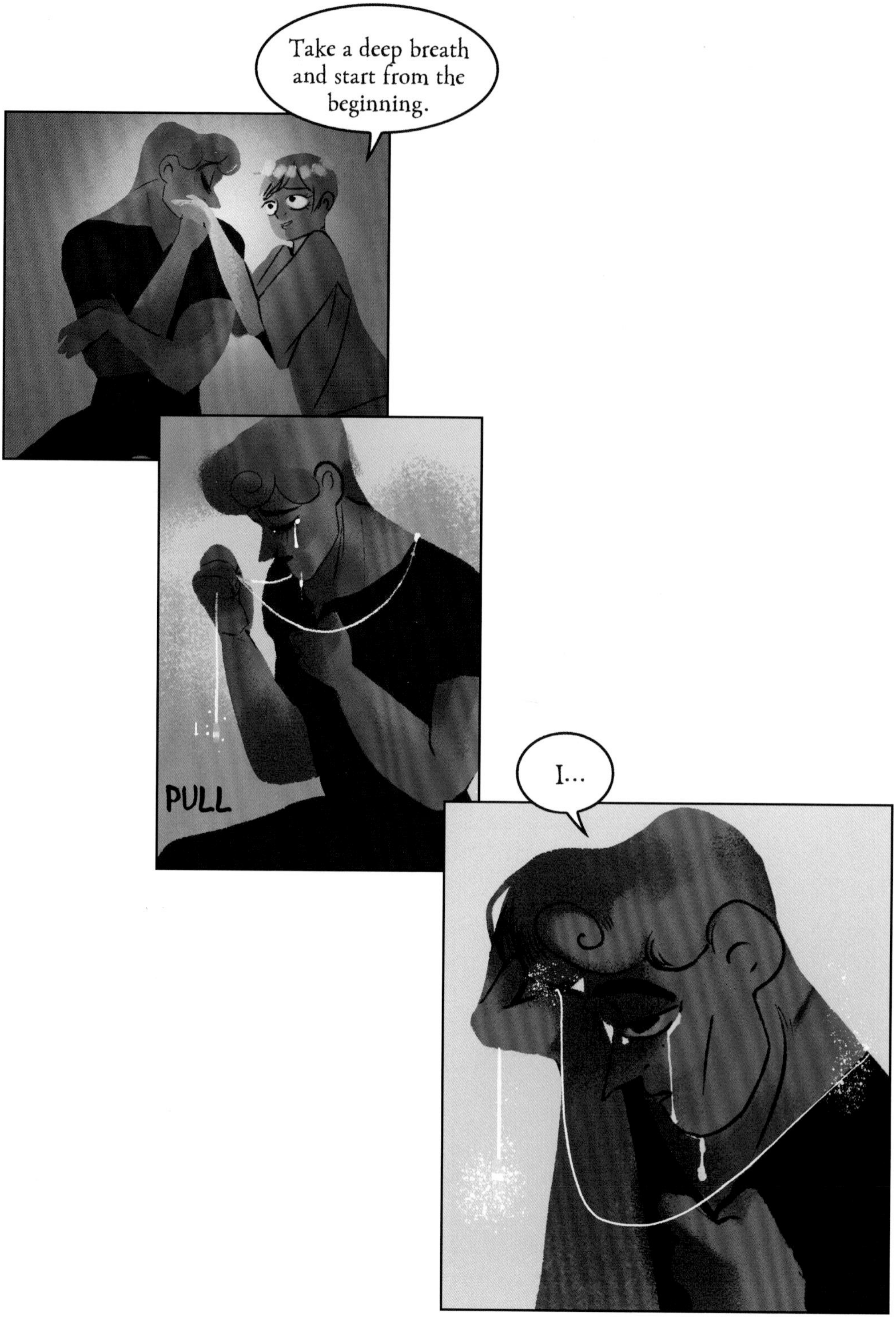
Take a deep breath and start from the beginning.
PULL
I...

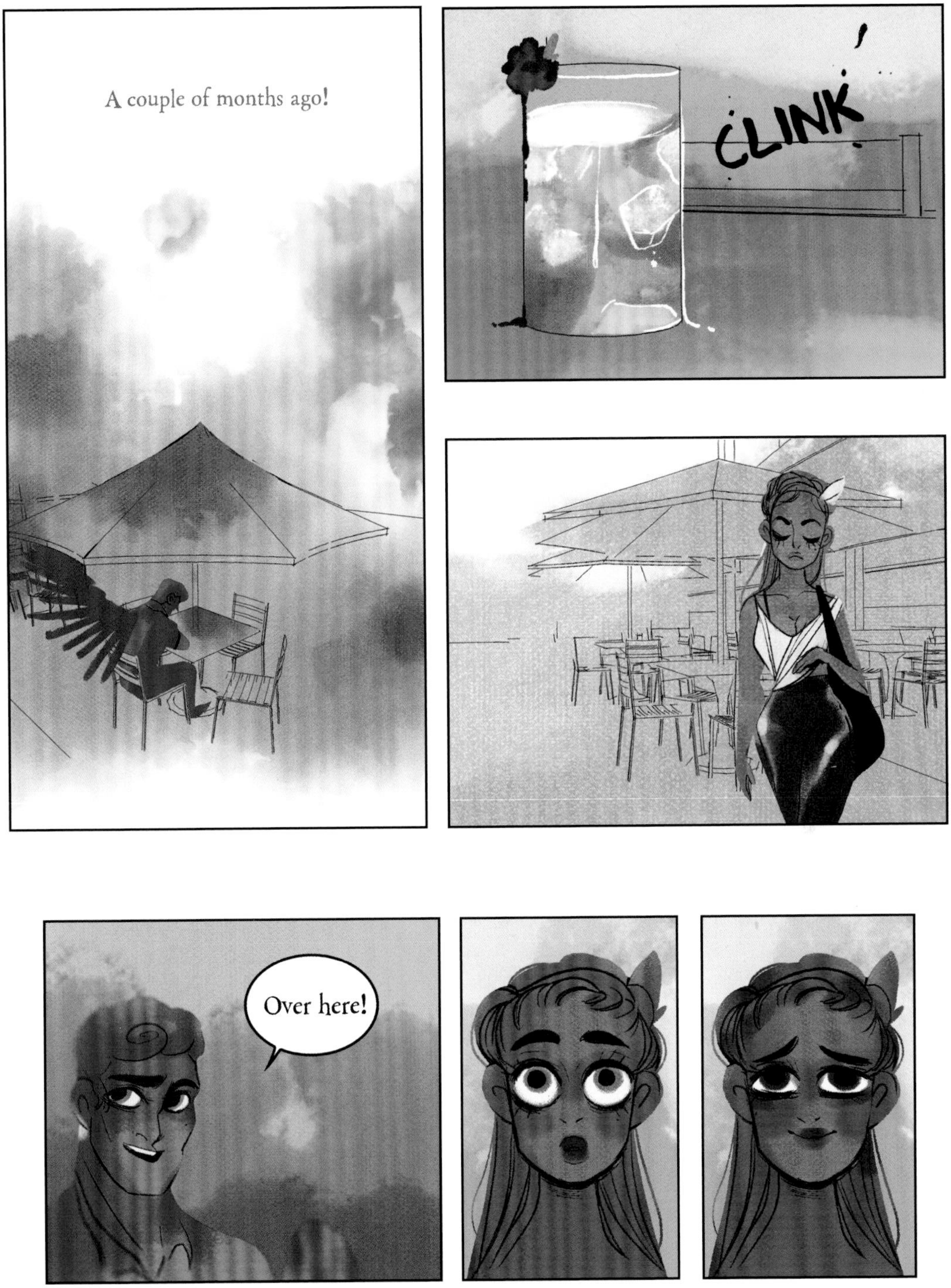
A couple of months ago!
CLINK
Over here!

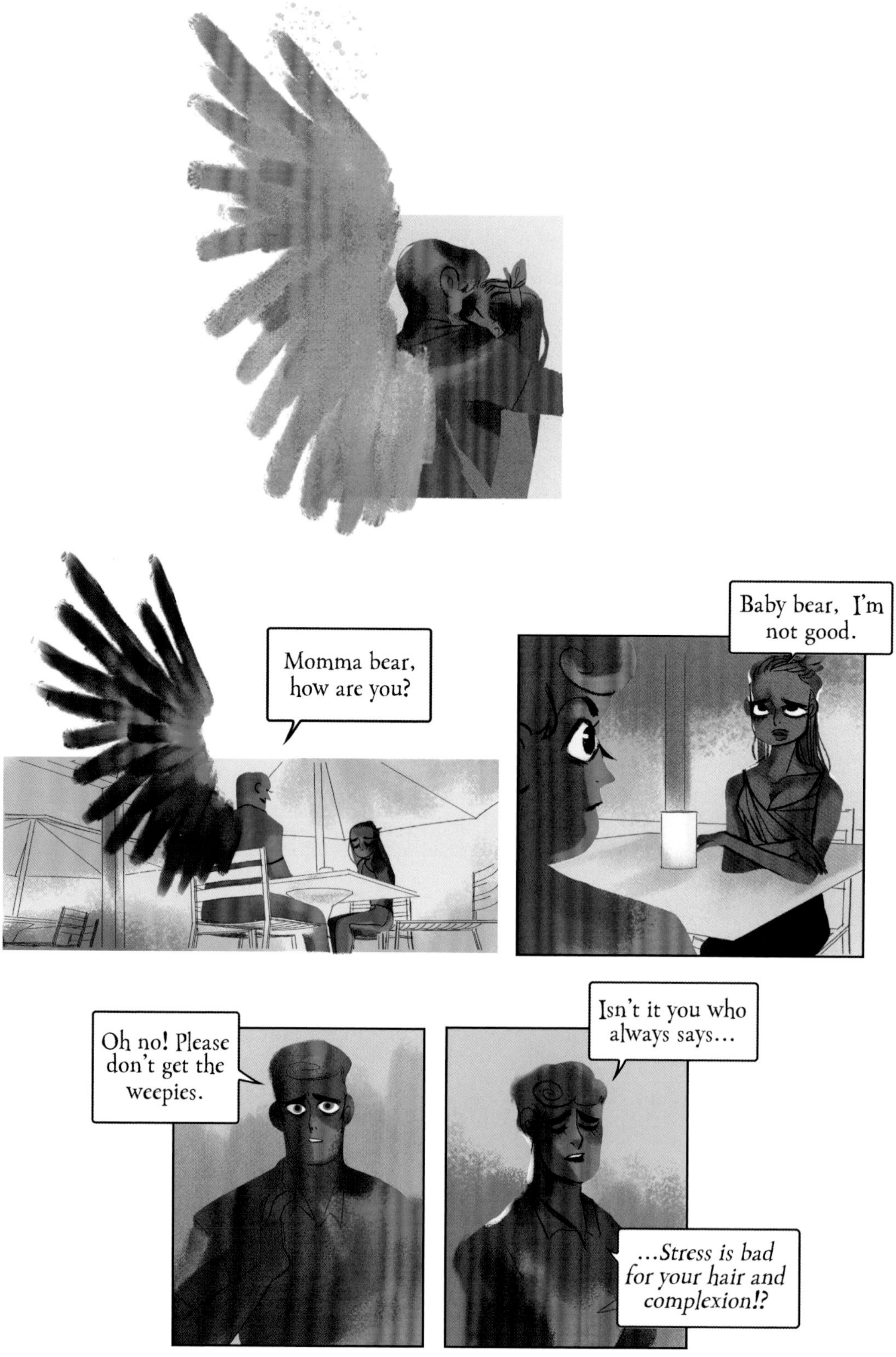
Momma bear,
how are you?
Baby bear, I'm
not good.
Oh no! Please
don't get the
weepies.
Isn't it you who
always says...
...Stress is bad
for your hair and
complexion!?

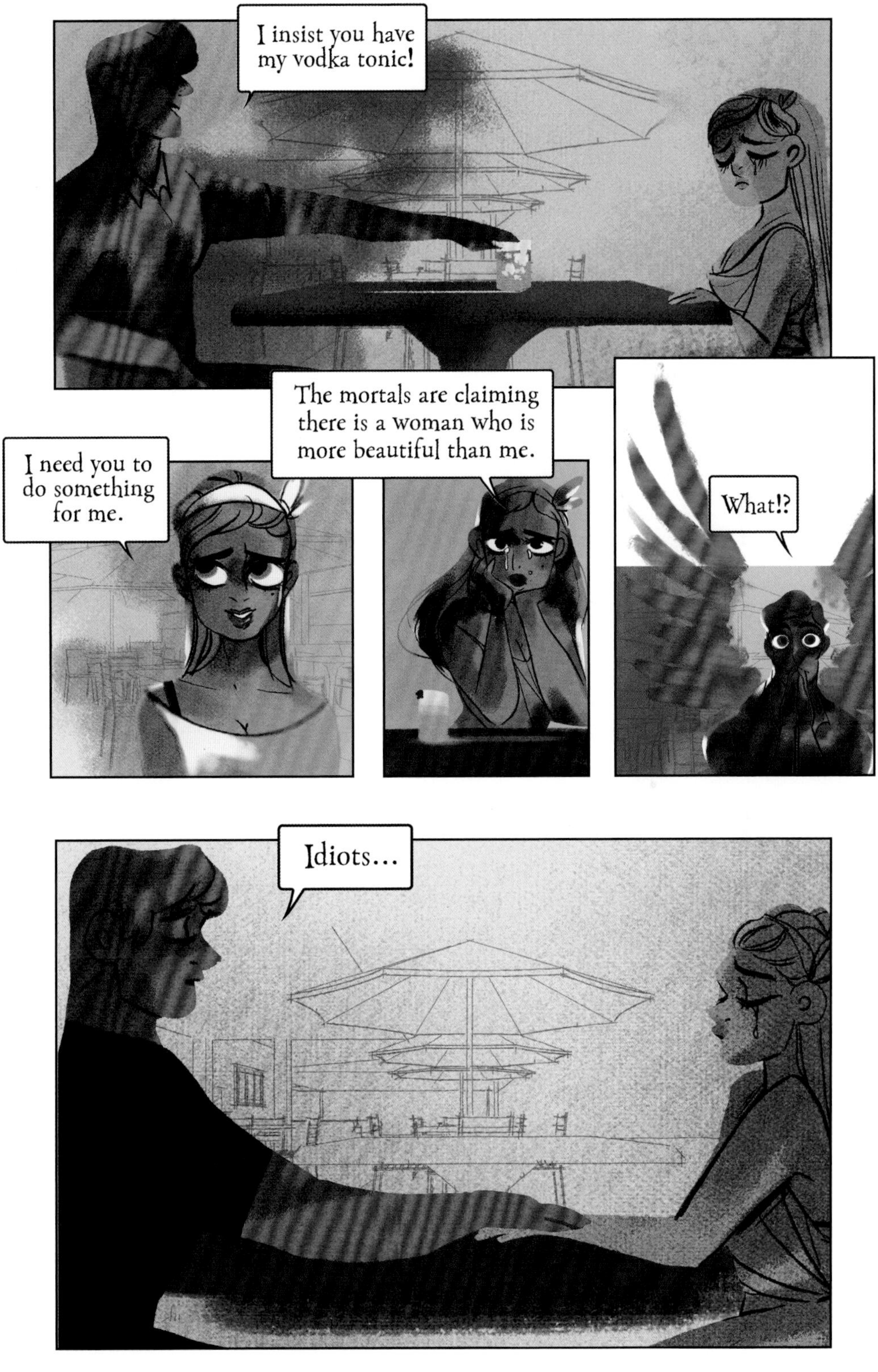
I insist you have my vodka tonic!
I need you to do something for me.
The mortals are claiming there is a woman who is more beautiful than me.
What!?
Idiots...

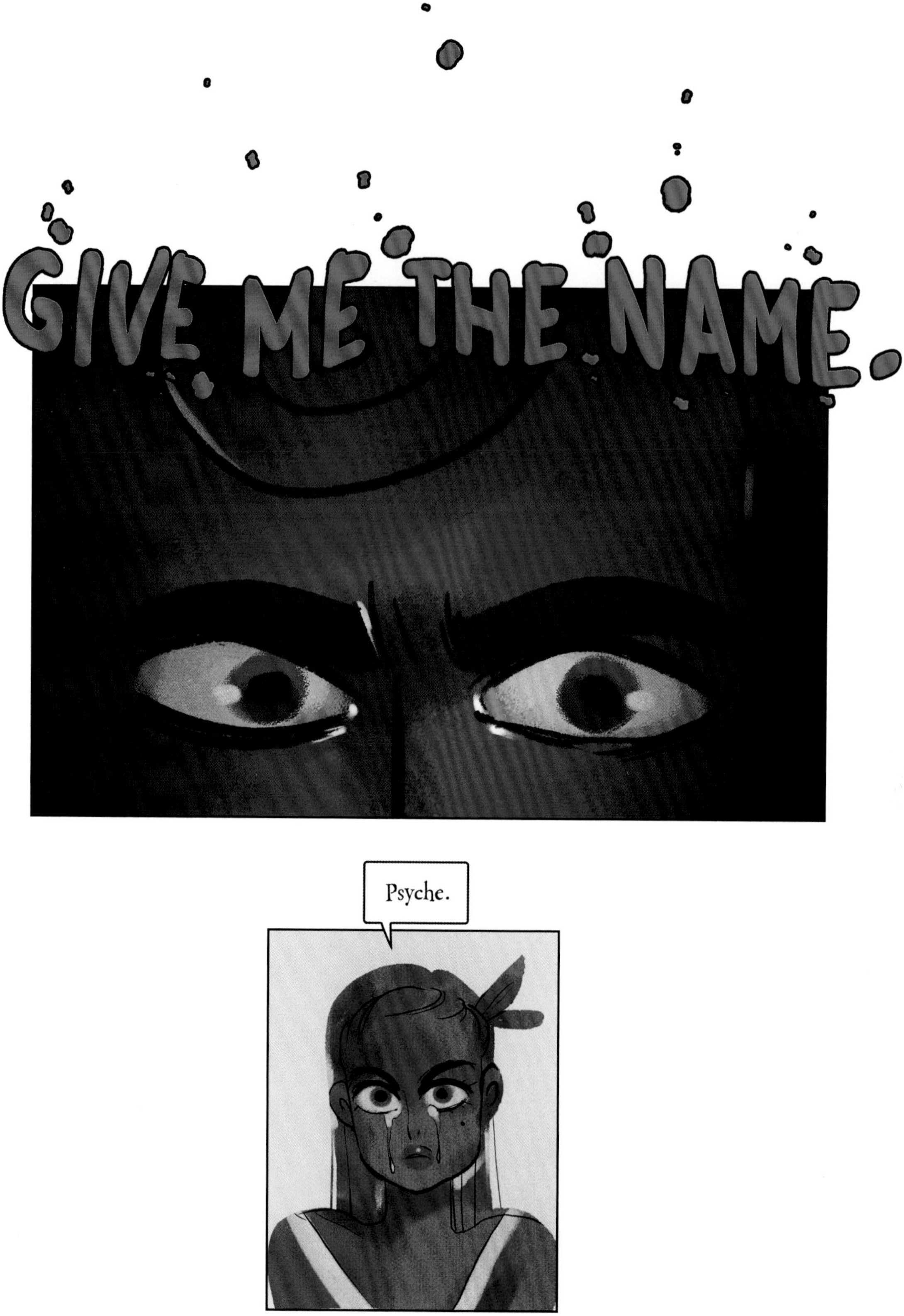
GIVE ME THE NAME.
Psyche.

EPISODE 13: MAMA'S BOY

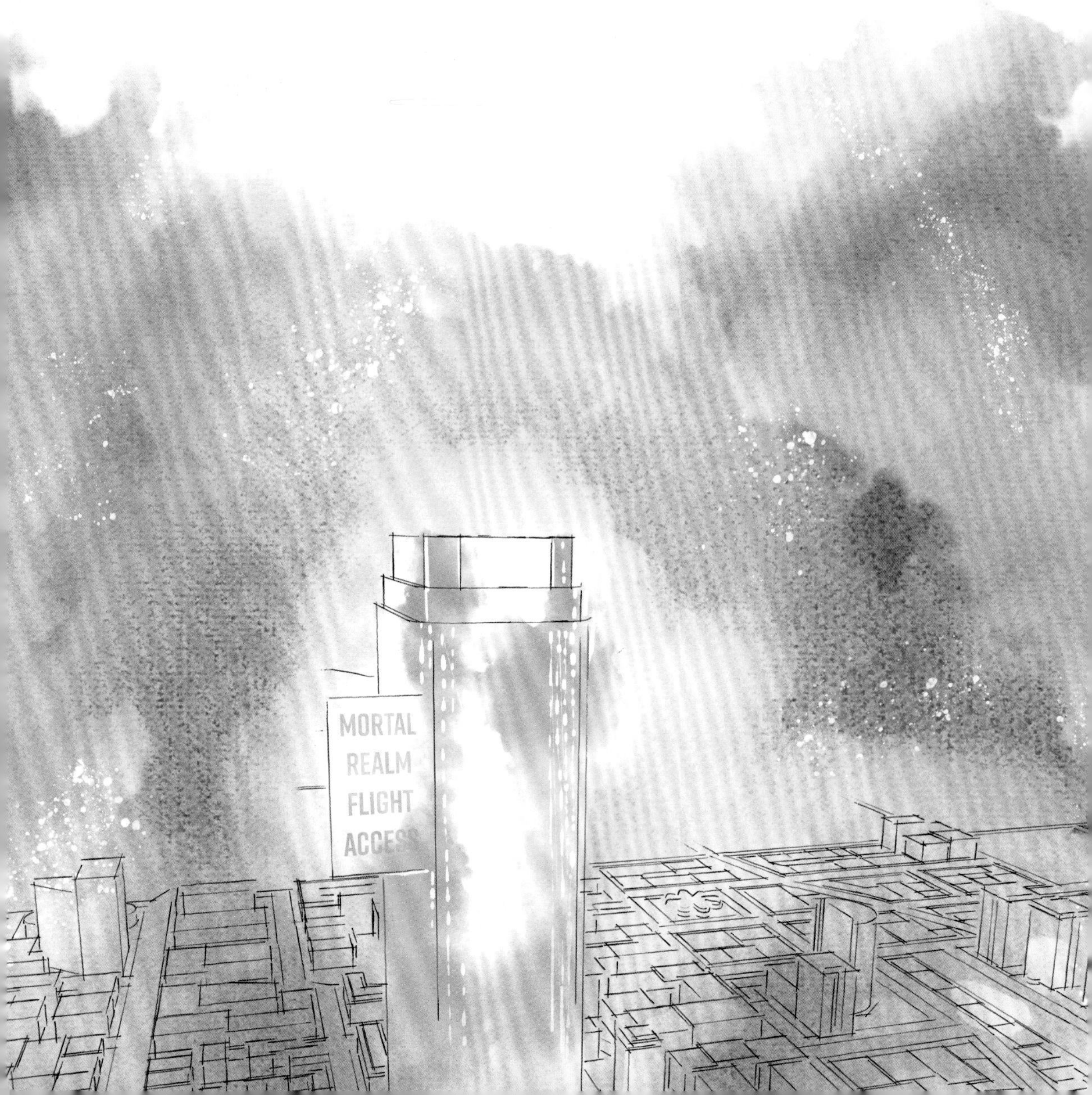
MORTAL
REALM
FLIGHT
ACCESS

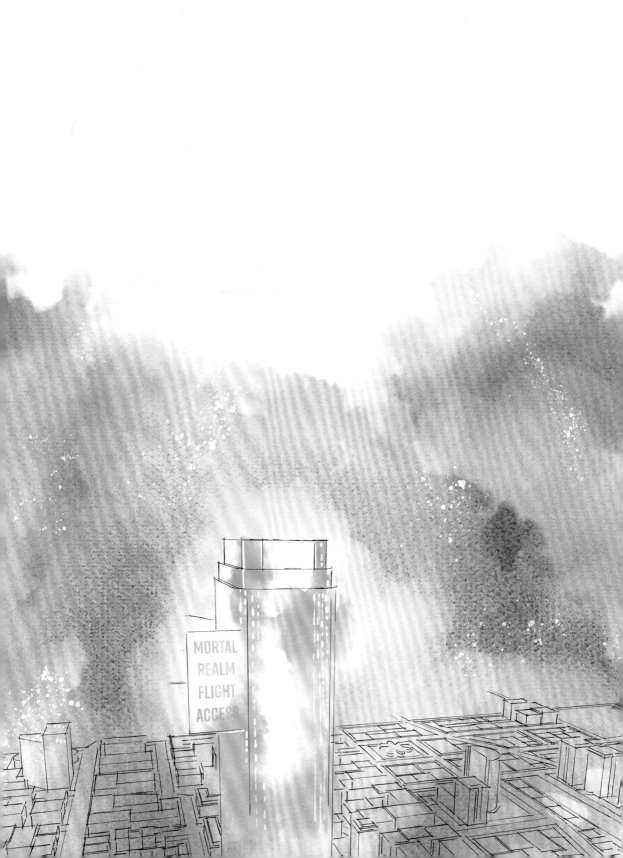

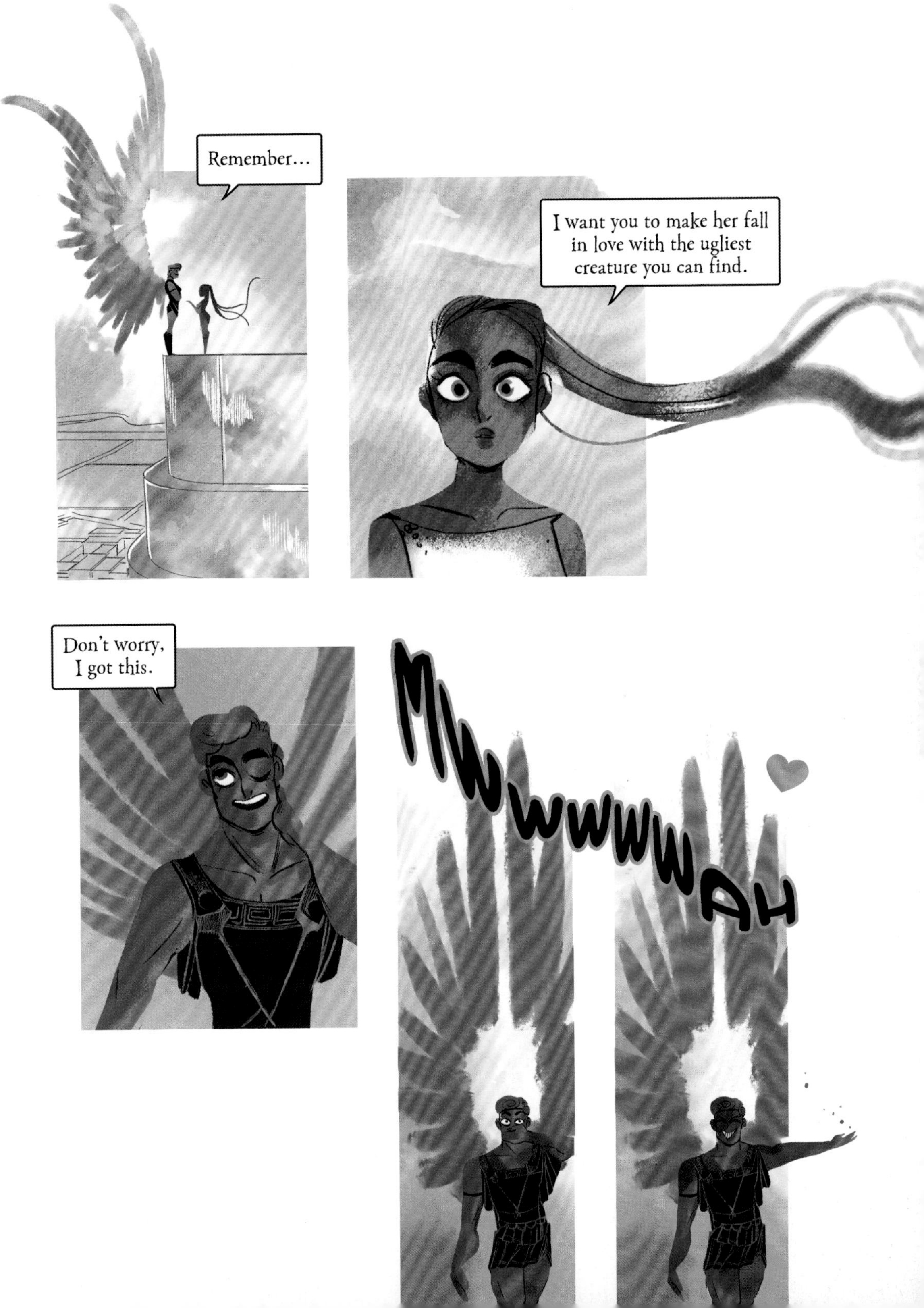
Remember...
I want you to make her fall in love with the ugliest creature you can find.
Don't worry, I got this.
MWWWWWWAH

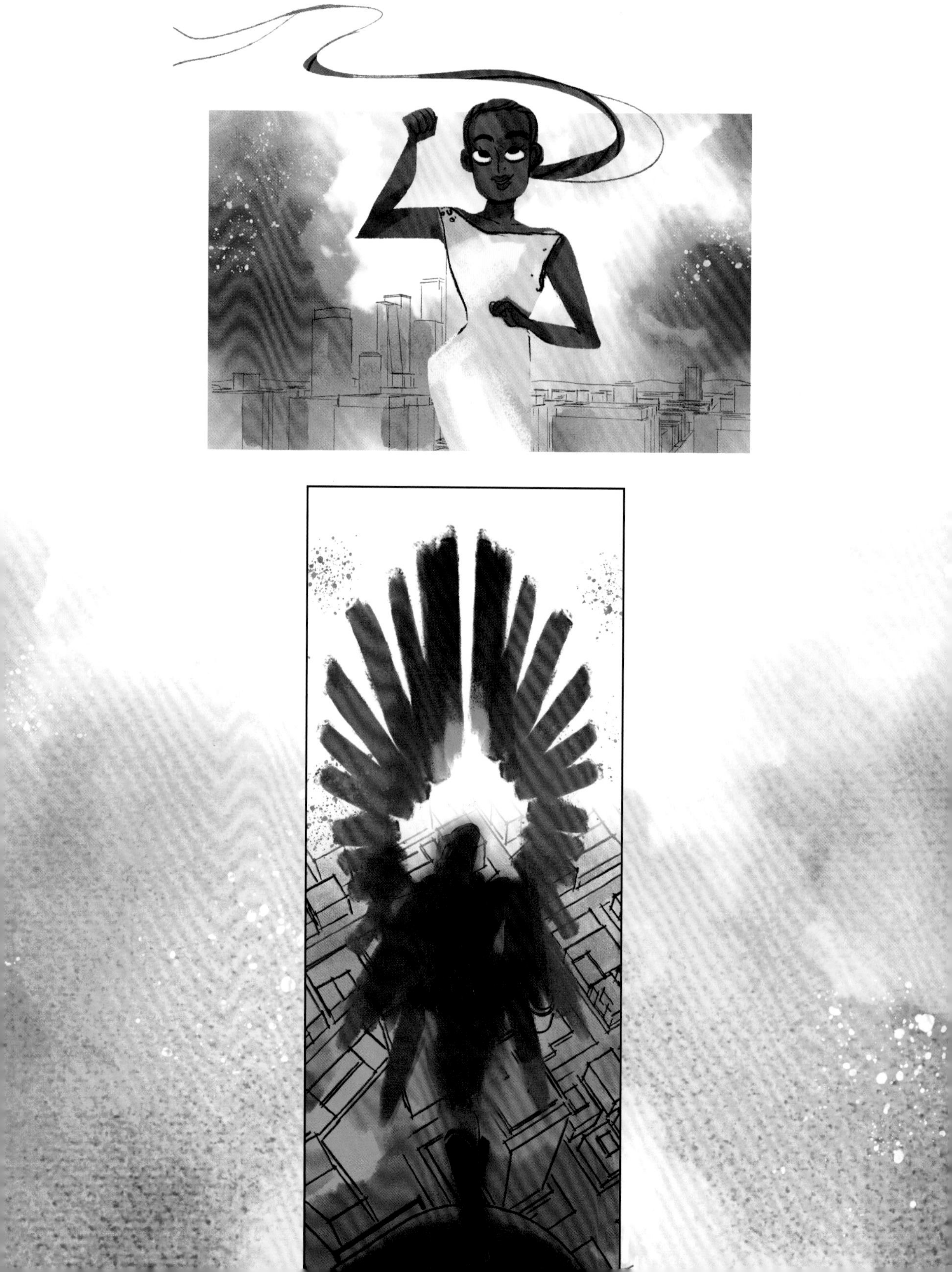

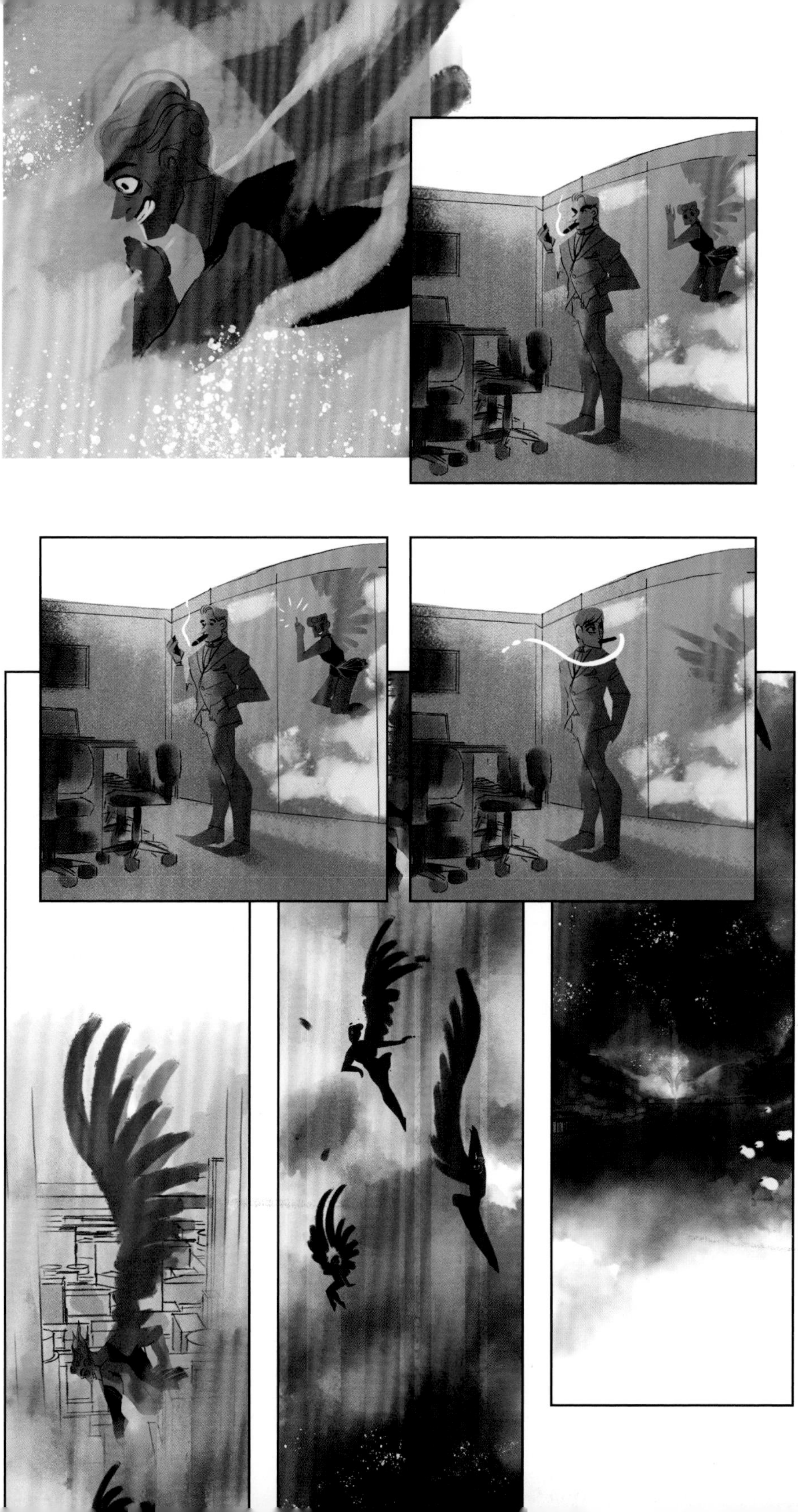

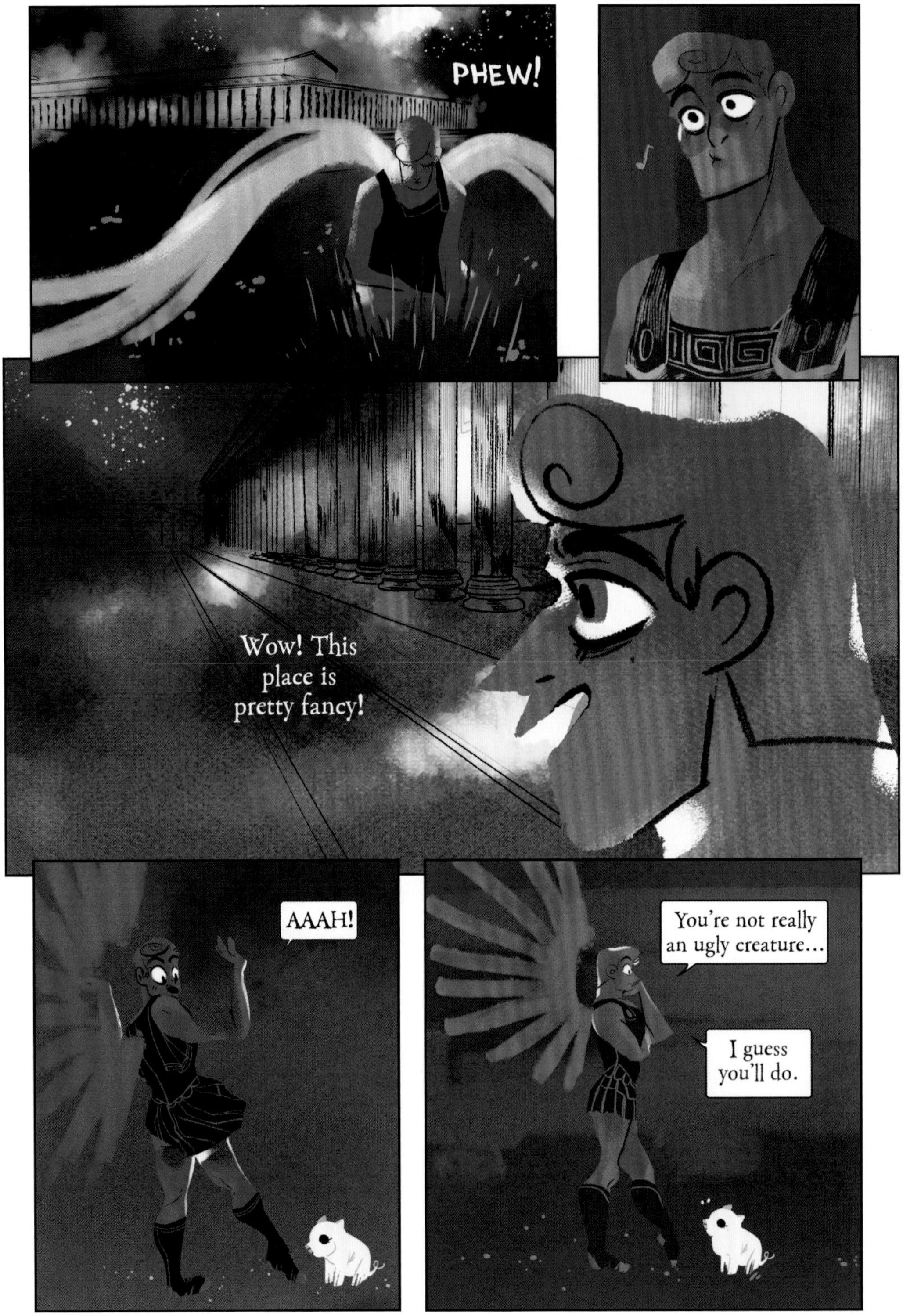
PHEW!
Wow! This place is pretty fancy!
AAAH!
You're not really an ugly creature...
I guess you'll do.

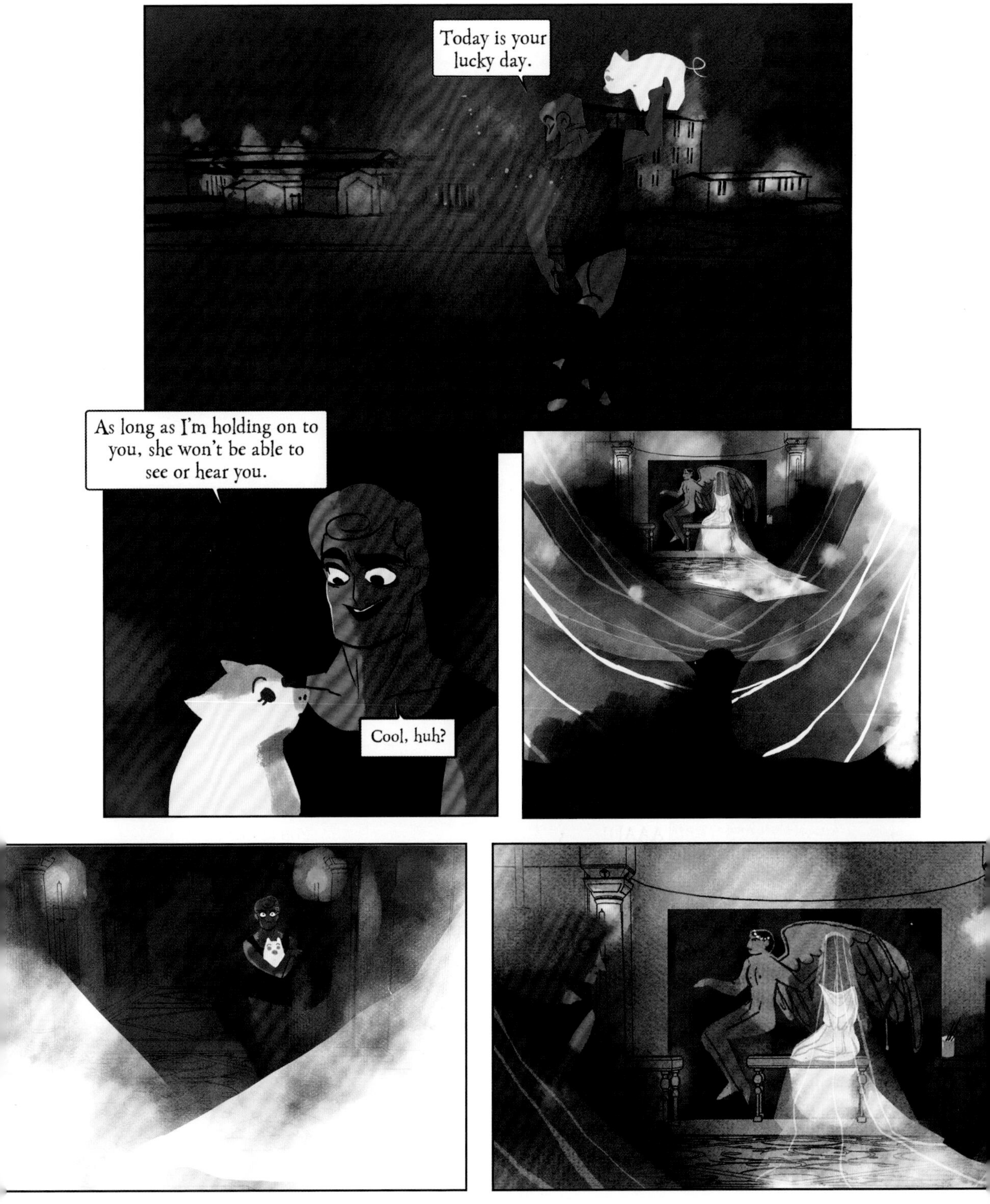
Today is your lucky day.
As long as I'm holding on to you, she won't be able to see or hear you.
Cool, huh?

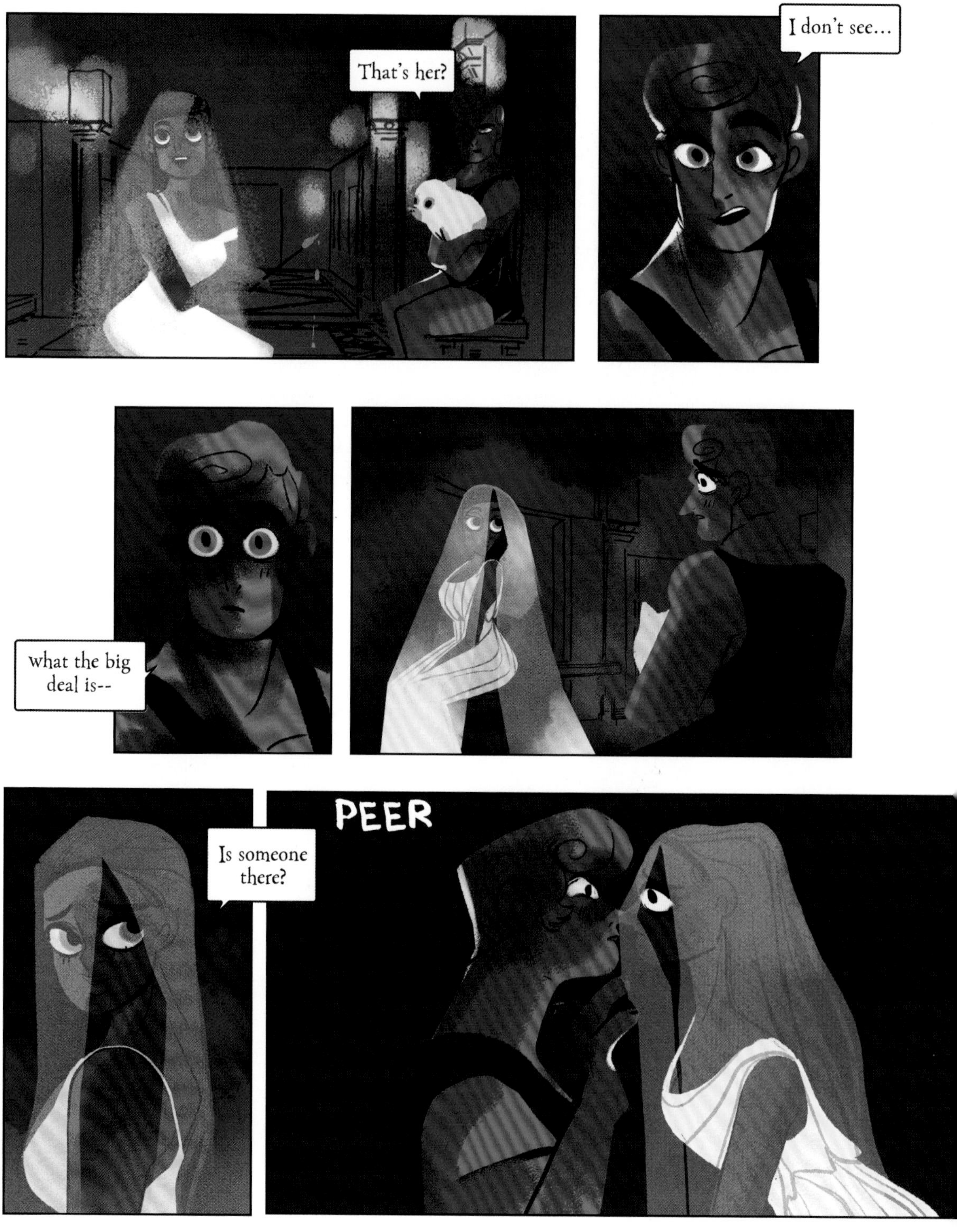
That's her?
I don't see...
what the big deal is--
Is someone there?
PEER

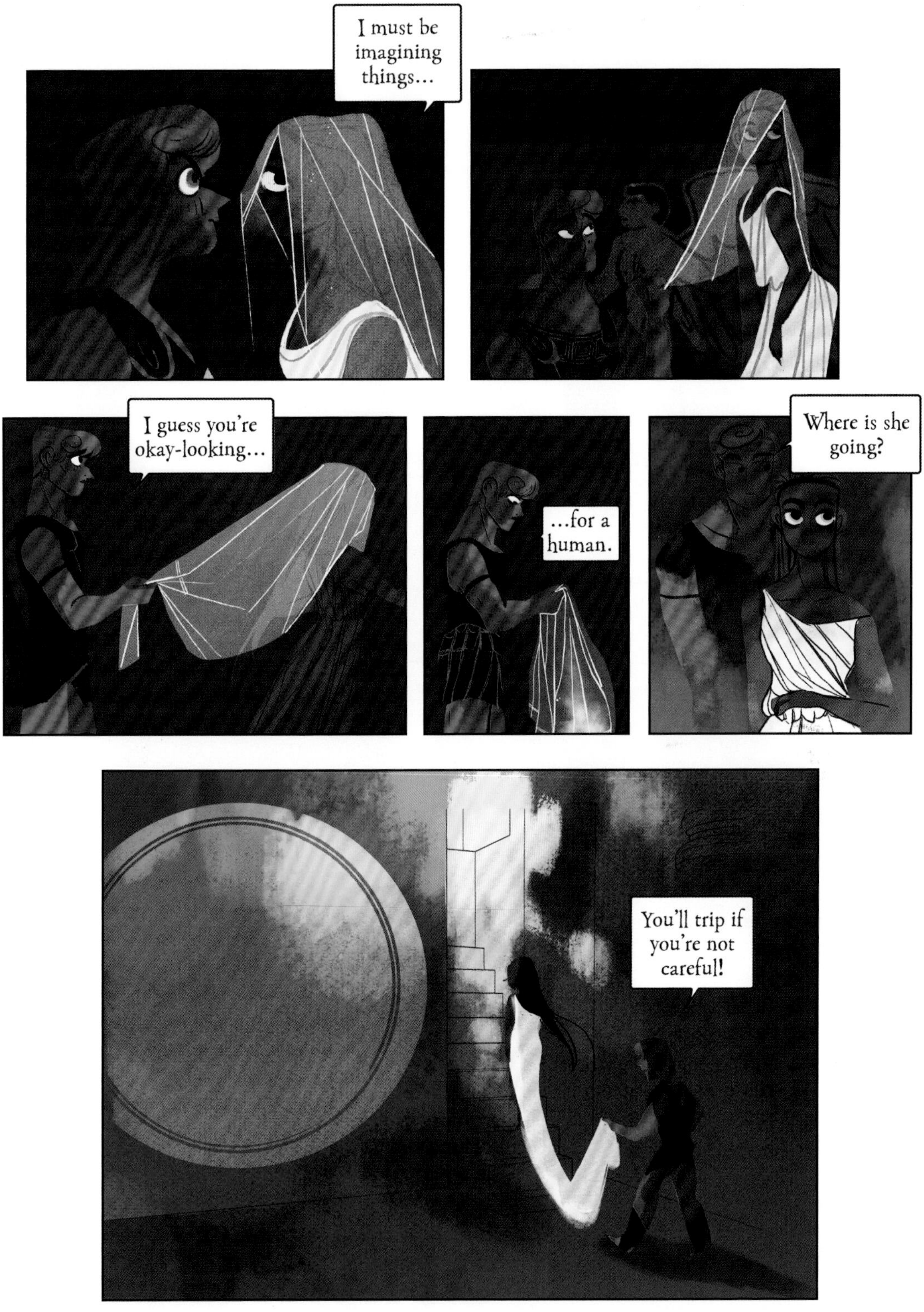
I must be imagining things...
I guess you're okay-looking...
...for a human.
Where is she going?
You'll trip if you're not careful!

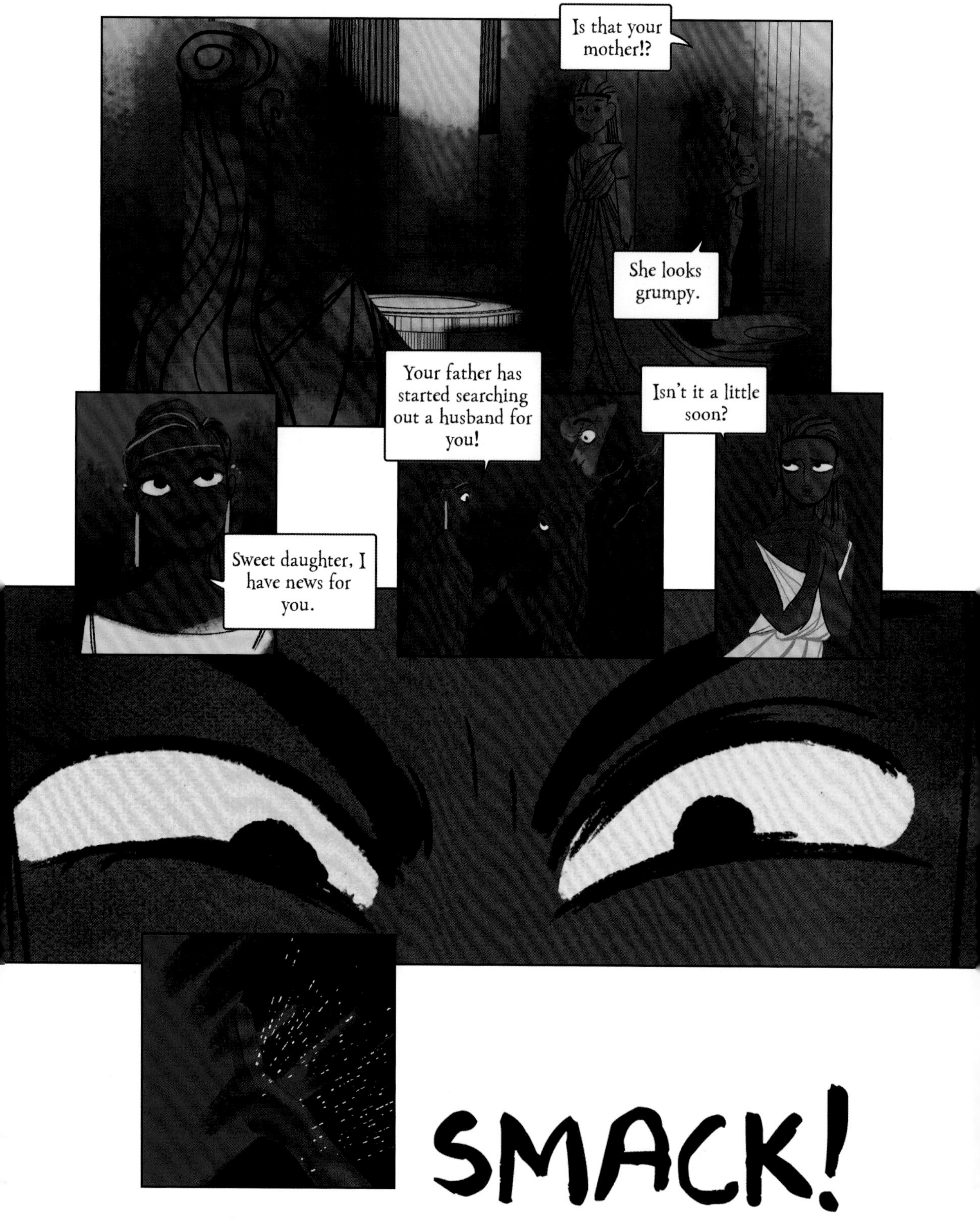
Is that your mother!?
She looks grumpy.
Sweet daughter, I have news for you.
Your father has started searching out a husband for you!
Isn't it a little soon?
SMACK!

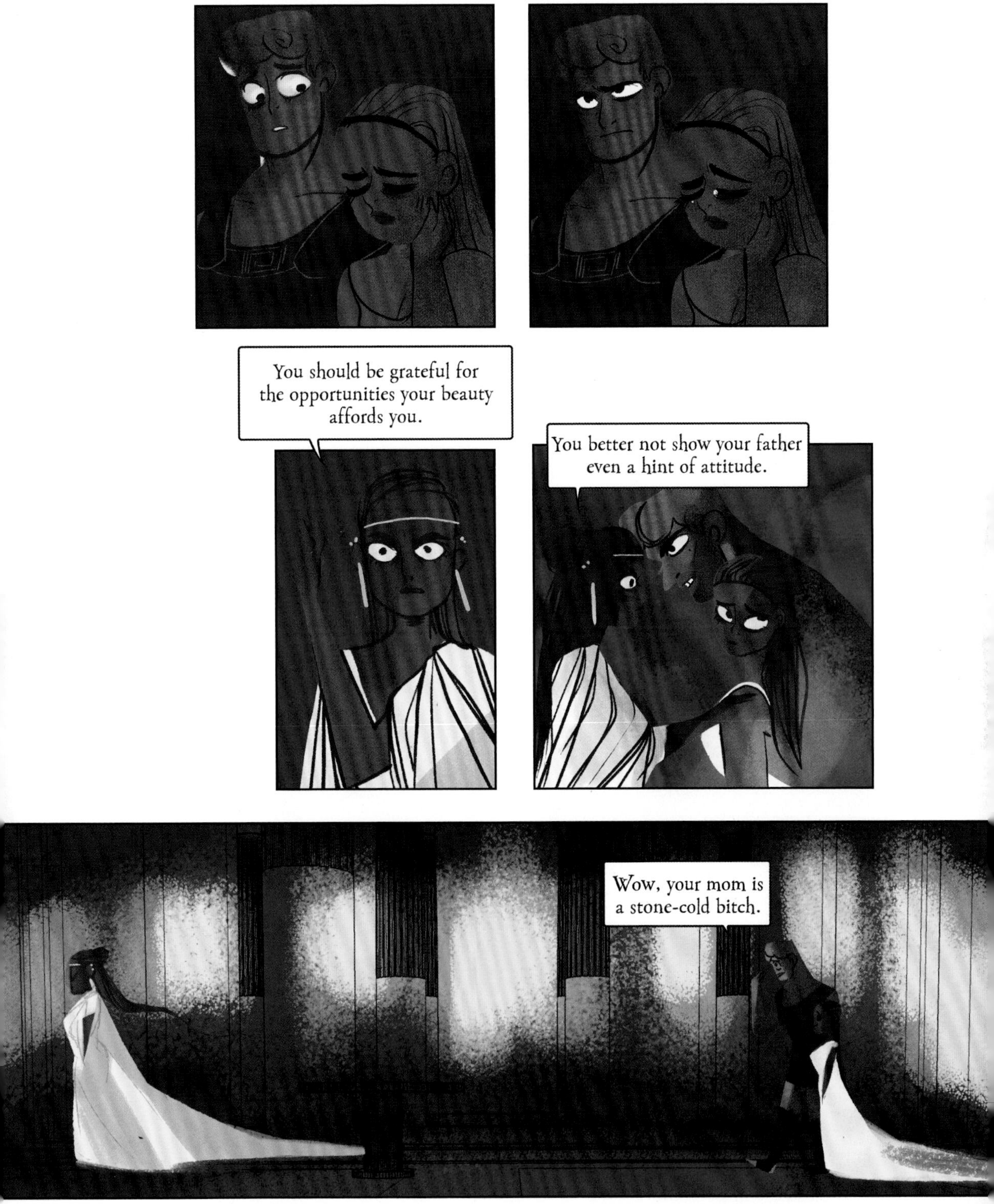
You should be grateful for the opportunities your beauty affords you.
You better not show your father even a hint of attitude.
Wow, your mom is a stone-cold bitch.

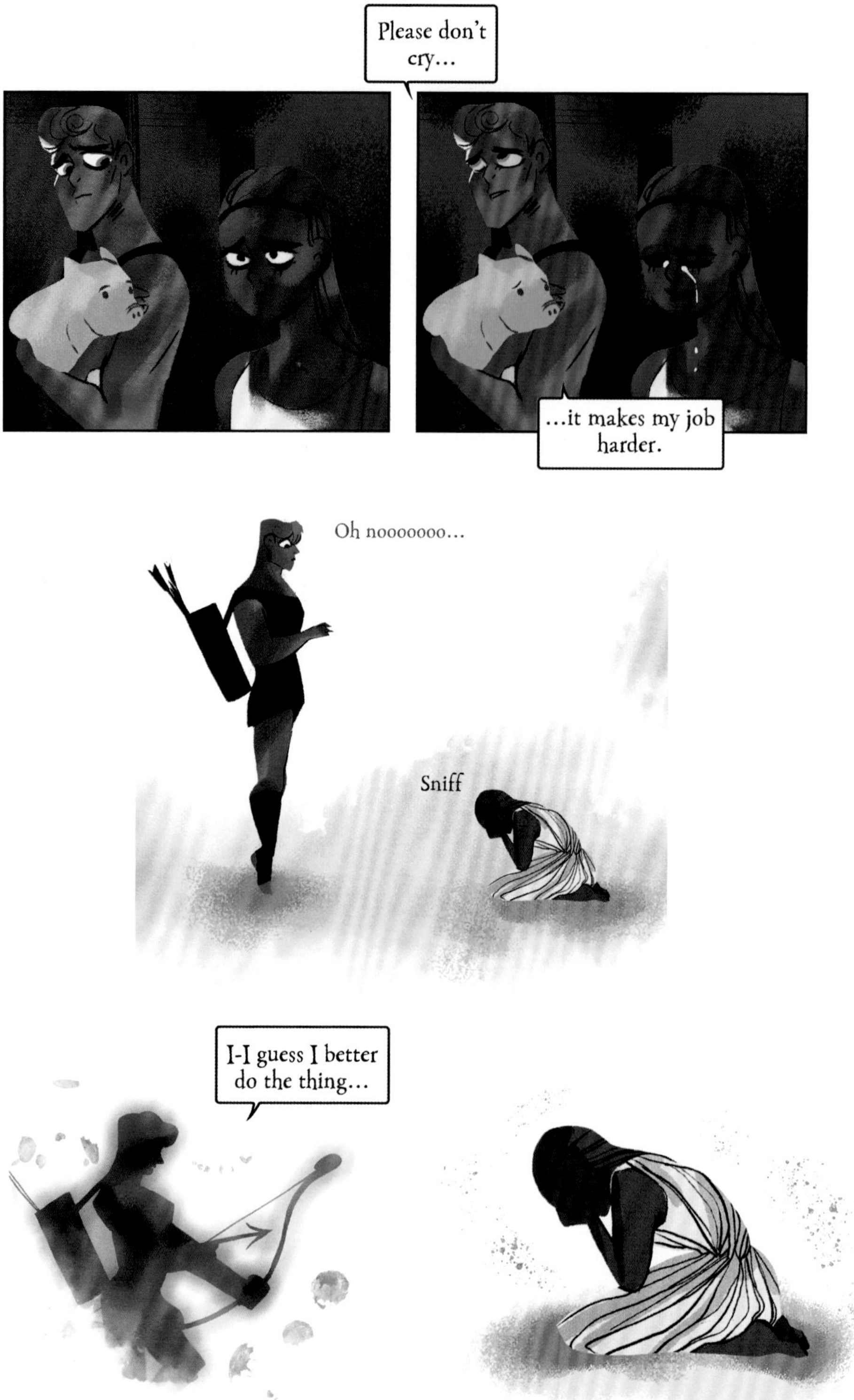
Please don't cry…
…it makes my job harder.
Oh noooooo…
Sniff
I-I guess I better do the thing…

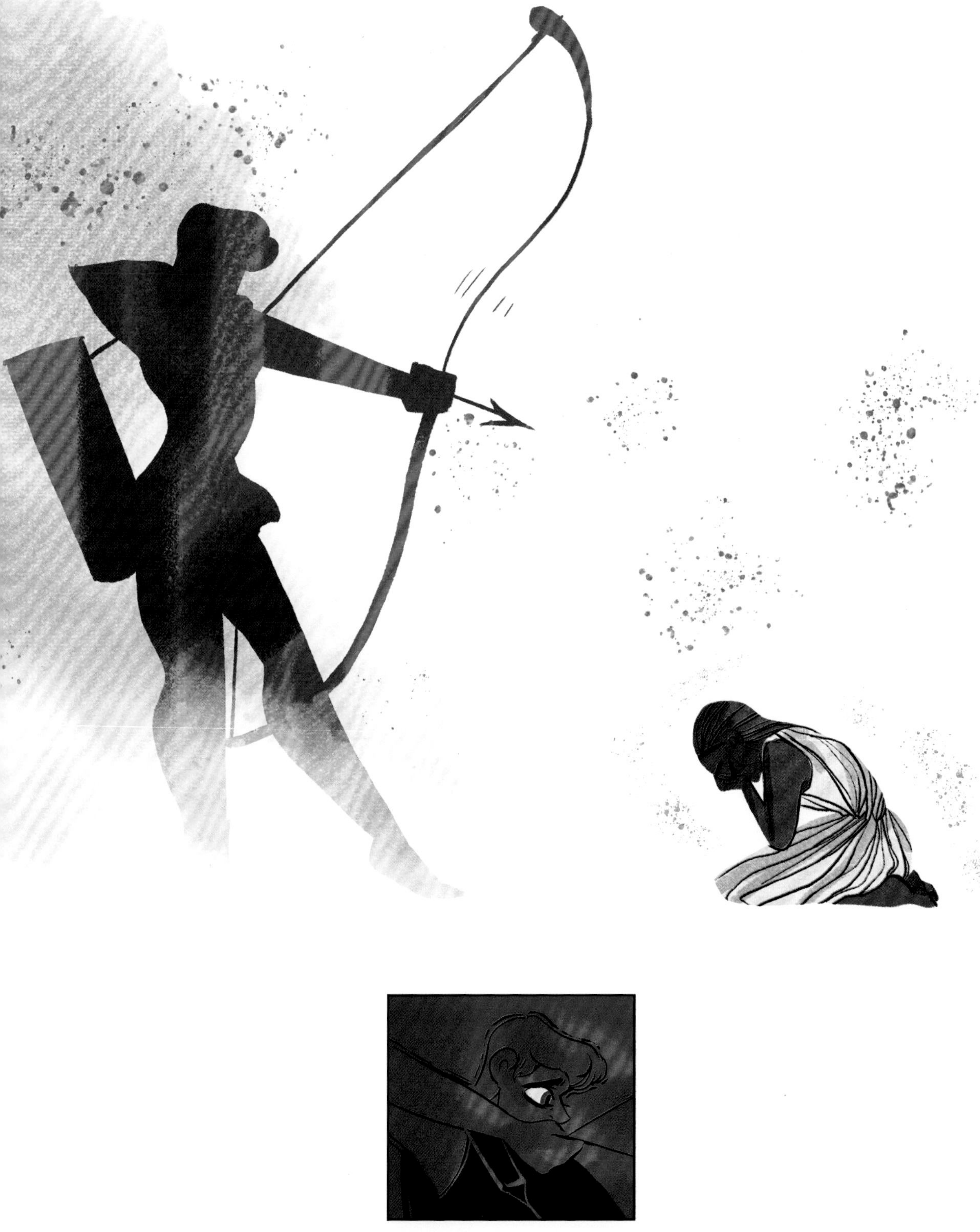

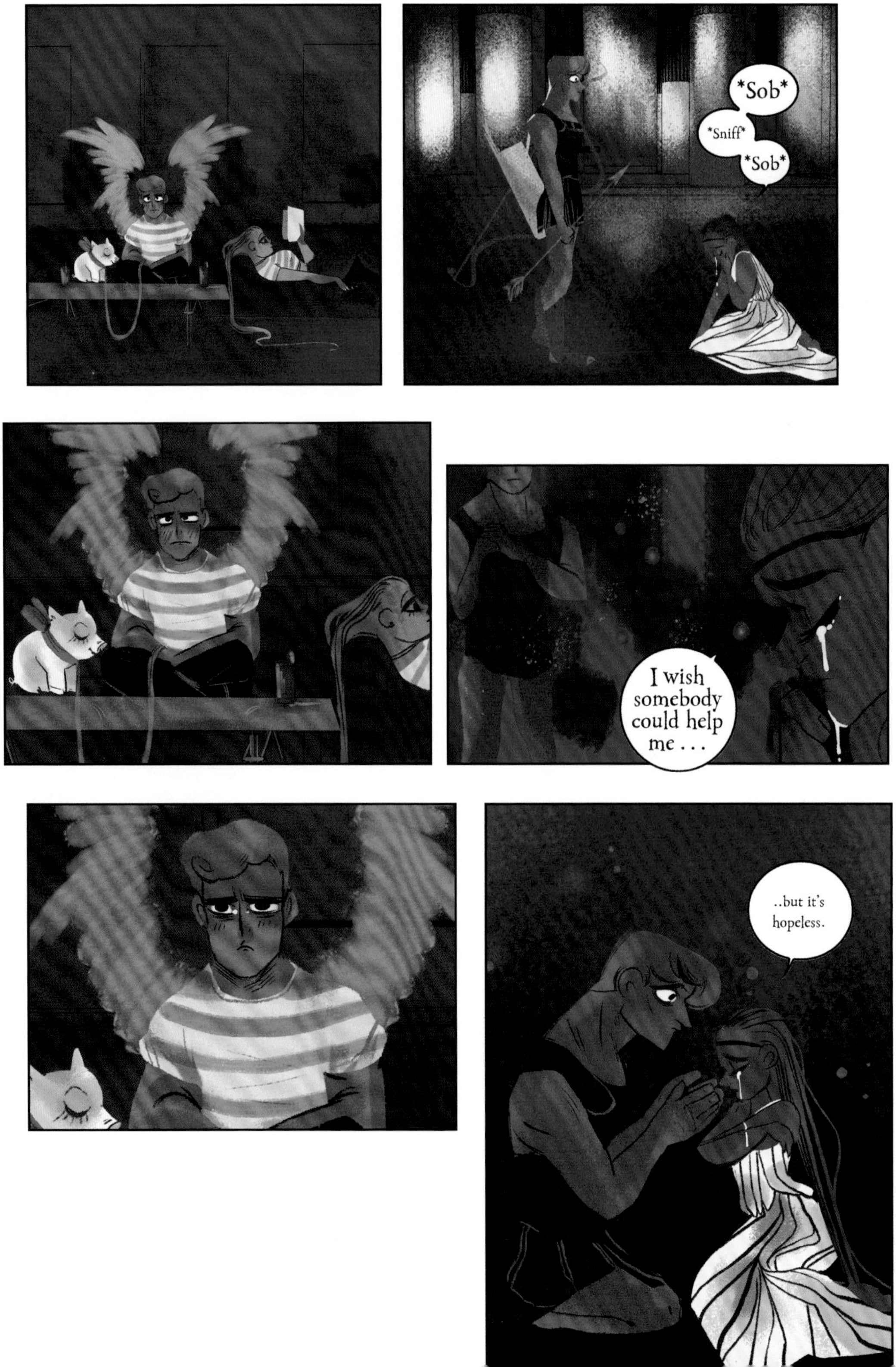
Sob
Sniff
Sob
I wish somebody could help me . . .
..but it's hopeless.

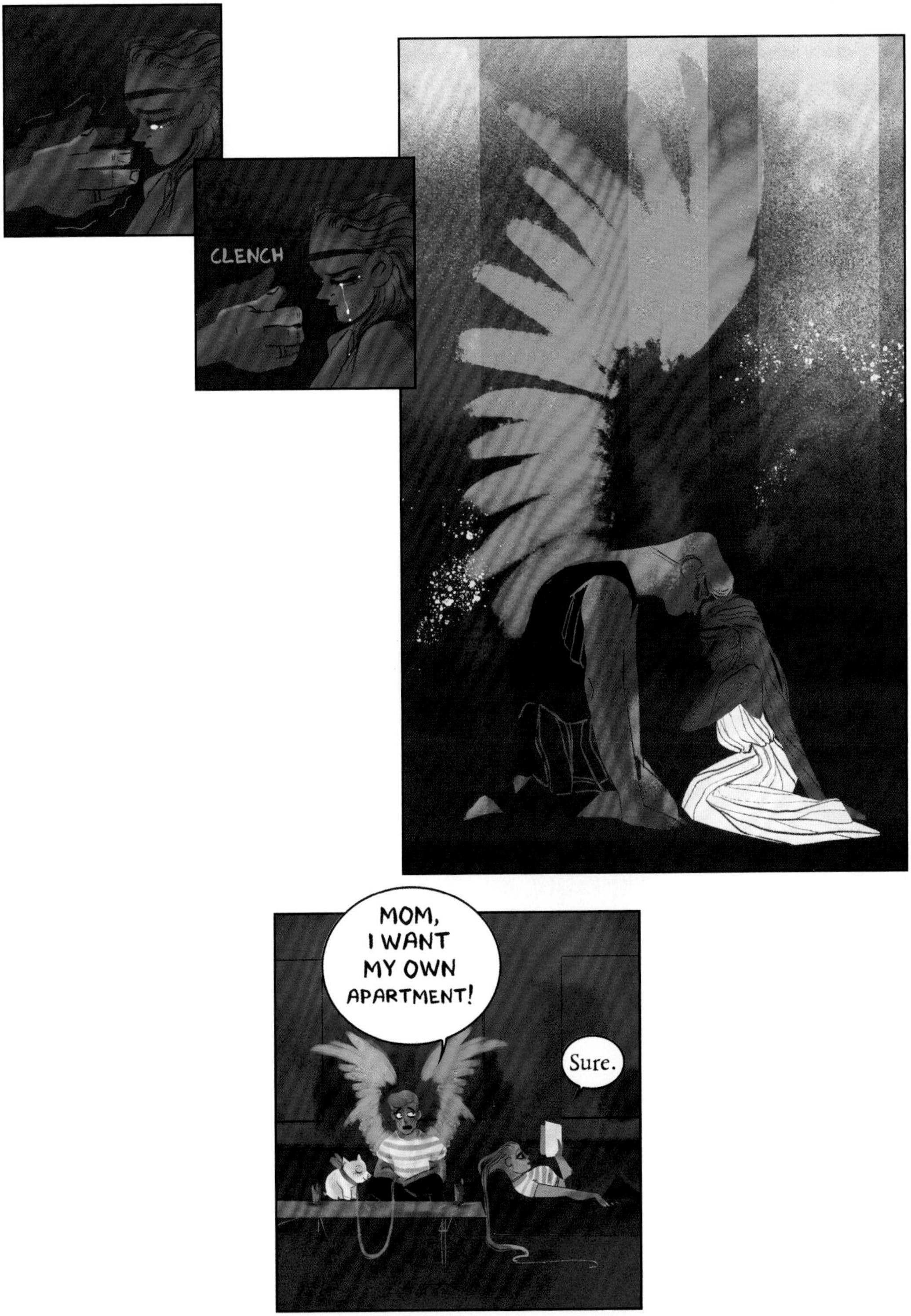
CLENCH
MOM, I WANT MY OWN APARTMENT!
Sure.

EPISODE 14: MONSTER BOY

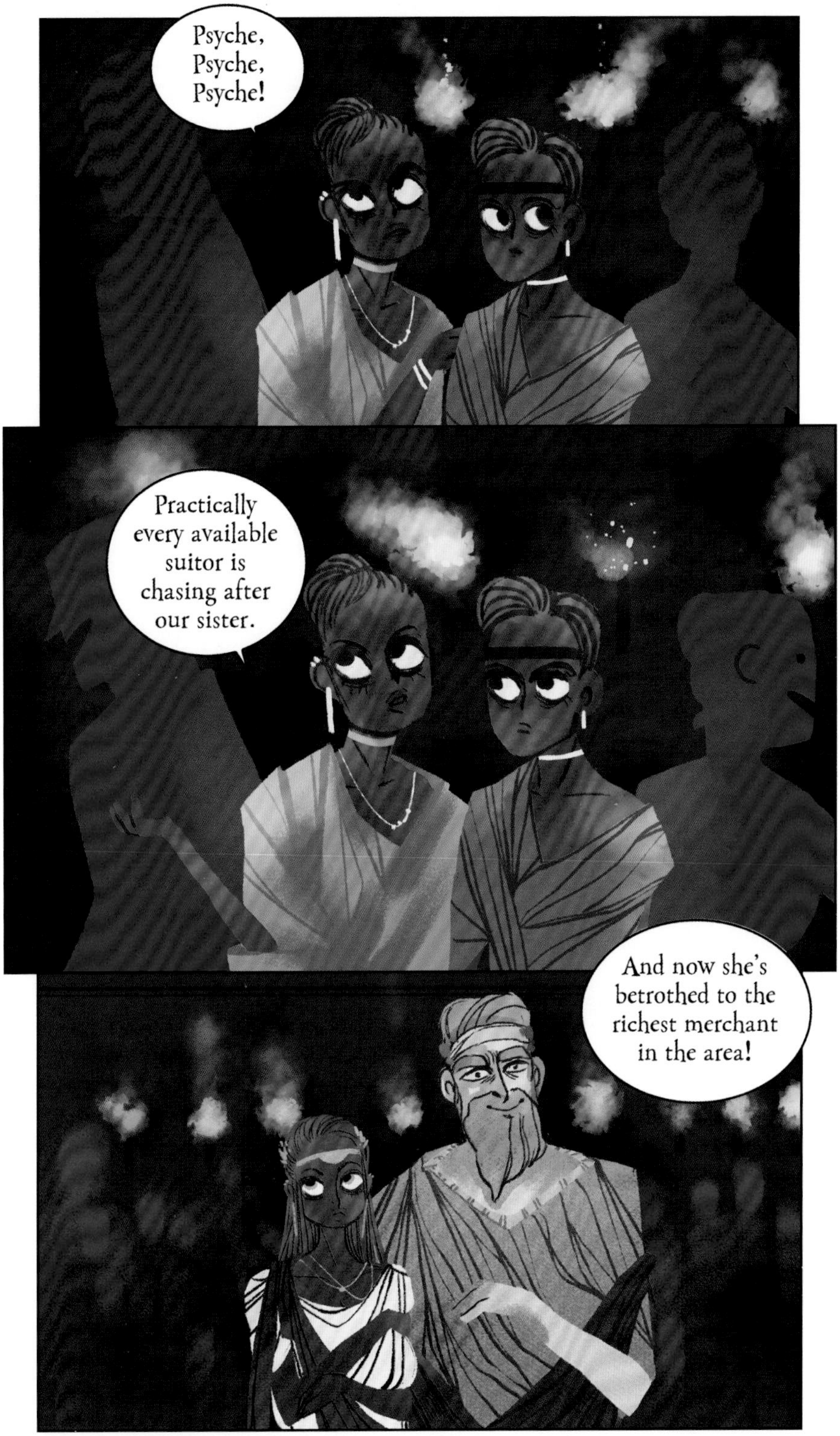
Psyche, Psyche, Psyche!
Practically every available suitor is chasing after our sister.
And now she's betrothed to the richest merchant in the area!

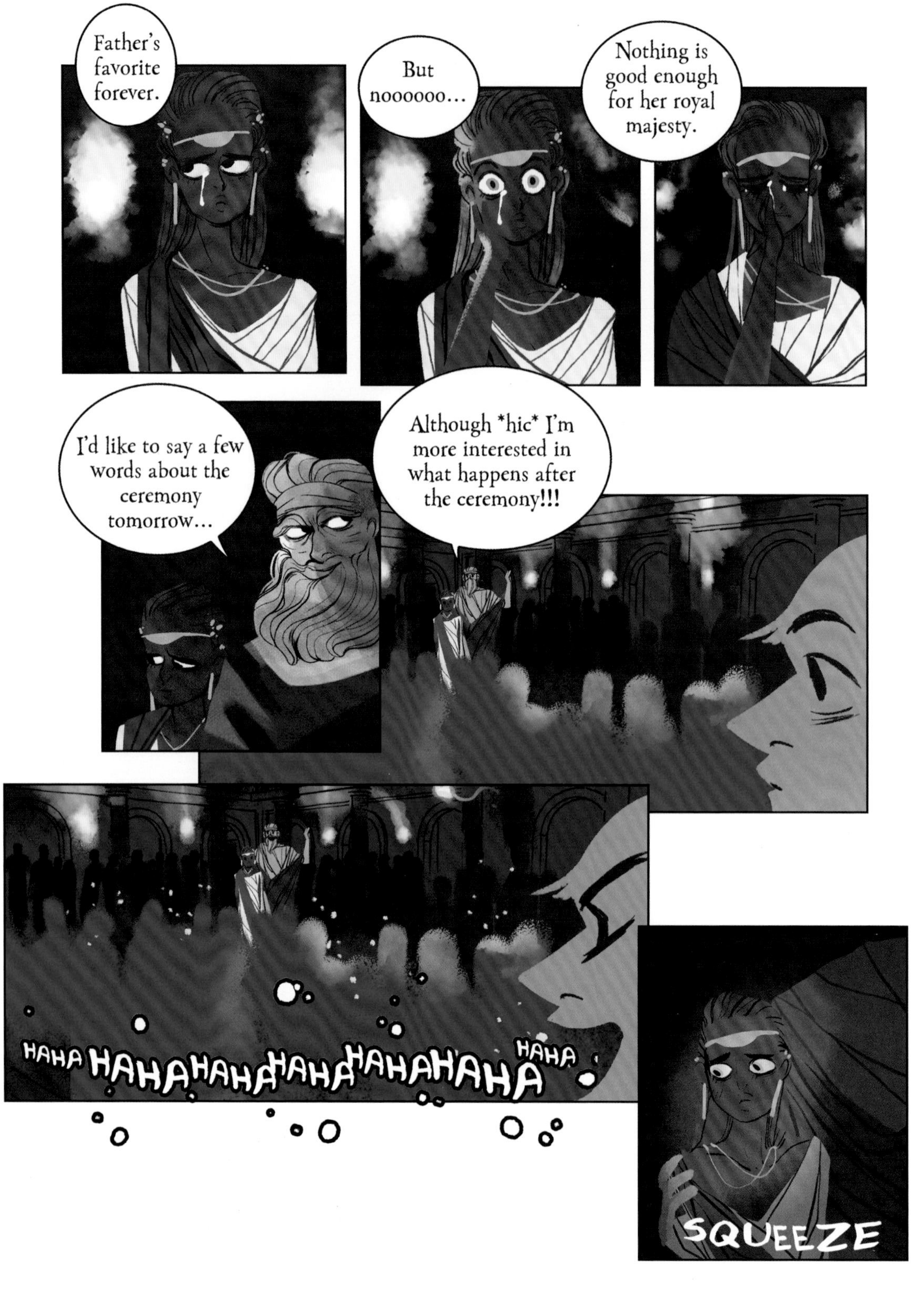

Father's favorite forever.
But noooooo...
Nothing is good enough for her royal majesty.
I'd like to say a few words about the ceremony tomorrow...
Although *hic* I'm more interested in what happens after the ceremony!!!
HAHA HAHAHAHAHAHAHAHAHAHA HAHA
SQUEEZE

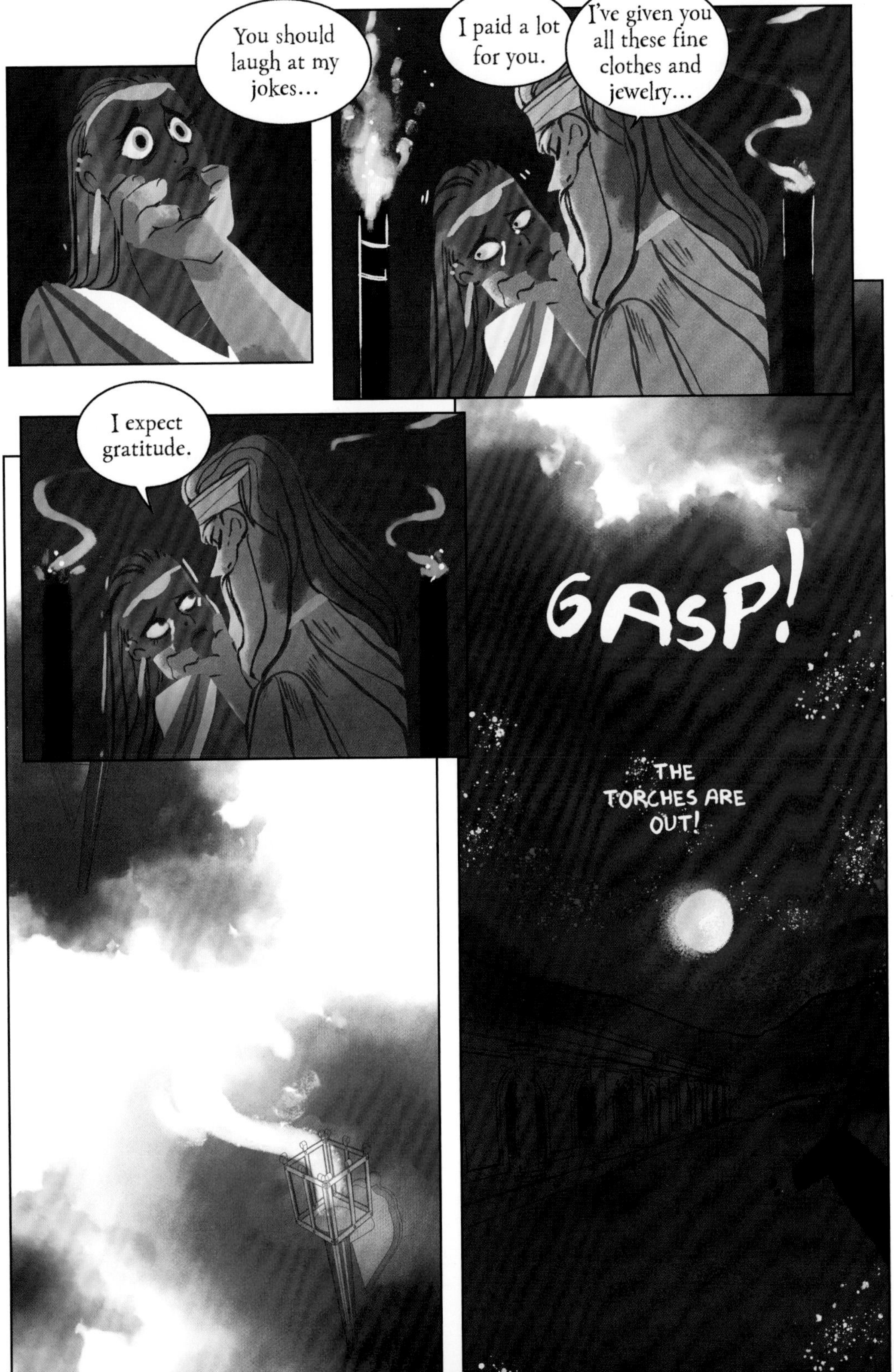
You should laugh at my jokes…
I paid a lot for you.
I've given you all these fine clothes and jewelry…
I expect gratitude.
GASP!
THE TORCHES ARE OUT!

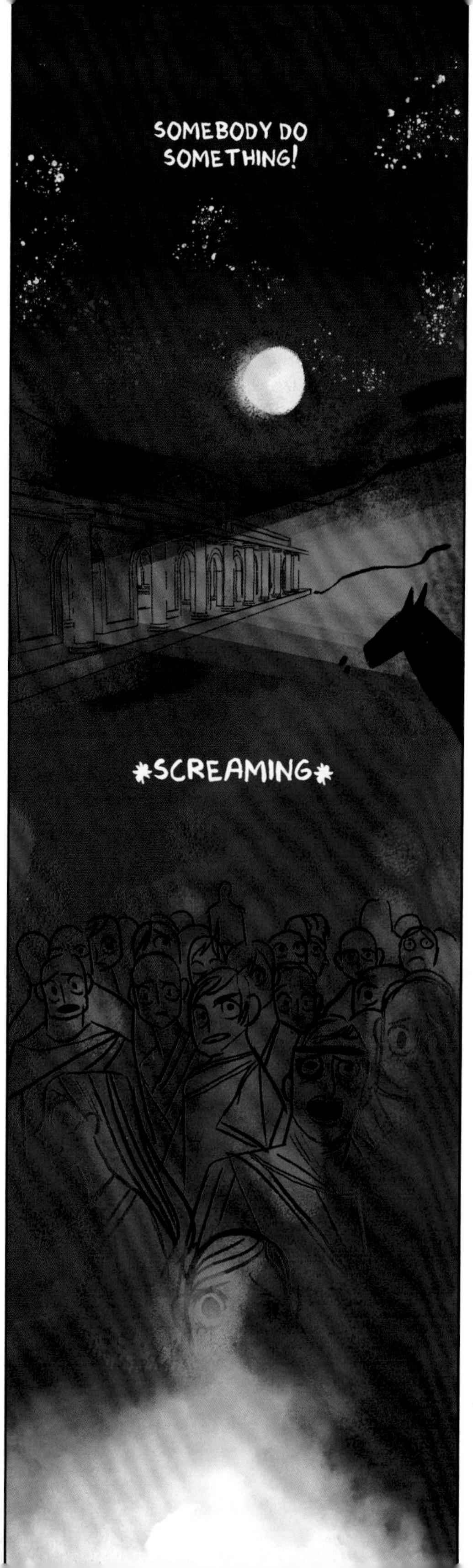
SOMEBODY DO SOMETHING!
SCREAMING
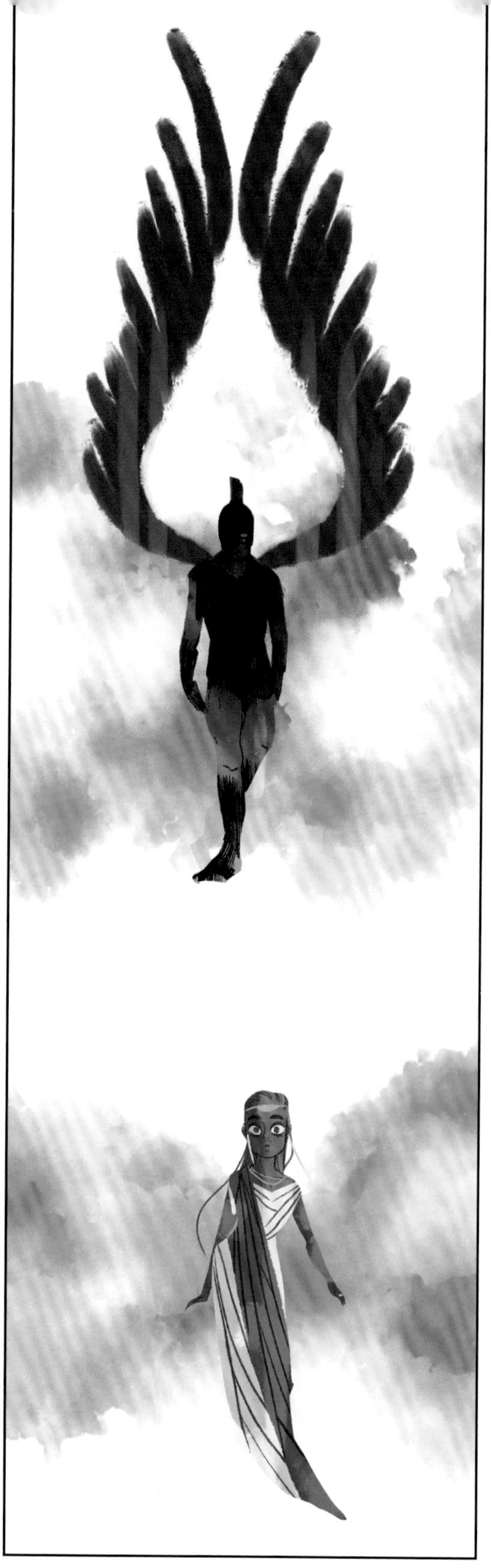

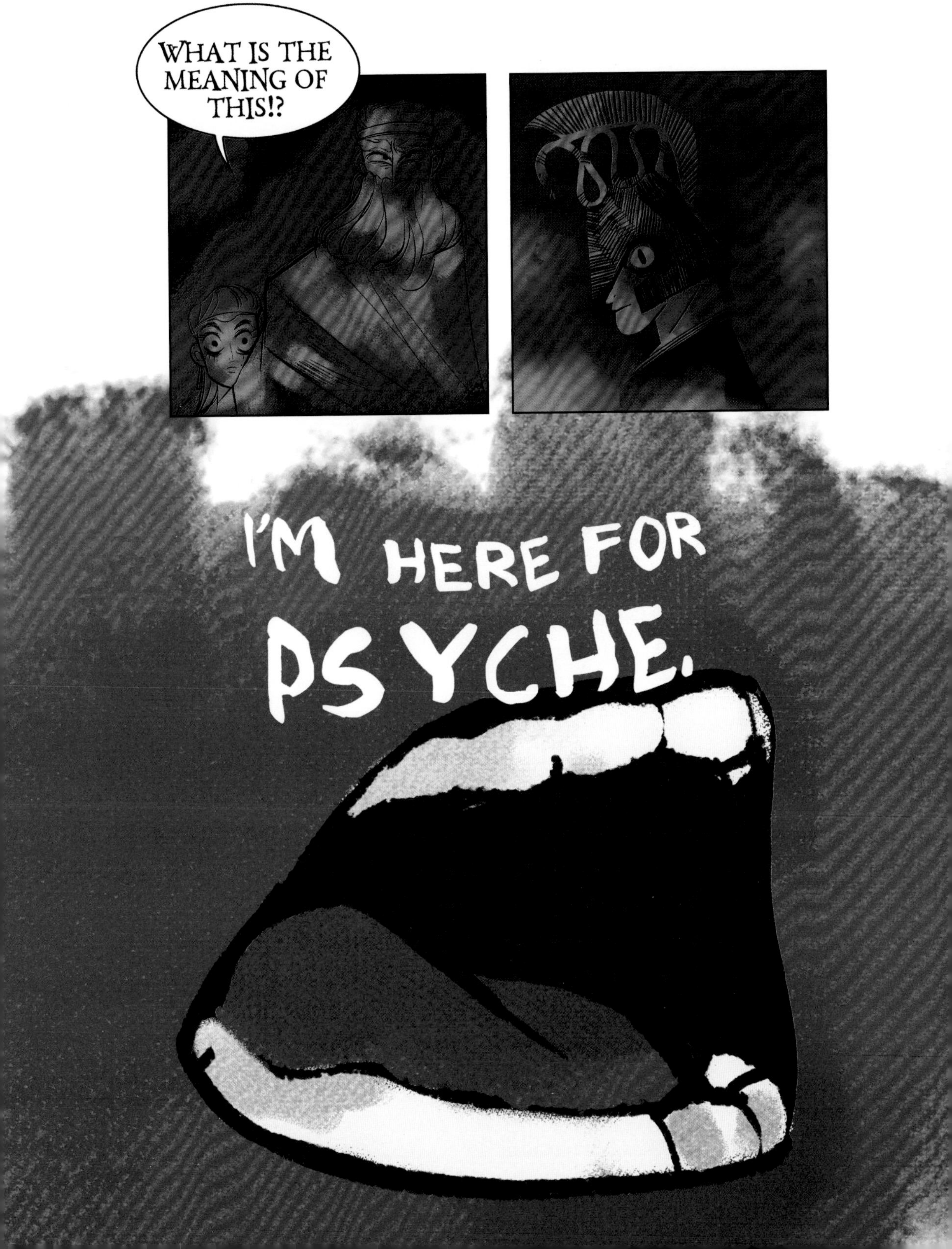
WHAT IS THE MEANING OF THIS!?
I'M HERE FOR PSYCHE.

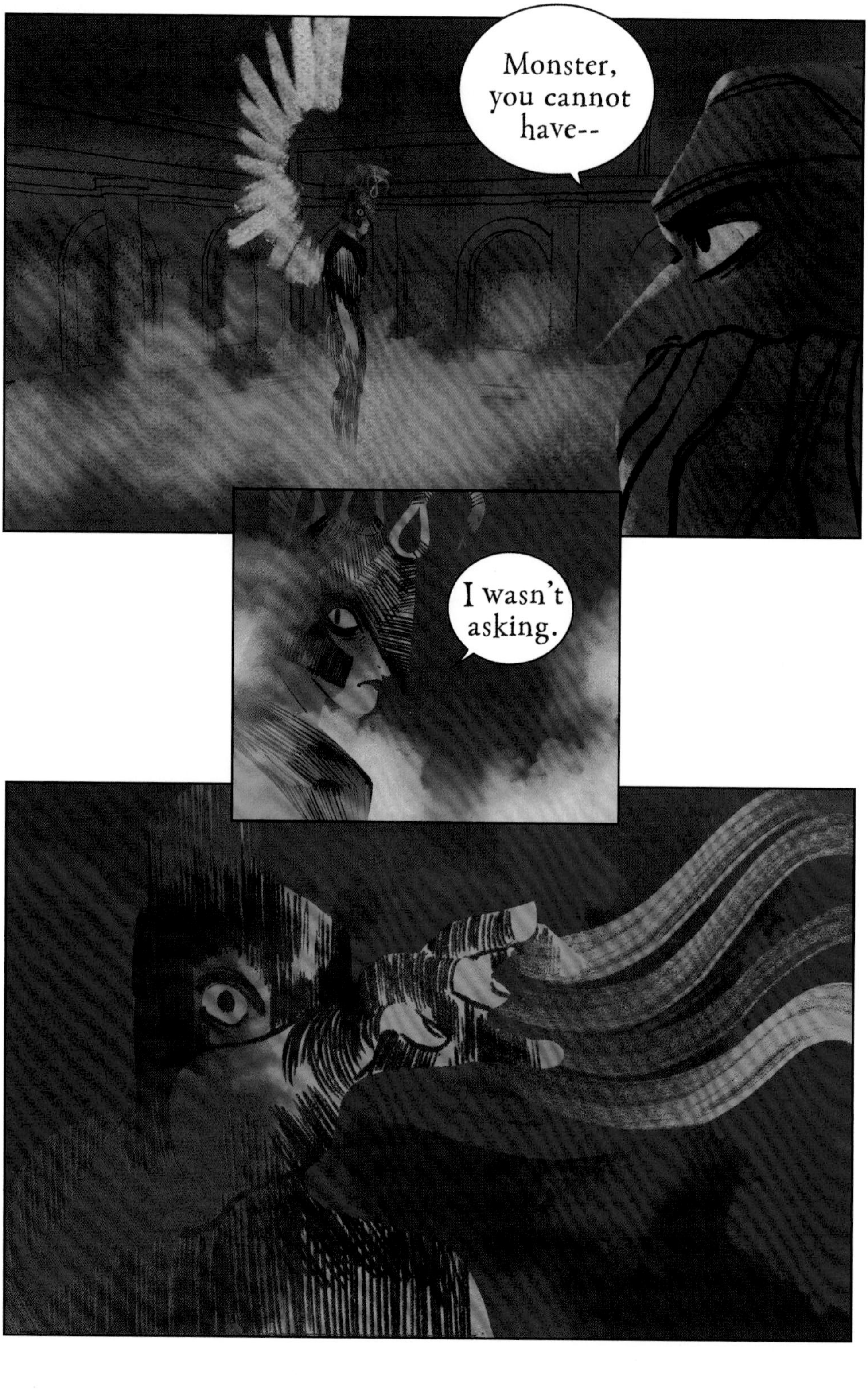
Monster, you cannot have--
I wasn't asking.

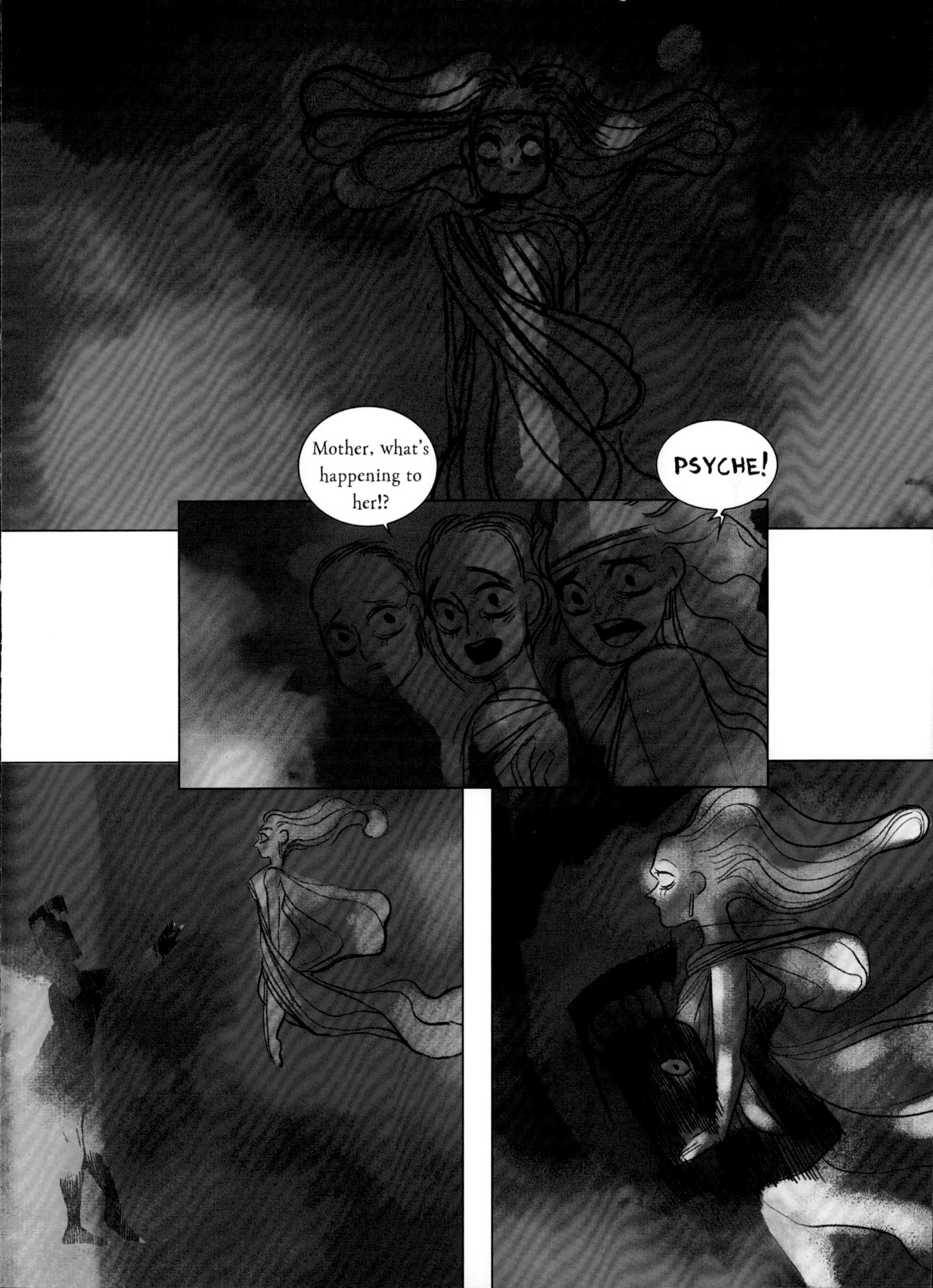
Mother, what's happening to her!?
PSYCHE!

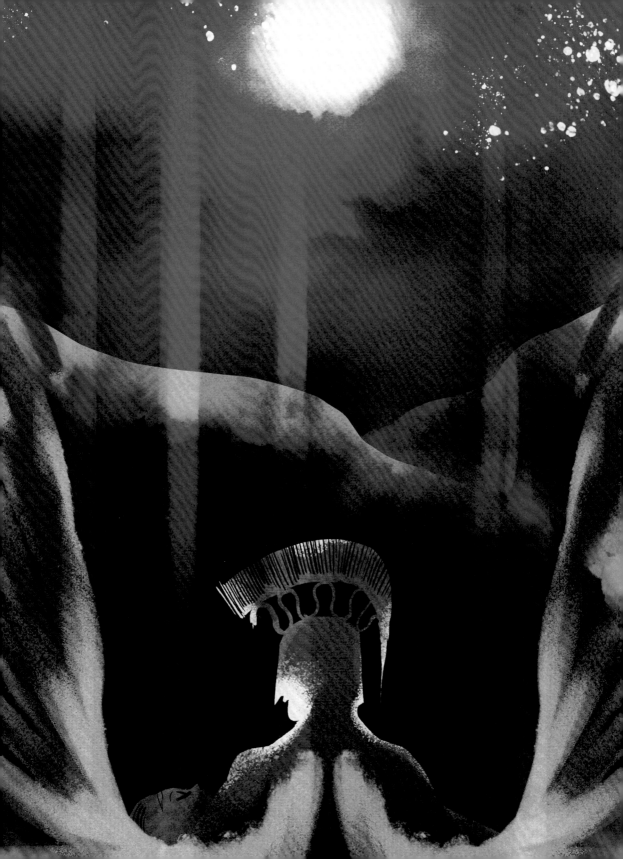

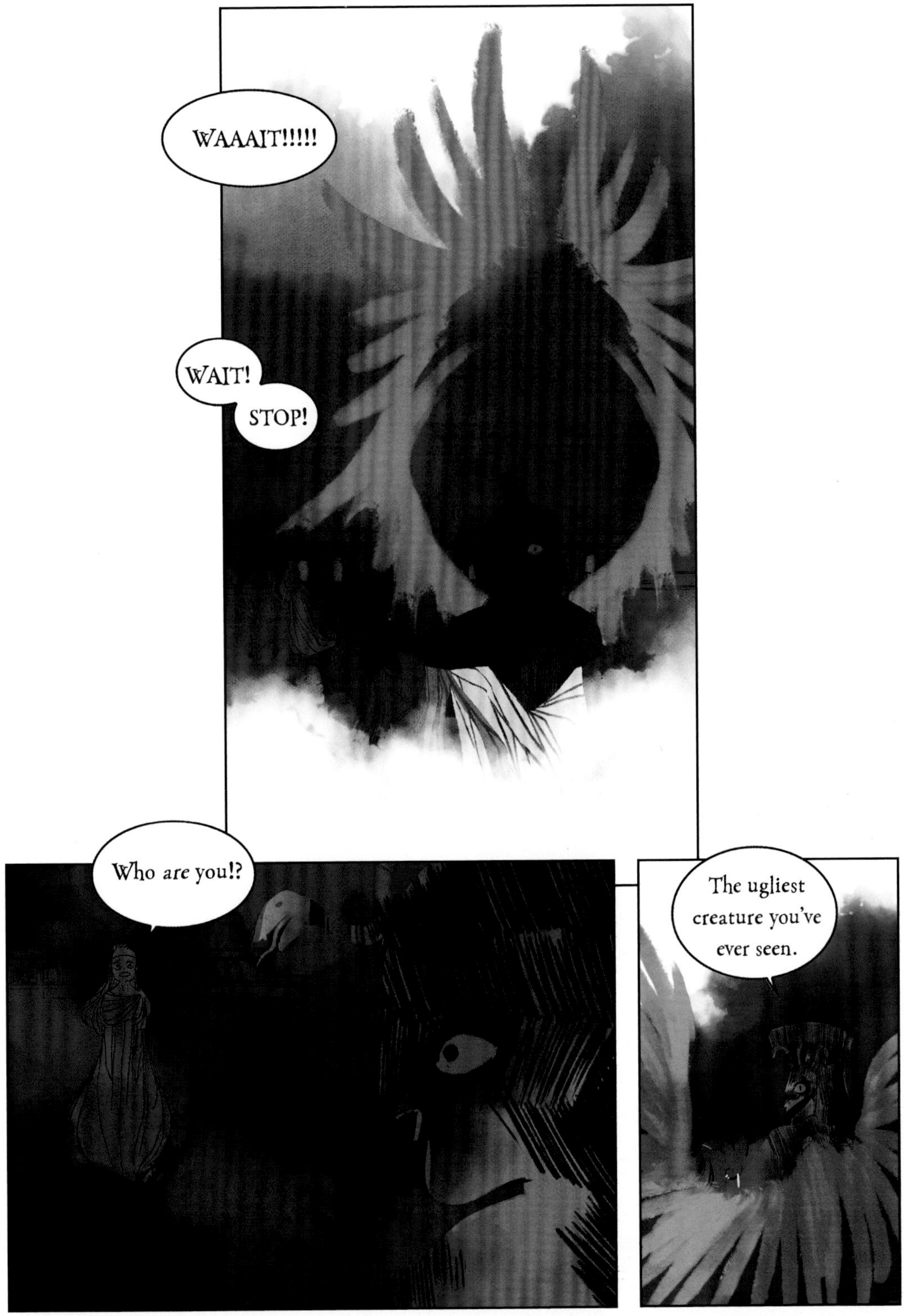
WAAAIT!!!!!
WAIT!
STOP!
Who are you!?
The ugliest creature you've ever seen.

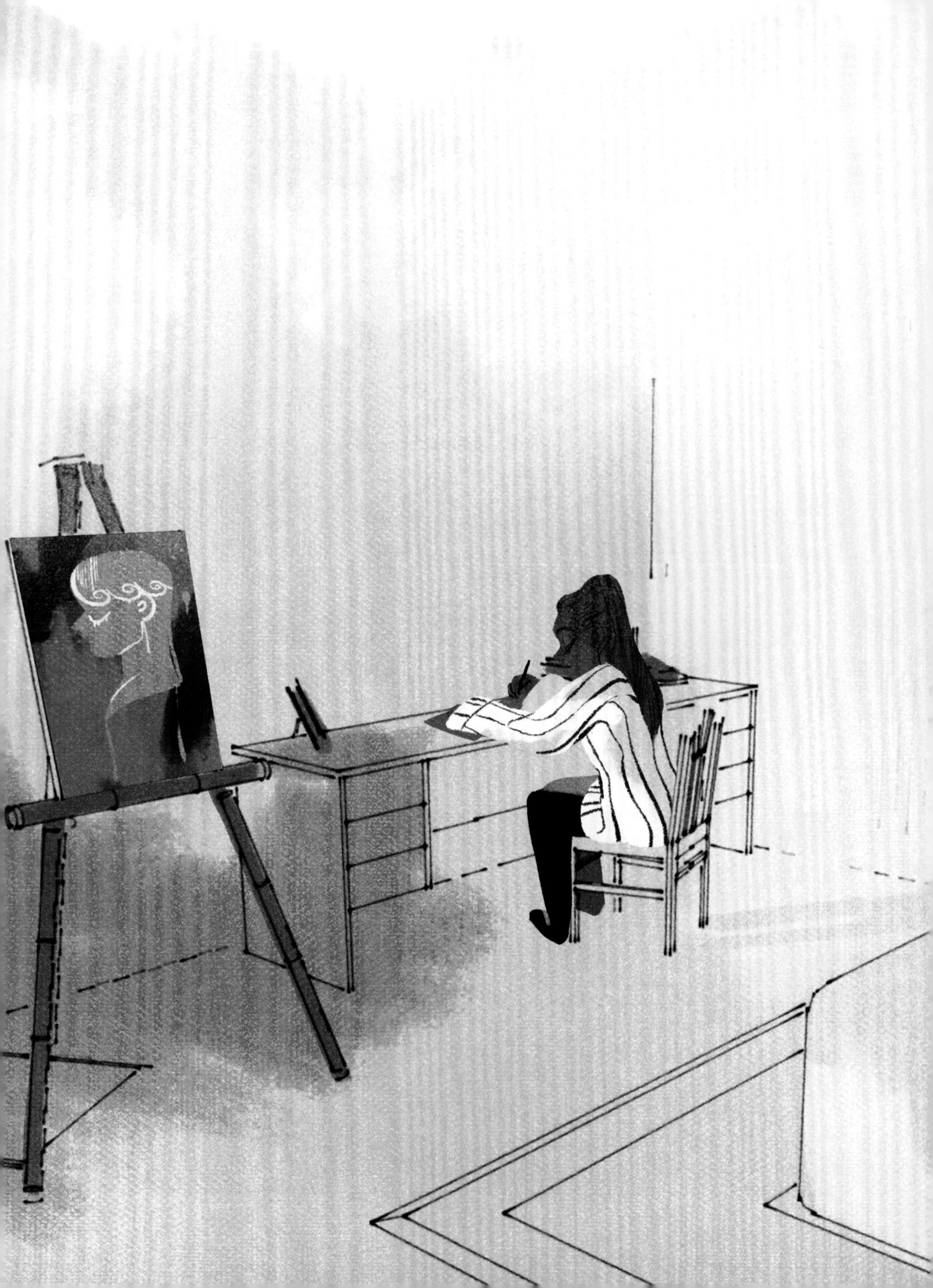

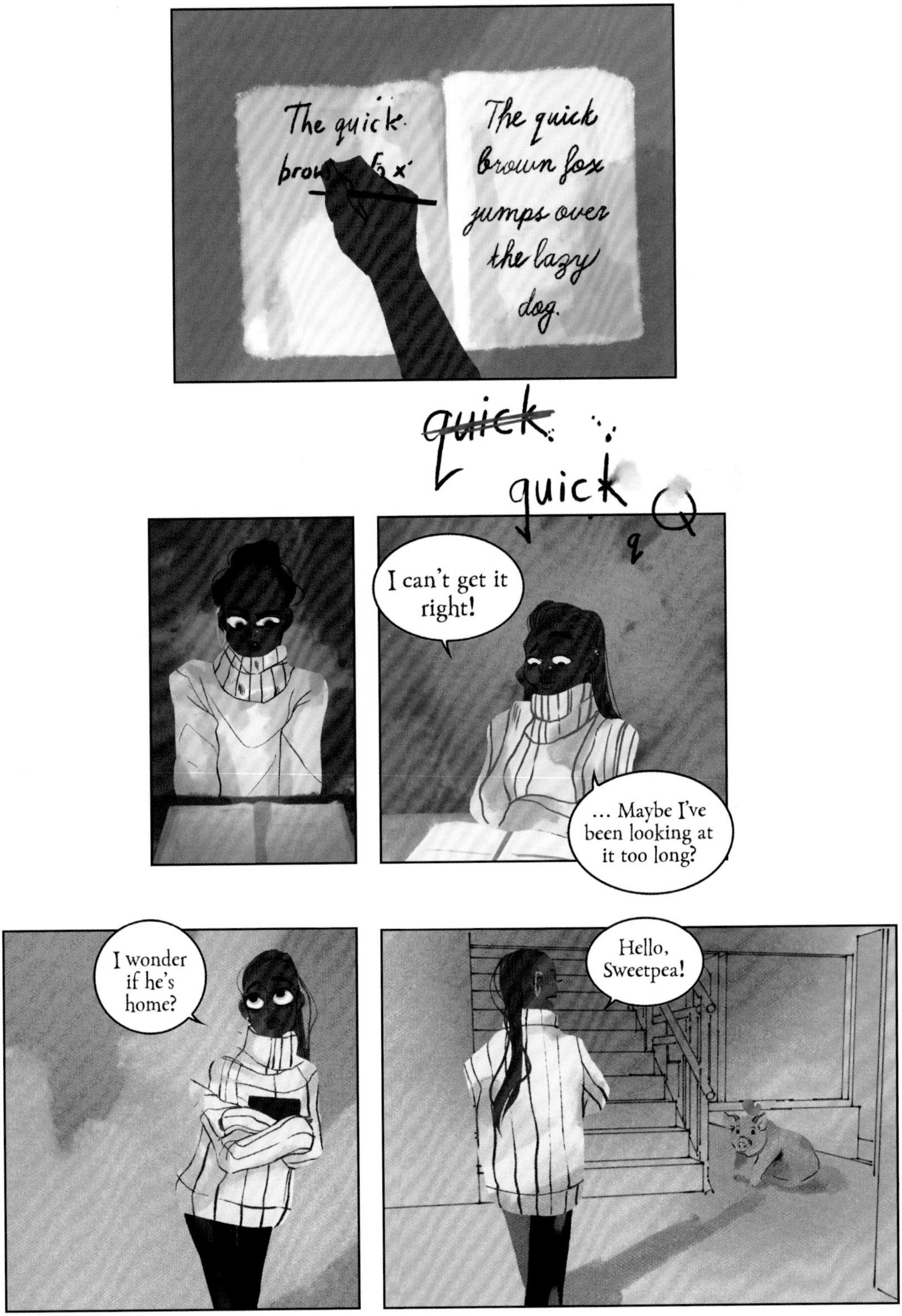

The quick
The quick brown fox jumps over the lazy dog.
~~quick~~
quick
Q
q
I can't get it right!
… Maybe I've been looking at it too long?
I wonder if he's home?
Hello, Sweetpea!

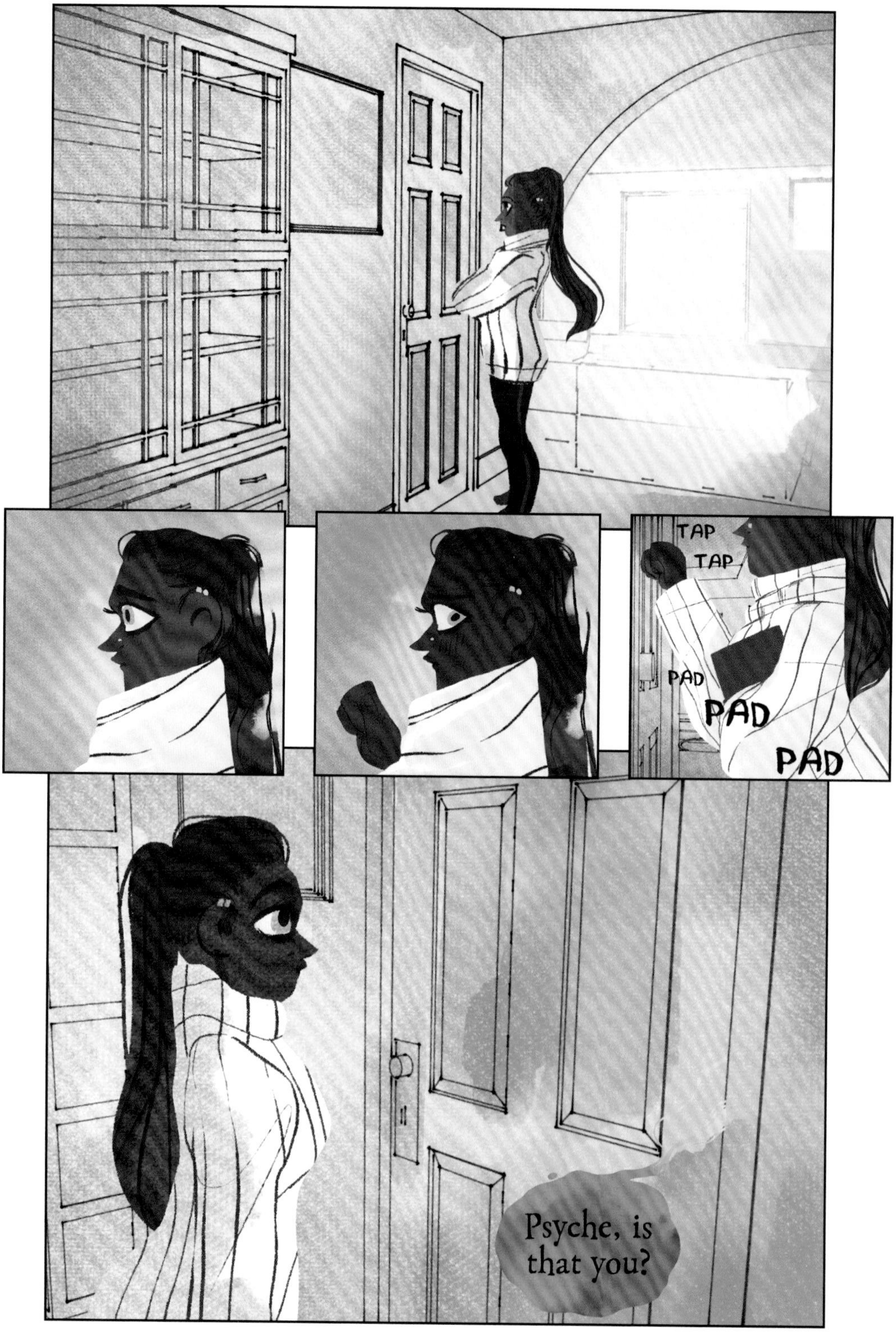
TAP
TAP
PAD
PAD
PAD
Psyche, is that you?

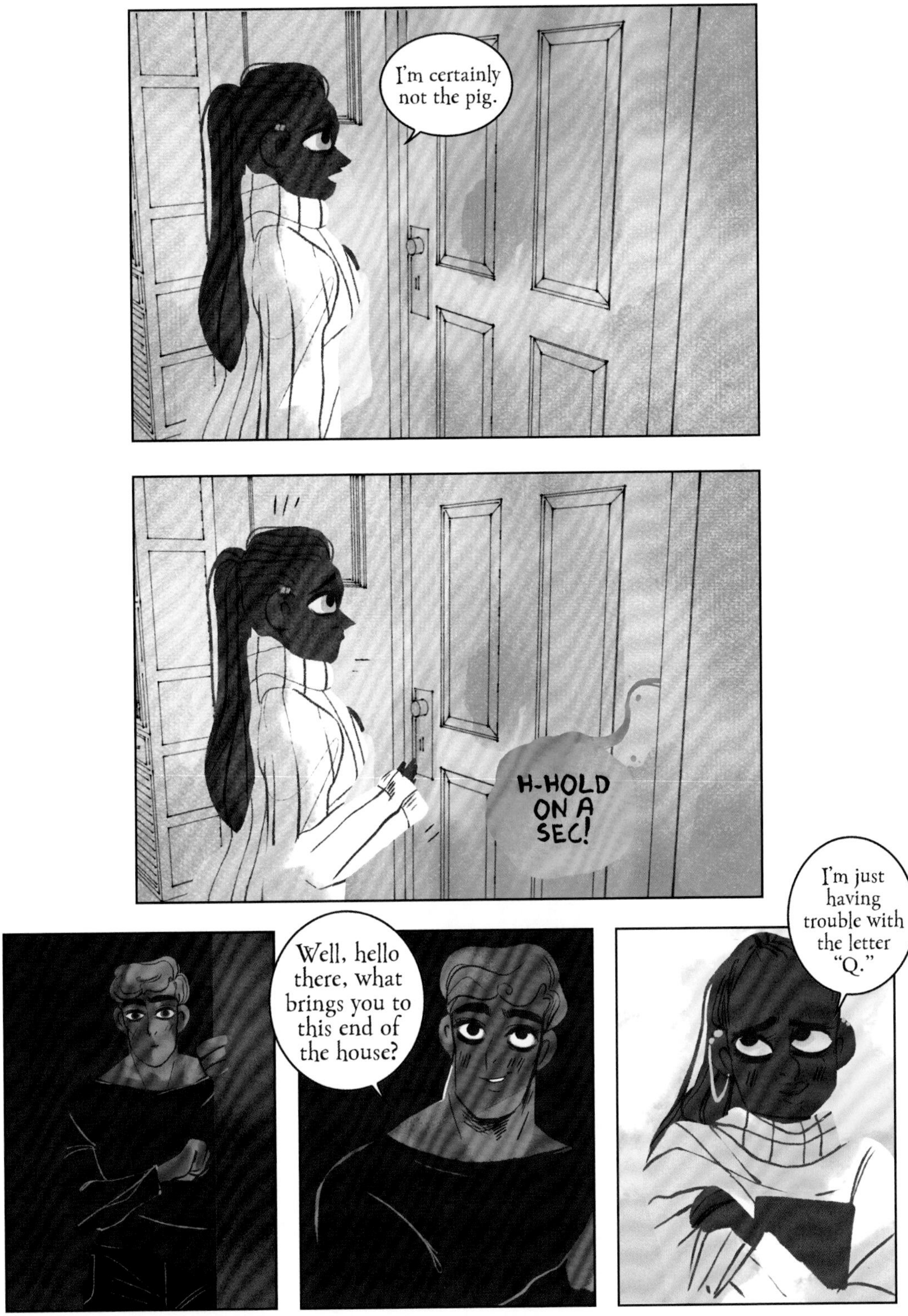
I'm certainly not the pig.
H-HOLD ON A SEC!
Well, hello there, what brings you to this end of the house?
I'm just having trouble with the letter "Q."

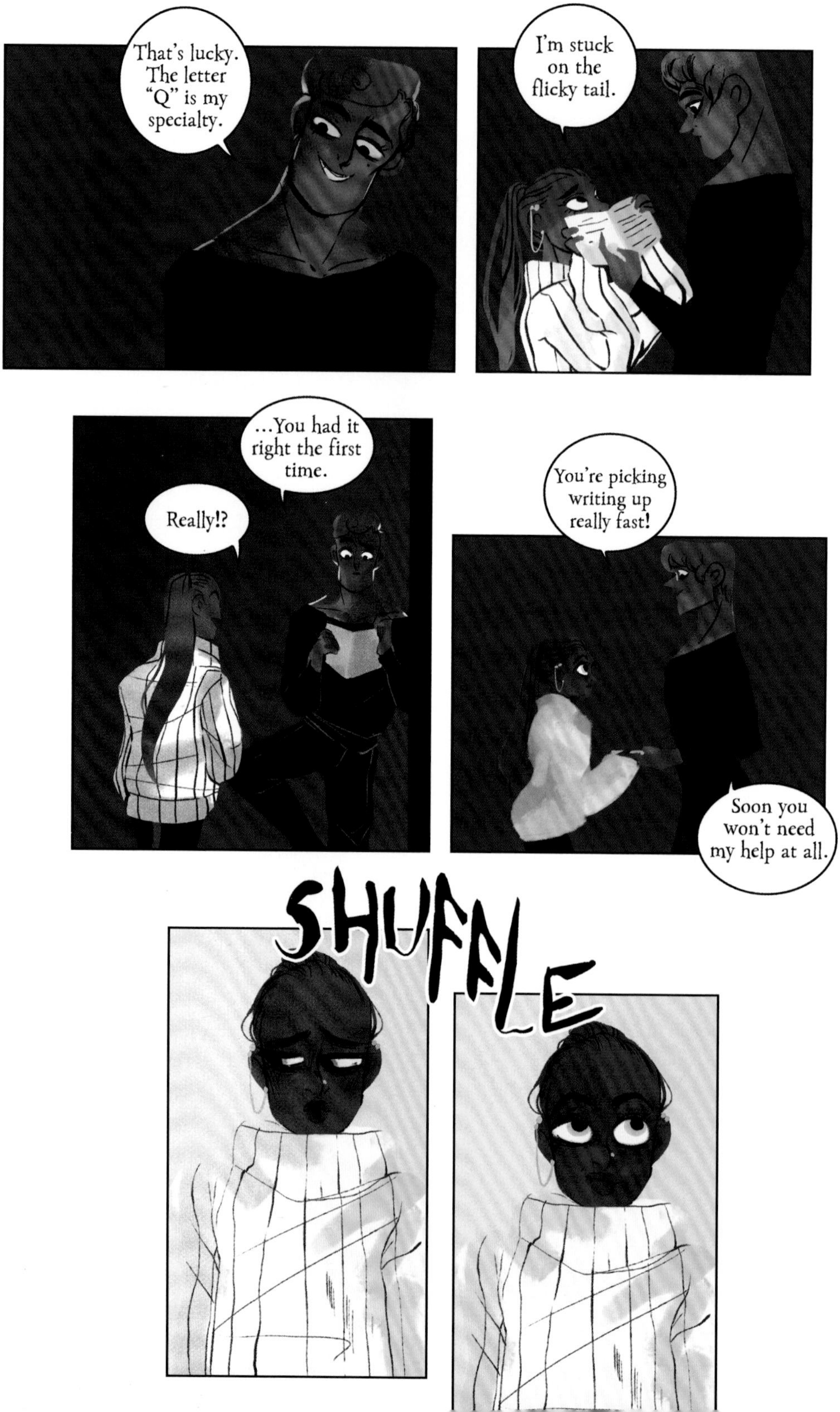
That's lucky. The letter "Q" is my specialty.
I'm stuck on the flicky tail.
...You had it right the first time.
Really!?
You're picking writing up really fast!
Soon you won't need my help at all.
SHUFFLE

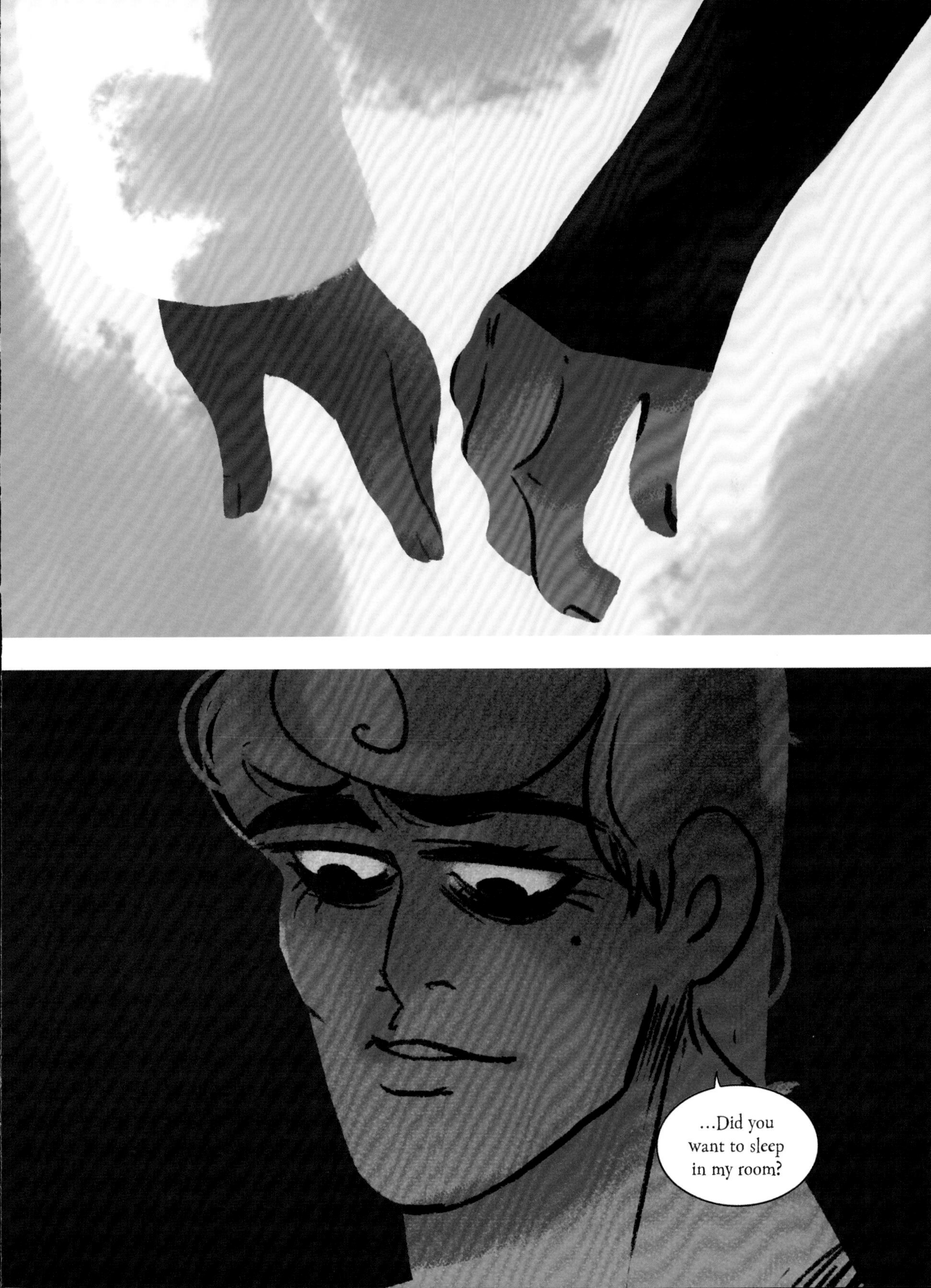
...Did you want to sleep in my room?

EPISODE 15: LOVER BOY

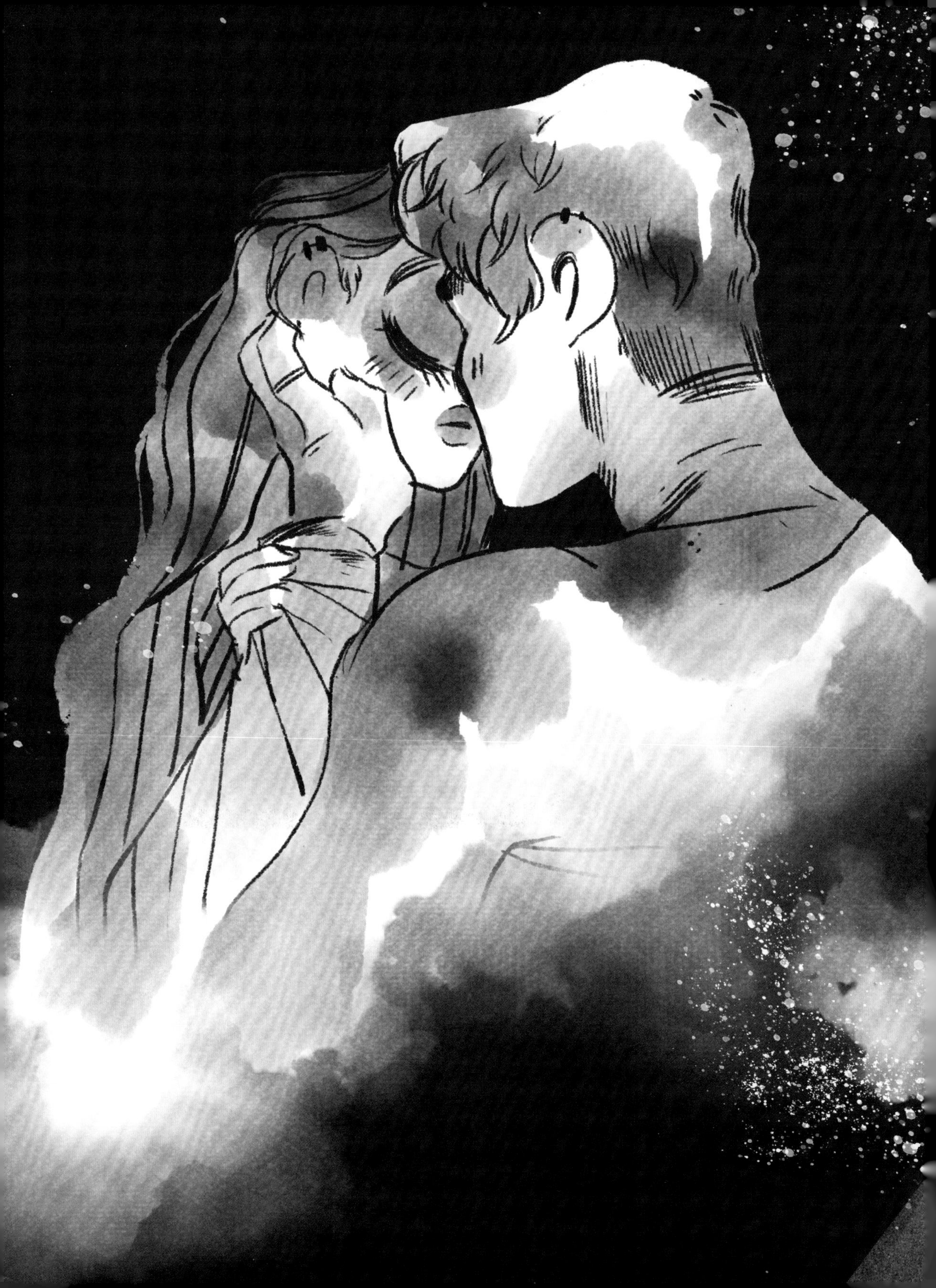

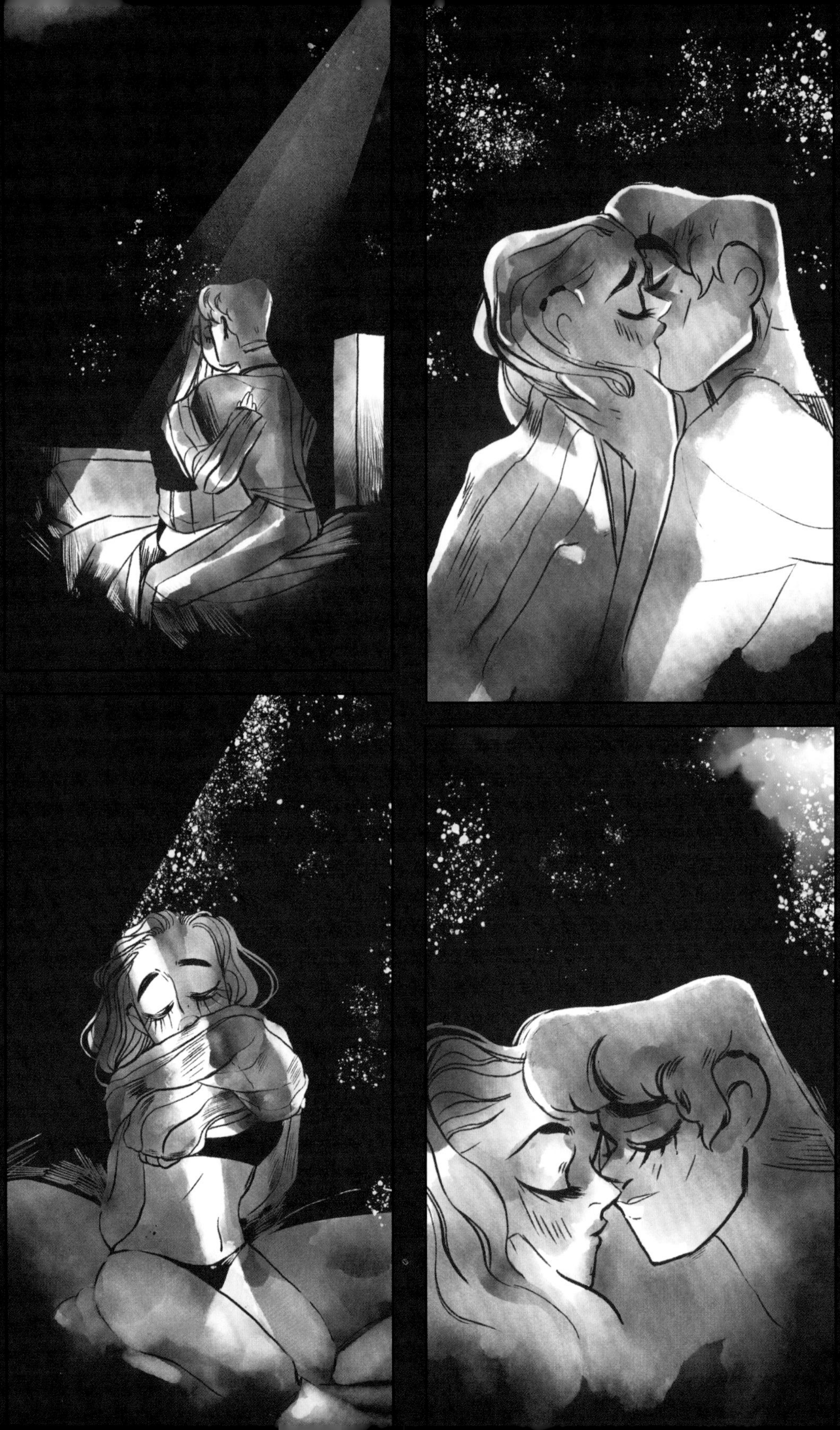

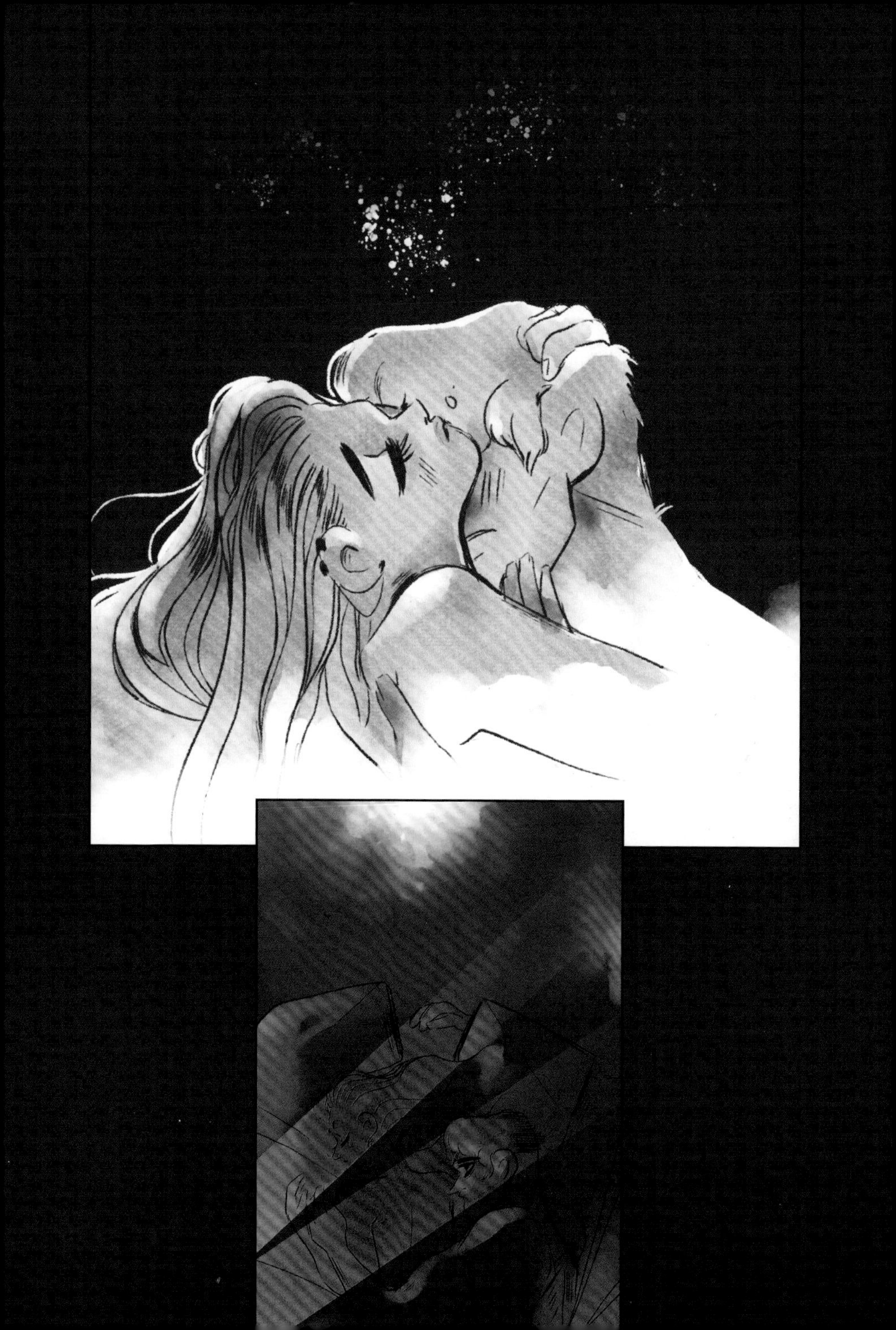

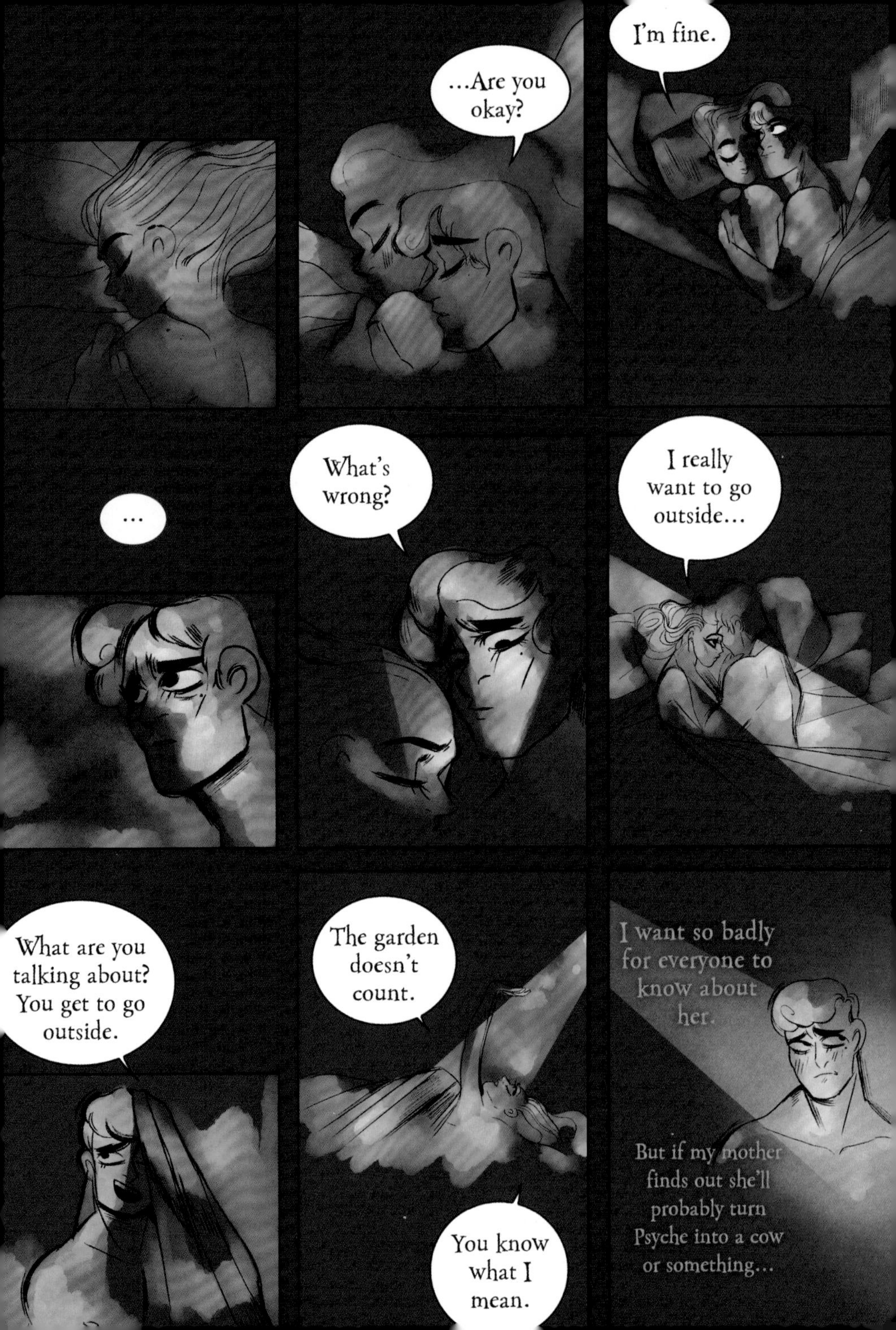

...Are you okay?
I'm fine.
...
What's wrong?
I really want to go outside...
What are you talking about? You get to go outside.
The garden doesn't count.
You know what I mean.
I want so badly for everyone to know about her.
But if my mother finds out she'll probably turn Psyche into a cow or something...

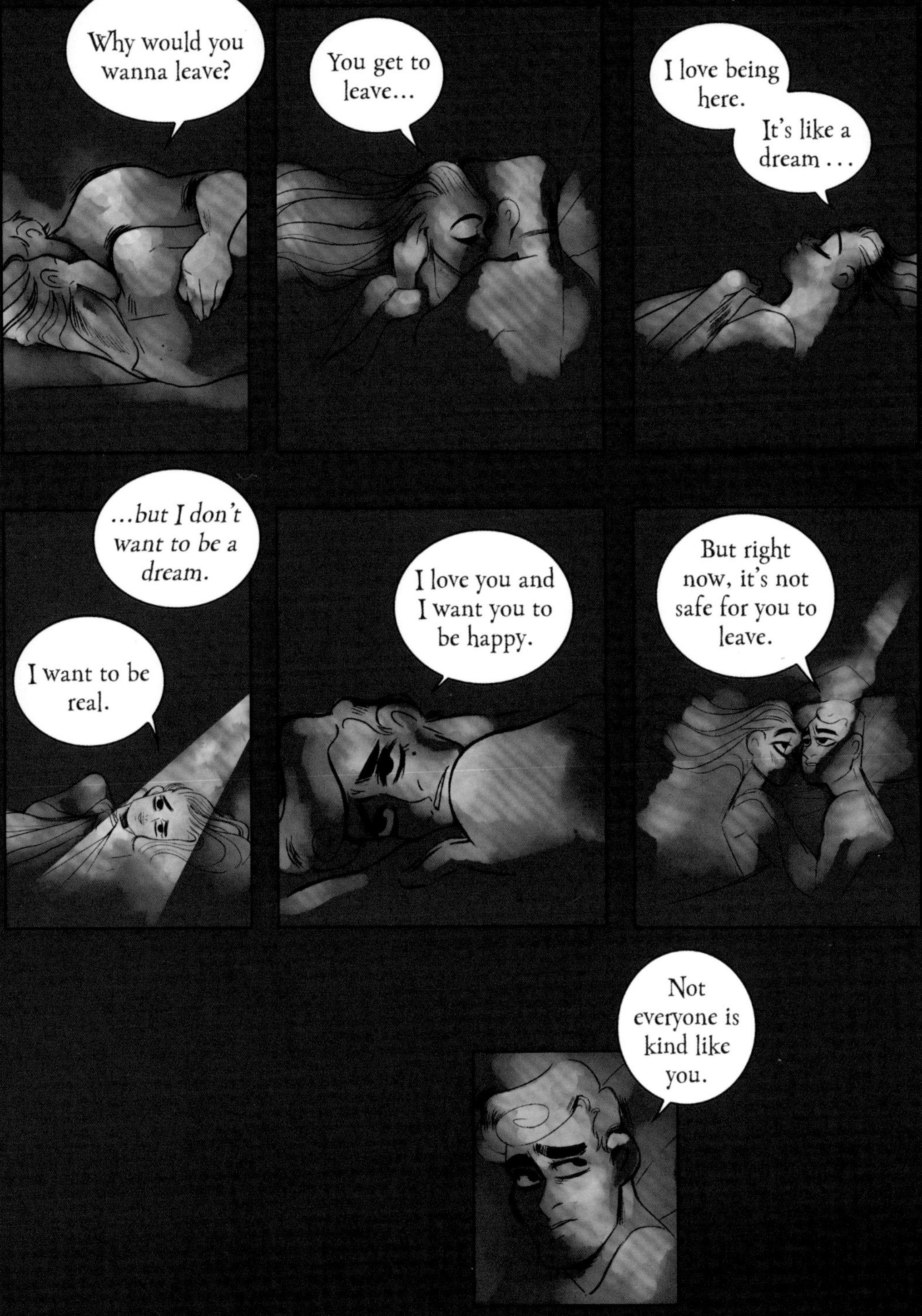
Why would you wanna leave?
You get to leave...
I love being here.
It's like a dream . . .
...but I don't want to be a dream.
I want to be real.
I love you and I want you to be happy.
But right now, it's not safe for you to leave.
Not everyone is kind like you.

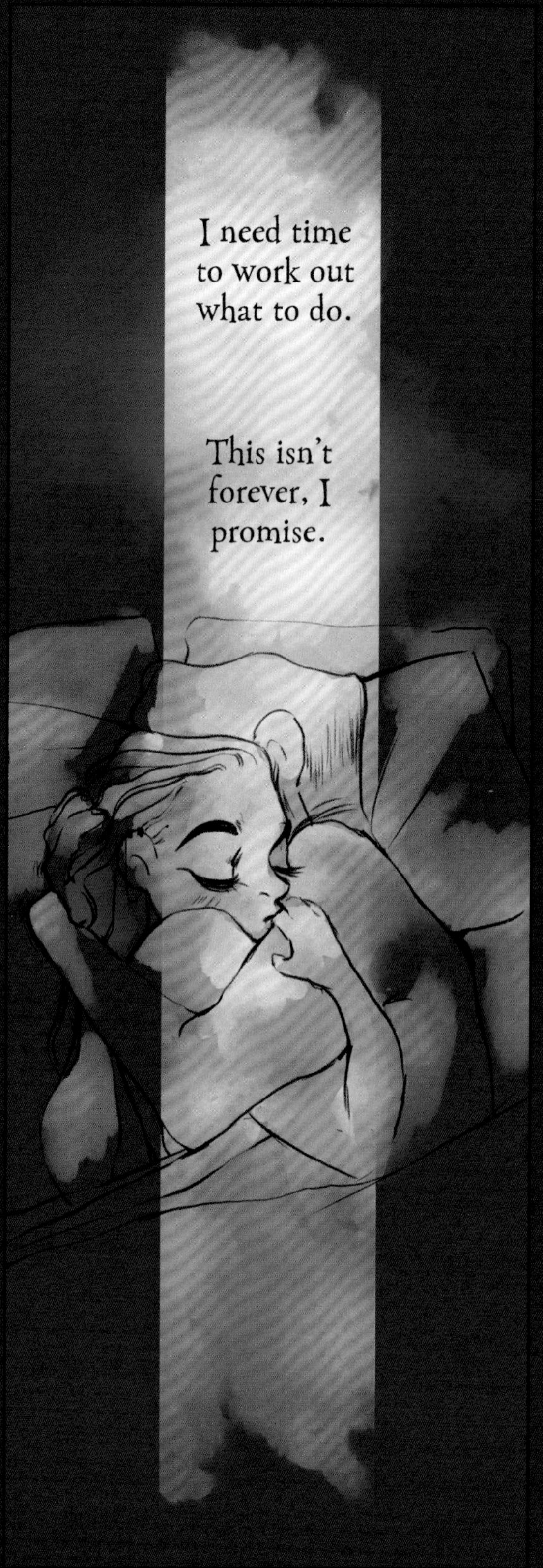
I need time to work out what to do.
This isn't forever, I promise.

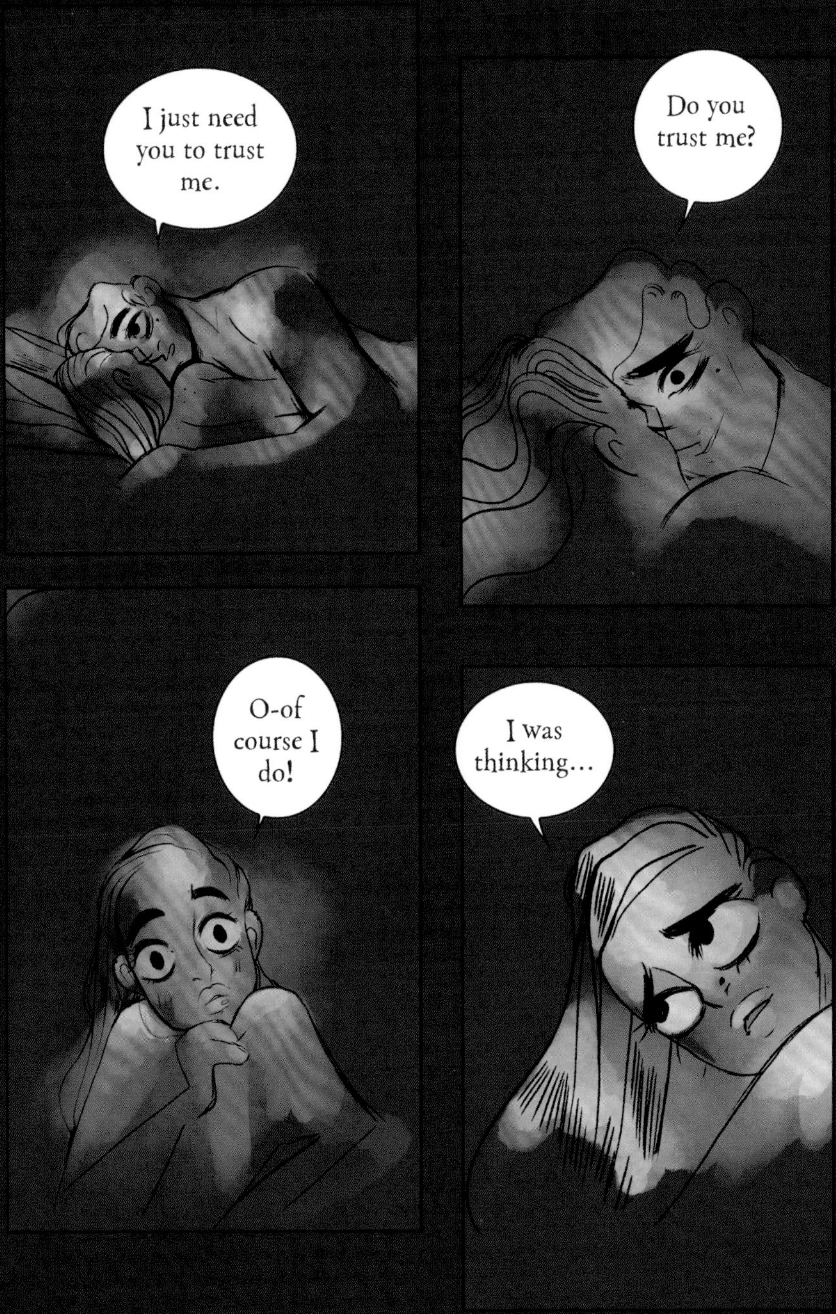
I just need you to trust me.
Do you trust me?
O-of course I do!
I was thinking...

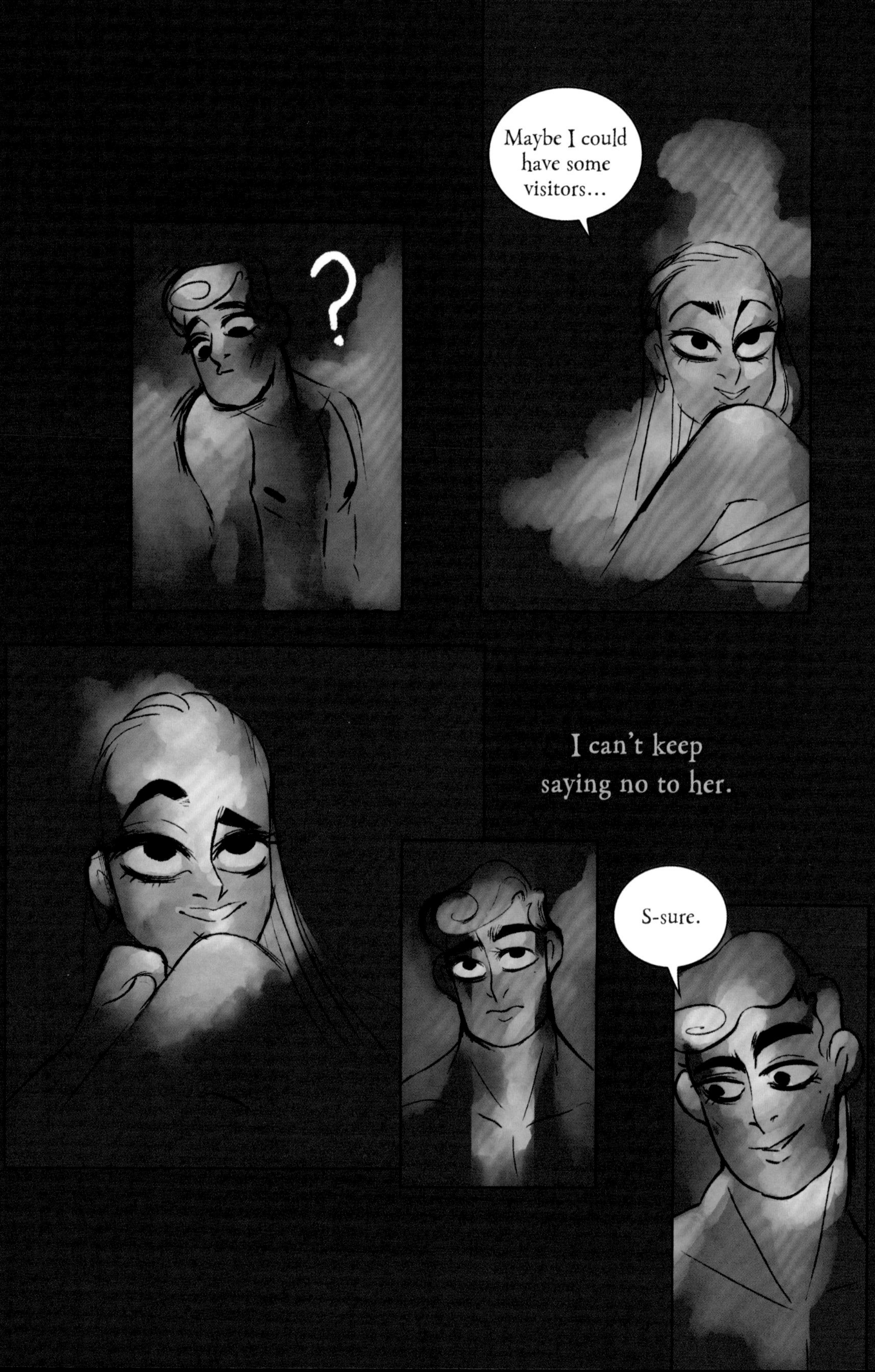

Maybe I could have some visitors…
?
I can't keep saying no to her.
S-sure.

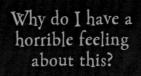

Why do I have a
horrible feeling
about this?

EPISODE 16: STUPID BOY

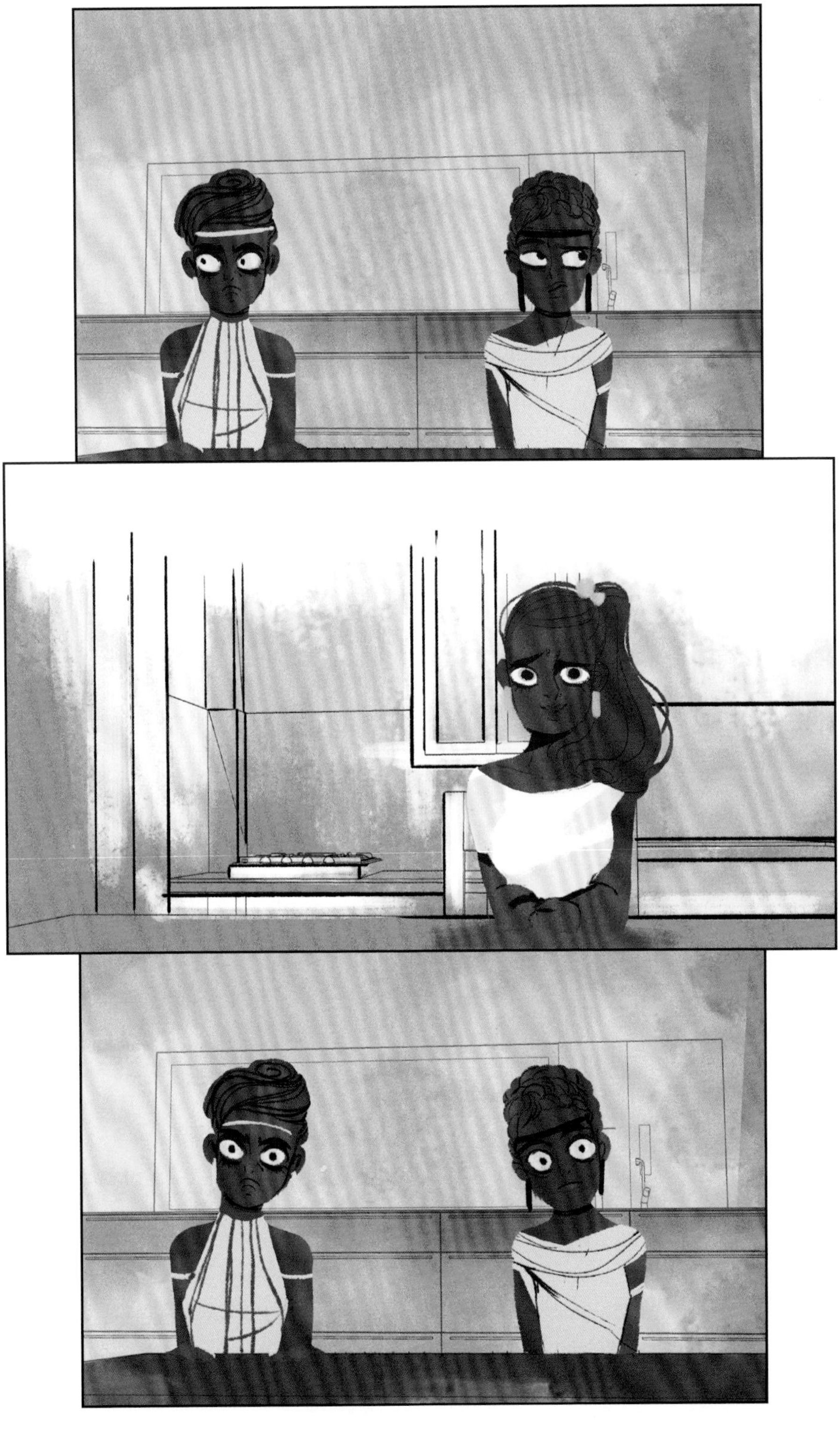

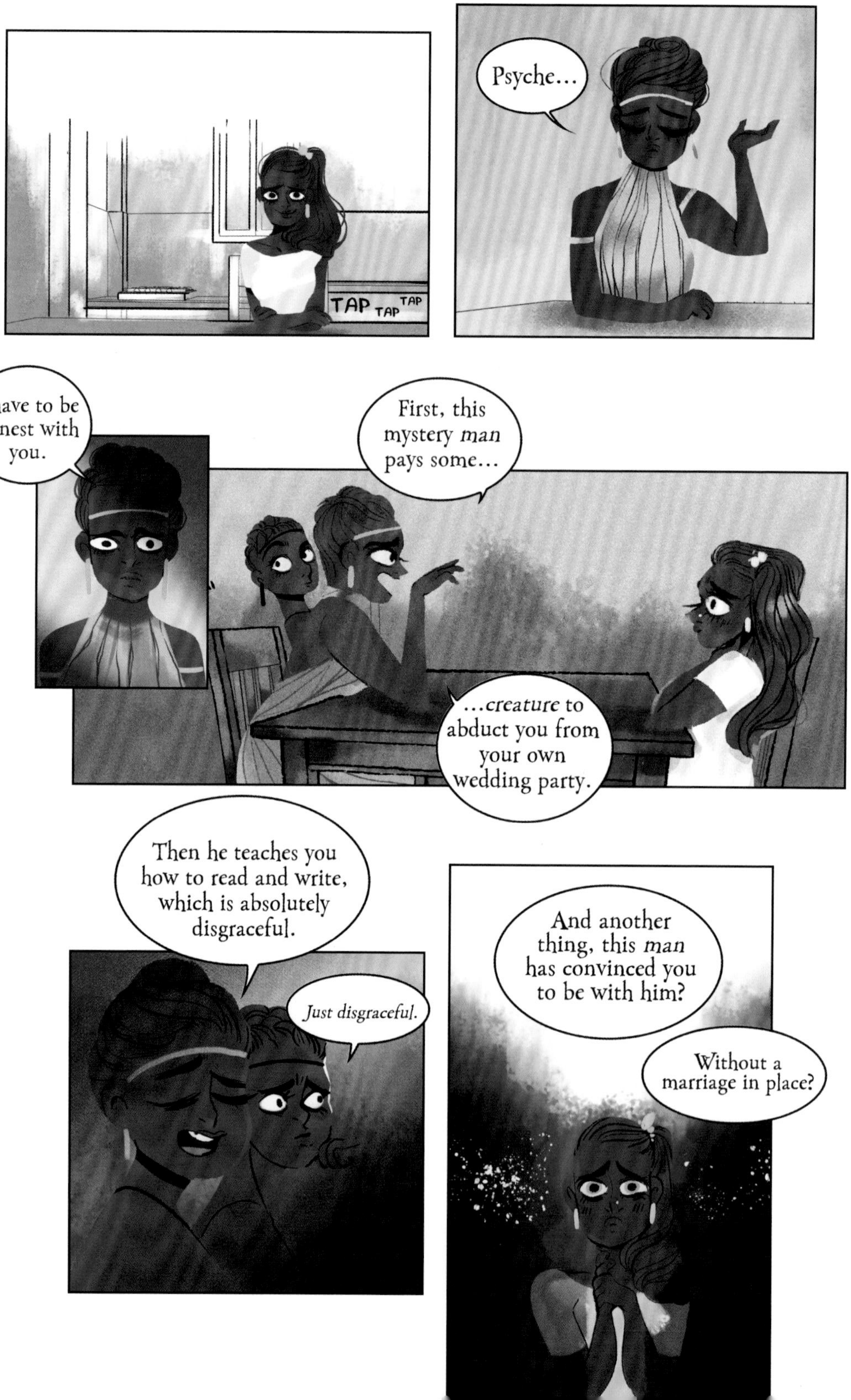
TAP TAP TAP
Psyche...
I have to be honest with you.
First, this mystery *man* pays some...
...*creature* to abduct you from your own wedding party.
Then he teaches you how to read and write, which is absolutely disgraceful.
Just disgraceful.
And another thing, this *man* has convinced you to be with him?
Without a marriage in place?

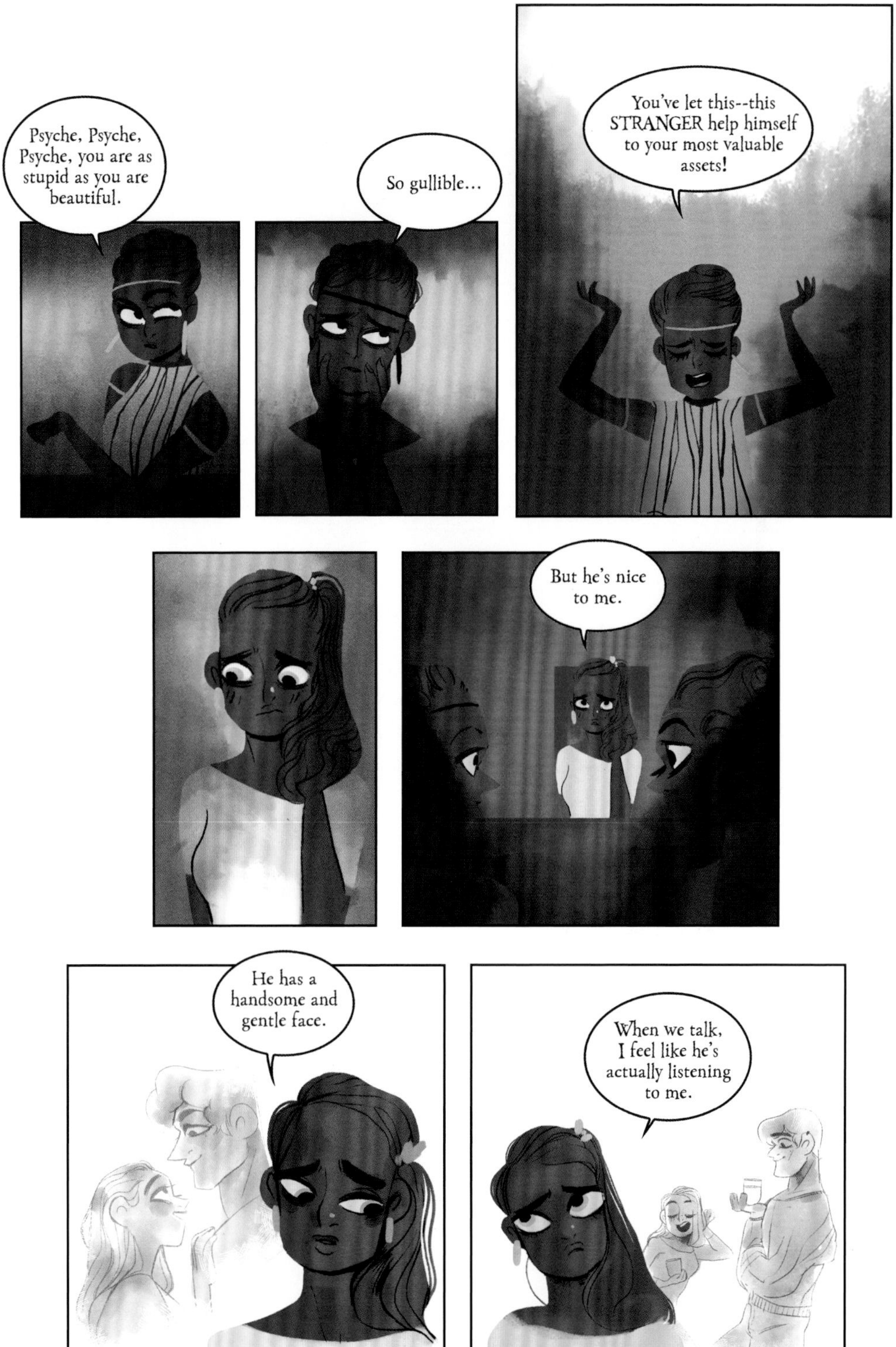
Psyche, Psyche, Psyche, you are as stupid as you are beautiful.
So gullible...
You've let this--this STRANGER help himself to your most valuable assets!
But he's nice to me.
He has a handsome and gentle face.
When we talk, I feel like he's actually listening to me.

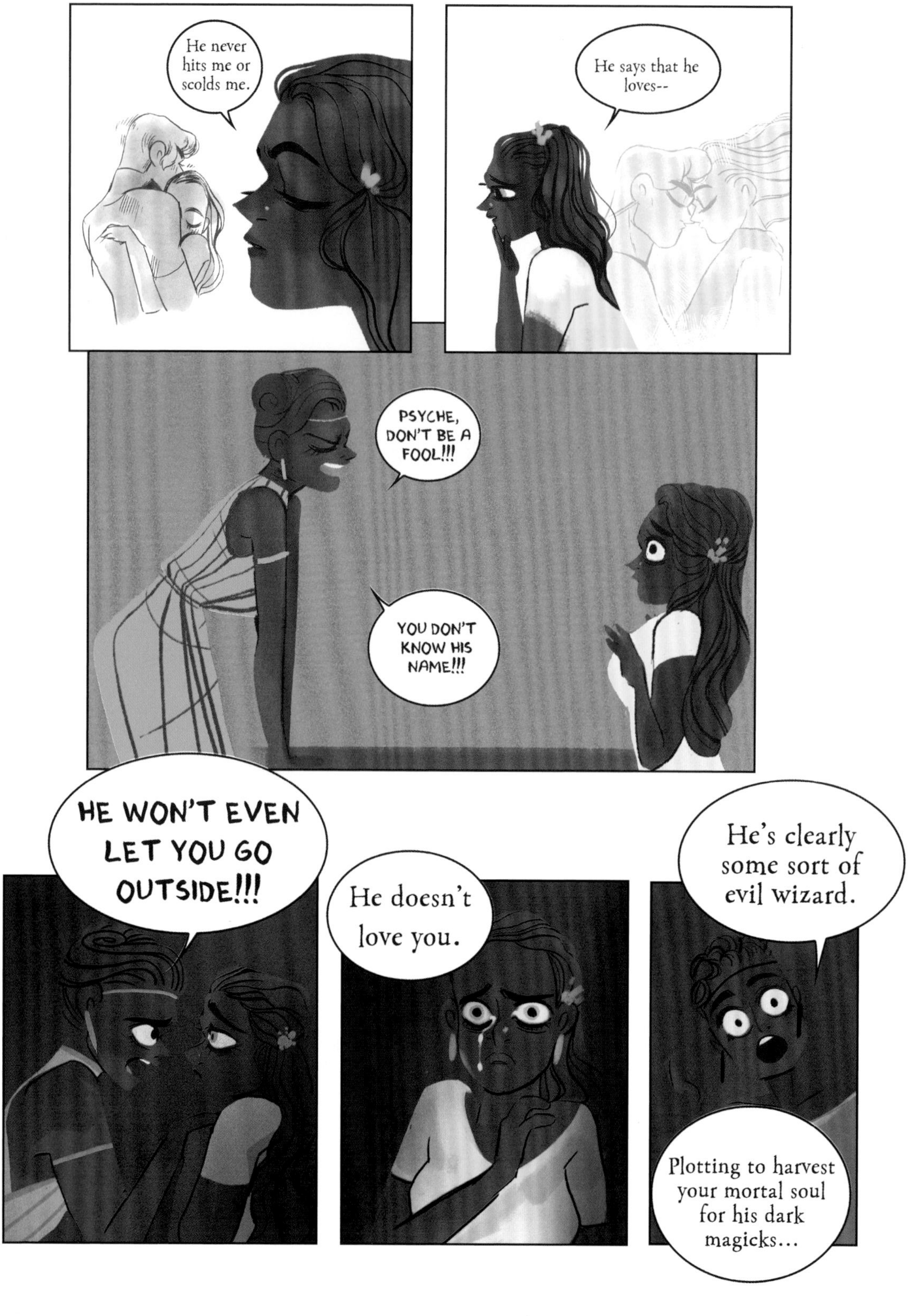
He never hits me or scolds me.
He says that he loves--
PSYCHE, DON'T BE A FOOL!!!
YOU DON'T KNOW HIS NAME!!!
HE WON'T EVEN LET YOU GO OUTSIDE!!!
He doesn't love you.
He's clearly some sort of evil wizard.
Plotting to harvest your mortal soul for his dark magicks...

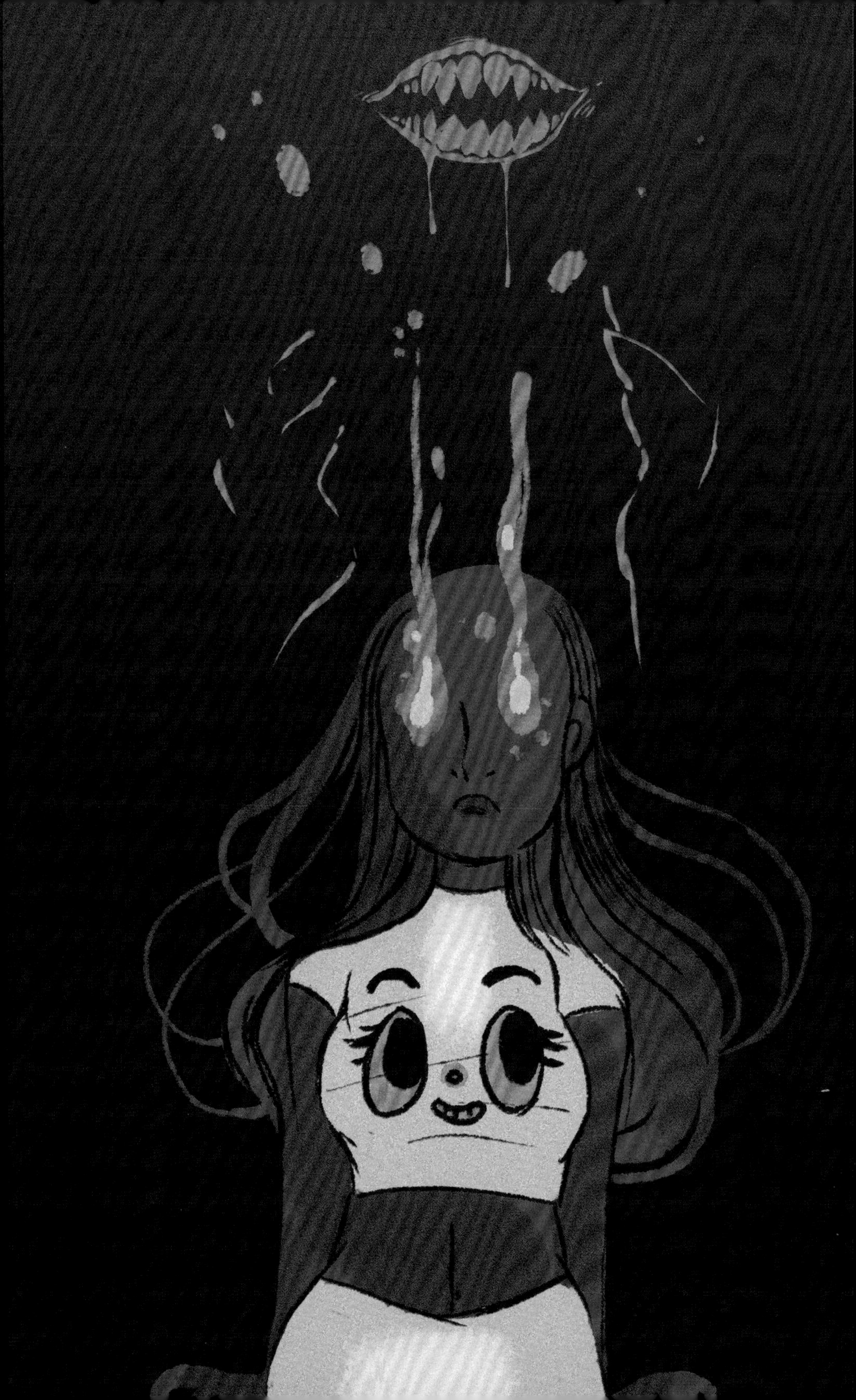

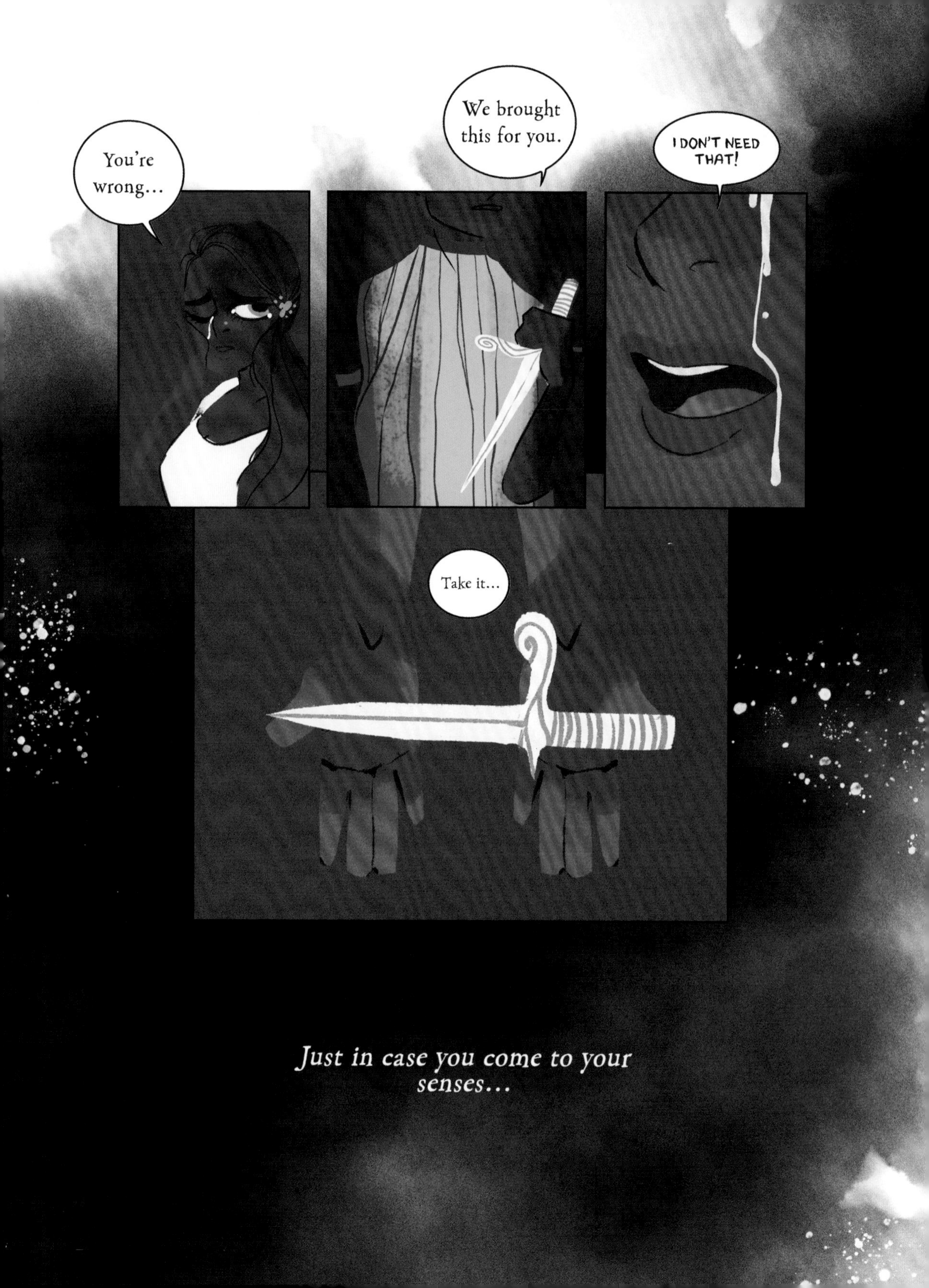
You're wrong...
We brought this for you.
I DON'T NEED THAT!
Take it...
Just in case you come to your senses...

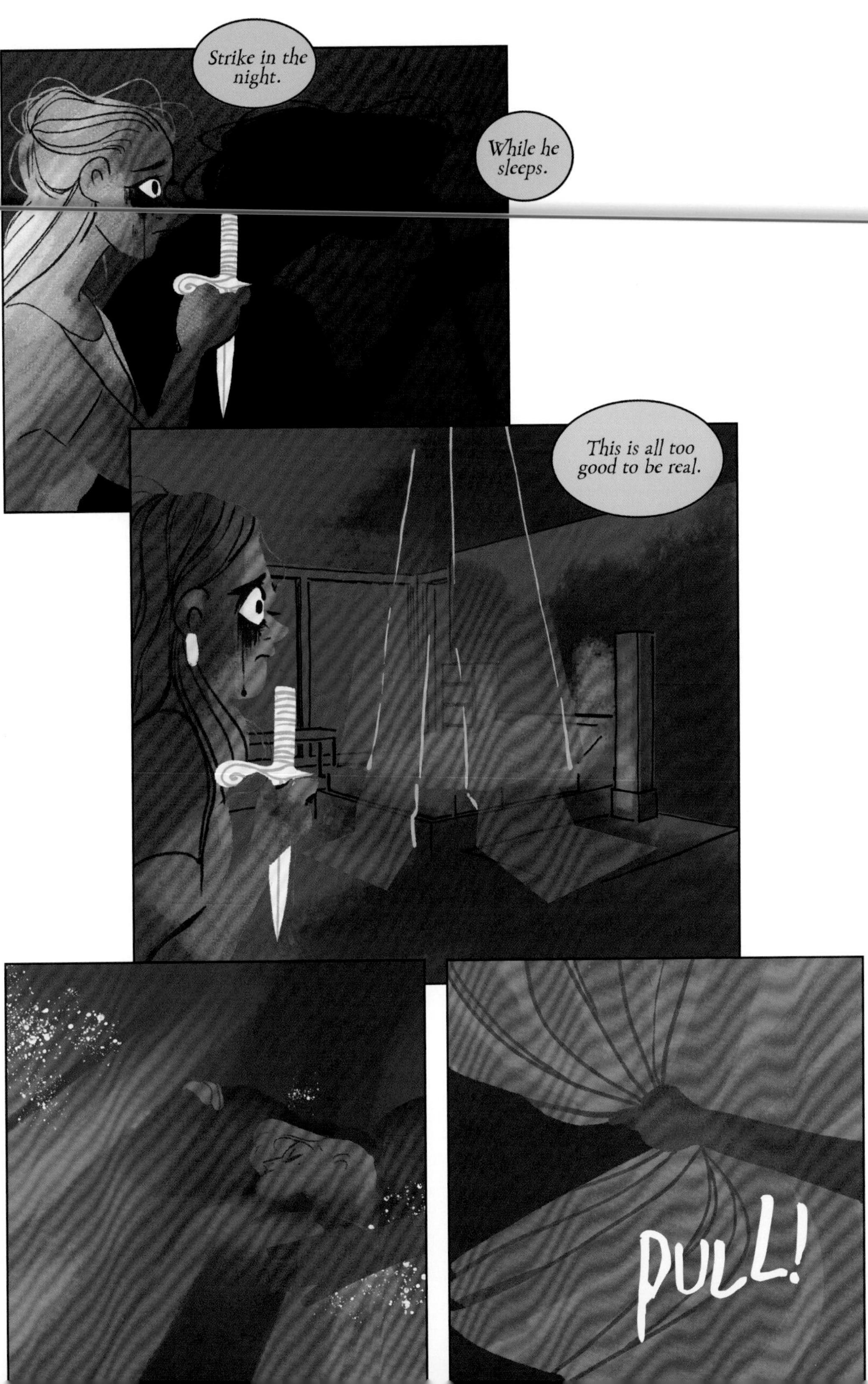
Strike in the night.
While he sleeps.
This is all too good to be real.
PULL!

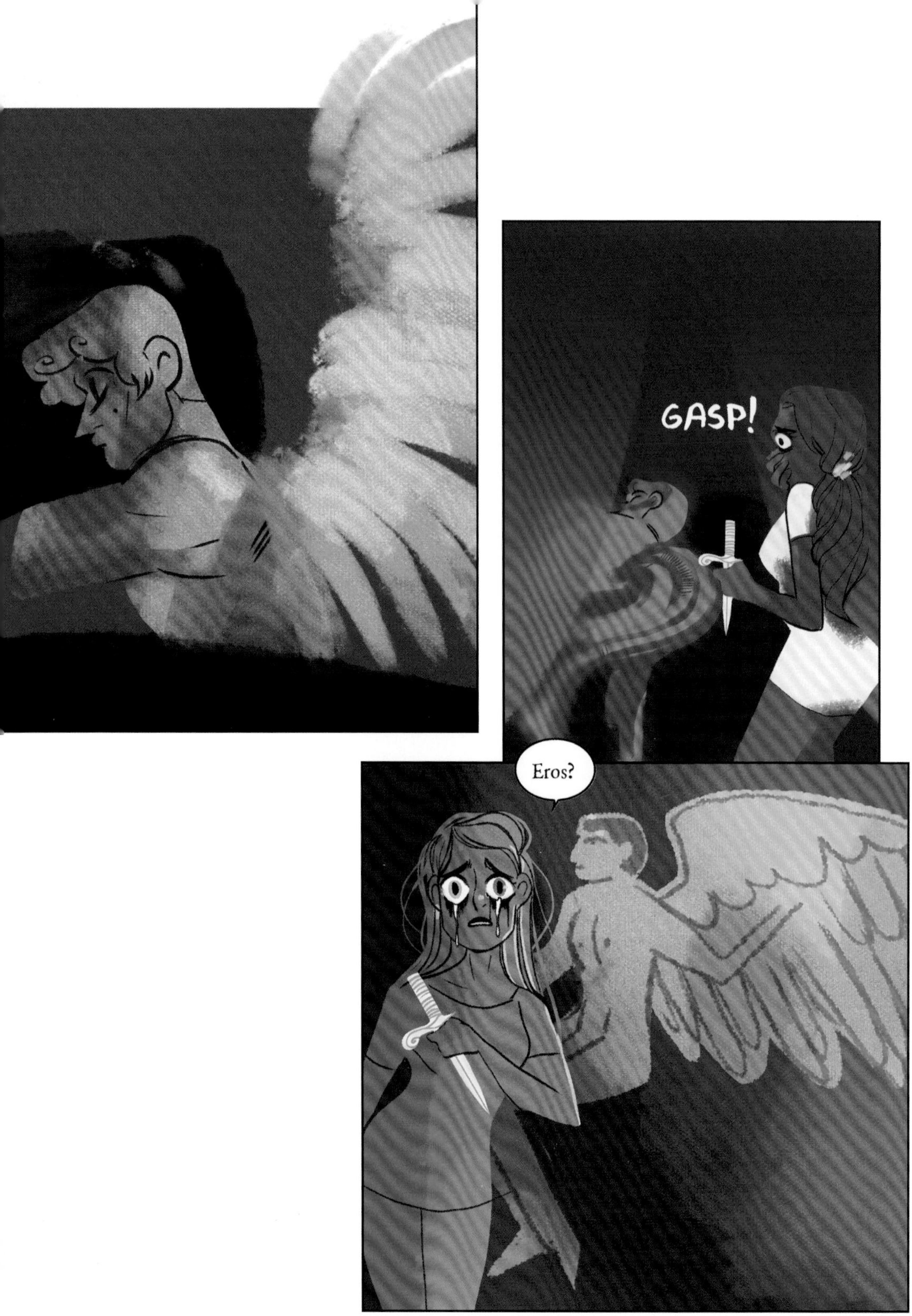
GASP!
Eros?

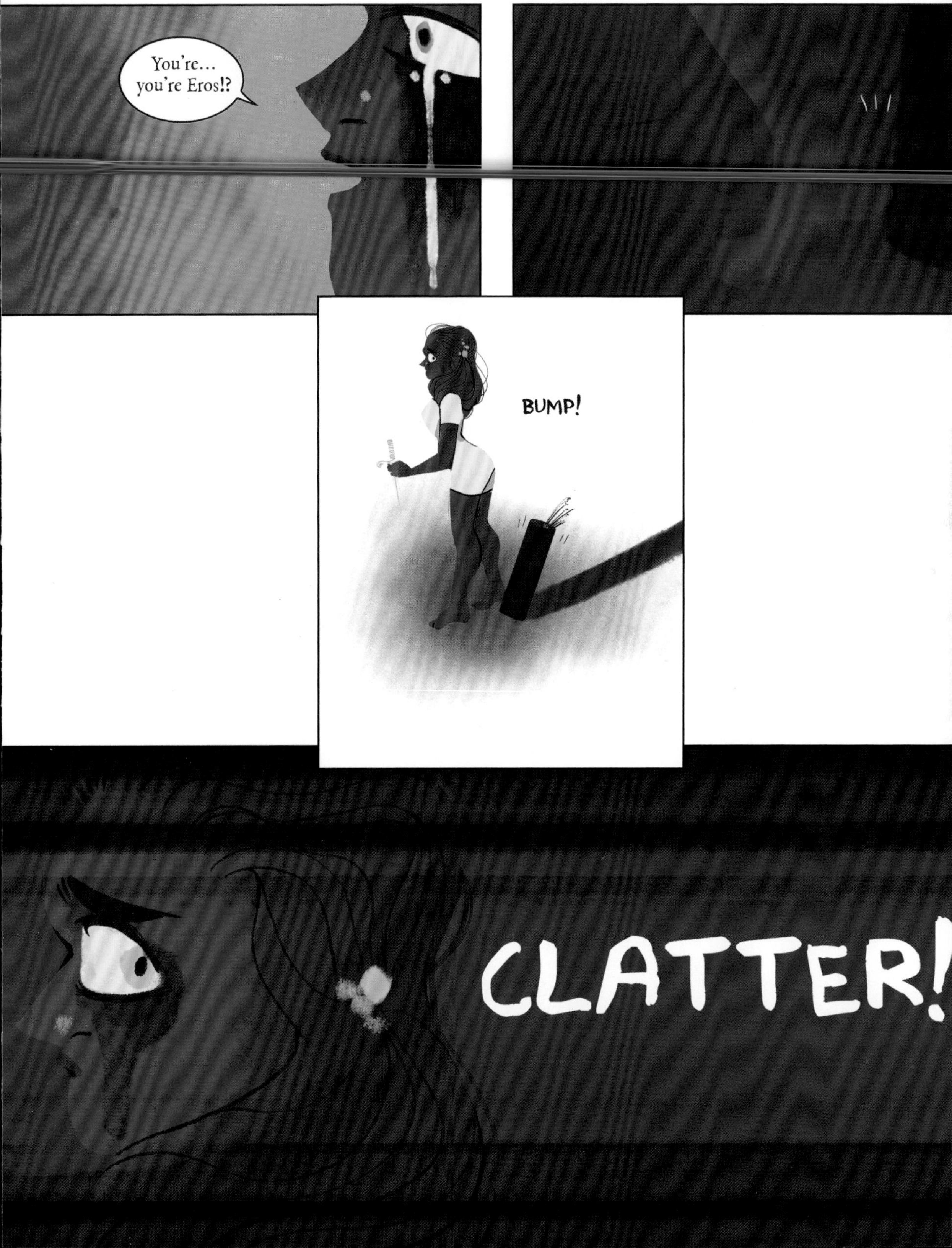
You're... you're Eros!?
BUMP!
CLATTER!

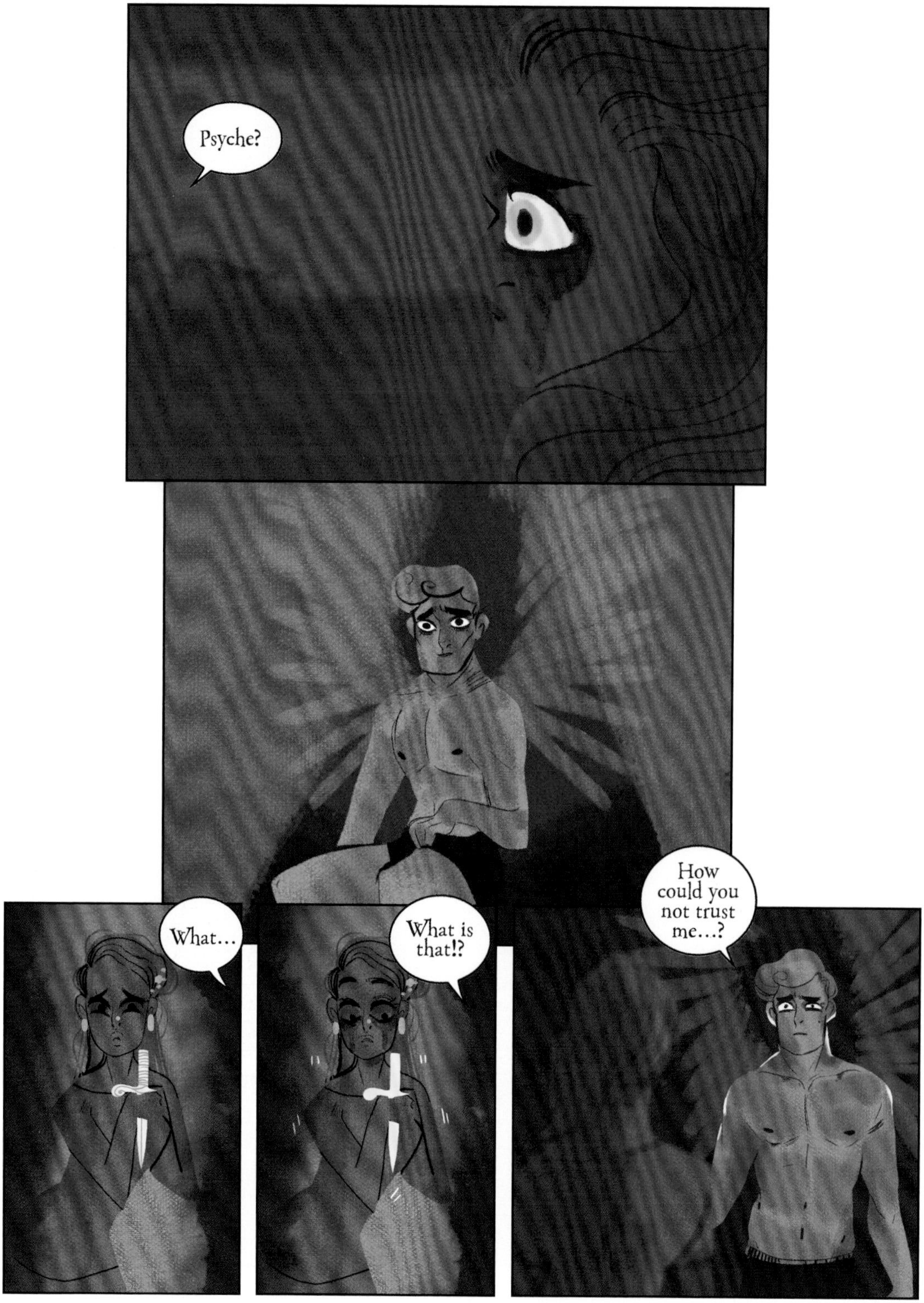
Psyche?
What...
What is that!?
How could you not trust me...?

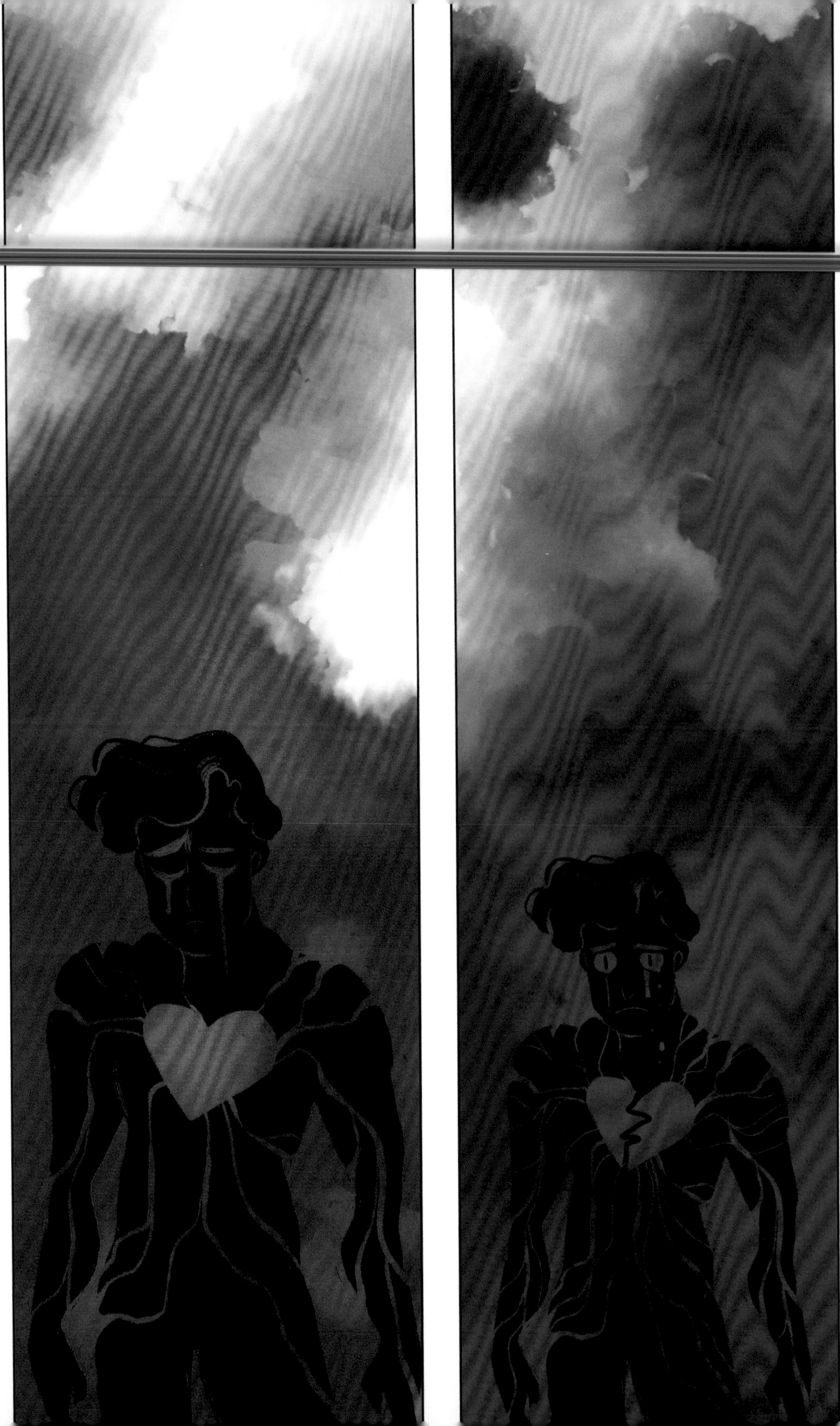

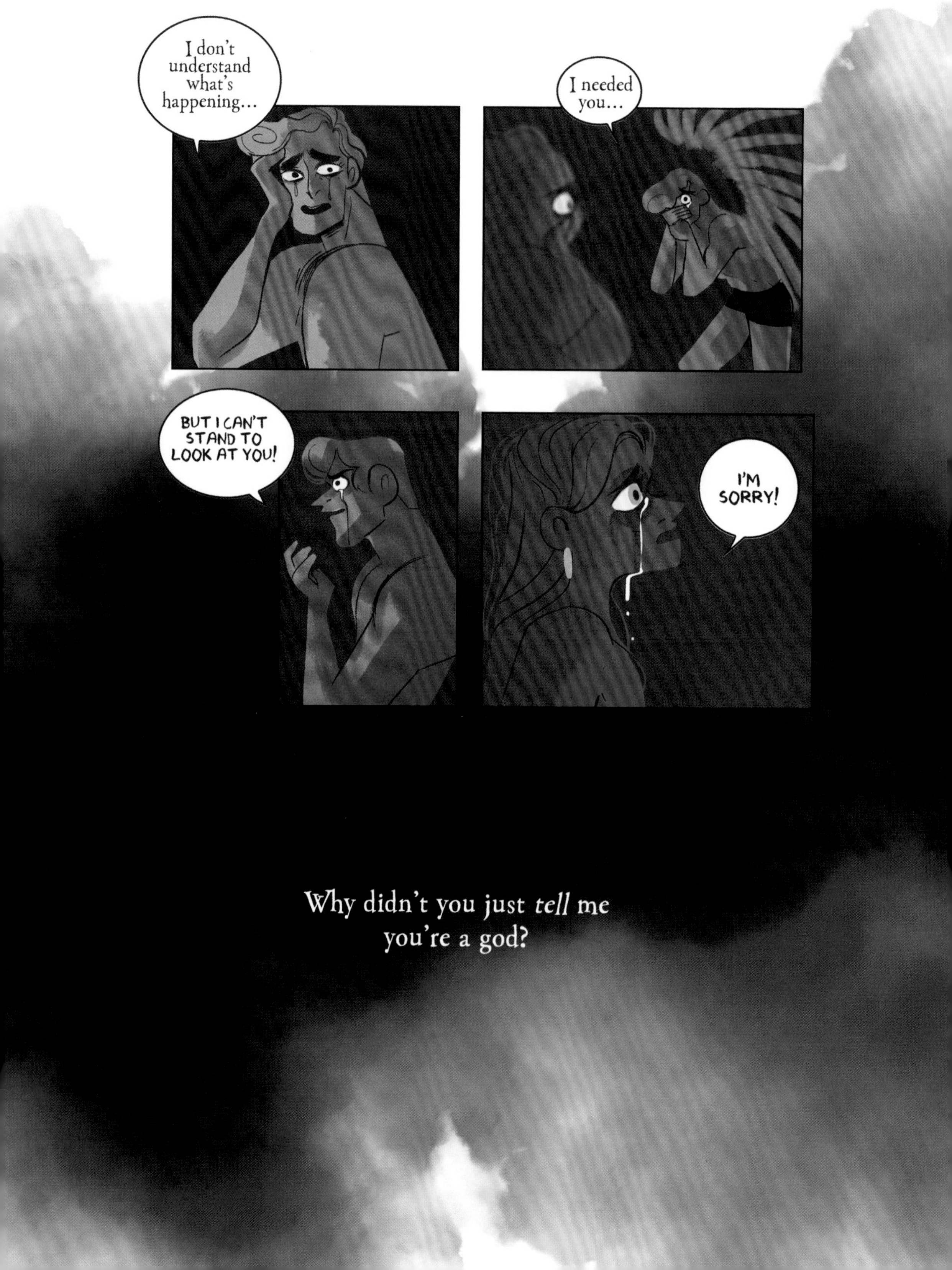
I don't understand what's happening...
I needed you...
BUT I CAN'T STAND TO LOOK AT YOU!
I'M SORRY!
Why didn't you just *tell* me you're a god?

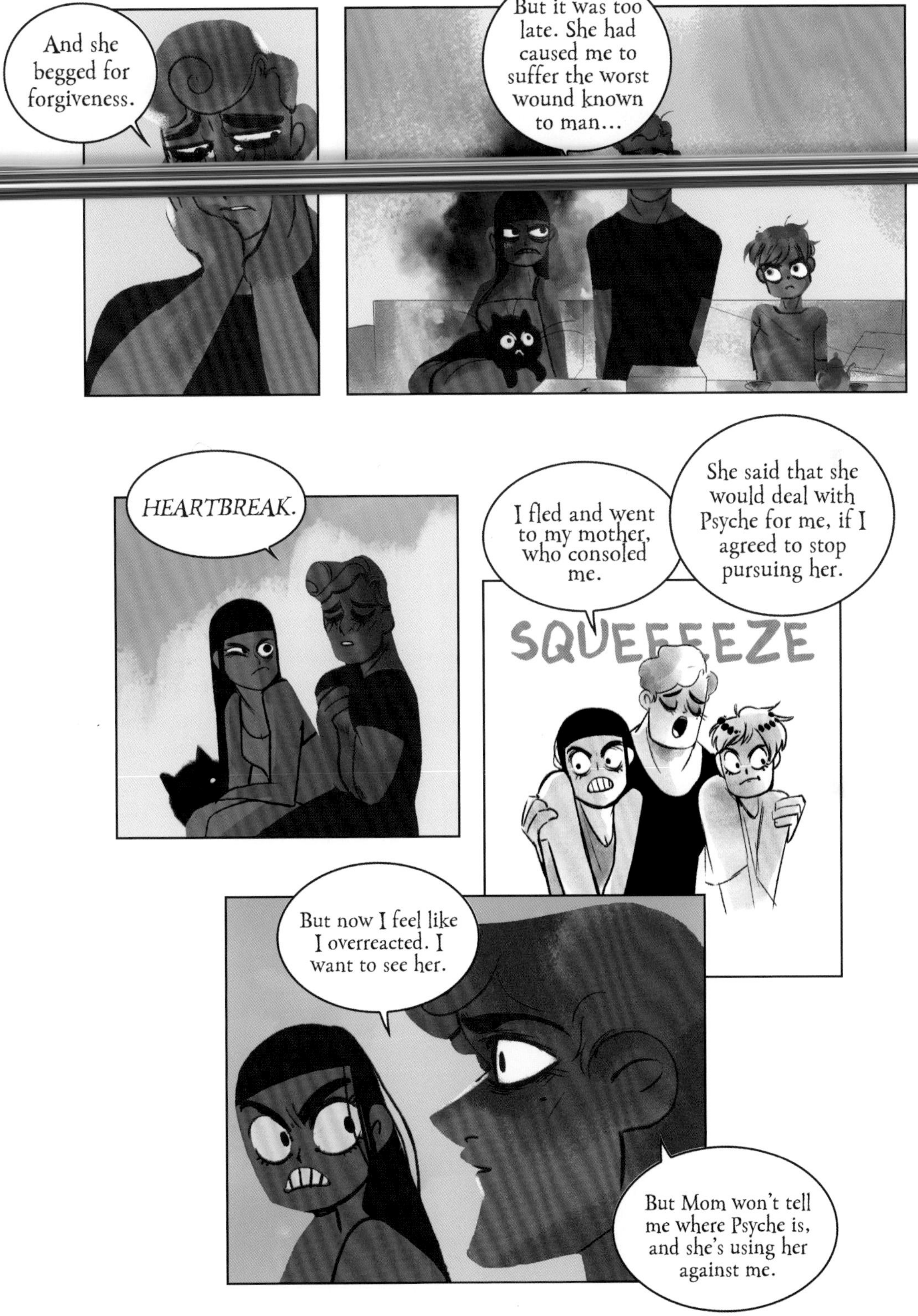
And she begged for forgiveness.
But it was too late. She had caused me to suffer the worst wound known to man...
HEARTBREAK.
I fled and went to my mother, who consoled me.
She said that she would deal with Psyche for me, if I agreed to stop pursuing her.
SQUEEEEZE
But now I feel like I overreacted. I want to see her.
But Mom won't tell me where Psyche is, and she's using her against me.

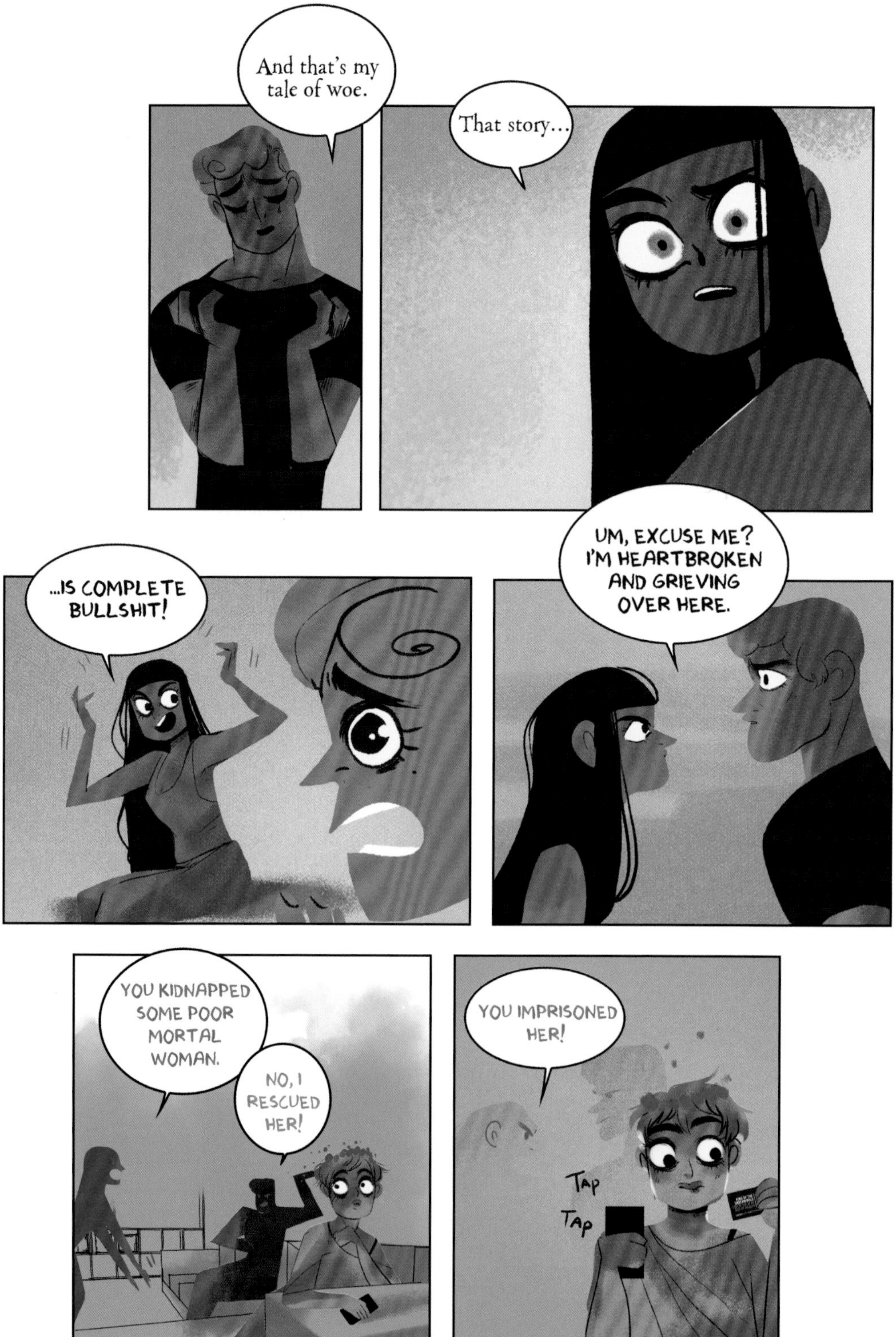
And that's my tale of woe.
That story…
…IS COMPLETE BULLSHIT!
UM, EXCUSE ME? I'M HEARTBROKEN AND GRIEVING OVER HERE.
YOU KIDNAPPED SOME POOR MORTAL WOMAN.
NO, I RESCUED HER!
YOU IMPRISONED HER!
TAP
TAP

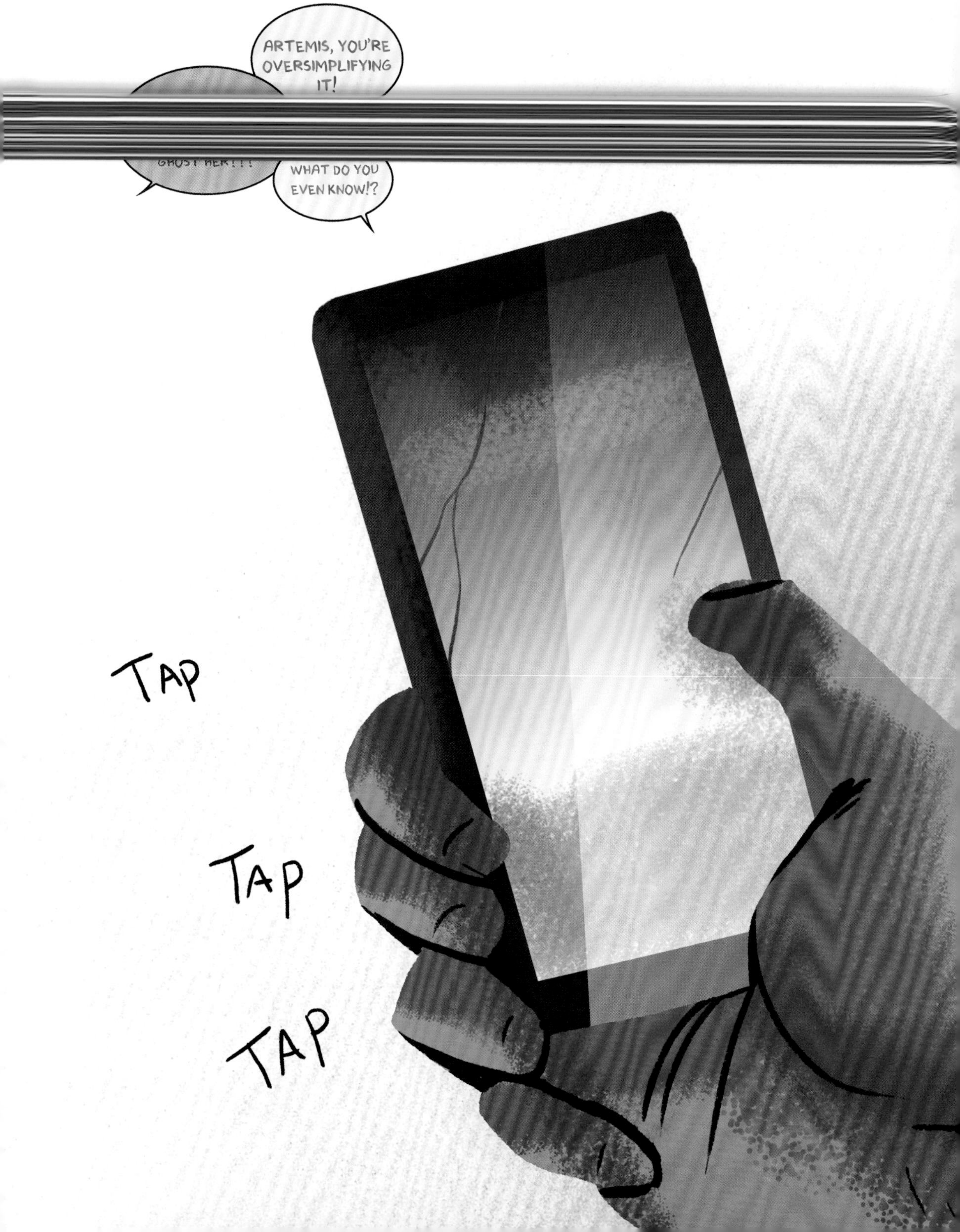
ARTEMIS, YOU'RE OVERSIMPLIFYING IT!
GHOST HER!!!
WHAT DO YOU EVEN KNOW!?
TAP
TAP
TAP

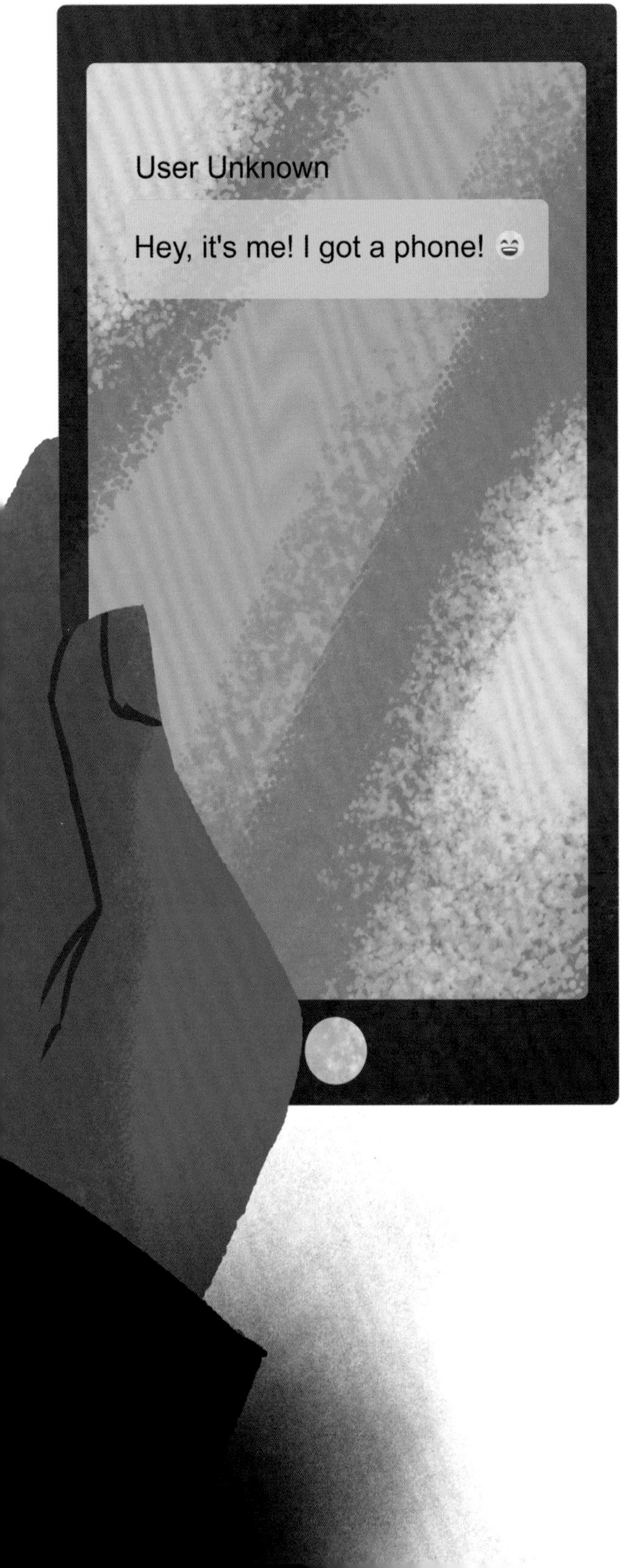
User Unknown
Hey, it's me! I got a phone! 😁

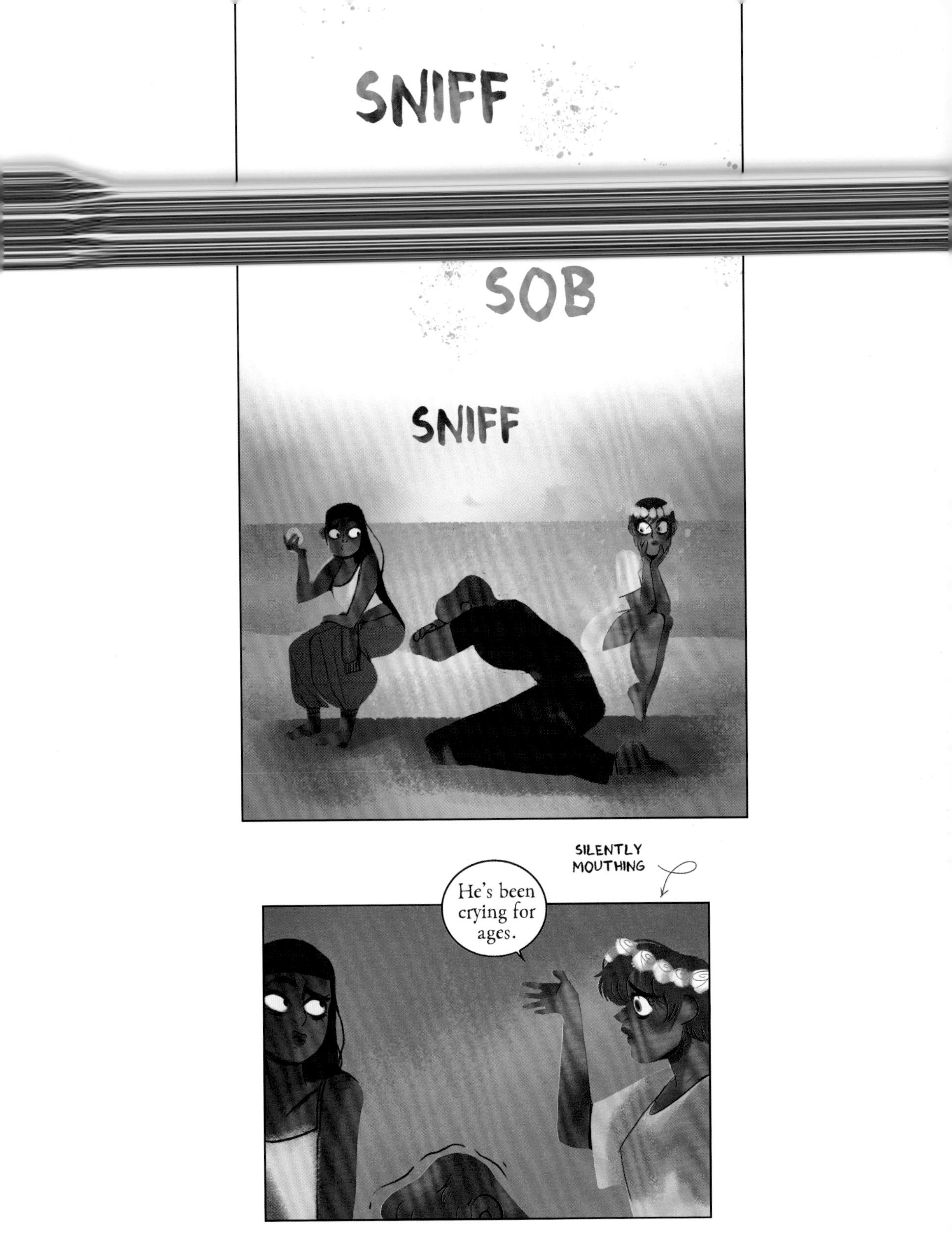
SNIFF
SOB
SNIFF
SILENTLY MOUTHING
He's been crying for ages.

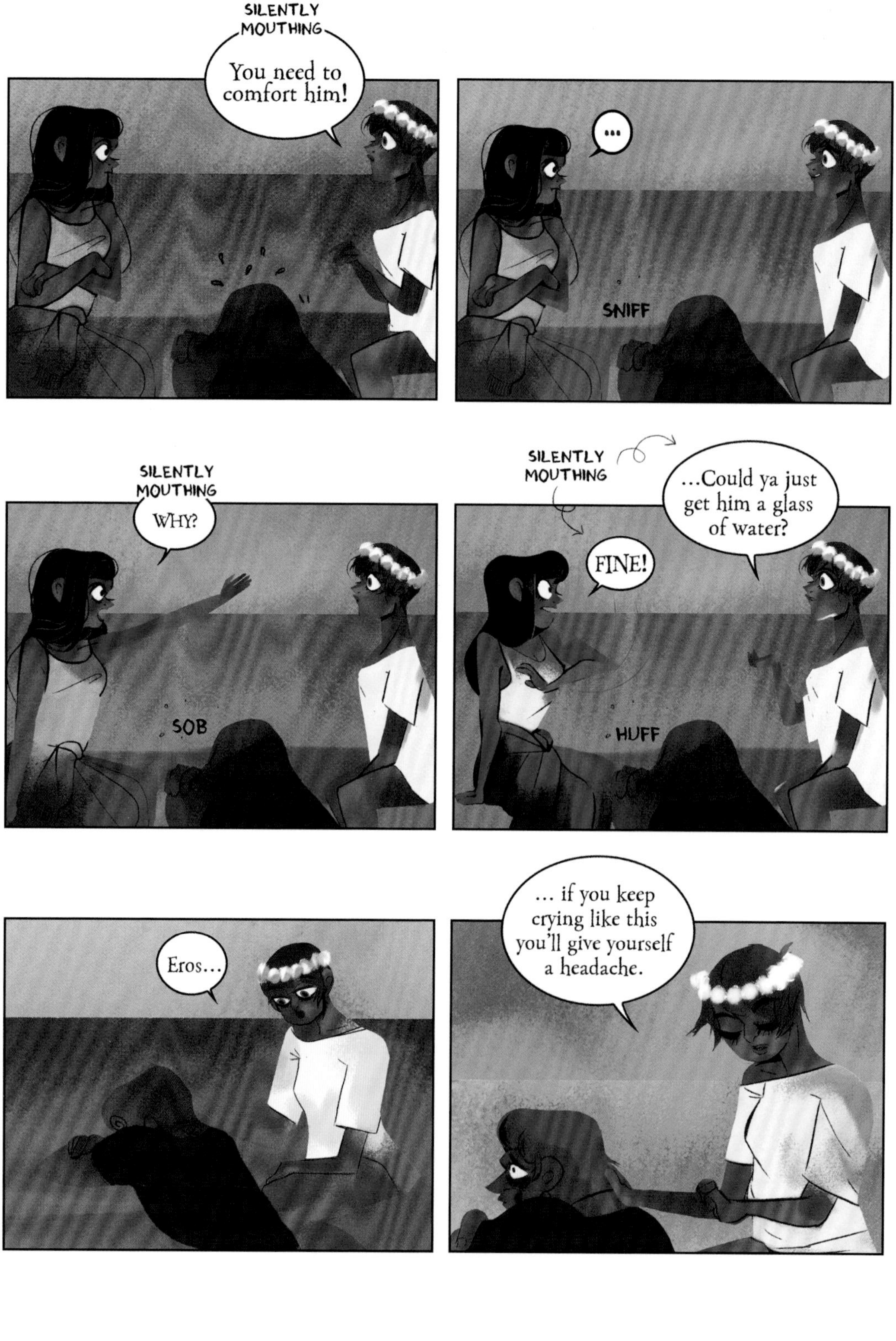
SILENTLY MOUTHING
You need to comfort him!
...
SNIFF
SILENTLY MOUTHING
WHY?
SOB
SILENTLY MOUTHING
...Could ya just get him a glass of water?
FINE!
HUFF
Eros...
... if you keep crying like this you'll give yourself a headache.

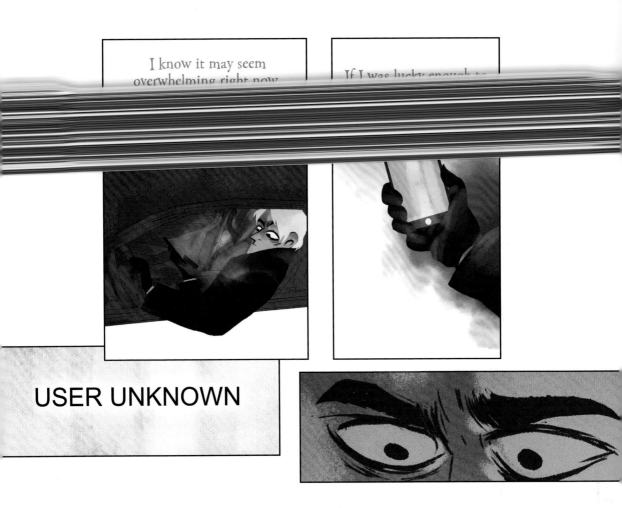

I know it may seem
overwhelming right now.

If I was lucky enough to

USER UNKNOWN

I would try everything to make
it work.

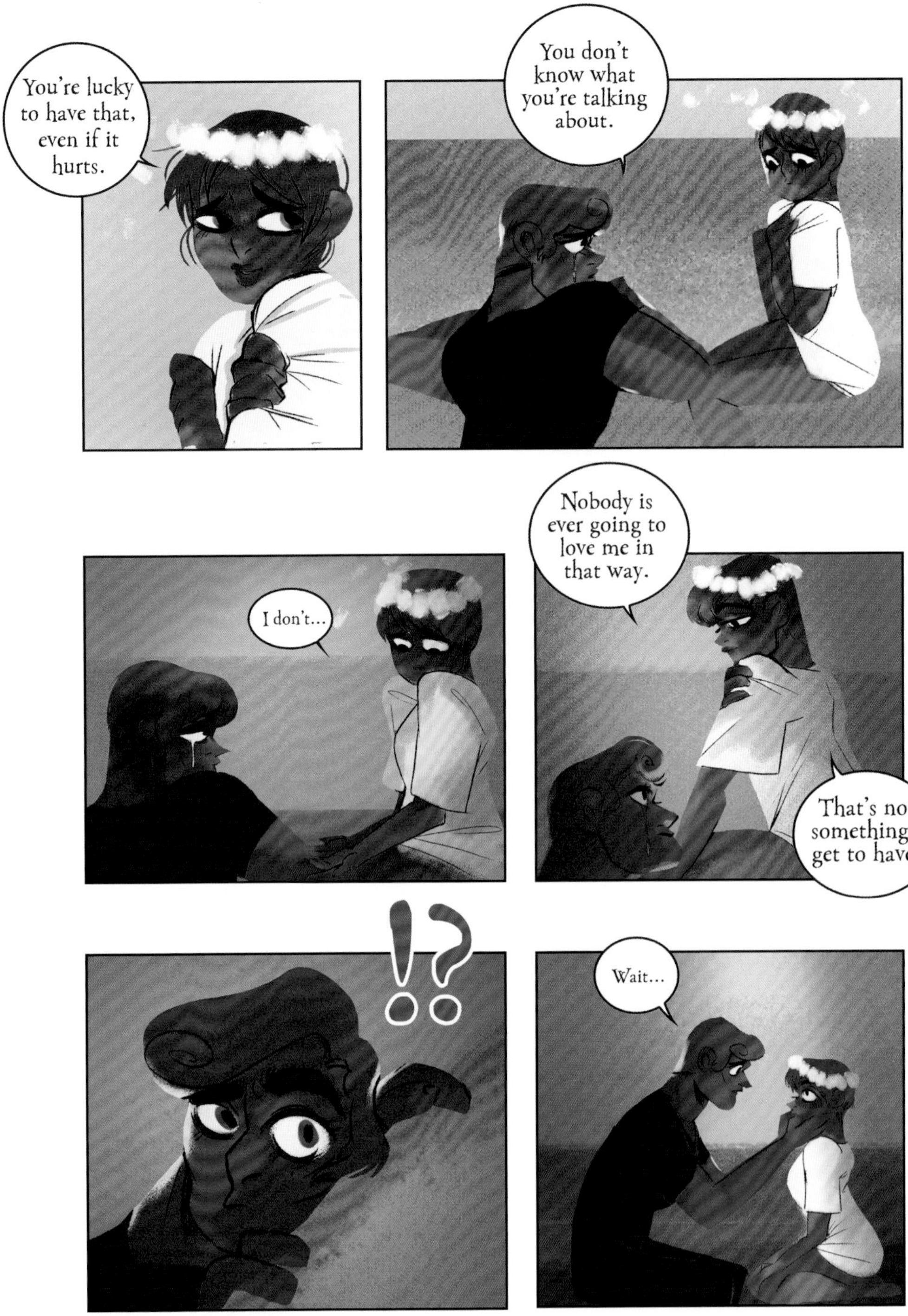
You're lucky to have that, even if it hurts.
You don't know what you're talking about.
I don't...
Nobody is ever going to love me in that way.
That's not something I get to have.
!?
Wait...

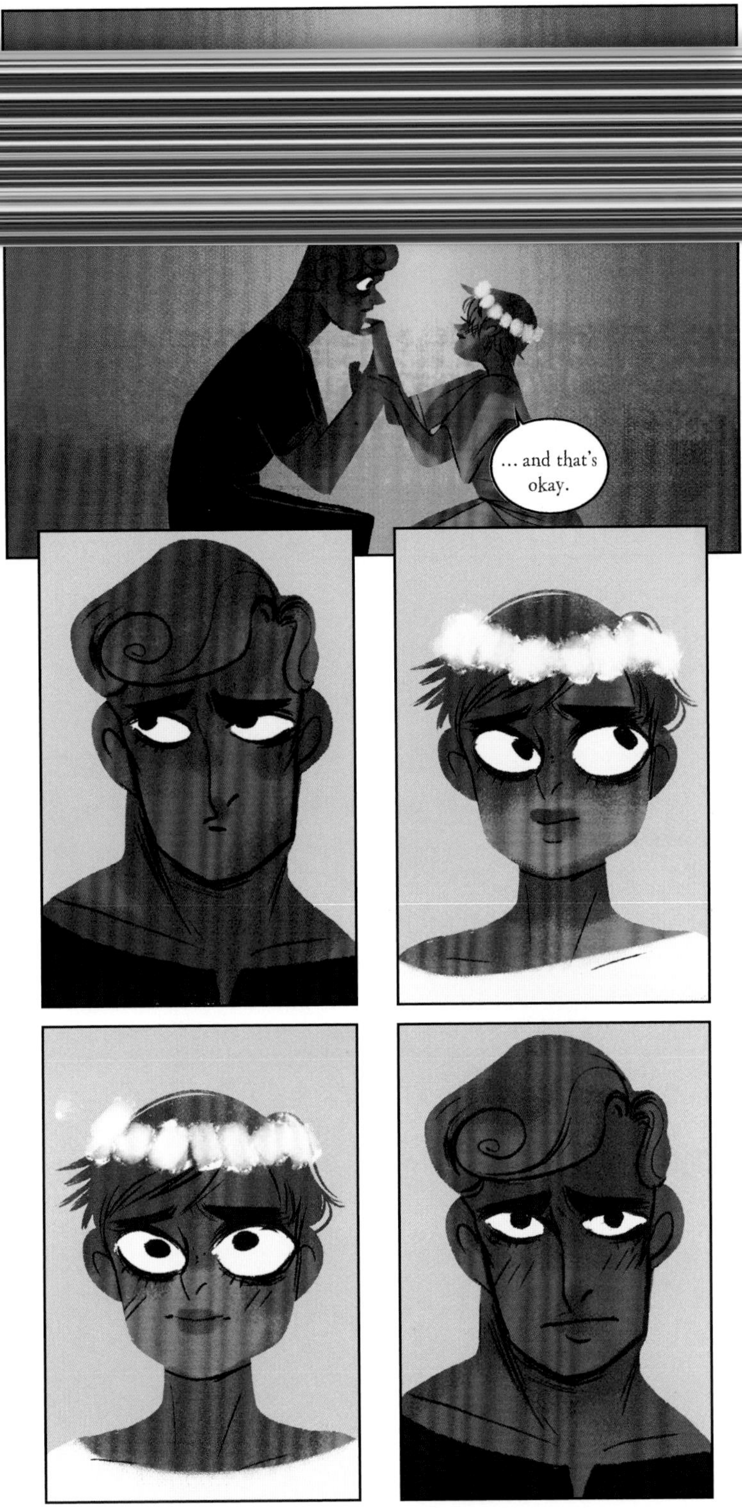
... and that's okay.

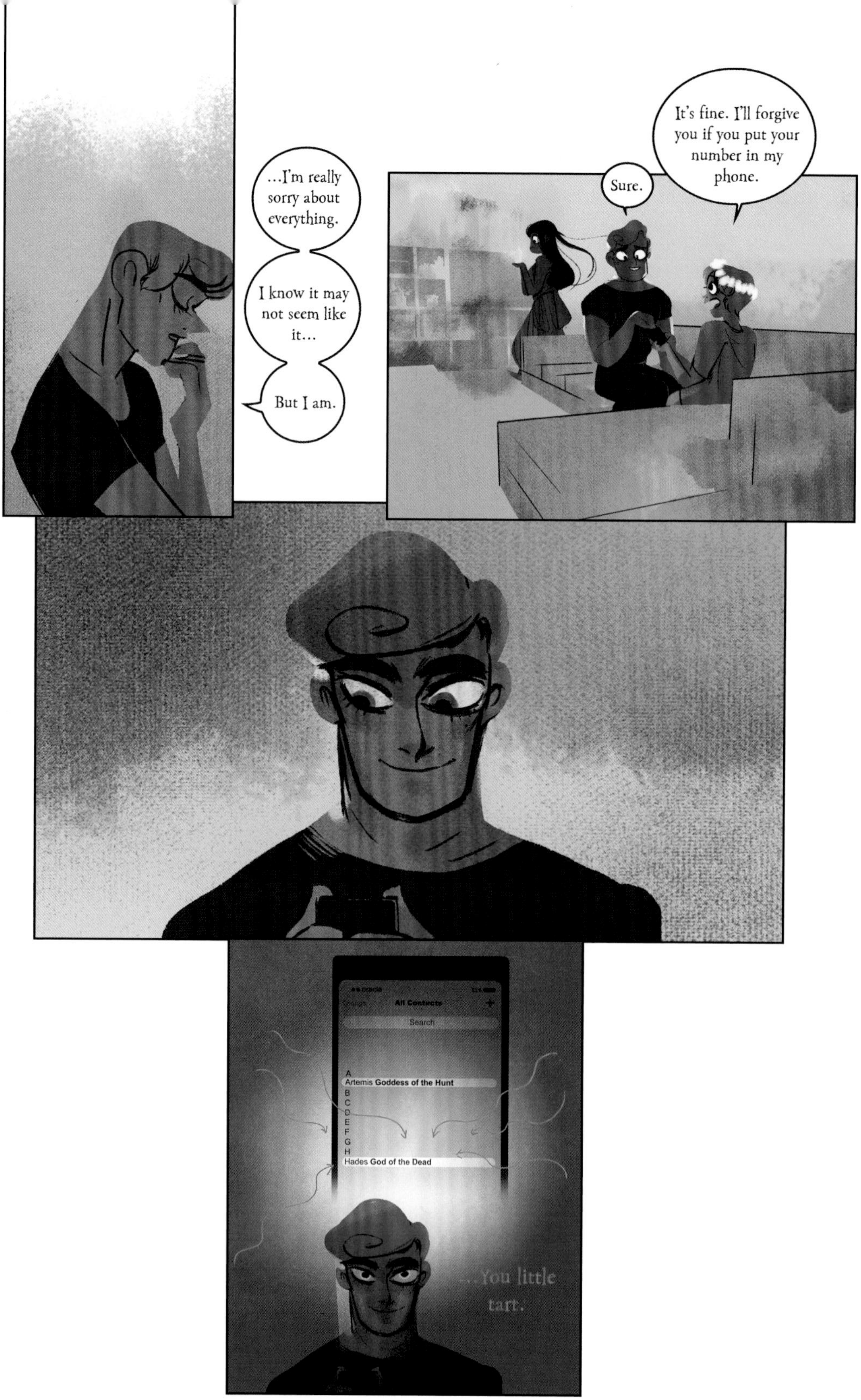
...I'm really sorry about everything.
I know it may not seem like it...
But I am.
It's fine. I'll forgive you if you put your number in my phone.
Sure.
All Contacts
Search
A
Artemis Goddess of the Hunt
B
C
D
E
F
G
H
Hades God of the Dead
...You little tart.

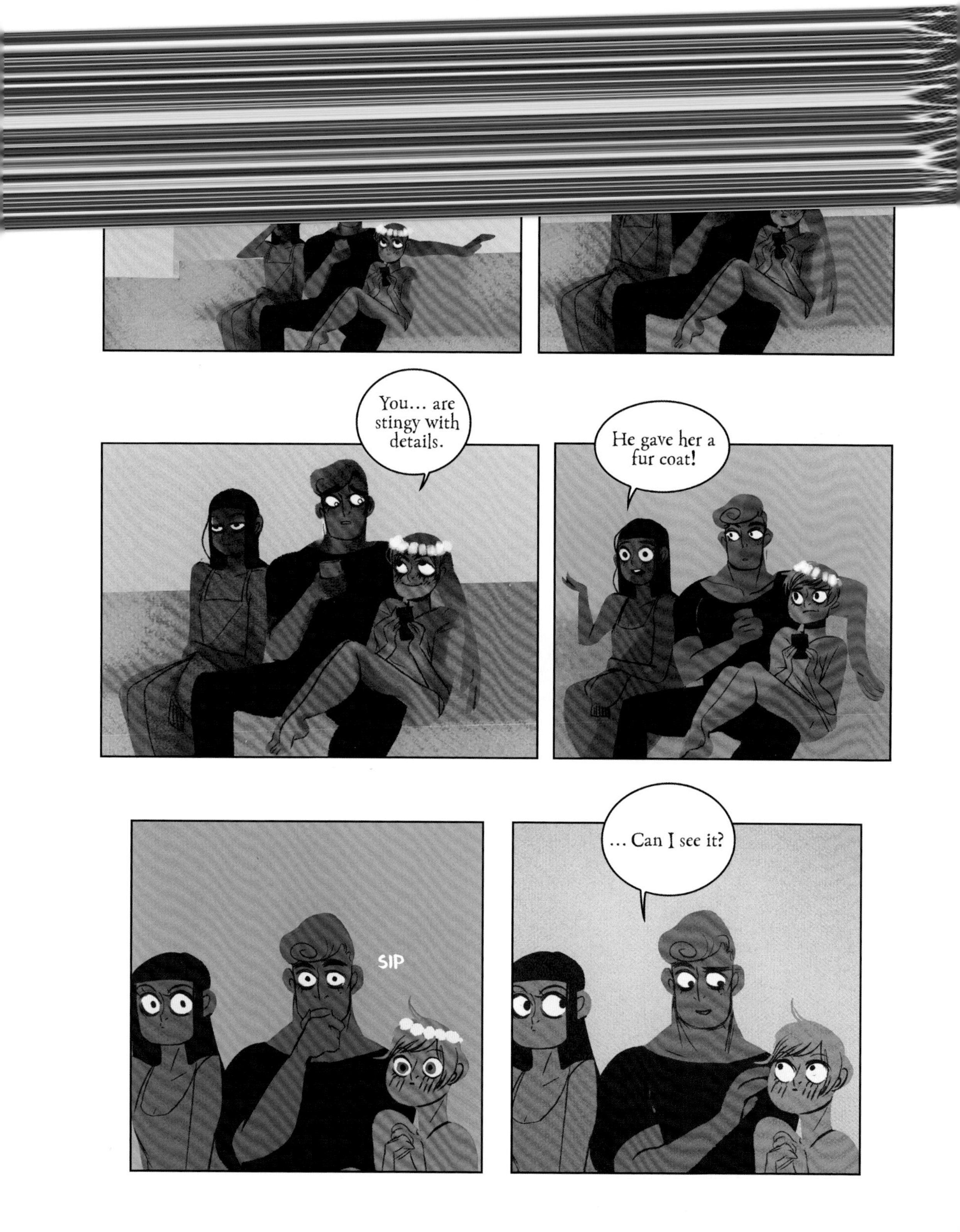

You… are stingy with details.
He gave her a fur coat!
SIP
… Can I see it?

OH MY GODS!

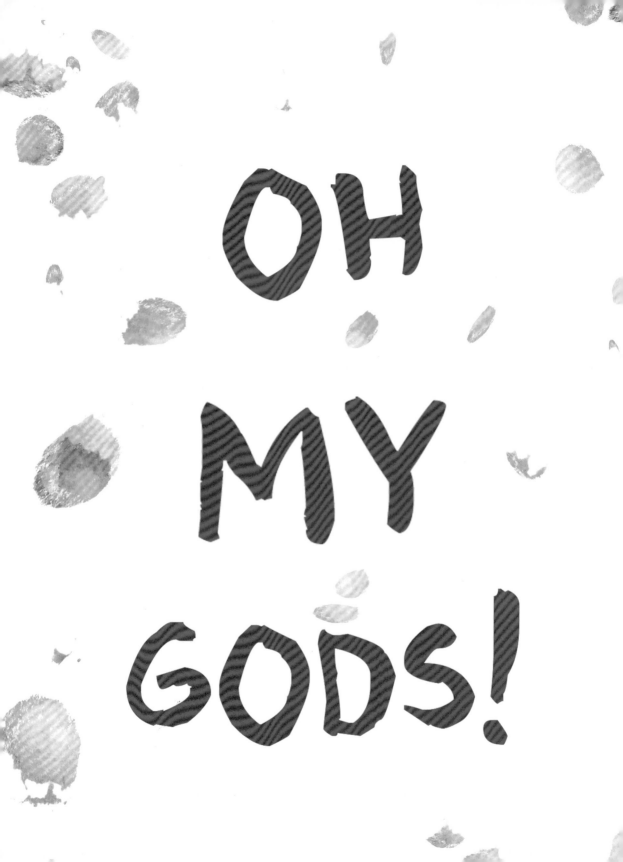

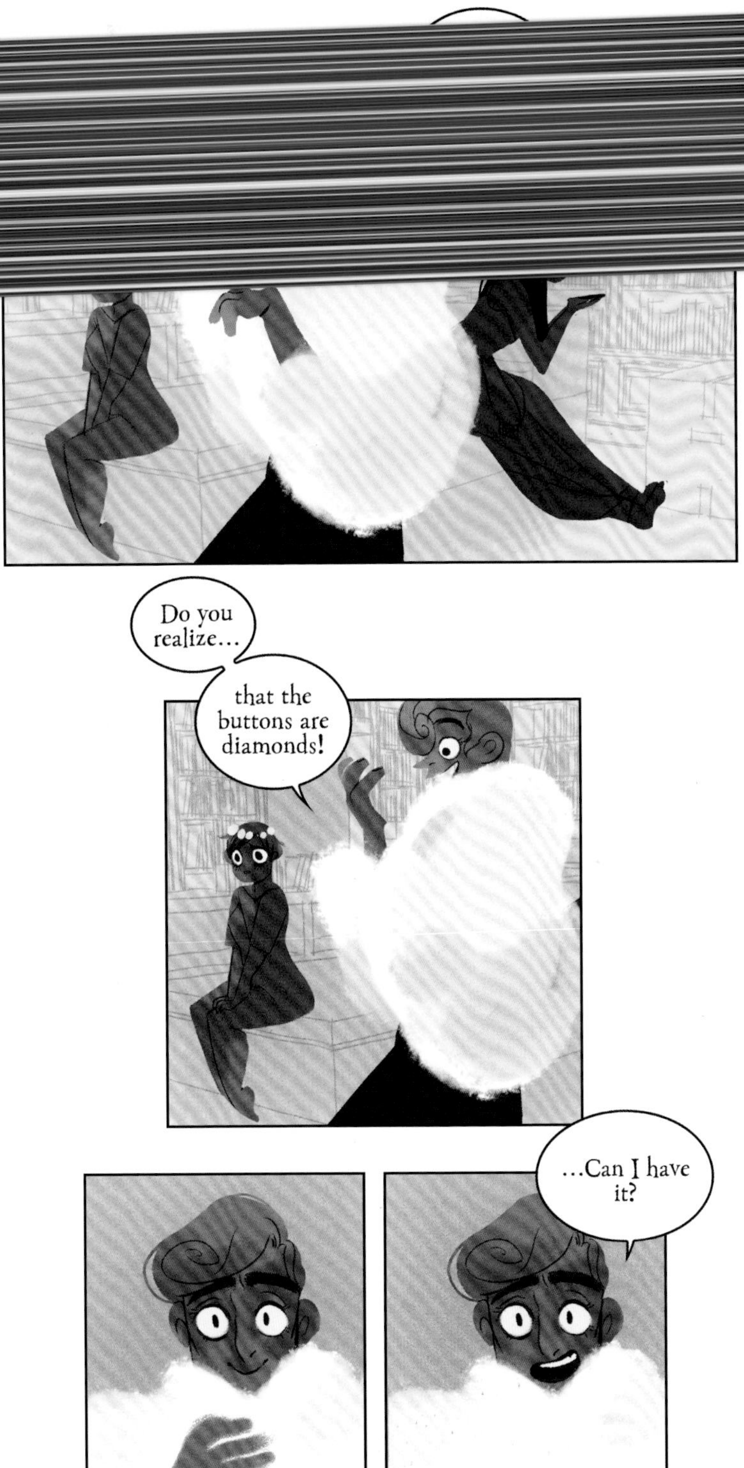
Do you realize…
that the buttons are diamonds!
…Can I have it?

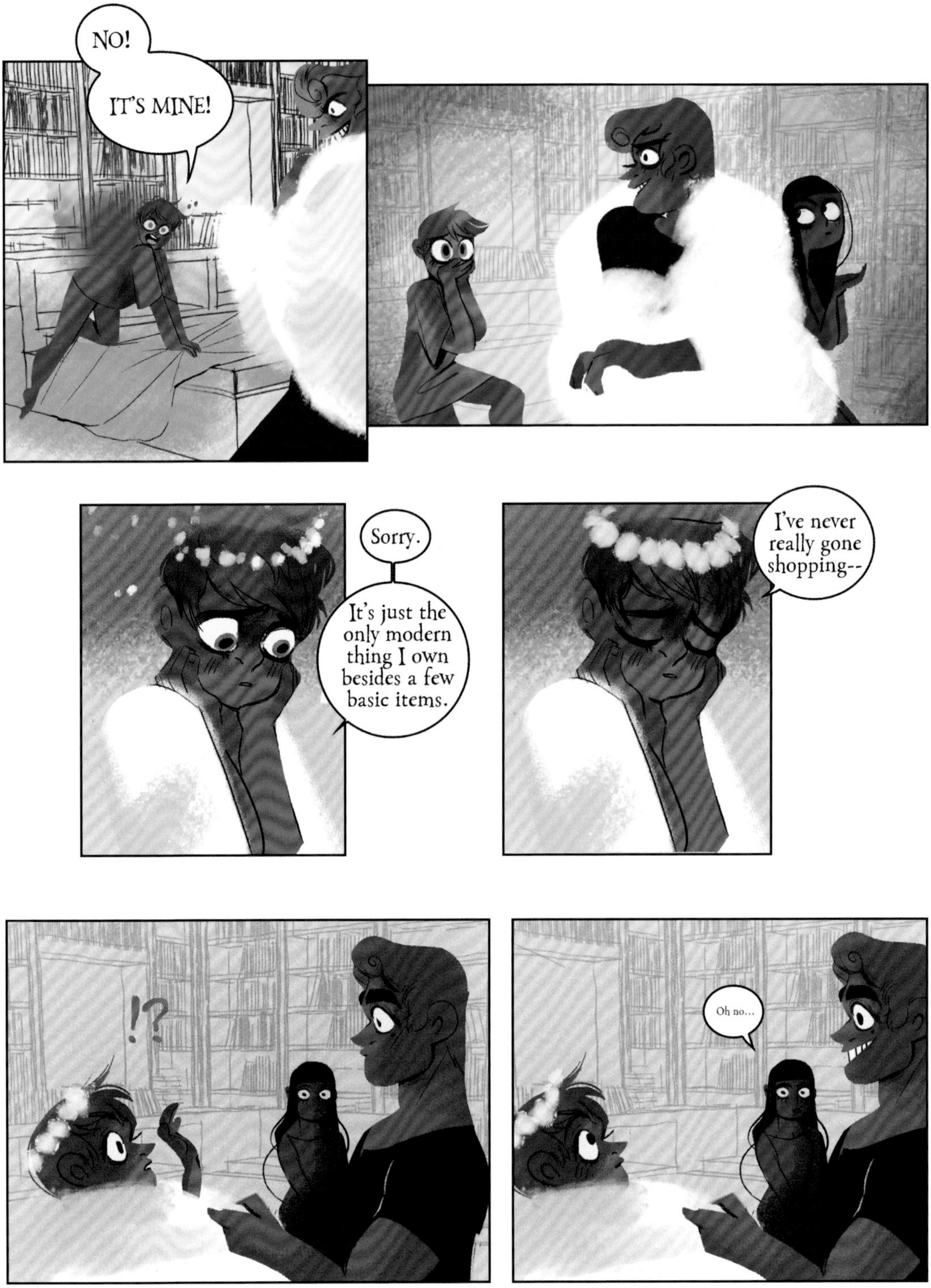
NO!
IT'S MINE!
Sorry.
It's just the only modern thing I own besides a few basic items.
I've never really gone shopping--
!?
Oh no...

EPISODE 17: GET IN

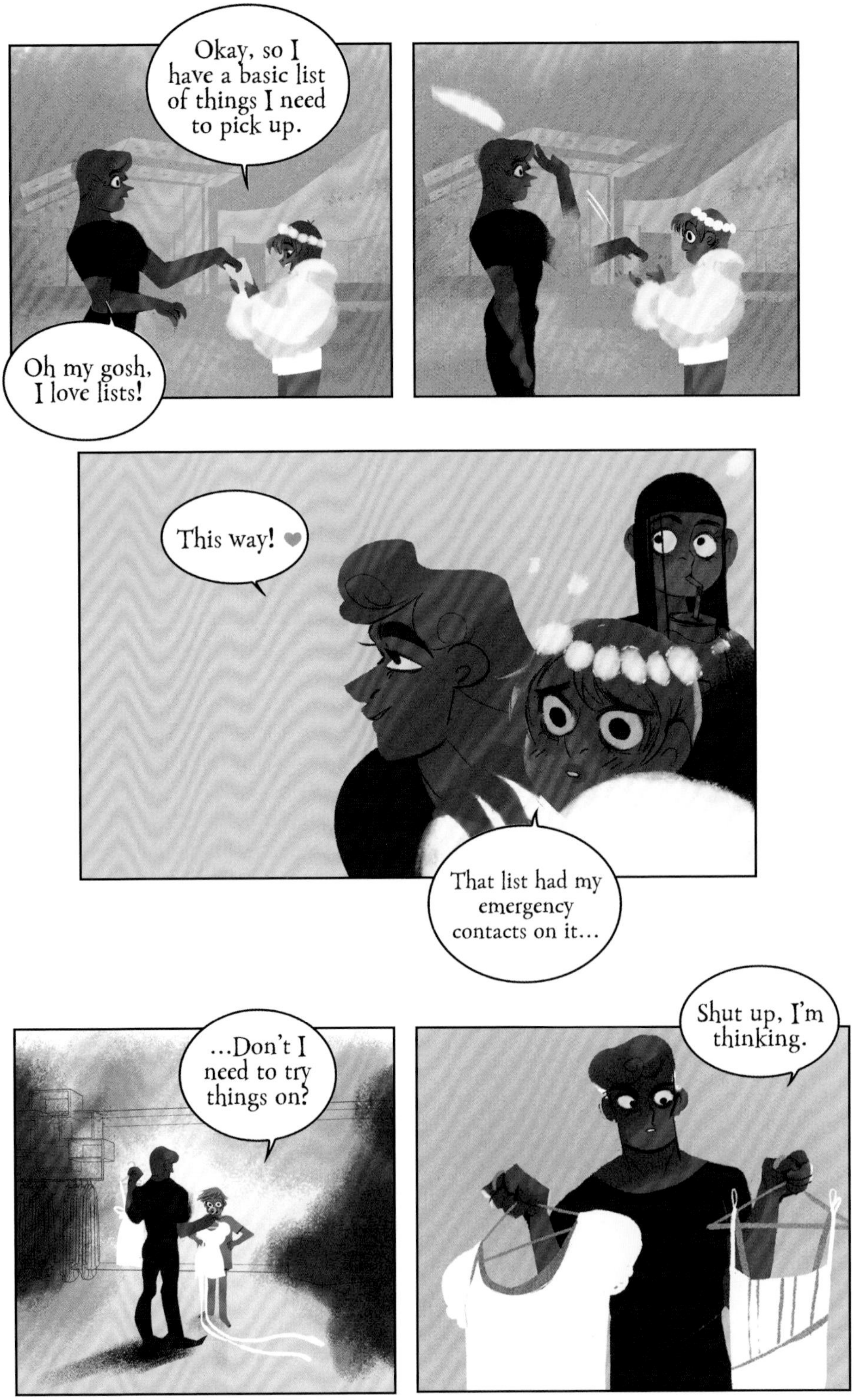
Okay, so I have a basic list of things I need to pick up.
Oh my gosh, I love lists!
This way!
That list had my emergency contacts on it...
...Don't I need to try things on?
Shut up, I'm thinking.

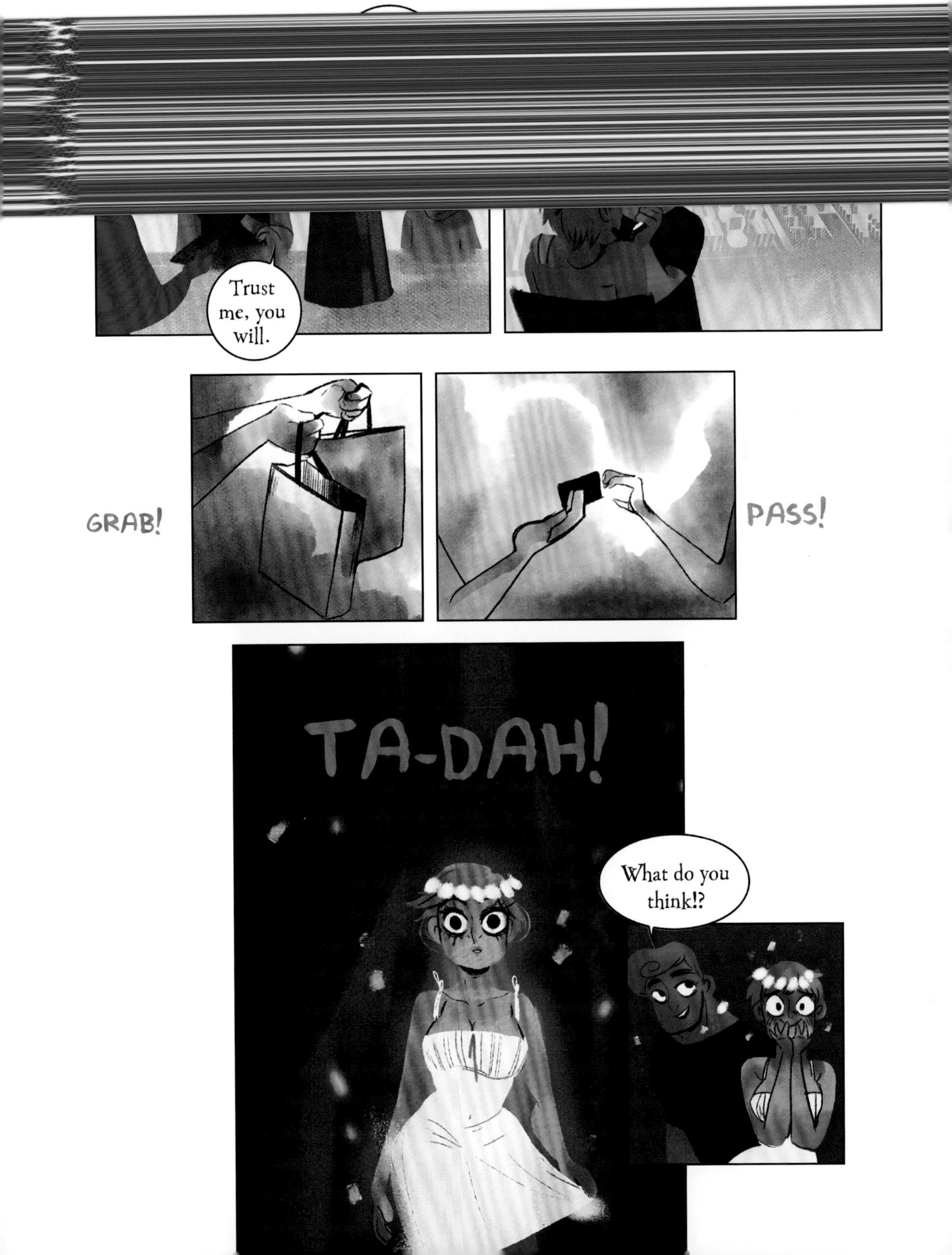
Trust me, you will.
GRAB!
PASS!
TA-DAH!
What do you think!?

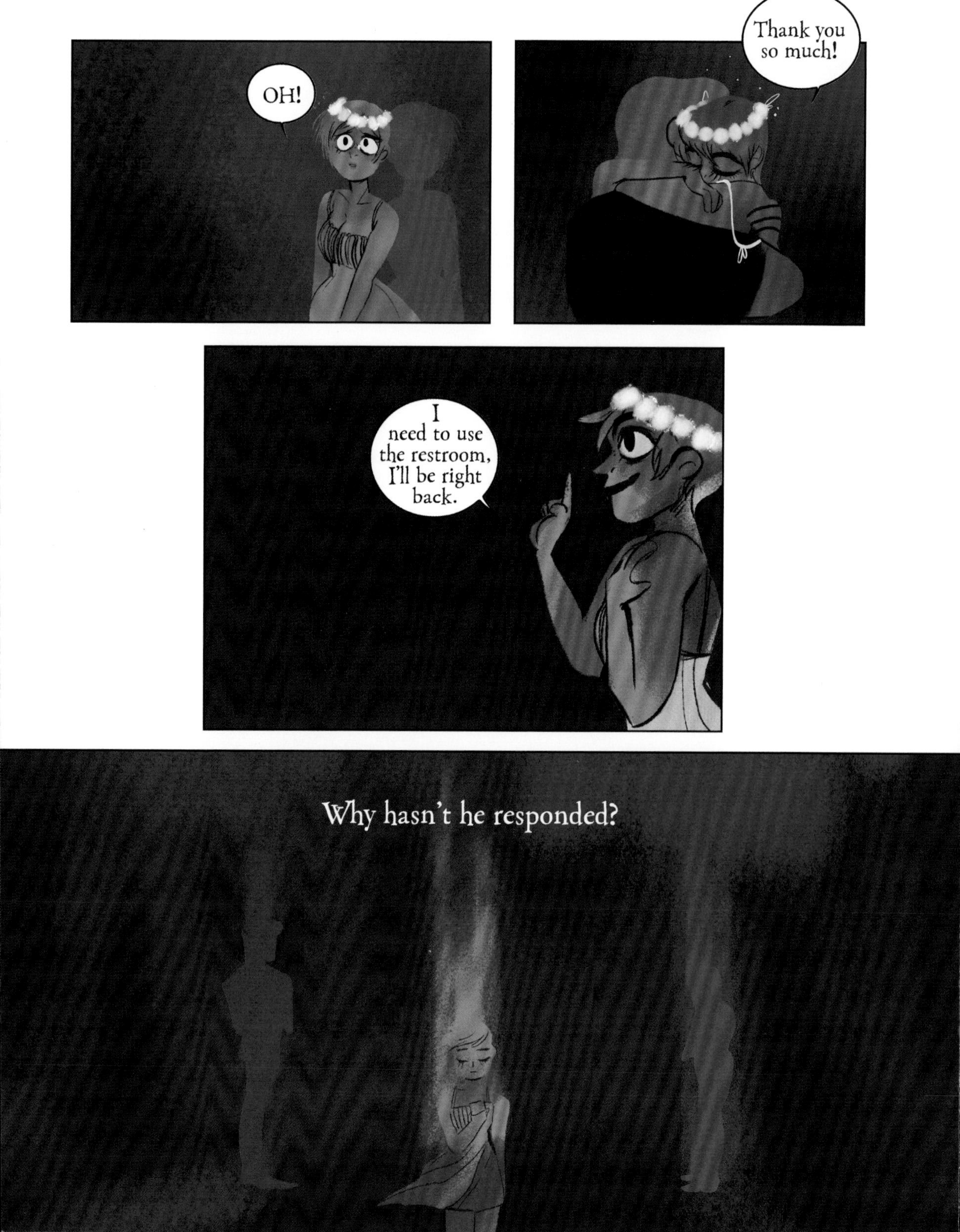
OH!
Thank you so much!
I need to use the restroom, I'll be right back.
Why hasn't he responded?

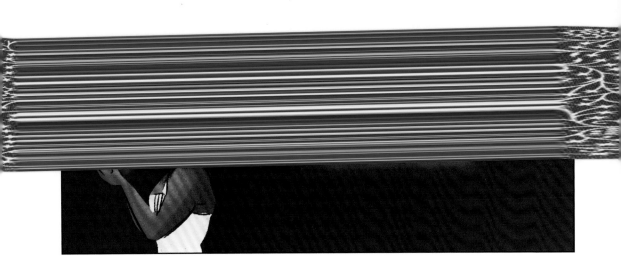

Did I write the number wrong?

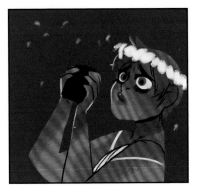

Was he just humoring me?

Maybe he doesn't want
to be my friend?

What am I even trying
to achieve anyway?

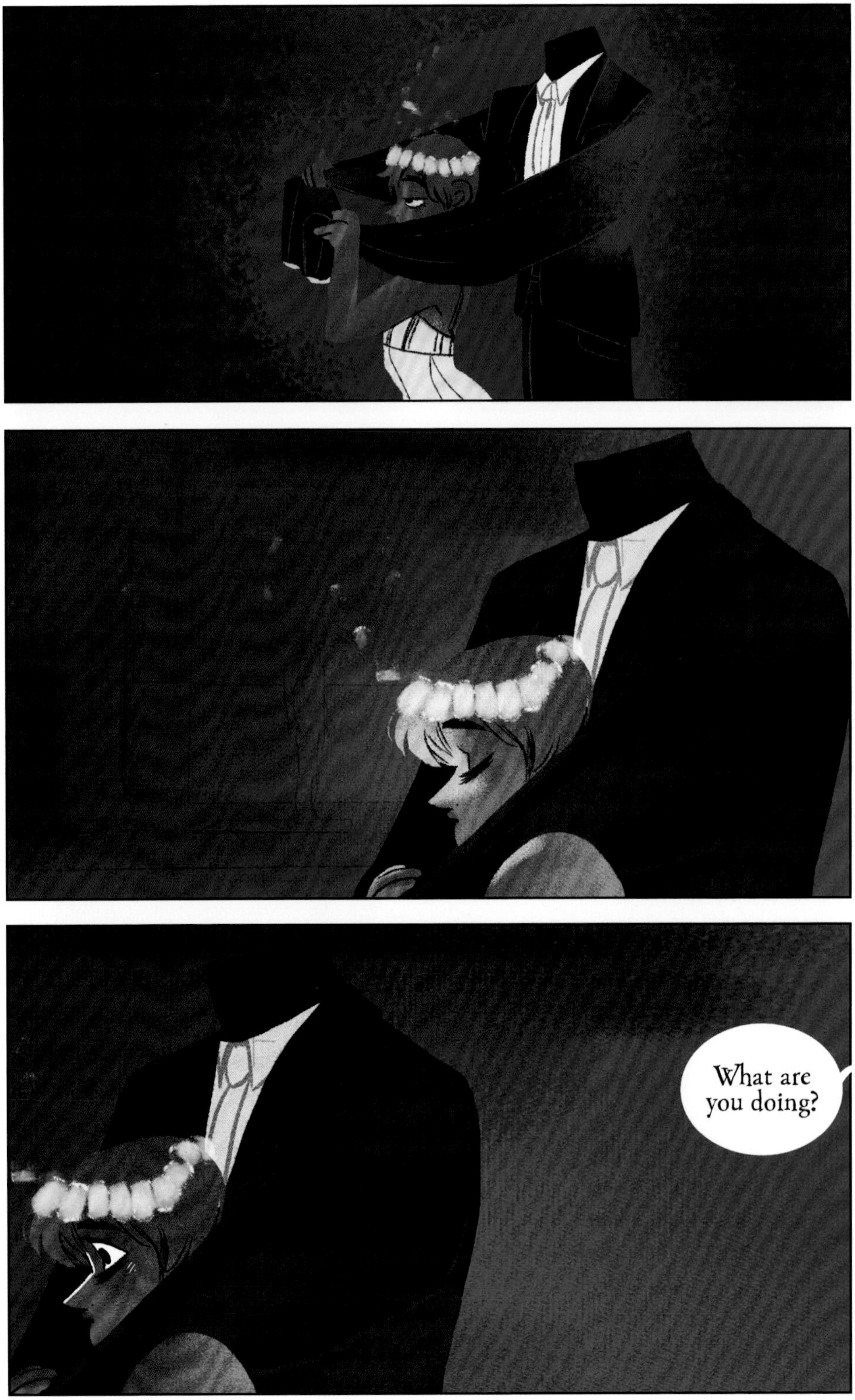
What are you doing?

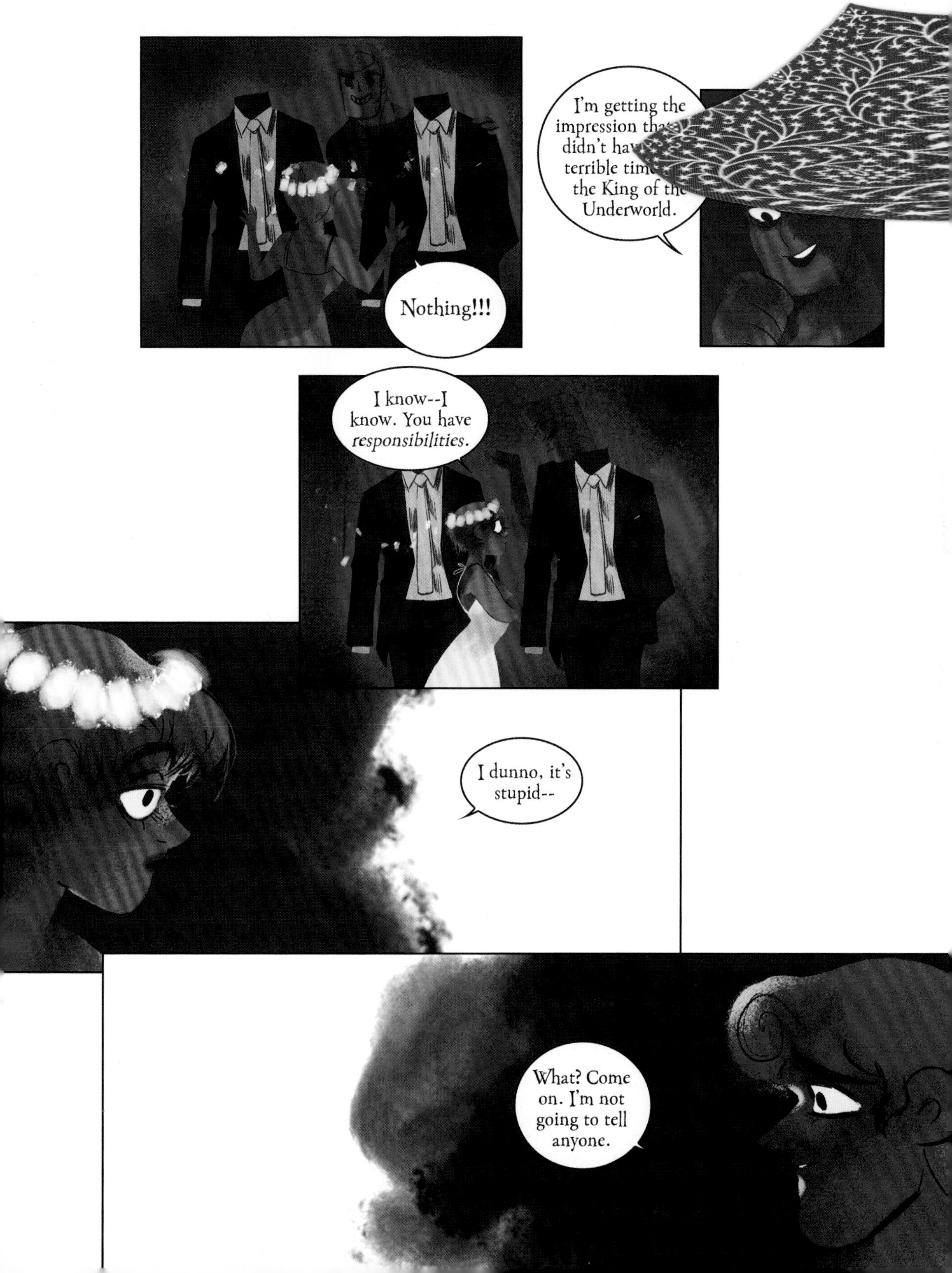
Nothing!!!
I'm getting the impression th didn't hav terrible tim the King of th Underworld.
I know--I know. You have *responsibilities*.
I dunno, it's stupid--
What? Come on. I'm not going to tell anyone.

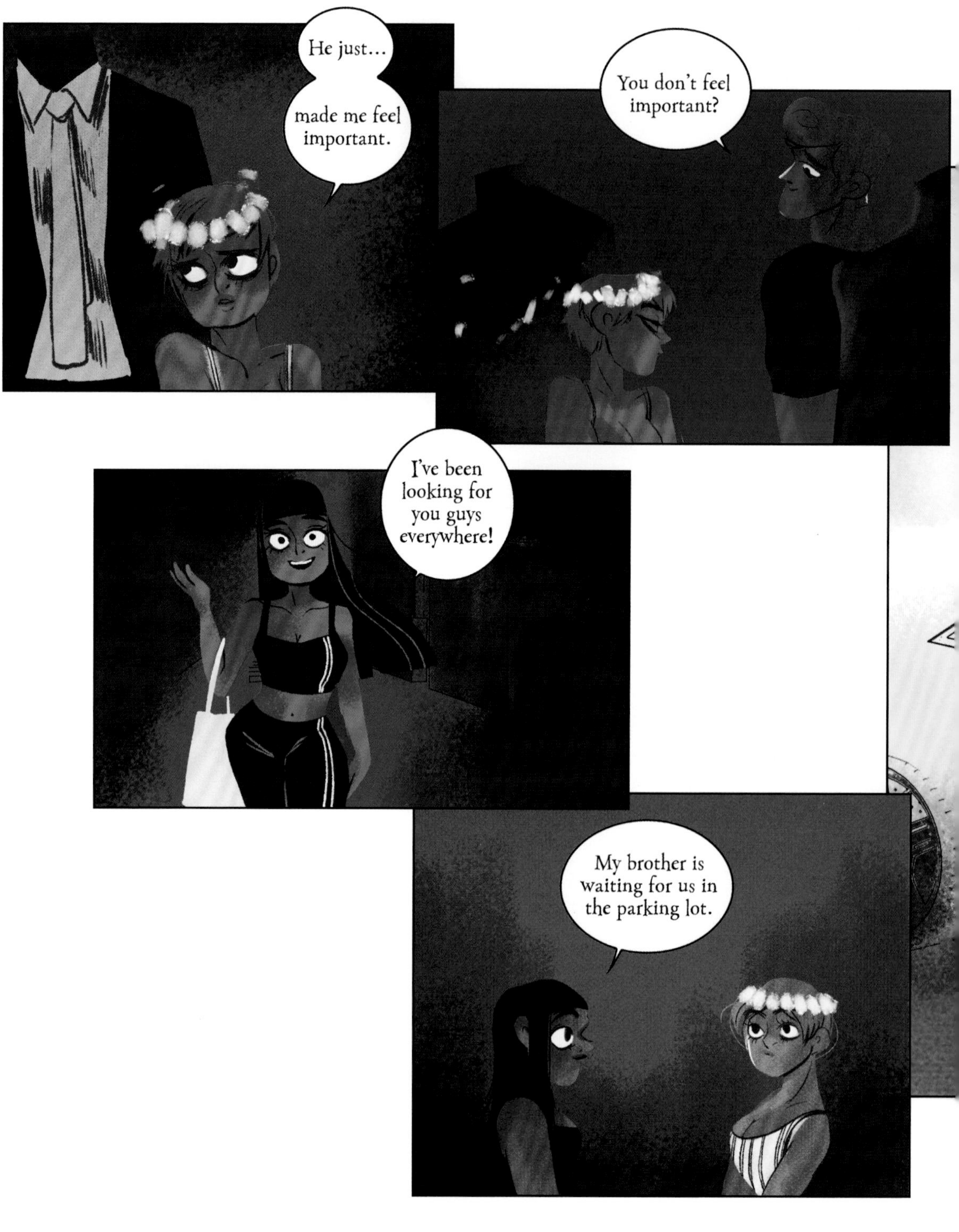
He just...
made me feel important.
You don't feel important?
I've been looking for you guys everywhere!
My brother is waiting for us in the parking lot.

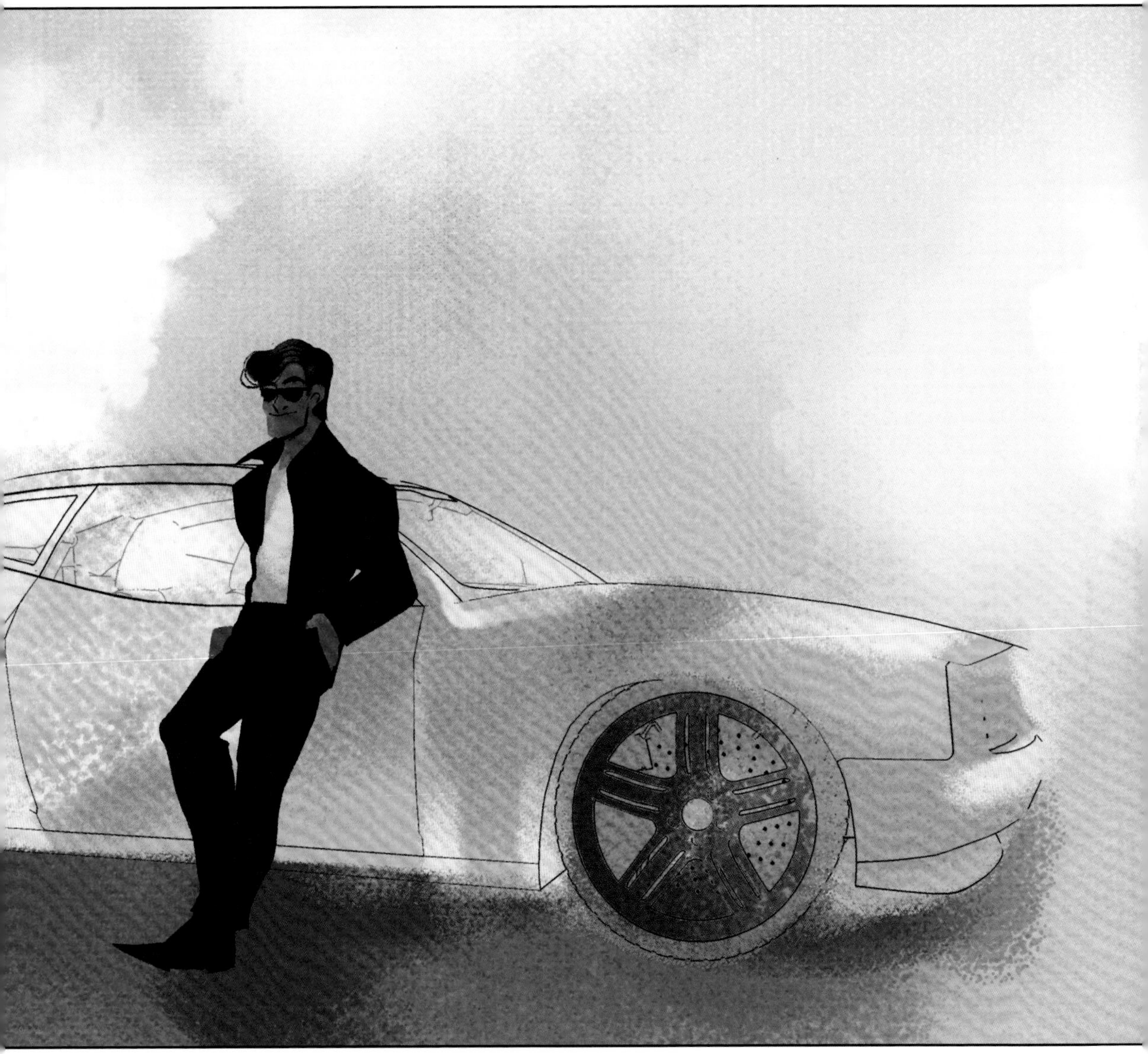

He's coming over for dinner.

You'll get a chance to meet him.

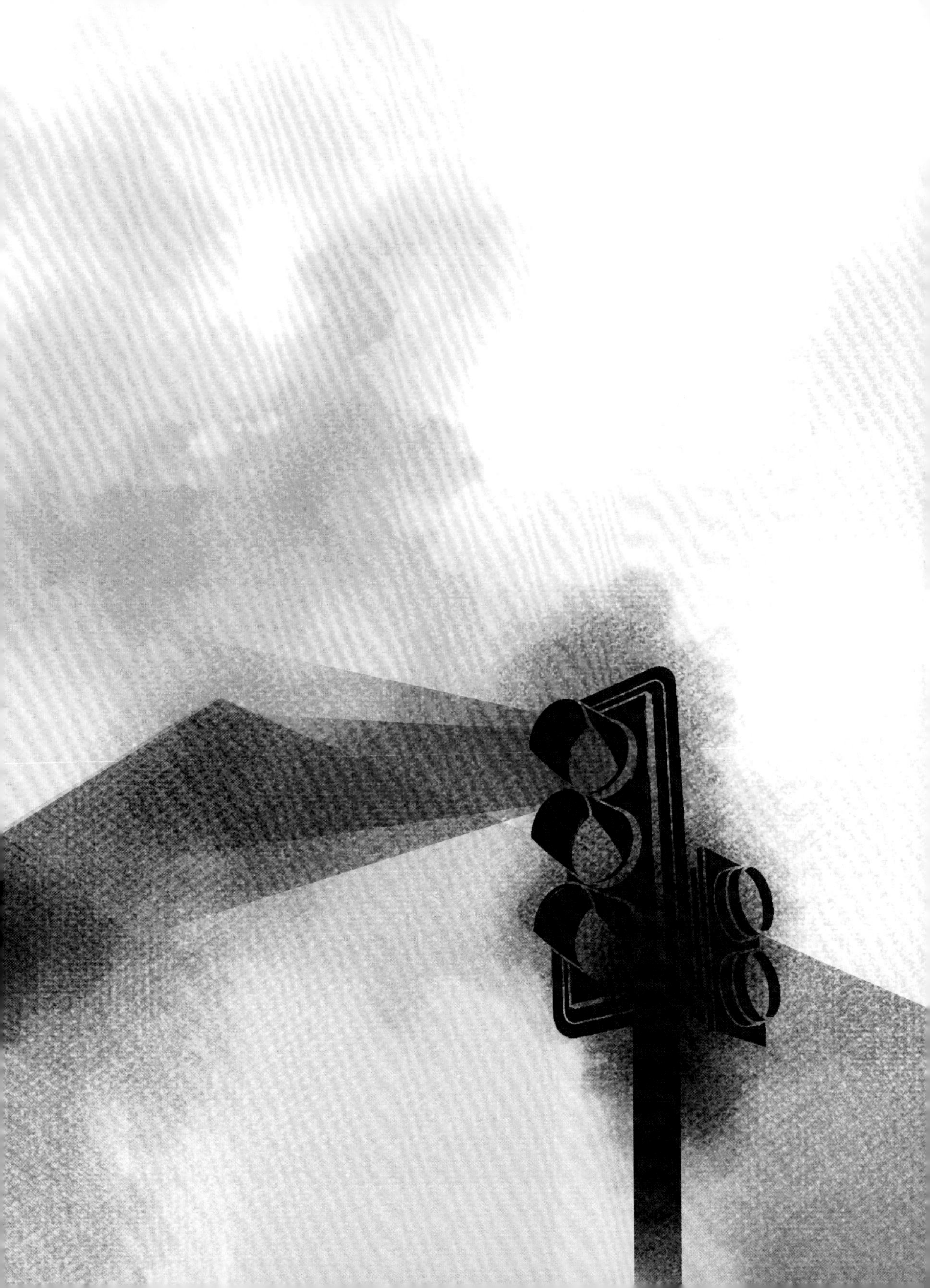

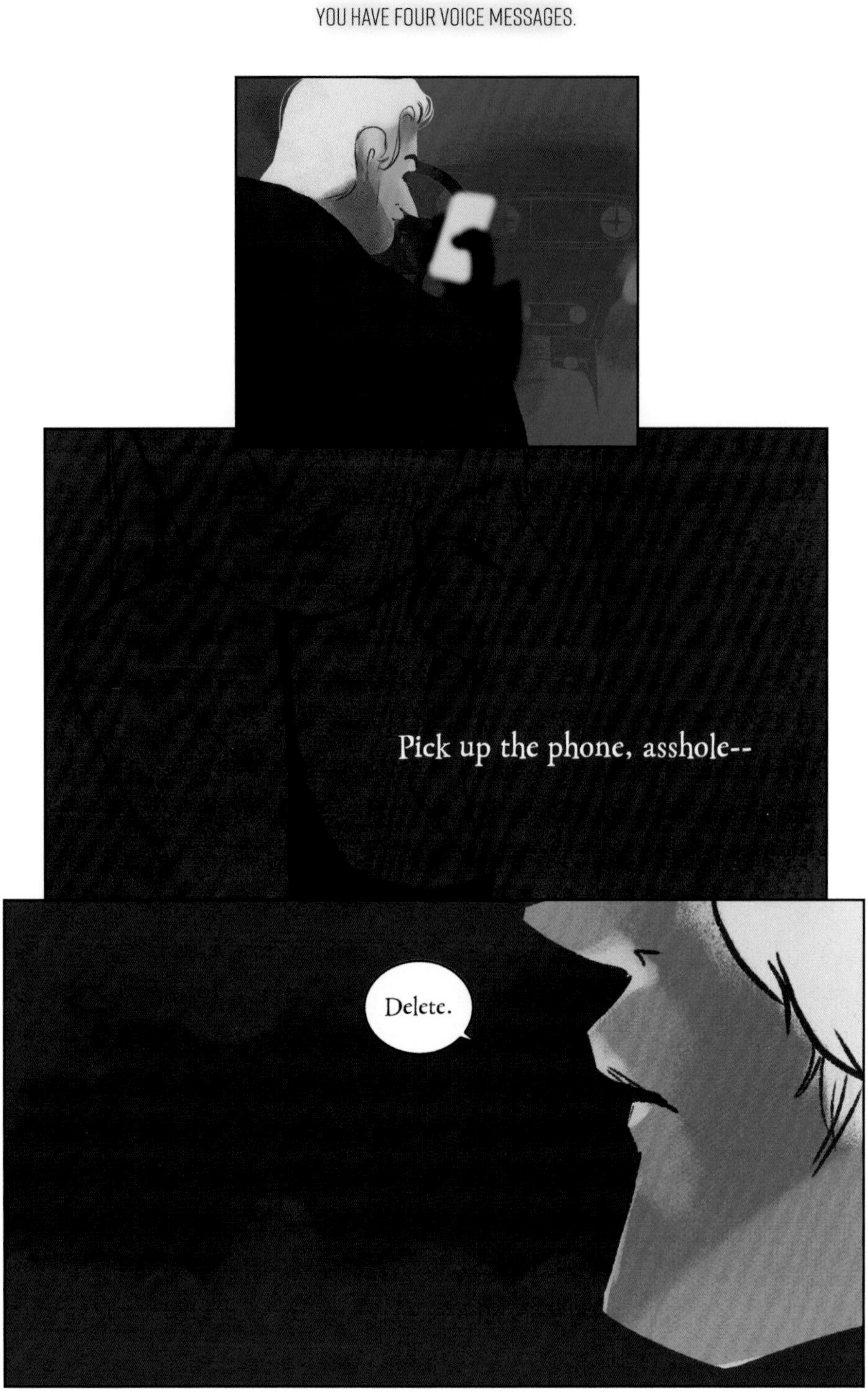
YOU HAVE FOUR VOICE MESSAGES.
Pick up the phone, asshole--
Delete.

I thought you were going to come over after the party--

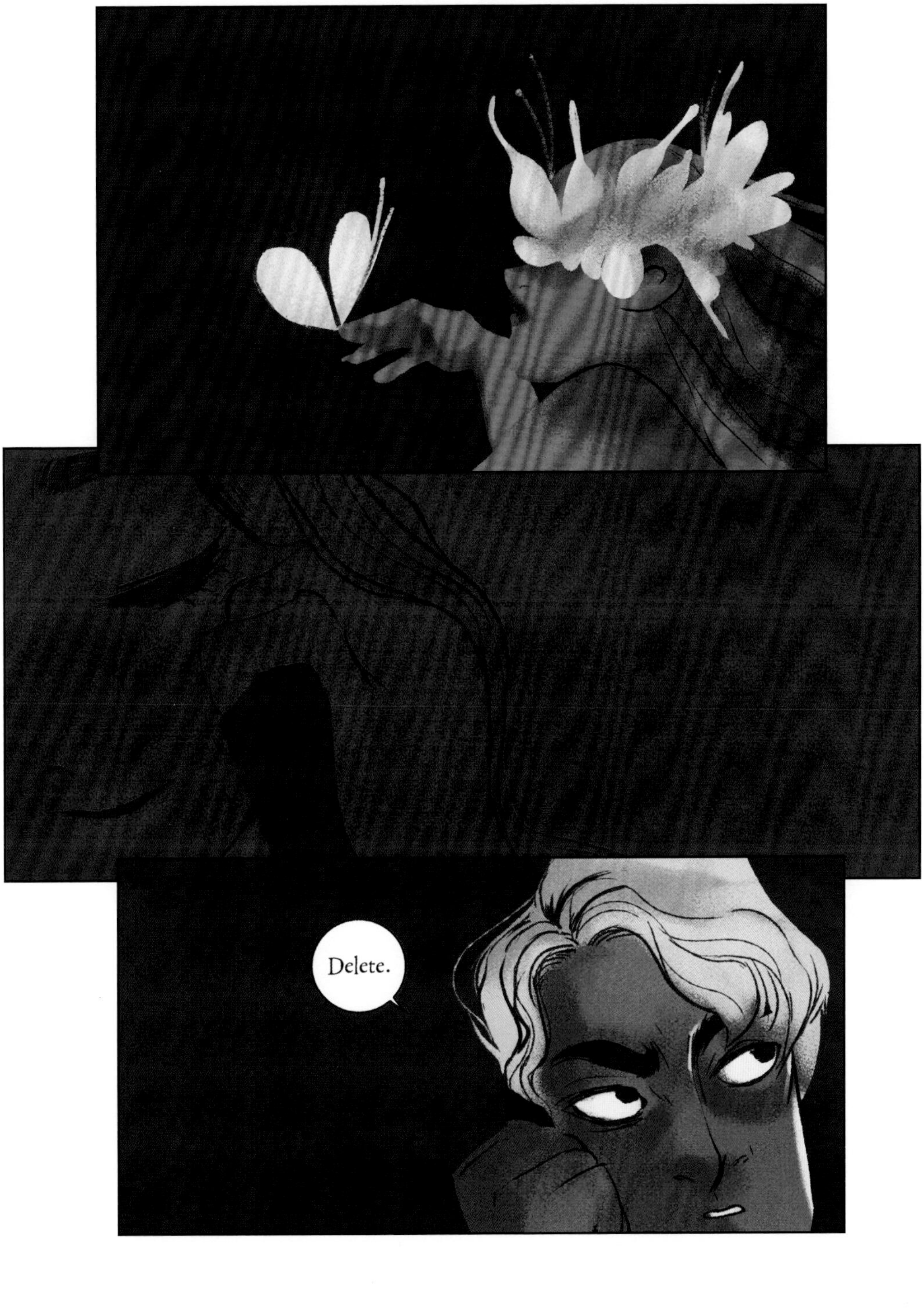
Delete.

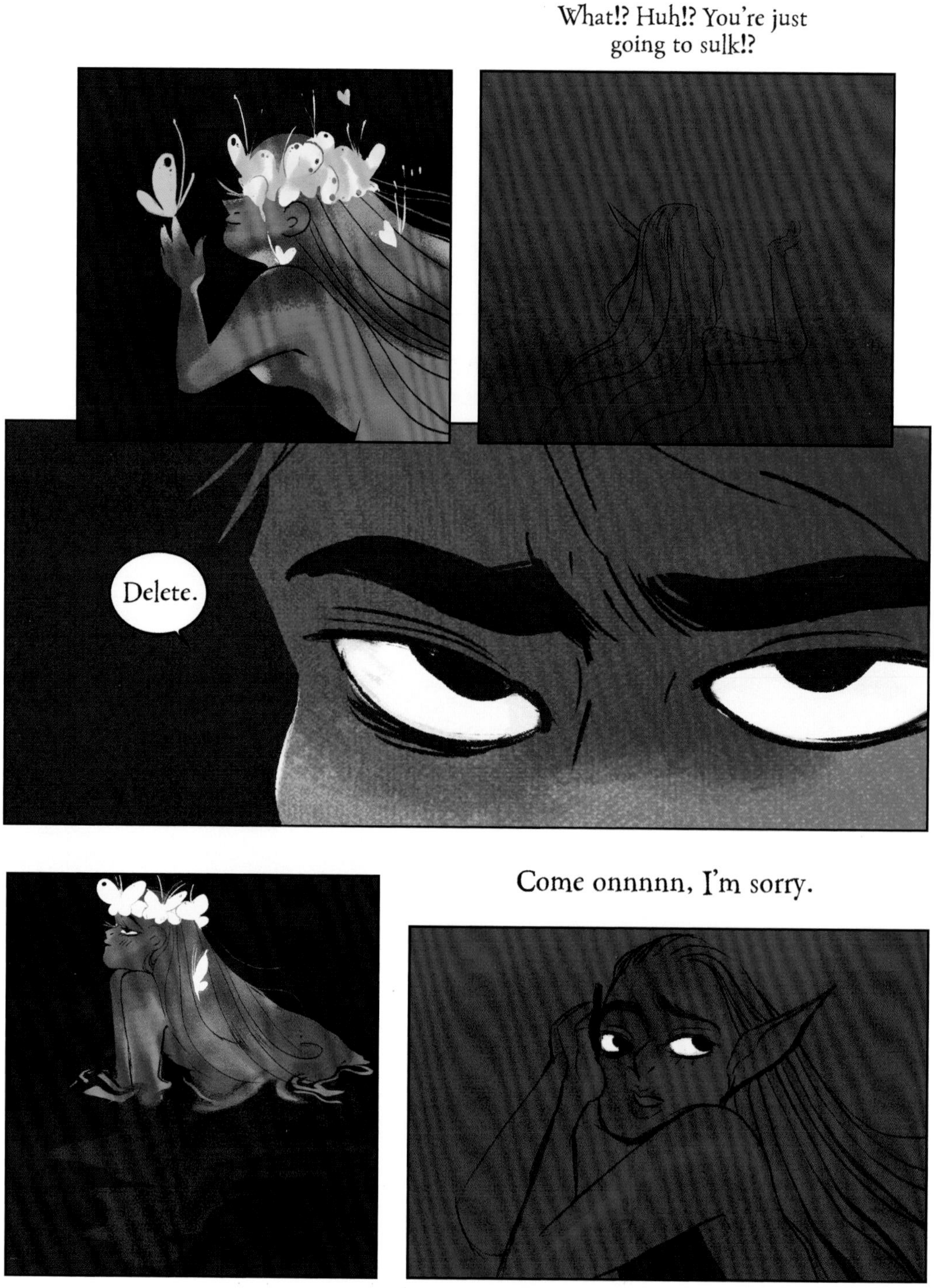
What!? Huh!? You're just going to sulk!?
Delete.
Come onnnnn, I'm sorry.

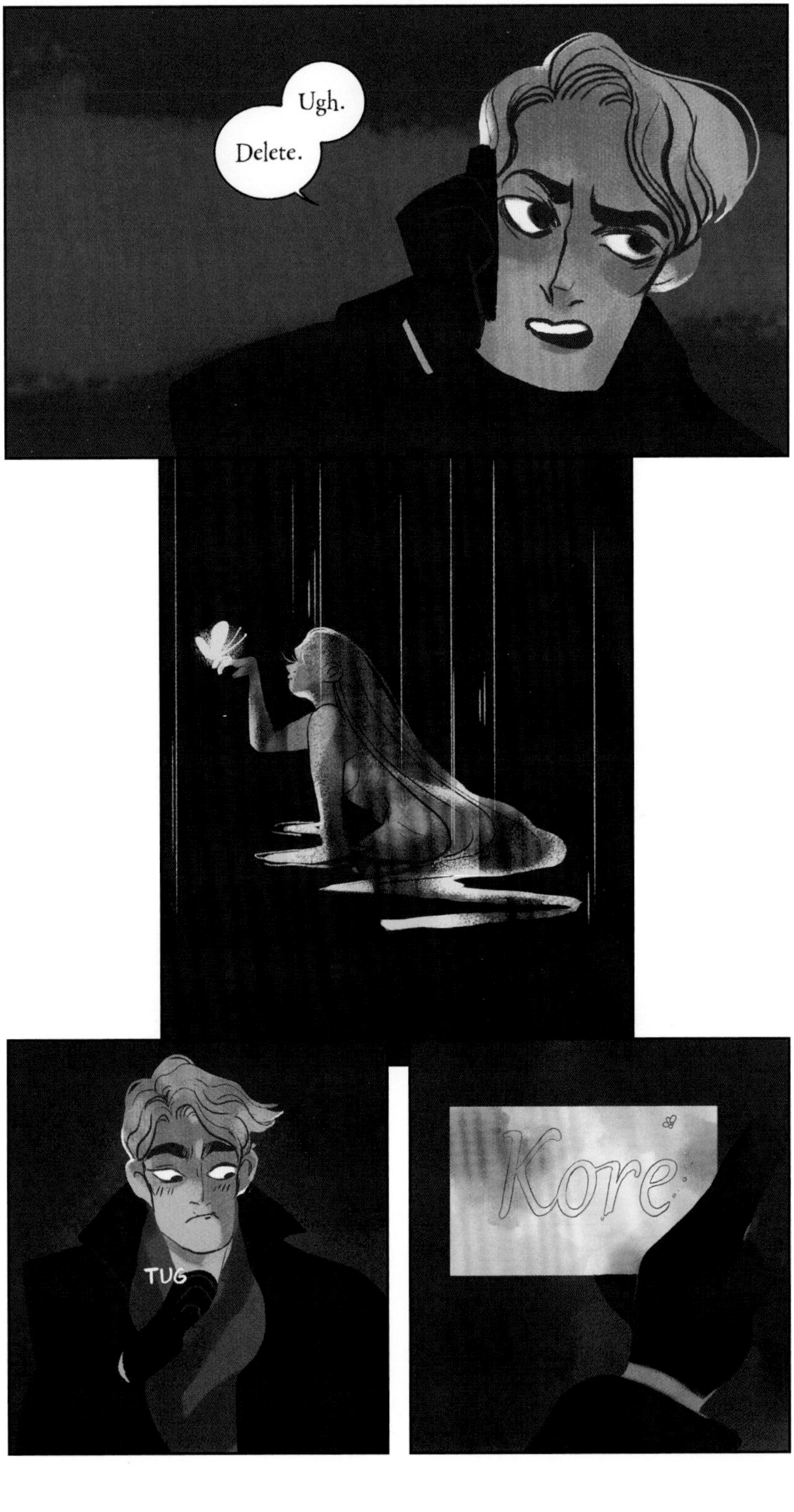
Ugh.
Delete.
TUG
Kore.

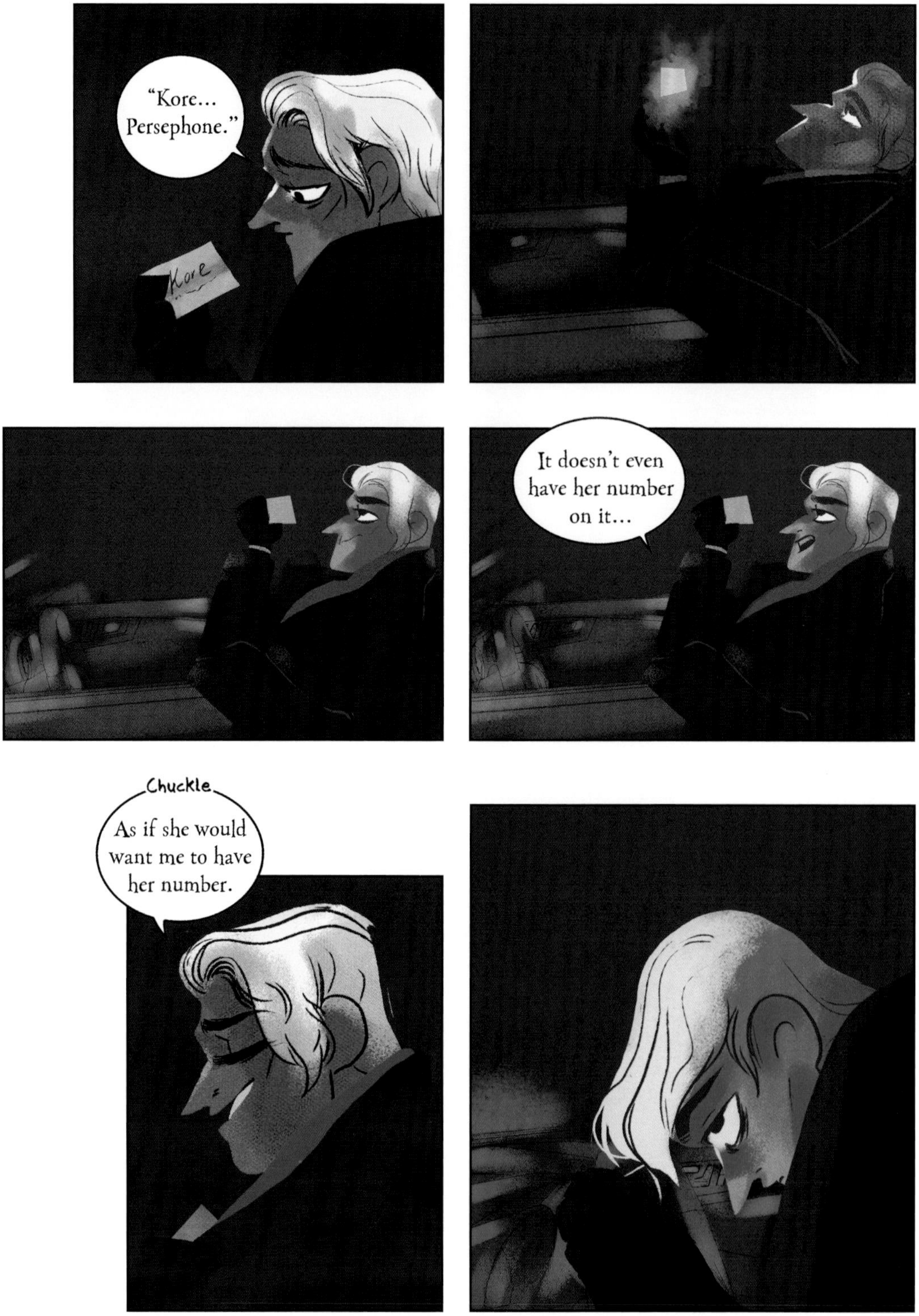
"Kore...
Persephone."
Kore
It doesn't even have her number on it...
Chuckle
As if she would want me to have her number.

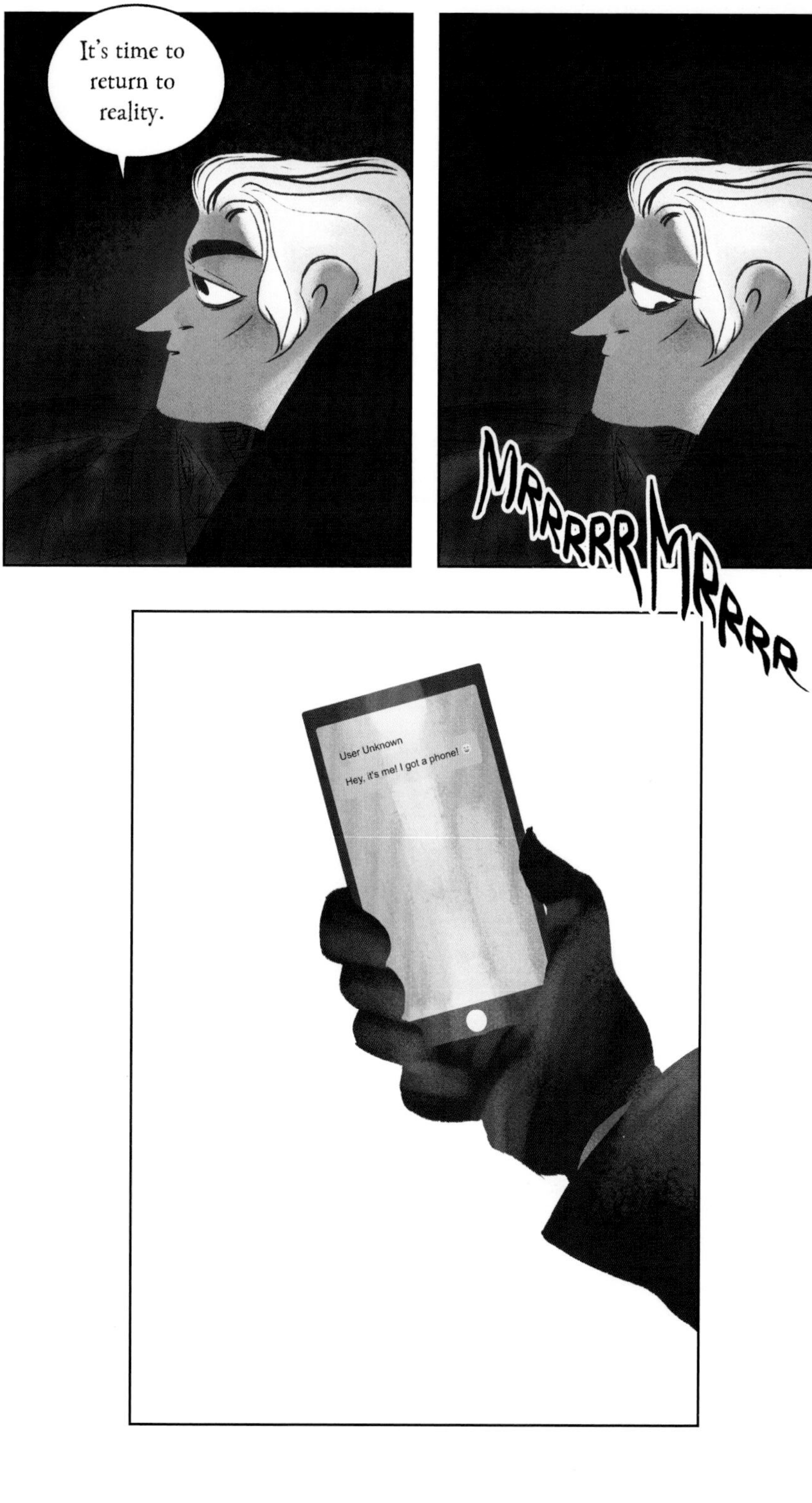
It's time to return to reality.
MRRRRR MRRRRR
User Unknown
Hey, it's me! I got a phone!

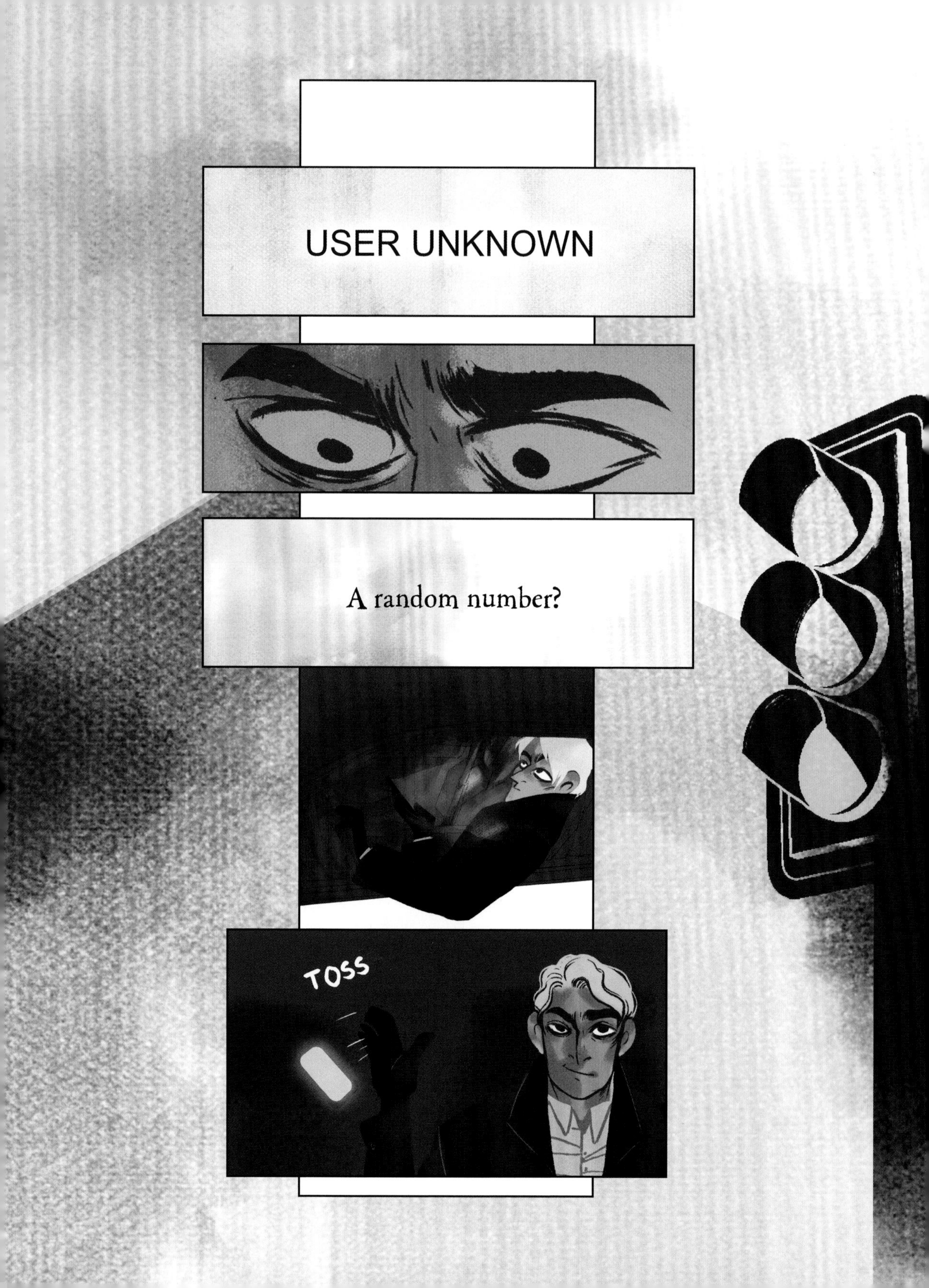
USER UNKNOWN
A random number?
TOSS

EPISODE 18: FOREST FOR THE TREES

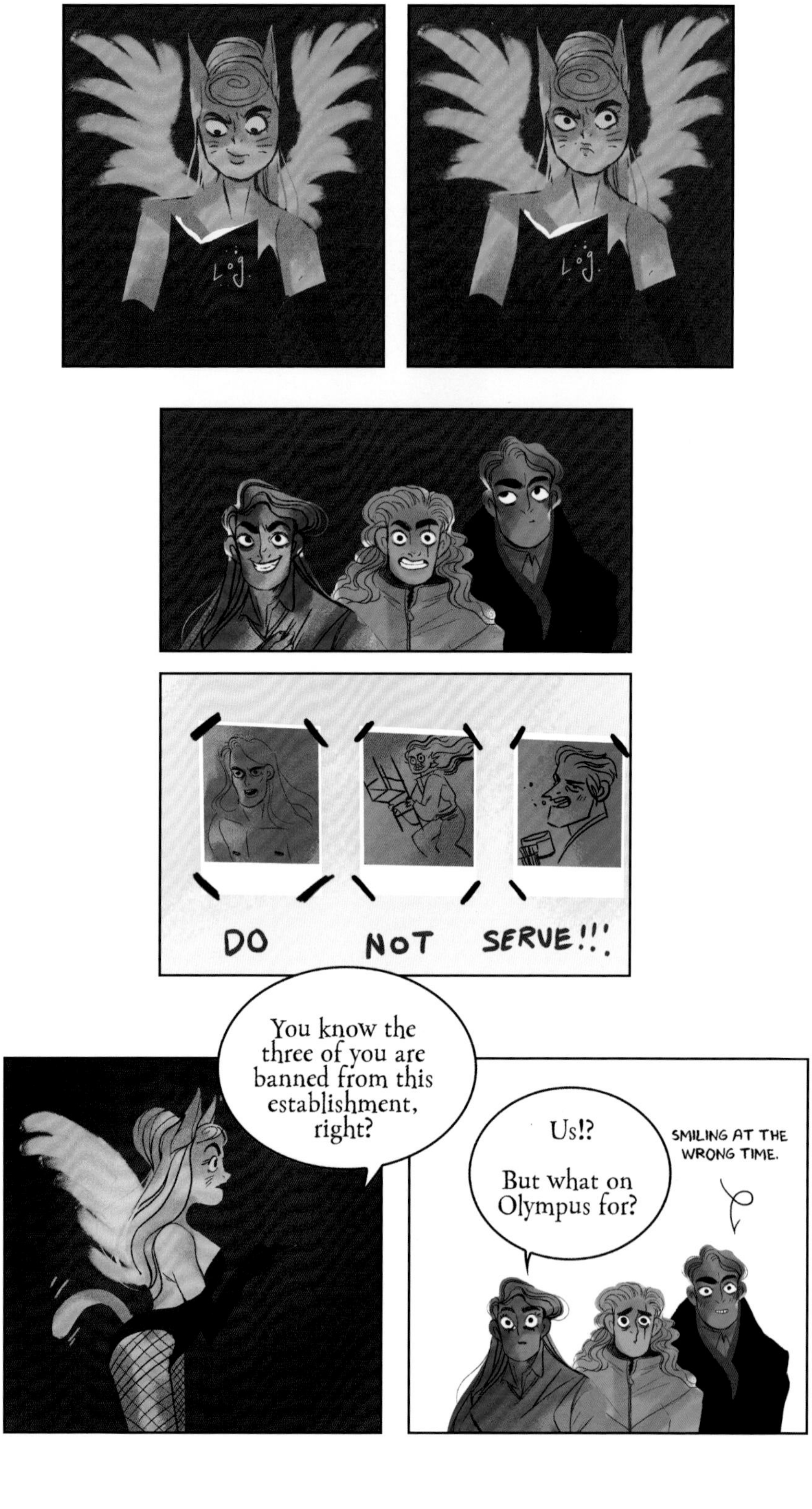
Log.
Log.
DO NOT SERVE!!!
You know the three of you are banned from this establishment, right?
Us!? But what on Olympus for?
SMILING AT THE WRONG TIME.

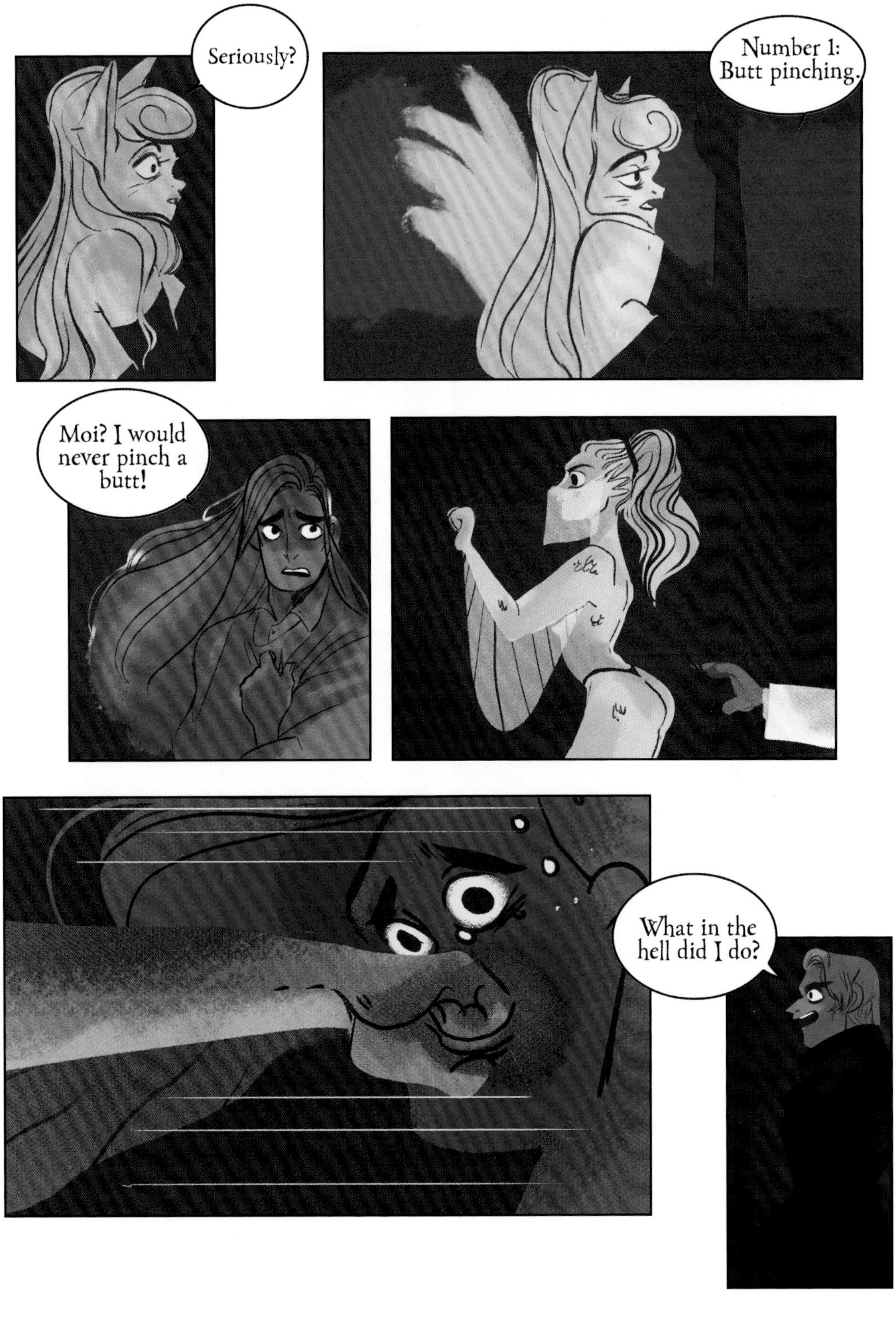
Seriously?
Number 1: Butt pinching.
Moi? I would never pinch a butt!
What in the hell did I do?

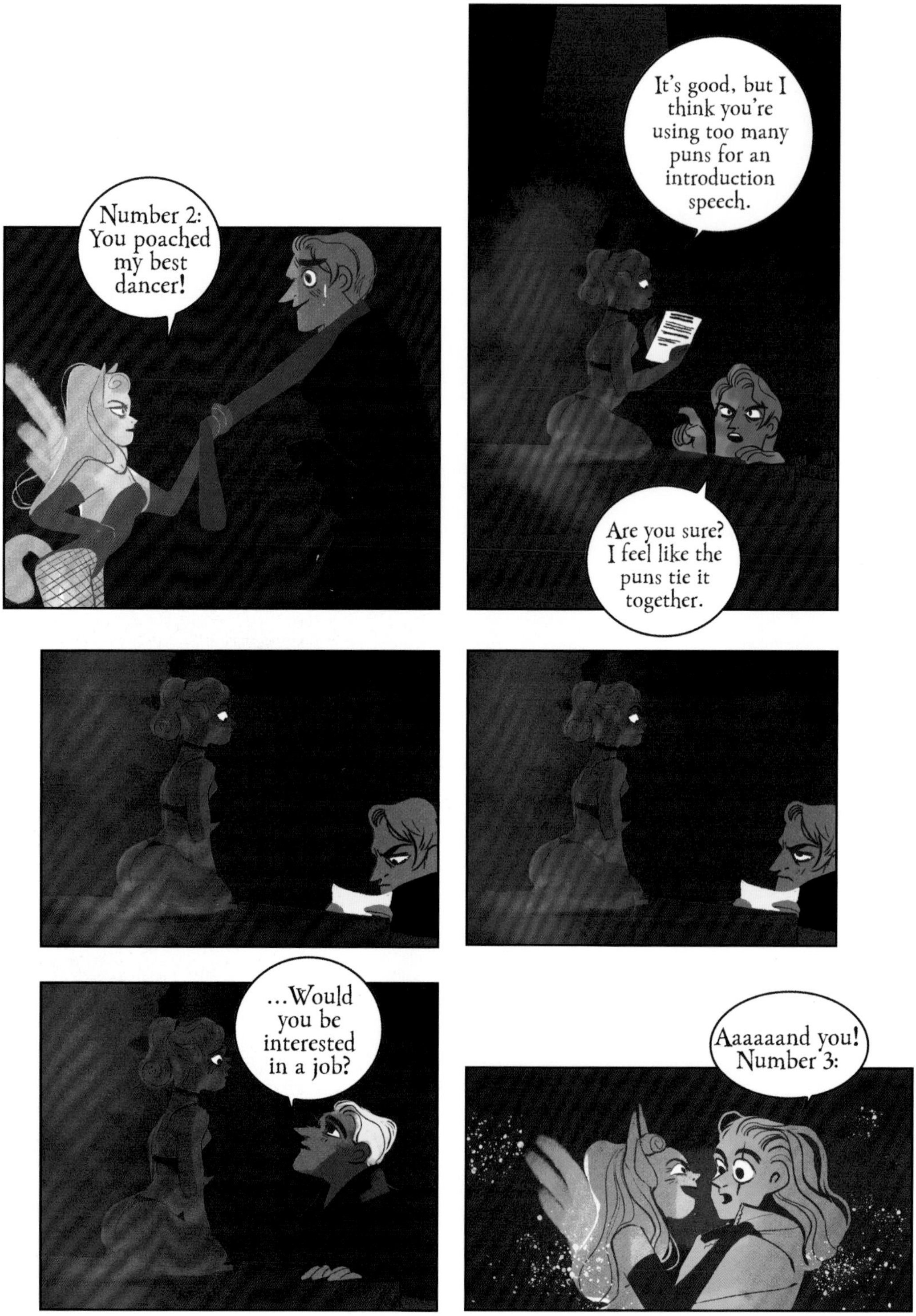
It's good, but I think you're using too many puns for an introduction speech.
Are you sure? I feel like the puns tie it together.
Number 2: You poached my best dancer!
...Would you be interested in a job?
Aaaaaand you! Number 3:

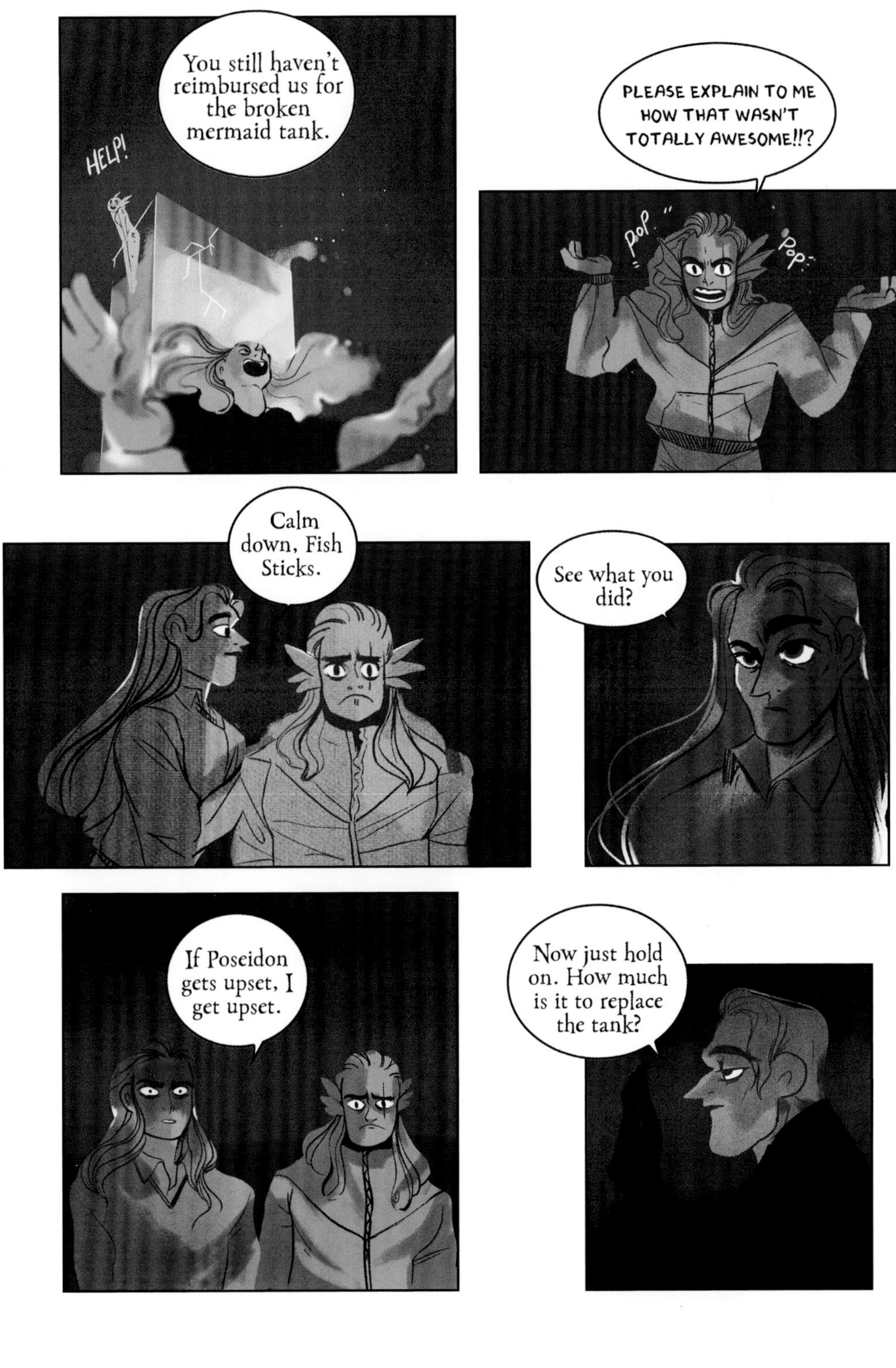
You still haven't reimbursed us for the broken mermaid tank.
HELP!
PLEASE EXPLAIN TO ME HOW THAT WASN'T TOTALLY AWESOME!!?
POP
POP
Calm down, Fish Sticks.
See what you did?
If Poseidon gets upset, I get upset.
Now just hold on. How much is it to replace the tank?

MMM...
2000 drachmas!
Do you take diamonds?

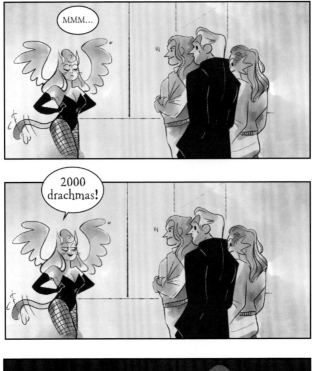

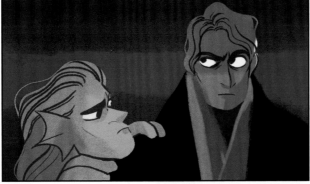

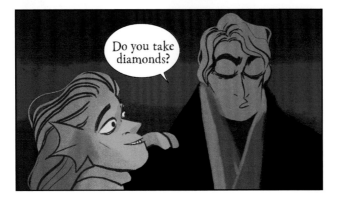

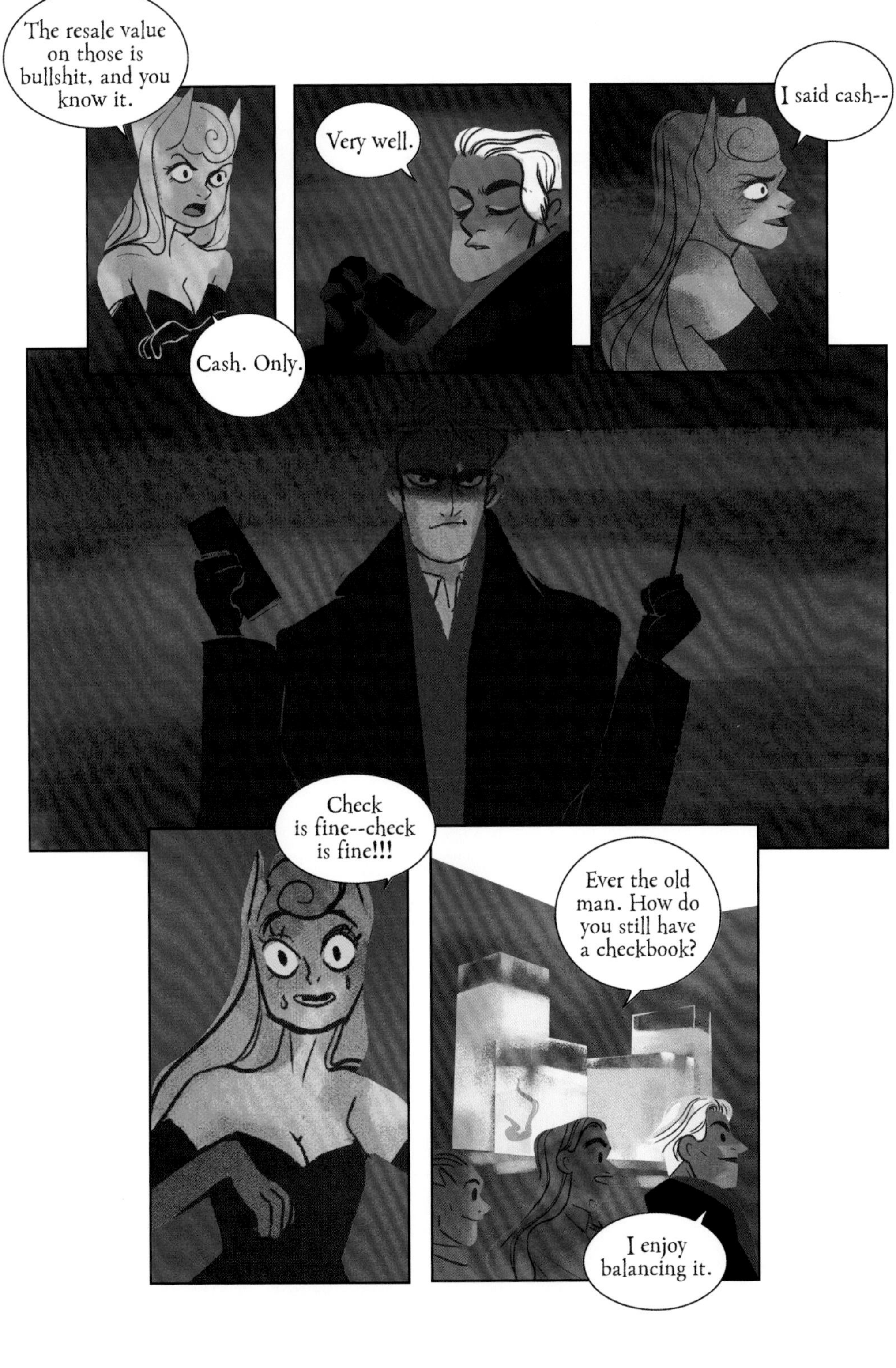
The resale value on those is bullshit, and you know it.
Cash. Only.
Very well.
I said cash--
Check is fine--check is fine!!!
Ever the old man. How do you still have a checkbook?
I enjoy balancing it.

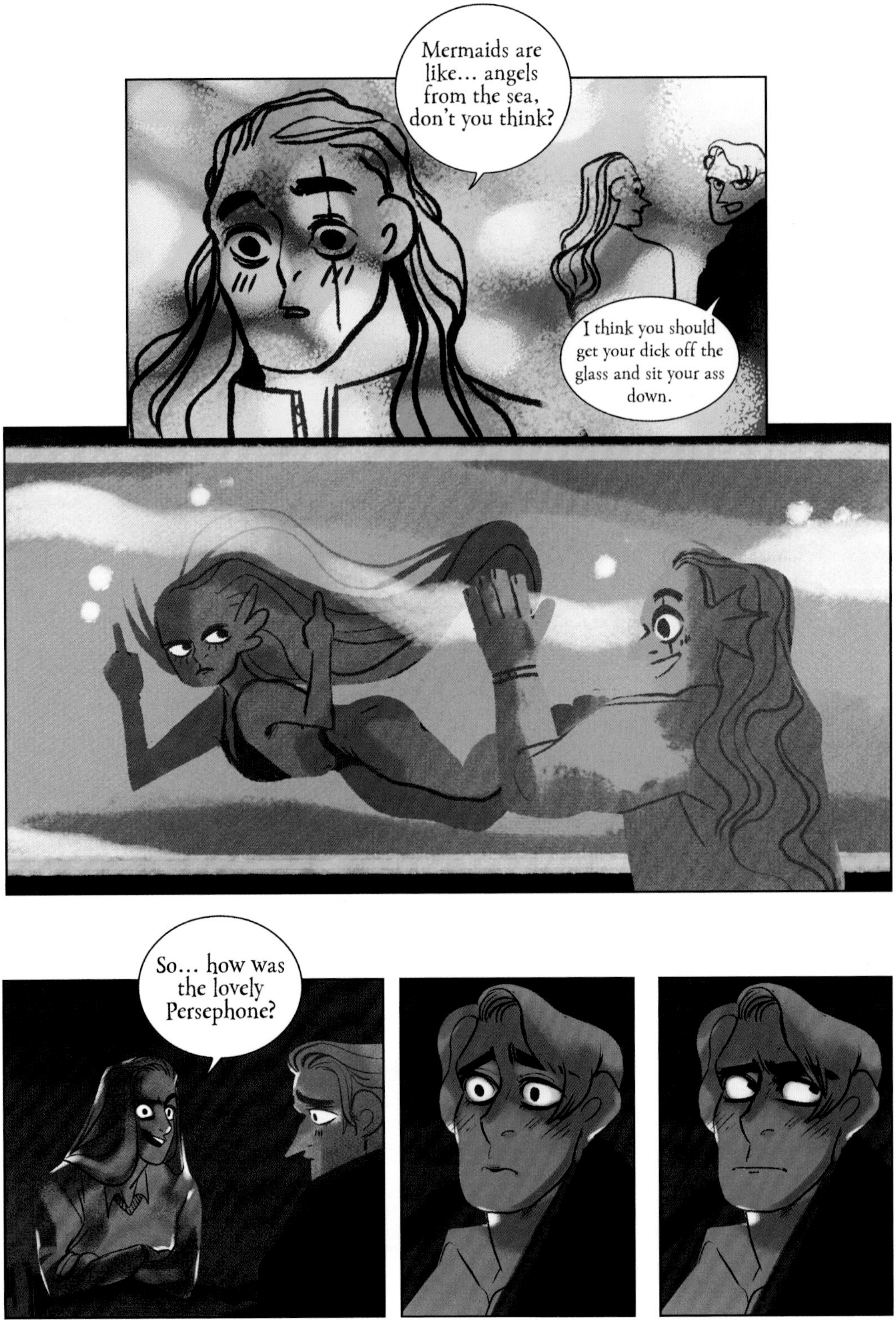
Mermaids are like... angels from the sea, don't you think?
I think you should get your dick off the glass and sit your ass down.
So... how was the lovely Persephone?

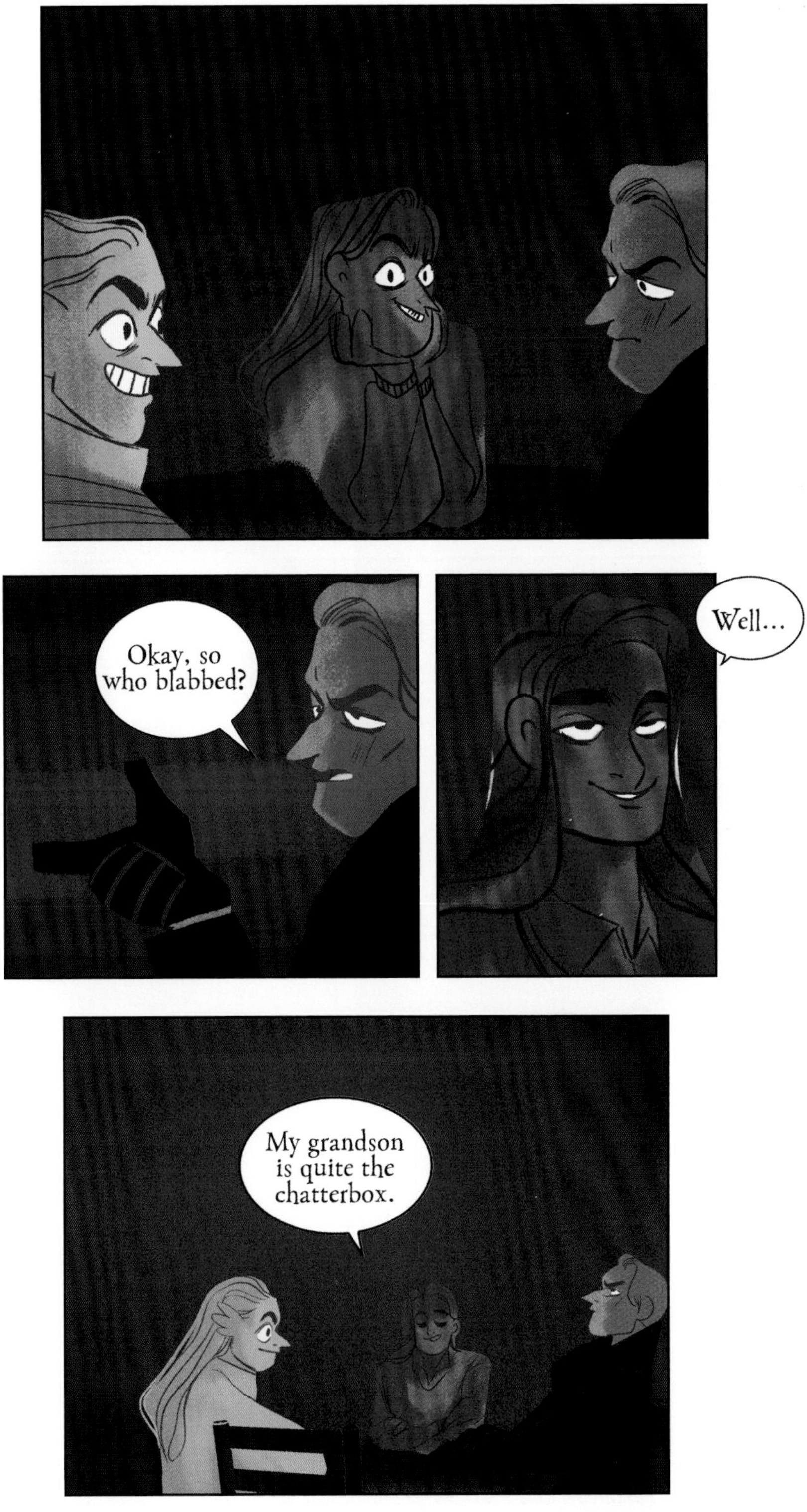
Okay, so who blabbed?
Well...
My grandson is quite the chatterbox.

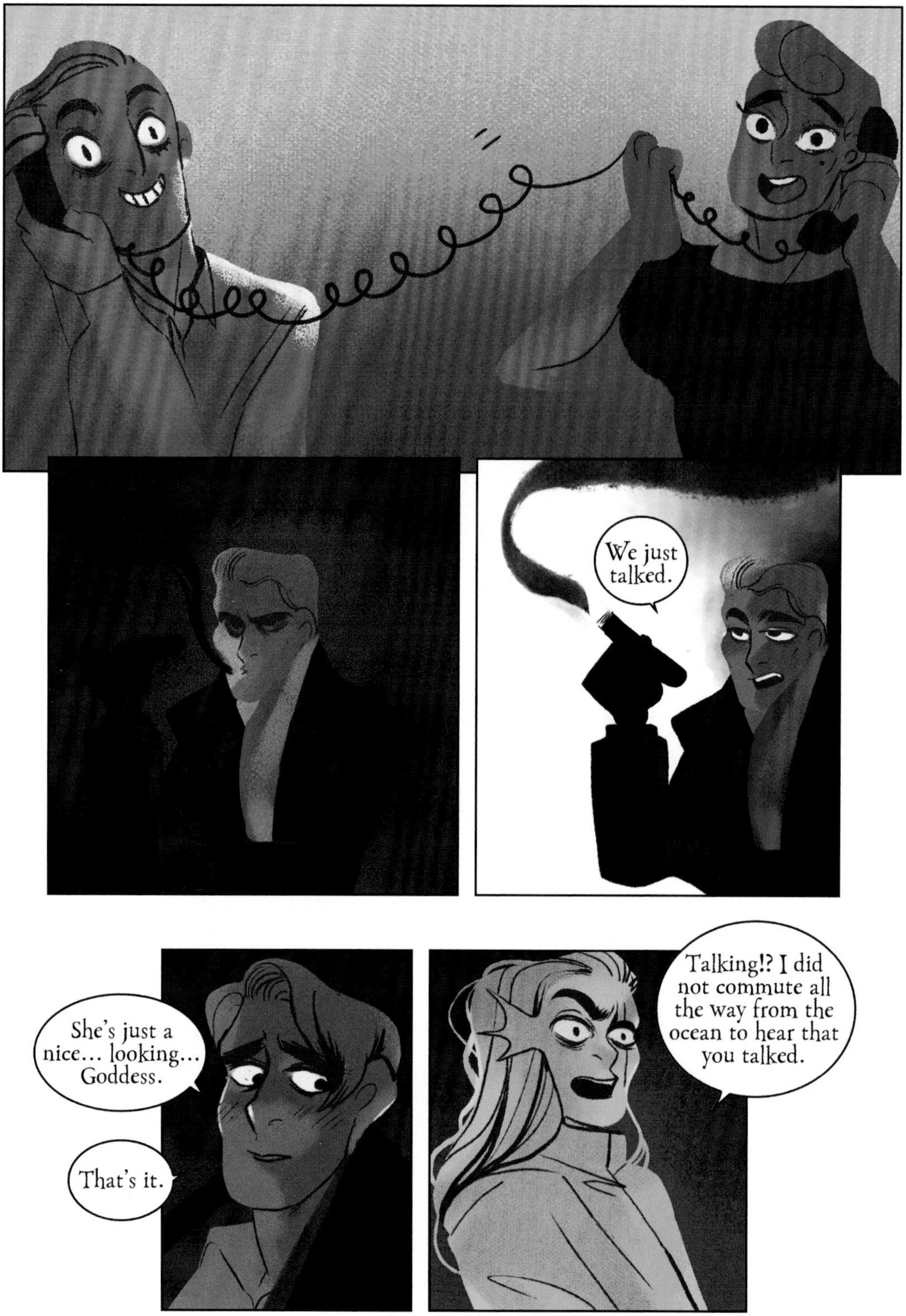
We just talked.
She's just a nice… looking… Goddess.
That's it.
Talking!? I did not commute all the way from the ocean to hear that you talked.

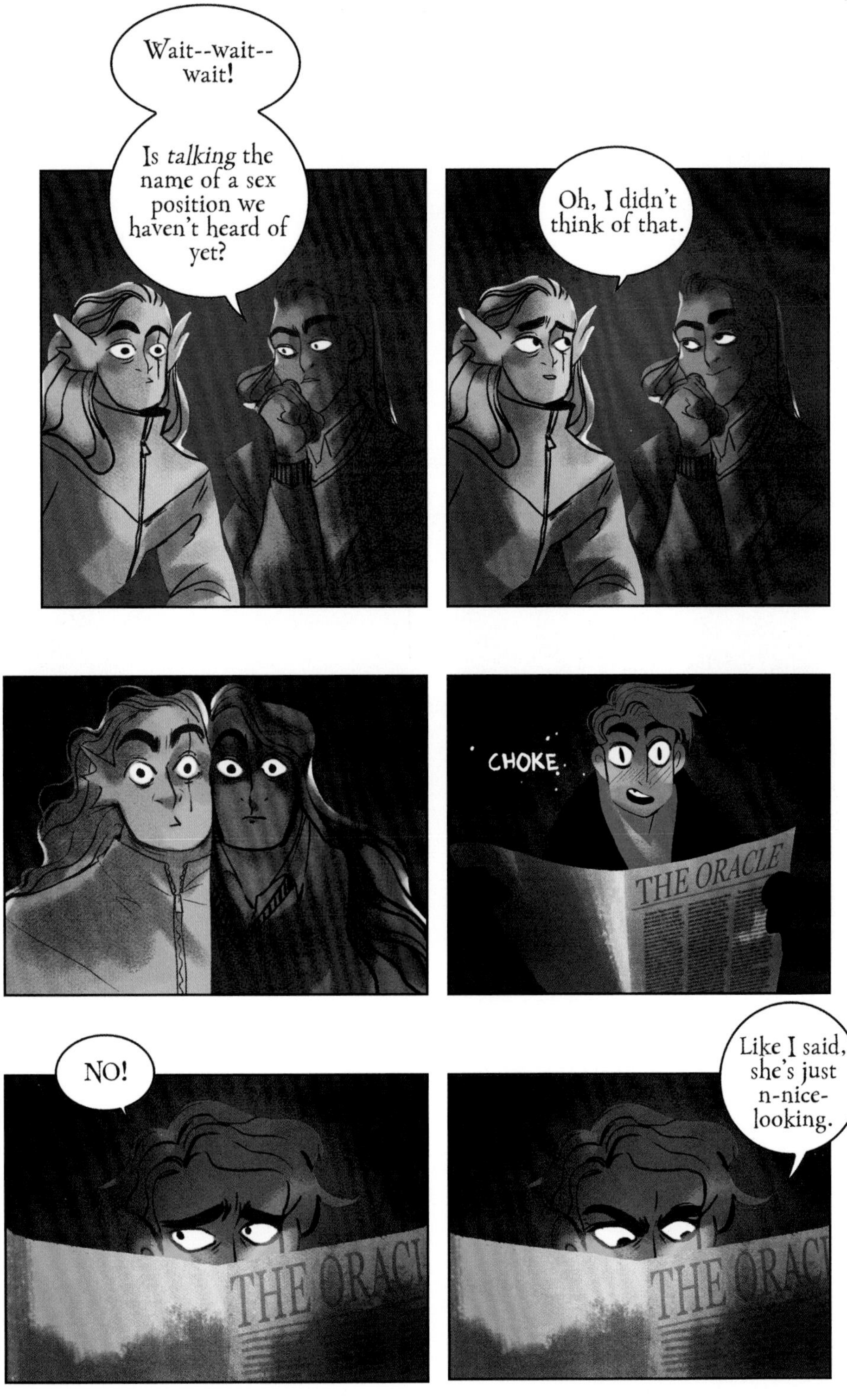
Wait--wait--wait!
Is *talking* the name of a sex position we haven't heard of yet?
Oh, I didn't think of that.
CHOKE
THE ORACLE
NO!
THE ORACL
Like I said, she's just n-nice-looking.
THE ORAC

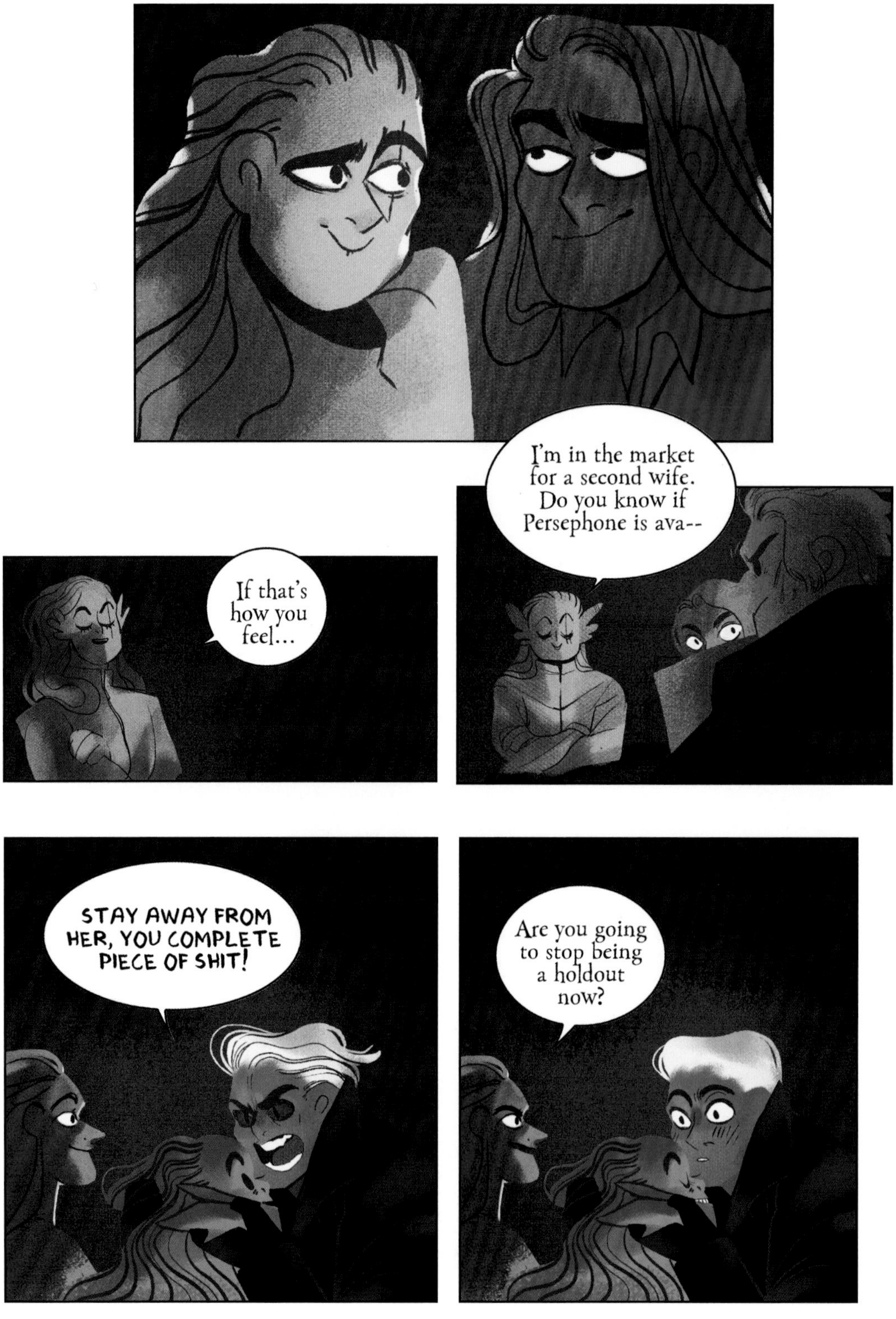
If that's how you feel...
I'm in the market for a second wife. Do you know if Persephone is ava--
STAY AWAY FROM HER, YOU COMPLETE PIECE OF SHIT!
Are you going to stop being a holdout now?

EPISODE 19: A FIFTH OF GIN

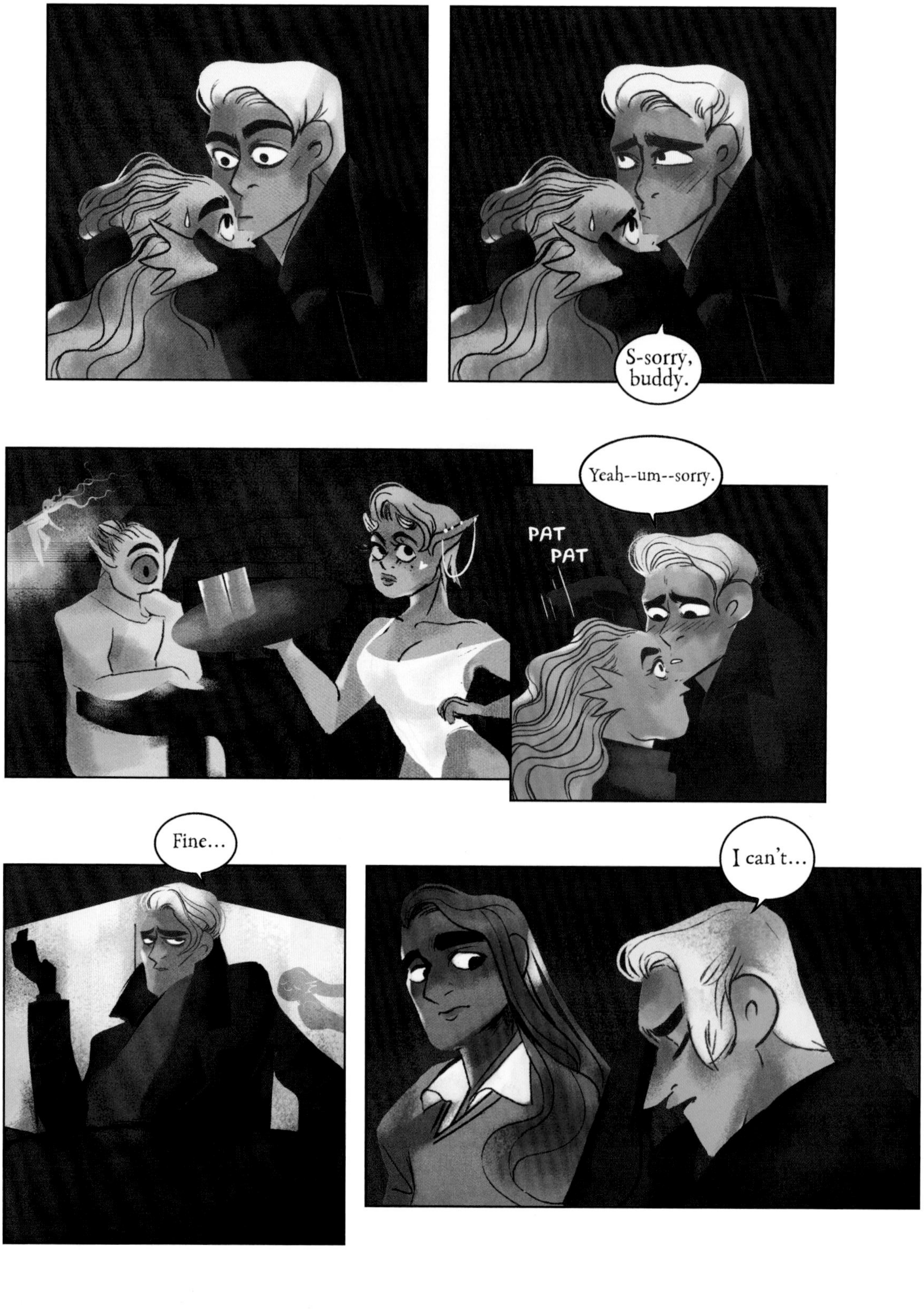

S-sorry, buddy.
Yeah--um--sorry.
PAT PAT
Fine...
I can't...

HESITATE

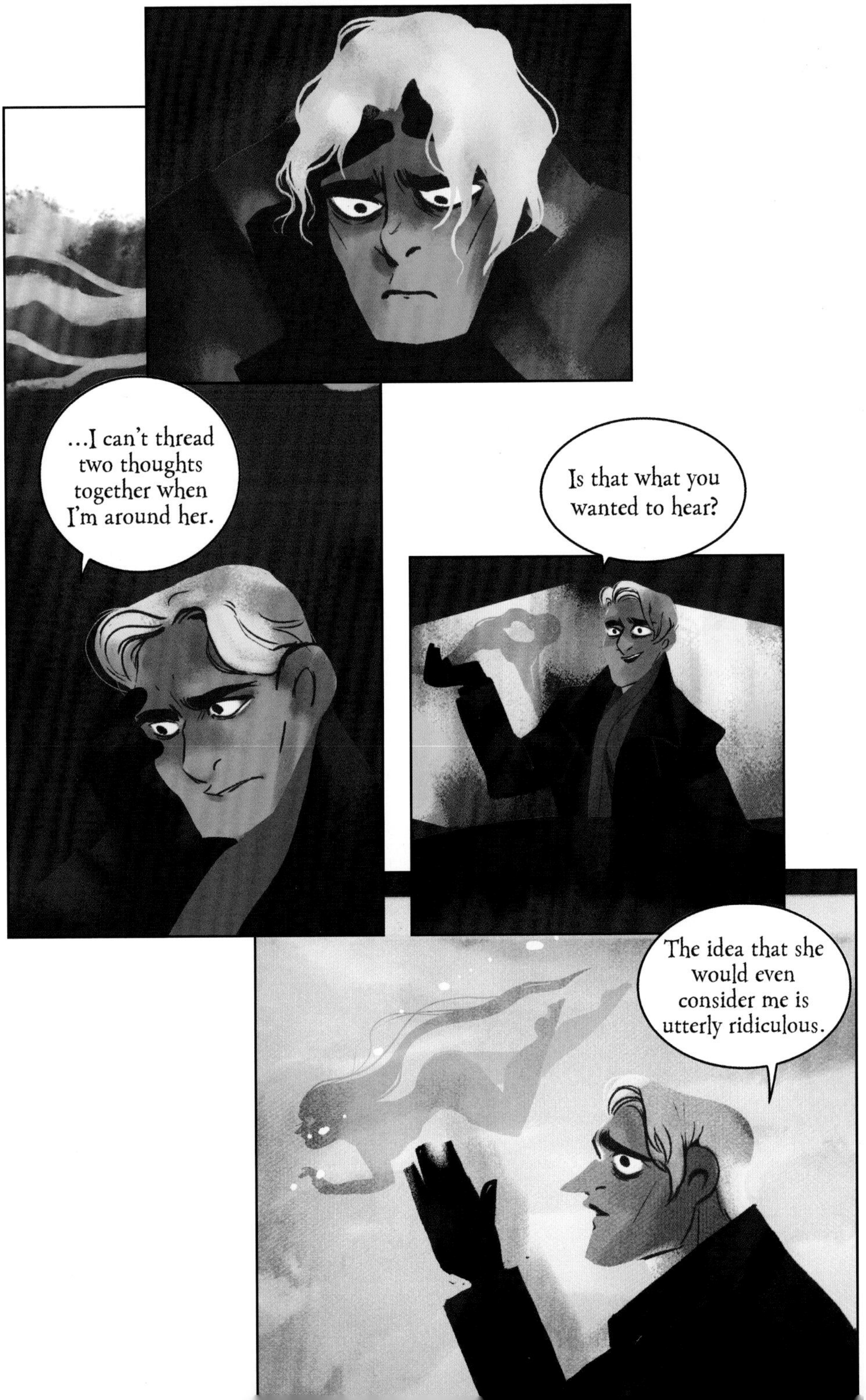

...I can't thread two thoughts together when I'm around her.
Is that what you wanted to hear?
The idea that she would even consider me is utterly ridiculous.

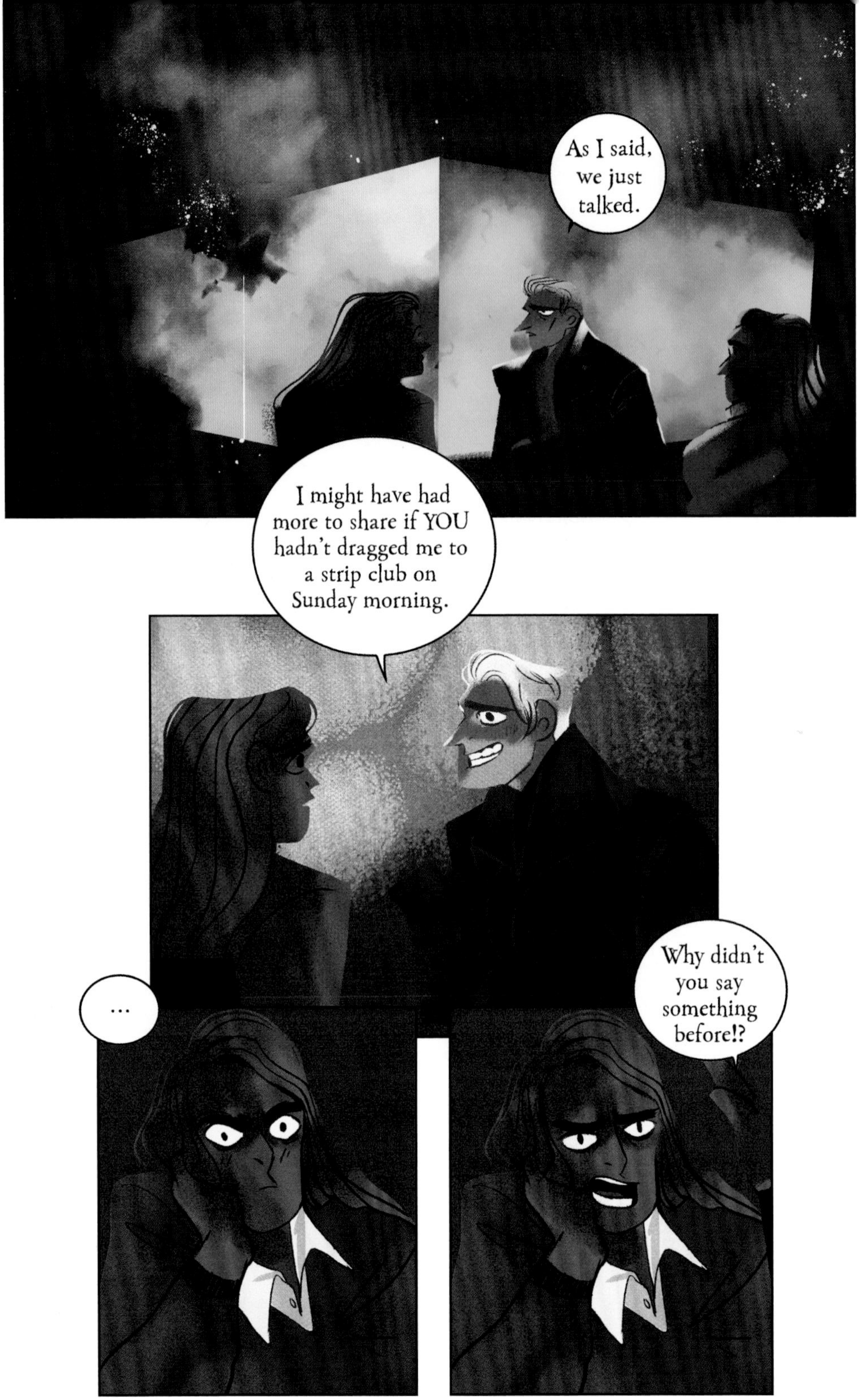
As I said, we just talked.
I might have had more to share if YOU hadn't dragged me to a strip club on Sunday morning.
...
Why didn't you say something before!?

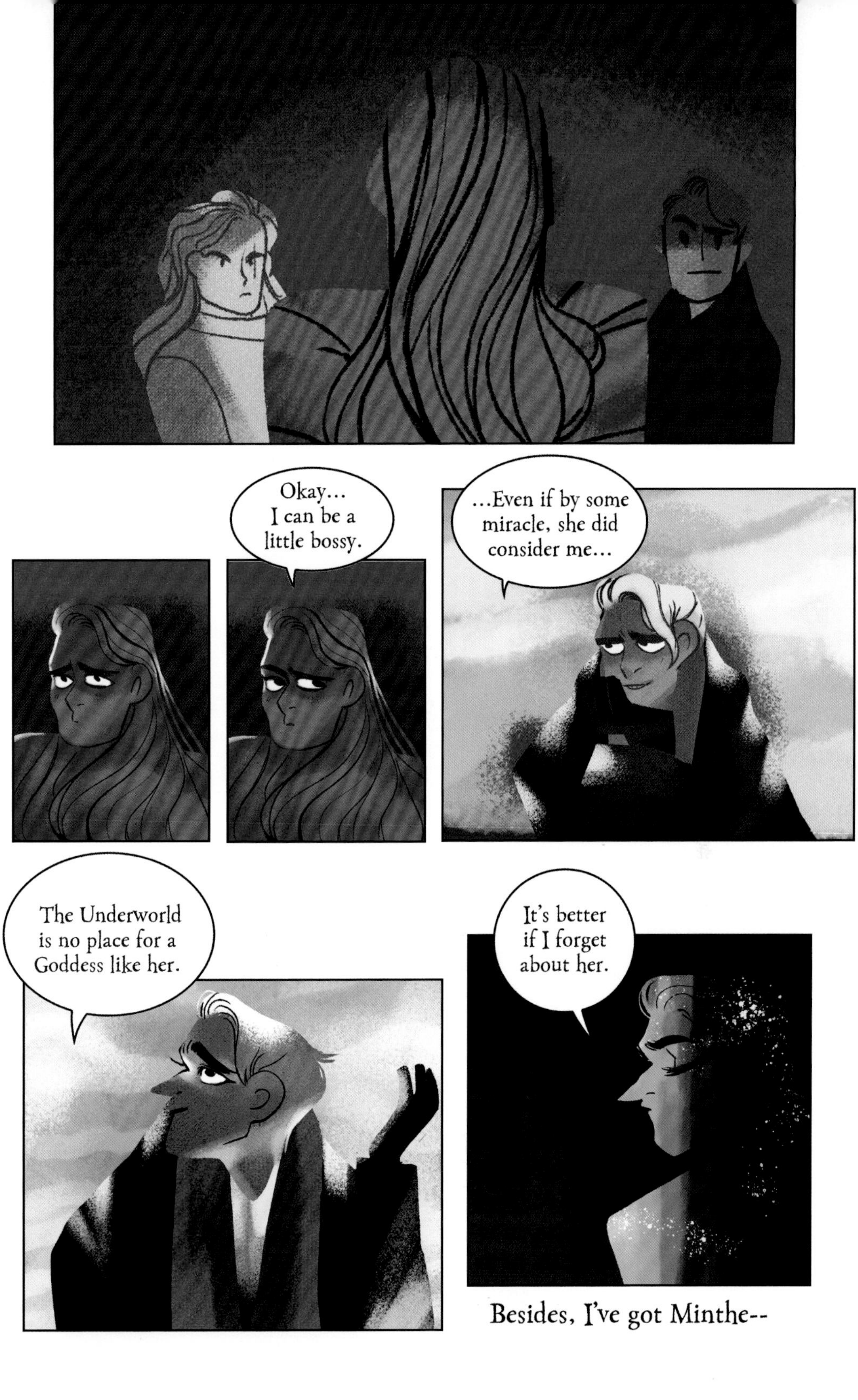
Okay... I can be a little bossy.
...Even if by some miracle, she did consider me...
The Underworld is no place for a Goddess like her.
It's better if I forget about her.
Besides, I've got Minthe--

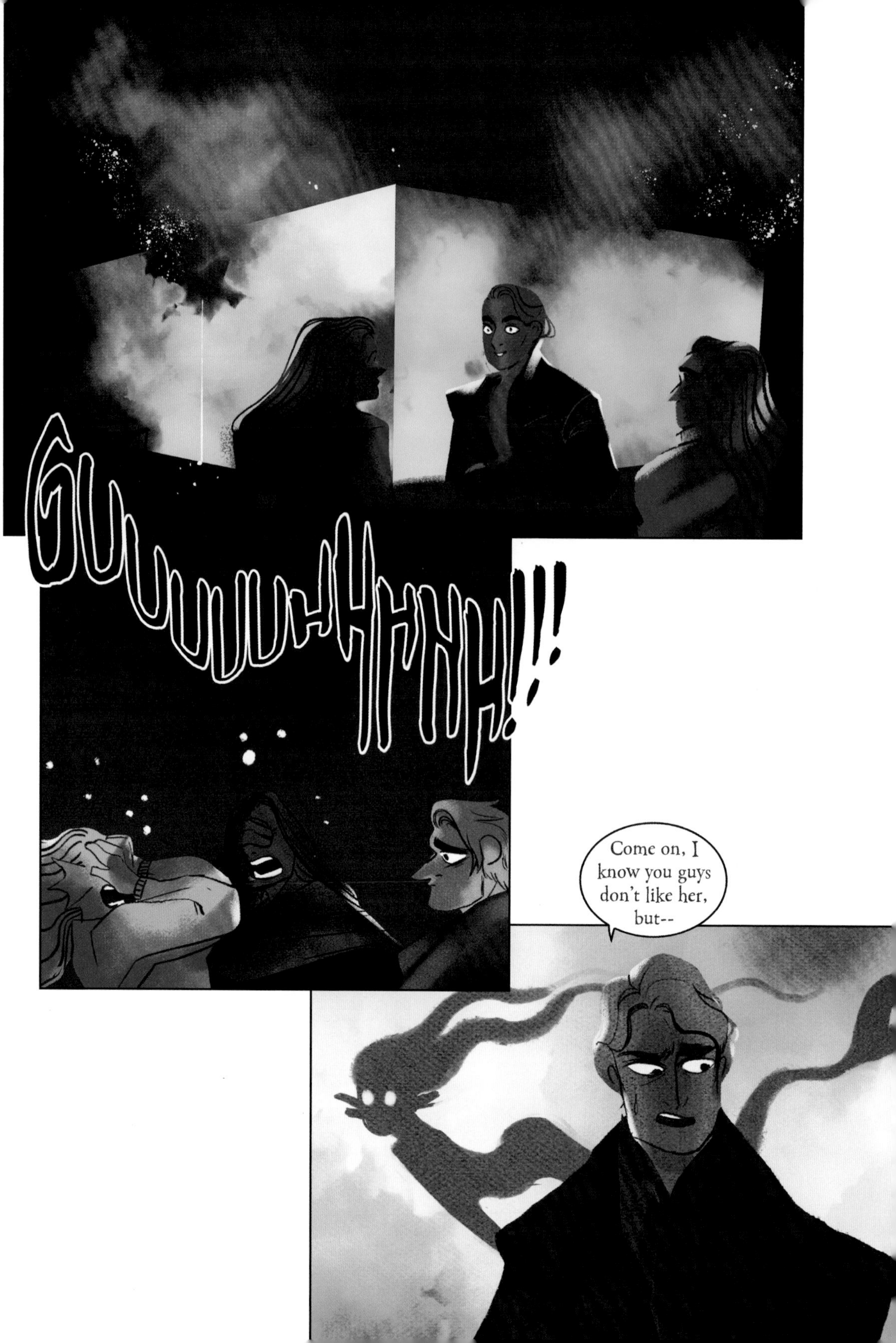
GUUUUUHHHH!!
Come on, I know you guys don't like her, but--

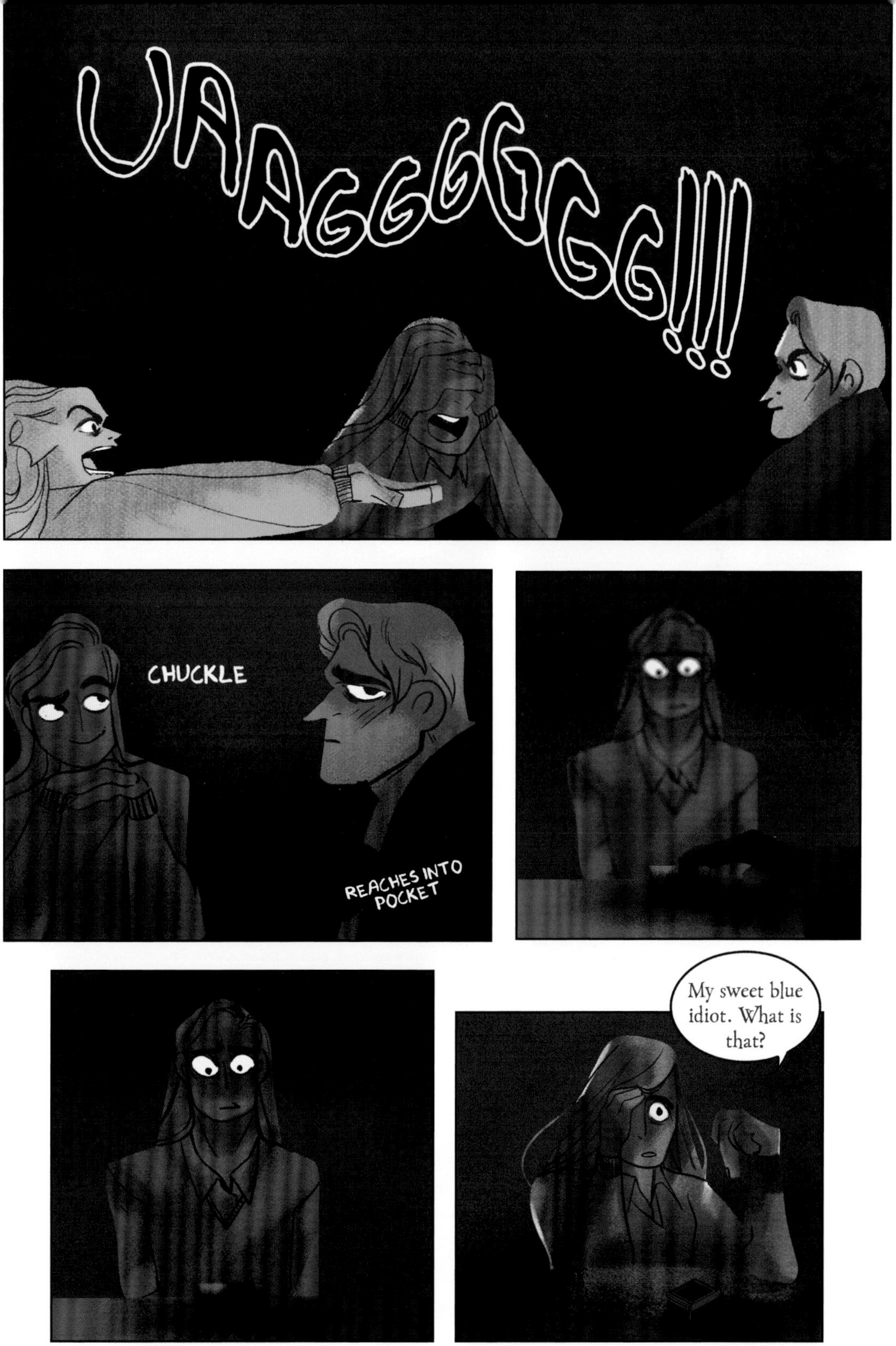
UAAGGGGGG!!!
CHUCKLE
REACHES INTO POCKET
My sweet blue idiot. What is that?

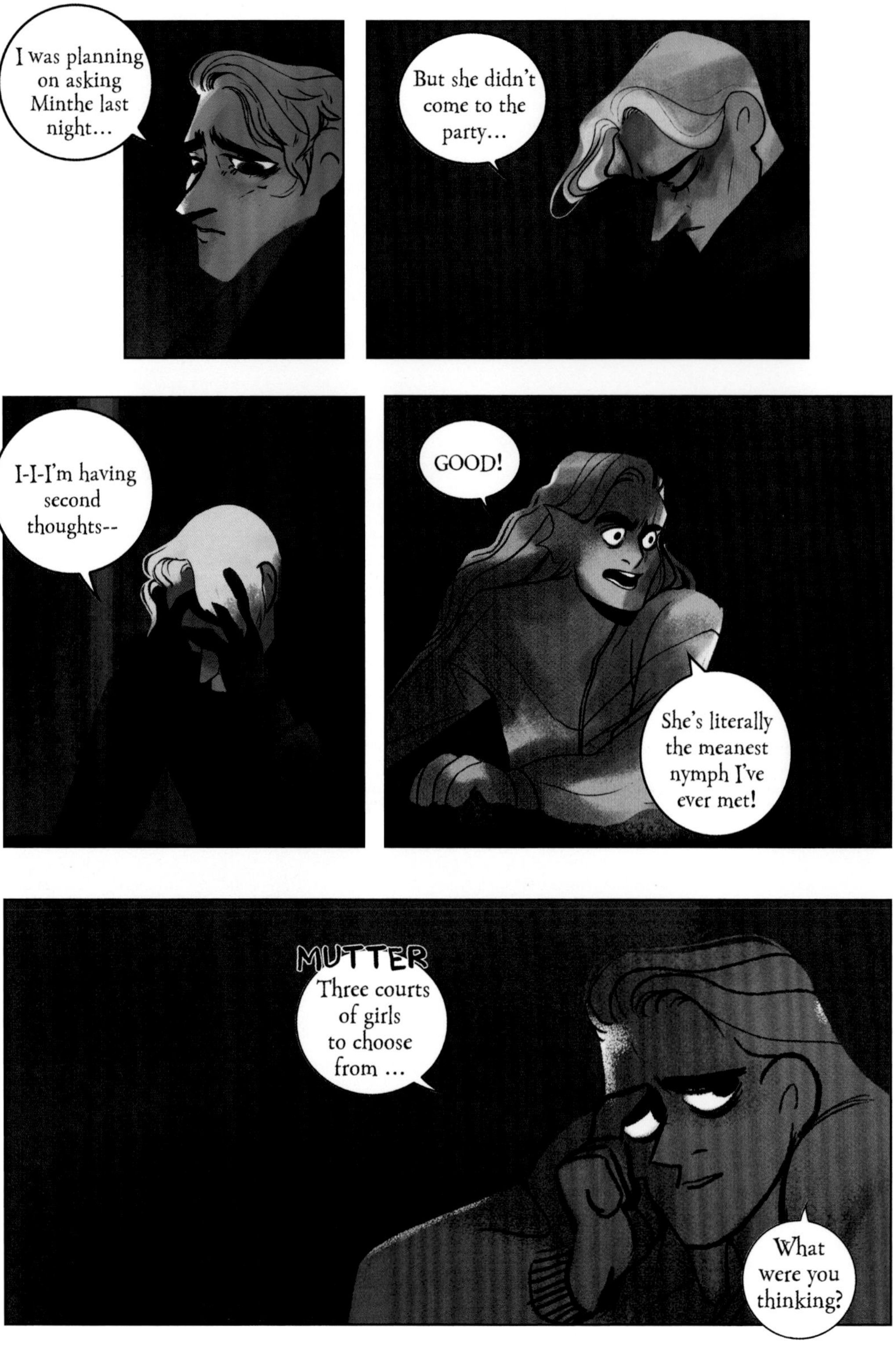
I was planning on asking Minthe last night...
But she didn't come to the party...
I-I-I'm having second thoughts--
GOOD!
She's literally the meanest nymph I've ever met!
MUTTER
Three courts of girls to choose from ...
What were you thinking?

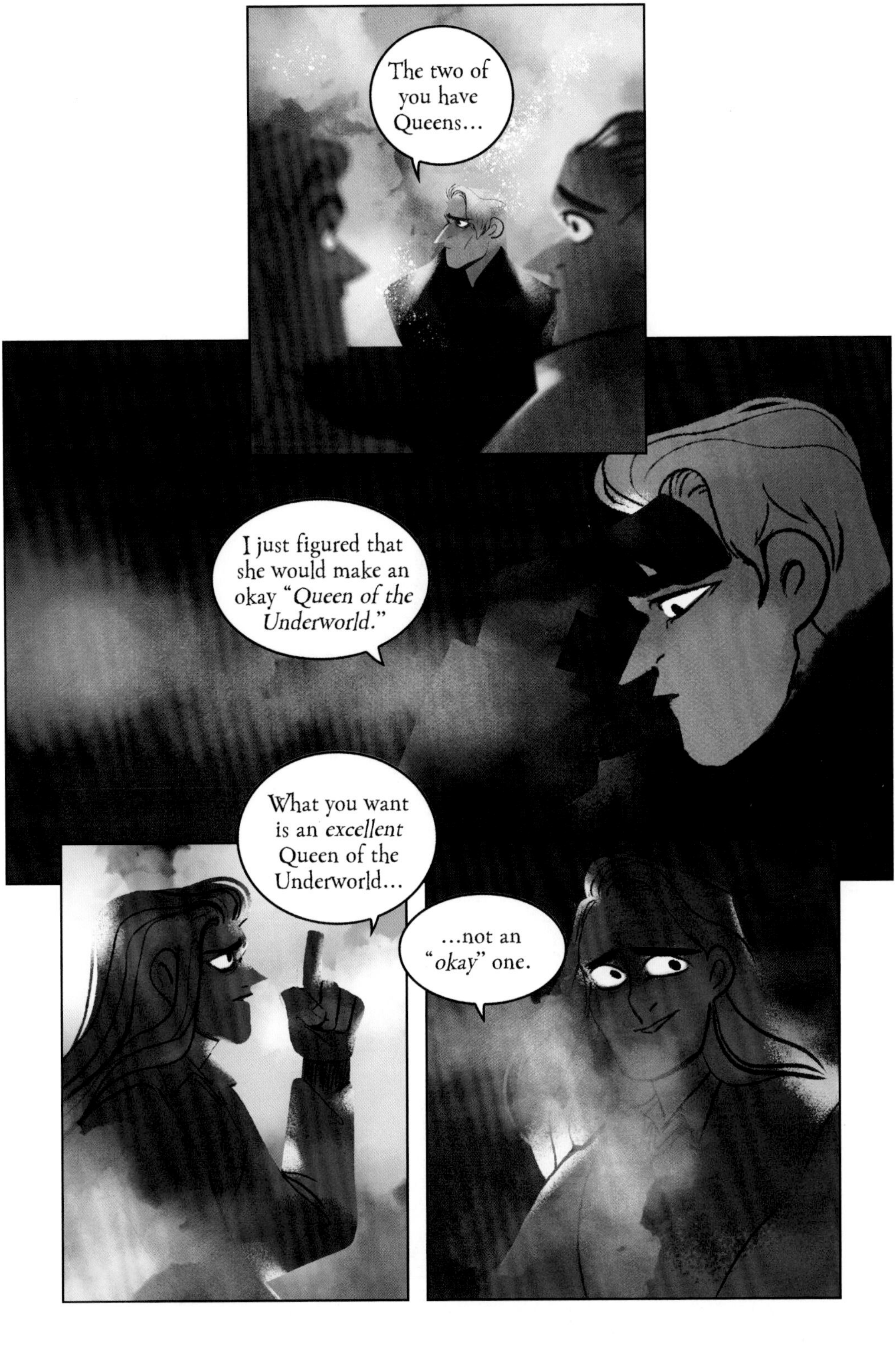
The two of you have Queens...
I just figured that she would make an okay *"Queen of the Underworld."*
What you want is an *excellent* Queen of the Underworld...
...not an *"okay"* one.

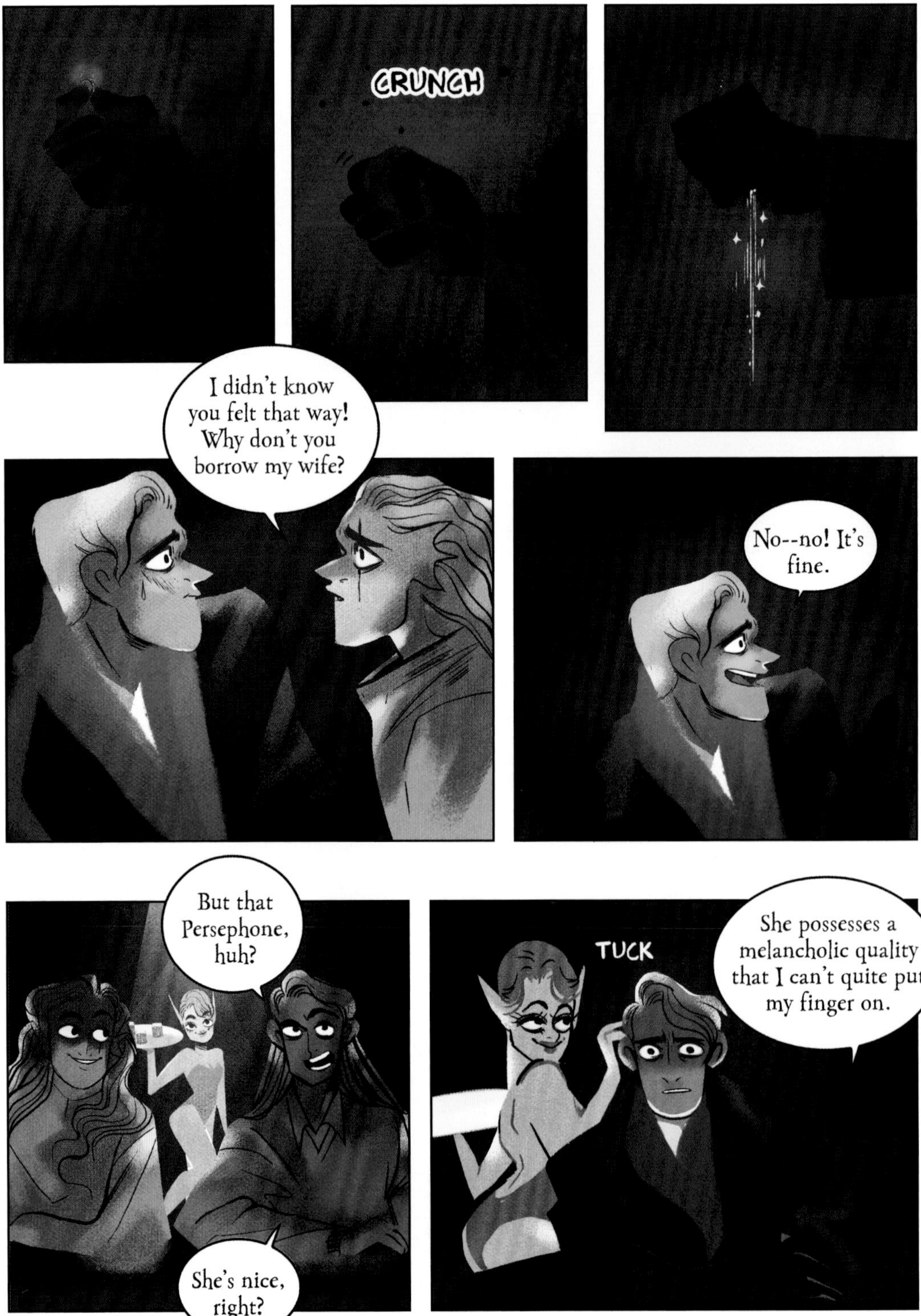
CRUNCH
I didn't know you felt that way! Why don't you borrow my wife?
No--no! It's fine.
But that Persephone, huh?
She's nice, right?
TUCK
She possesses a melancholic quality that I can't quite put my finger on.

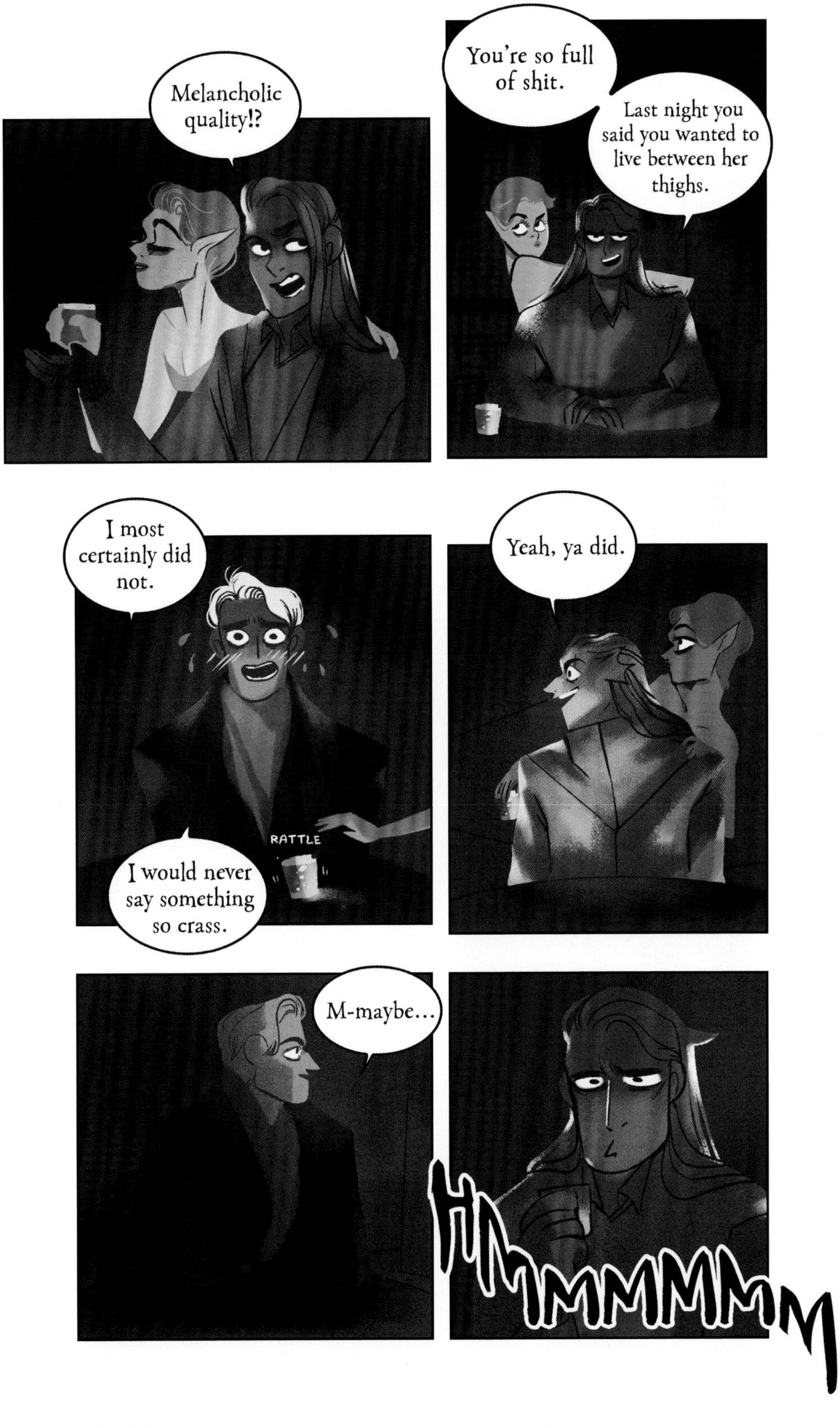
Melancholic quality!?
You're so full of shit.
Last night you said you wanted to live between her thighs.
I most certainly did not.
RATTLE
I would never say something so crass.
Yeah, ya did.
M-maybe...
HMMMMMM

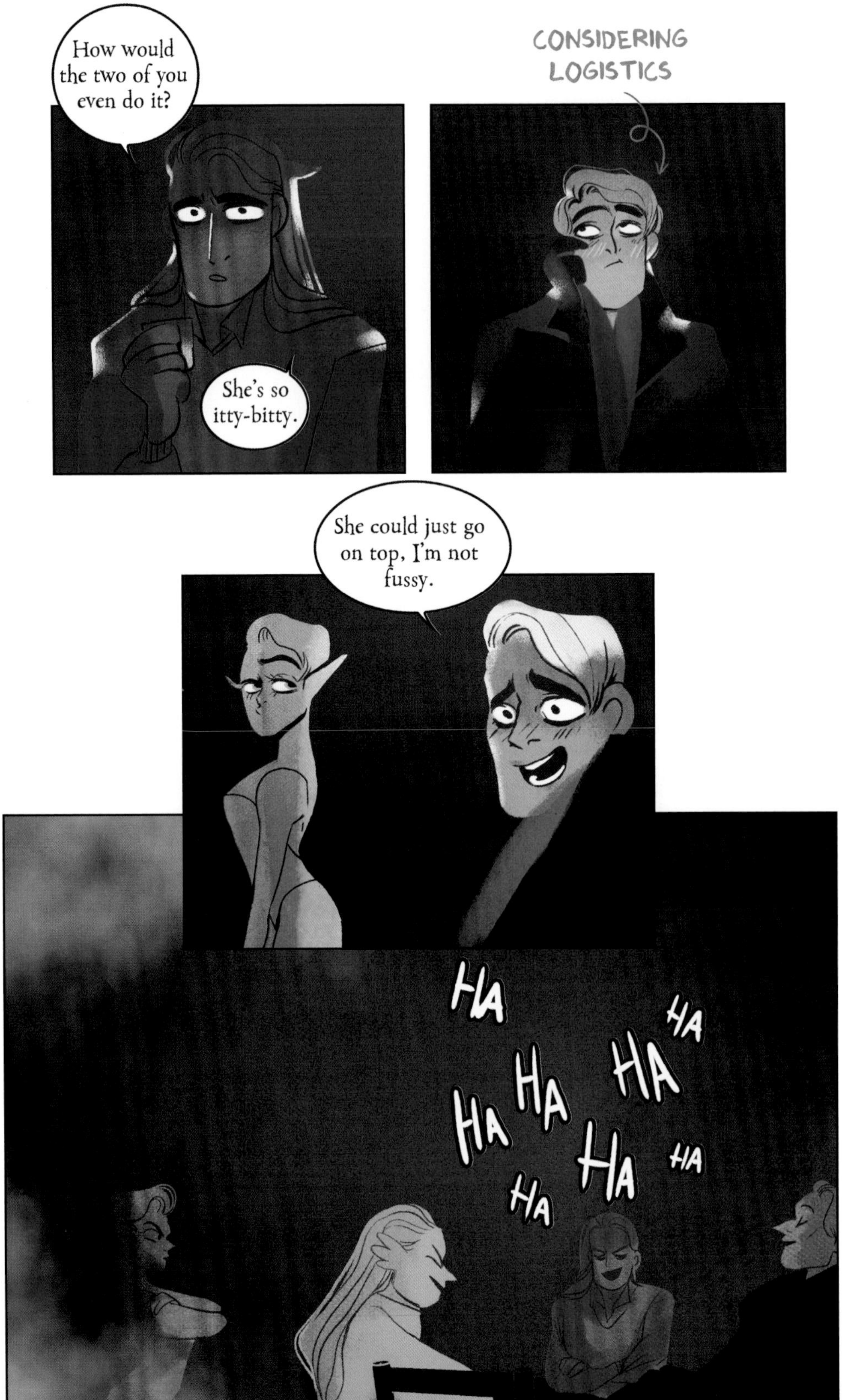
How would the two of you even do it?
She's so itty-bitty.
CONSIDERING LOGISTICS
She could just go on top, I'm not fussy.
HA HA HA HA HA HA HA HA HA

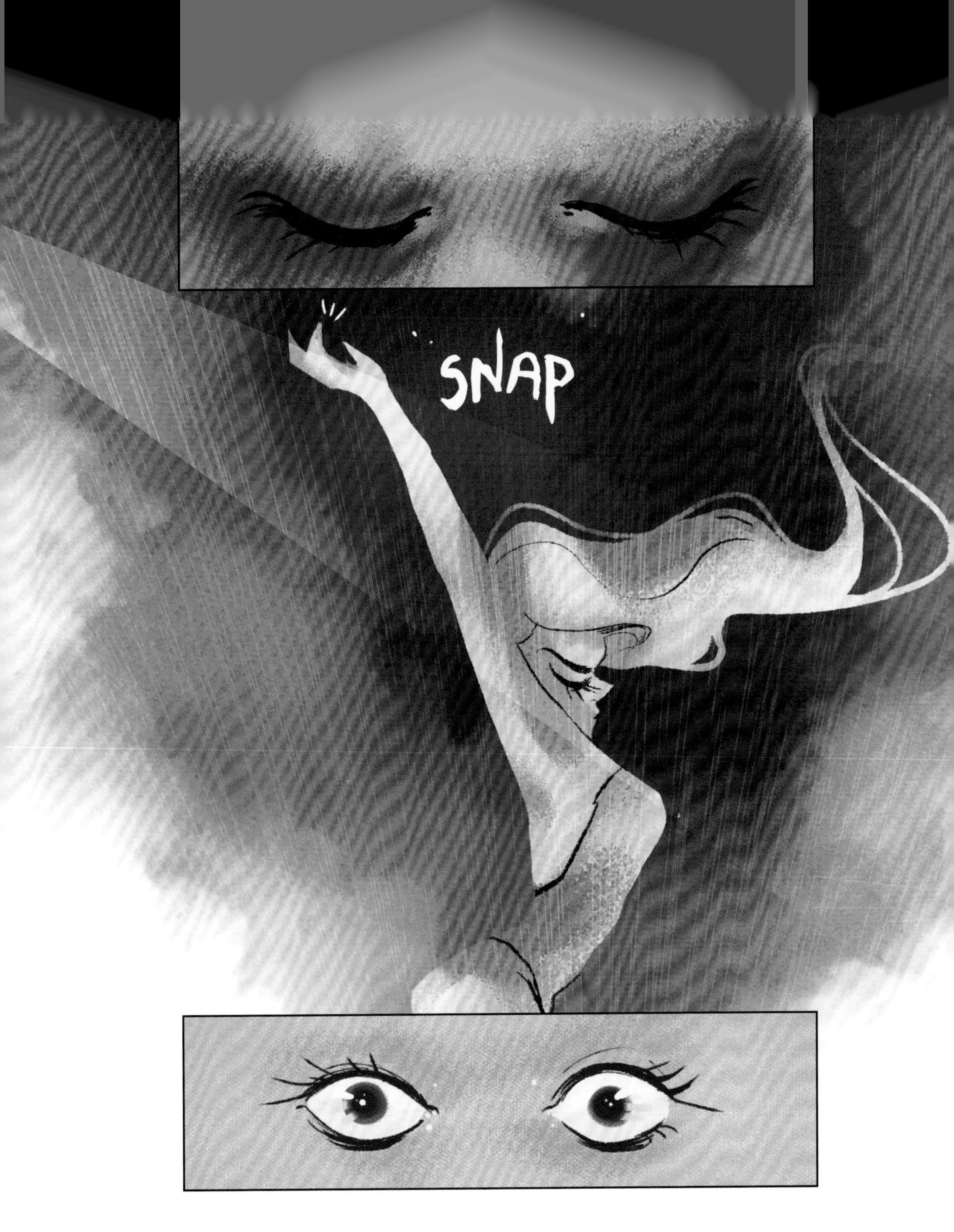
SNAP

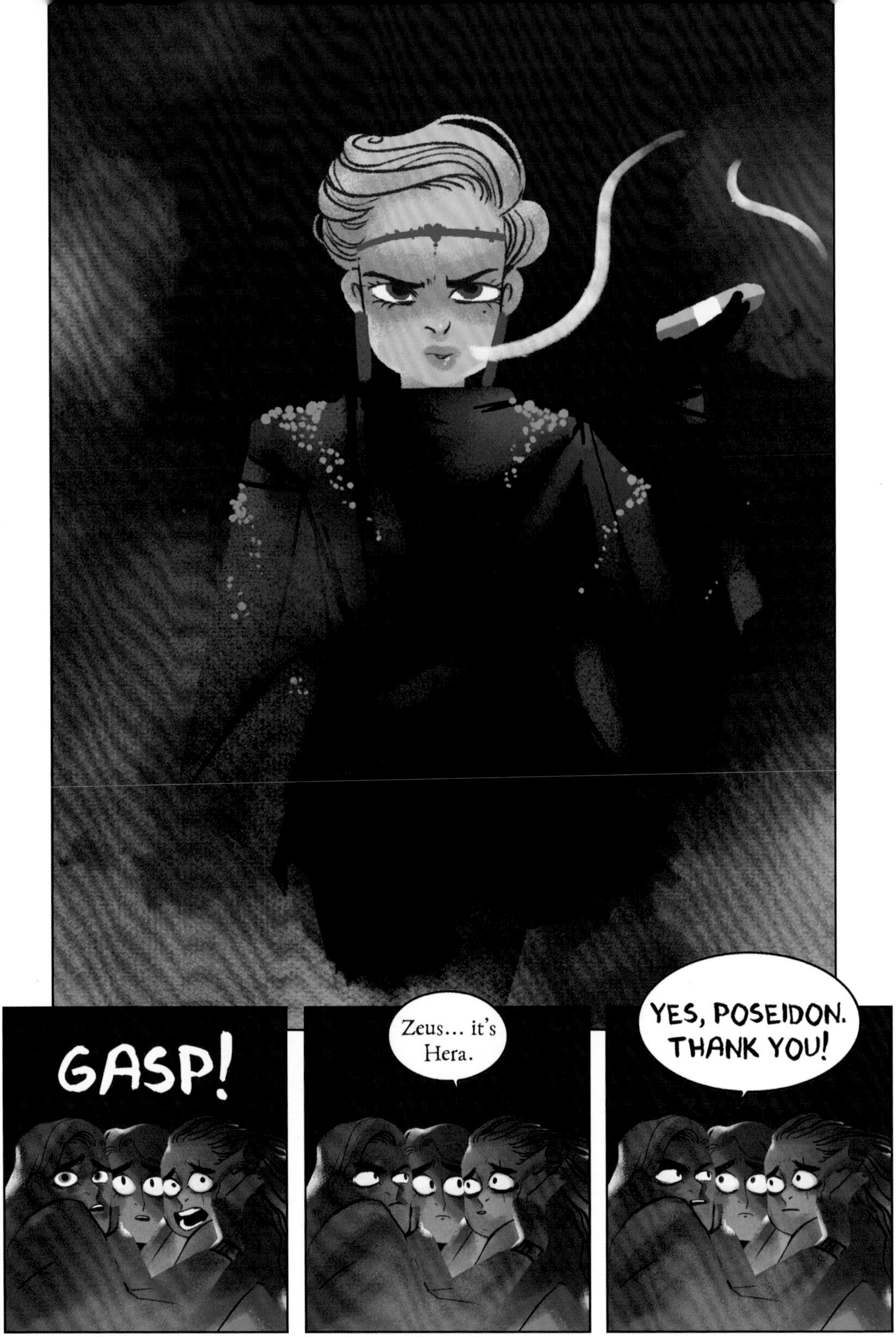
GASP!
Zeus… it's Hera.
YES, POSEIDON. THANK YOU!

Some time ago!

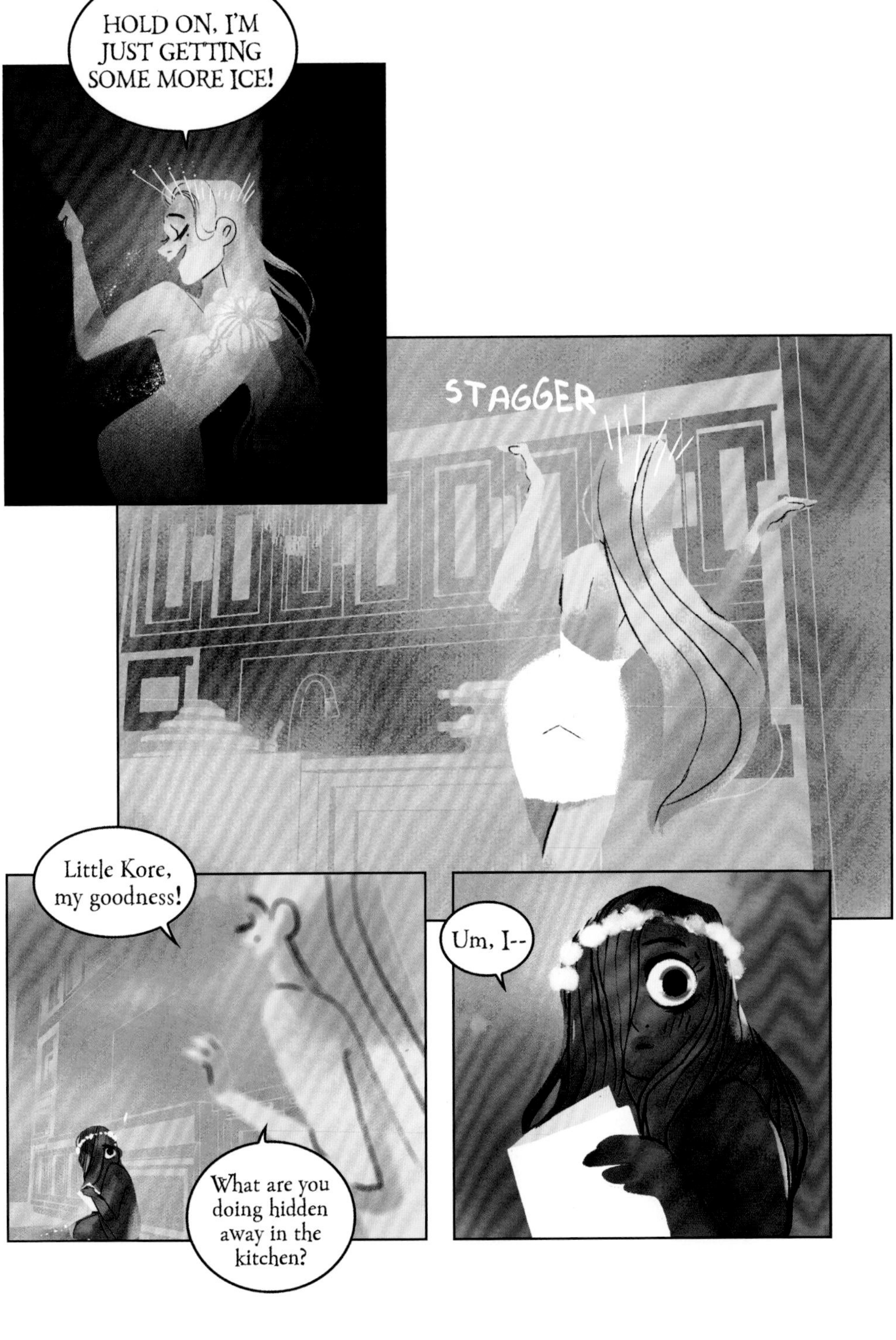

HOLD ON, I'M JUST GETTING SOME MORE ICE!
STAGGER
Little Kore, my goodness!
What are you doing hidden away in the kitchen?
Um, I--

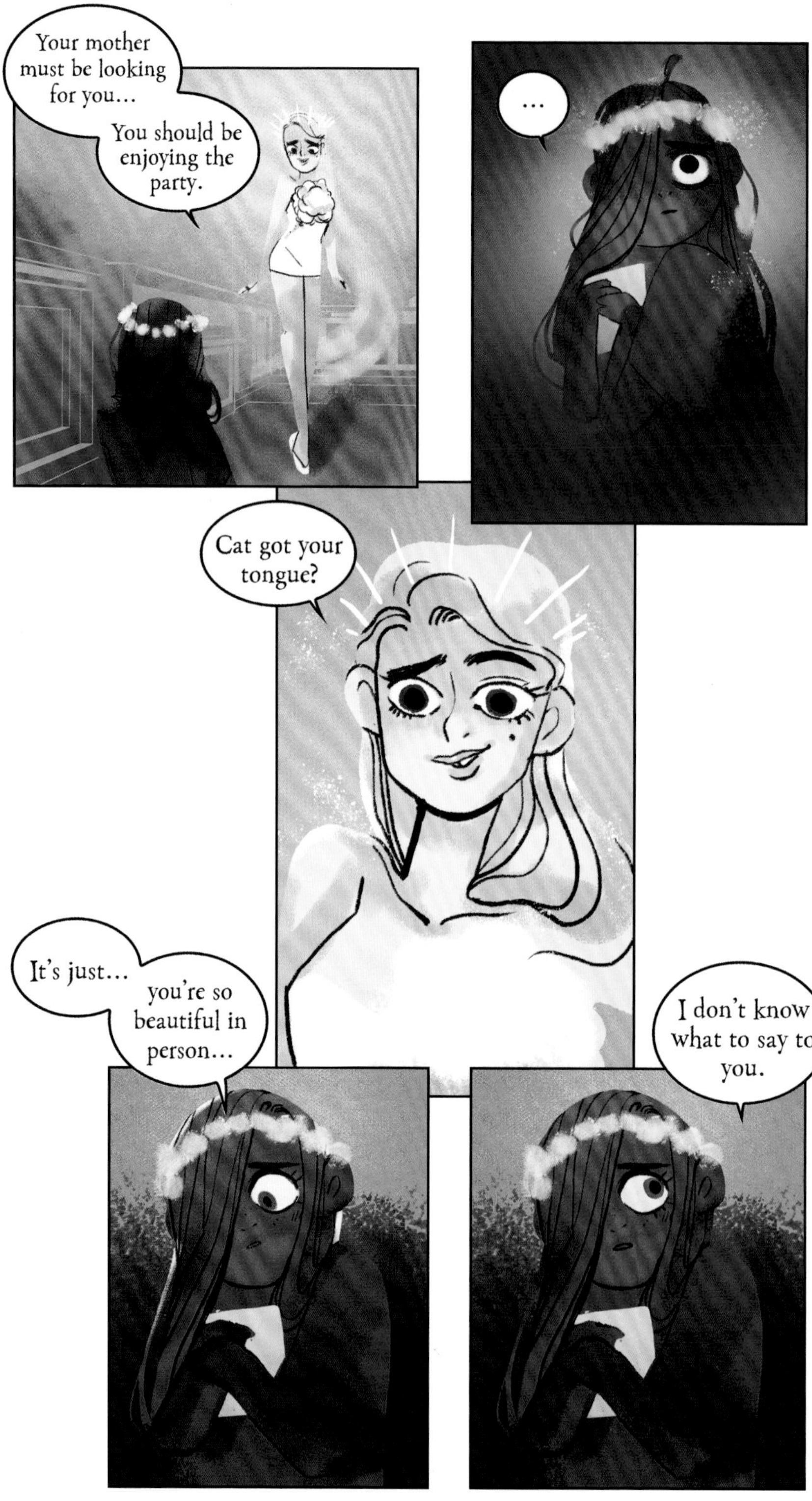
Your mother must be looking for you...
You should be enjoying the party.
...
Cat got your tongue?
It's just... you're so beautiful in person...
I don't know what to say to you.

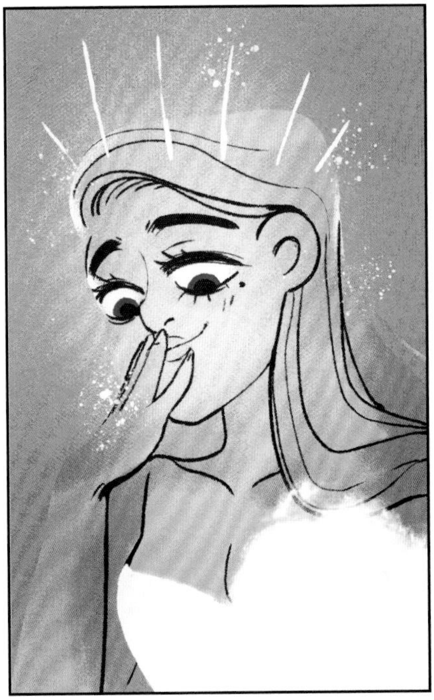

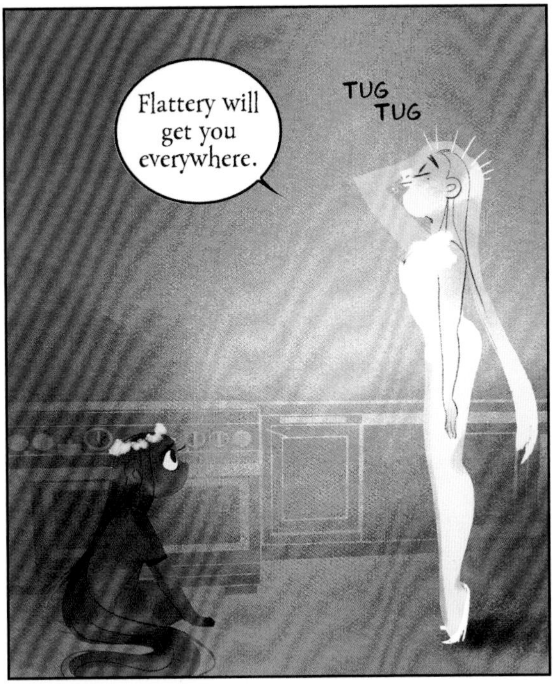
Flattery will get you everywhere.
TUG TUG

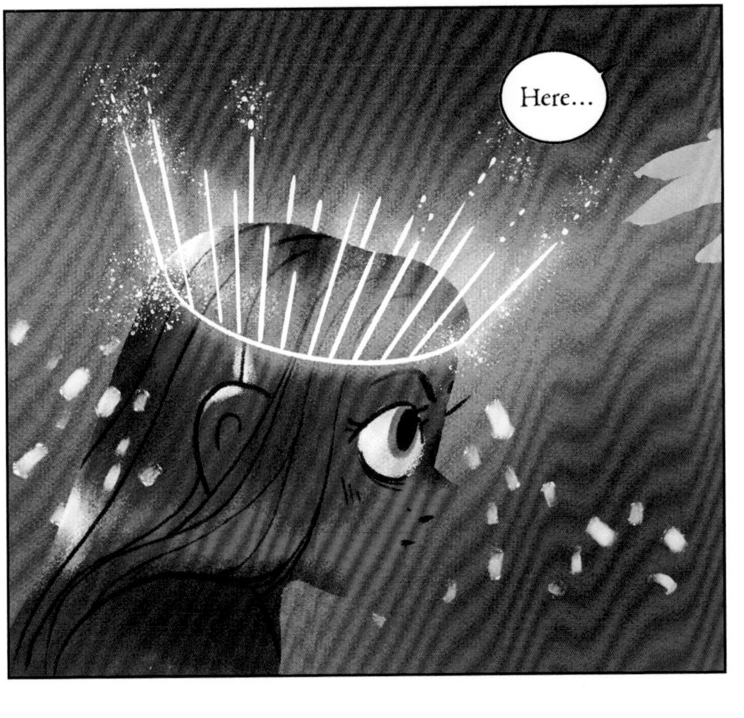
Here...

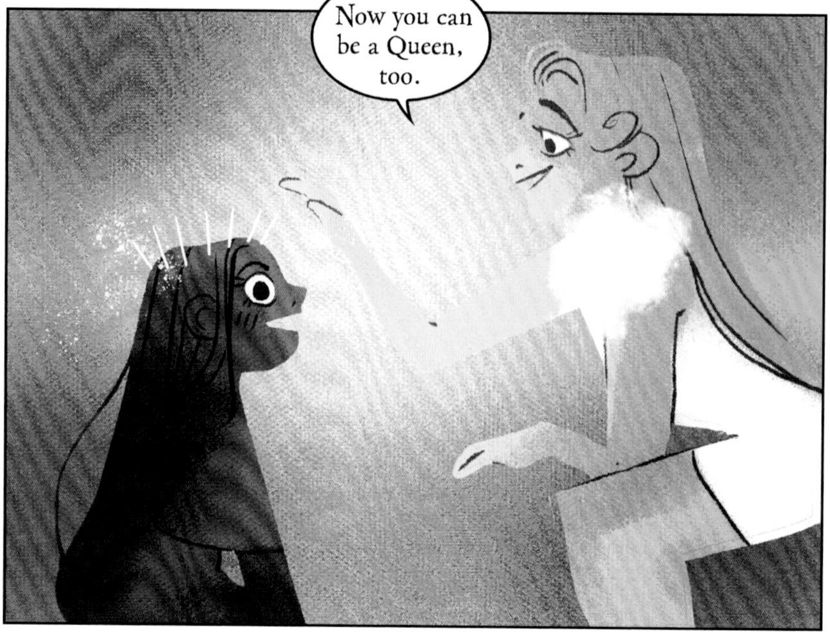
Now you can be a Queen, too.

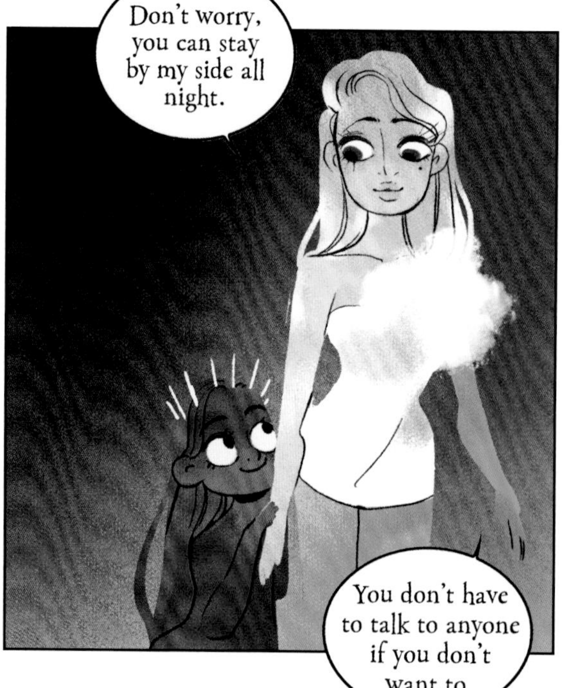
Don't worry, you can stay by my side all night.
You don't have to talk to anyone if you don't want to.

EPISODE 20: TREAT

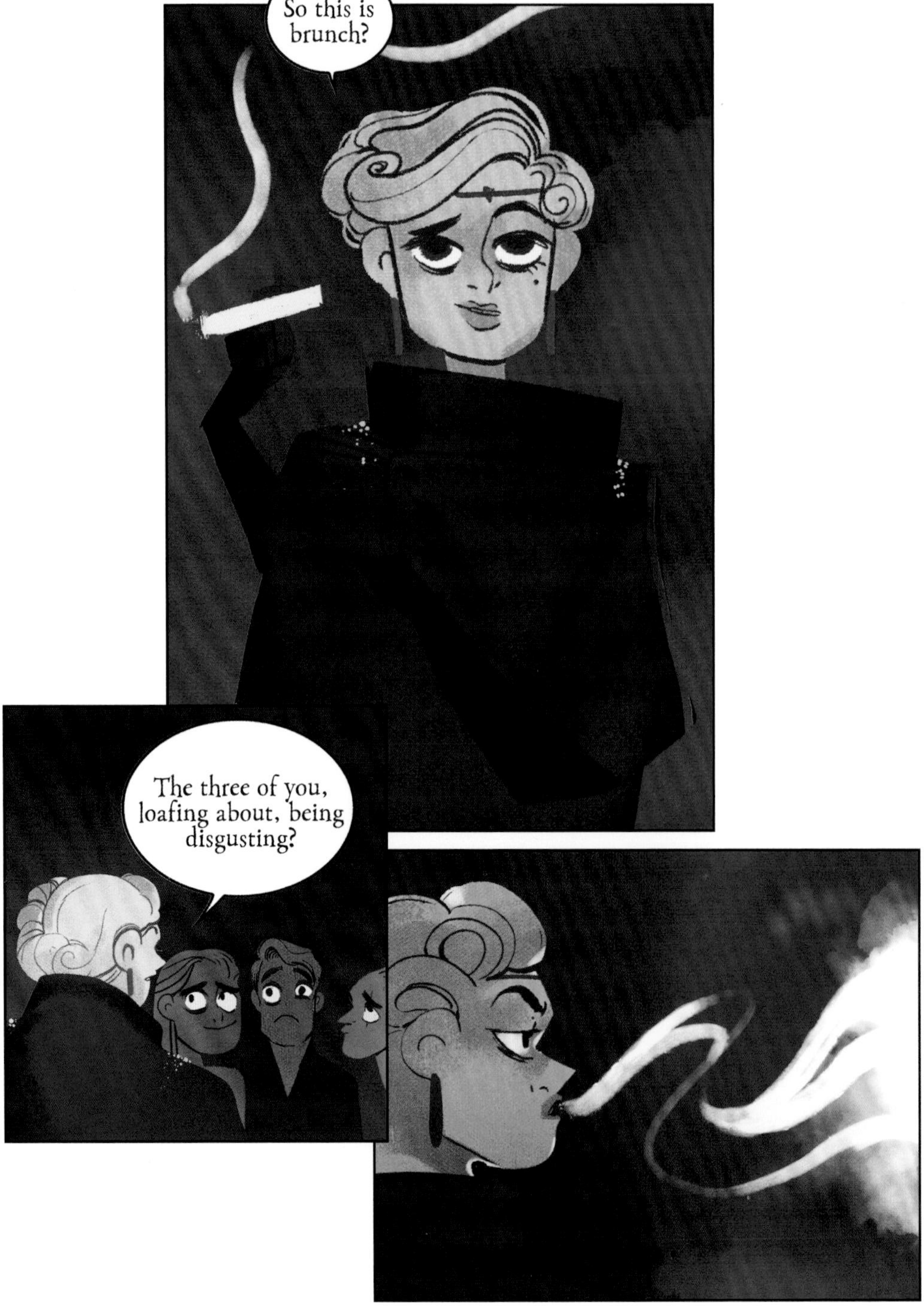
So this is brunch?
The three of you, loafing about, being disgusting?

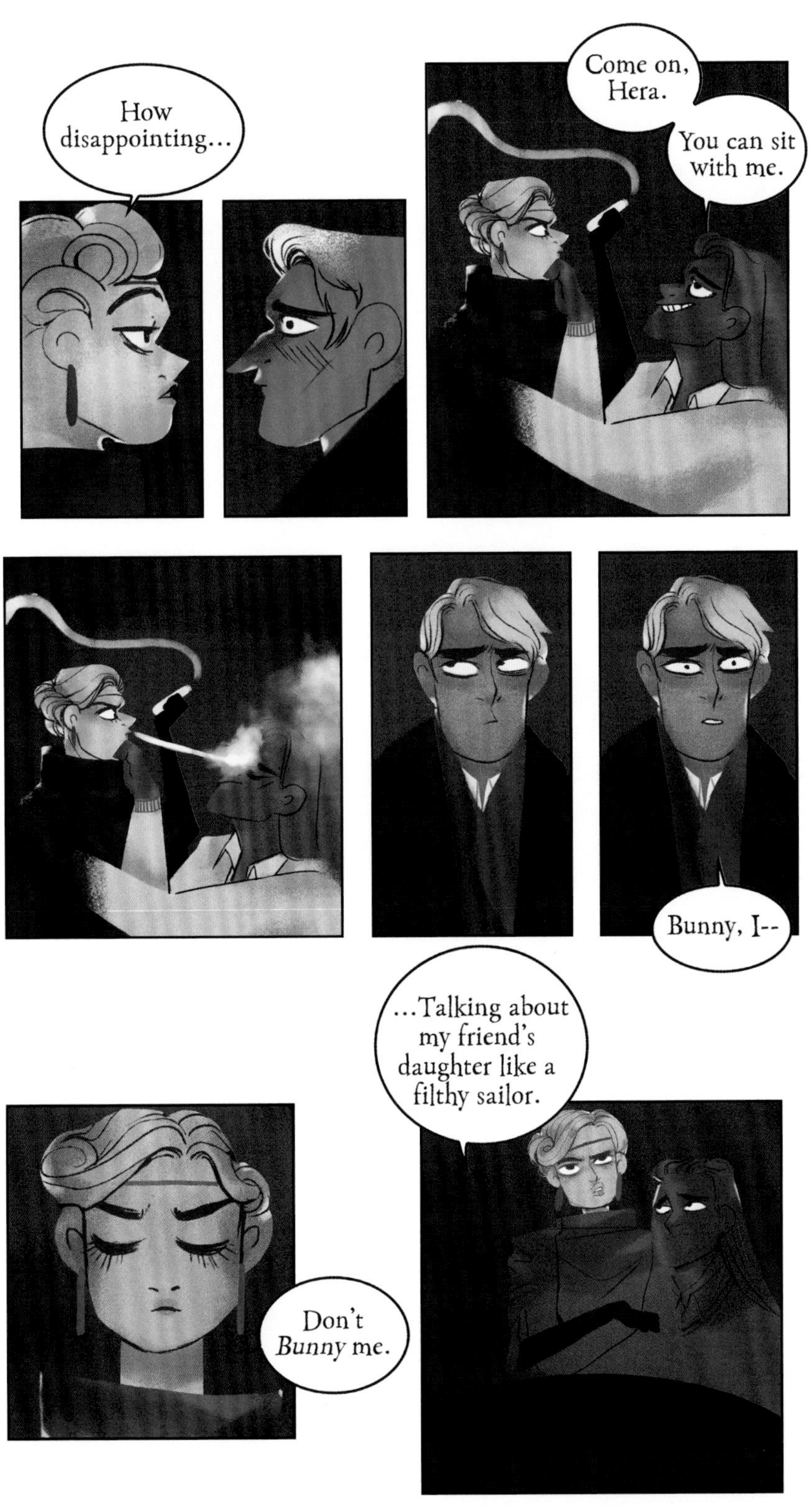
How disappointing...
Come on, Hera.
You can sit with me.
Bunny, I--
...Talking about my friend's daughter like a filthy sailor.
Don't *Bunny* me.

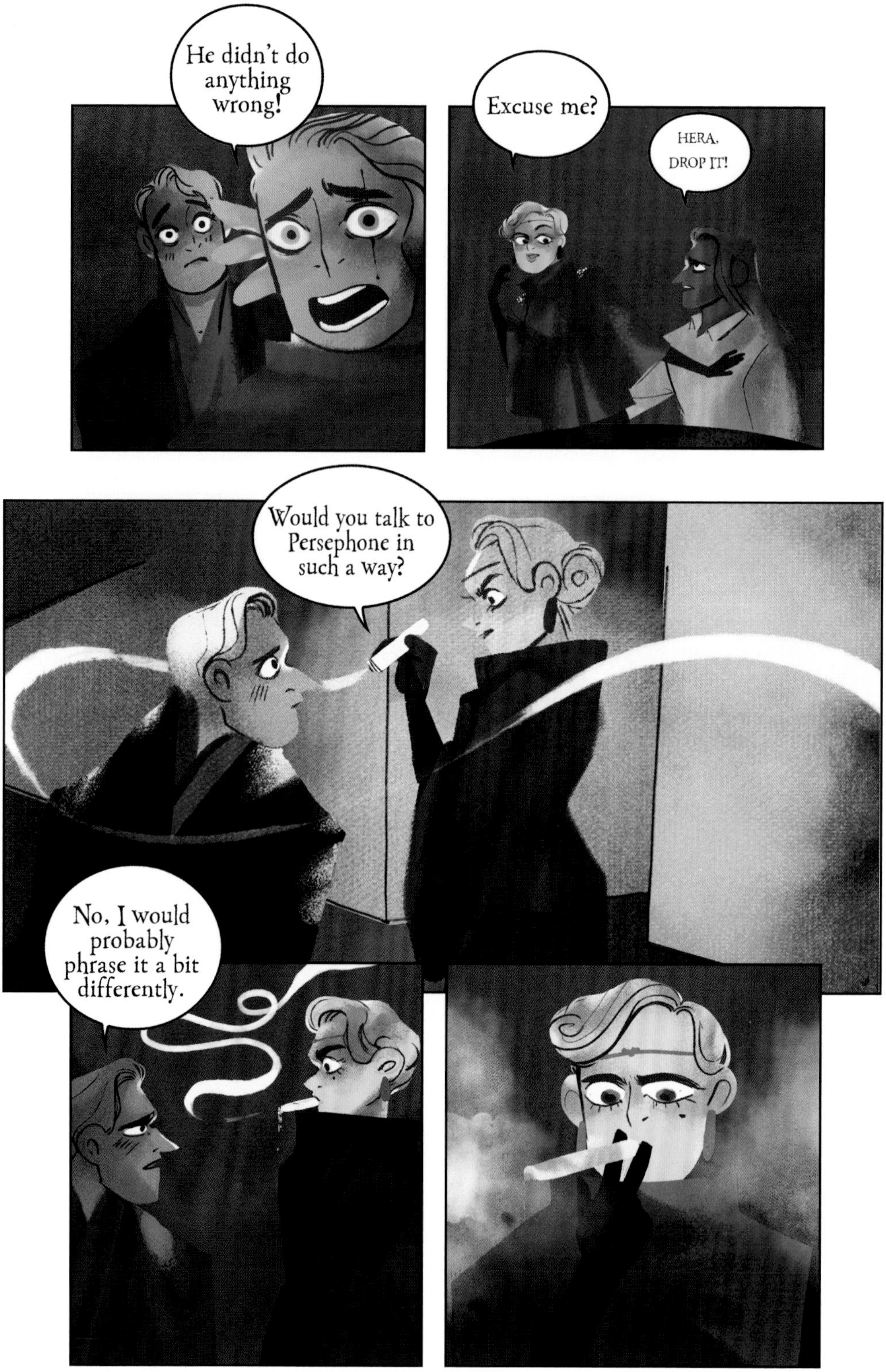
He didn't do anything wrong!
Excuse me?
HERA, DROP IT!
Would you talk to Persephone in such a way?
No, I would probably phrase it a bit differently.

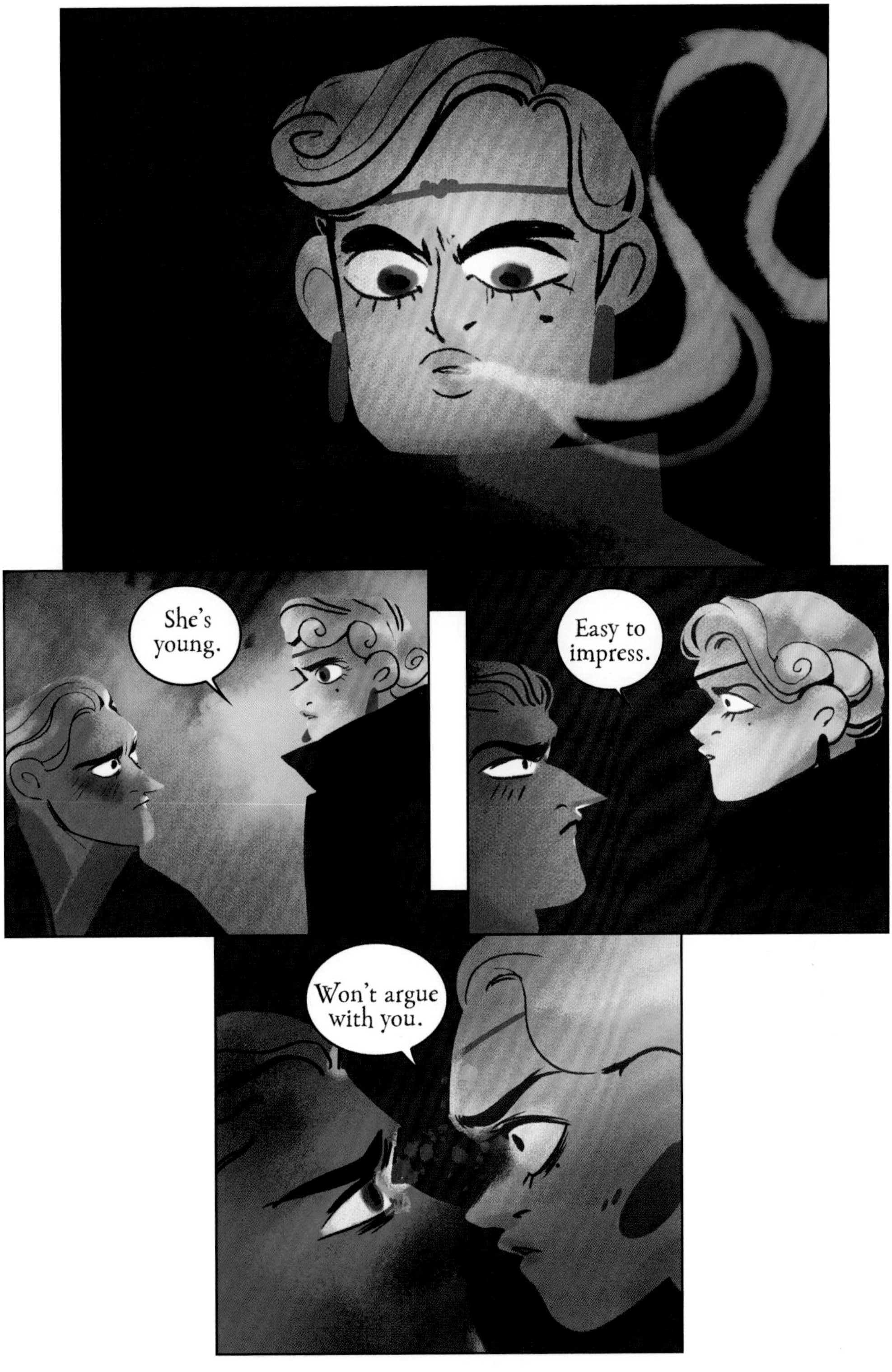
She's young.
Easy to impress.
Won't argue with you.

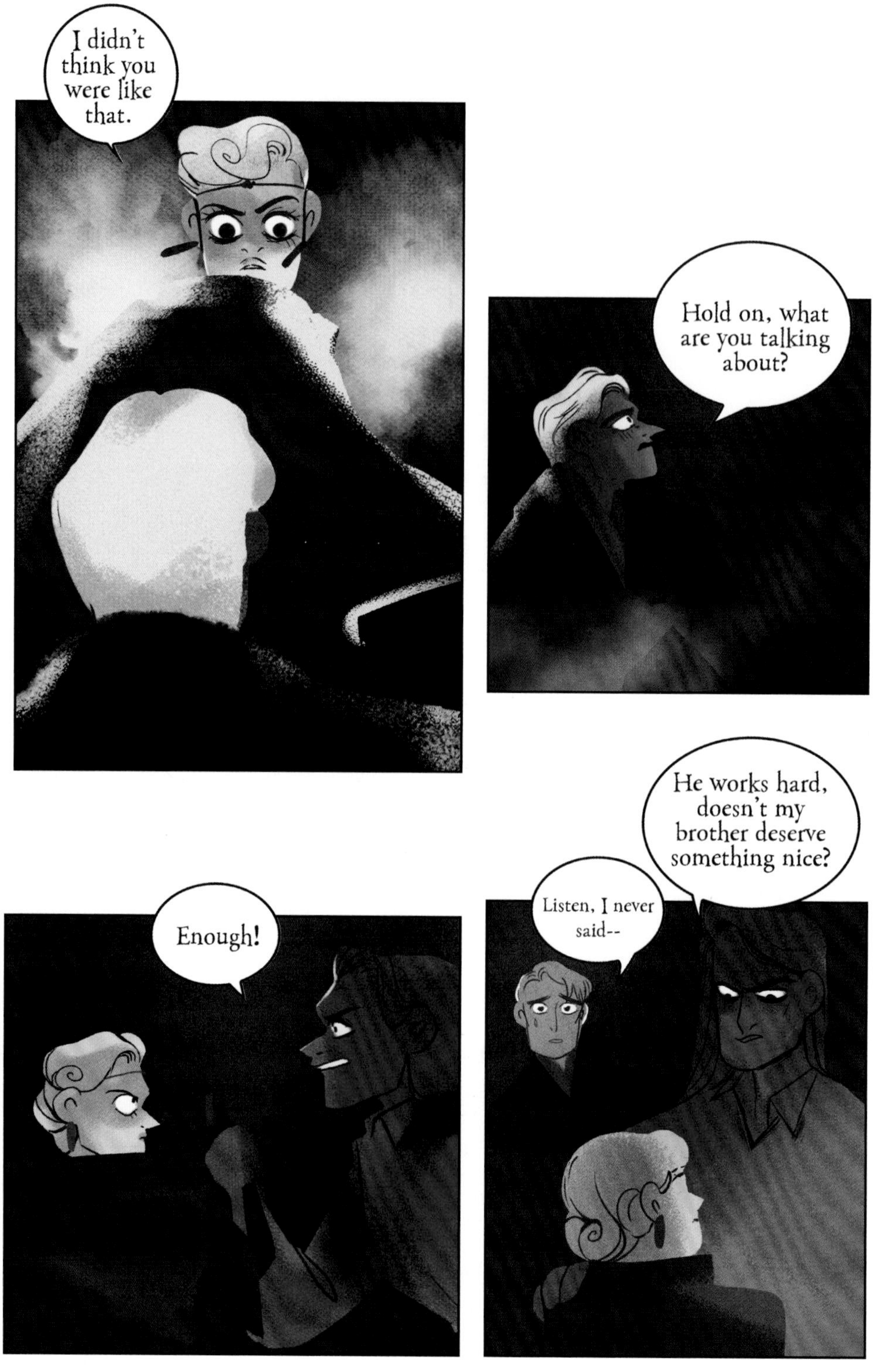
I didn't think you were like that.
Hold on, what are you talking about?
Enough!
He works hard, doesn't my brother deserve something nice?
Listen, I never said--

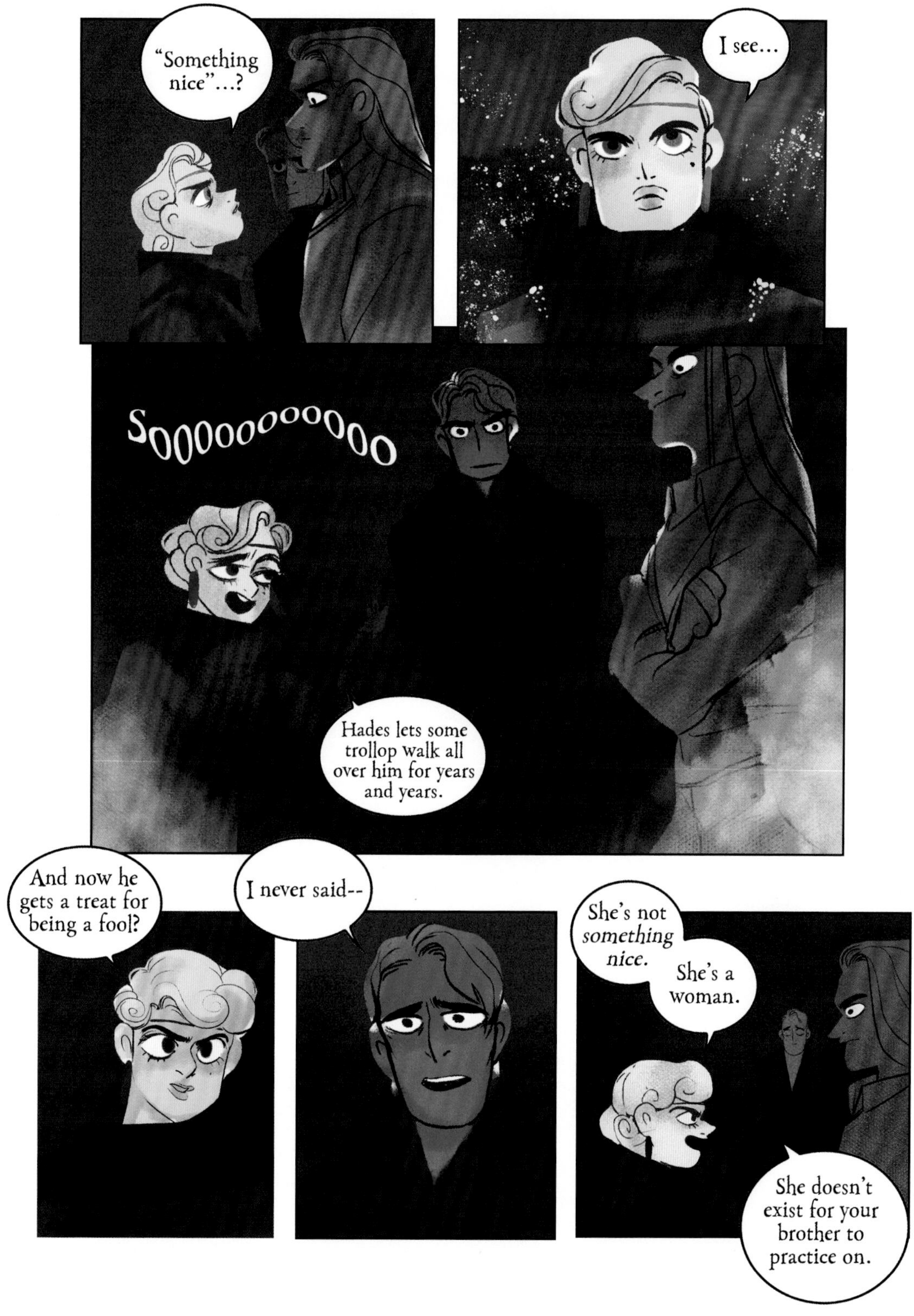
"Something nice"...?
I see...
Sooooooooooo
Hades lets some trollop walk all over him for years and years.
And now he gets a treat for being a fool?
I never said--
She's not *something nice.*
She's a woman.
She doesn't exist for your brother to practice on.

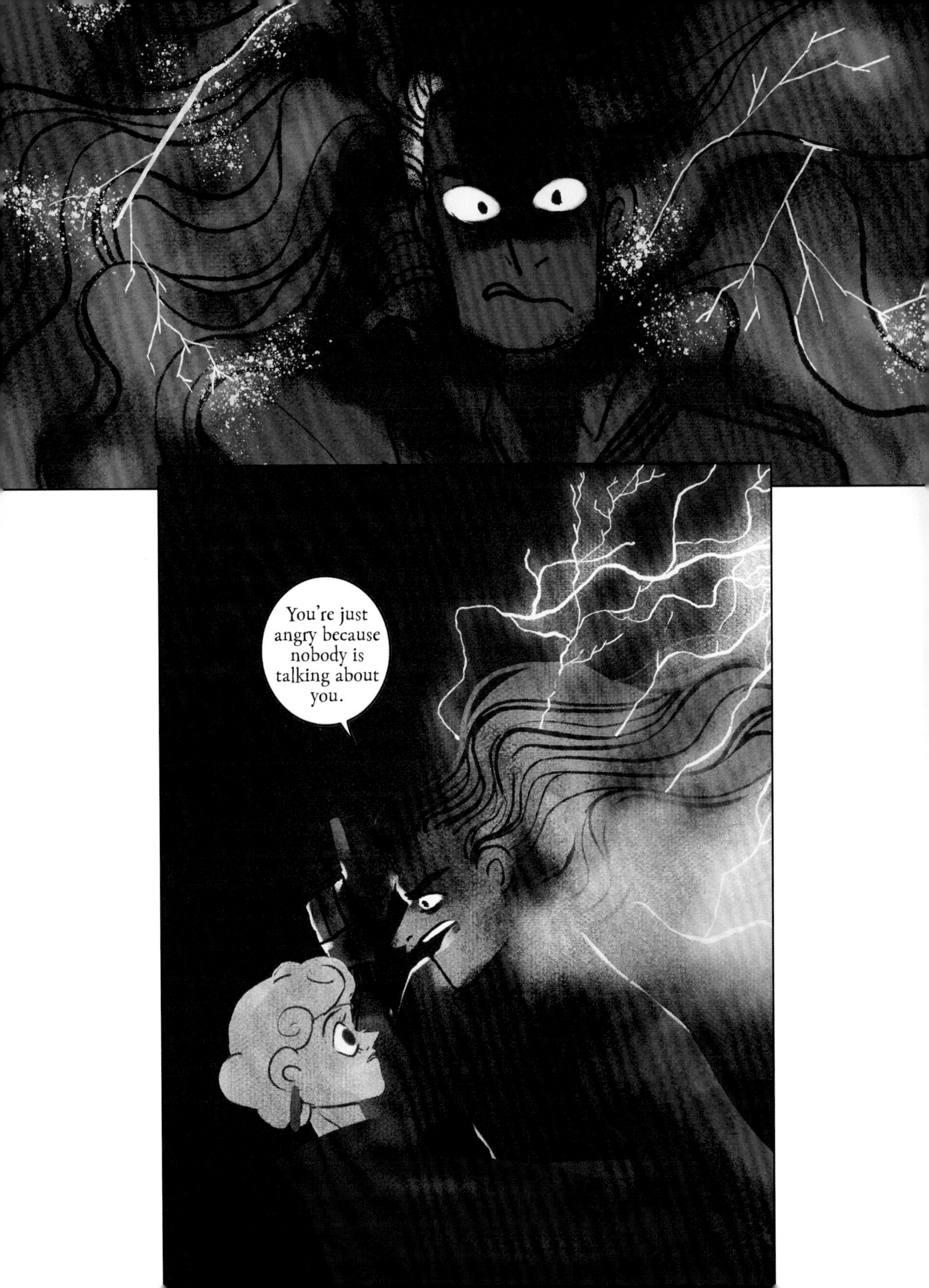
You're just angry because nobody is talking about you.

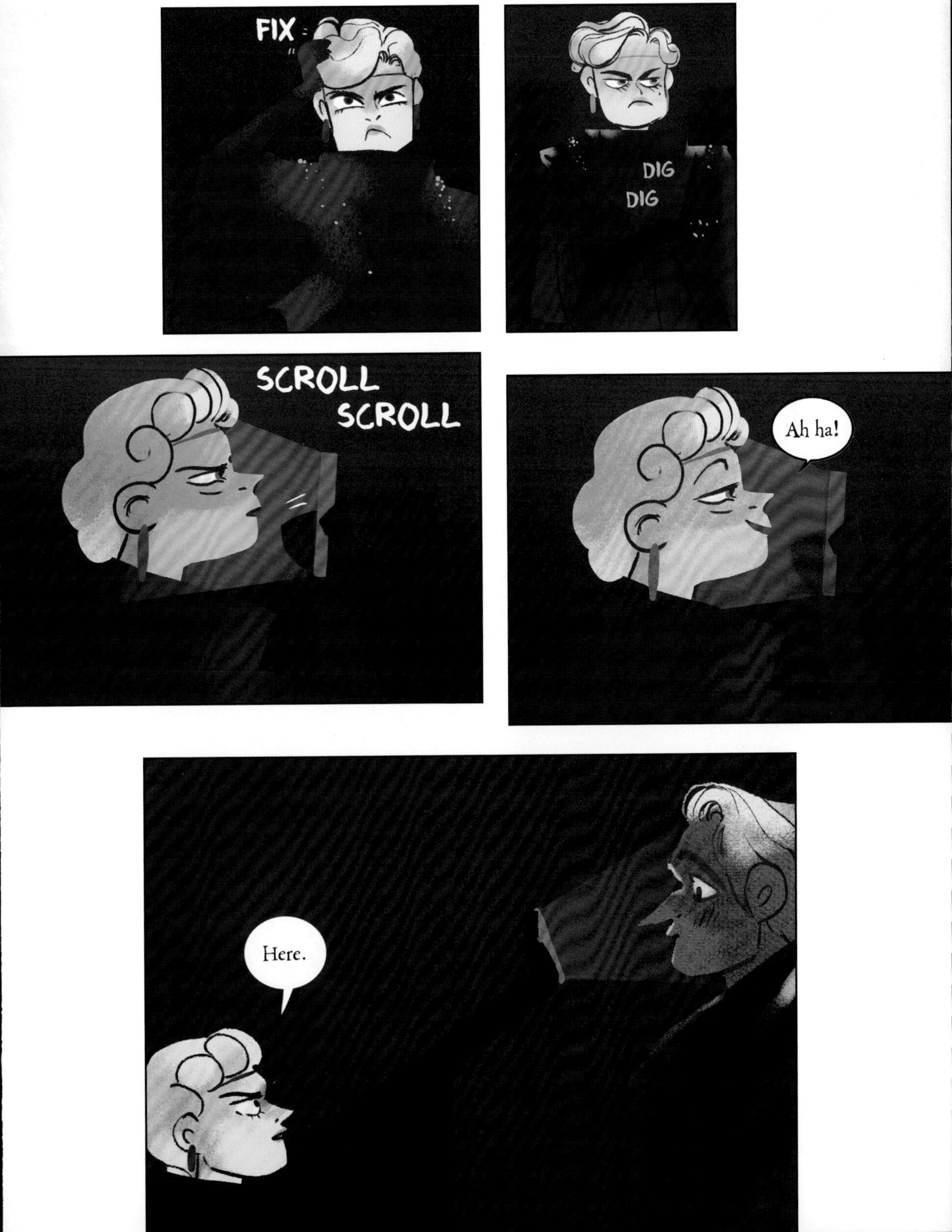
FIX
DIG
DIG
SCROLL
SCROLL
Ah ha!
Here.

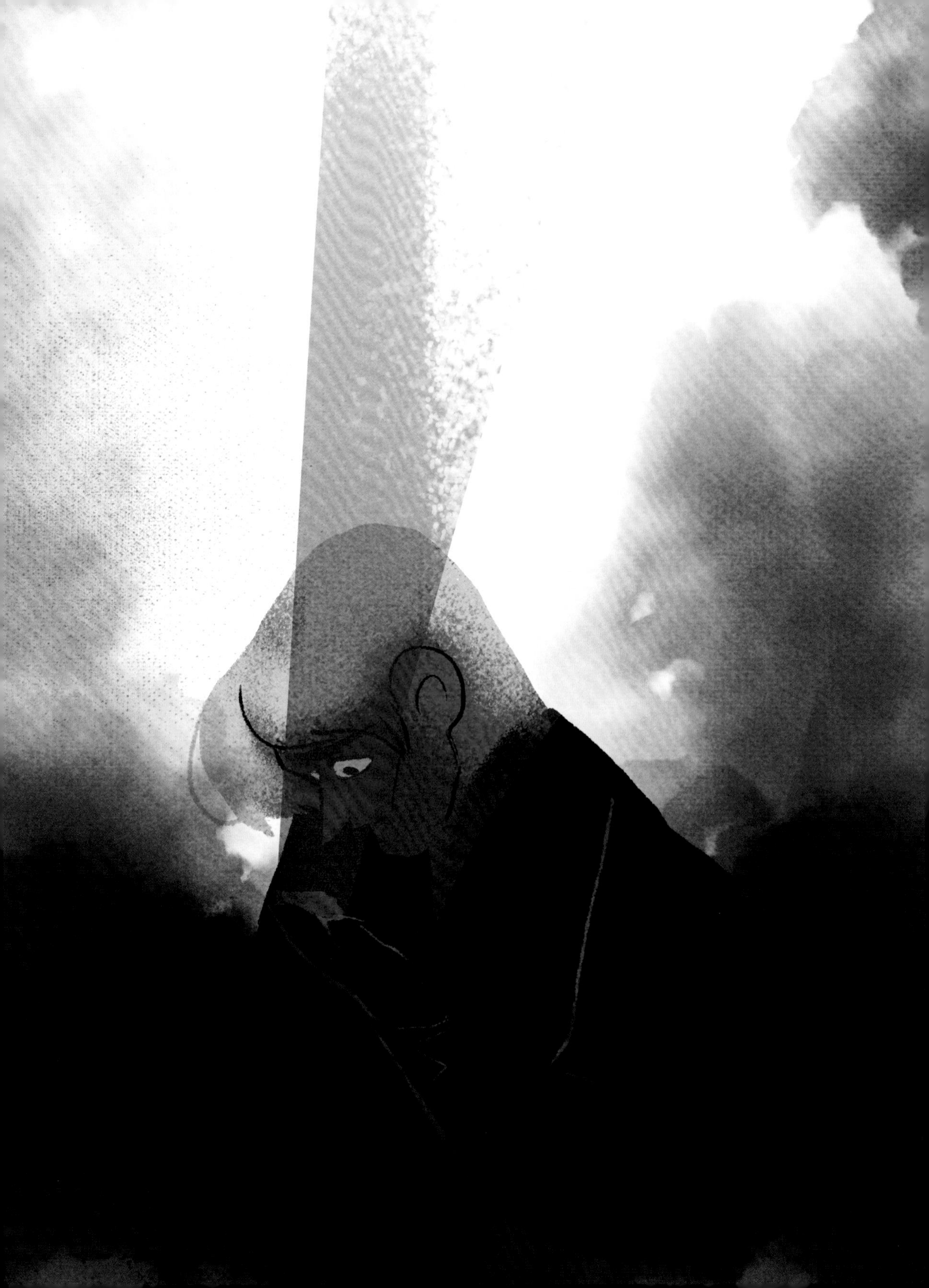

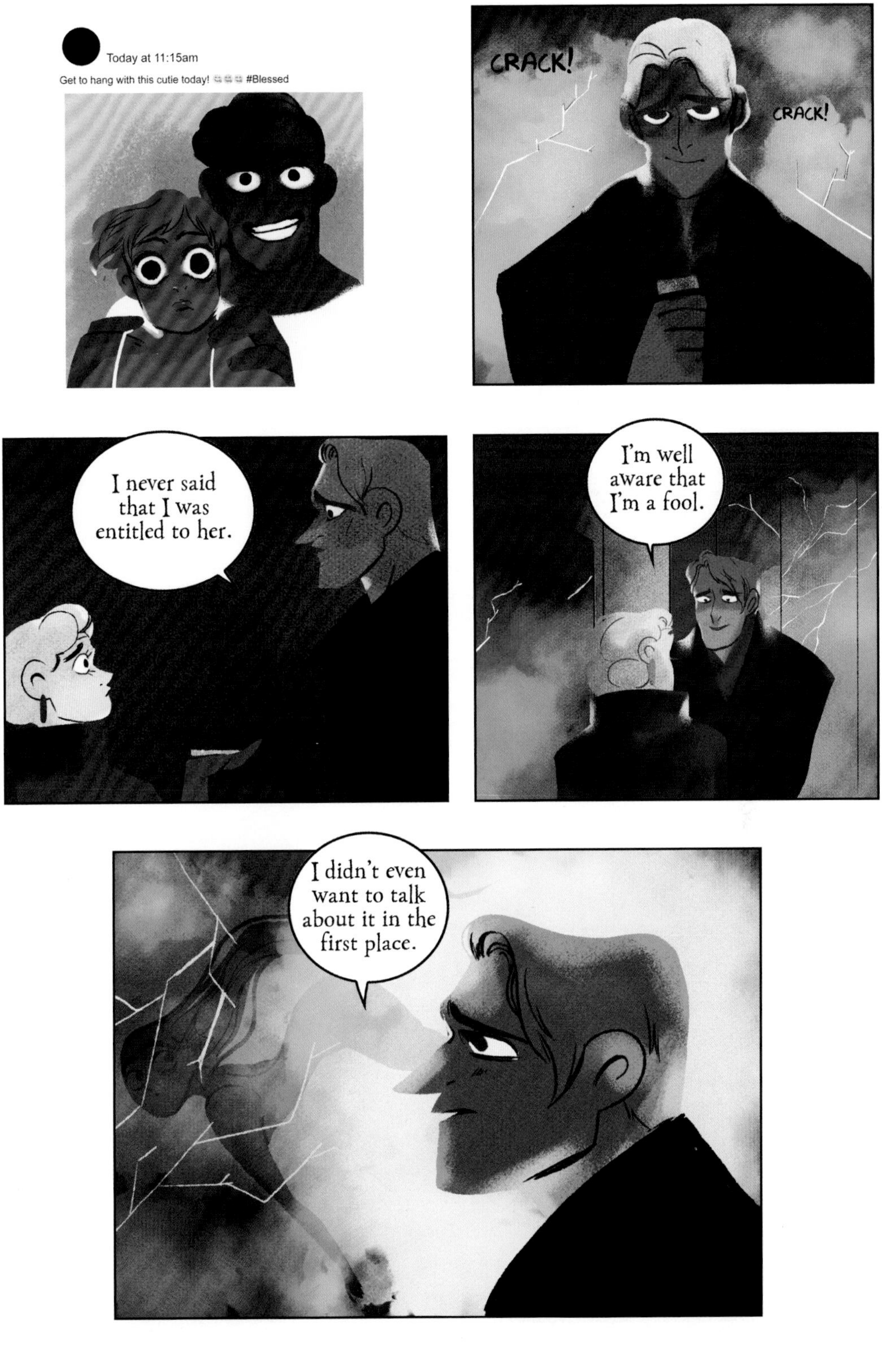
Today at 11:15am
Get to hang with this cutie today! #Blessed
CRACK!
CRACK!
I never said that I was entitled to her.
I'm well aware that I'm a fool.
I didn't even want to talk about it in the first place.

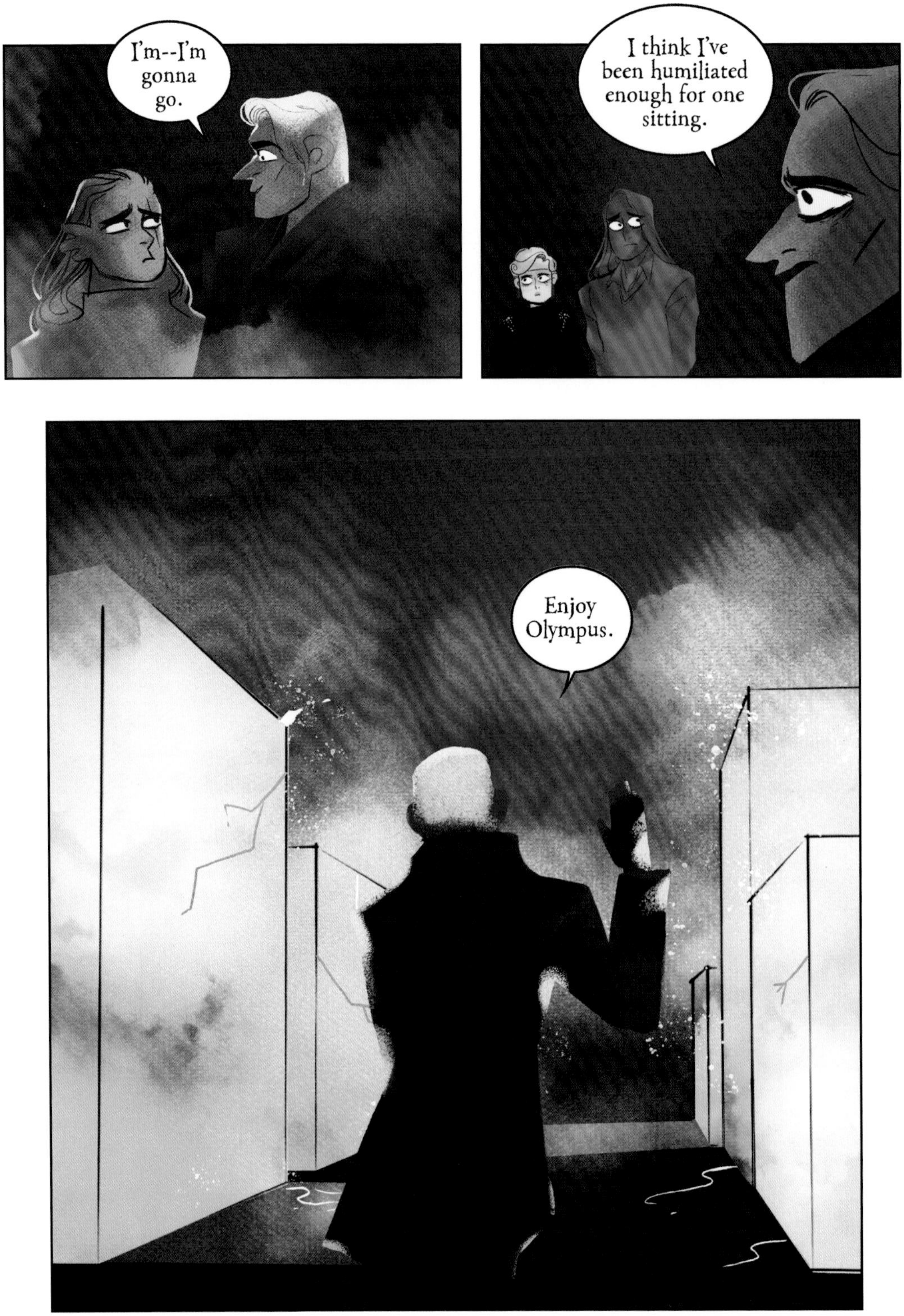
I'm--I'm gonna go.
I think I've been humiliated enough for one sitting.
Enjoy Olympus.

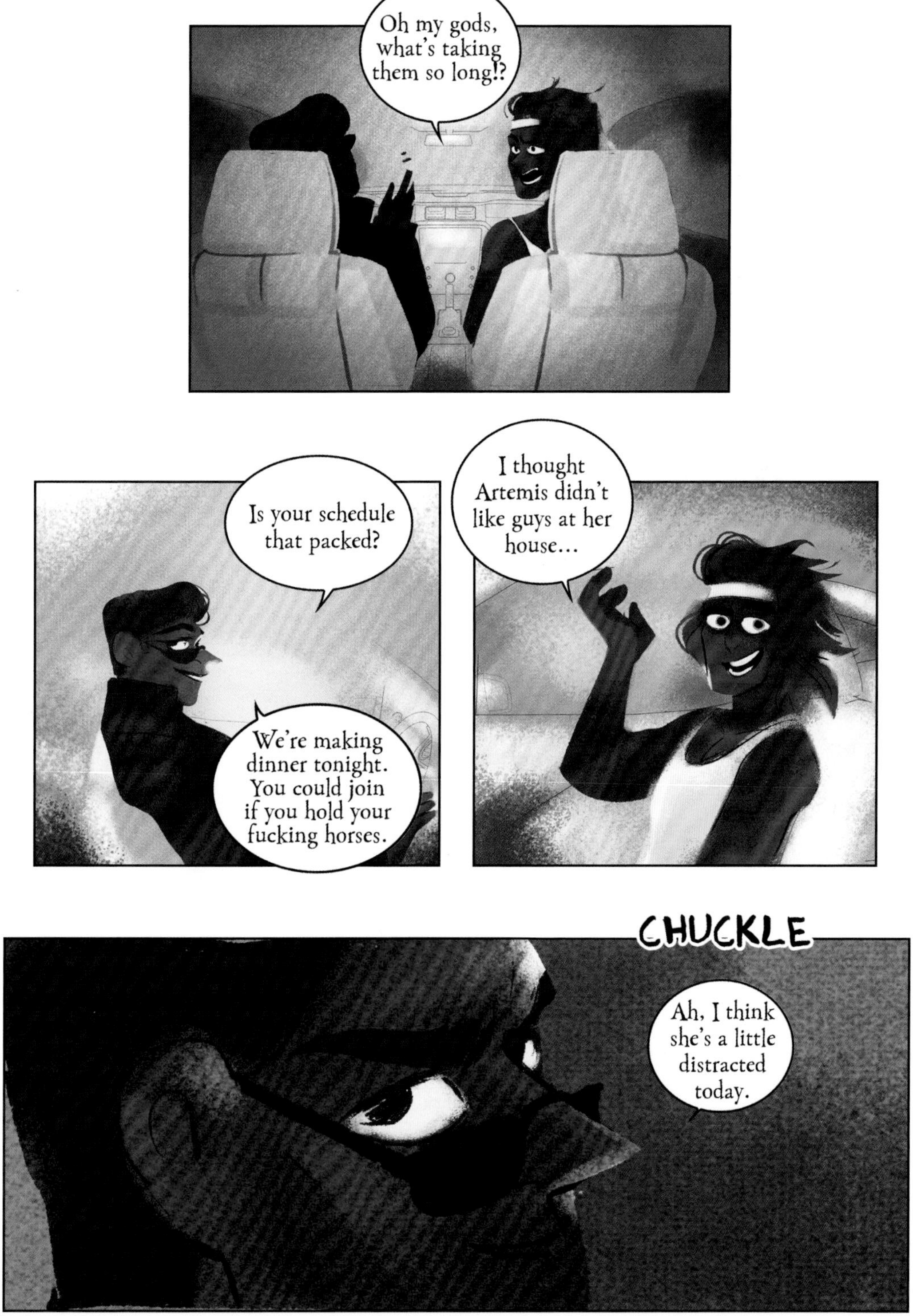
Oh my gods, what's taking them so long!?
Is your schedule that packed?
We're making dinner tonight. You could join if you hold your fucking horses.
I thought Artemis didn't like guys at her house...
CHUCKLE
Ah, I think she's a little distracted today.

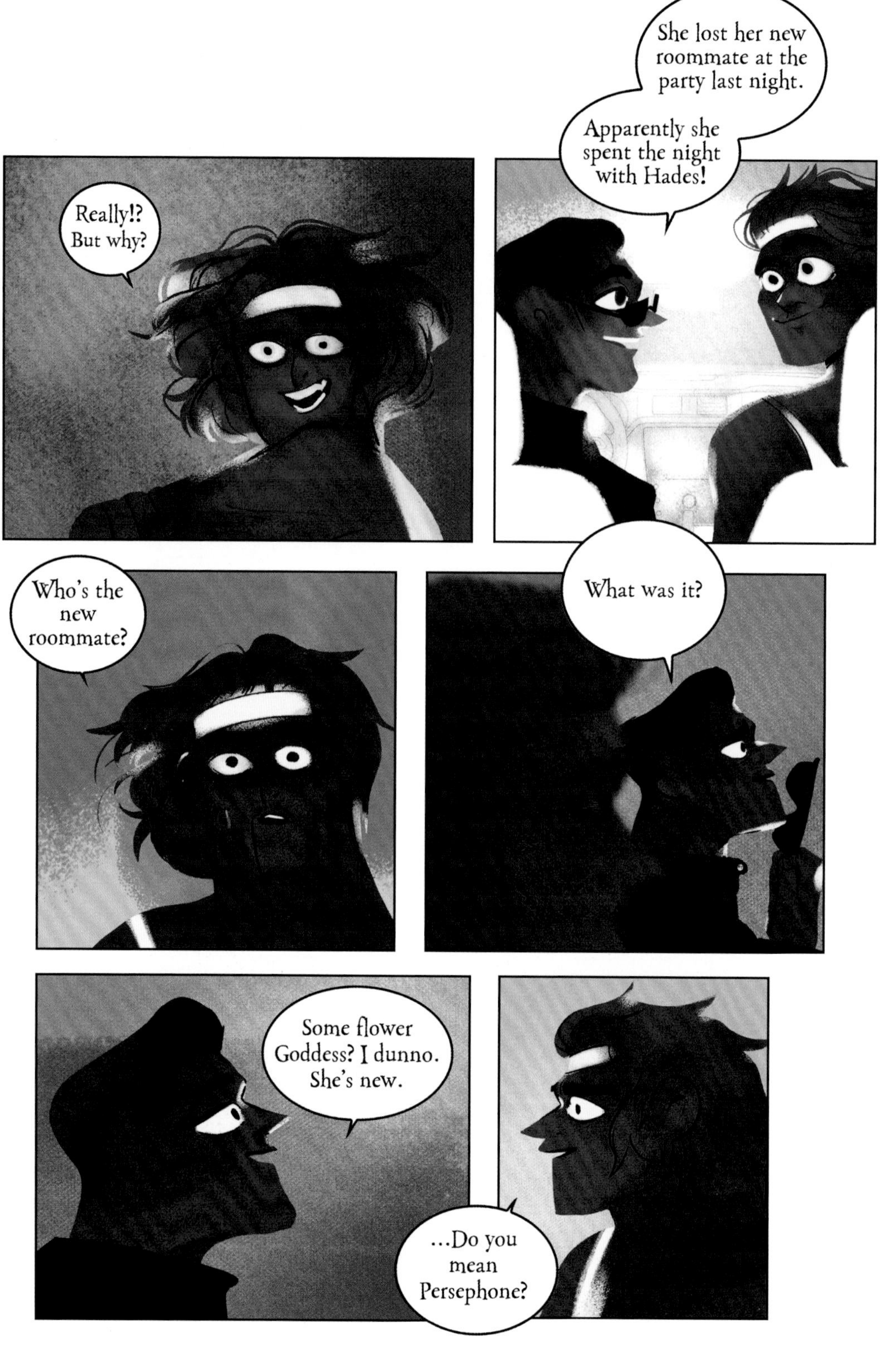
Really!? But why?
She lost her new roommate at the party last night.
Apparently she spent the night with Hades!
Who's the new roommate?
What was it?
Some flower Goddess? I dunno. She's new.
...Do you mean Persephone?

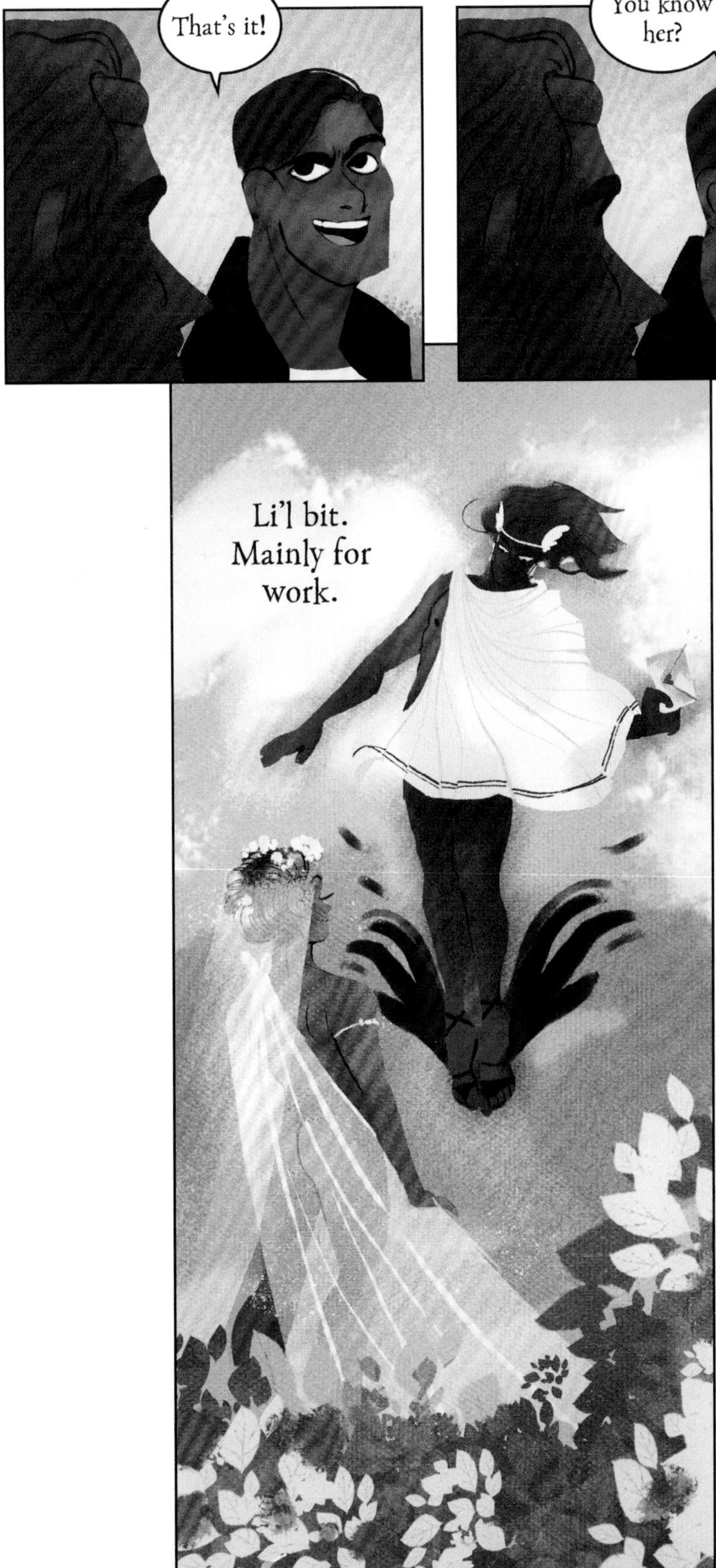
That's it!
You know her?
Li'l bit. Mainly for work.

Demeter sends her A LOT of letters...

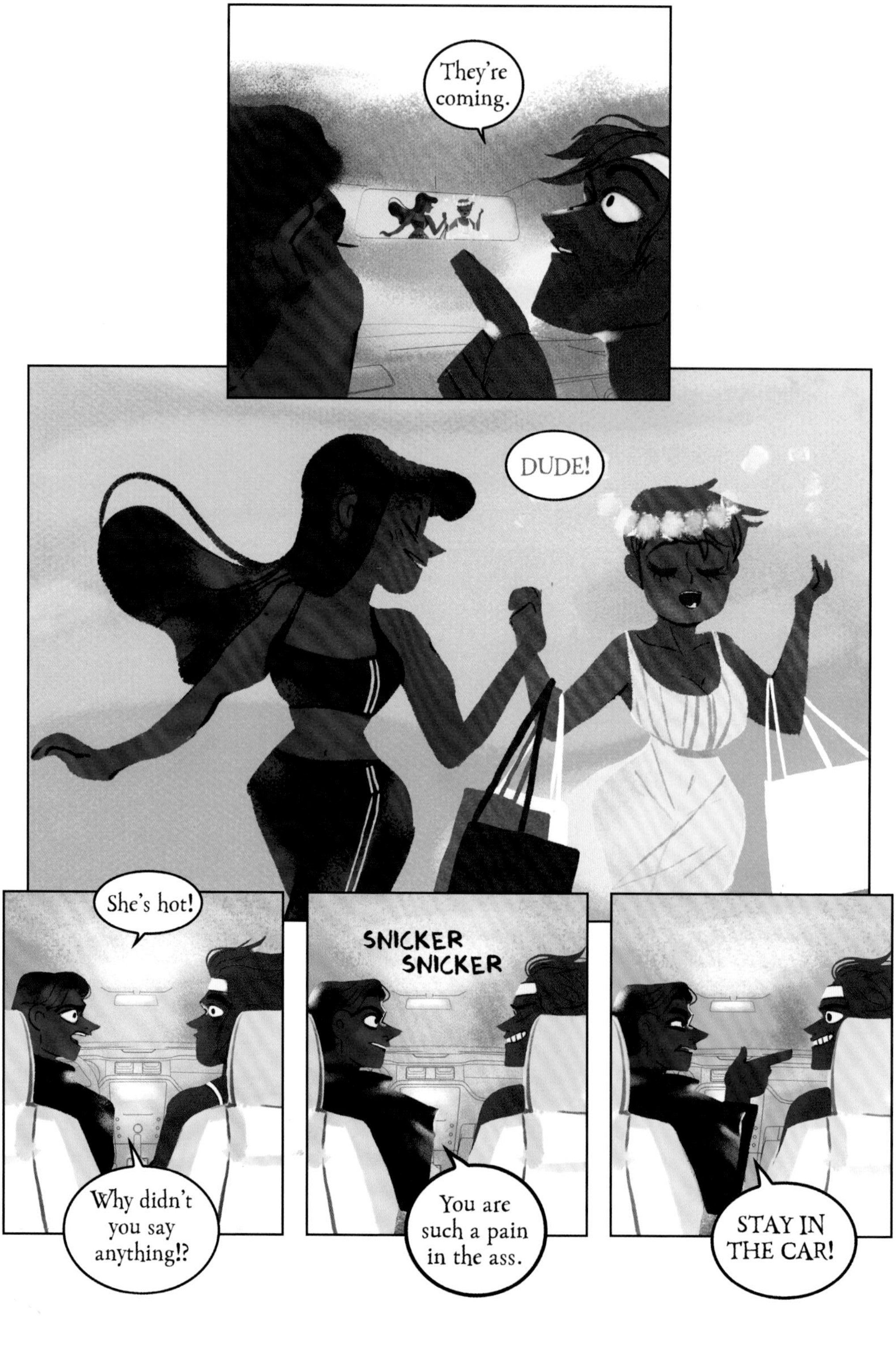
They're coming.
DUDE!
She's hot!
Why didn't you say anything!?
SNICKER SNICKER
You are such a pain in the ass.
STAY IN THE CAR!

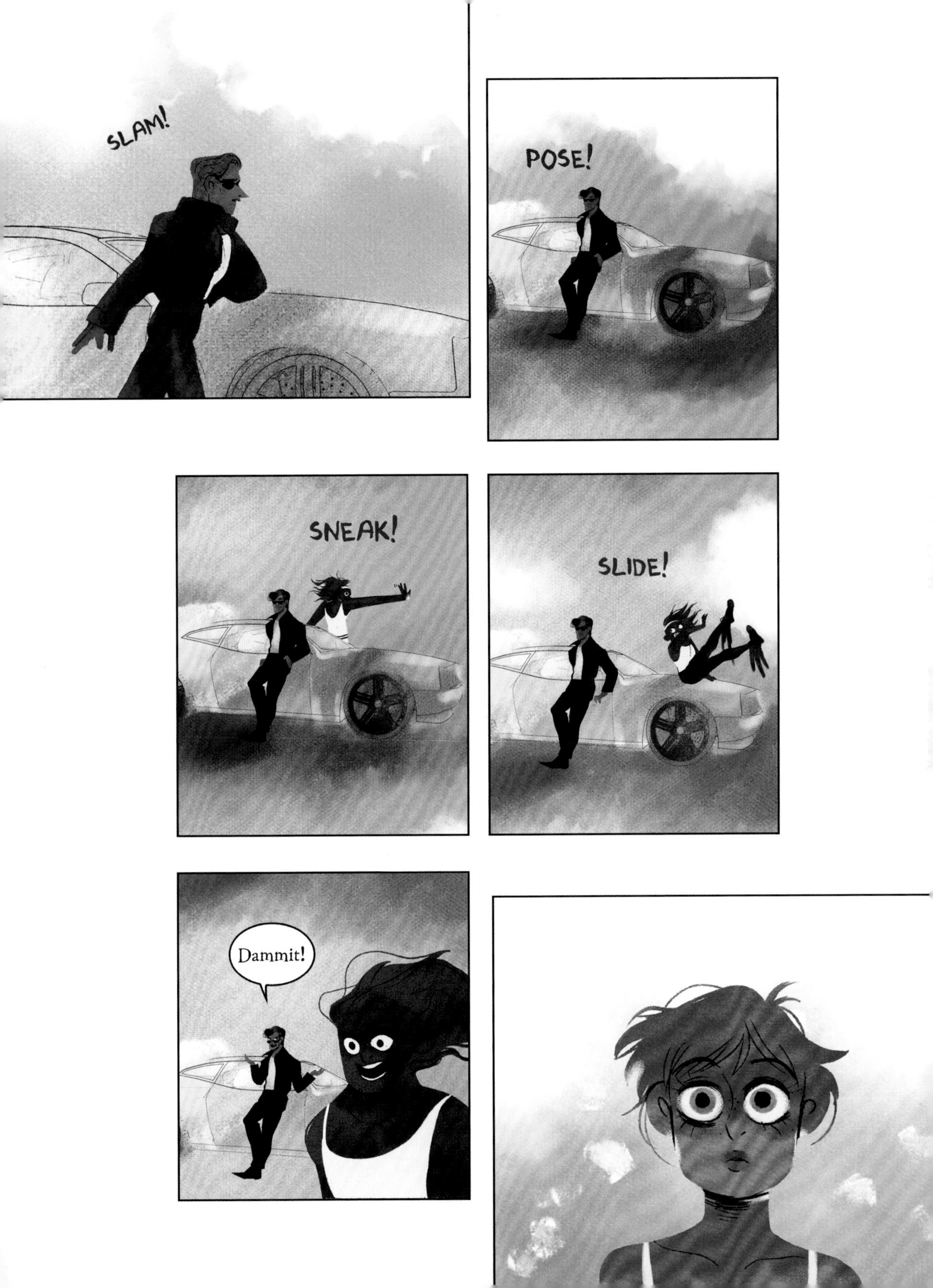
SLAM!
POSE!
SNEAK!
SLIDE!
Dammit!

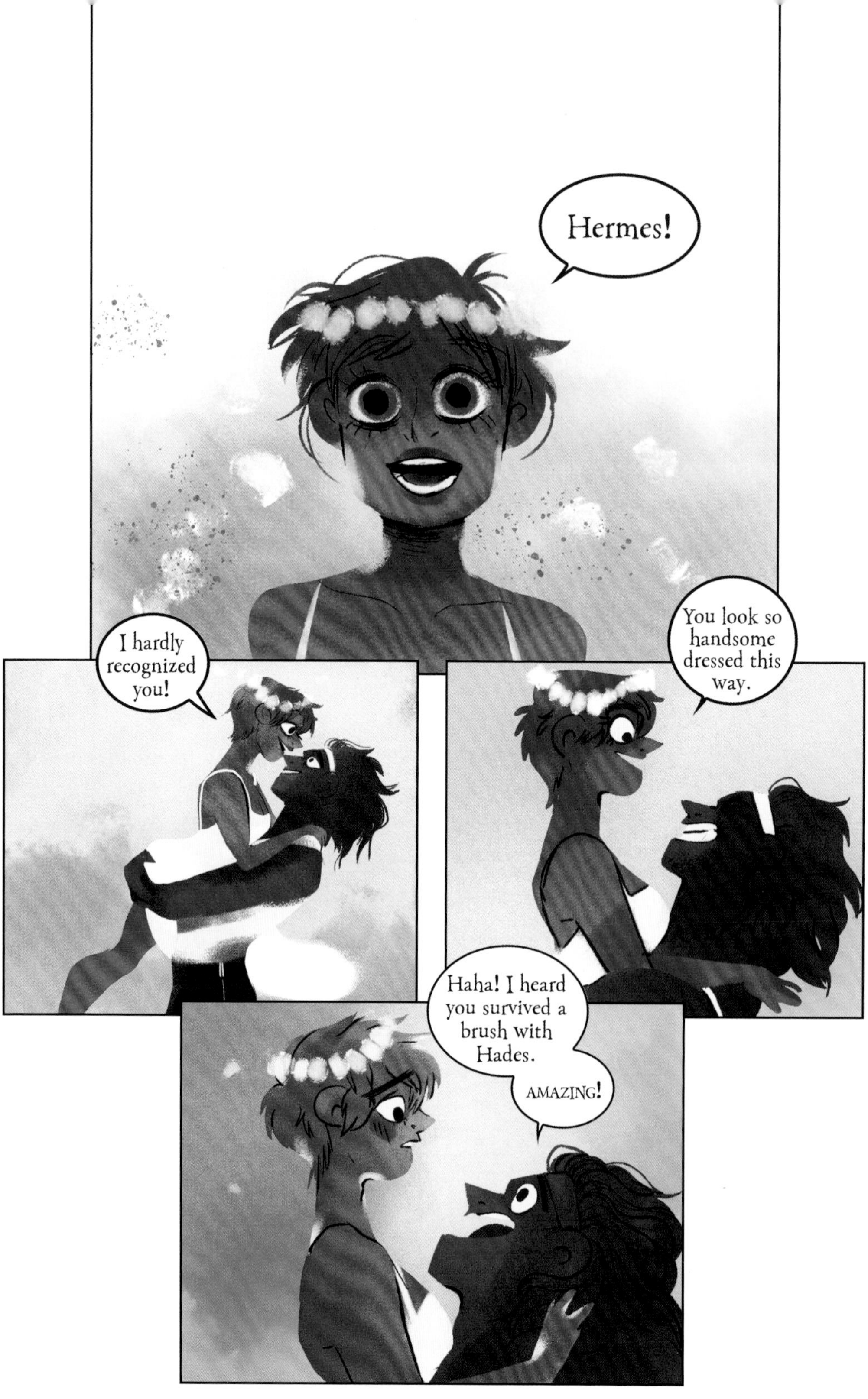
Hermes!
I hardly recognized you!
You look so handsome dressed this way.
Haha! I heard you survived a brush with Hades.
AMAZING!

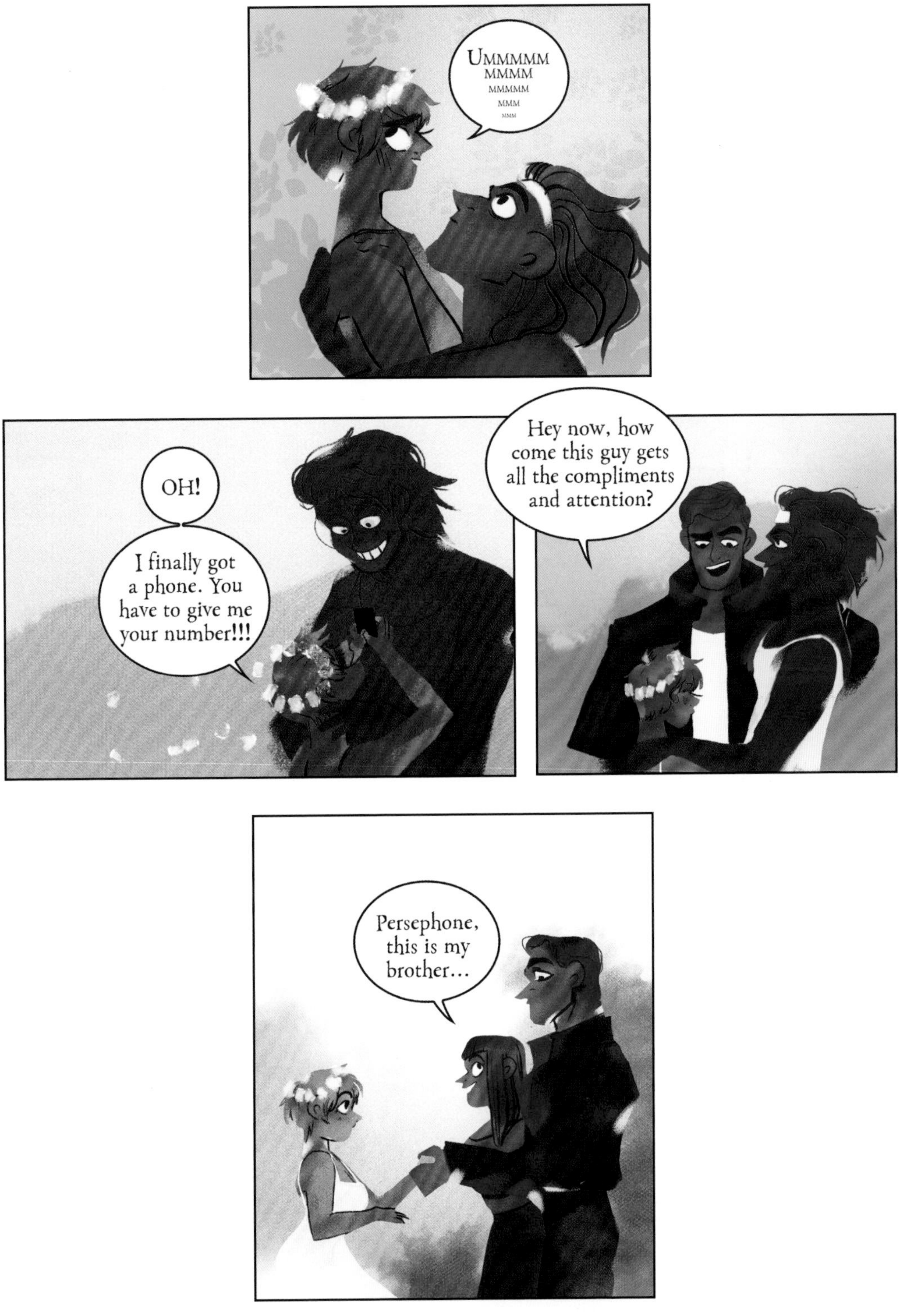
UMMMMM
MMMM
MMMMM
MMM
MMM
OH!
I finally got a phone. You have to give me your number!!!
Hey now, how come this guy gets all the compliments and attention?
Persephone, this is my brother...

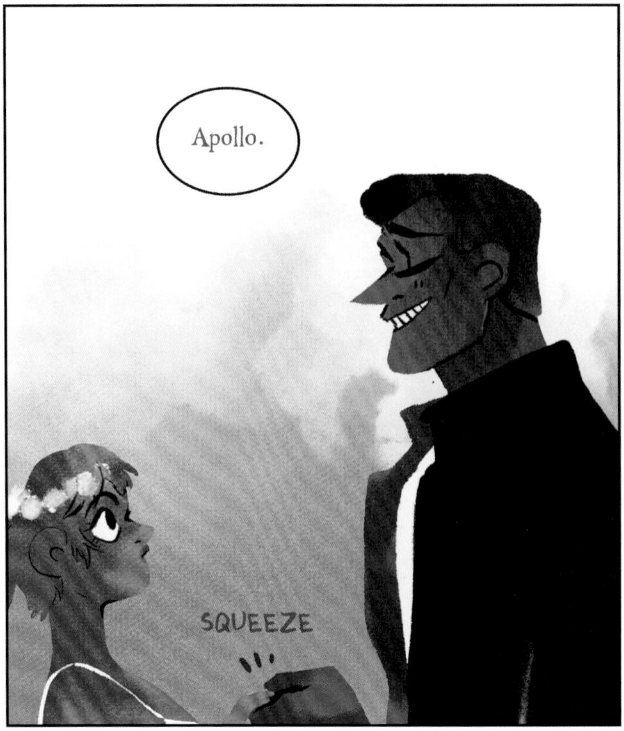
Apollo.
SQUEEZE

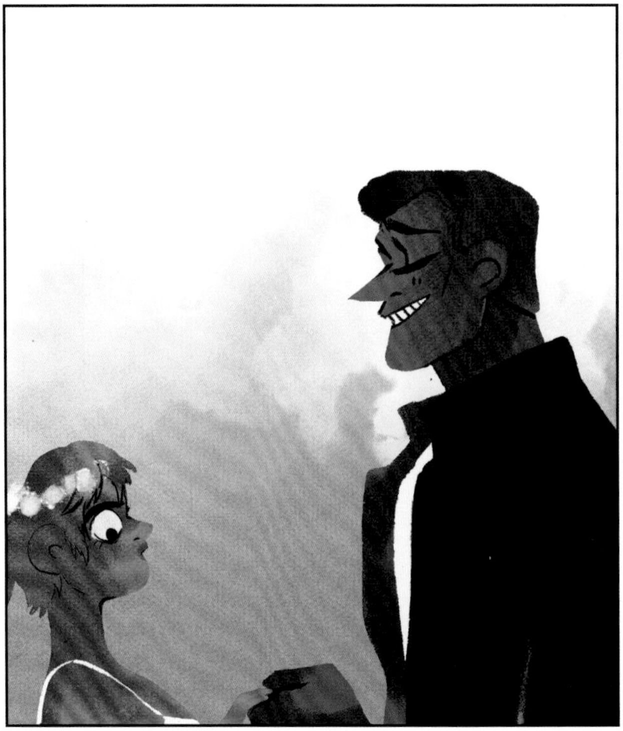

EPISODE 21: THANKS BUT NAH

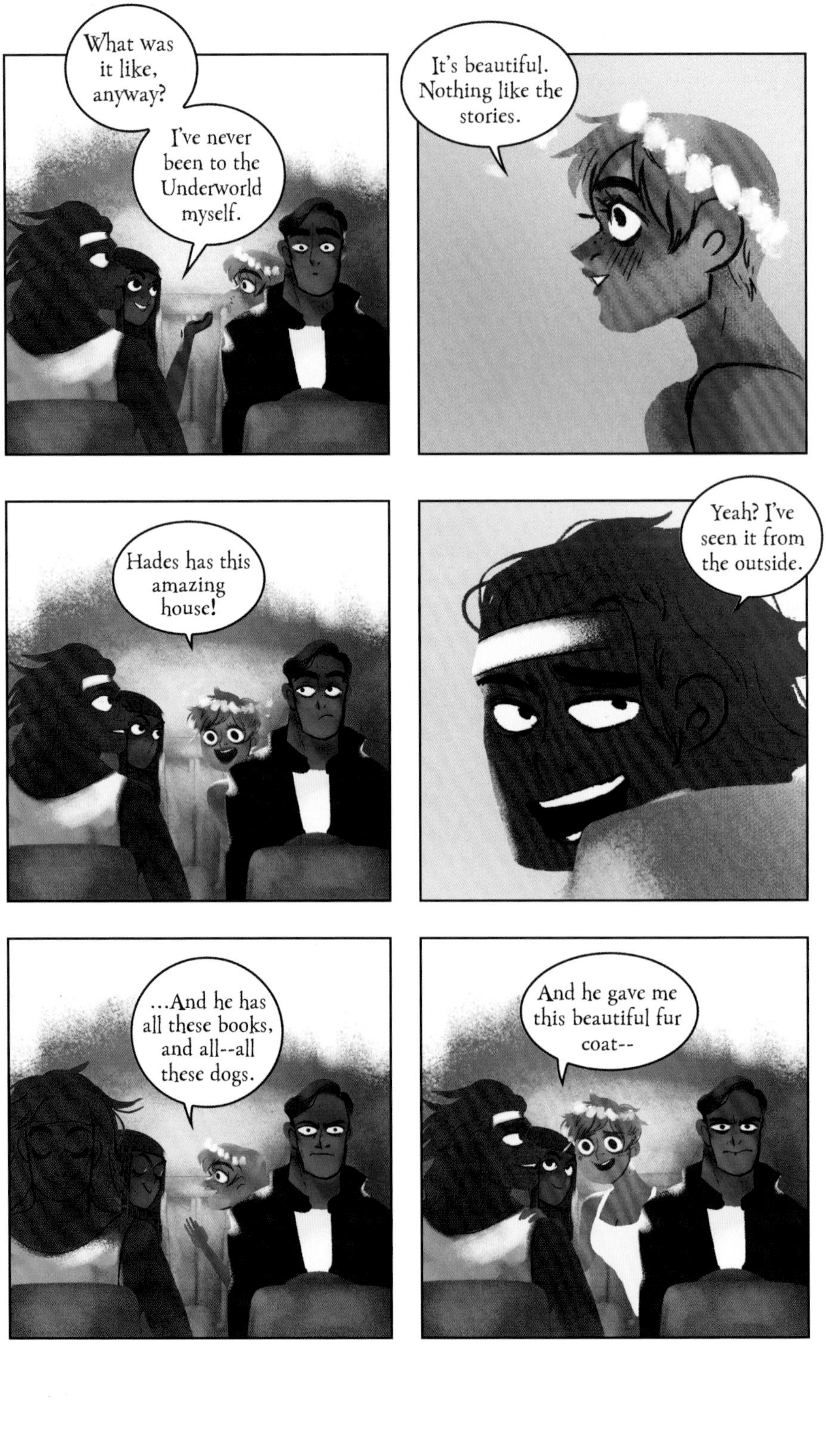
What was it like, anyway?
I've never been to the Underworld myself.
It's beautiful. Nothing like the stories.
Hades has this amazing house!
Yeah? I've seen it from the outside.
...And he has all these books, and all--all these dogs.
And he gave me this beautiful fur coat--

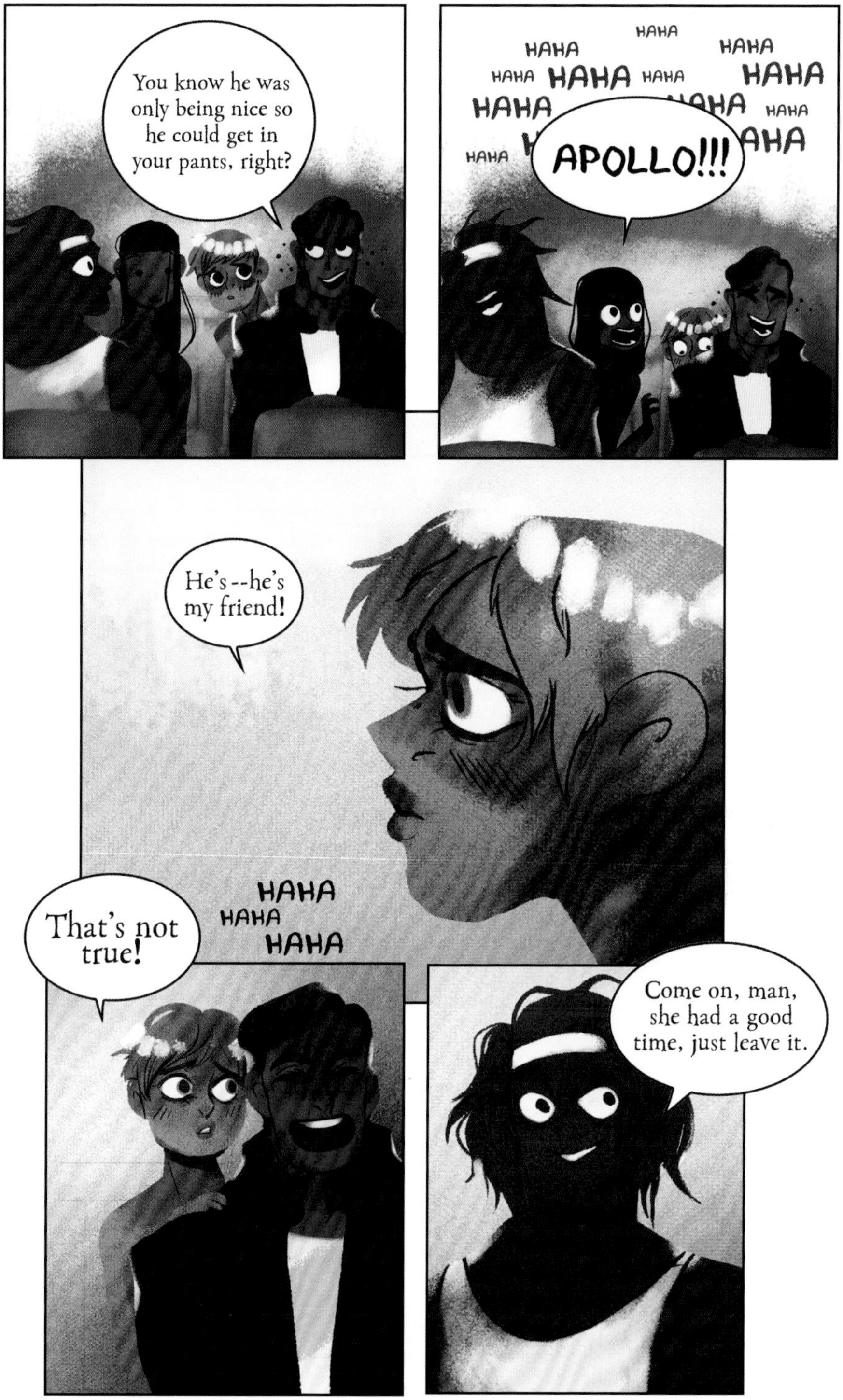

You know he was only being nice so he could get in your pants, right?
HAHA HAHA HAHA HAHA HAHA HAHA HAHA HAHA HAHA HAHA HAHA HAHA
APOLLO!!!
He's--he's my friend!
HAHA HAHA HAHA
That's not true!
Come on, man, she had a good time, just leave it.

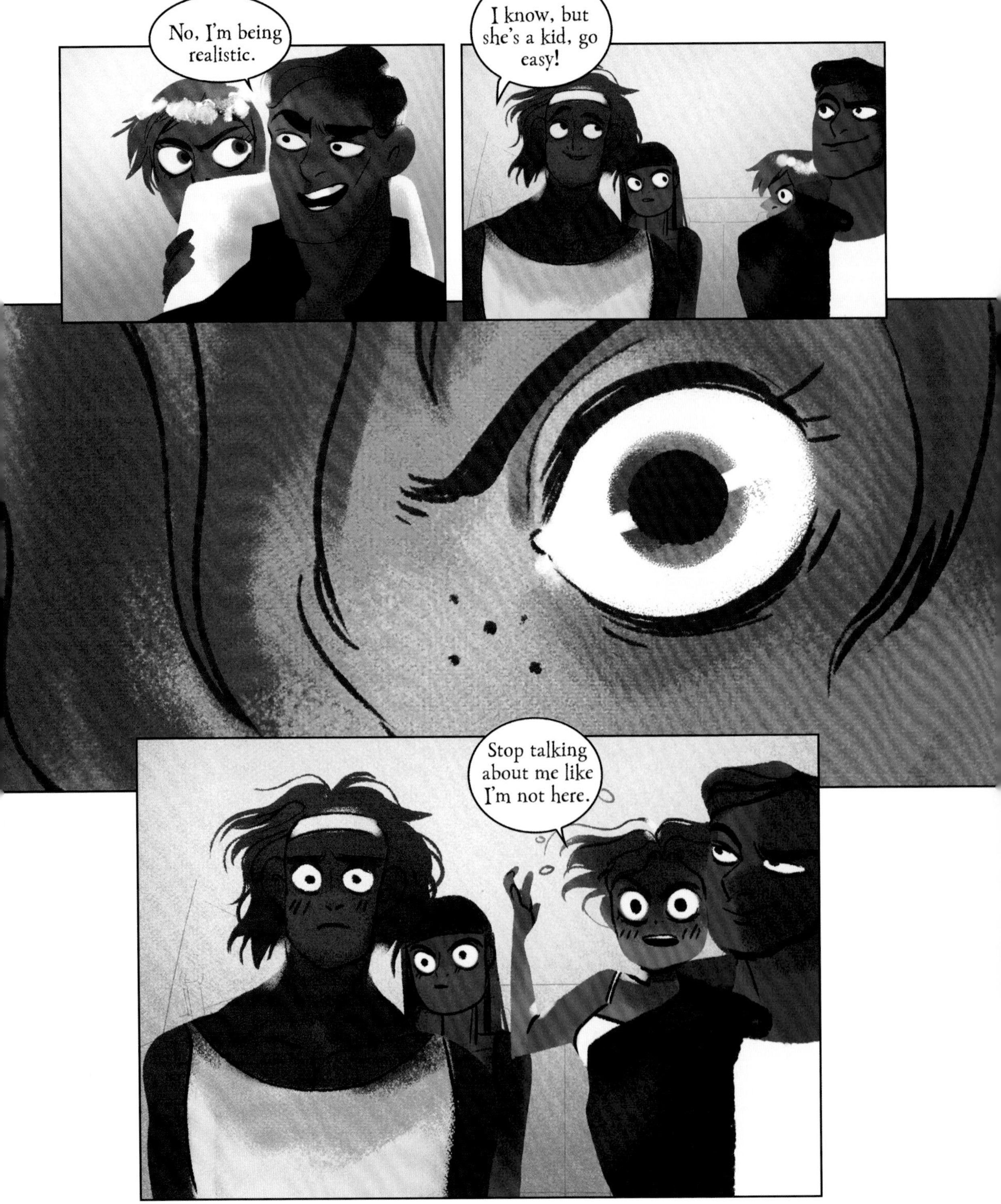
No, I'm being realistic.
I know, but she's a kid, go easy!
Stop talking about me like I'm not here.

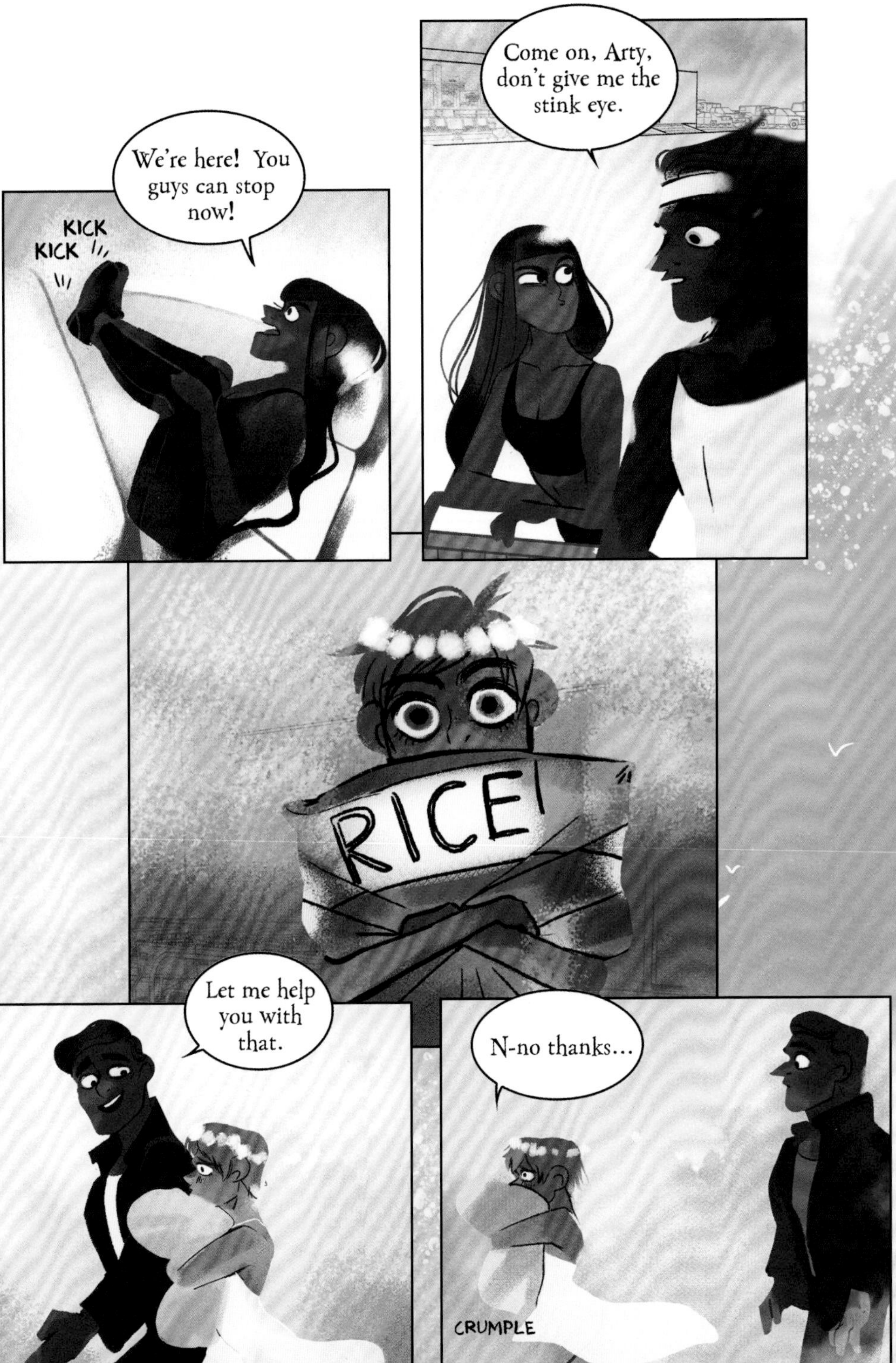

KICK
KICK
We're here! You guys can stop now!
Come on, Arty, don't give me the stink eye.
RICE
Let me help you with that.
N-no thanks...
CRUMPLE

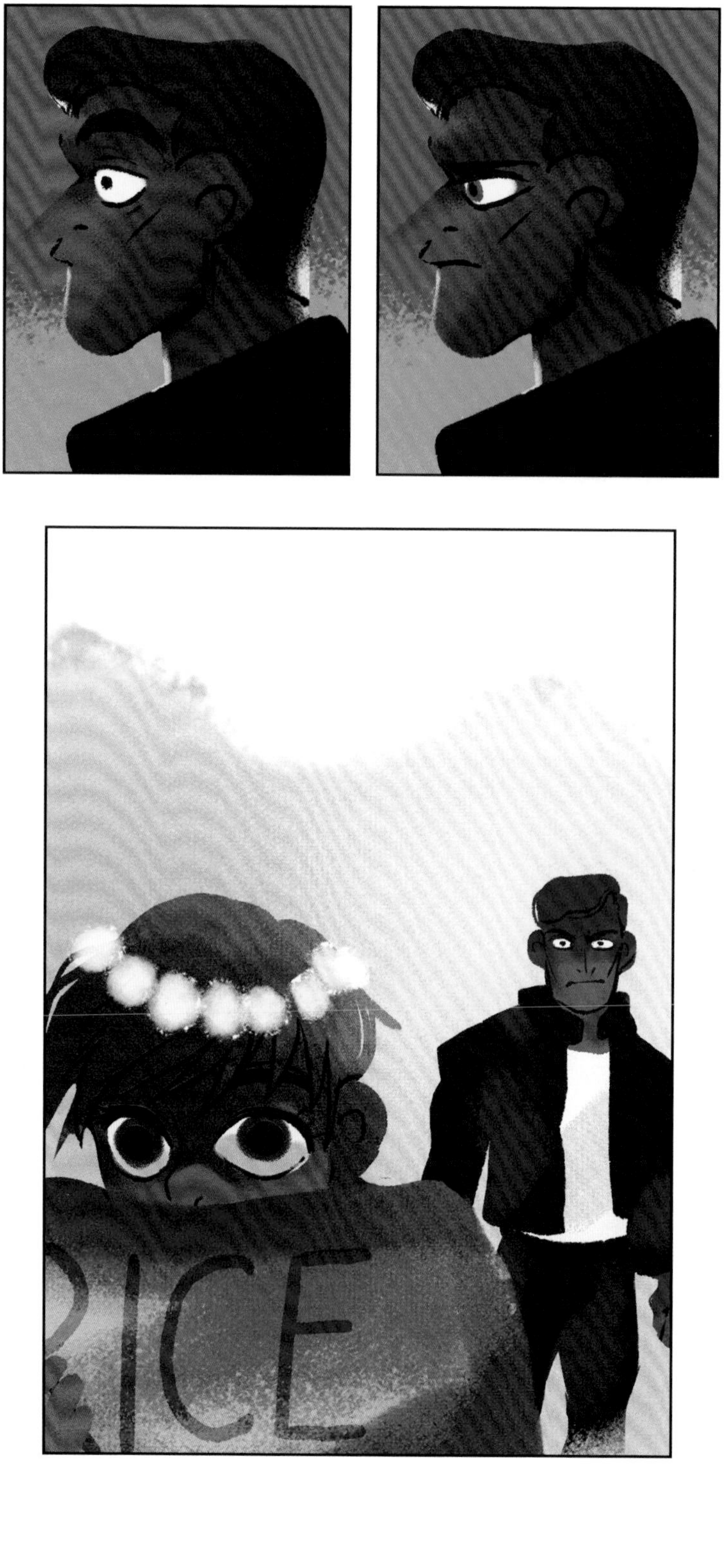
ICE

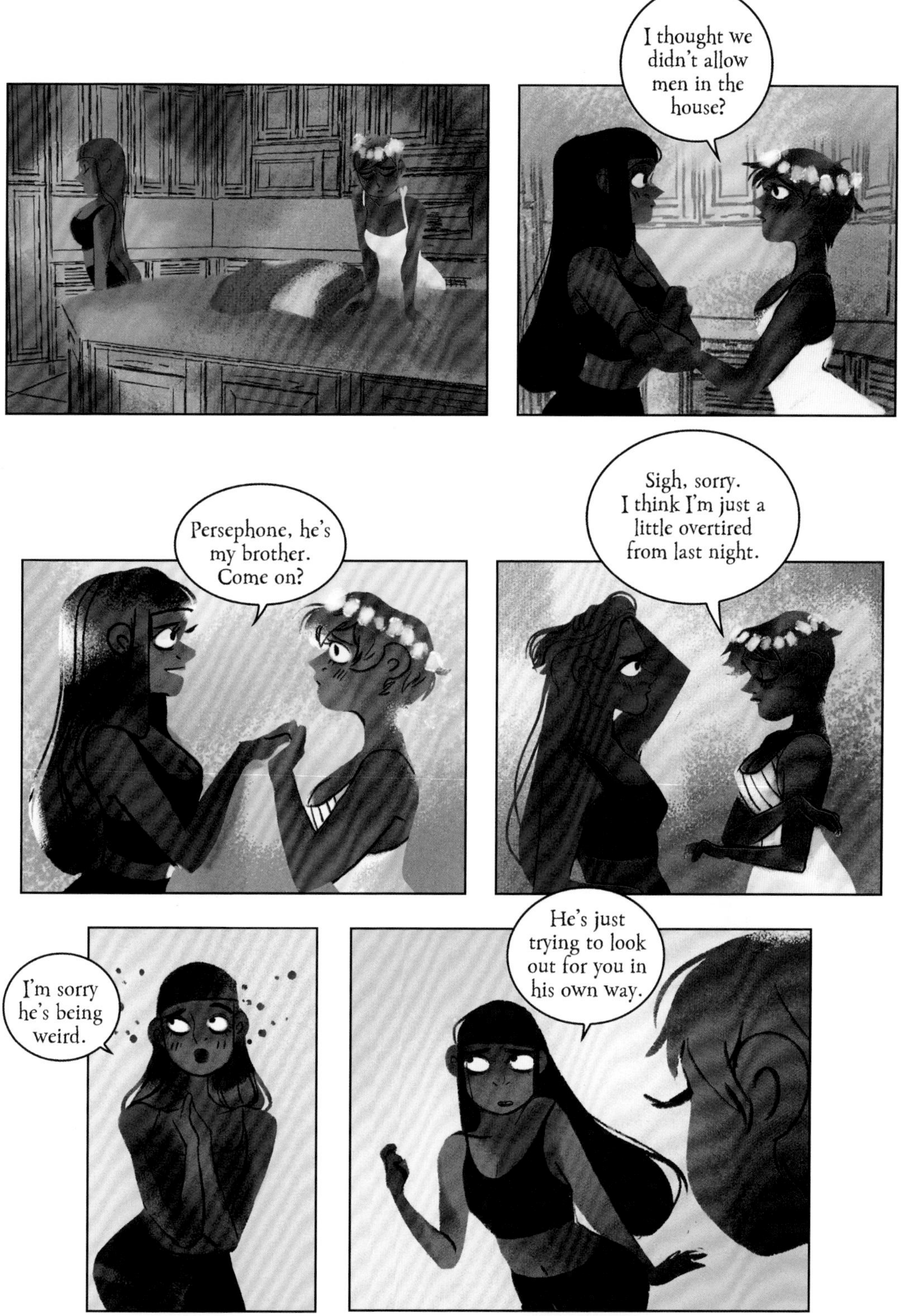
I thought we didn't allow men in the house?
Persephone, he's my brother. Come on?
Sigh, sorry. I think I'm just a little overtired from last night.
I'm sorry he's being weird.
He's just trying to look out for you in his own way.

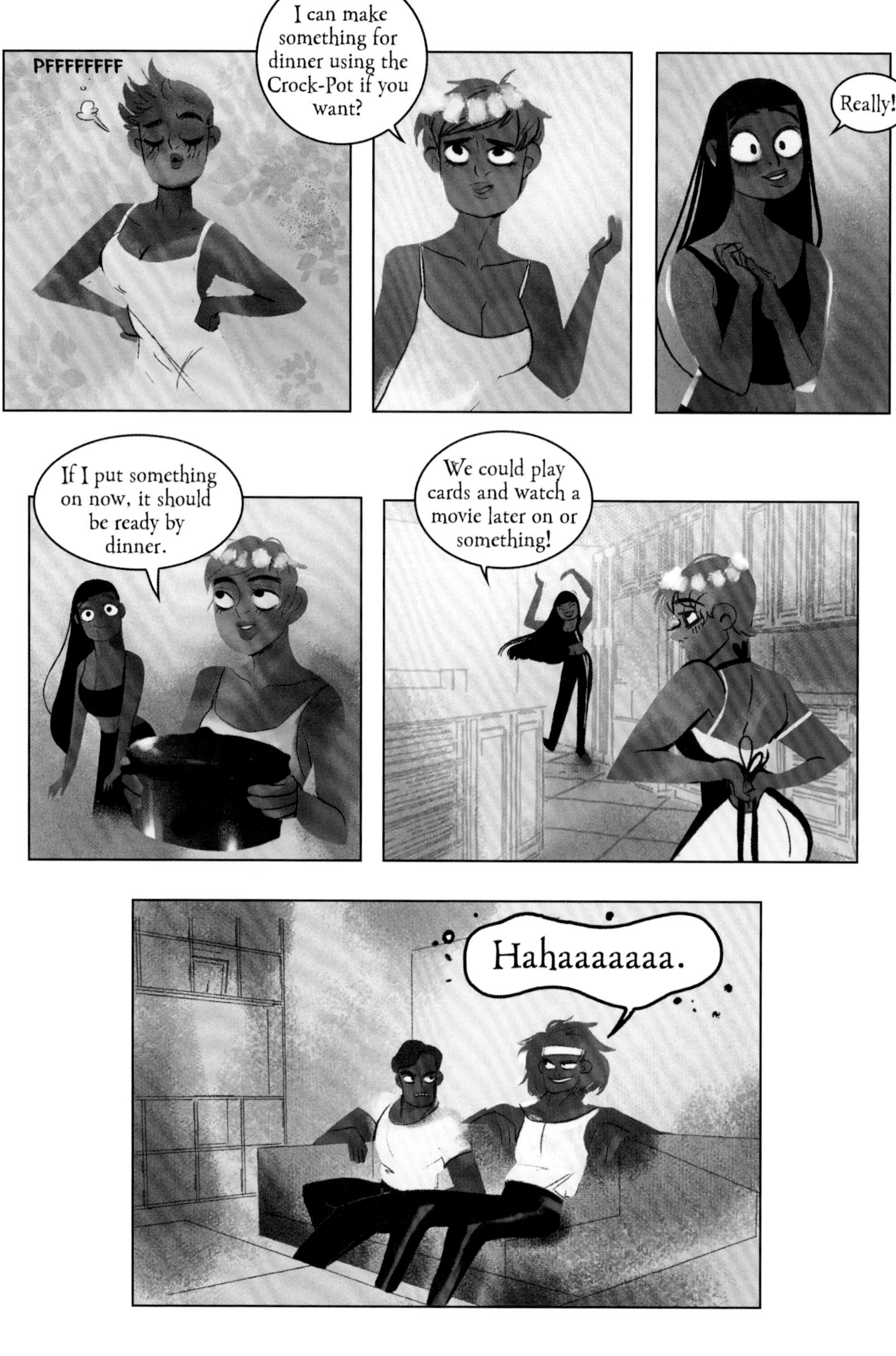
PFFFFFFFF
I can make something for dinner using the Crock-Pot if you want?
Really!?
If I put something on now, it should be ready by dinner.
We could play cards and watch a movie later on or something!
Hahaaaaaaa.

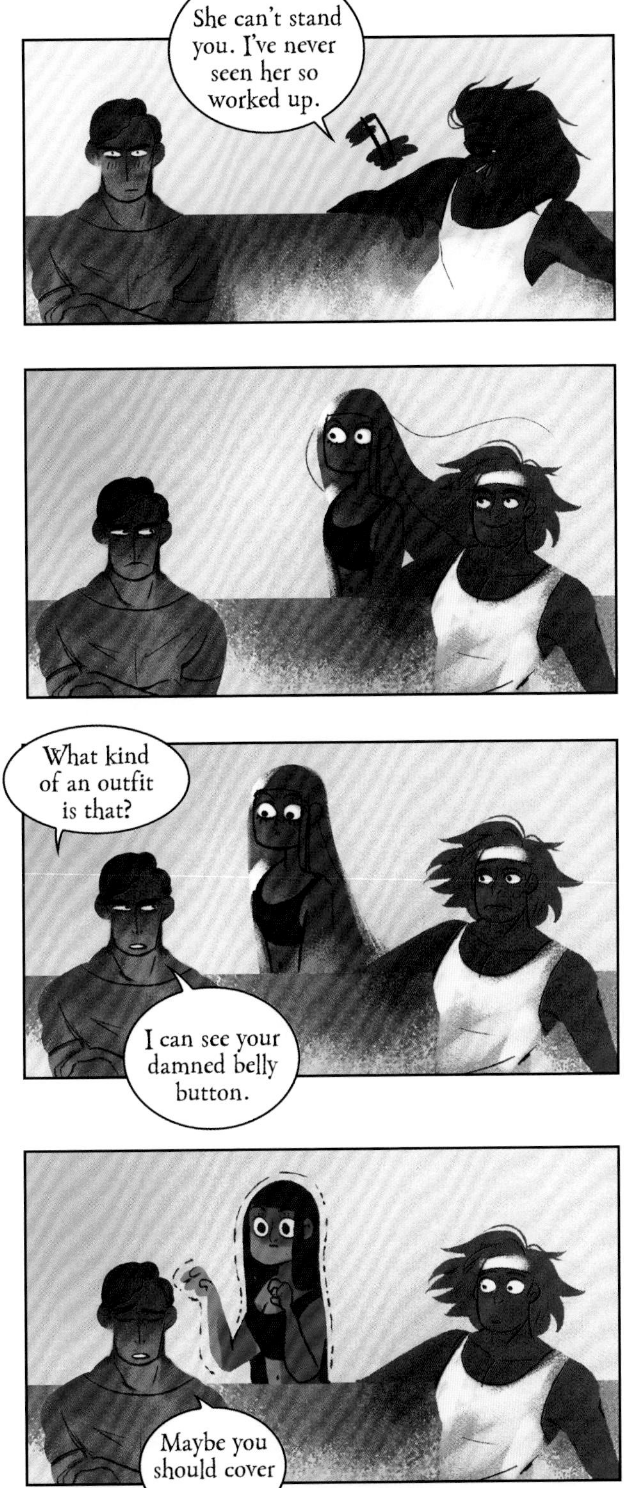
She can't stand you. I've never seen her so worked up.
What kind of an outfit is that?
I can see your damned belly button.
Maybe you should cover up.

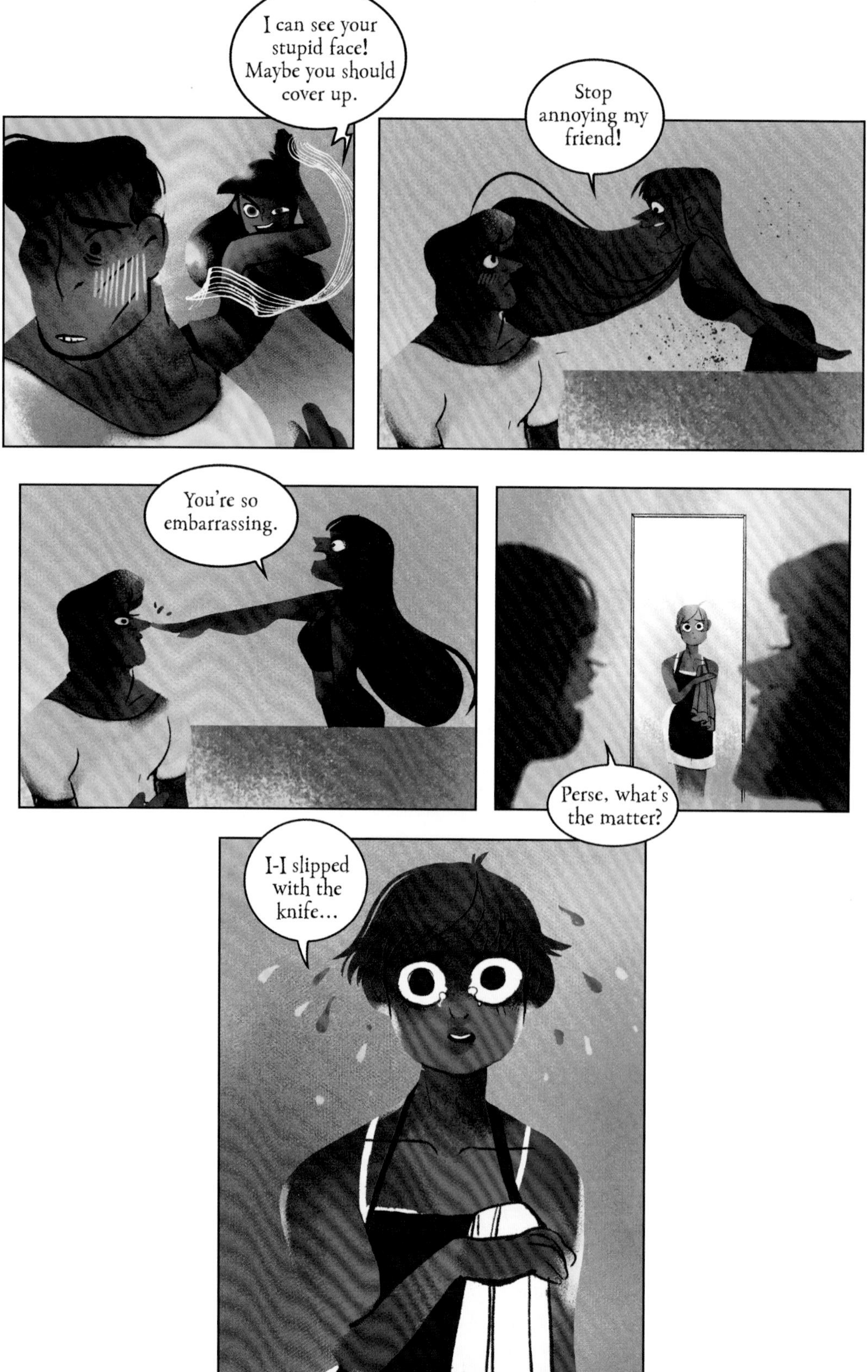
I can see your stupid face! Maybe you should cover up.
Stop annoying my friend!
You're so embarrassing.
Perse, what's the matter?
I-I slipped with the knife...

EPISODE 22: A WOLF IN THE HENHOUSE (PART I)

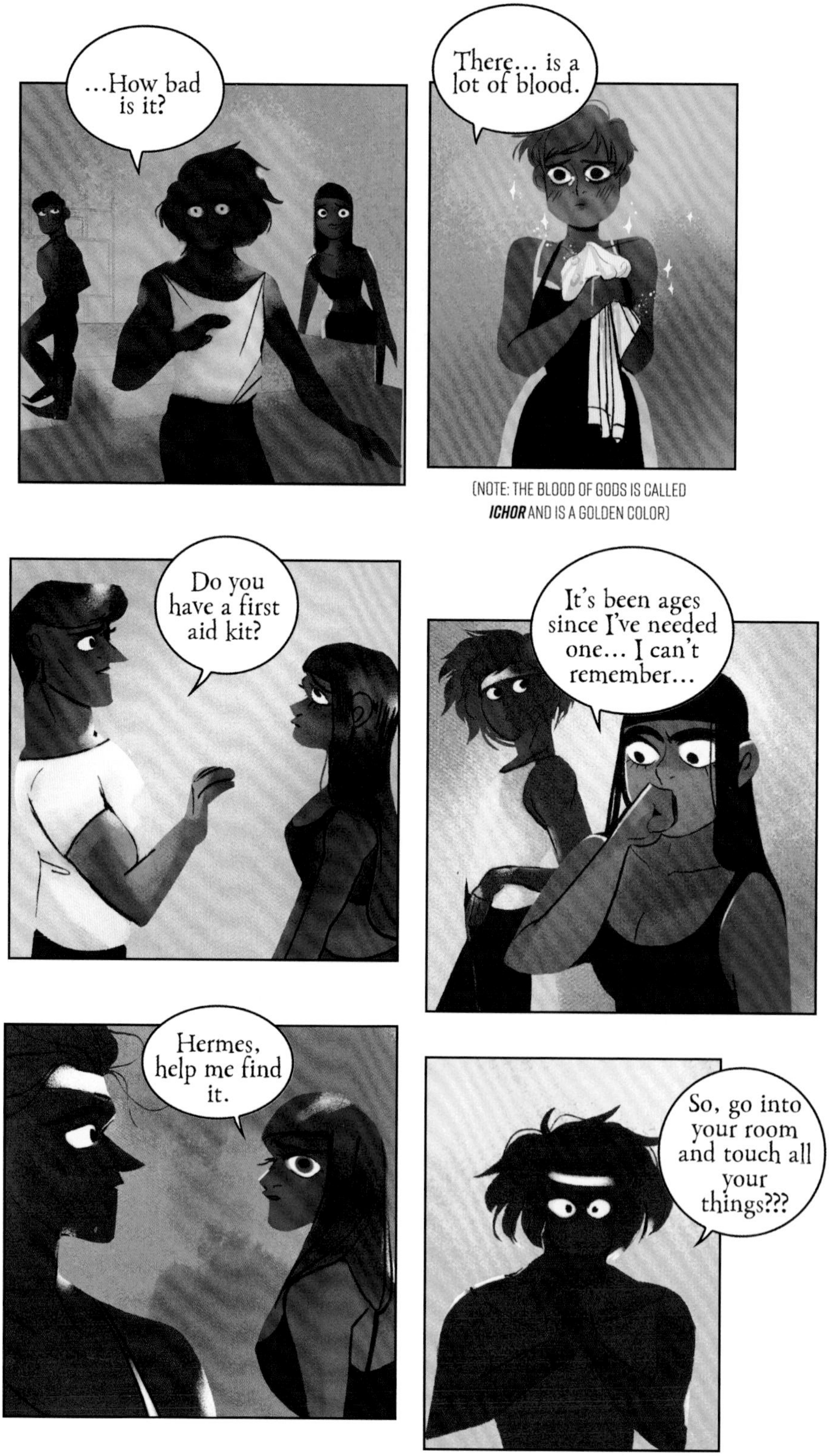
...How bad is it?
There... is a lot of blood.
(NOTE: THE BLOOD OF GODS IS CALLED ICHOR AND IS A GOLDEN COLOR)
Do you have a first aid kit?
It's been ages since I've needed one... I can't remember...
Hermes, help me find it.
So, go into your room and touch all your things???

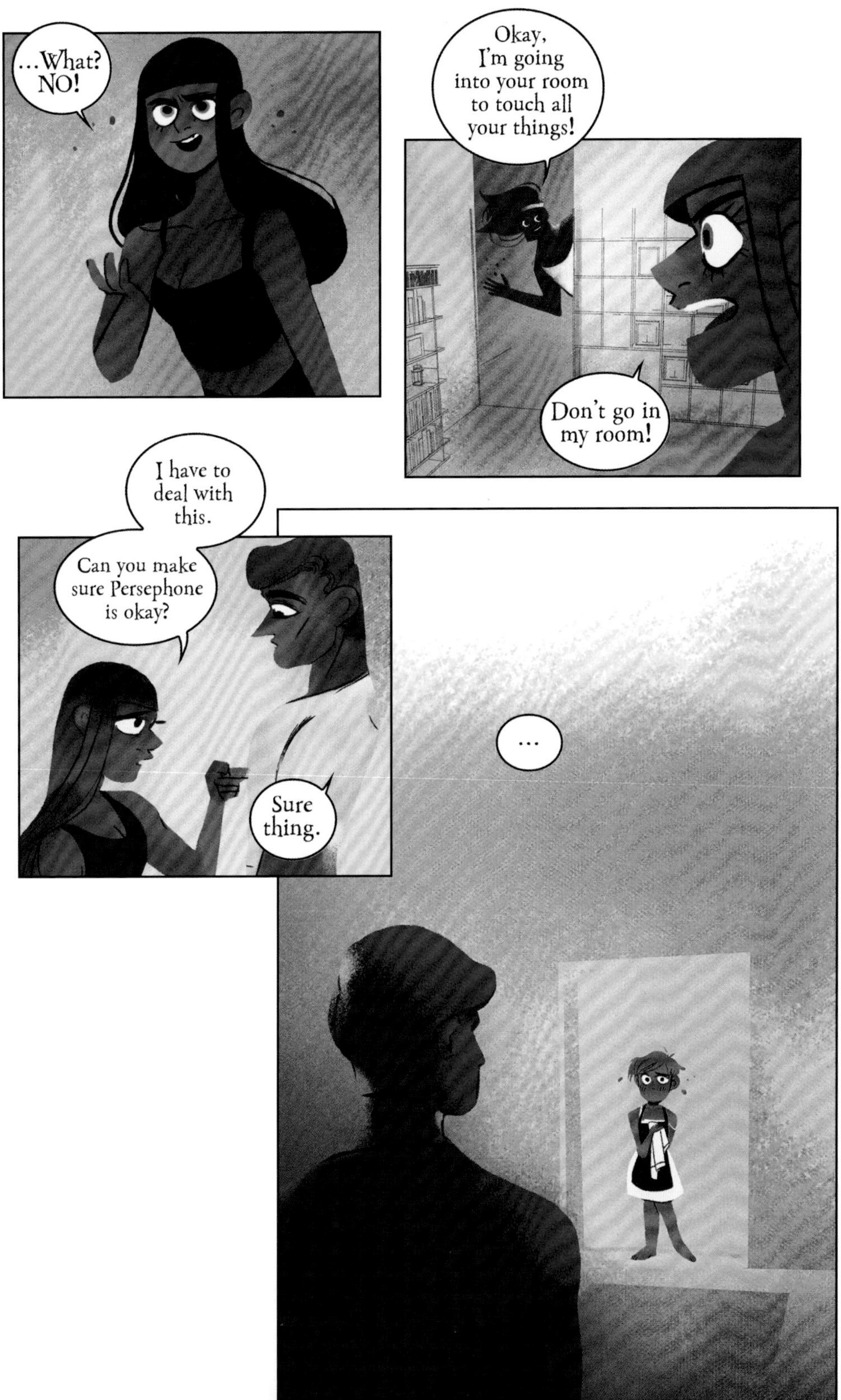
...What? NO!
Okay, I'm going into your room to touch all your things!
Don't go in my room!
I have to deal with this.
Can you make sure Persephone is okay?
Sure thing.
...

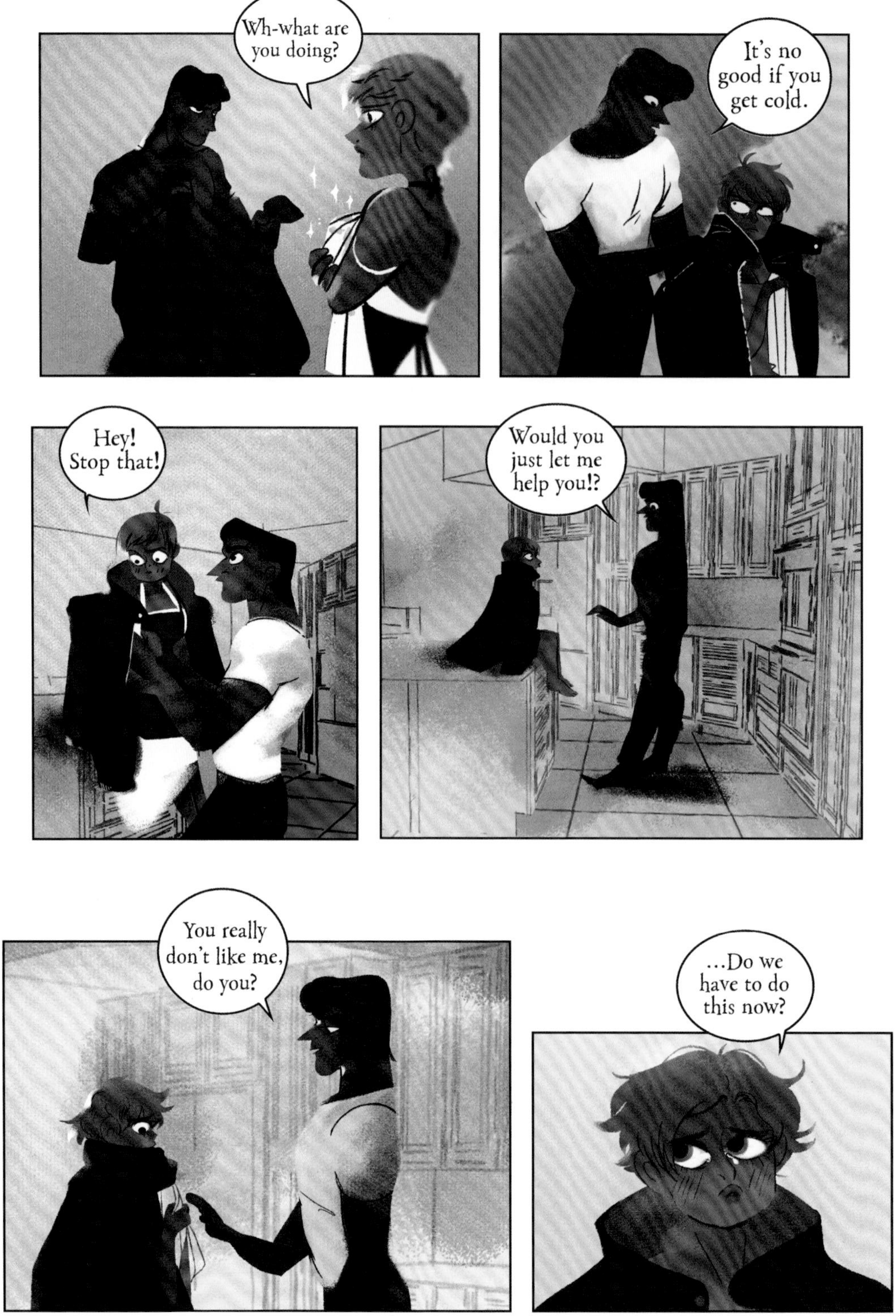
Wh-what are you doing?
It's no good if you get cold.
Hey! Stop that!
Would you just let me help you!?
You really don't like me, do you?
...Do we have to do this now?

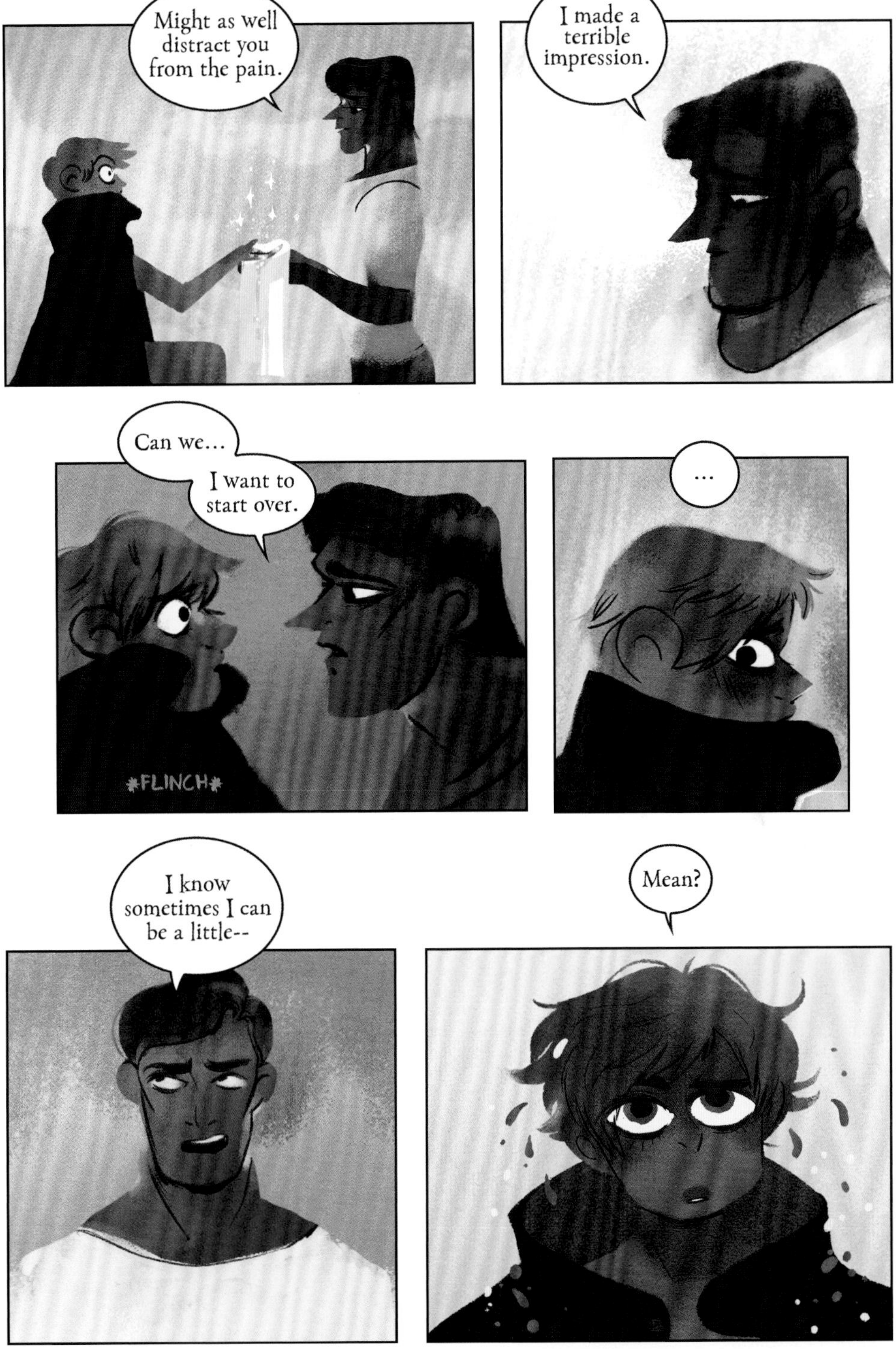
Might as well distract you from the pain.
I made a terrible impression.
Can we...
I want to start over.
FLINCH
...
I know sometimes I can be a little--
Mean?

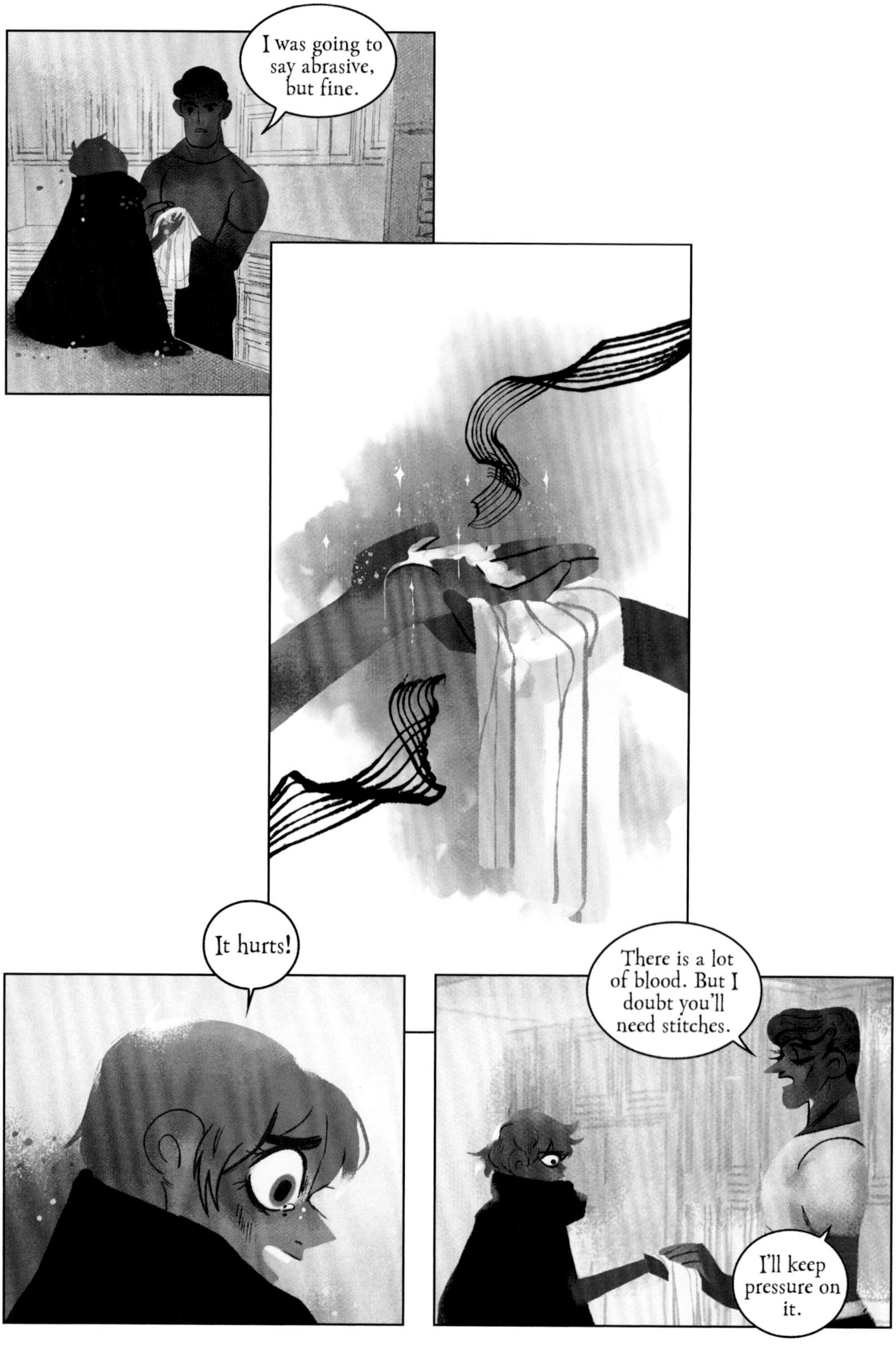
I was going to say abrasive, but fine.
It hurts!
There is a lot of blood. But I doubt you'll need stitches.
I'll keep pressure on it.

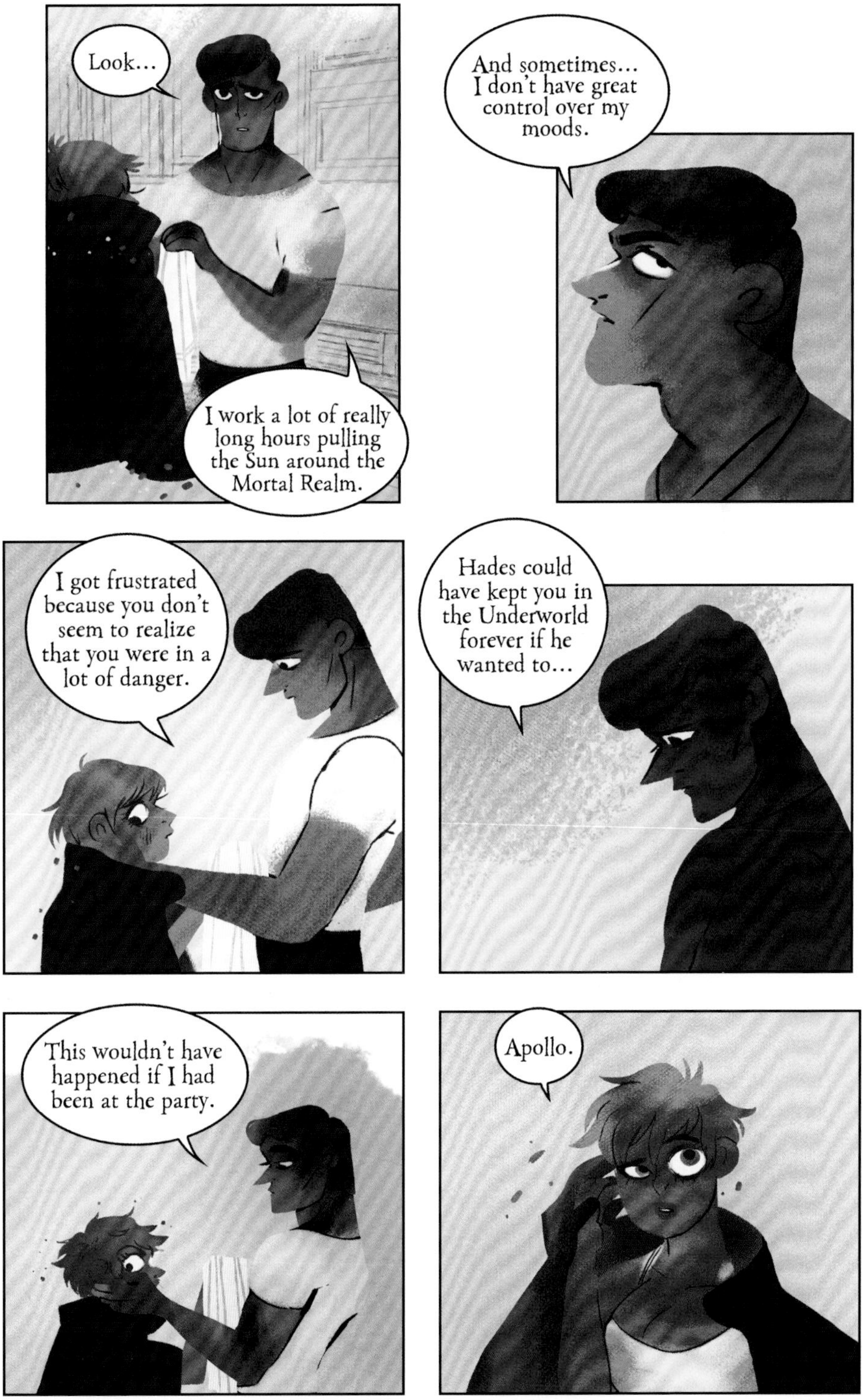
Look…
I work a lot of really long hours pulling the Sun around the Mortal Realm.
And sometimes… I don't have great control over my moods.
I got frustrated because you don't seem to realize that you were in a lot of danger.
Hades could have kept you in the Underworld forever if he wanted to…
This wouldn't have happened if I had been at the party.
Apollo.

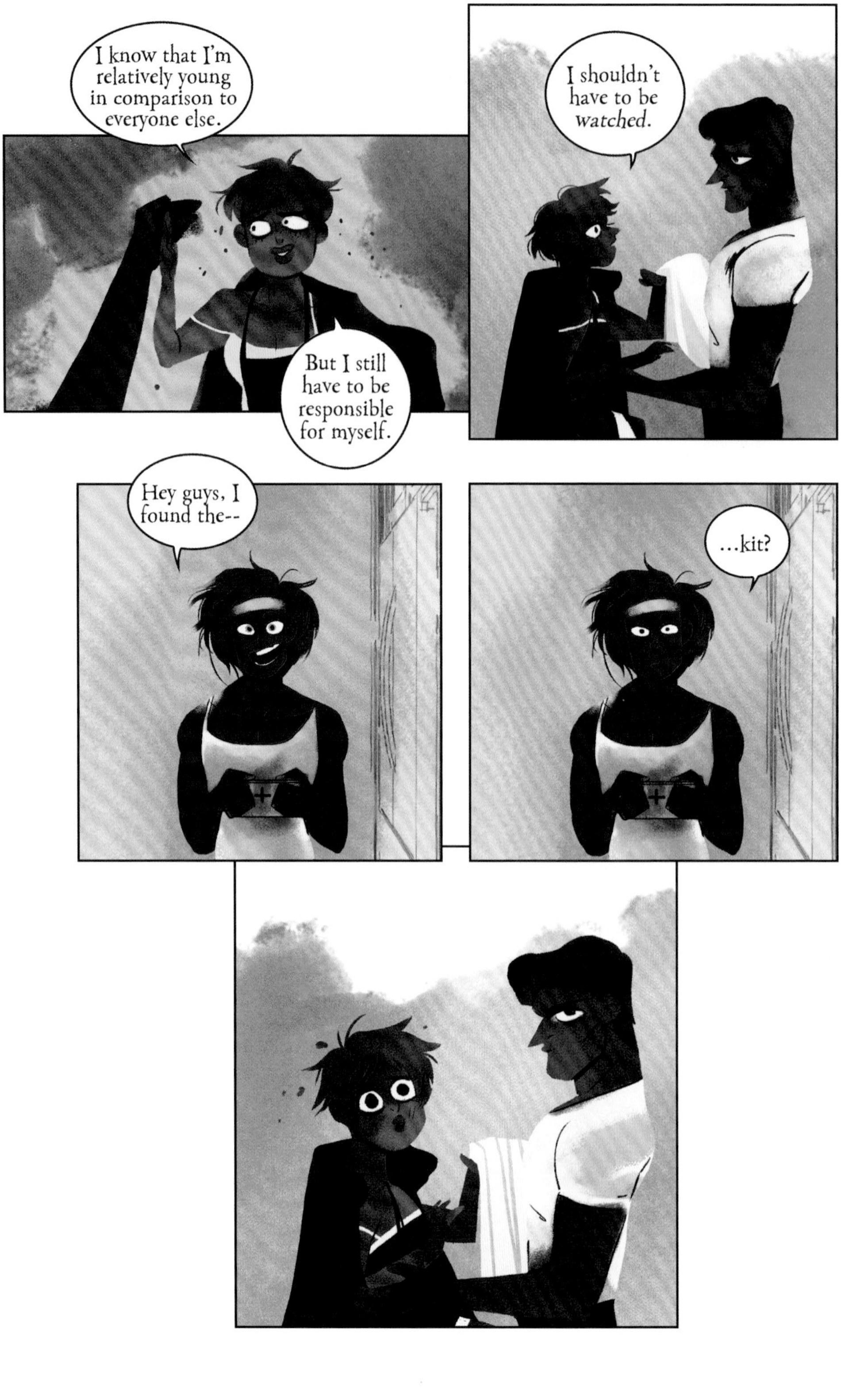
I know that I'm relatively young in comparison to everyone else.
But I still have to be responsible for myself.
I shouldn't have to be *watched*.
Hey guys, I found the--
...kit?

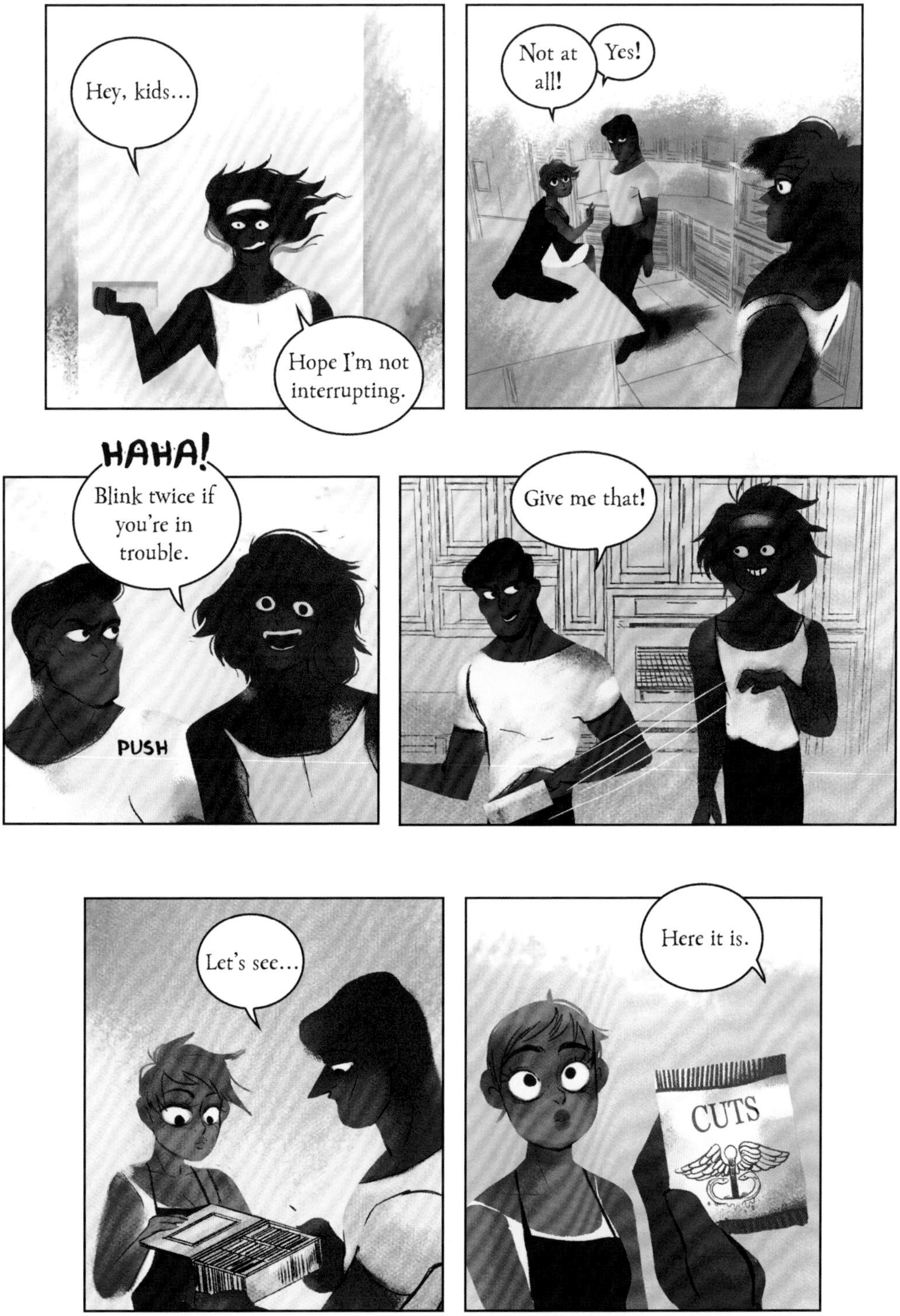
Hey, kids...
Hope I'm not interrupting.
Not at all!
Yes!
HAHA!
Blink twice if you're in trouble.
PUSH
Give me that!
Let's see...
Here it is.
CUTS

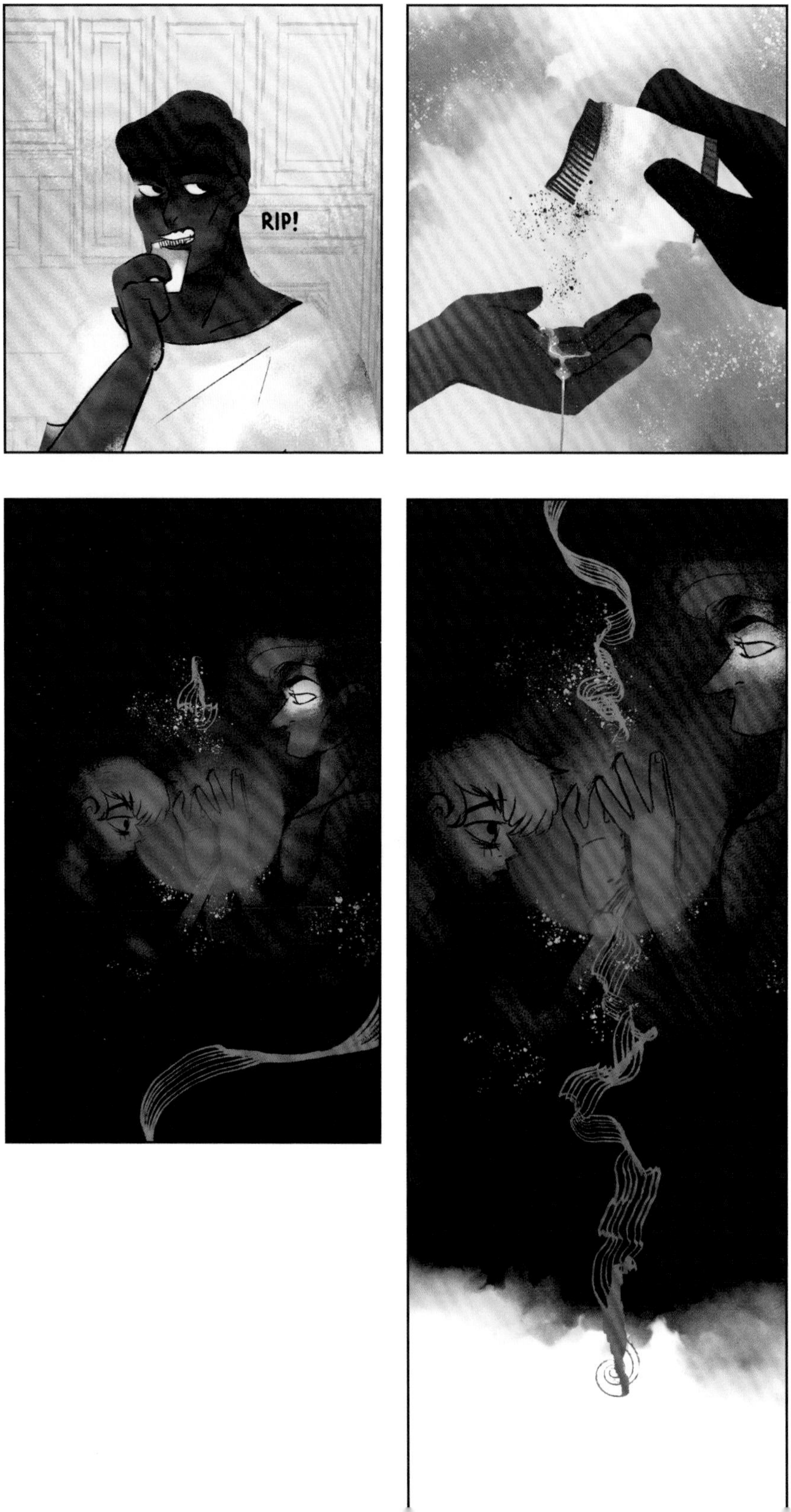
RIP!

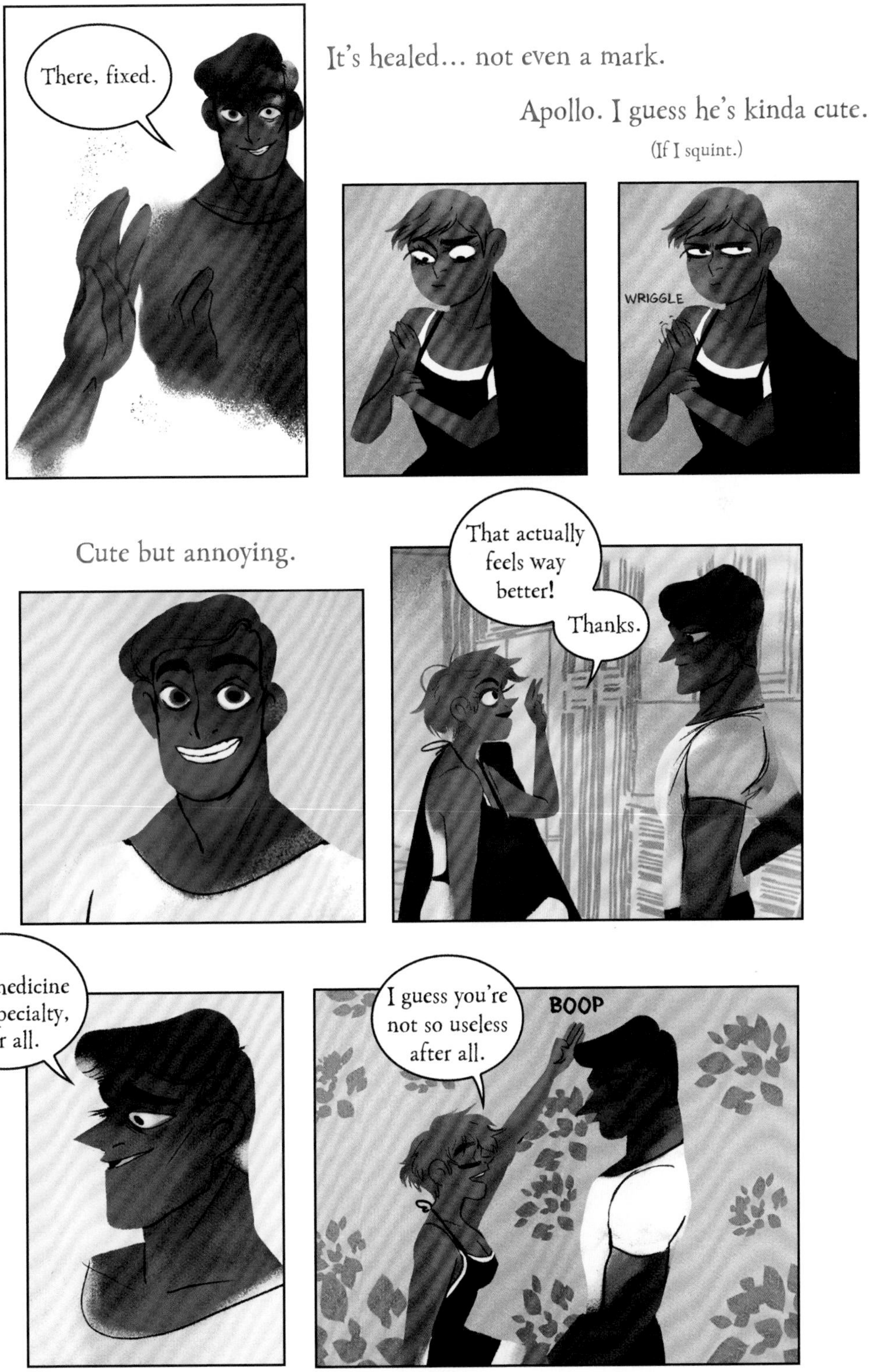
There, fixed.
It's healed... not even a mark.
Apollo. I guess he's kinda cute.
(If I squint.)
WRIGGLE
Cute but annoying.
That actually feels way better!
Thanks.
Well, medicine is my specialty, after all.
I guess you're not so useless after all.
BOOP

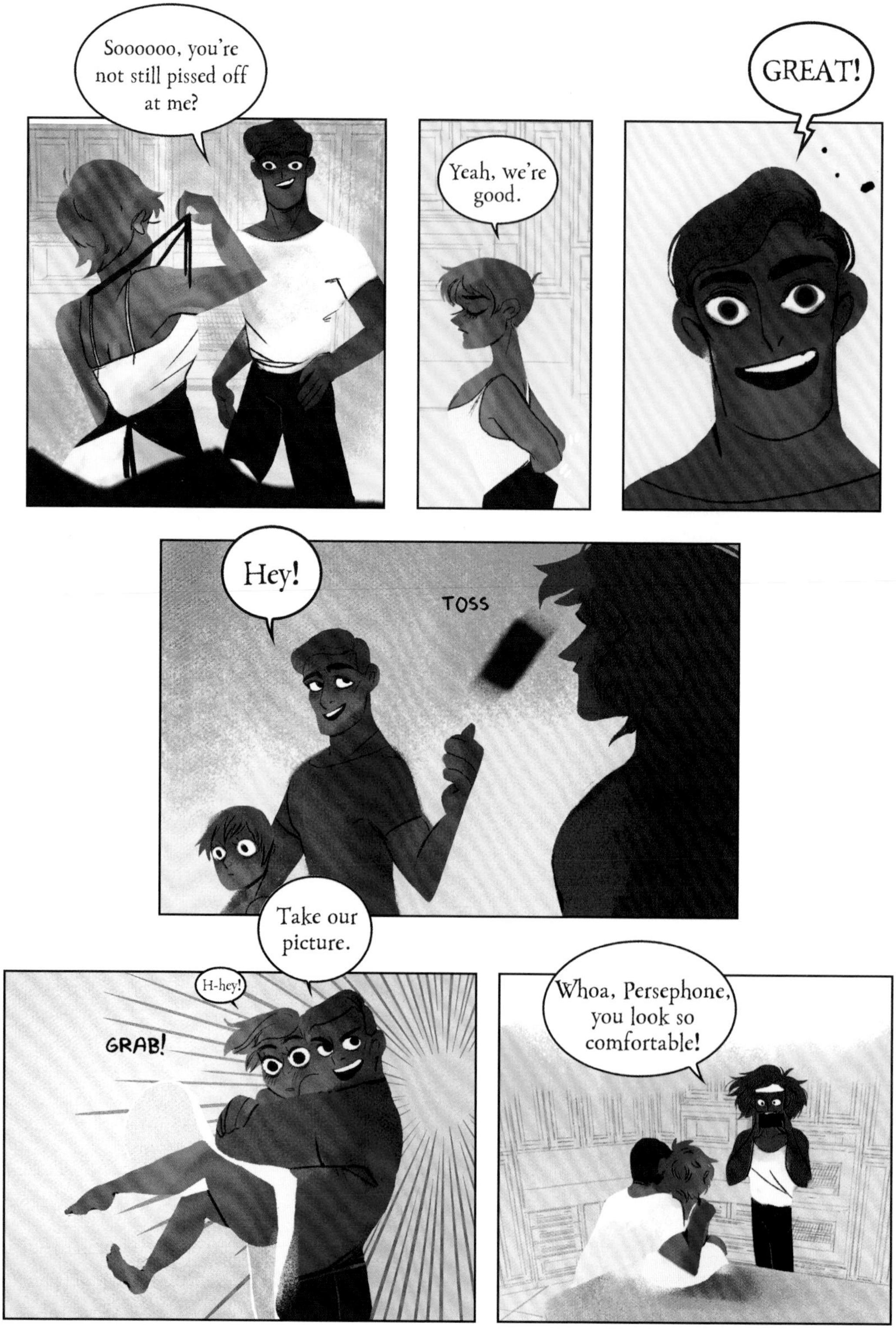
Soooooo, you're not still pissed off at me?
Yeah, we're good.
GREAT!
Hey!
TOSS
Take our picture.
H-hey!
GRAB!
Whoa, Persephone, you look so comfortable!

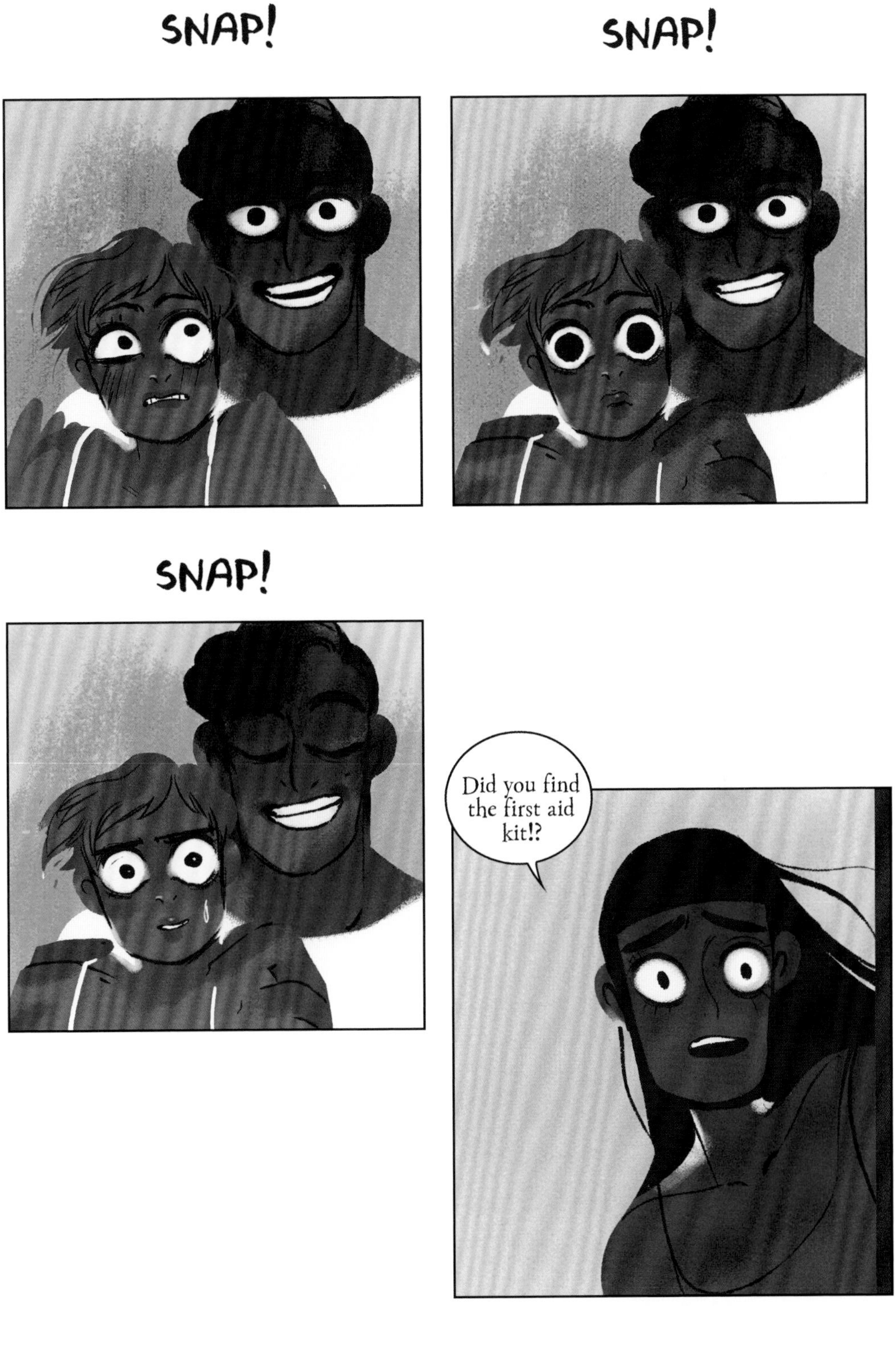
SNAP!
SNAP!
SNAP!
Did you find the first aid kit!?

FIXED!

EPISODE 23: A WOLF IN THE HENHOUSE (PART 2)

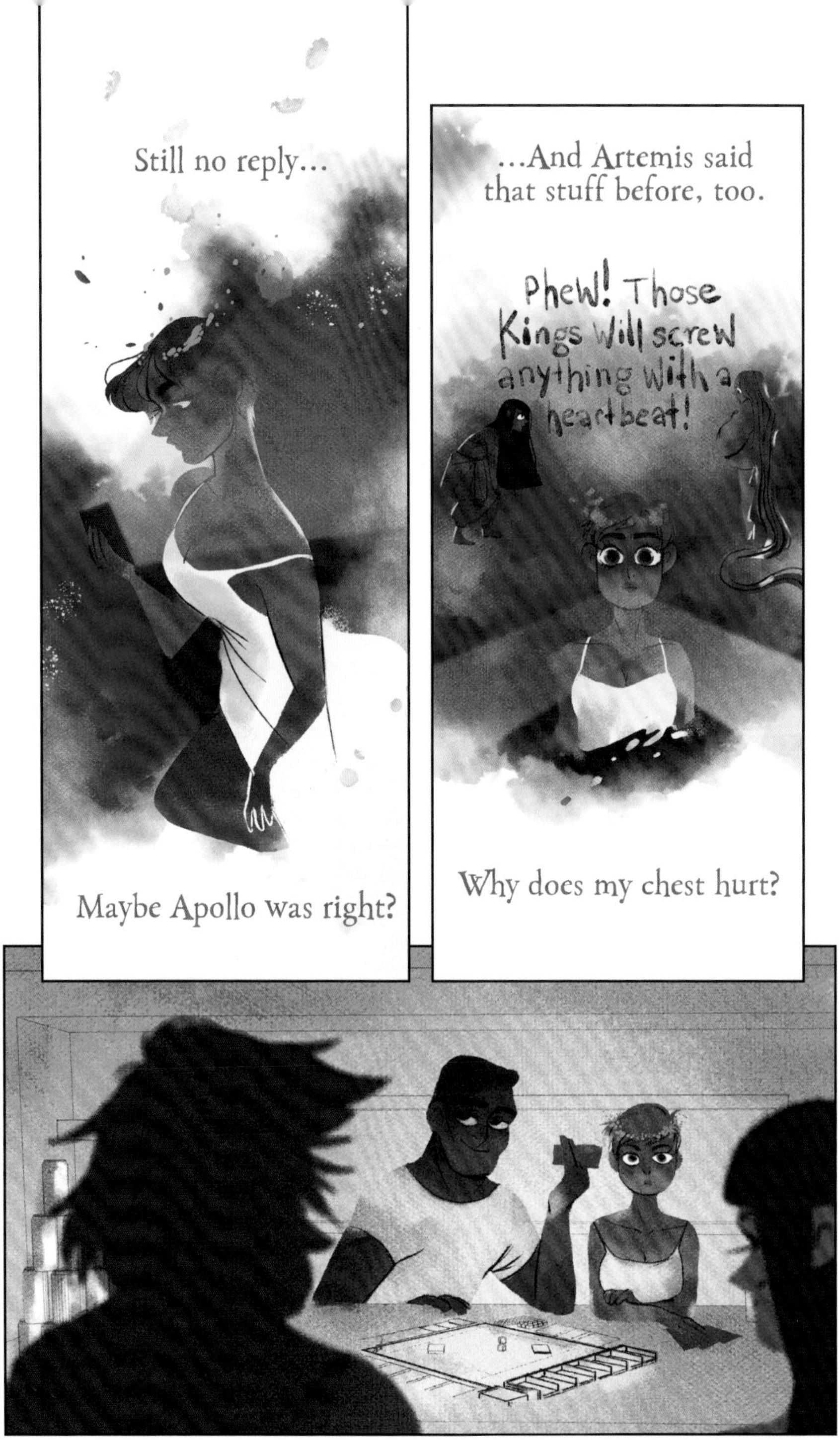
Still no reply...
Maybe Apollo was right?
...And Artemis said that stuff before, too.
Phew! Those Kings will screw anything with a heartbeat!
Why does my chest hurt?

Do they have a point?

All I ever hear about
are Zeus's and Poseidon's escapades.

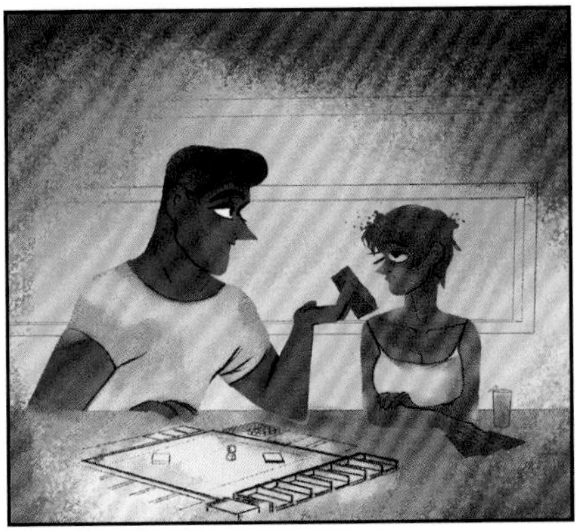

Is Hades the same?

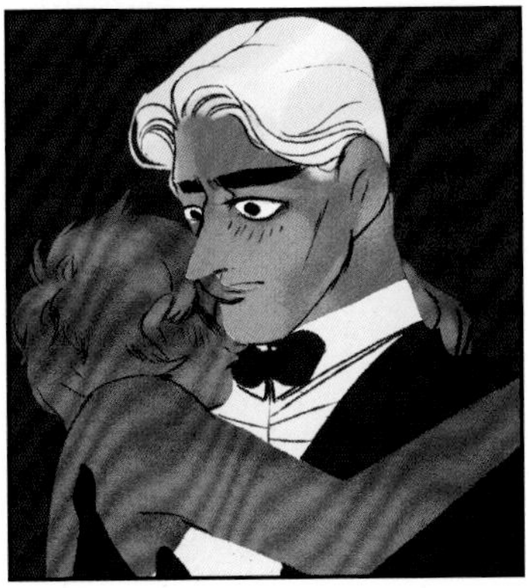

He didn't seem that way.

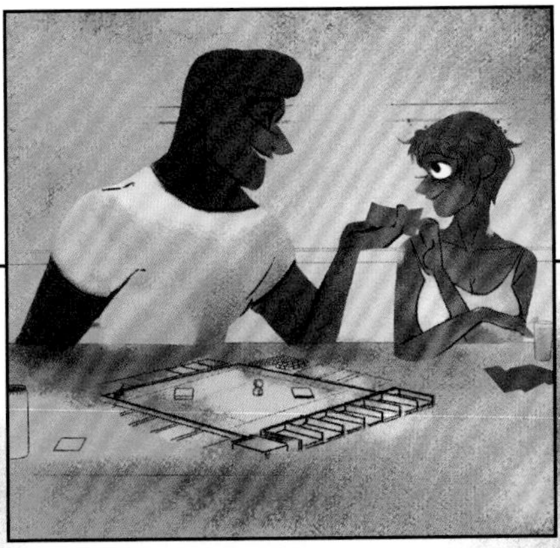

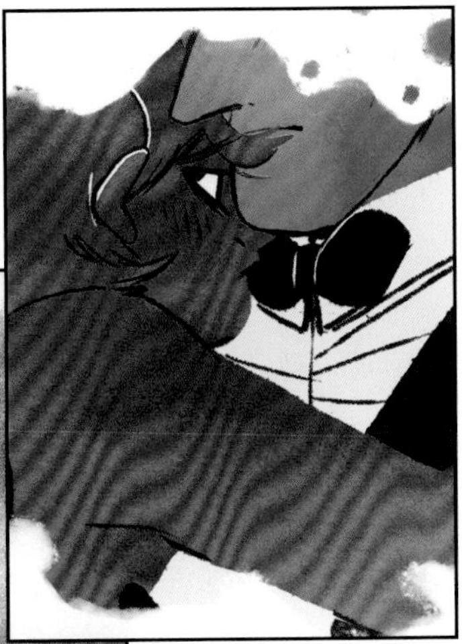

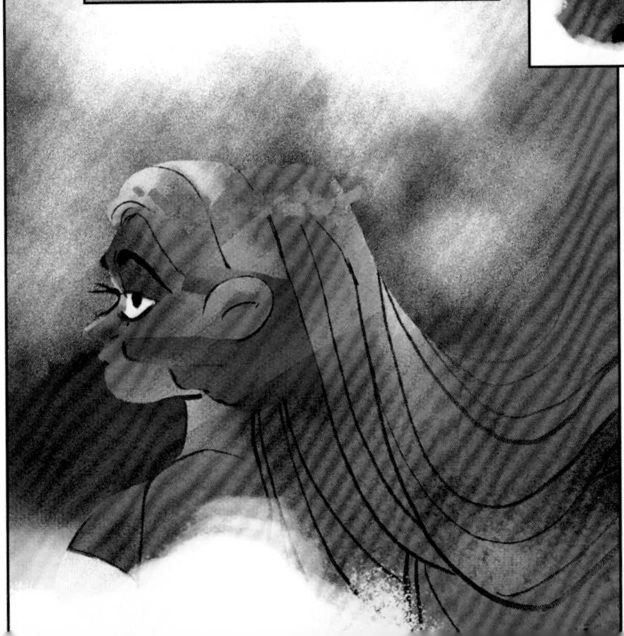

I'd be lying if I said I didn't find
the attention exciting.

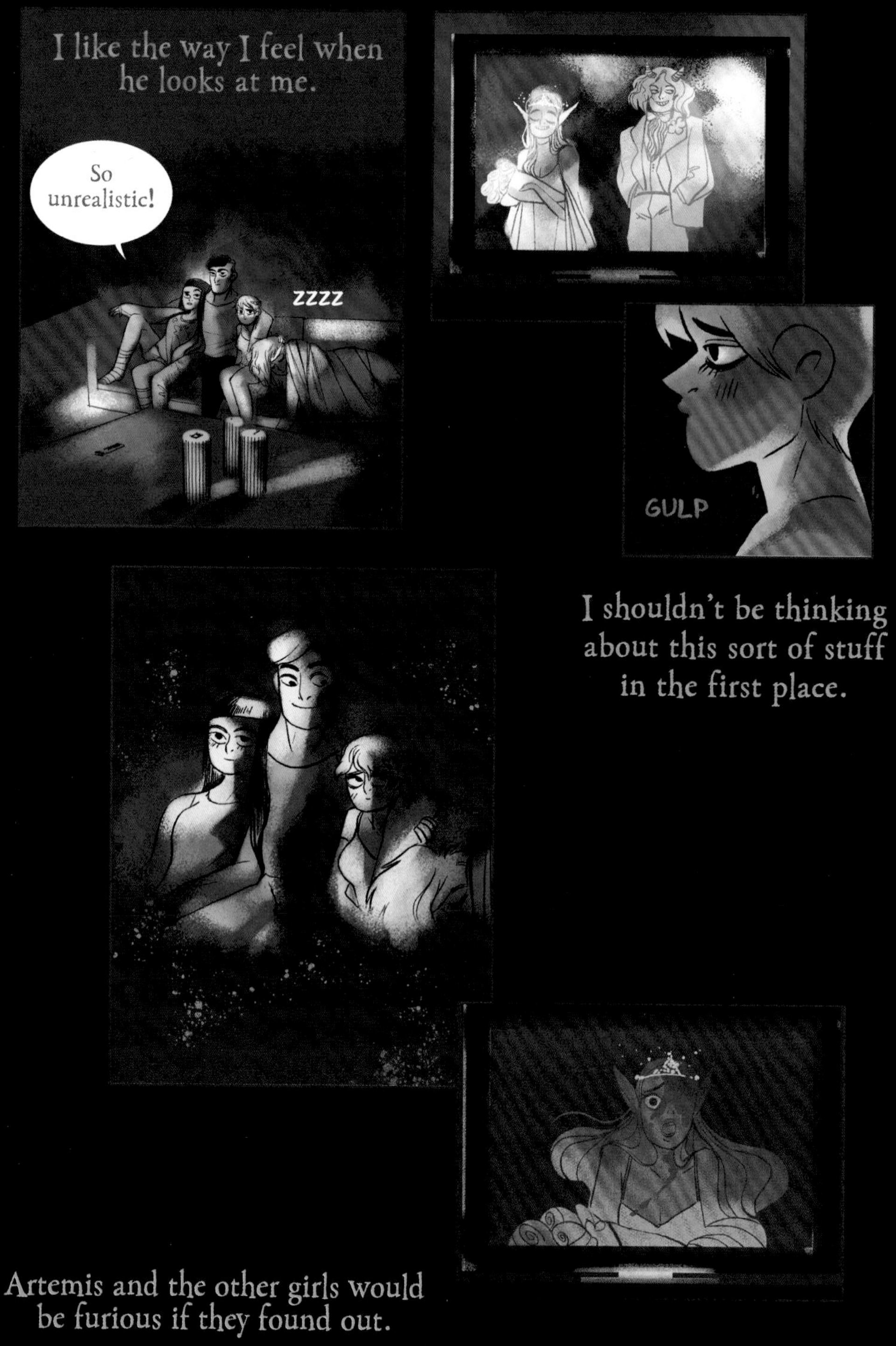
I like the way I feel when he looks at me.
So unrealistic!
ZZZZ
GULP
I shouldn't be thinking about this sort of stuff in the first place.
Artemis and the other girls would be furious if they found out.

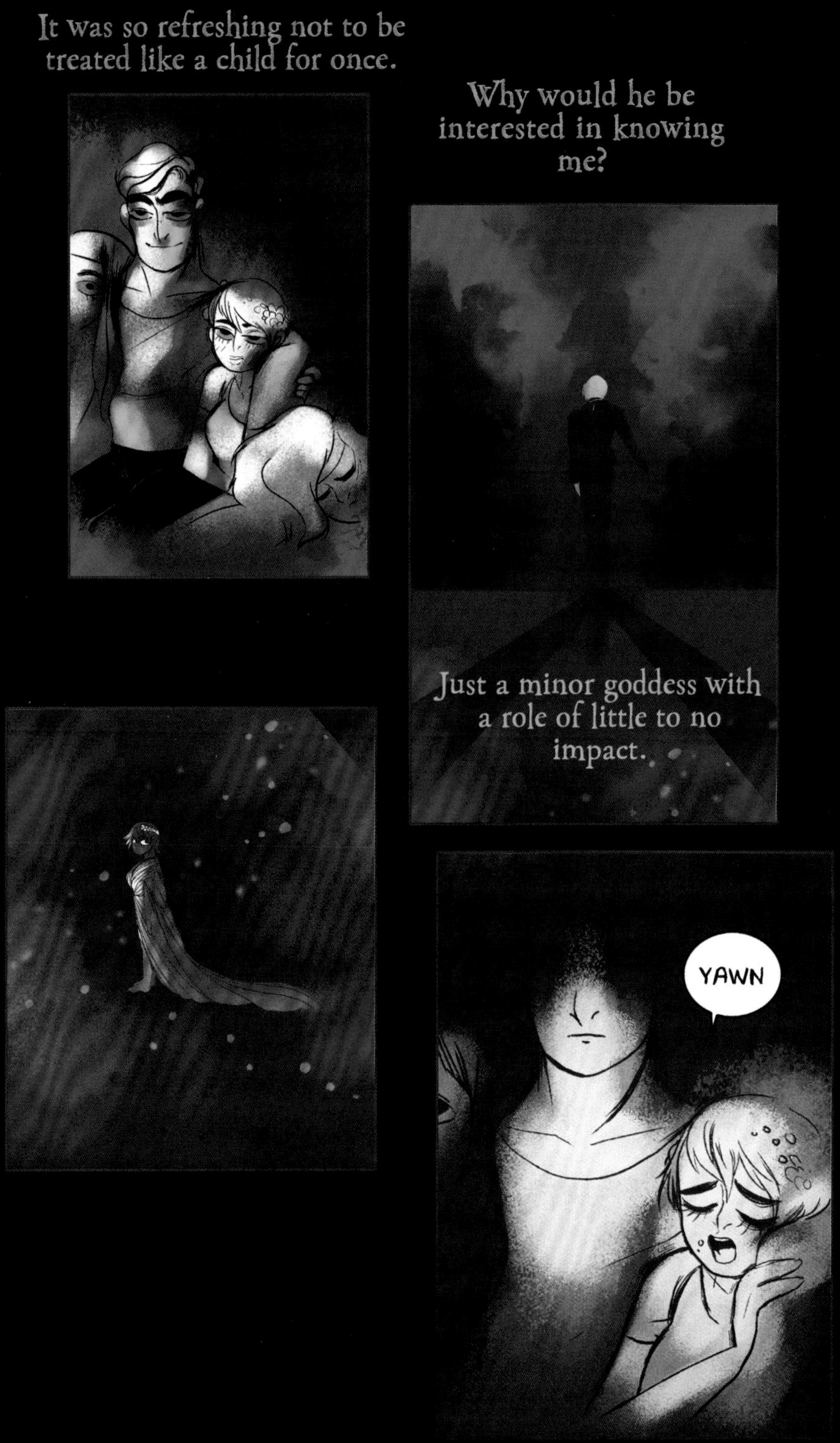
It was so refreshing not to be treated like a child for once.
Why would he be interested in knowing me?
Just a minor goddess with a role of little to no impact.
YAWN

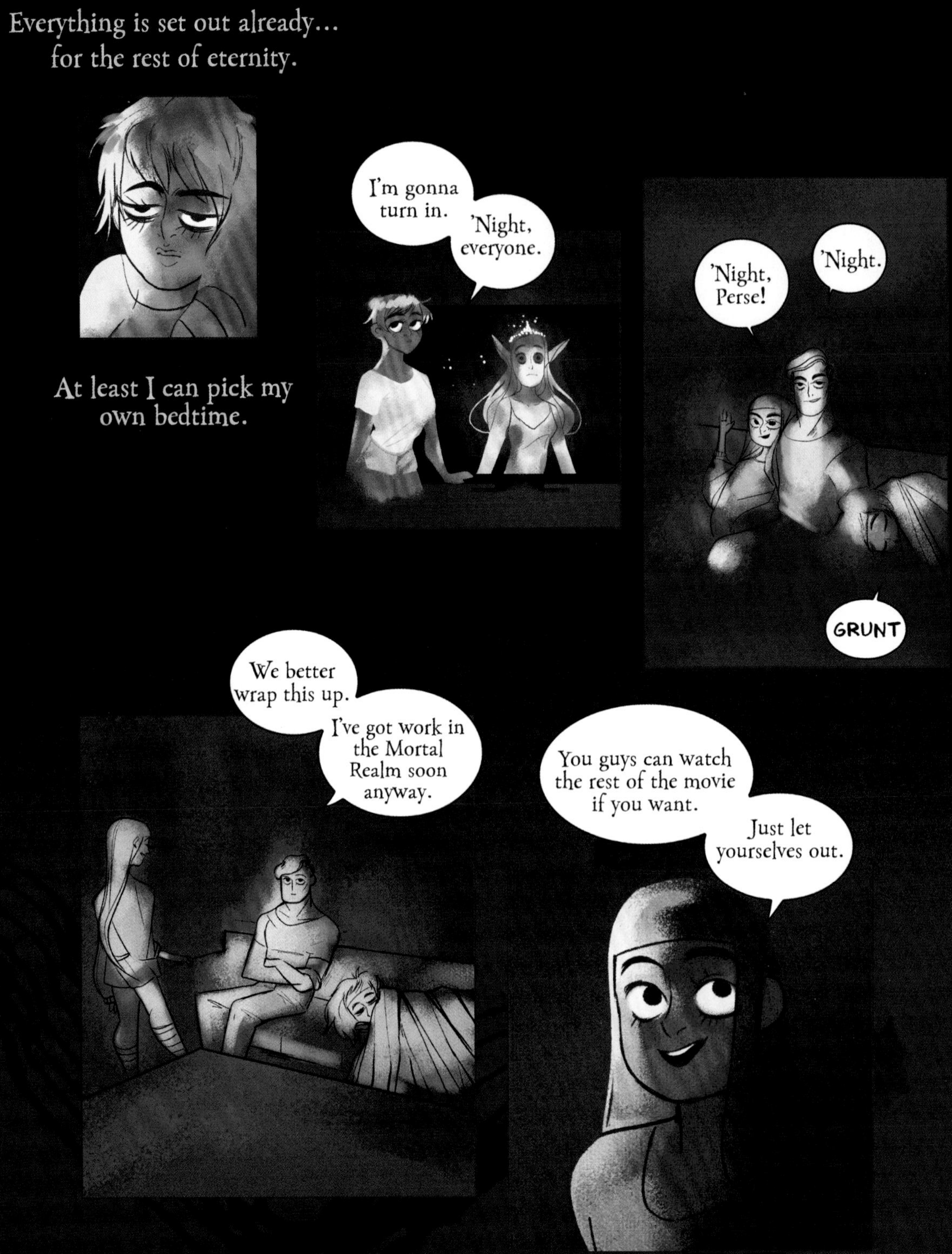
Everything is set out already... for the rest of eternity.
At least I can pick my own bedtime.
I'm gonna turn in.
'Night, everyone.
'Night, Perse!
'Night.
GRUNT
We better wrap this up.
I've got work in the Mortal Realm soon anyway.
You guys can watch the rest of the movie if you want.
Just let yourselves out.

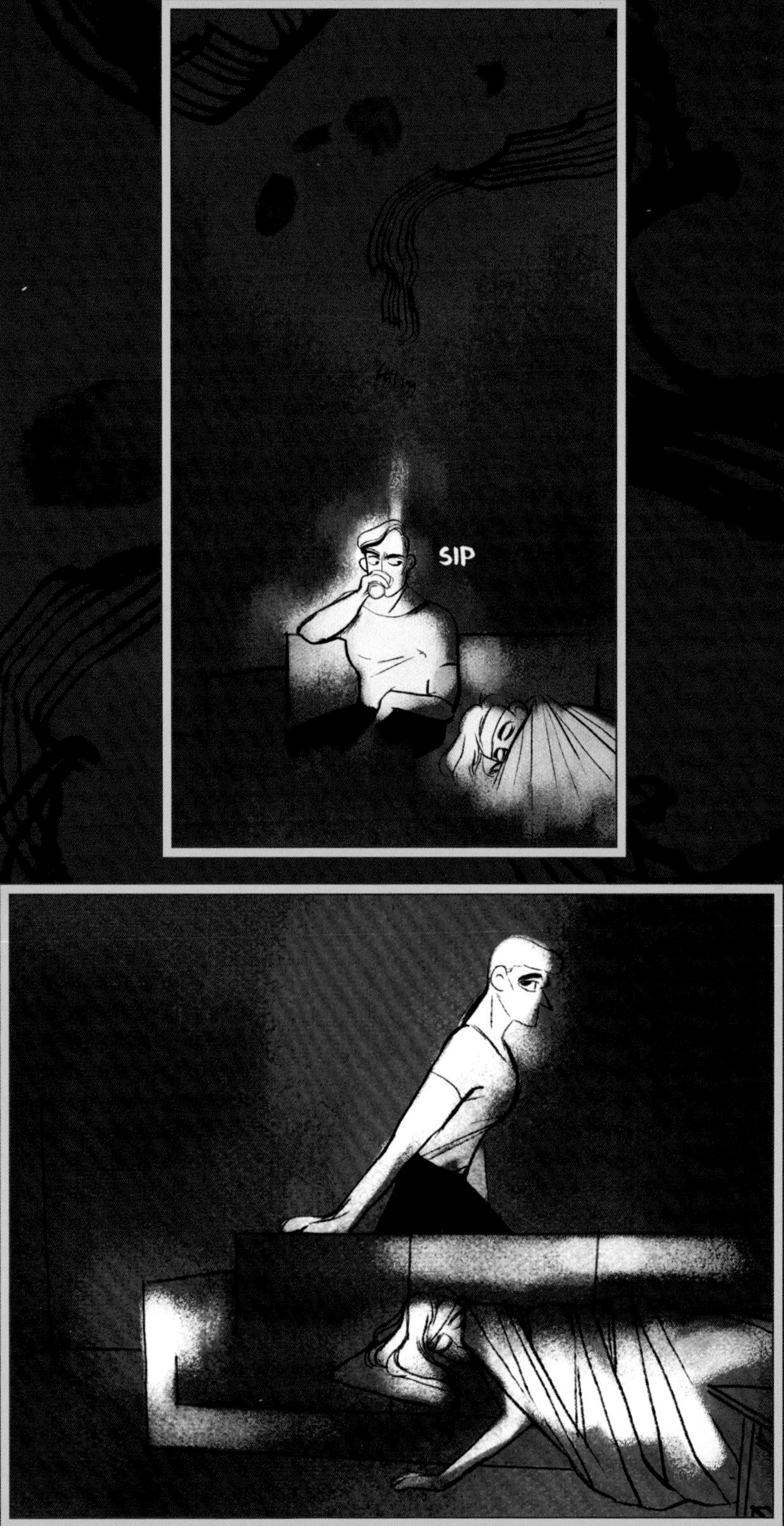
SIP

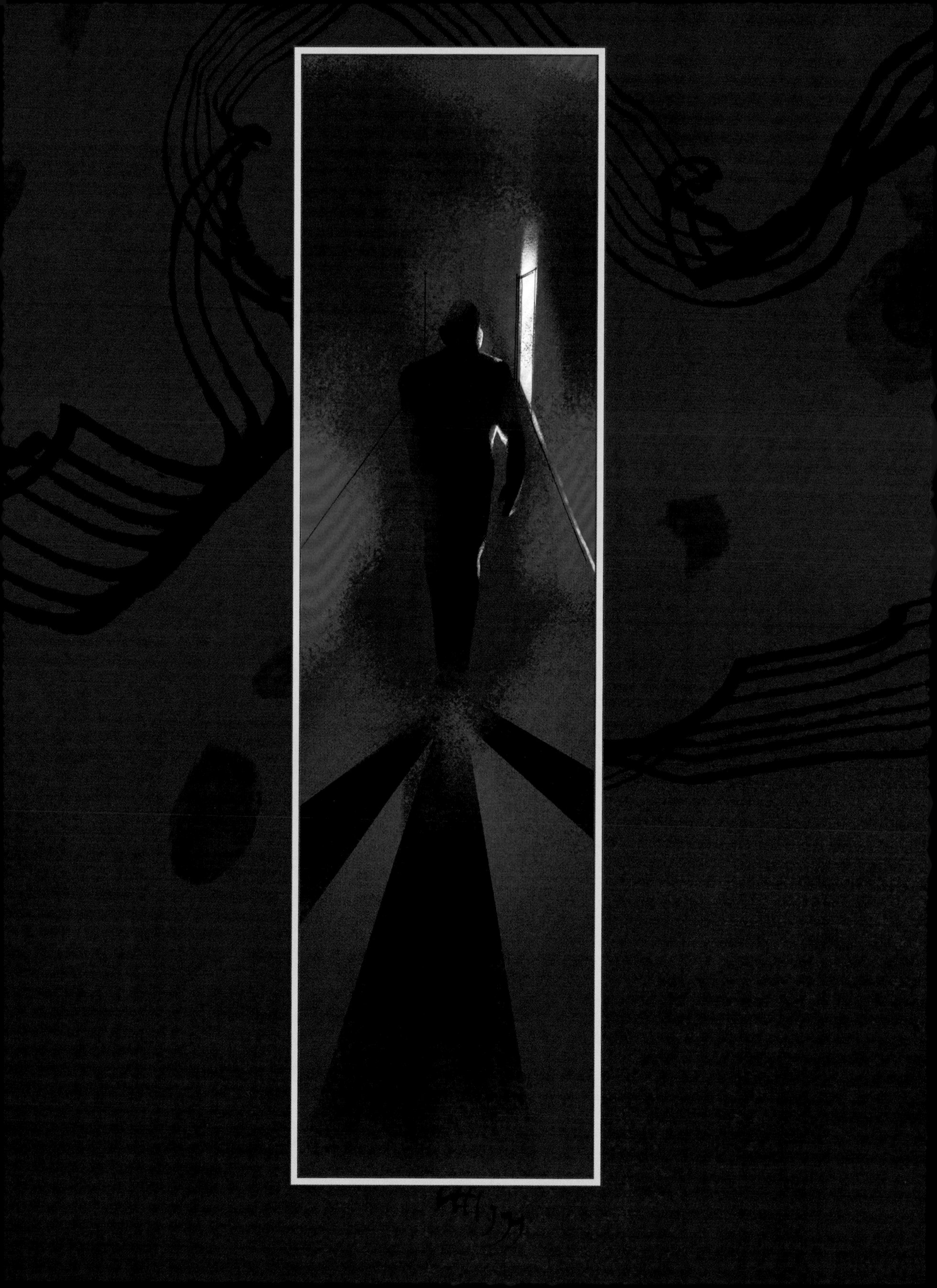

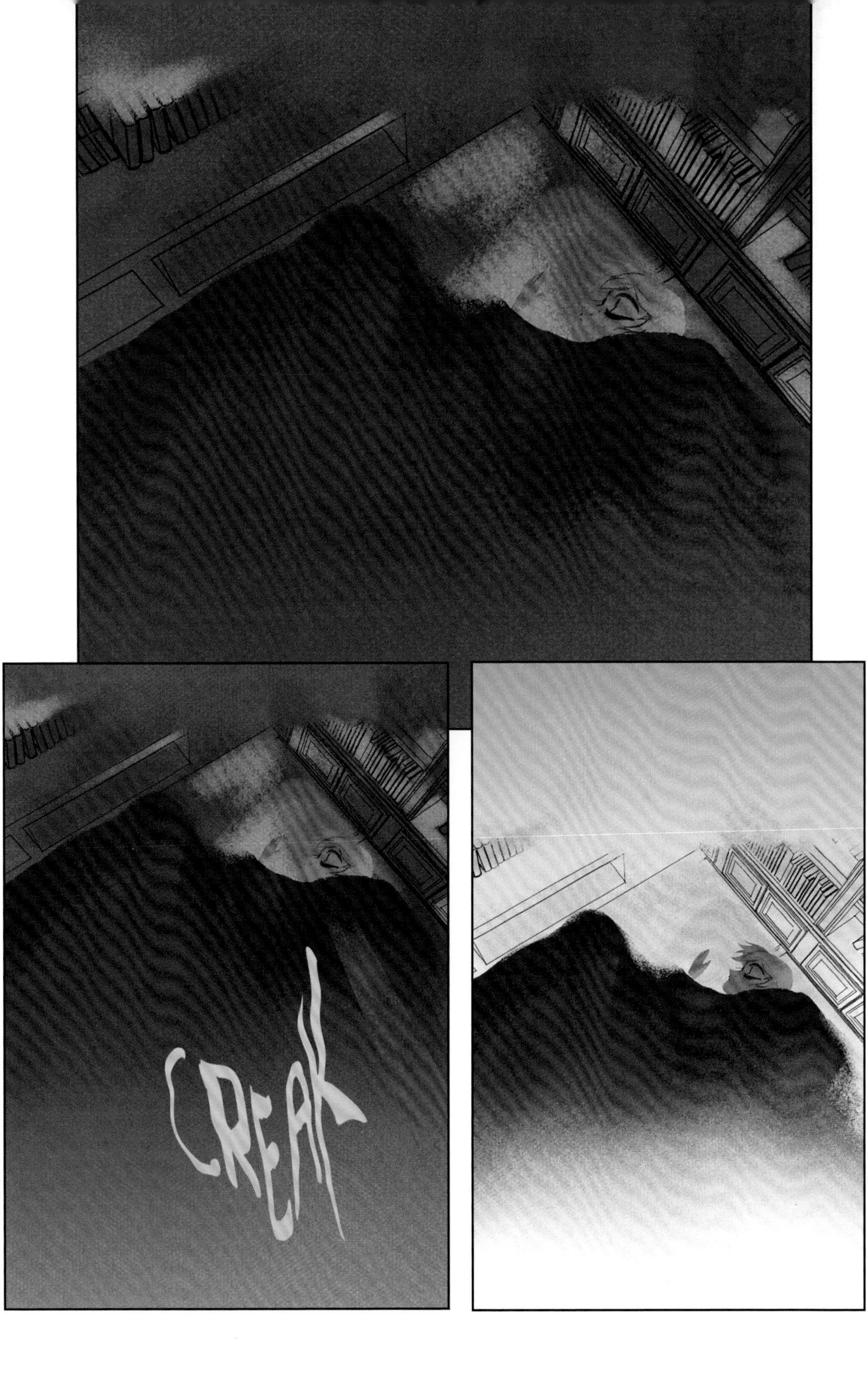
CREAK

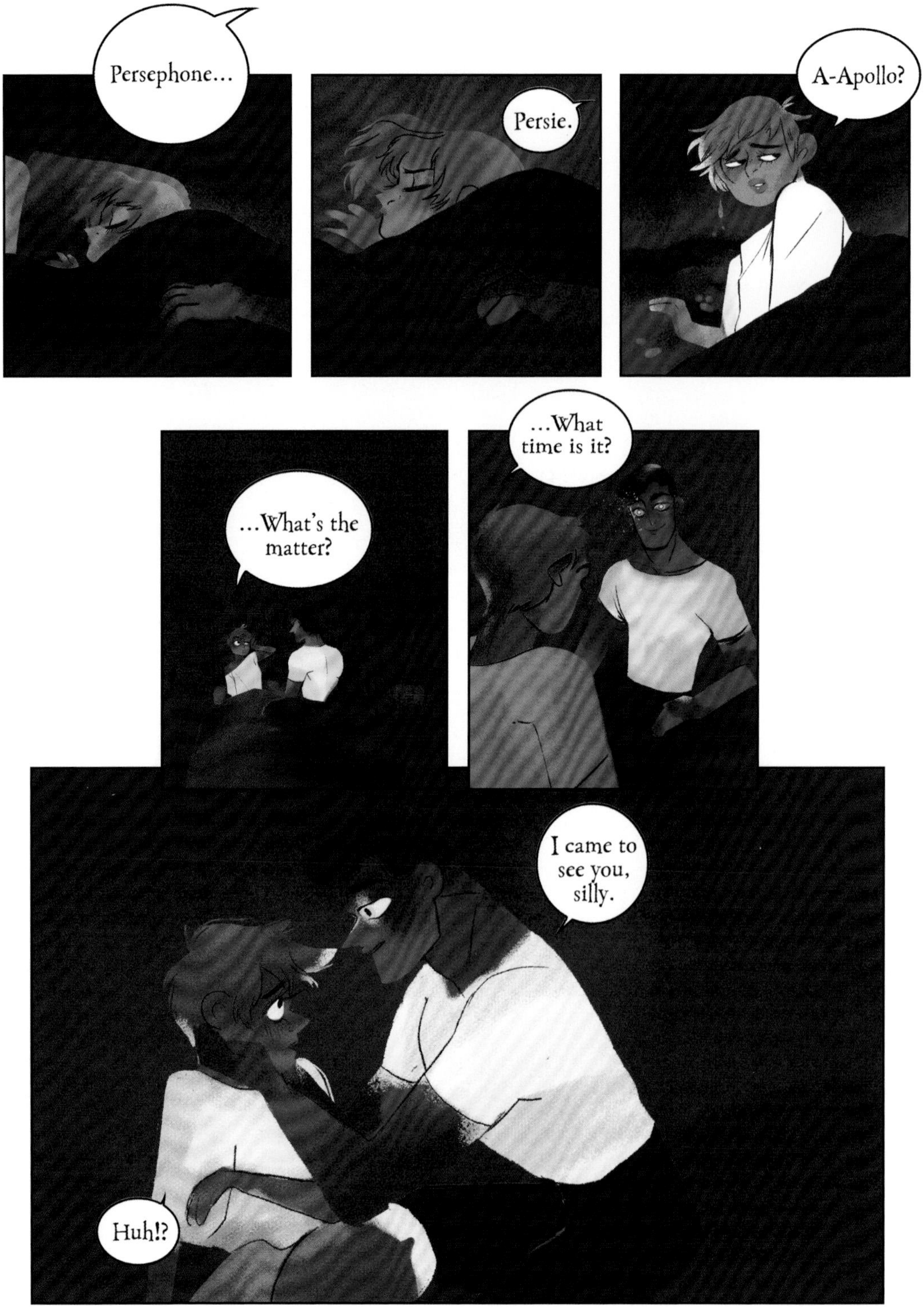
Persephone...
Persie.
A-Apollo?
...What's the matter?
...What time is it?
I came to see you, silly.
Huh!?

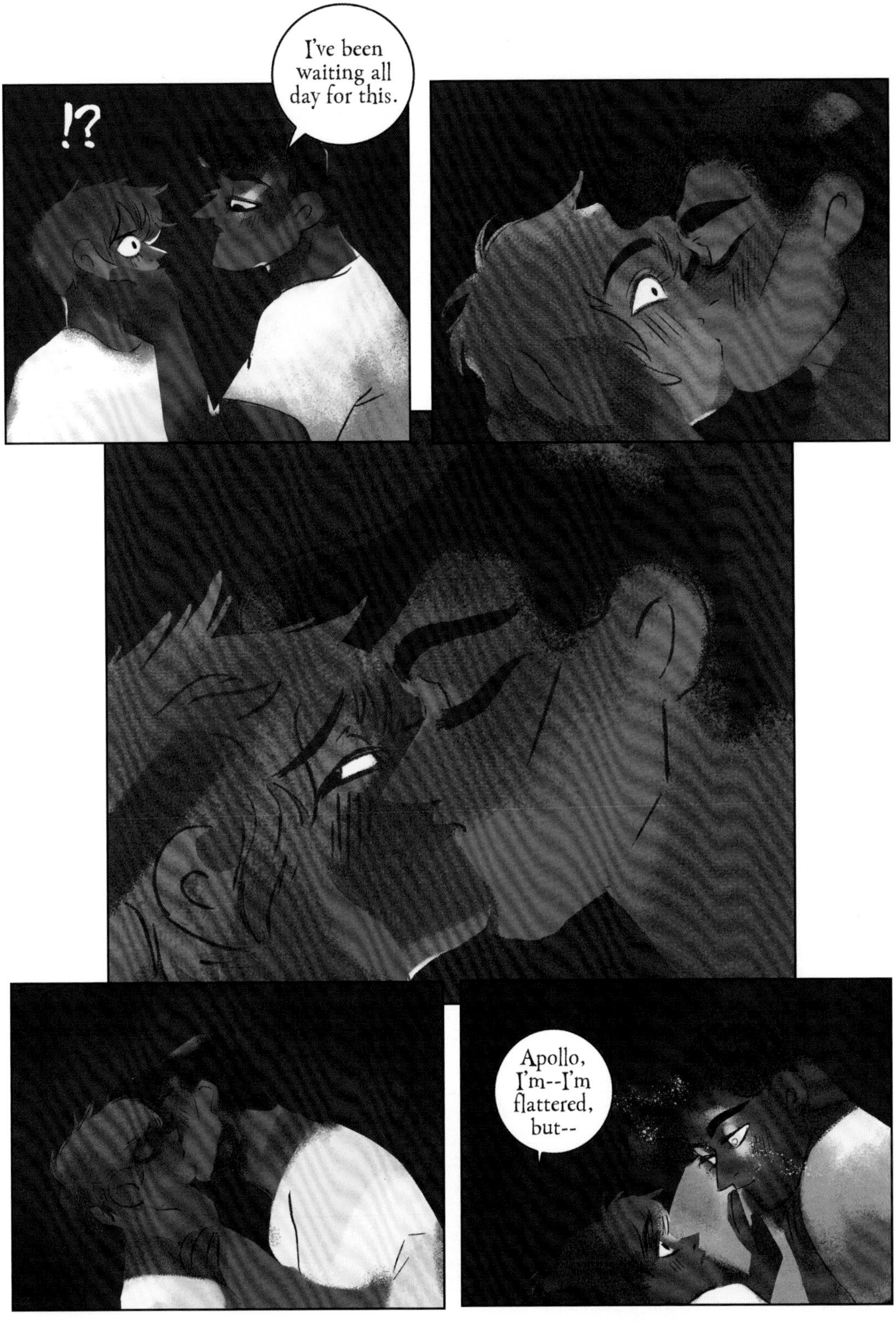
!?
I've been waiting all day for this.
Apollo, I'm--I'm flattered, but--

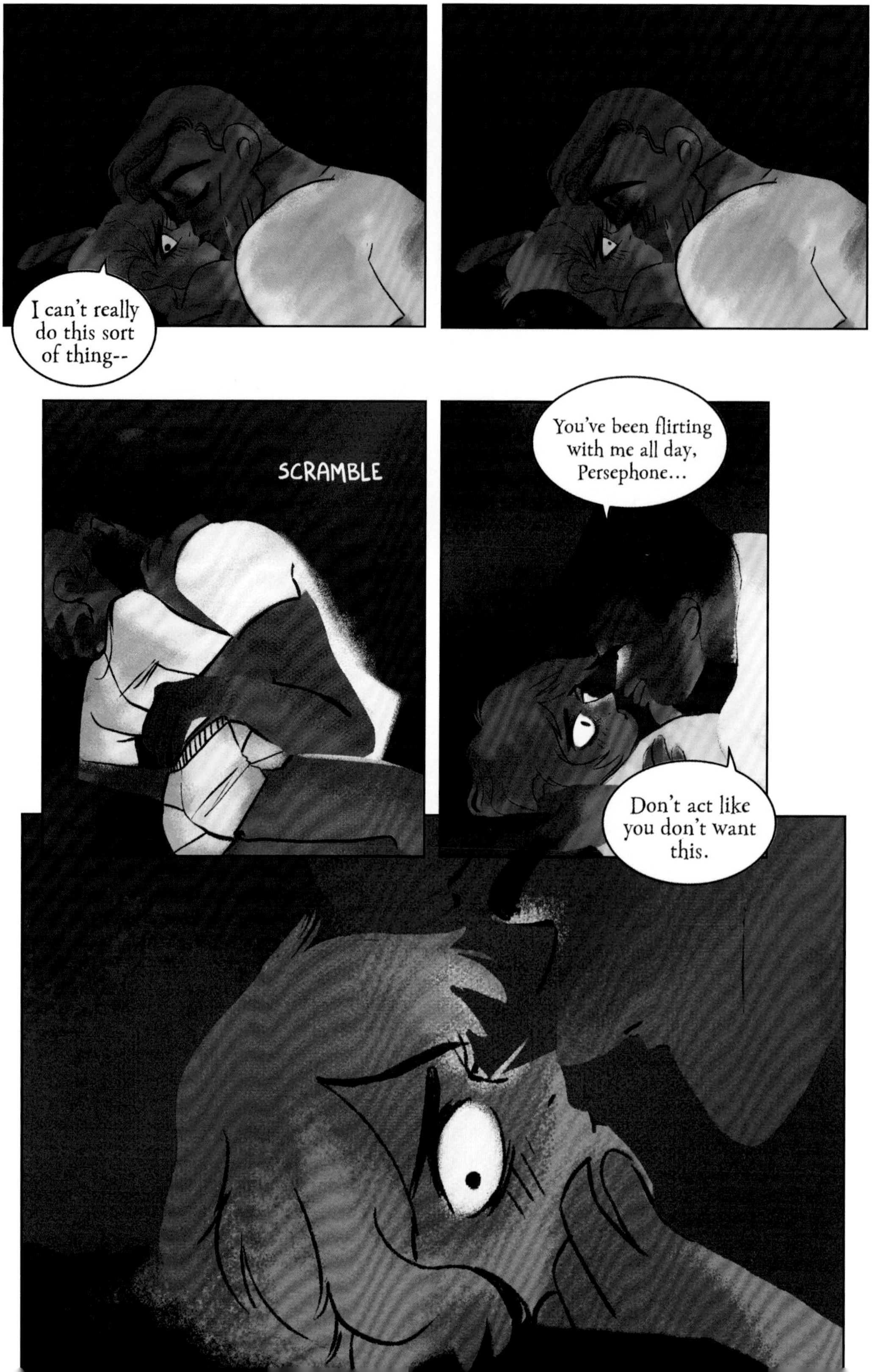
I can't really do this sort of thing--
SCRAMBLE
You've been flirting with me all day, Persephone...
Don't act like you don't want this.

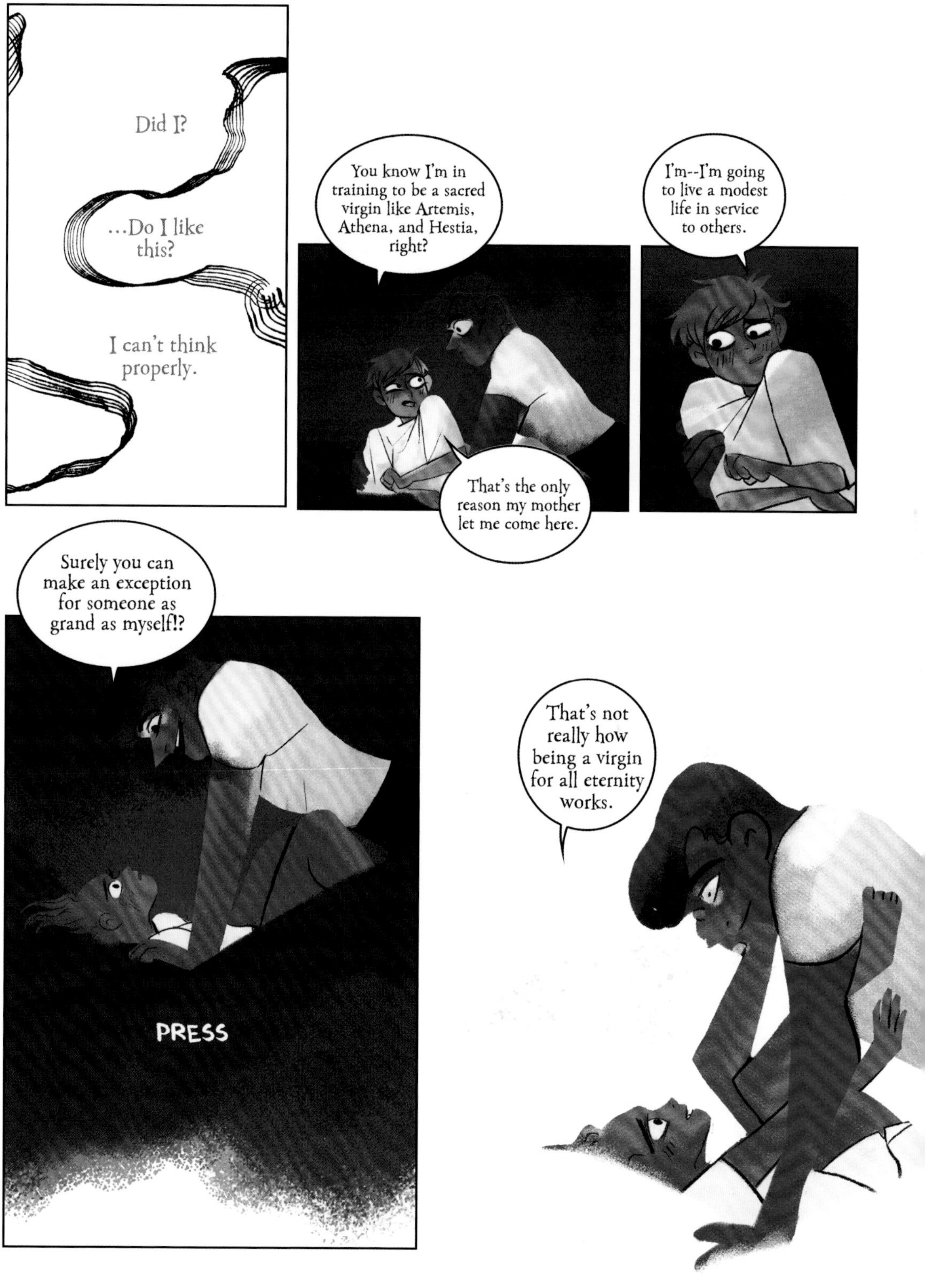
Did I?
...Do I like this?
I can't think properly.
You know I'm in training to be a sacred virgin like Artemis, Athena, and Hestia, right?
That's the only reason my mother let me come here.
I'm--I'm going to live a modest life in service to others.
Surely you can make an exception for someone as grand as myself!?
PRESS
That's not really how being a virgin for all eternity works.

All eternity.

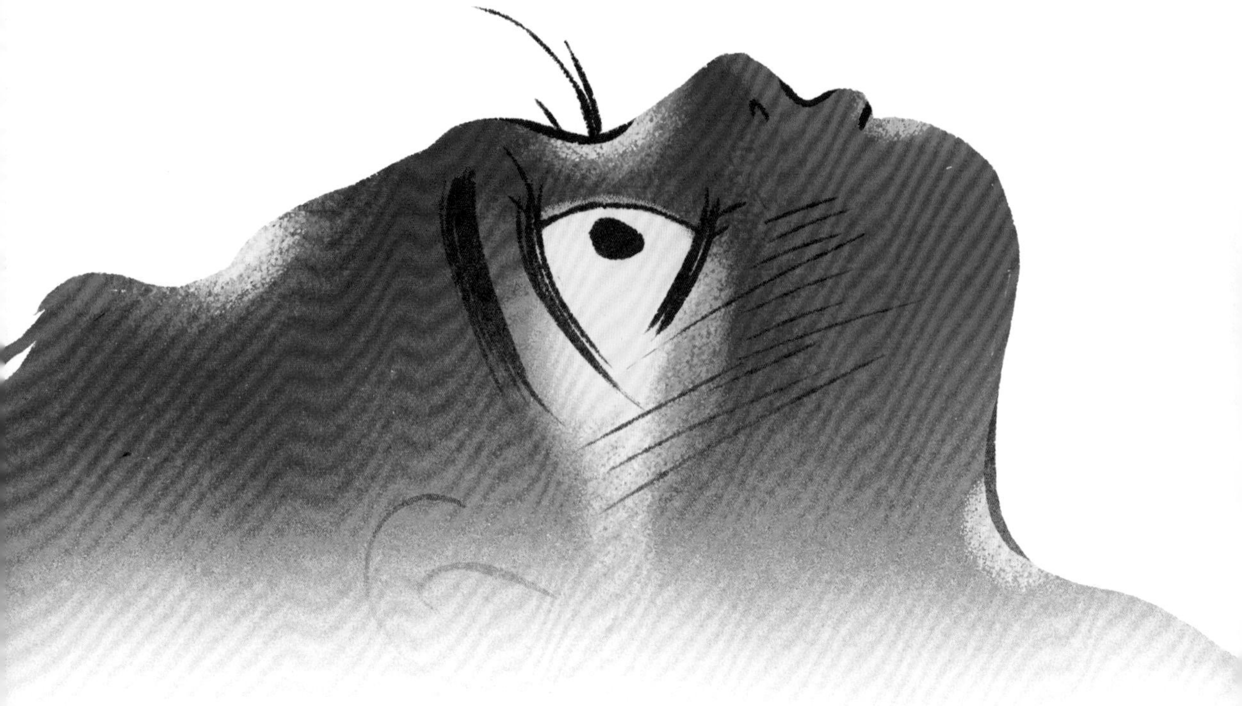

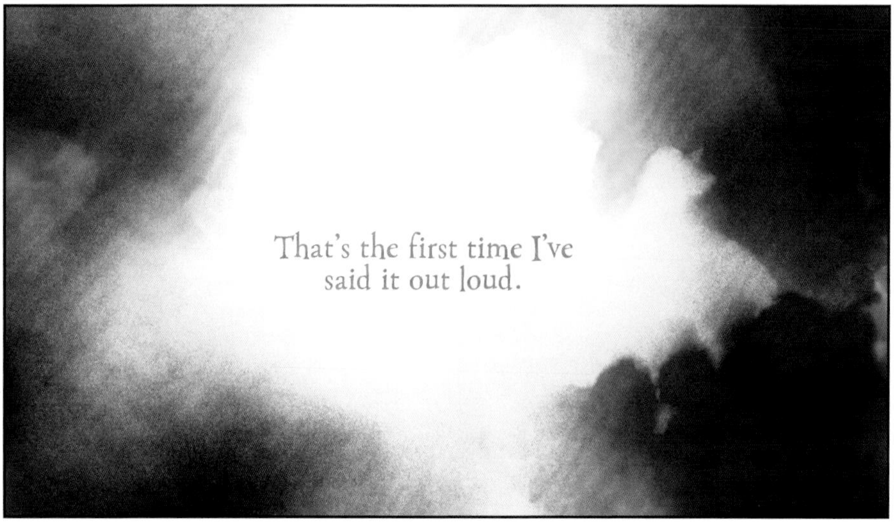
That's the first time I've said it out loud.

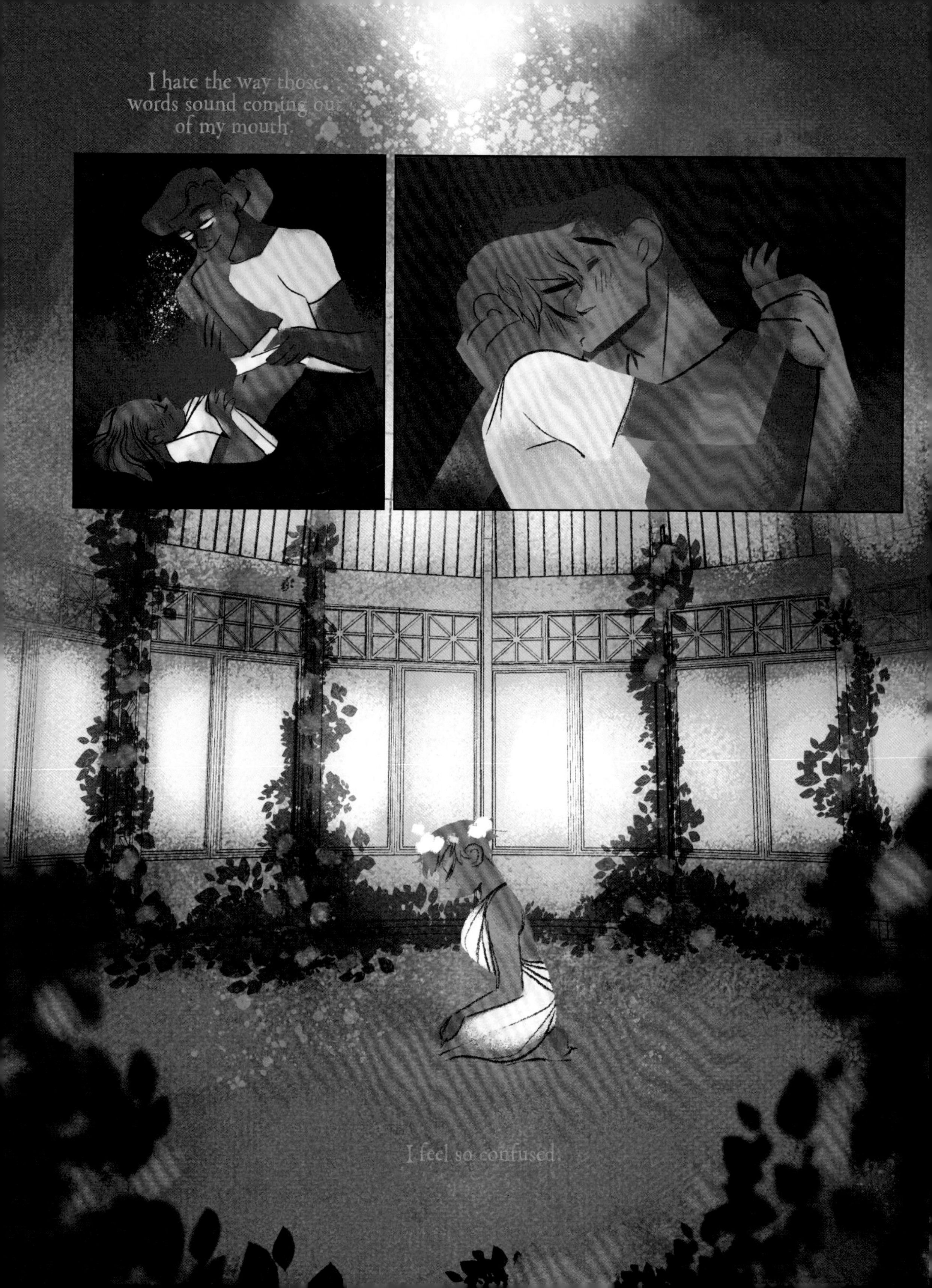
I hate the way those words sound coming out of my mouth.
I feel so confused.

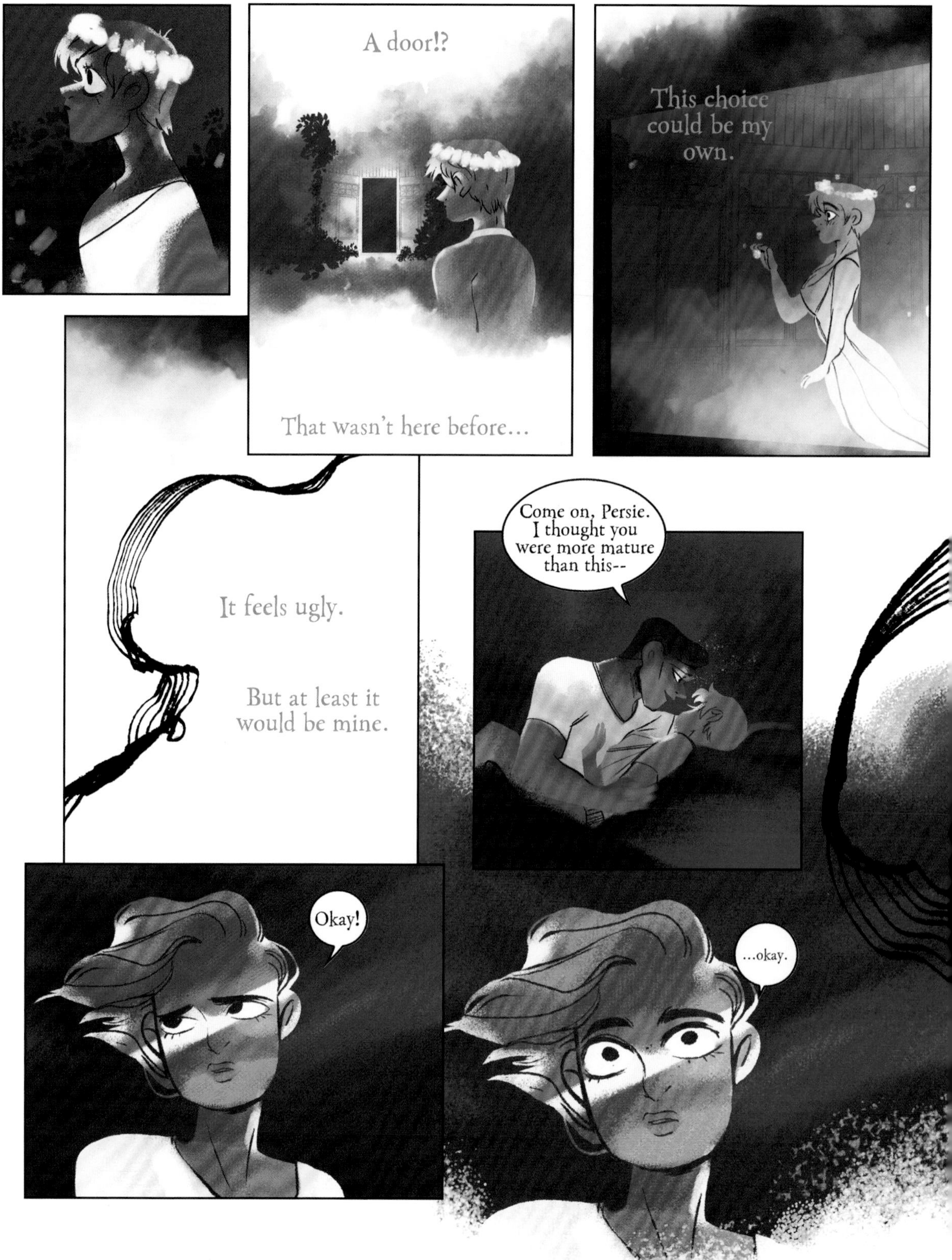
A door!?
That wasn't here before...
This choice could be my own.
It feels ugly.
But at least it would be mine.
Come on, Persie. I thought you were more mature than this--
Okay!
...okay.

EPISODE 24: A WOLF IN THE HENHOUSE (PART 3)

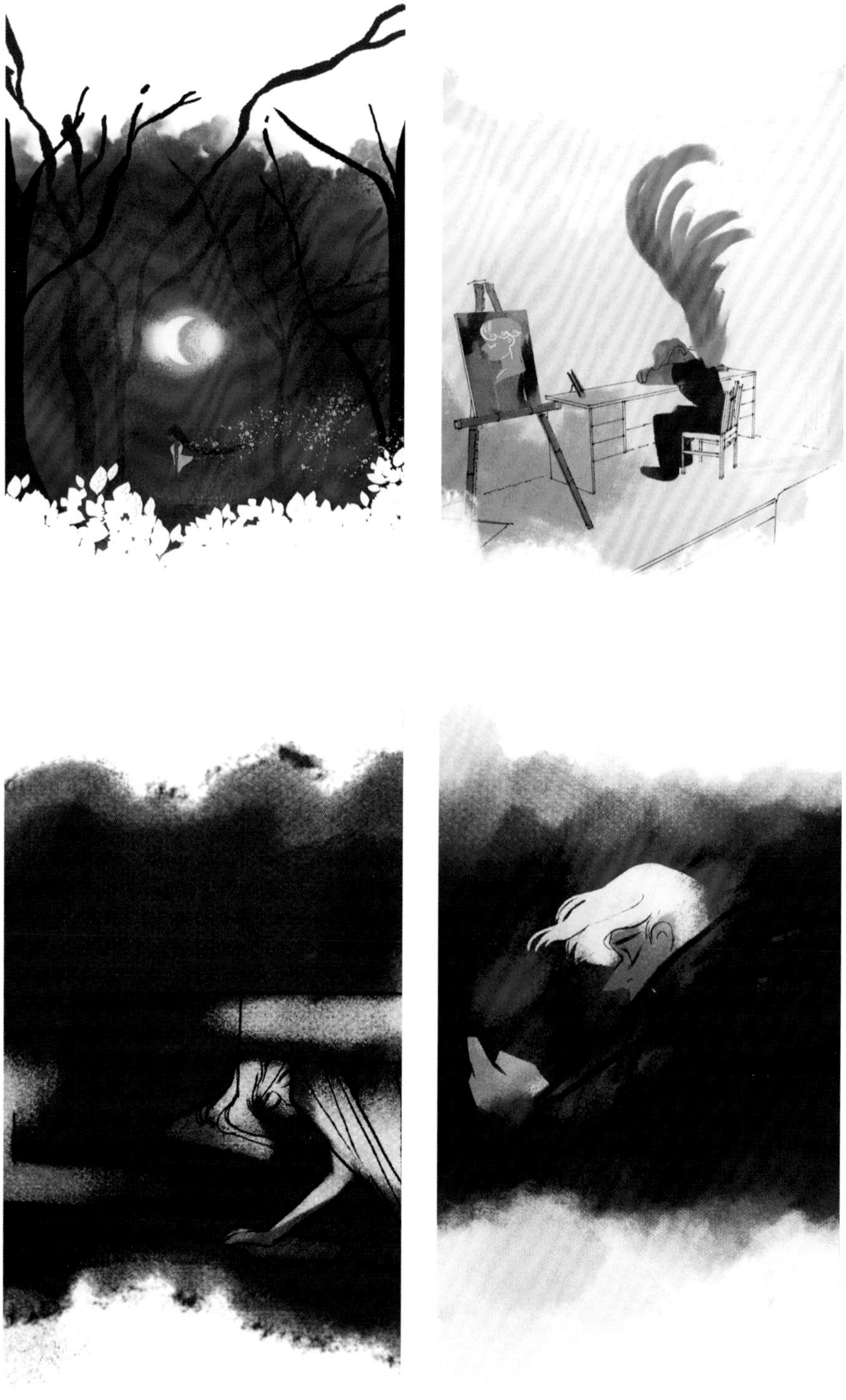

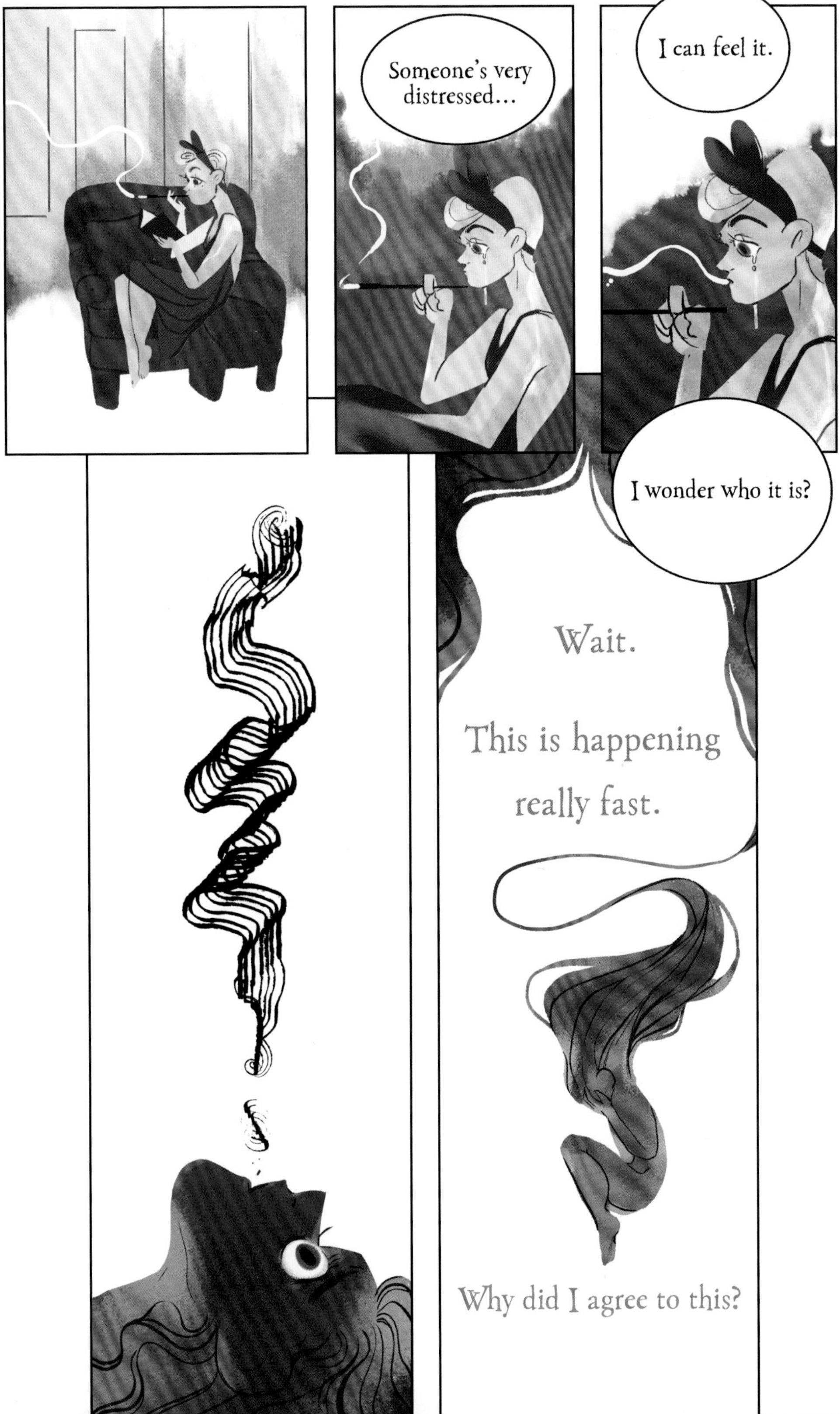
Someone's very distressed...
I can feel it.
I wonder who it is?
Wait.
This is happening really fast.
Why did I agree to this?

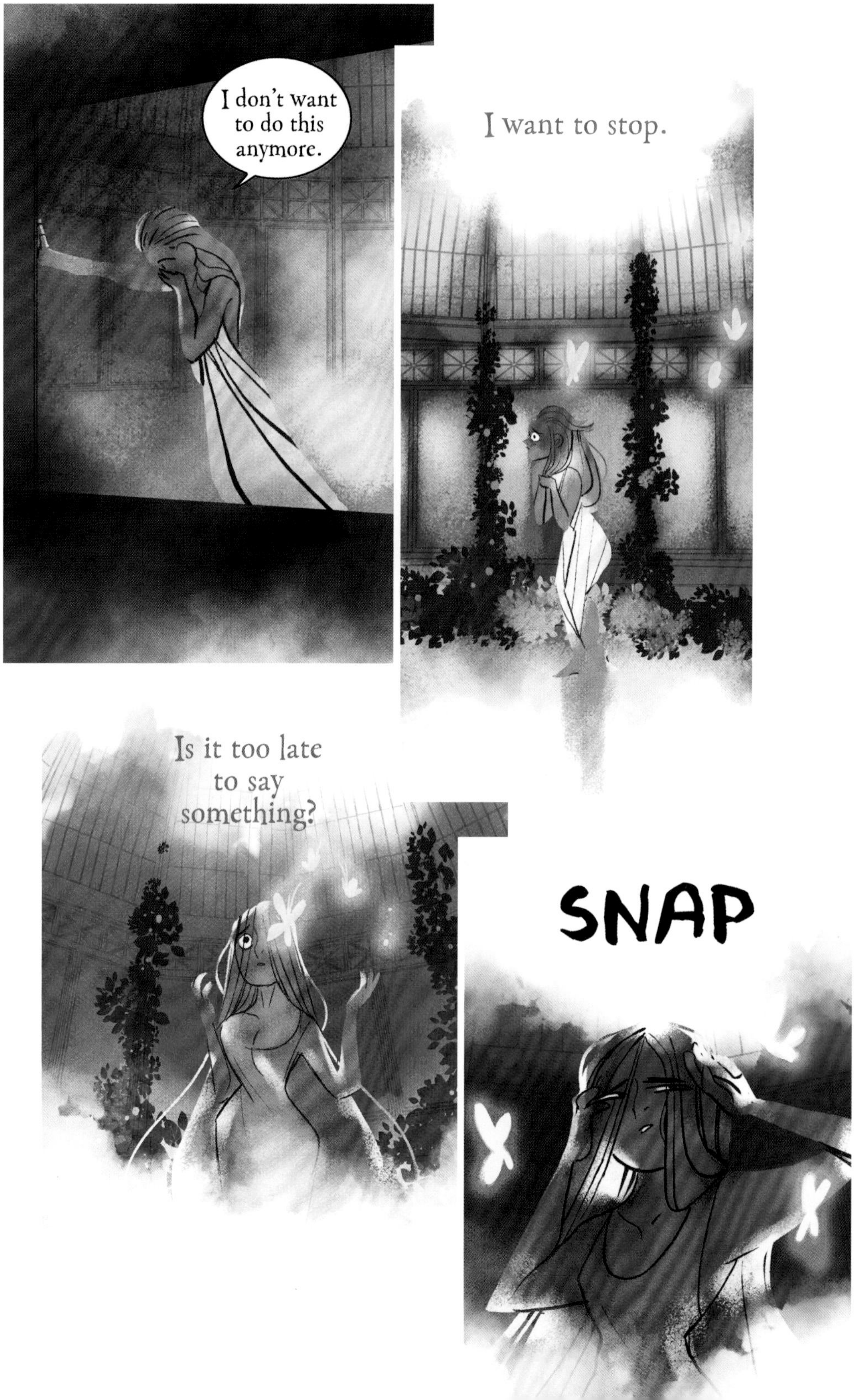
I don't want to do this anymore.
I want to stop.
Is it too late to say something?
SNAP

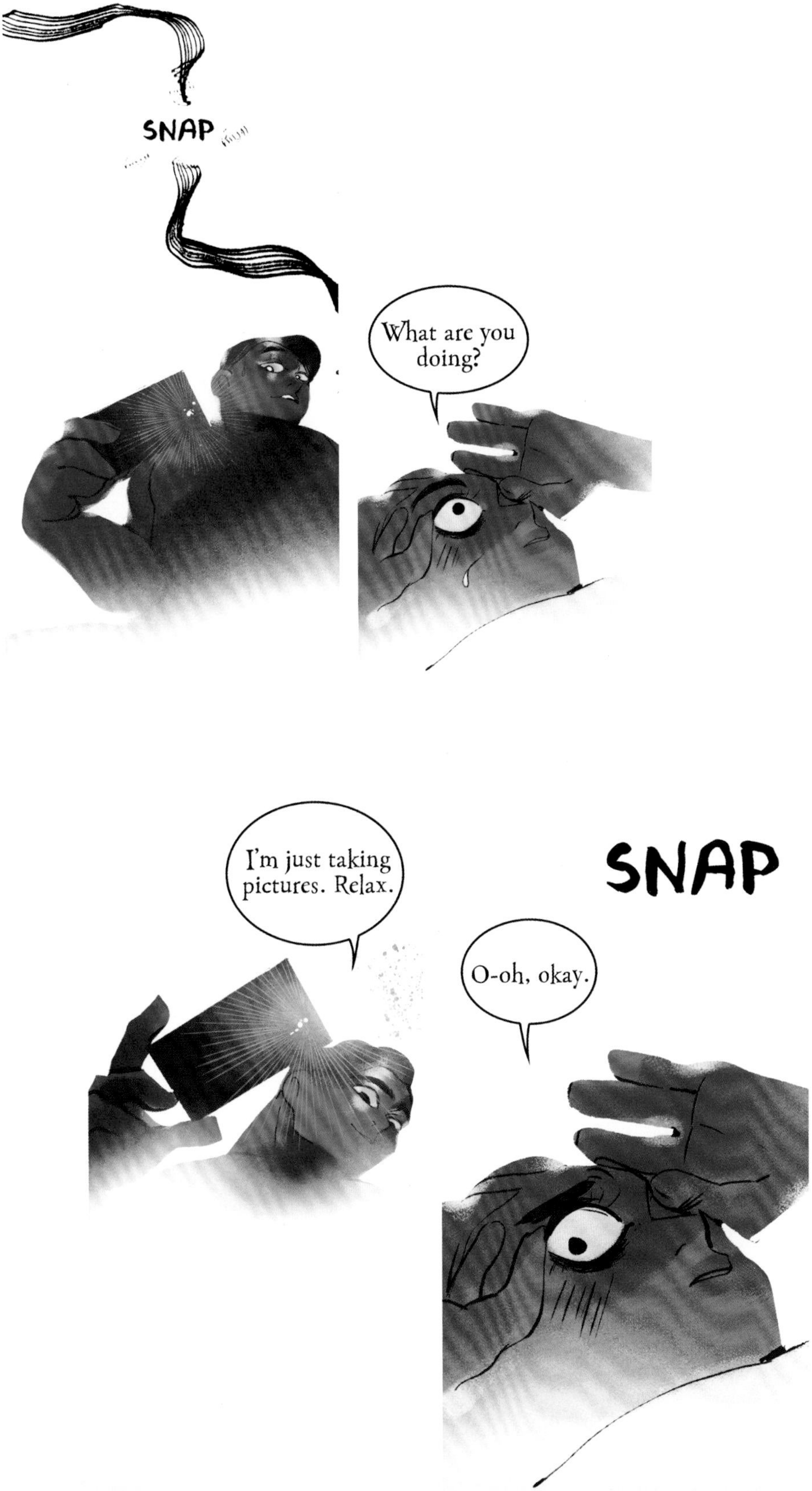
SNAP
What are you doing?
I'm just taking pictures. Relax.
SNAP
O-oh, okay.

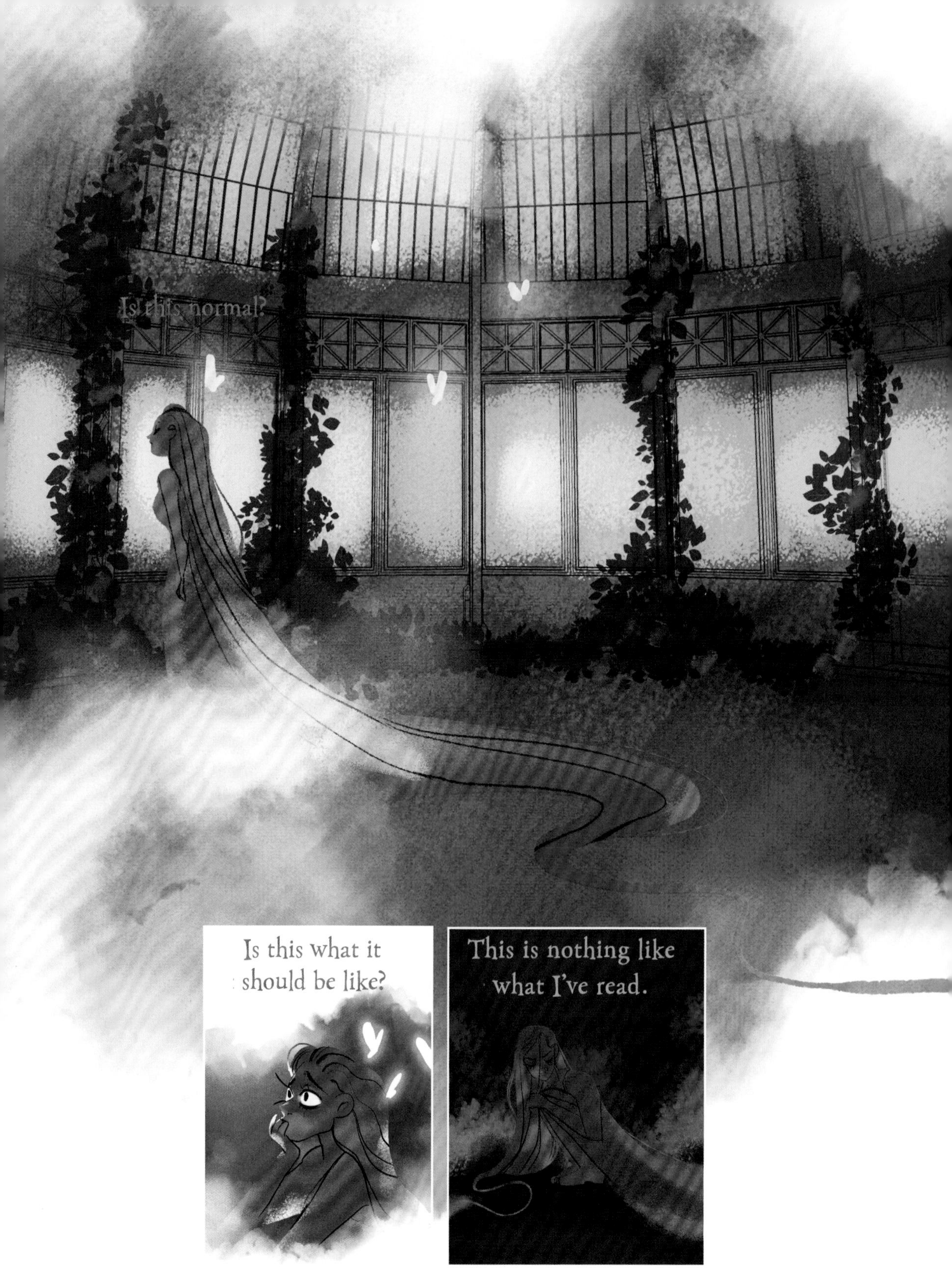
Is this normal?
Is this what it should be like?
This is nothing like what I've read.

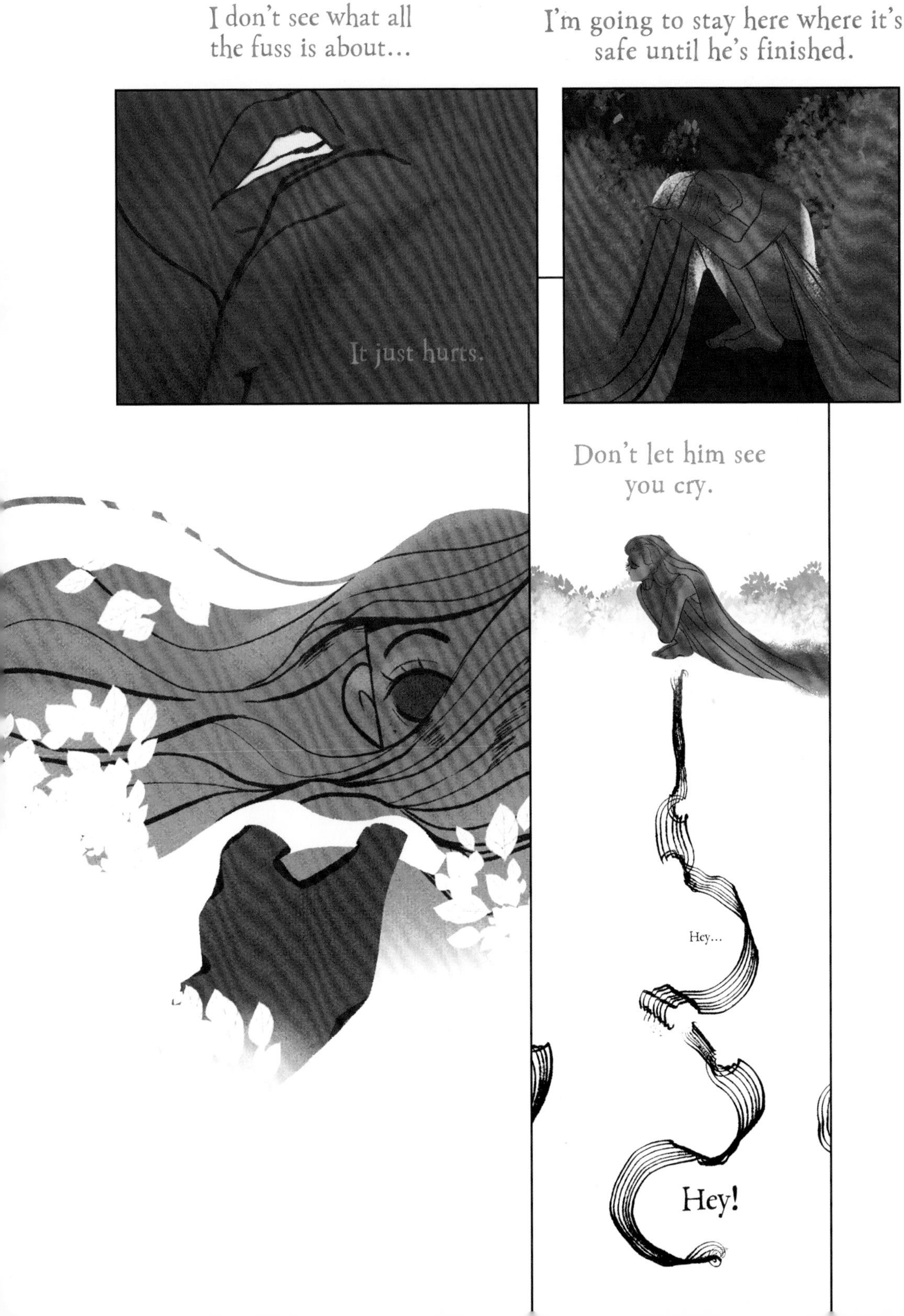
I don't see what all the fuss is about...
It just hurts.
I'm going to stay here where it's safe until he's finished.
Don't let him see you cry.
Hey...
Hey!

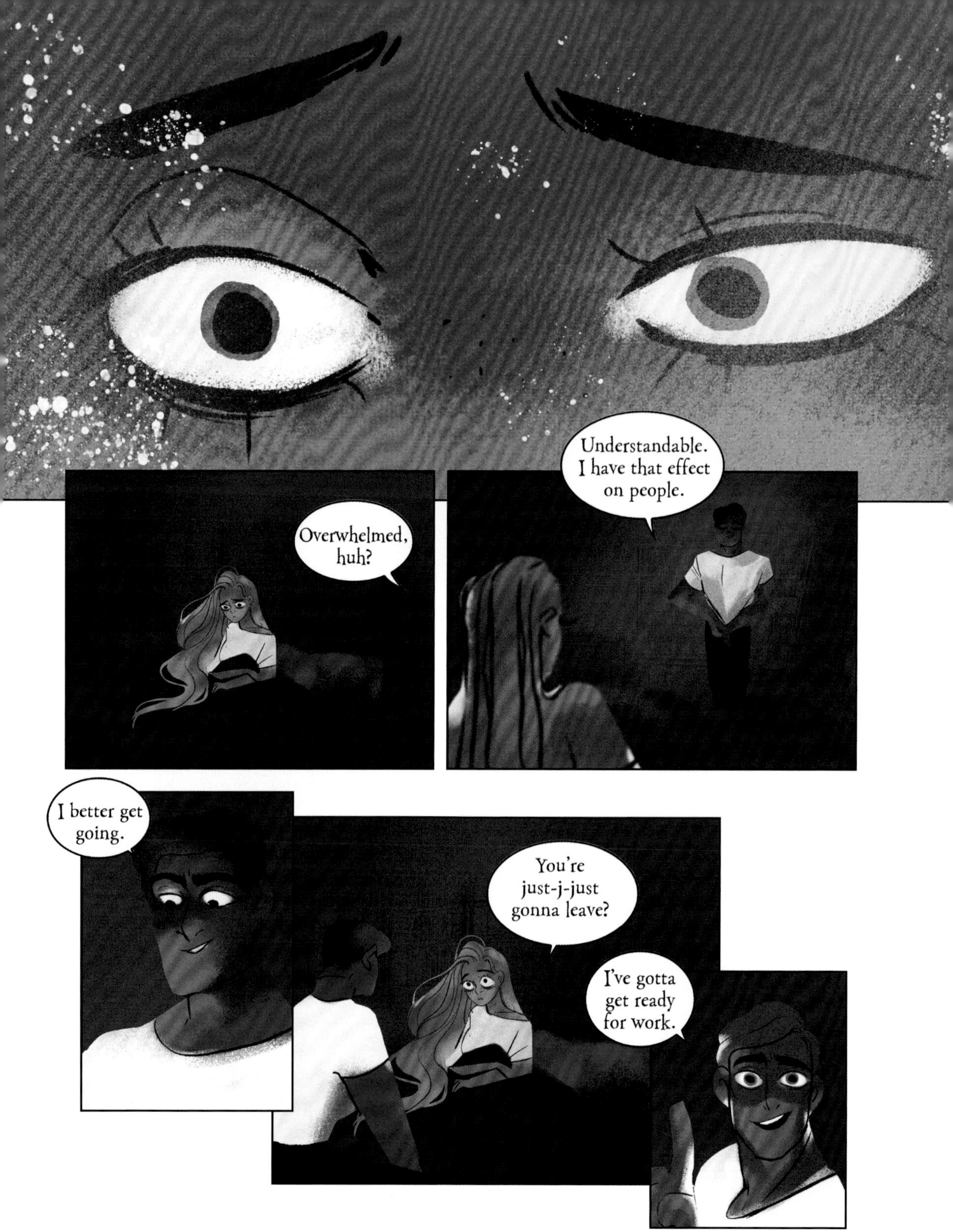
Overwhelmed, huh?
Understandable. I have that effect on people.
I better get going.
You're just-j-just gonna leave?
I've gotta get ready for work.

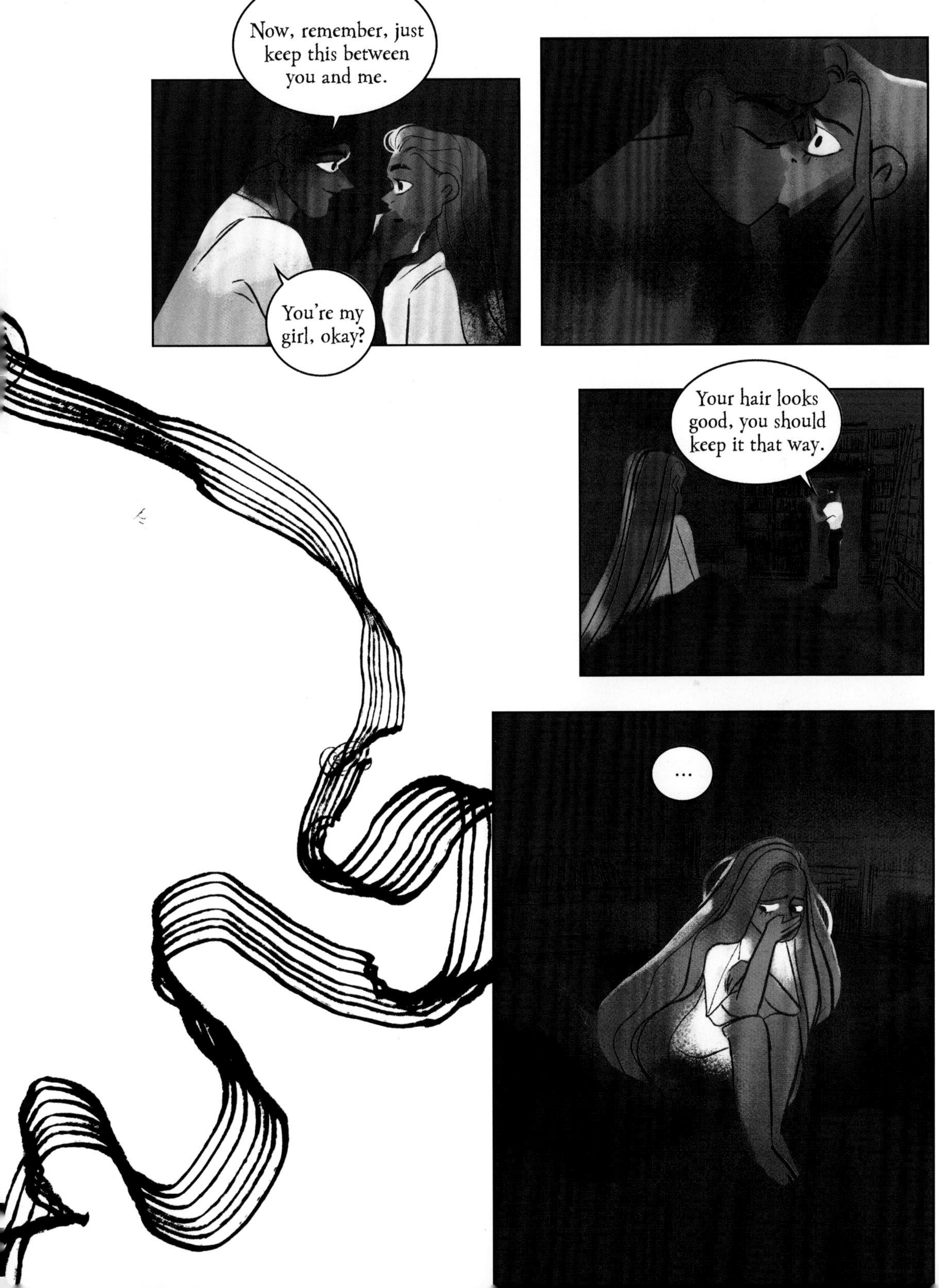
Now, remember, just keep this between you and me.
You're my girl, okay?
Your hair looks good, you should keep it that way.
...

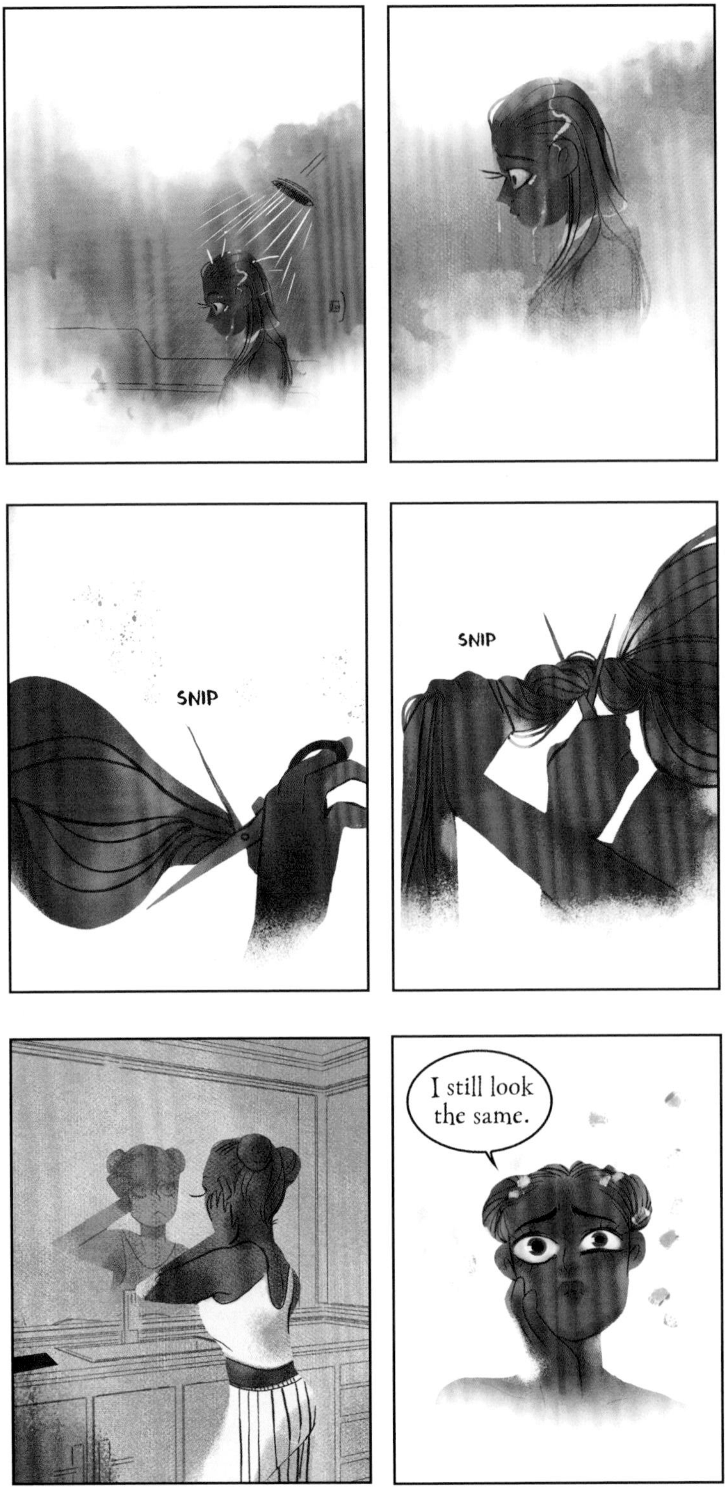
SNIP
SNIP
I still look the same.

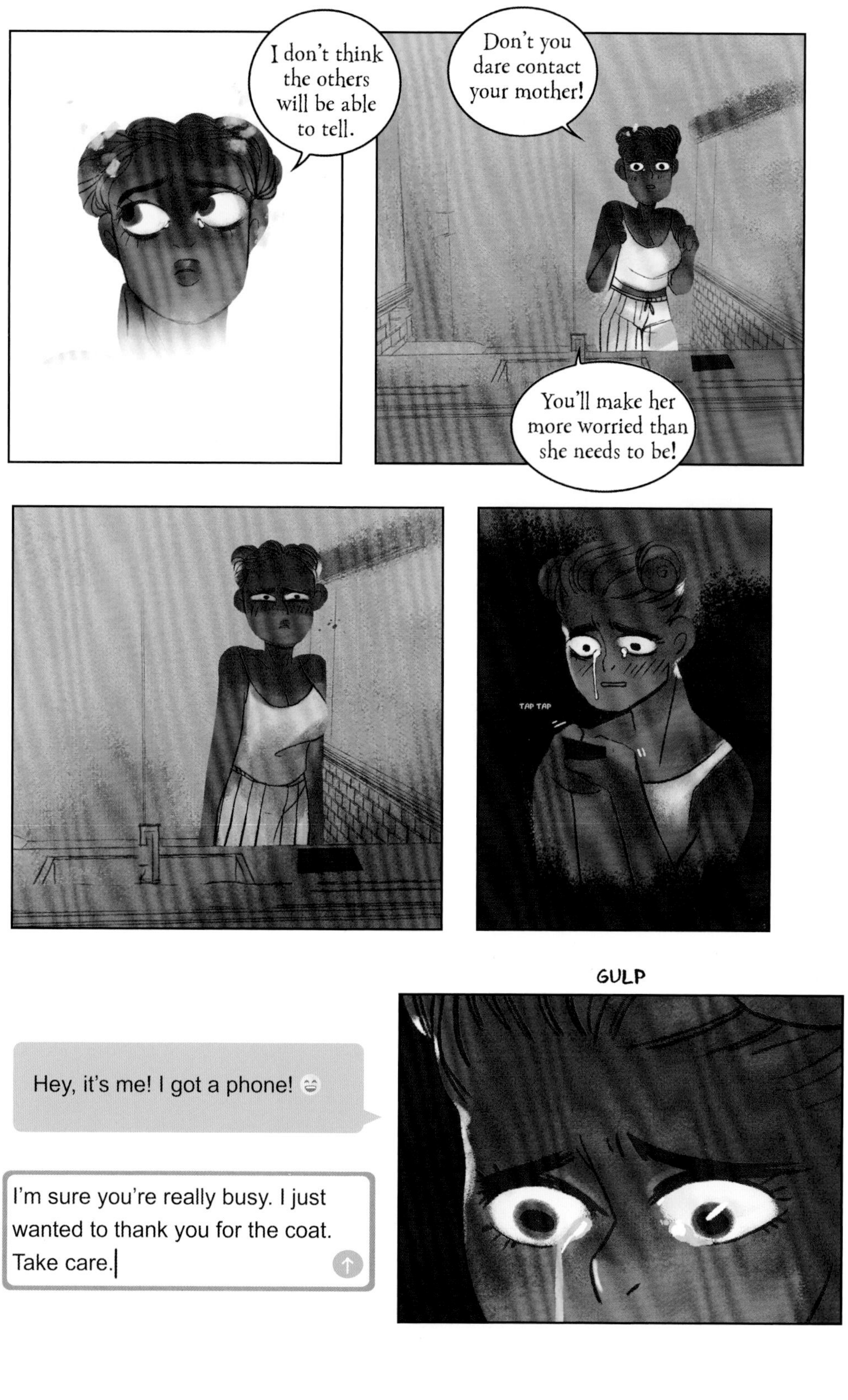
I don't think the others will be able to tell.
Don't you dare contact your mother!
You'll make her more worried than she needs to be!
TAP TAP
GULP
Hey, it's me! I got a phone!
I'm sure you're really busy. I just wanted to thank you for the coat. Take care.

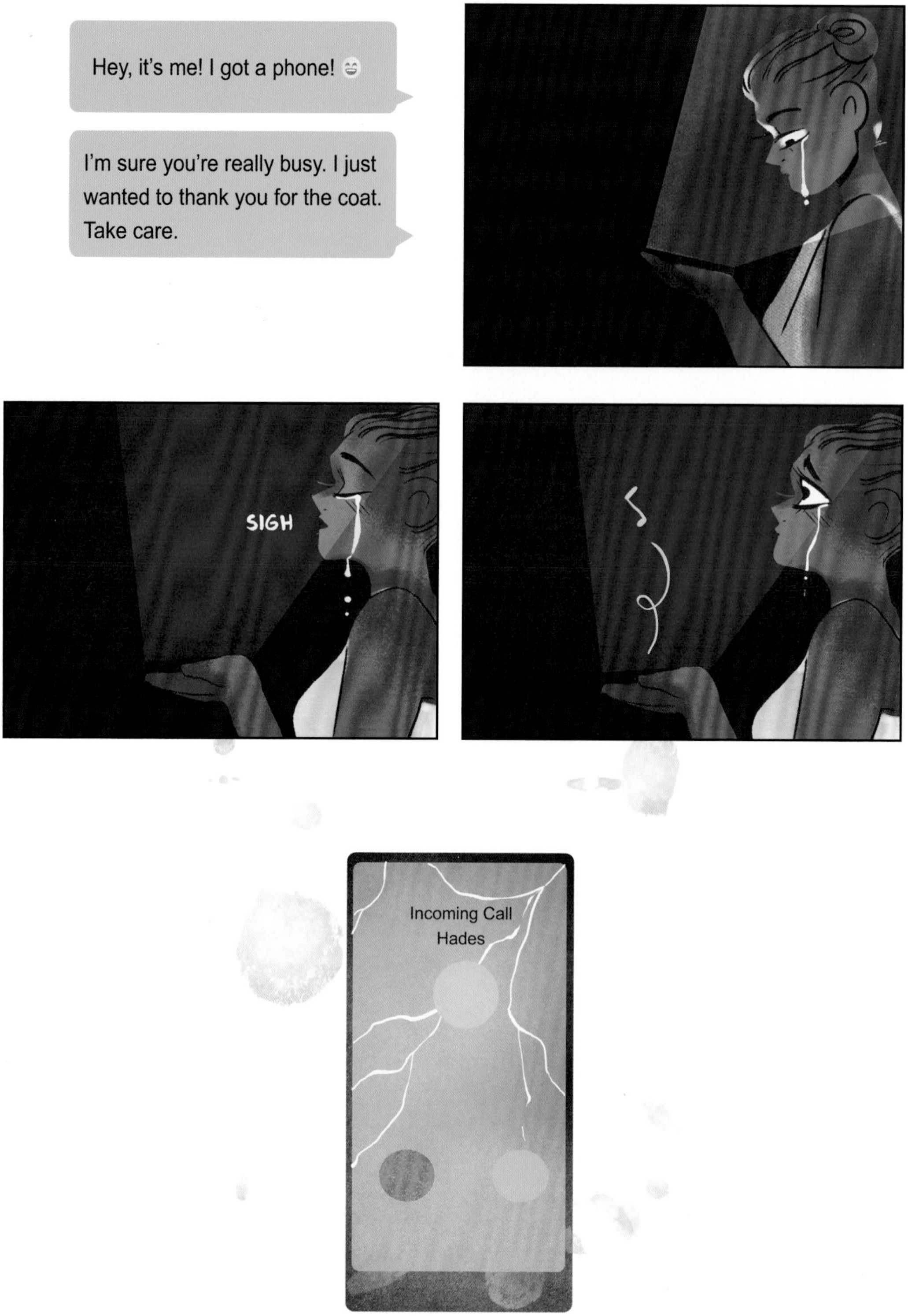
Hey, it's me! I got a phone! 😁
I'm sure you're really busy. I just wanted to thank you for the coat. Take care.
SIGH
Incoming Call
Hades

EPISODE 25: AIDONEUS

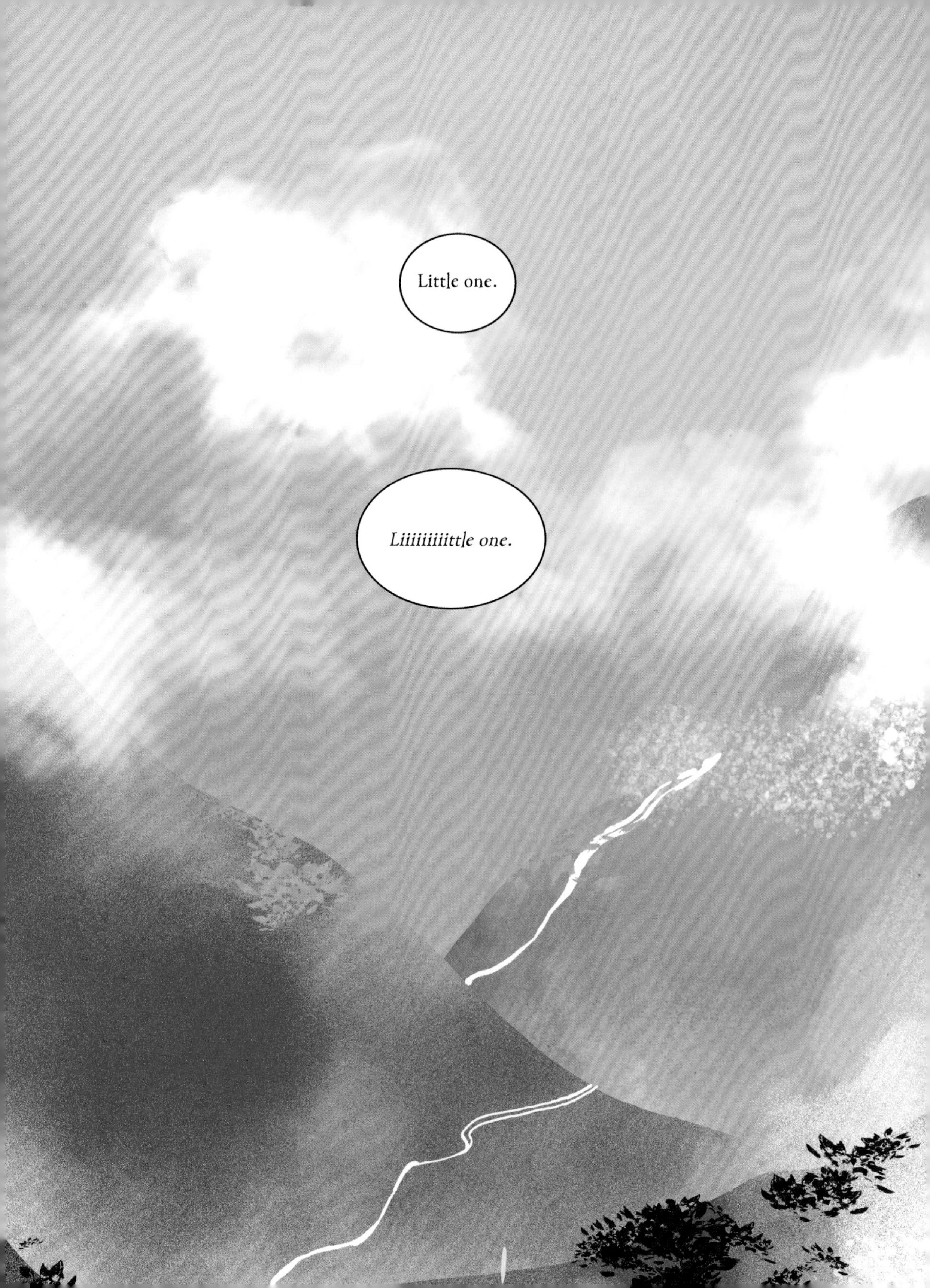
Little one.
Liiiiiiiiittle one.

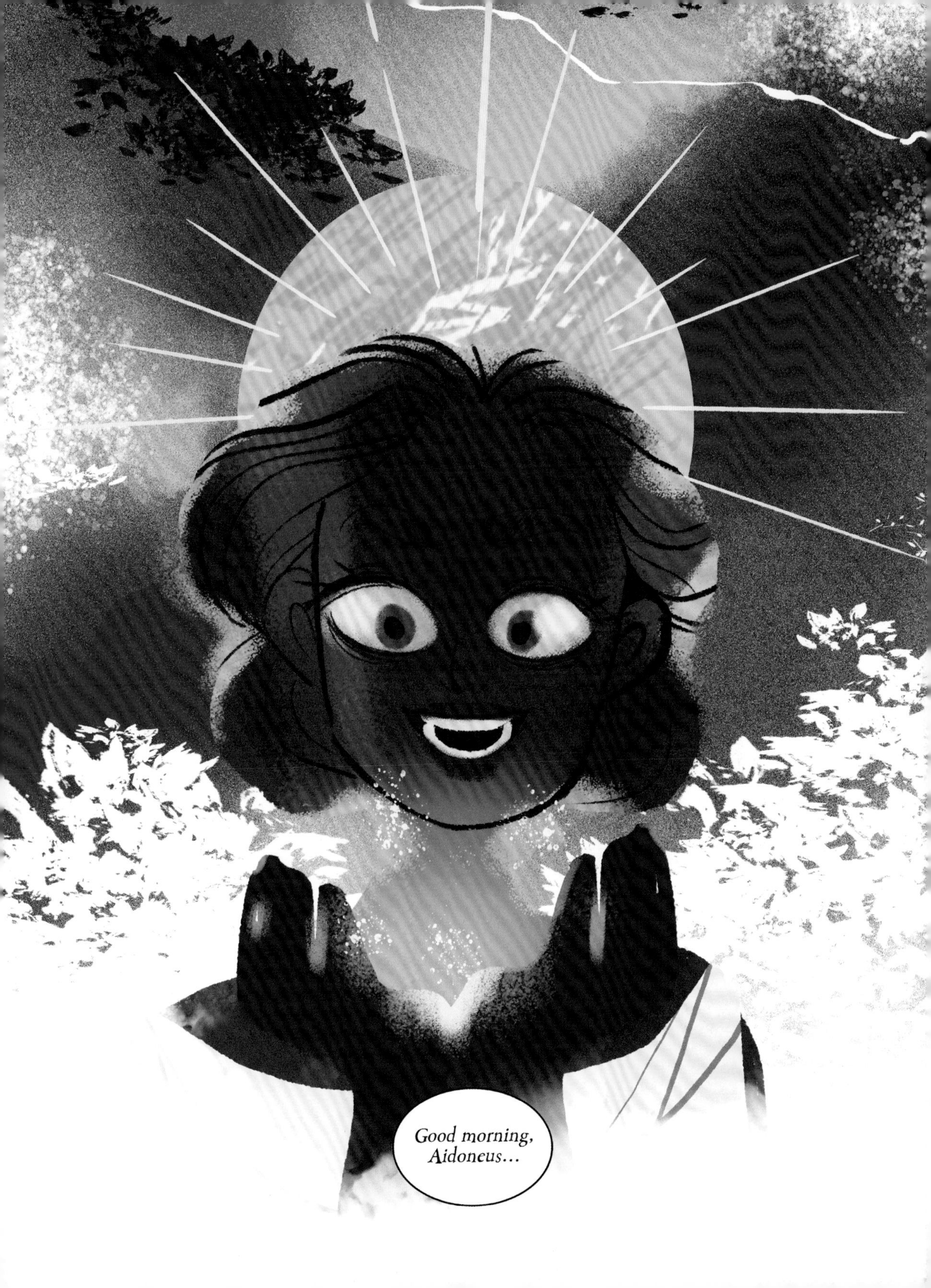
Good morning, Aidoneus...

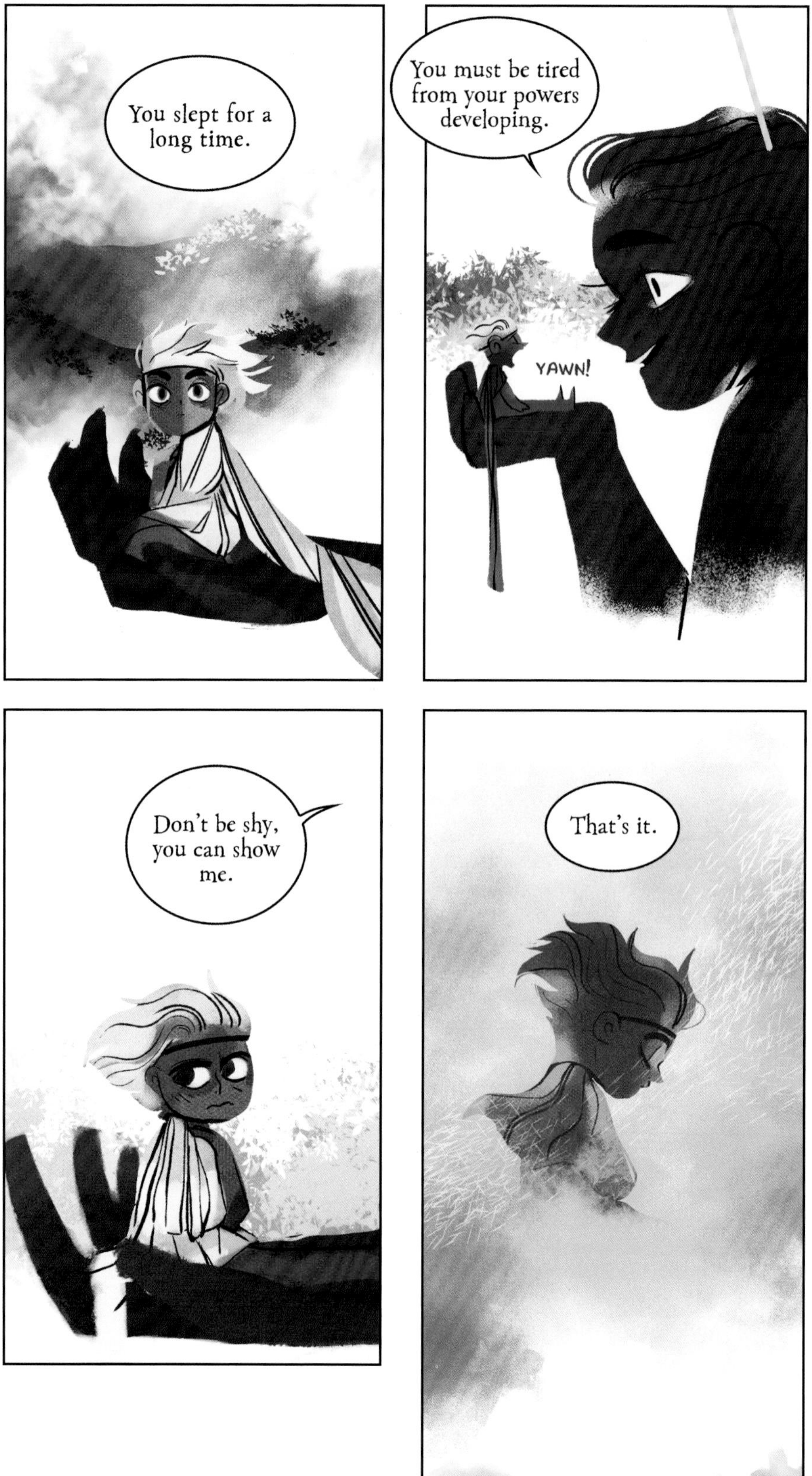
You slept for a long time.
You must be tired from your powers developing.
YAWN!
Don't be shy, you can show me.
That's it.

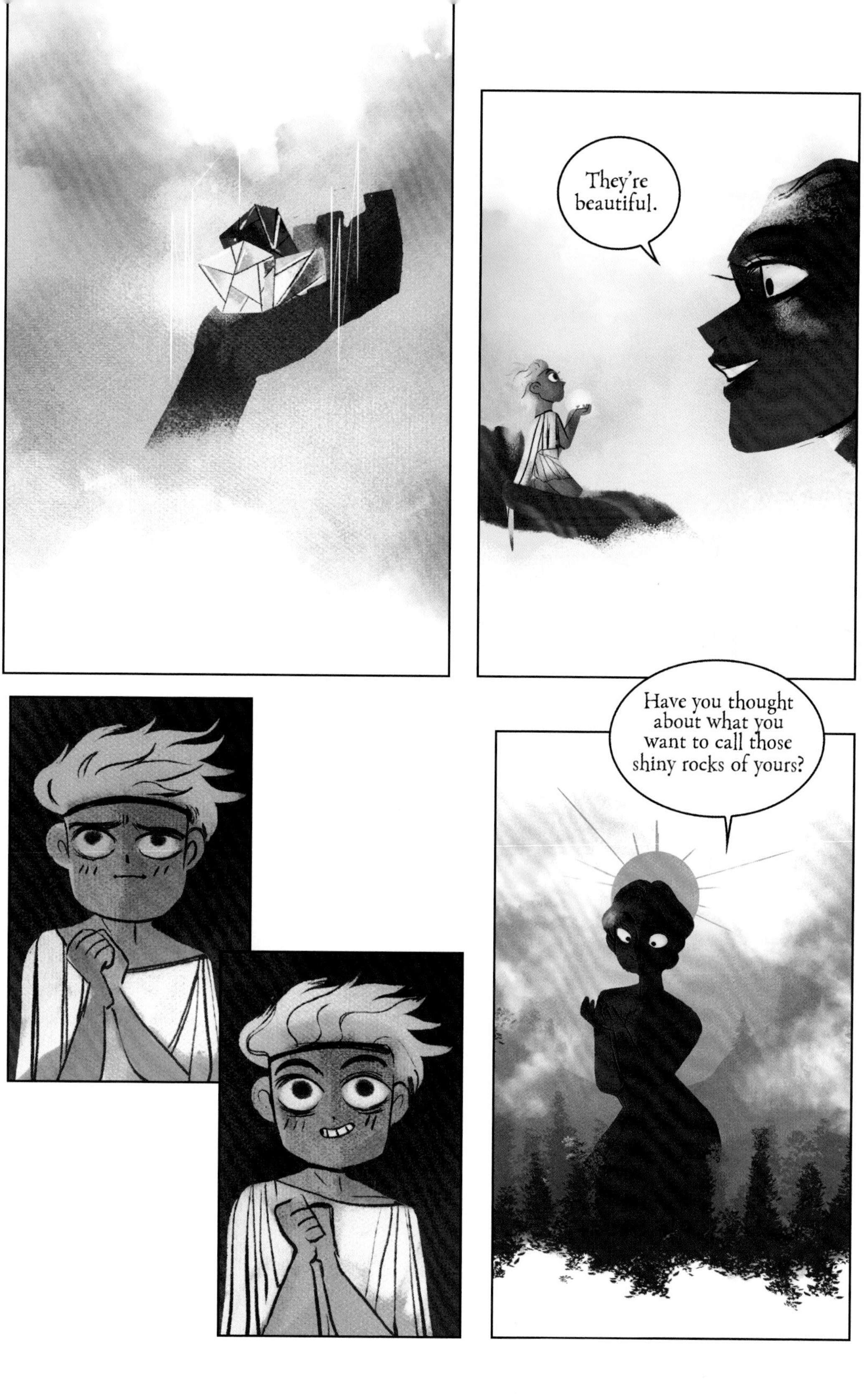
They're beautiful.
Have you thought about what you want to call those shiny rocks of yours?

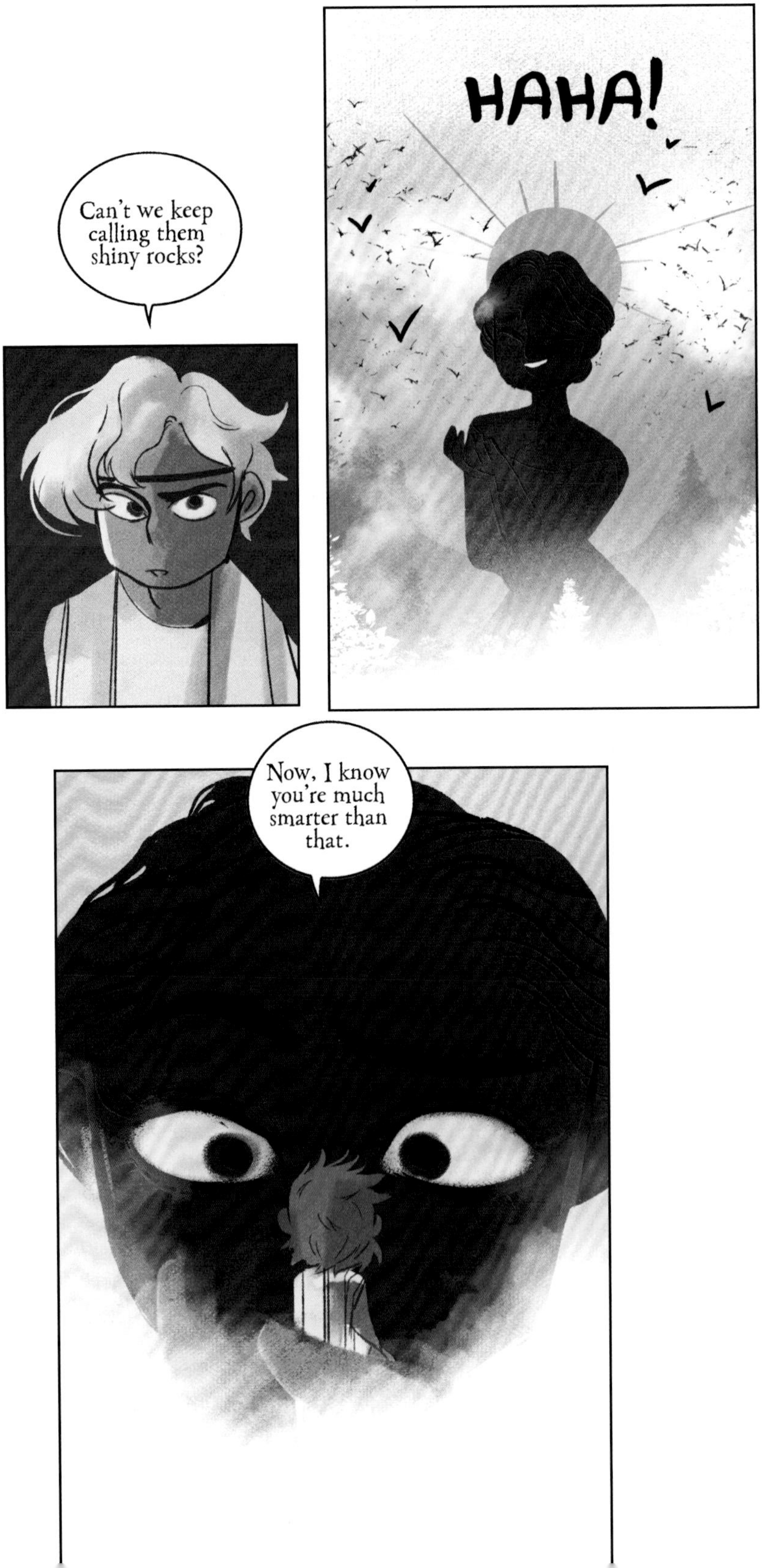
Can't we keep calling them shiny rocks?
HAHA!
Now, I know you're much smarter than that.

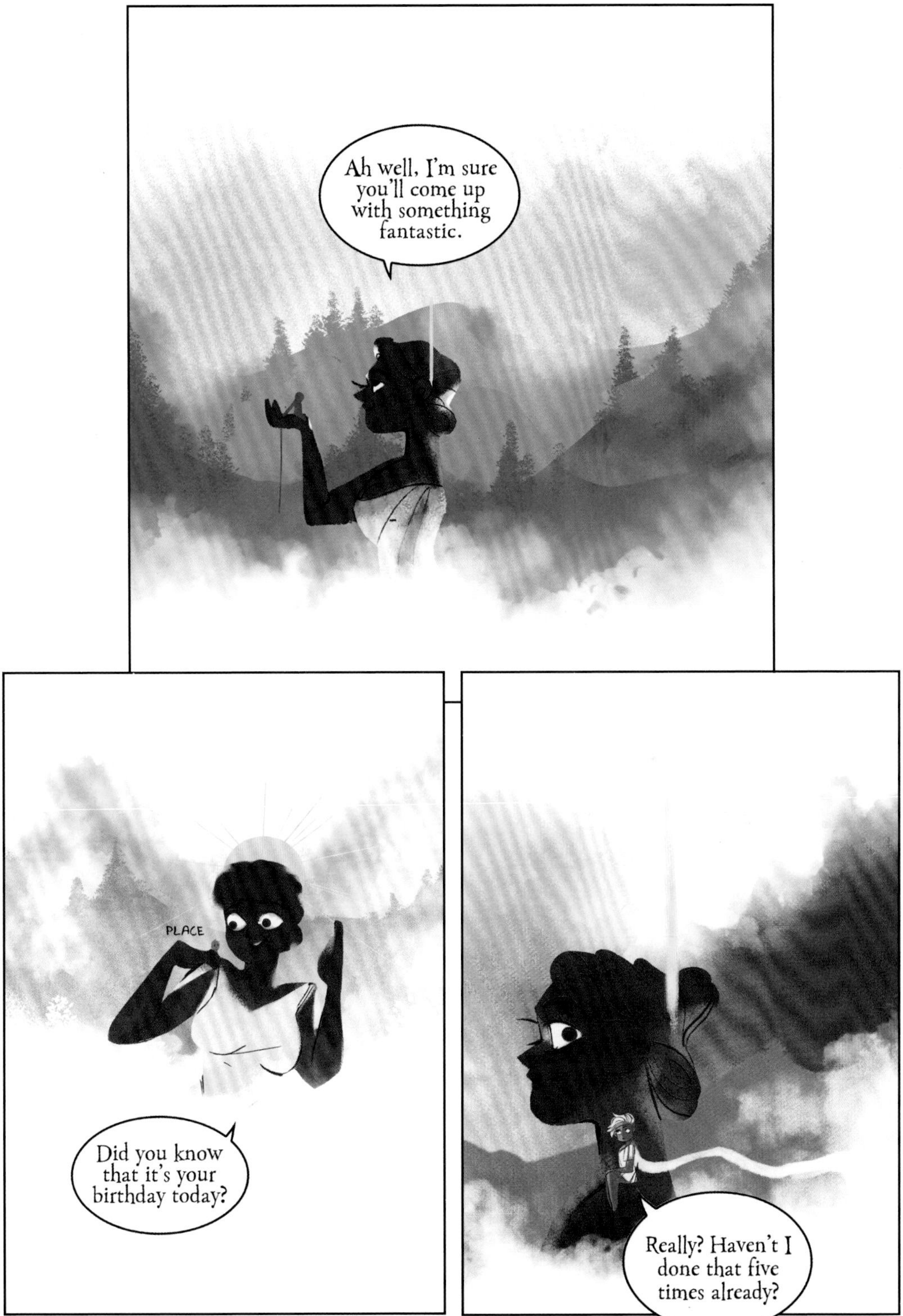
Ah well, I'm sure you'll come up with something fantastic.
PLACE
Did you know that it's your birthday today?
Really? Haven't I done that five times already?

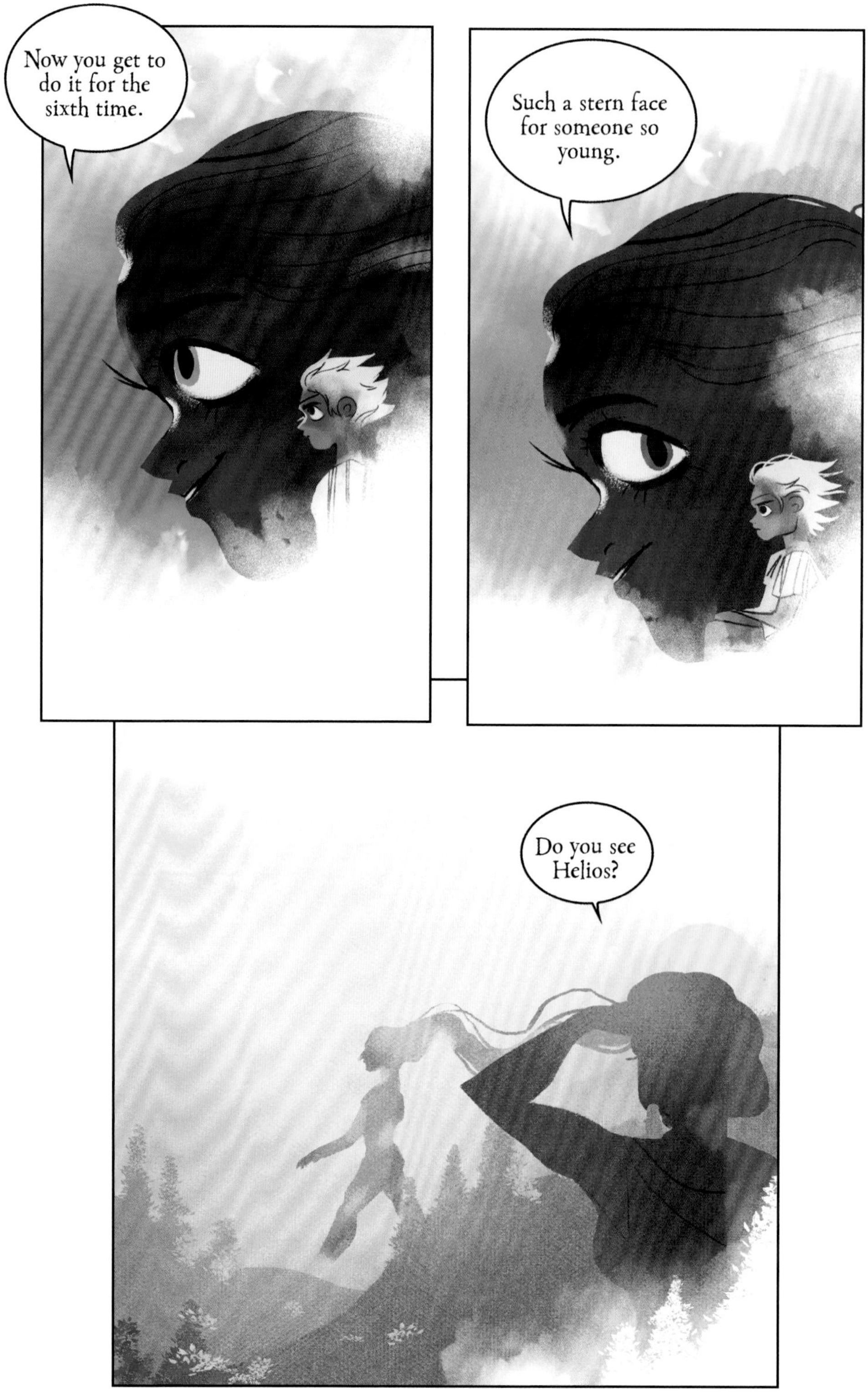
Now you get to do it for the sixth time.
Such a stern face for someone so young.
Do you see Helios?

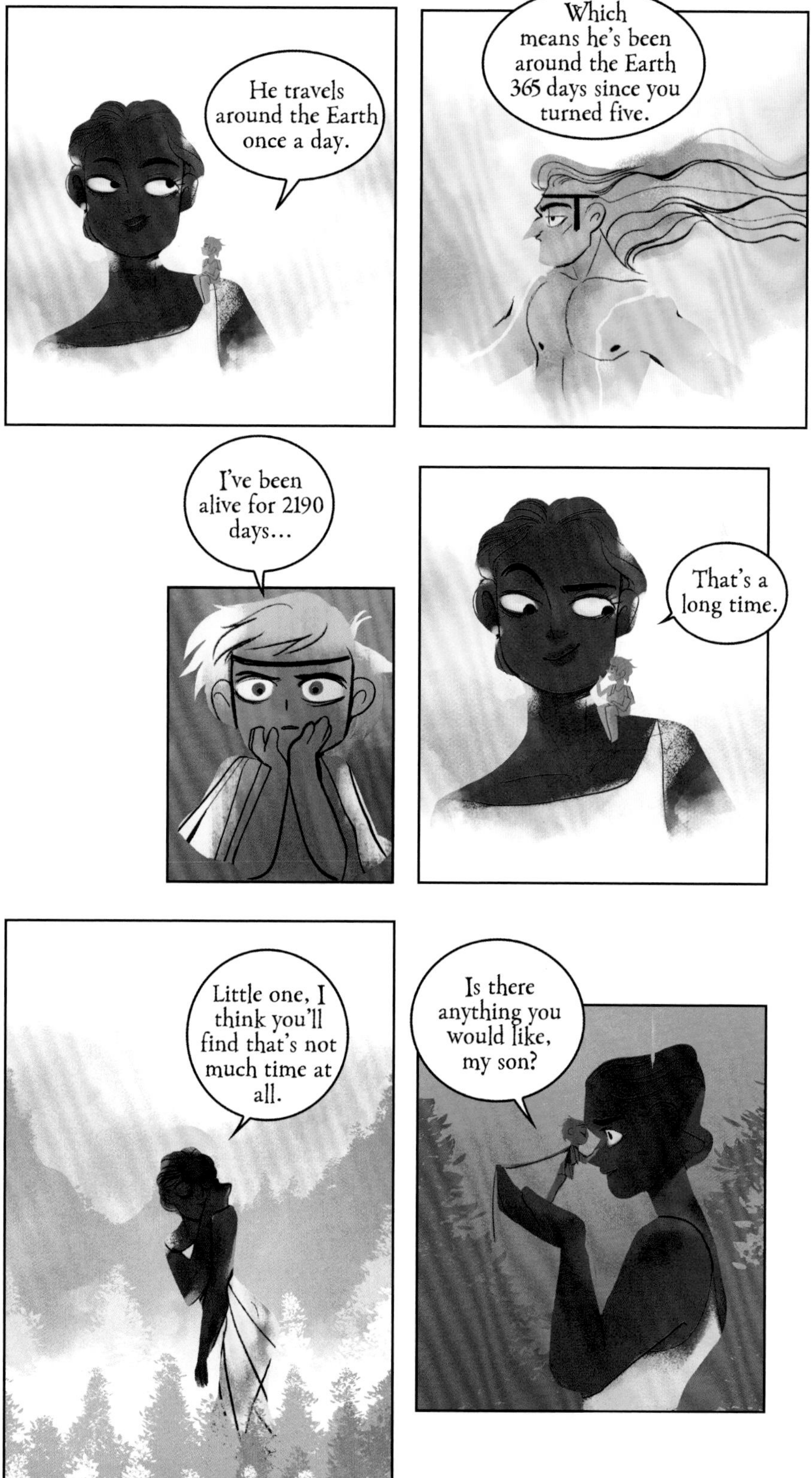
He travels around the Earth once a day.
Which means he's been around the Earth 365 days since you turned five.
I've been alive for 2190 days...
That's a long time.
Little one, I think you'll find that's not much time at all.
Is there anything you would like, my son?

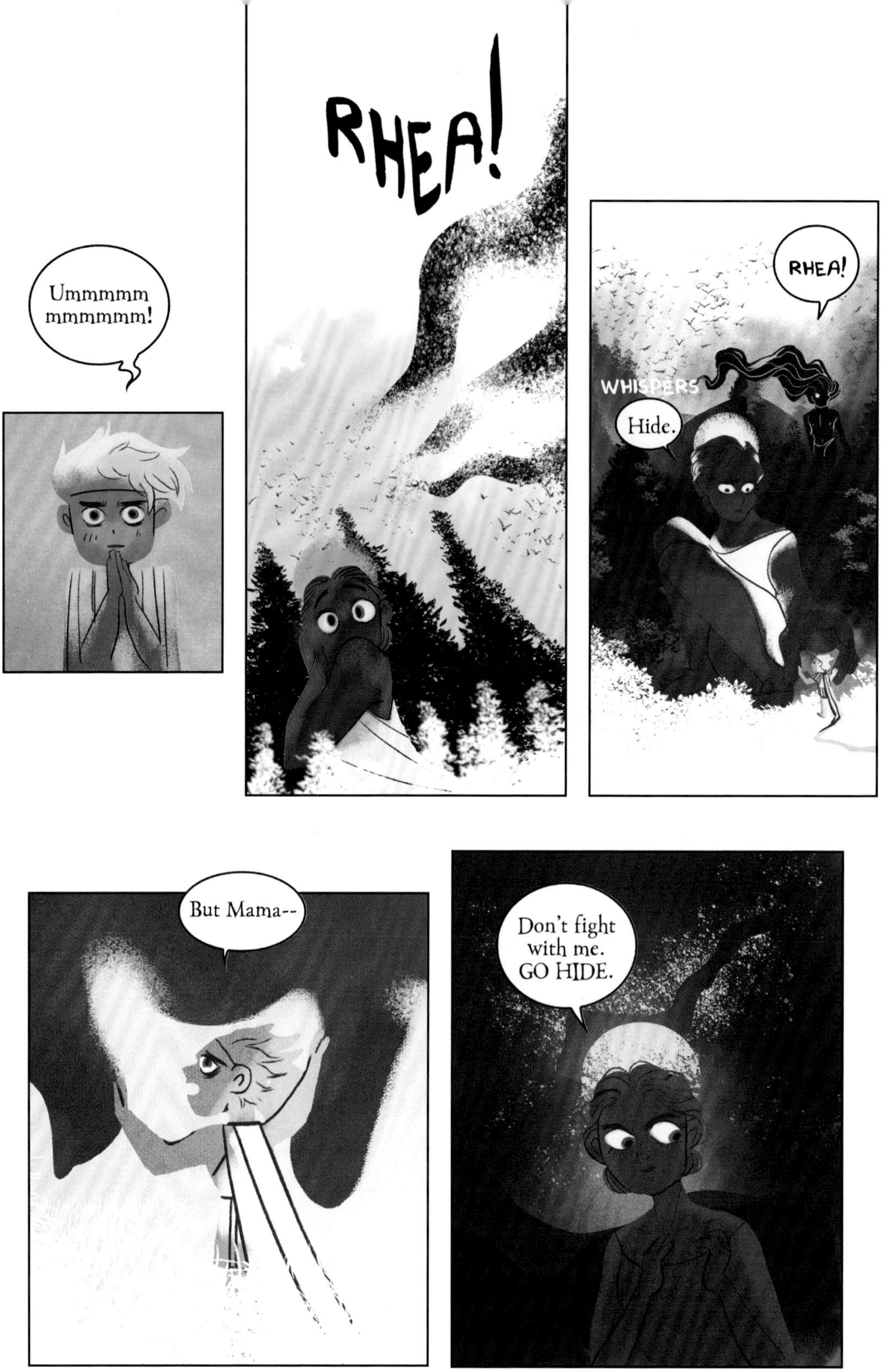
Ummmmm mmmmmm!
RHEA!
RHEA!
WHISPERS
Hide.
But Mama--
Don't fight with me. GO HIDE.

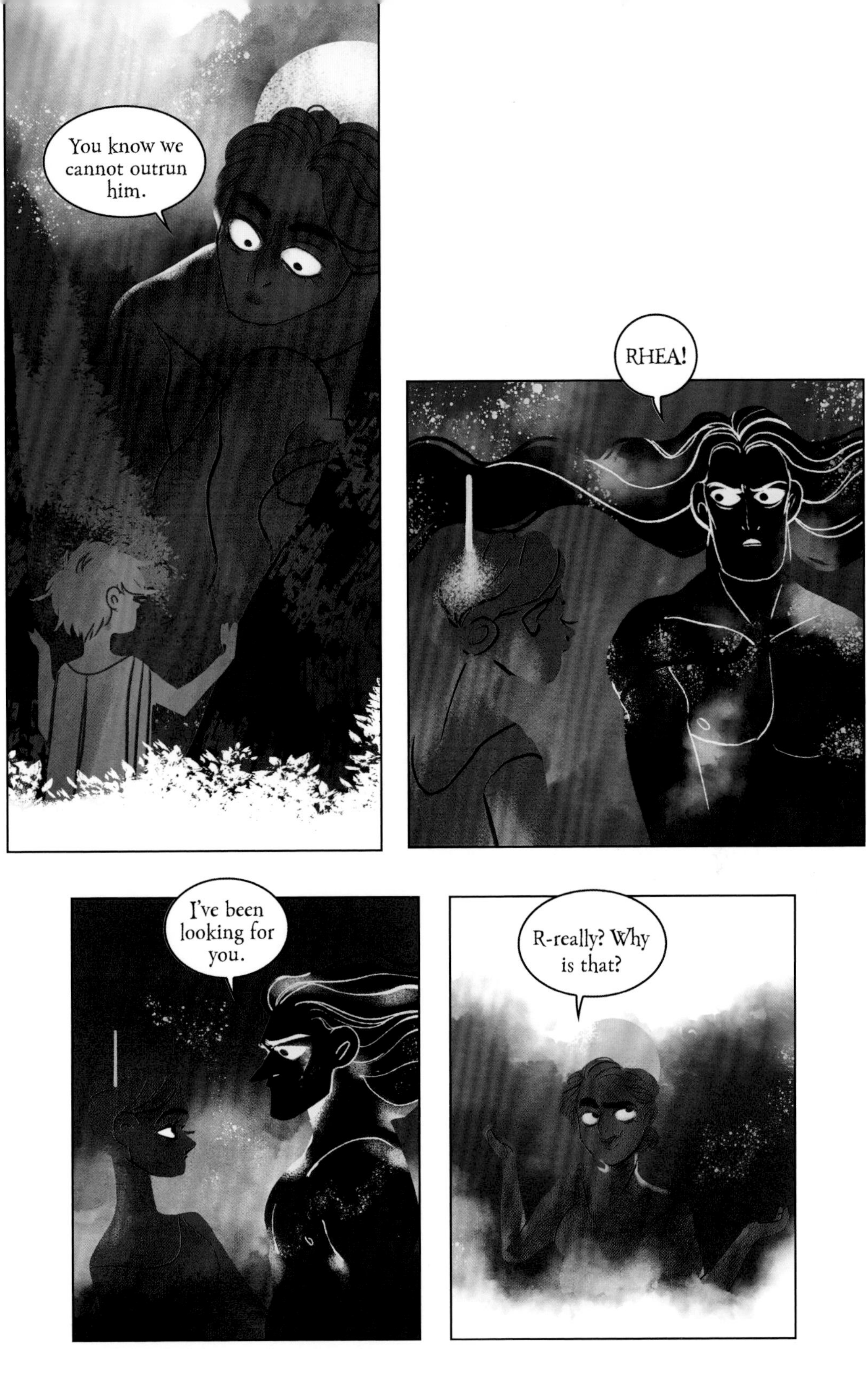
You know we cannot outrun him.
RHEA!
I've been looking for you.
R-really? Why is that?

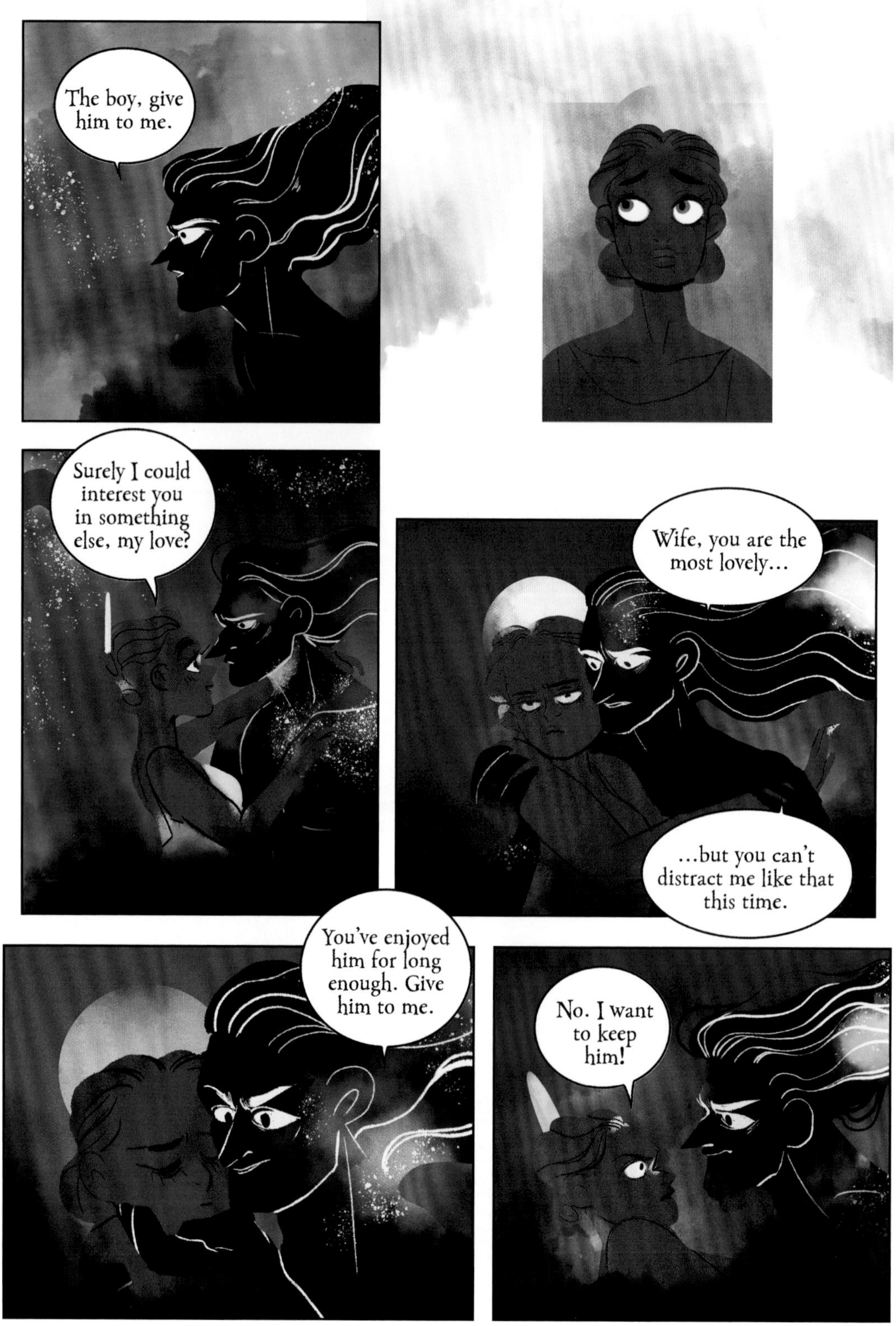
The boy, give him to me.
Surely I could interest you in something else, my love?
Wife, you are the most lovely...
...but you can't distract me like that this time.
You've enjoyed him for long enough. Give him to me.
No. I want to keep him!

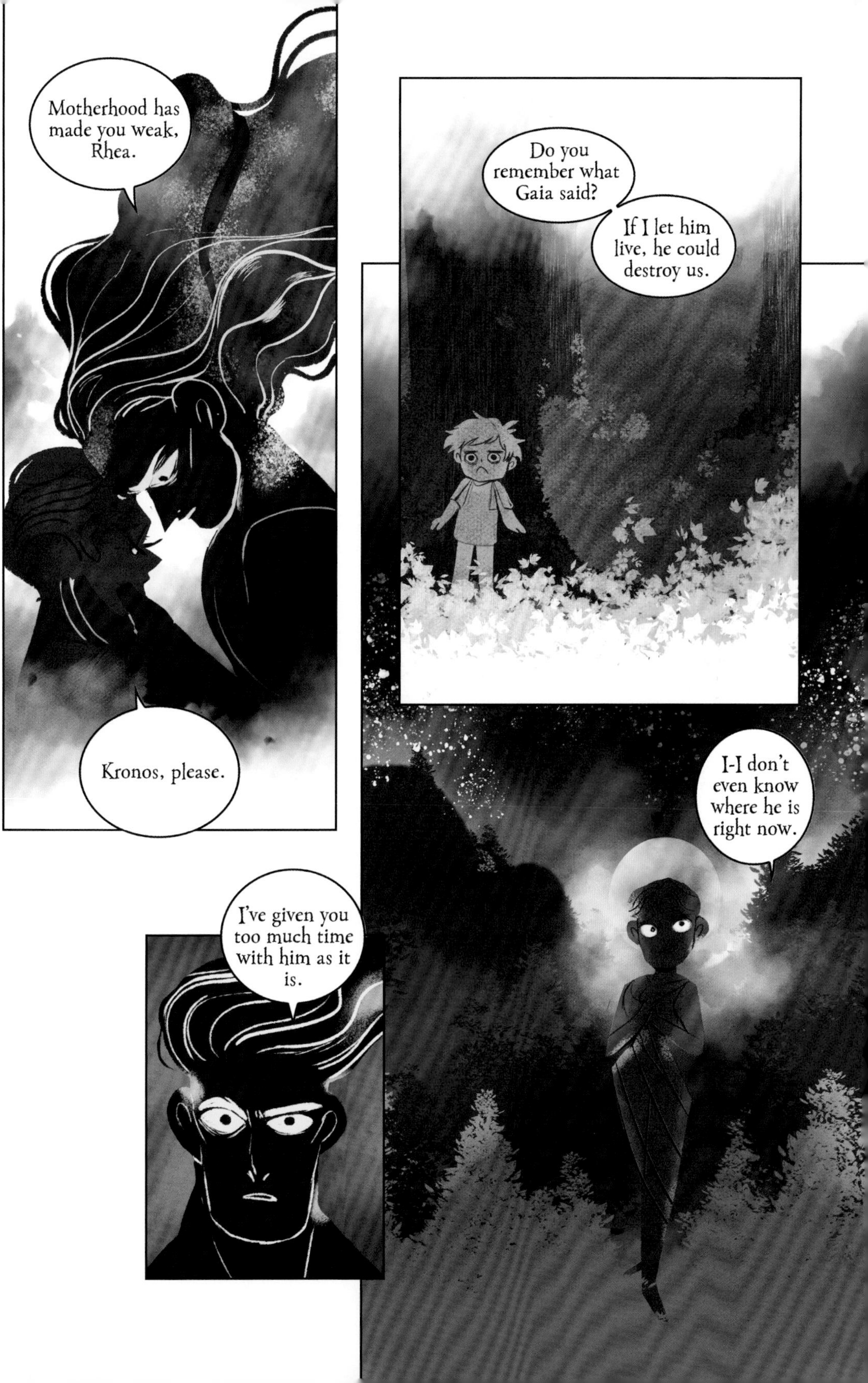
Motherhood has made you weak, Rhea.
Kronos, please.
Do you remember what Gaia said?
If I let him live, he could destroy us.
I've given you too much time with him as it is.
I-I don't even know where he is right now.

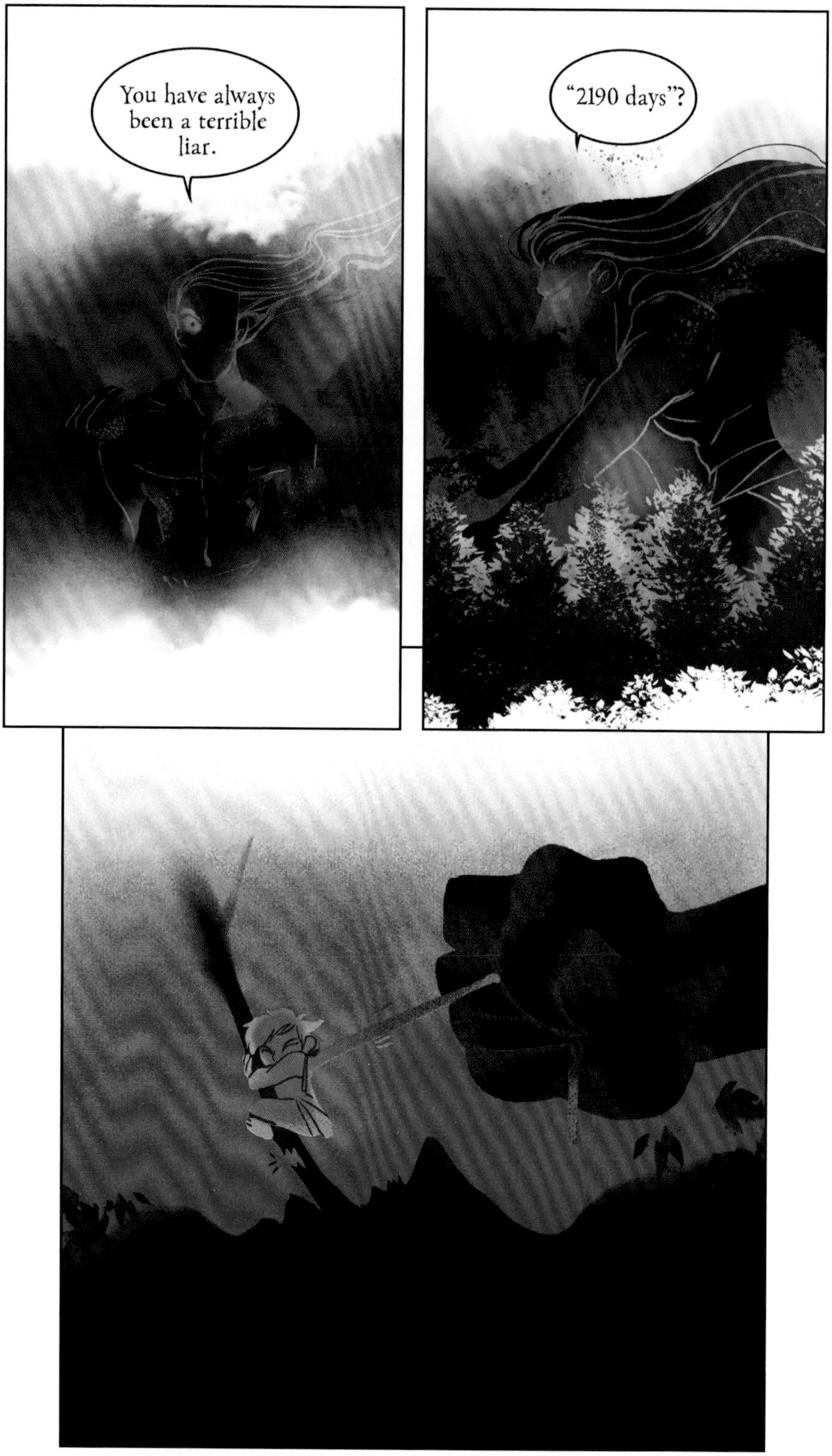
You have always been a terrible liar.
"2190 days"?

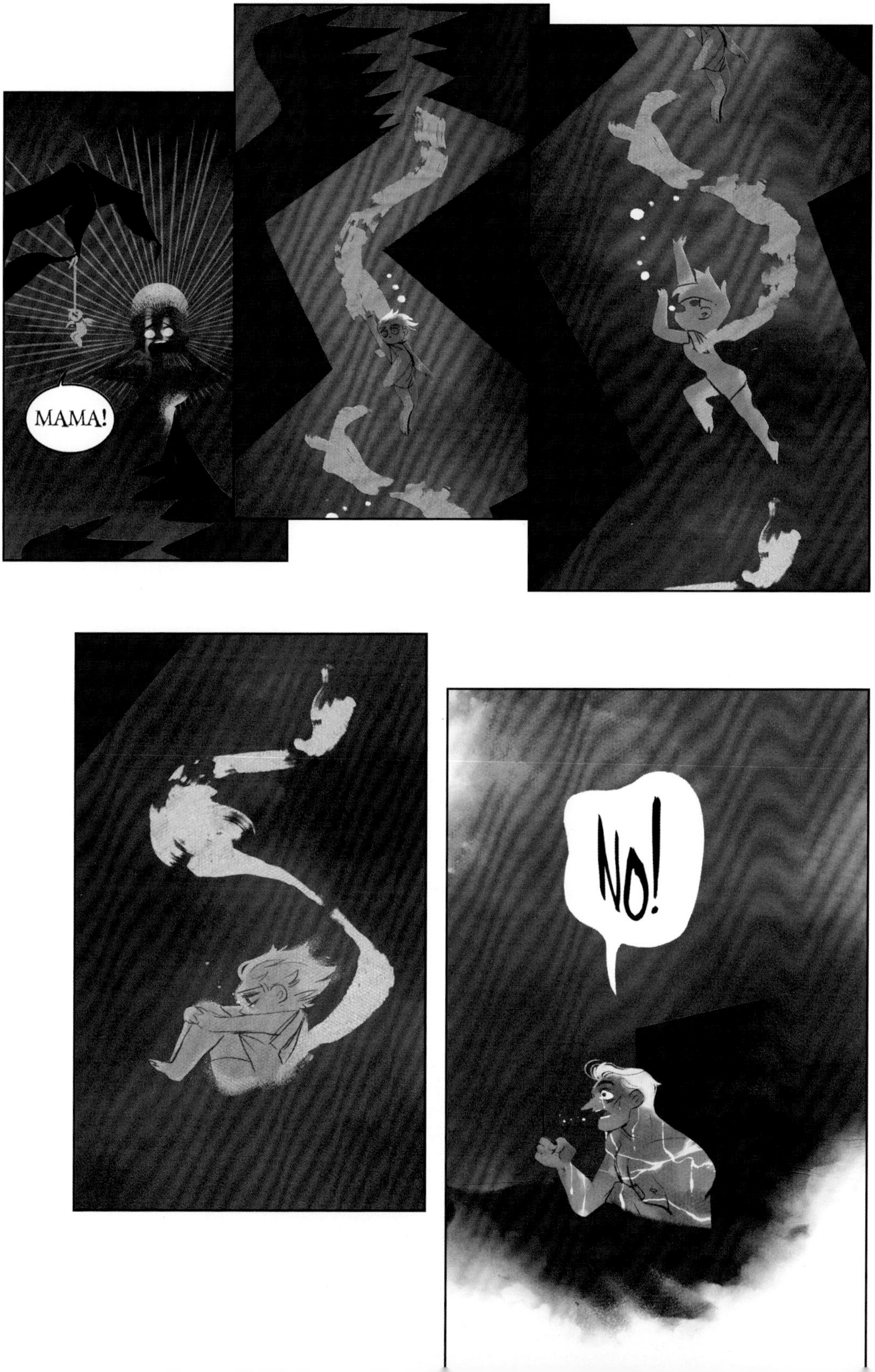
MAMA!
NO!

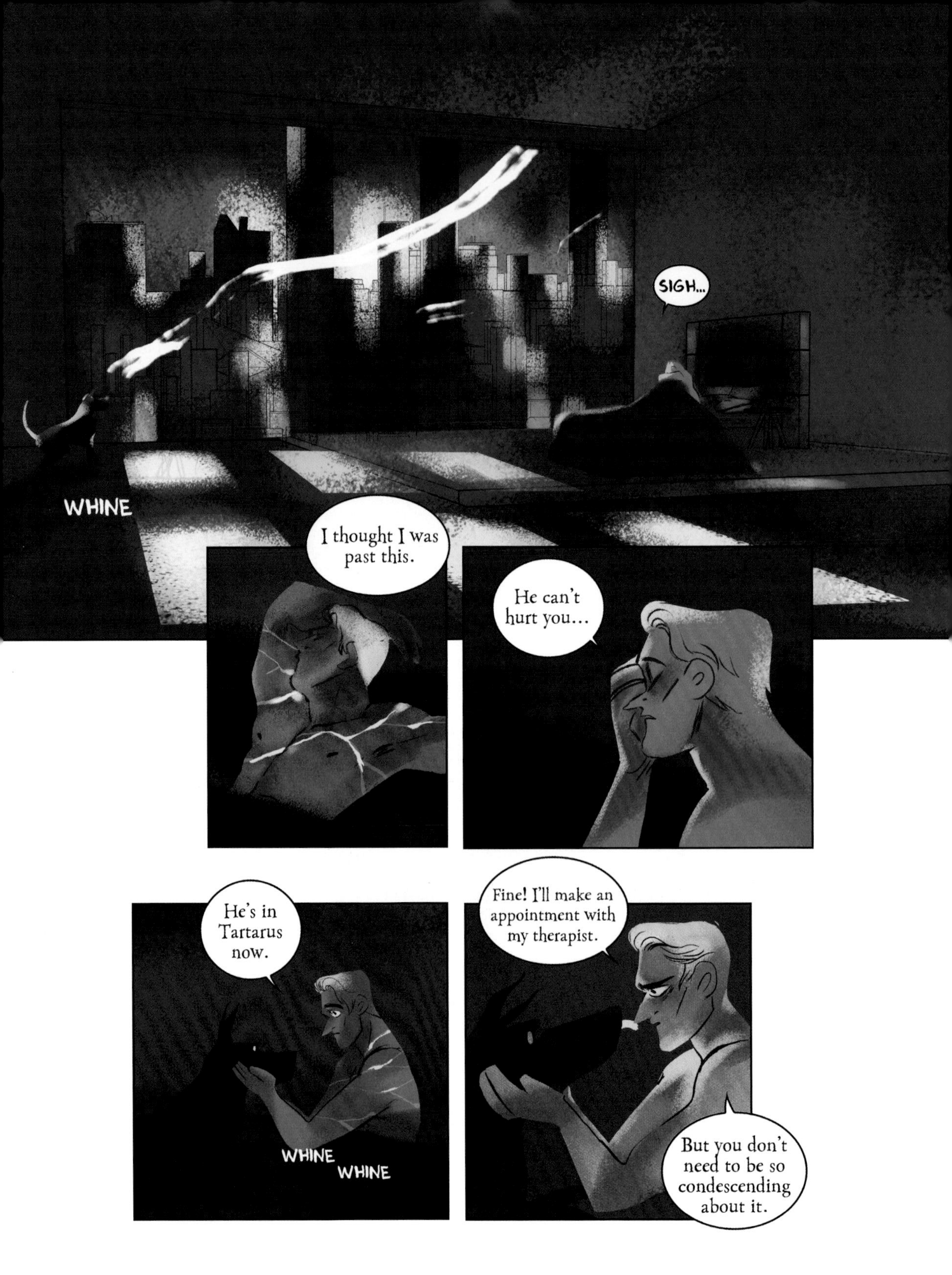
SIGH...
WHINE
I thought I was past this.
He can't hurt you...
He's in Tartarus now.
WHINE
WHINE
Fine! I'll make an appointment with my therapist.
But you don't need to be so condescending about it.

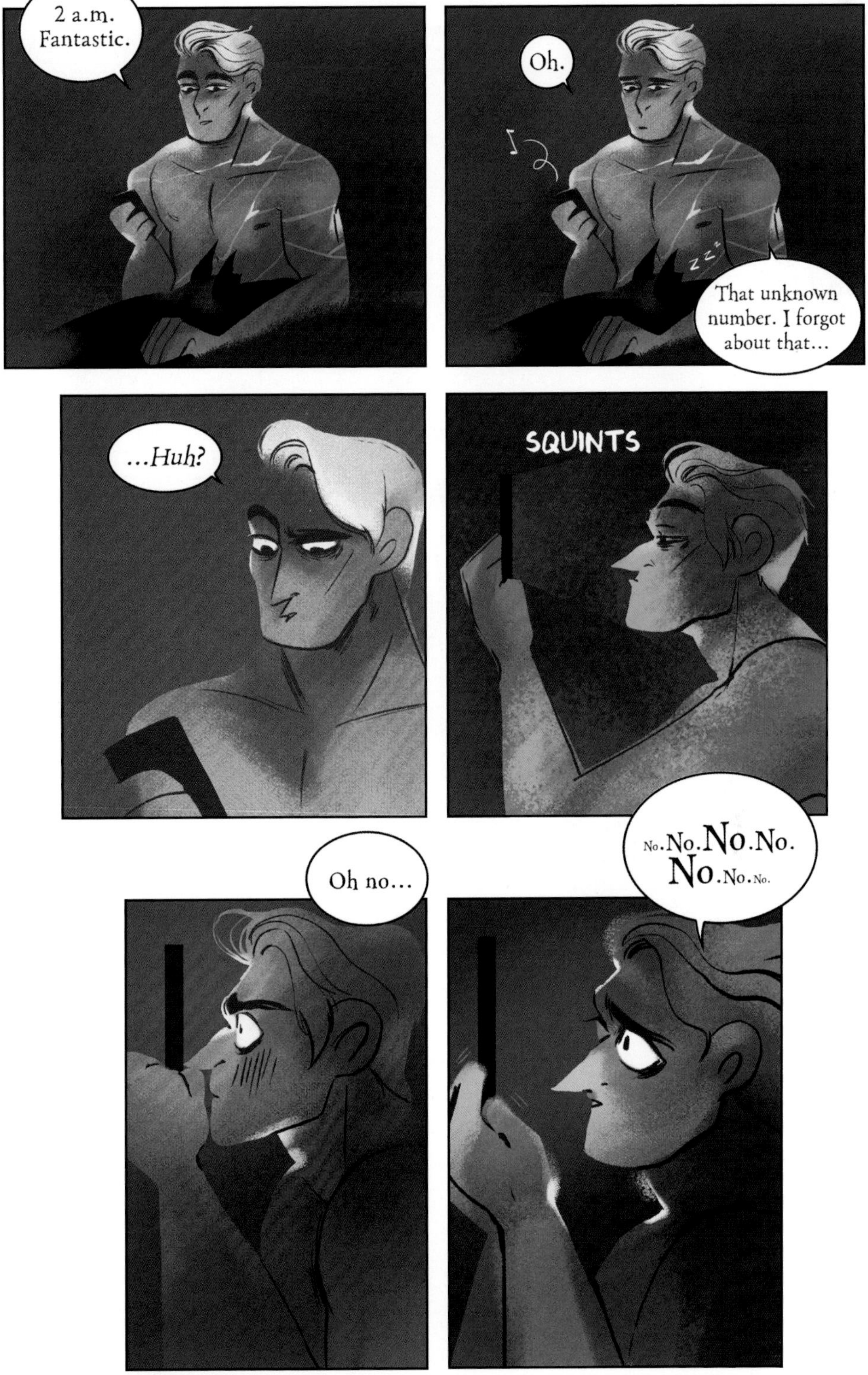
2 a.m.
Fantastic.
Oh.
That unknown number. I forgot about that…
…Huh?
SQUINTS
Oh no…
No. No. No. No.
No. No. No.

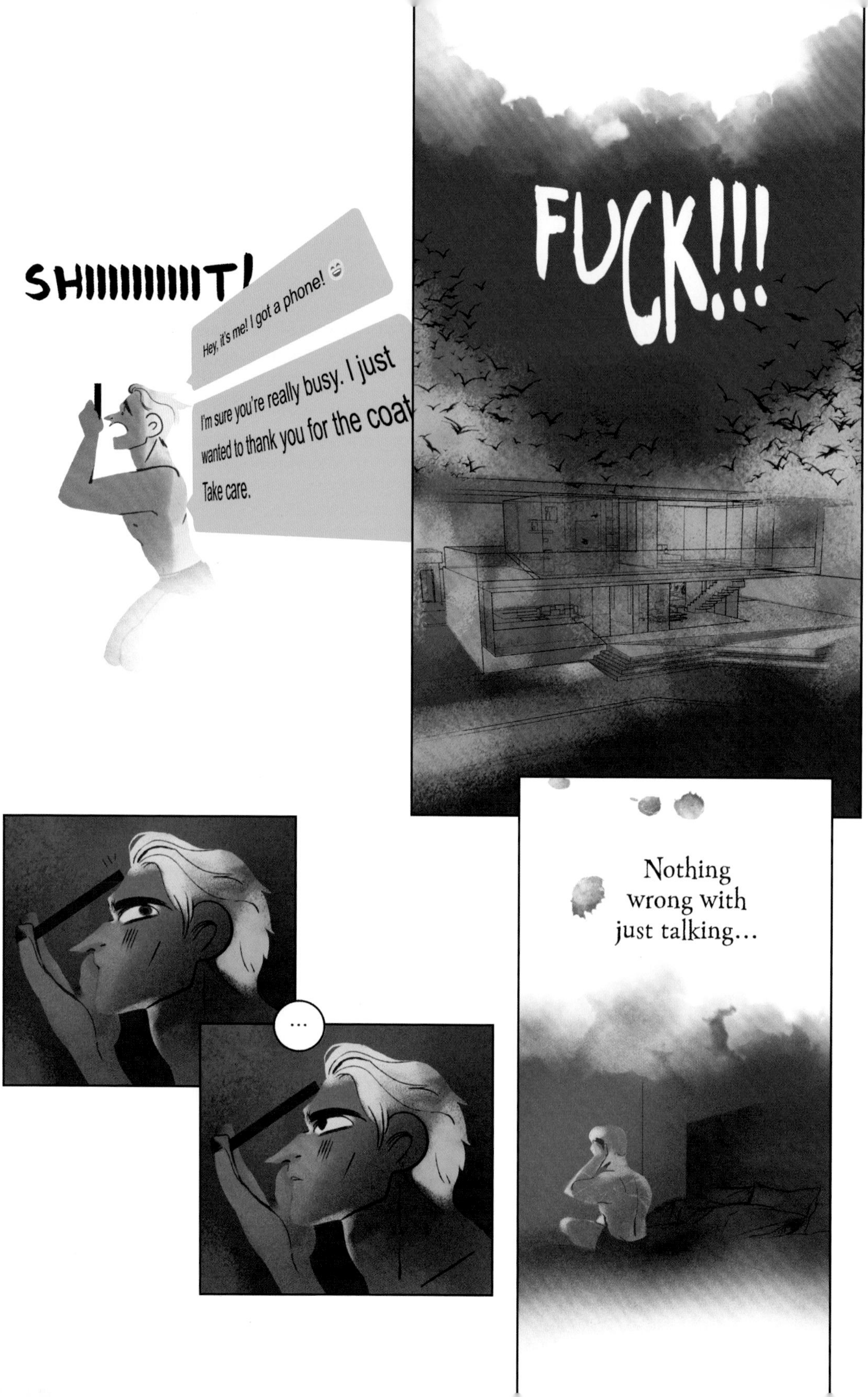
SHIIIIIIIIIIT!
Hey, it's me! I got a phone!
I'm sure you're really busy. I just wanted to thank you for the coat
Take care.
FUCK!!!
...
Nothing wrong with just talking...

I originally wrote this chapter to be episode 10 of *Lore Olympus*. However, after a discussion with my editor at the time we decided that the first Hera-focused chapter shouldn't be about Hades (which is fair). The spot was filled with an episode where Persephone and Hades go for a drive, which suited the narrative better at that time and meant that Hera wasn't defined by her relationship with Hades.

Ultimately, the chapter I had written for Hera didn't fit naturally into the flow of the story and ended up in the story-beat graveyard.

With this publication, I'm glad to have the opportunity to share this moment.

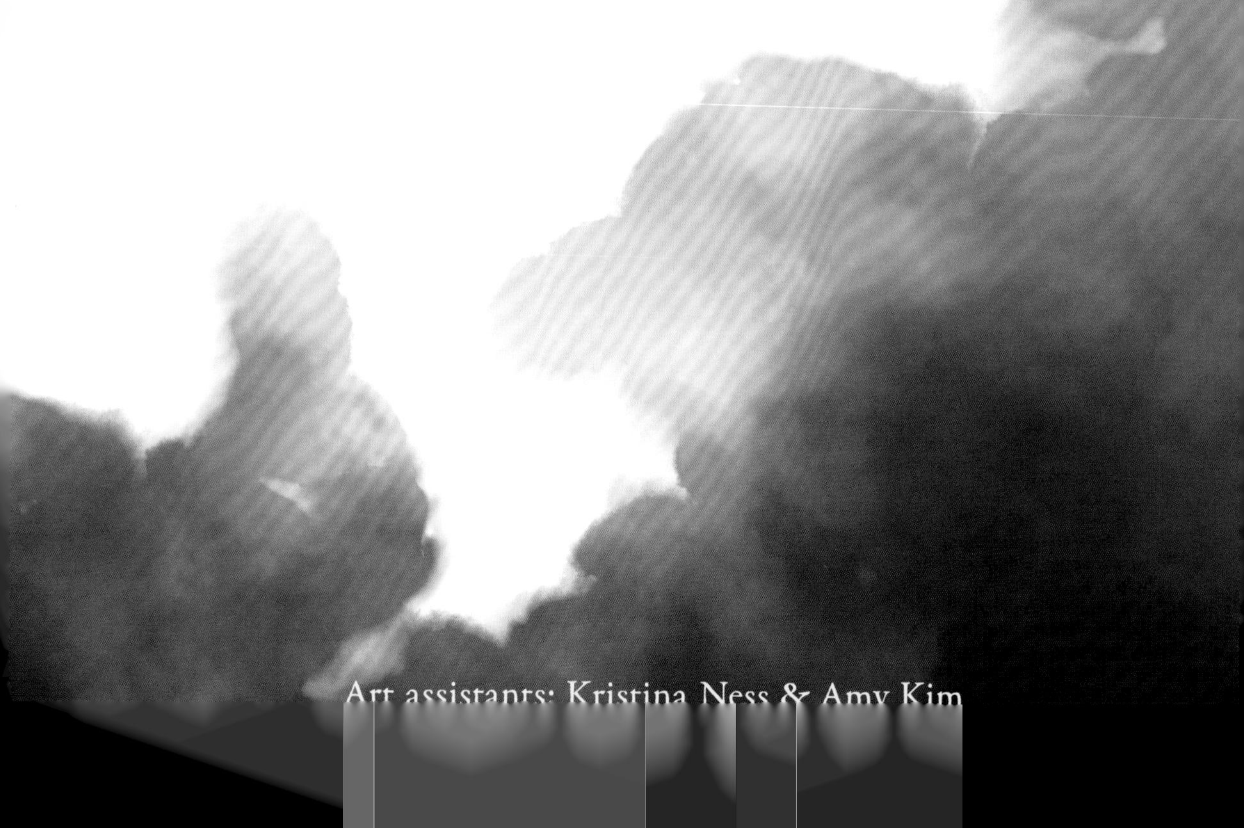

Art assistants: Kristina Ness & Amy Kim

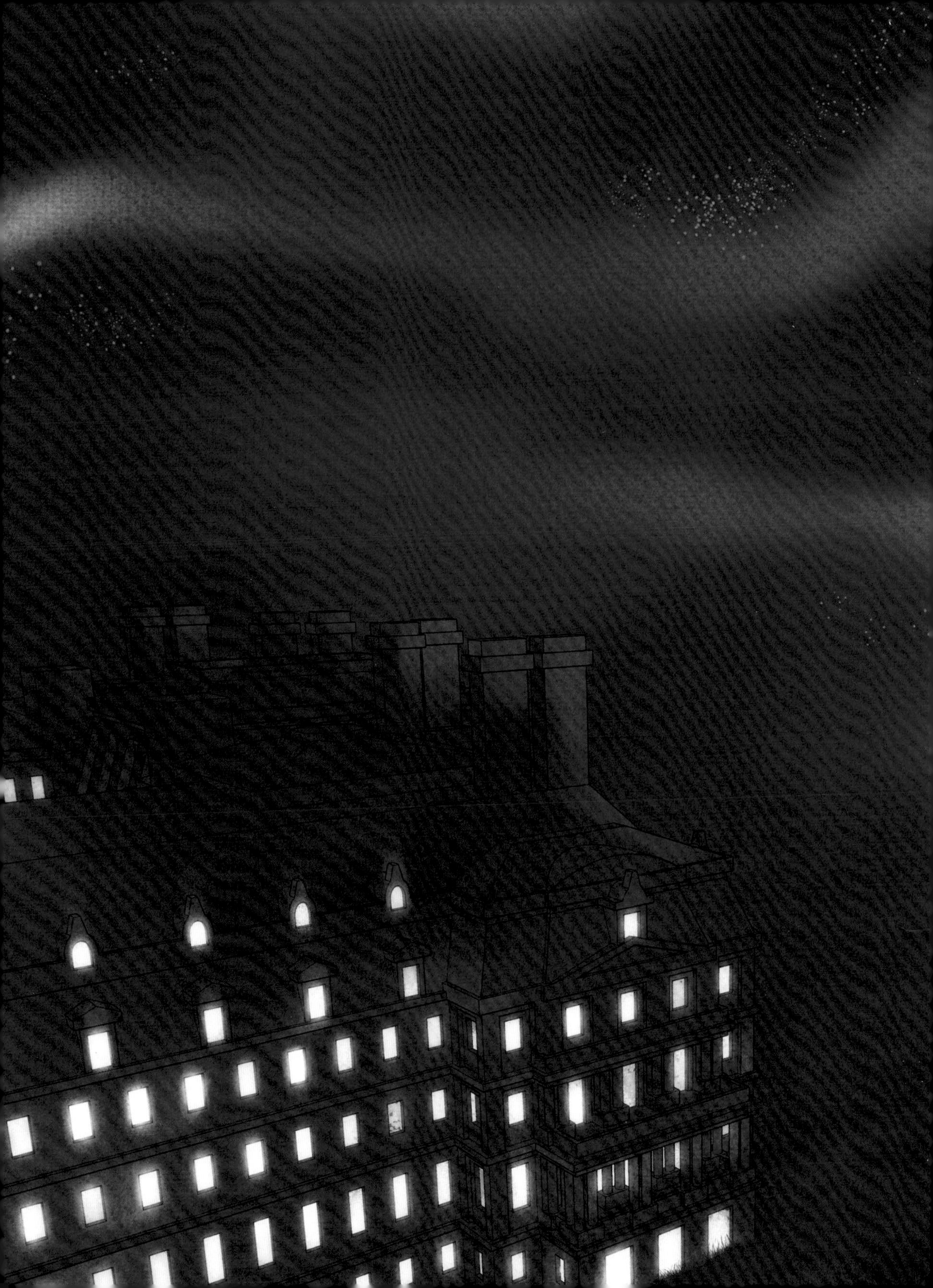

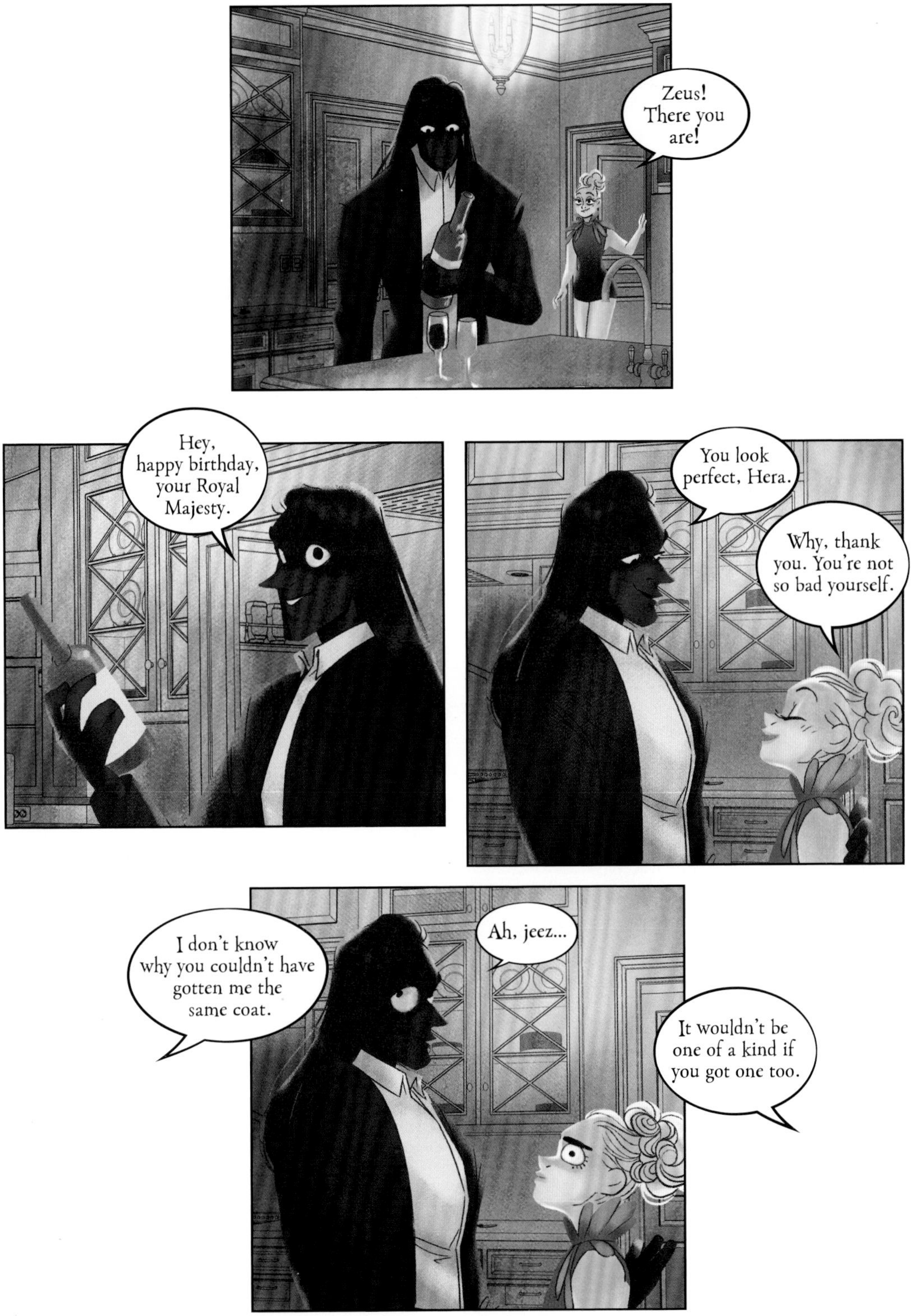
Zeus! There you are!
Hey, happy birthday, your Royal Majesty.
You look perfect, Hera.
Why, thank you. You're not so bad yourself.
I don't know why you couldn't have gotten me the same coat.
Ah, jeez...
It wouldn't be one of a kind if you got one too.

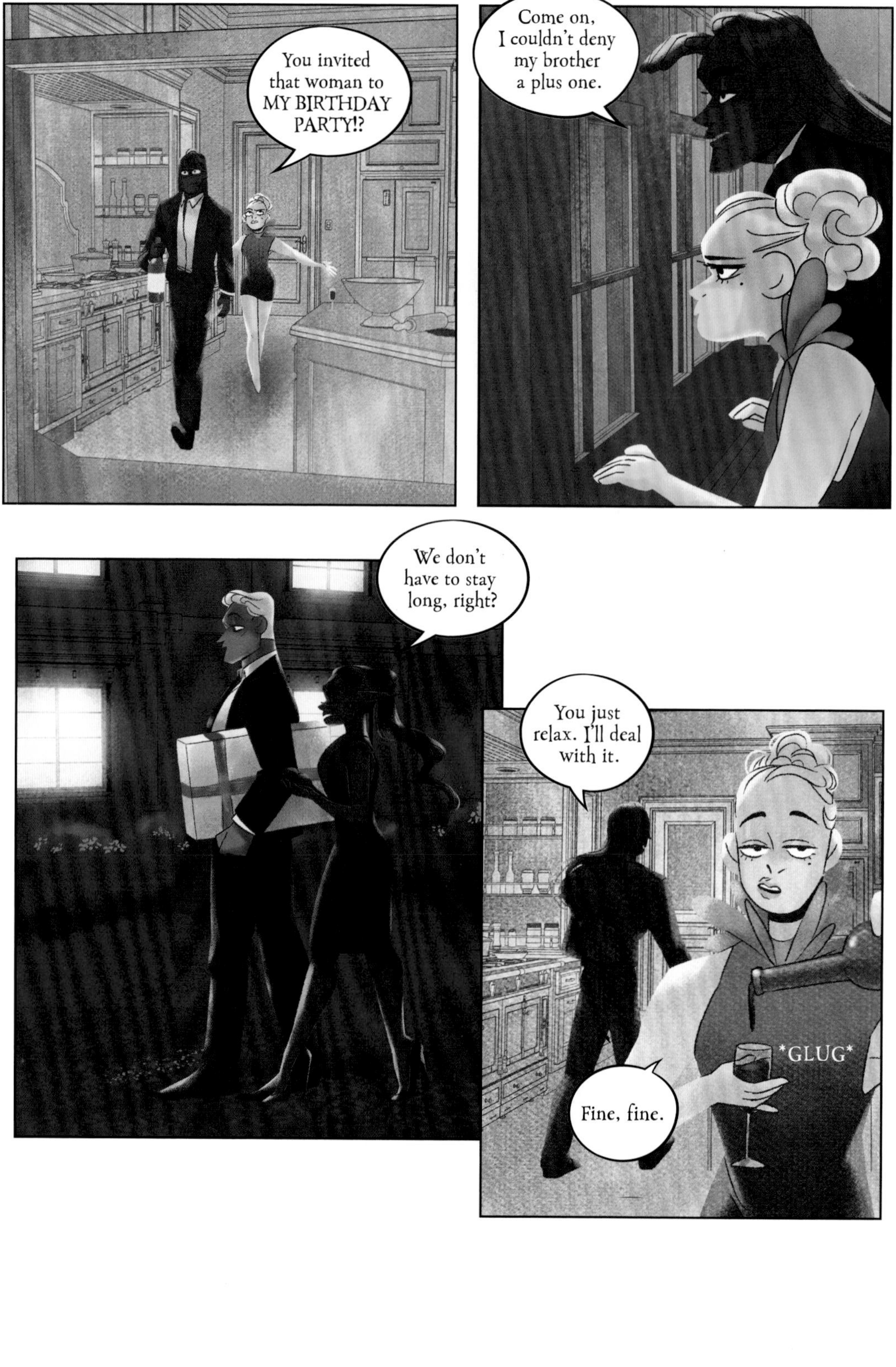
You invited that woman to MY BIRTHDAY PARTY!?
Come on, I couldn't deny my brother a plus one.
We don't have to stay long, right?
You just relax. I'll deal with it.
GLUG
Fine, fine.

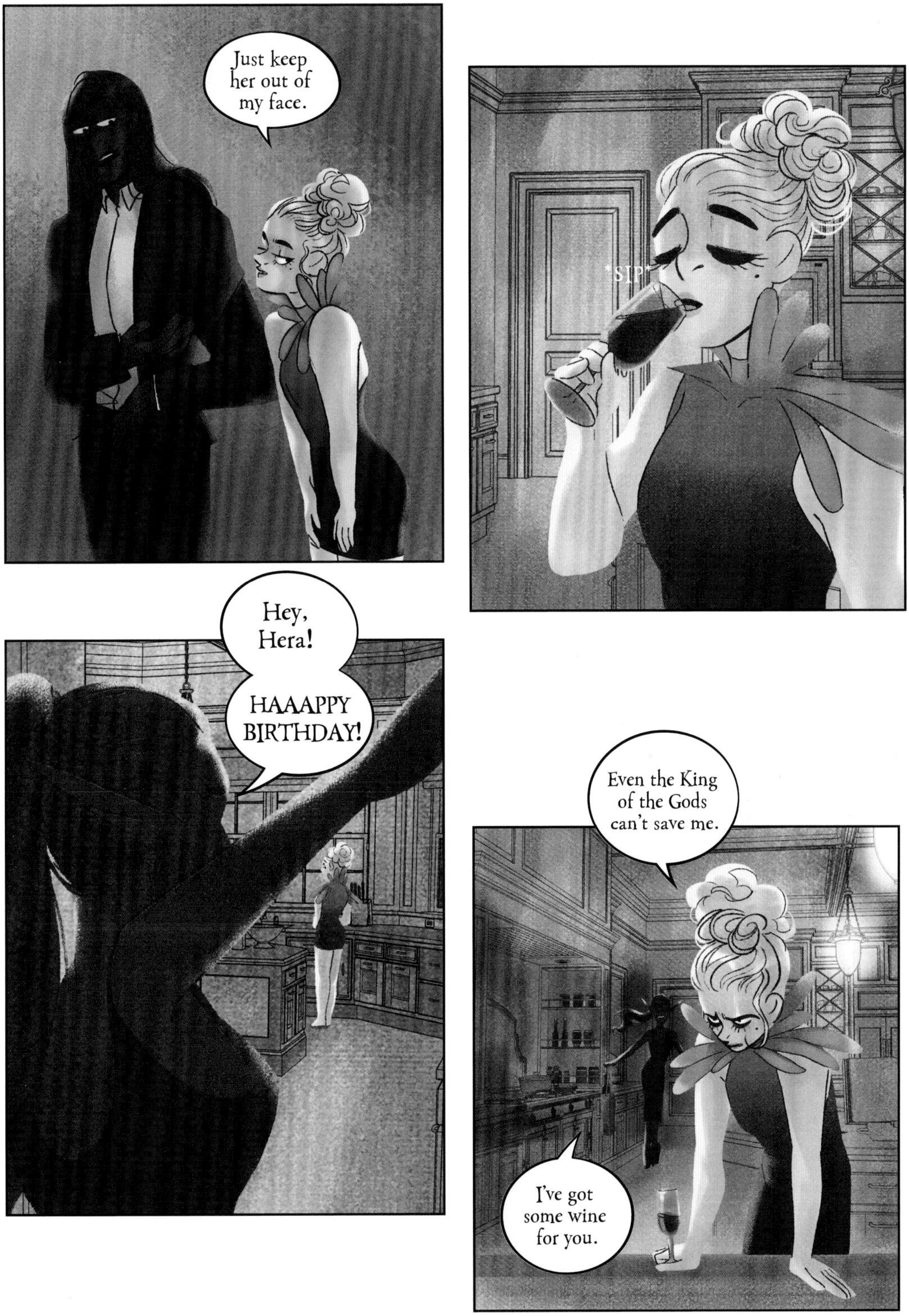
Just keep her out of my face.
SIP
Hey, Hera!
HAAAPPY BIRTHDAY!
Even the King of the Gods can't save me.
I've got some wine for you.

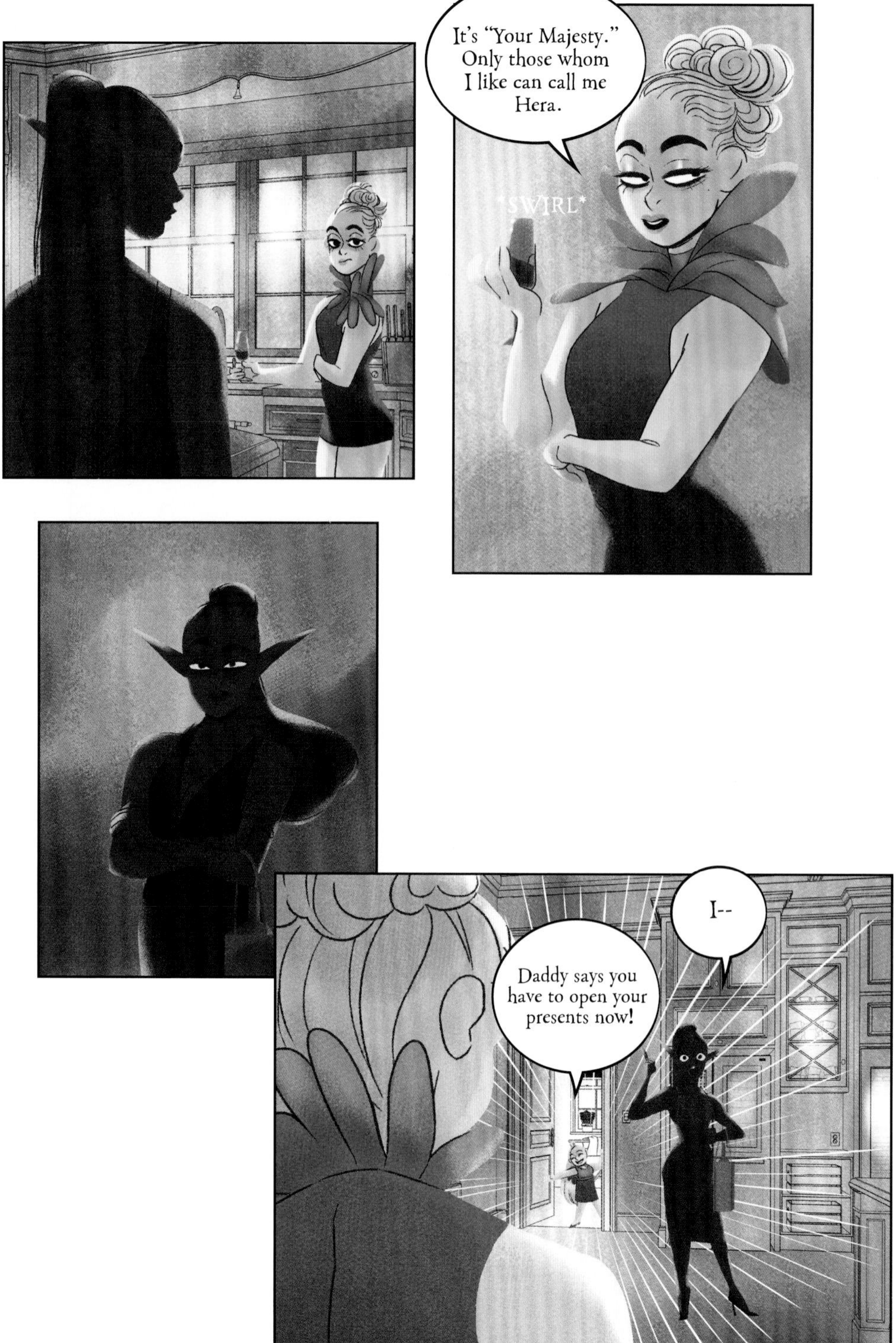
It's "Your Majesty." Only those whom I like can call me Hera.
SWIRL
I--
Daddy says you have to open your presents now!

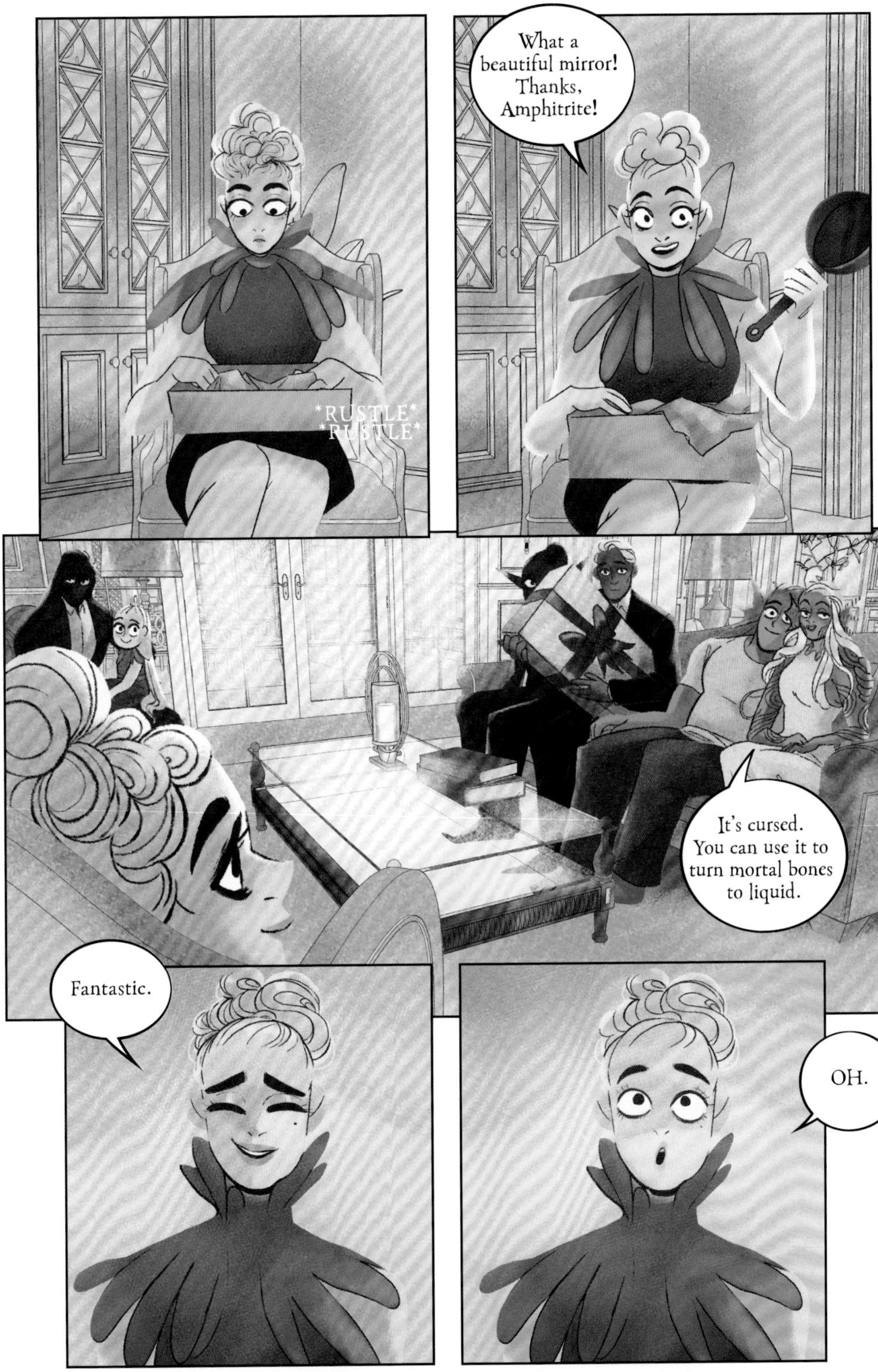
RUSTLE
RUSTLE
What a beautiful mirror! Thanks, Amphitrite!
It's cursed. You can use it to turn mortal bones to liquid.
Fantastic.
OH.

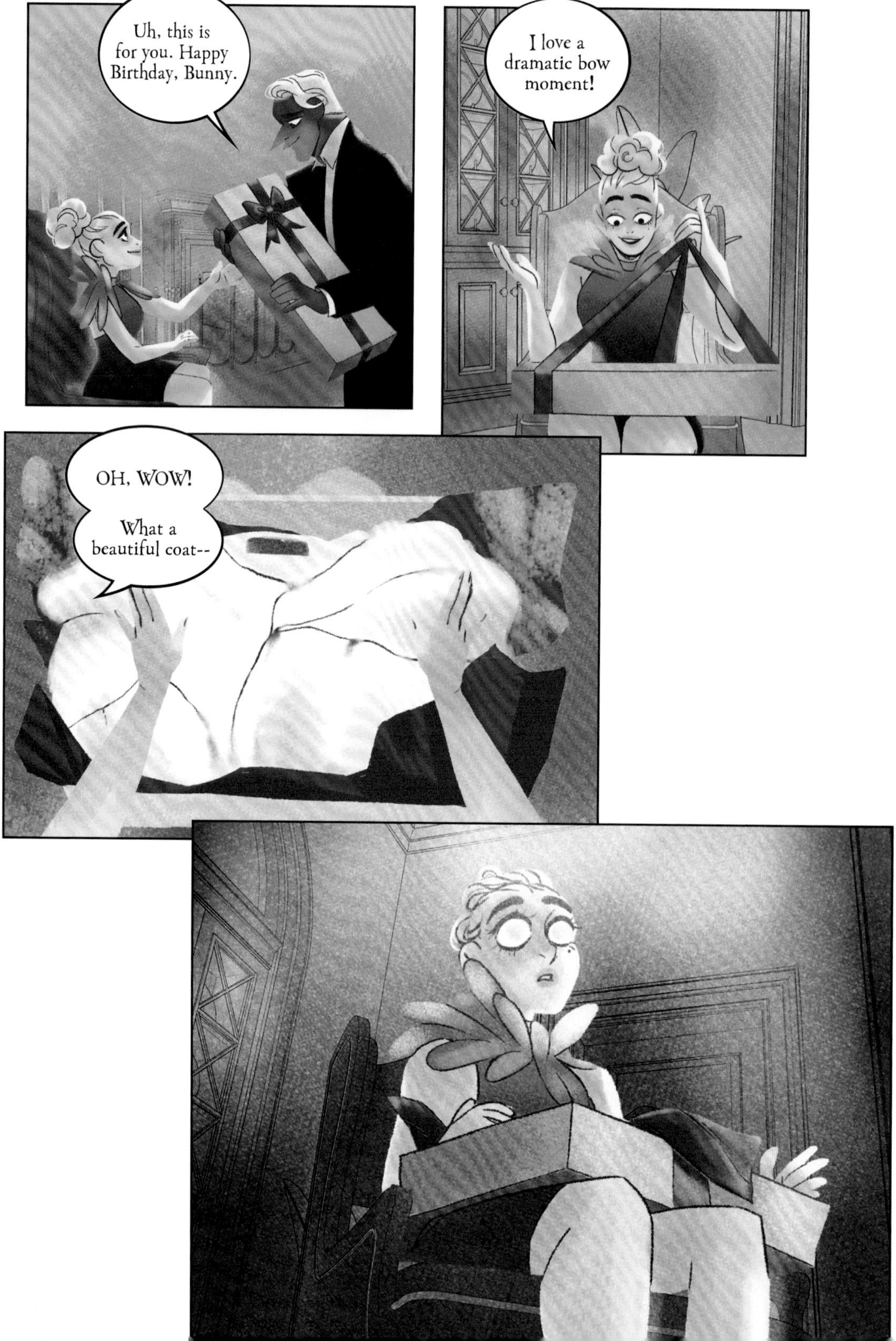
Uh, this is for you. Happy Birthday, Bunny.
I love a dramatic bow moment!
OH, WOW!
What a beautiful coat--

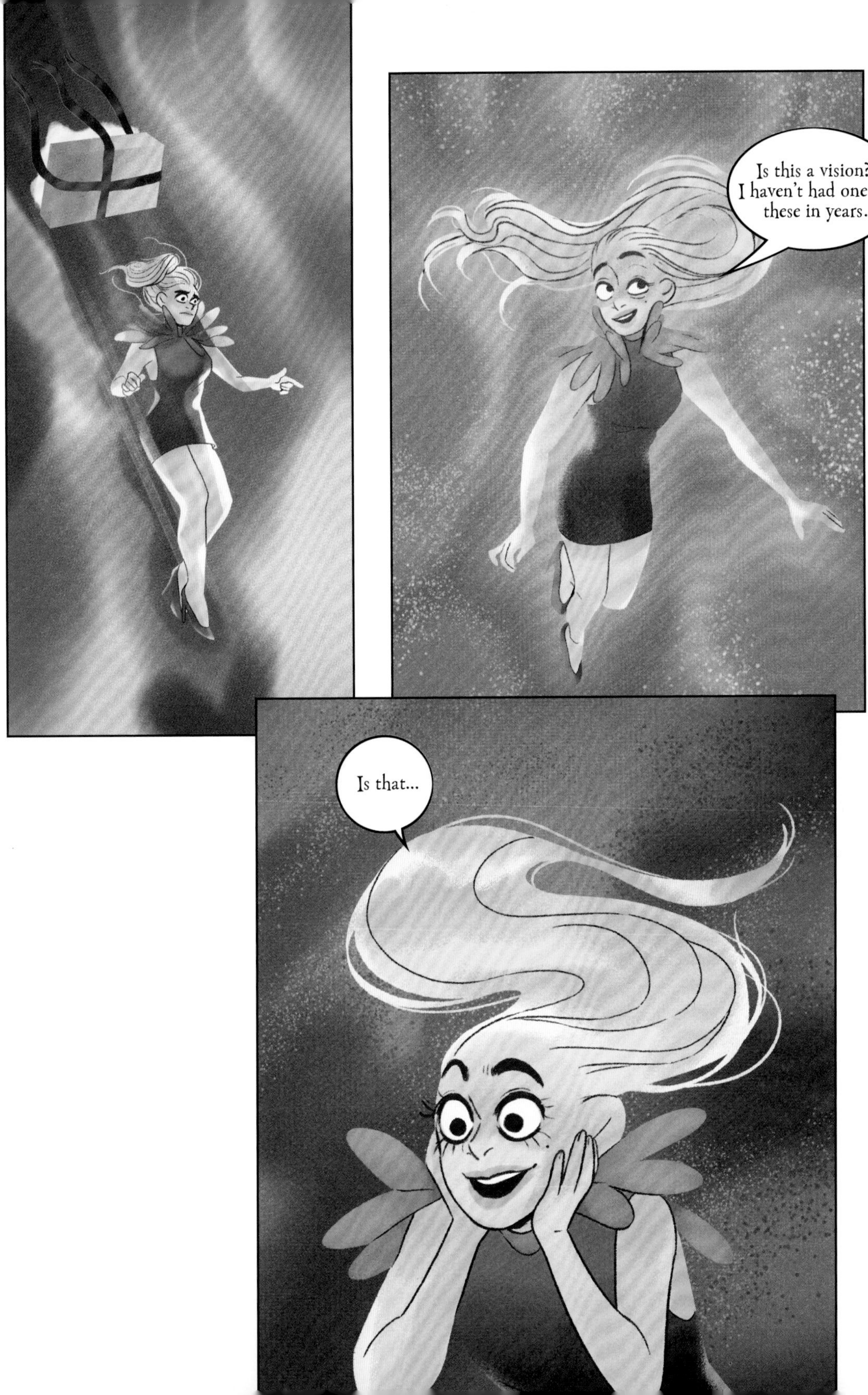
Is this a vision? I haven't had one of these in years.
Is that...

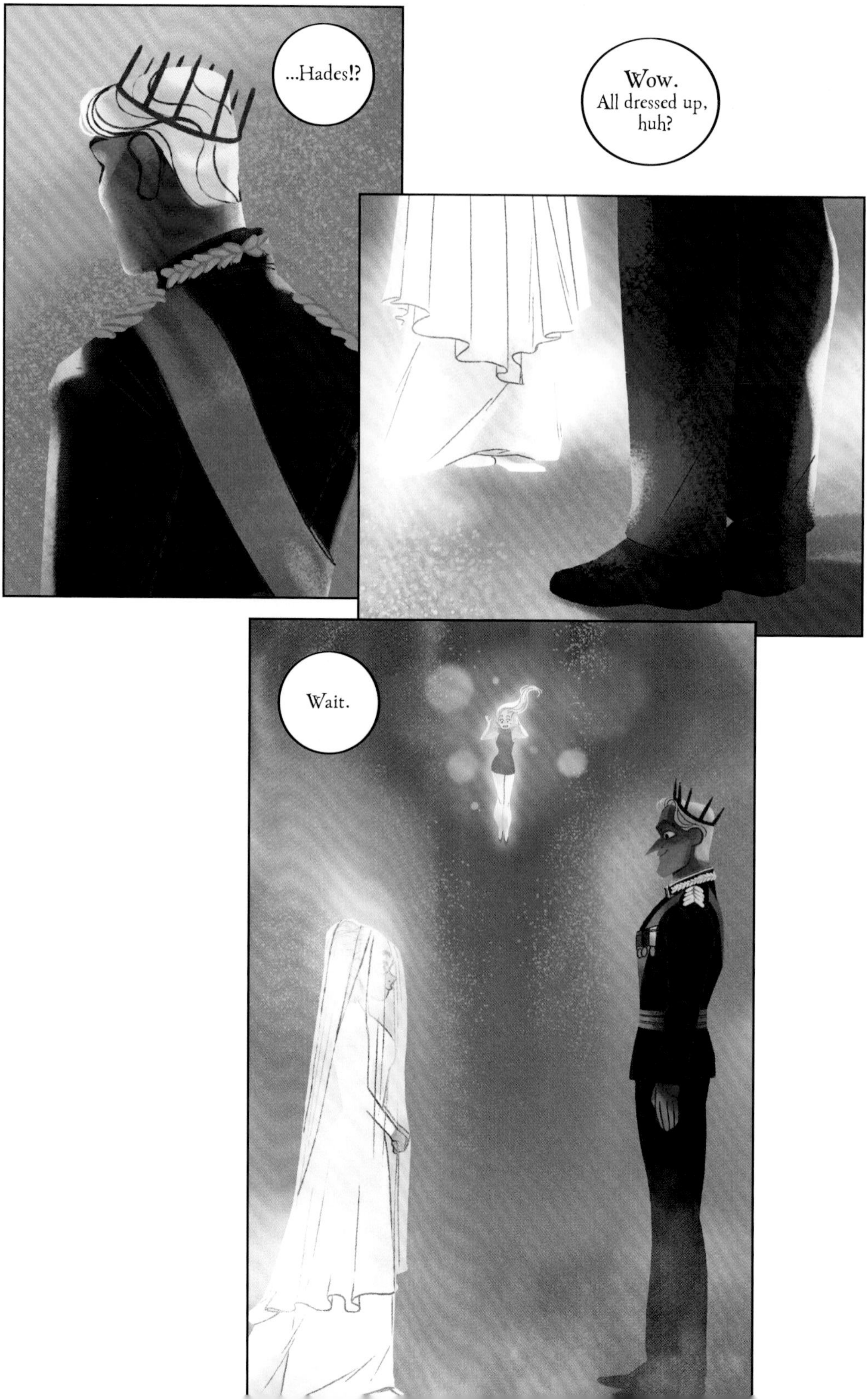
...Hades!?
Wow. All dressed up, huh?
Wait.

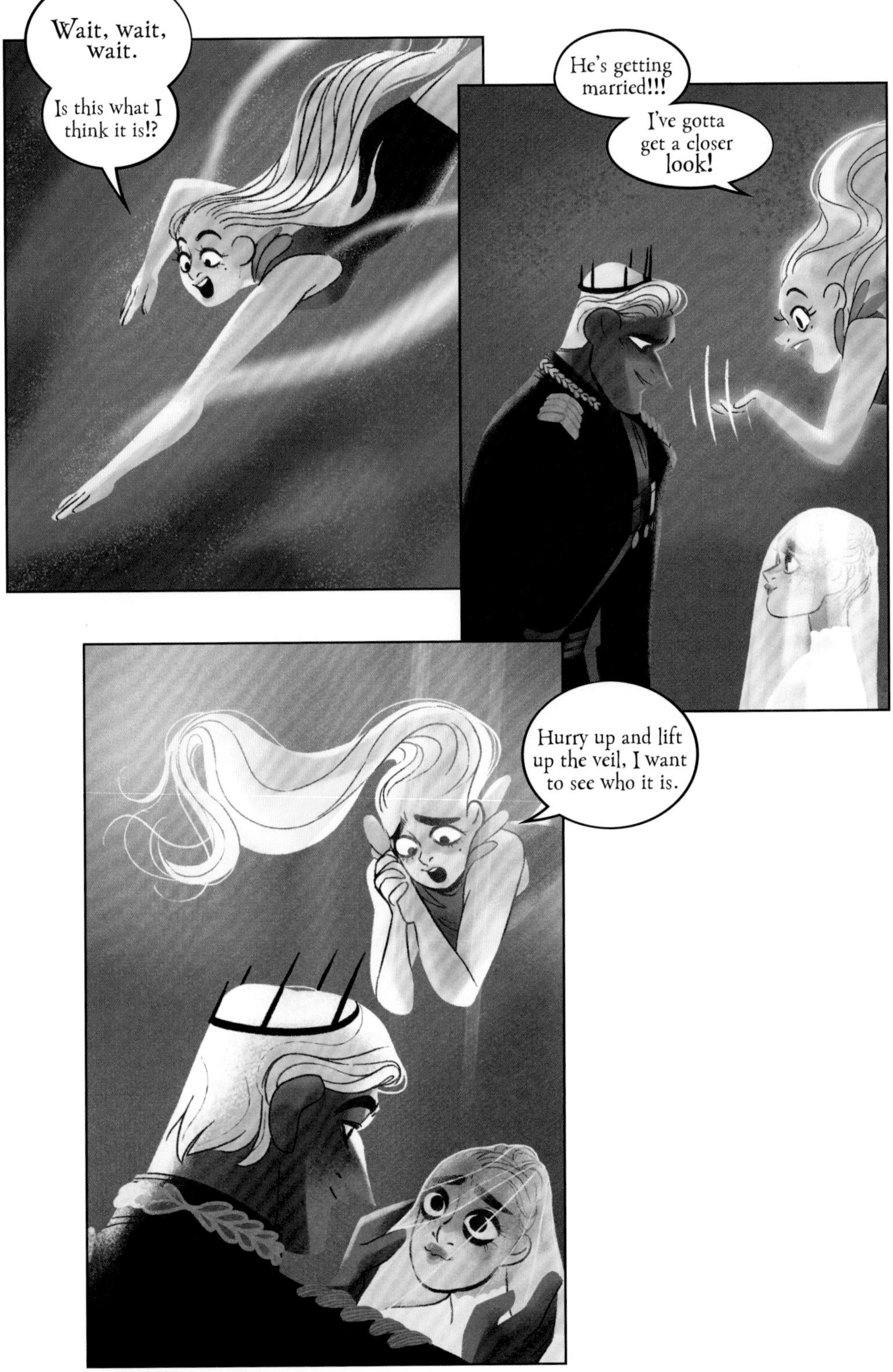
Wait, wait, wait.
Is this what I think it is!?
He's getting married!!!
I've gotta get a closer look!
Hurry up and lift up the veil, I want to see who it is.

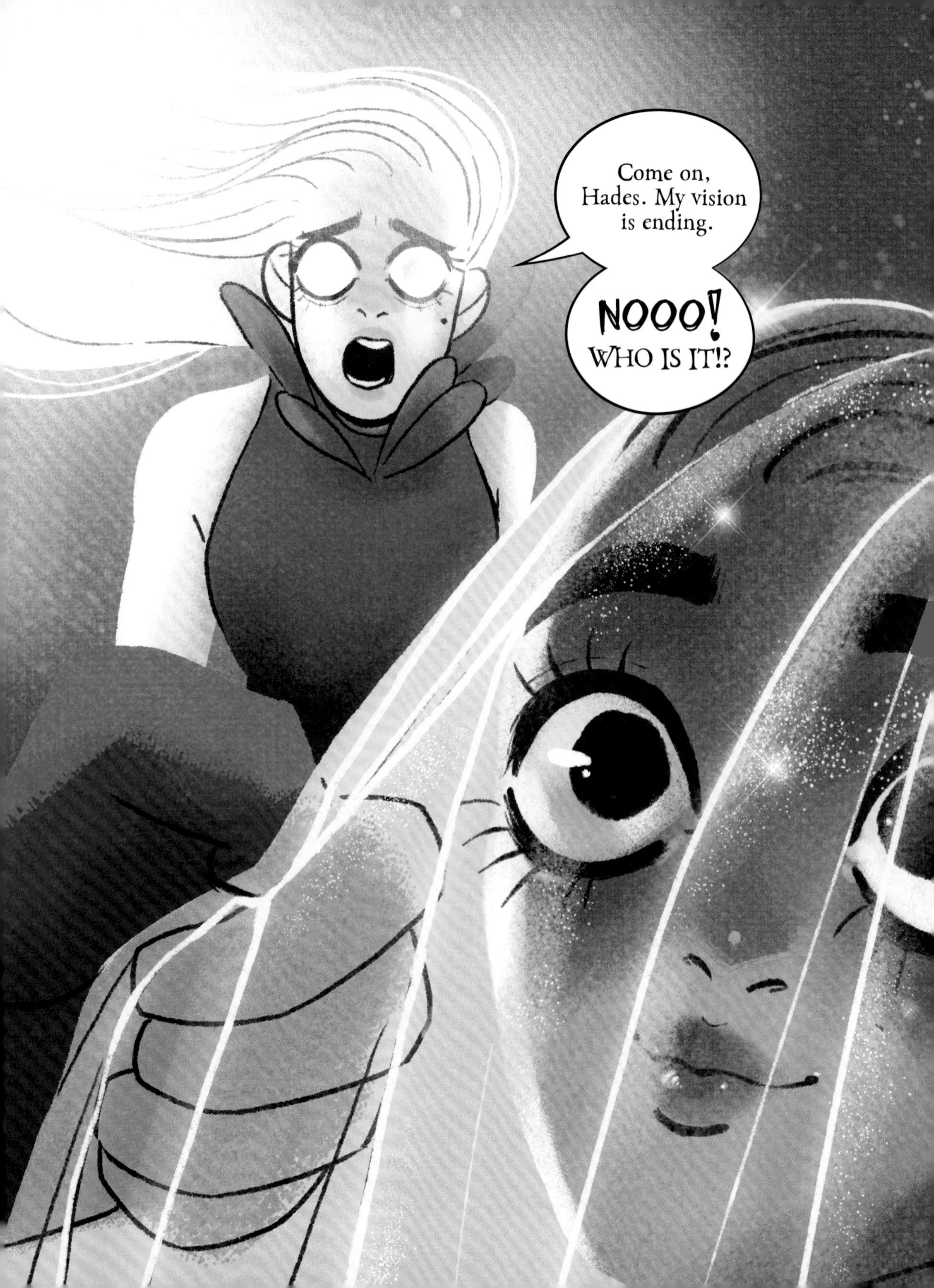
Come on, Hades. My vision is ending.
NOOO! WHO IS IT!?

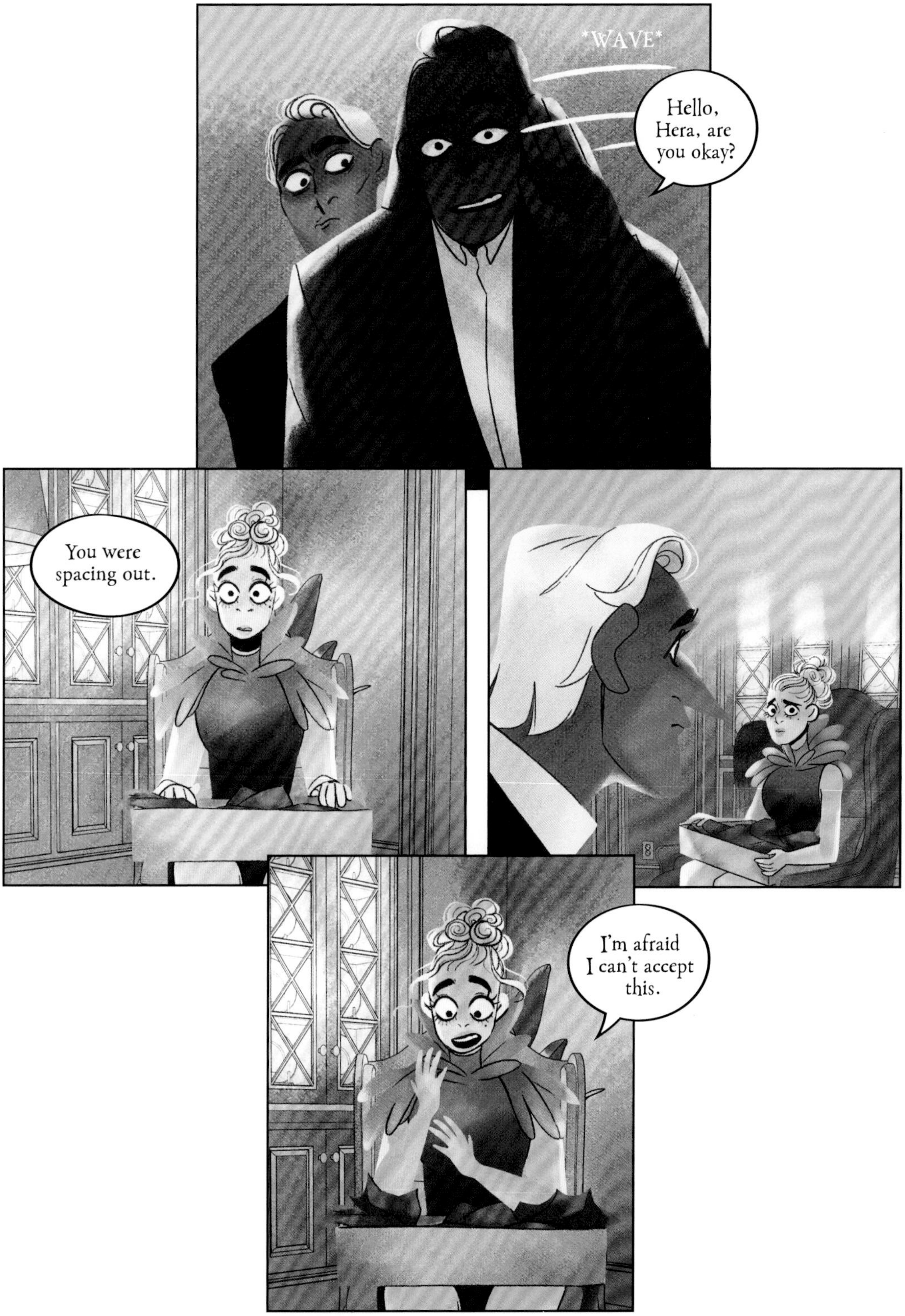
WAVE
Hello, Hera, are you okay?
You were spacing out.
I'm afraid I can't accept this.

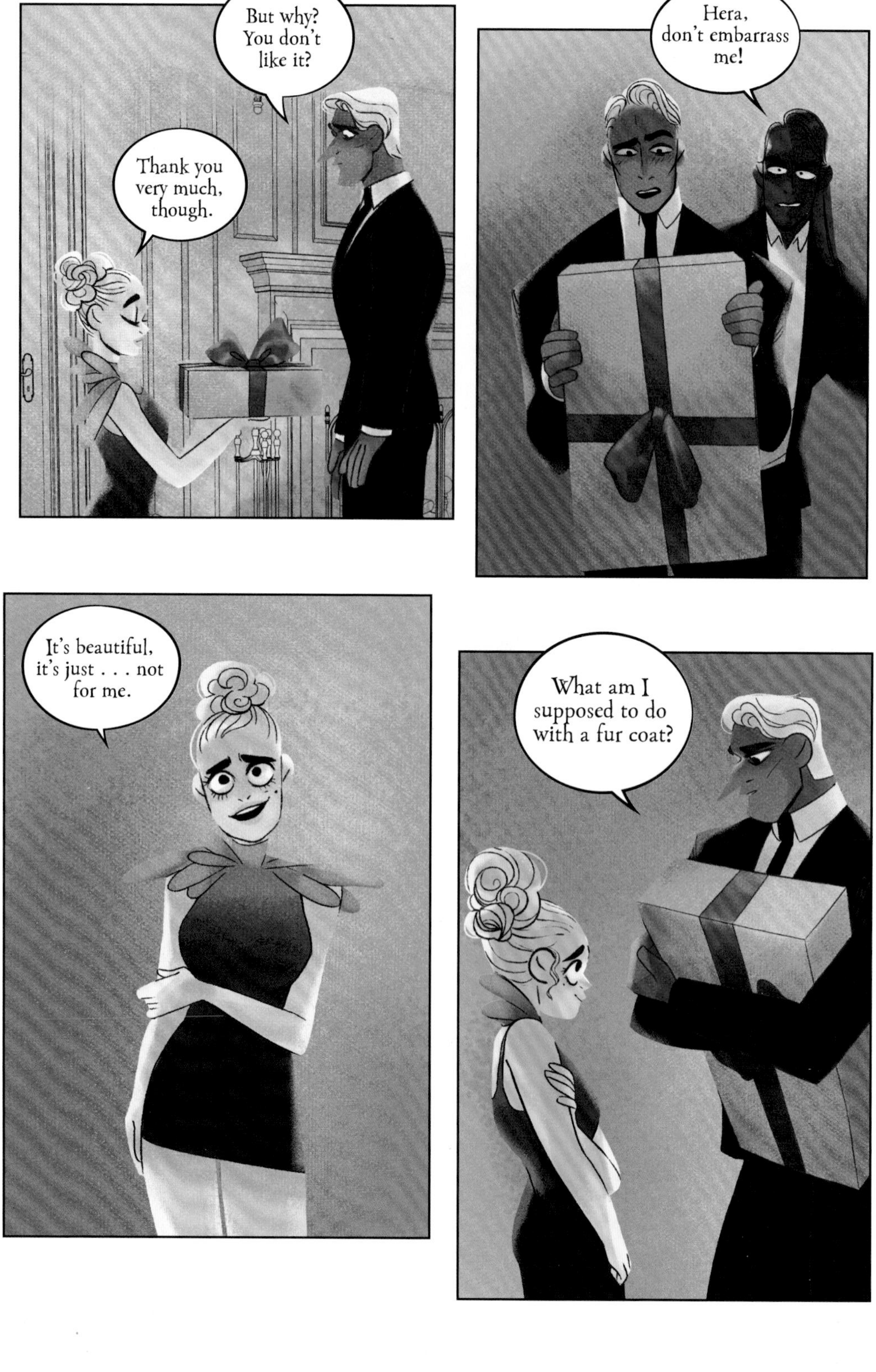
But why? You don't like it?
Thank you very much, though.
Hera, don't embarrass me!
It's beautiful, it's just . . . not for me.
What am I supposed to do with a fur coat?

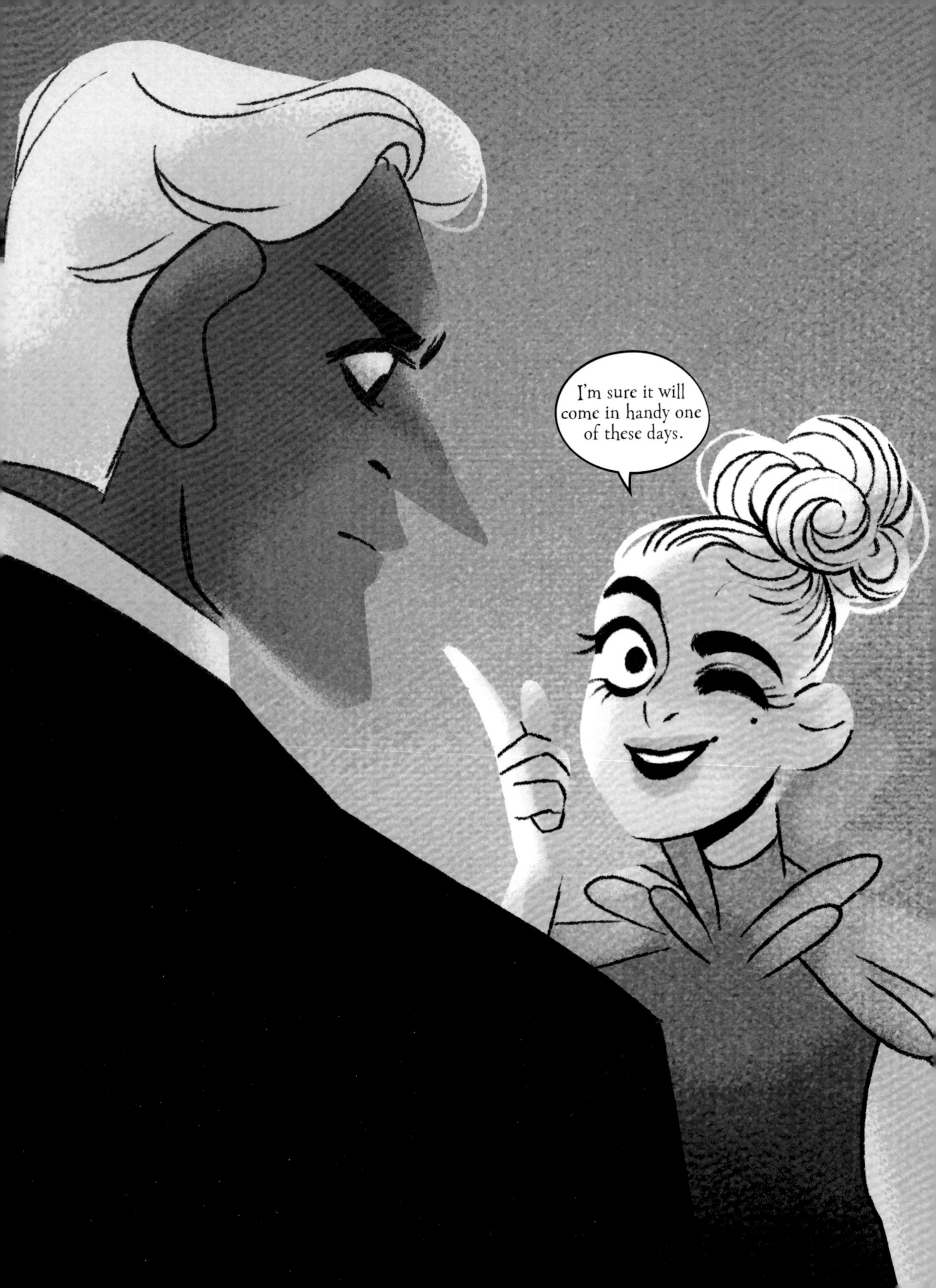
I'm sure it will come in handy one of these days.

ABOUT THE AUTHOR

RACHEL SMYTHE is the creator of the Eisner-nominated *Lore Olympus*, published via WEBTOON.

Twitter: @used_bandaid

Instagram: @usedbandaid

Facebook.com/Usedbandaidillustration

LoreOlympusBooks.com